THE COLLECTED STORIES OF

DEBORAH EISENBERG

ALSO BY DEBORAH EISENBERG

THE
COLLECTED STORIES OF
DEBORAH EISENBERG

PICADOR

Farrar, Straus and Giroux

NEW YORK

www.picadorusa.com

Picador® is a U.S. registered trademark and is used by Farrar, Straus and Giroux under license from Pan Books Limited.

For information on Picador Reading Group Guides, please contact Picador. E-mail: readinggroupguides@picadorusa.com

Designed by Jonathan D. Lippincott

Grateful acknowledgment is made to the following publications, in which these stories originally appeared: "Flotsam," "What It Was Like, Seeing Chris," "Transactions in a Foreign Currency," "Broken Glass," "A Cautionary Tale," "Under the 82nd Airborne," "Presents," and "The Custodian," in somewhat different form, in *The New Yorker.* "A Lesson in Traveling Light" in *Vanity Fair;* "The Robbery" and "In the Station" in *Bomb;* "Holy Week" in *Western Humanities Review;* "Across the Lake" and "Tlaloc's Paradise" in the *Voice Literary Supplement;* "Someone to Talk To," "Rosie Gets a Soul," and "The Girl Who Left Her Sock on the Floor" in *The New Yorker;* "Mermaids" first appeared in *The Yale Review;* "Twilight of the Superheroes" in *Final Edition;* "Some Other, Better Otto" in *The Yale Review;* "Like It or Not" in *The Threepenny Review;* "Window" and "Revenge of the Dinosaurs" in *Tin House;* and "The Flaw in the Design" in *The Virginia Quarterly Review.*

Library of Congress Cataloging-in-Publication Data

Eisenberg, Deborah.
   [Short stories. Selections]
   The collected stories of Deborah Eisenberg. — 1st Picador ed.
      p. cm.
   ISBN 978-0-312-42989-8
   I. Title.
   PS3555.I793A6   2010
   813'.54—dc22

                   2010002081

D 20 19 18 17 16 15 14 13 12 11

CONTENTS

THE COLLECTED STORIES OF

DEBORAH EISENBERG

TRANSACTIONS
IN A FOREIGN CURRENCY

For Wall, of course

FLOTSAM

The other evening, I was having a drink with a friend when the sight of two women at the next table caused me to stop speaking in midsentence. Both of the women were very young, and fashionable to an almost painful degree. They were drinking beer straight from the bottle, and they radiated a self-conscious, helpless daring, as if they had been made to enter some baffling contest and all eyes were upon them.

"Earth to Charlotte," my friend said. "Everything all right?"

"Fine," I said, and it was, but for a moment that seemed endless I had been pulled down into a forgotten period of my life when I, too, had strained to adhere to the slippery requirements of distant authorities.

I had just come to New York then, after breaking up with a man named Robert. At first, everything had gone well with Robert. We lived in Buffalo, on the ground floor of a large house, and while he taught at a local university and read and worked on his dissertation in the study, I tried to make things grow in our little patch of a garden and did some part-time research for a professor of political science. At night, we cooked dinner together or with other couples from Robert's department, or once in a while went dancing or to a movie, and I thought Robert was happy.

But after a while Robert seemed to lose interest in me,

and part of what I had been was torn from me as he pulled away. And the further he pulled away from me, increasingly the only thing I cared about was that he love me, and there was nothing I would not have done to be right for him. But although I tried and tried to figure out how I ought to be, my means for judging such a thing seemed to have split off with him. So while Robert seemed to grow finer and more fastidious—easily annoyed by things I said or did—I seemed to grow coarser and more unfocused, and even my athletic tallness, which Robert had admired when we met, with the dissolving of his affection came to feel like an untended sprawl, and my long blond hair, which I'd been proud of at one time, seemed insipid and childish—just another manifestation of how unequal to Robert I had proved to be. And after a time I was overtaken by a paralysis that spread through every area of my life, rapidly, like an illness.

One day, Robert and I had been sitting in the living room reading when I noticed that he had put down his book and was just staring out with a little frown. "What are you thinking about?" I said before I could stop myself.

"Nothing," he said.

"Sorry," I said. "I'm sorry."

"Then why did you ask, Charlotte?"

"Sorry," I said.

"Then why do you always ask? Always," he said.

I didn't say anything.

"You know what?" he said. "You're like the Blob. You remember that movie *The Blob*? You're sentient protoplasm, but you're as undifferentiated as sentient protoplasm can get. You're devoid of even taxonomic attributes."

"Robert," I said.

"Have you ever had an intention?" he said. "Have you ever

had a desire? Have you ever even had what could be accurately described as a reaction?"

My ears went strange, and I heard my voice say, "You always want me to be different. You want me to be some other person, but if you don't tell me what you want, how can I know what to do?"

"Jesus," Robert said. He looked at me, his eyes narrowed. The moment locked, and I felt a harsh tingling across the bridge of my nose, and I knew that if I didn't turn away fast Robert would hit me.

I went out carefully, as if trying not to startle something from a hedge, and drove to a drugstore where there was a telephone, and eventually I got a hold of my friend Fran.

"Sit right there," she said. "Don't move. I'll make some calls and get back to you."

So then I sat on the little wooden seat and waited. A pretty girl with dark hair came into the store, and I watched as she chose a lipstick at the counter, looking very pleased with herself. What was going to happen to me, I wondered. After a while, Fran called with the number of someone named Cinder, who lived in New York and was looking for a roommate.

"Great," Cinder said when I reached her. "I'm desperate. The girl who was living here disappeared a few weeks ago with about half my stuff. Ex-stuff now. I had to get myself a live-in junkie, right? And of course she stuck me for all of last month's rent. I know it's a sign that you called today, because I was just about to advertise, which I really hate to do, because you get these guys saying their name is Shirley and can they come over and shit in your ear or rupture your asshole, kind of thing."

"Well, I got your name from Franny Straub," I said. "Her friend Lauren took a design class with you."

"Whatever," Cinder said.

"Listen," I said. I felt ill with apprehension. "Could I move in tonight?"

"Sure," Cinder said. "You wouldn't be able to bring the rent in cash, would you?"

I'd never been to New York before, and I remember so clearly how the subway looked to me that night. How gaudy and festive it was, like a huge Chinese dragon, clanking and huffling through its glimmering cavern. Even though it was very late, the cars were full of people. They sat there, all together, and their expressions were eased in that subterranean lull between their different points of embarkation and destination. It seemed to me that I was the only newcomer.

Cinder came down and helped me lug my suitcase upstairs. She moved with brisk precision, and her blond hair was cut like a teddy bear's. "Cinder," I said. "It's an interesting name."

"Lucinda, actually," she said. "But—you know." She opened two bottles of beer and handed one to me. "So, hey, welcome to your new home, which is what my seventh-grade teacher said to our class the first day of junior high, scaring us all out of our *wits*. So you're just coming down from a bad thing, huh?"

"Yes," I said, looking around unsuccessfully for a glass. "Well, not exactly." I didn't know how to put into words to this able person my failure with Robert.

"Anyhow," she said, "tomorrow we'll talk and talk and talk, but there's some stuff I have to take care of now, and, besides, you probably want to sleep. If you go out before I'm up, just leave the rent on the kitchen table."

Cinder gave me a tiny room to myself, but I spent most of my time in the kitchen with her and men she was seeing and her friend Mitchell. Most of my belongings were in the kitchen, too, which had shelves and a closet and a bathtub in which things could be kept, and Cinder had told me to put anything I wanted on the walls. In a place of honor, looking down over the kitchen table, I tacked a snapshot I'd taken of Robert one day in our garden. He was smiling—a free, simple, lifted instant of a smile that I never saw again.

The apartment was in the East Village, and although the neighborhood had long since lost its notoriety, it glittered to me. Cinder and Mitchell seemed so comfortable there. Mitchell moved with an underwater languor that was due to a happy combination of grace and drugs, and his black hair was marvelously glossed. But even though he and Cinder were so different in appearance, they both dressed in meticulously calculated assemblages that reached from past decades far into the future. Together their individual impact was increased exponentially, like that of twins, owing to a similarity I now understand to be stylistic, in addition, of course, to whatever similarity underlies all acute and self-conscious beauty.

Next to them, I felt clumsy and hideous, but it seemed to me, I suppose, that the power of their self-assurance would protect me, that my own face and body would learn from it, and that soon things and people would alter in my path, as they did for Cinder and Mitchell. It seemed, in short, that I would become fit for Robert.

But nearly five months passed, during which I sat around Cinder's kitchen table under Robert's picture, and my face and body remained the same. And then I found one day, that what I'd become fit for was, in fact, something quite other than Robert.

Everything seemed to change on that one day, but really, I think, things had been changing and changing over the course of many previous days, and perhaps what eventually appears to be information always appears at first to be just flotsam, meaningless fragments, until enough flotsam accretes to manifest, when one notices it, a construction. In any case, there was a day when I started out as usual by going uptown to the office where I'd gotten a job as a secretary, and around lunchtime Cinder called. She was at her store, a tiny place around the corner from the apartment, where she sold clothes, some of which were used and some of which she designed and made herself, and she was in a terrible rage, having just had a big set-to with John Paul, a man she was going out with. "Can you come down?" she said. "I need you."

I was always gratified and astonished that it was I in whom Cinder confided and whose help she asked for, but when I arrived at the store that day Mitchell was already there, lying on the couch, and Cinder was laughing. "Charlotte!" Cinder said. "I know what this looks like, but I was an absolute wreck when Mitchell got here—wasn't I, Mitchell?—and he literally glued me back together. You know what we should do, though. I'm absolutely starving. We should get some pirogi. Hey, I've learned this interesting new fact about men. The more weight they make you gain, the more attractive it means they are. God. Why can't I be one of those little twitching things who shred their food when something goes wrong? I wish I were willowy and thin like you, Charlie."

"You are willowy and thin," I said. "I'm bony and big, like a dinosaur skeleton in a museum."

"Dinosaur skeleton." Mitchell centered me slowly in his gaze, and I faltered. "It's been a long, long time since I thought about one of those," he said.

"Mitchell, darling," Cinder said, straddling him to massage his shoulders, "how could I get you to go next door and get us some pirogi? Like three orders, with extra sour cream. I am *ravenous*."

"That stuff I glued you together with sort of absorbed my liquid assets," he said.

"I have money," I said, handing him a ten.

After Mitchell left, Cinder told me about her fight with John Paul. "He called and said he wouldn't be able to go to the concert tomorrow night, and I said why, and he said it was work, but I mean, how could I believe him, after all, Charlie? So he said, right, there was this girl, and then, stupid me, I got just incredibly pissed off, and naturally he ended up saying he didn't think we should see each other anymore. I mean, Charles, I really don't care, you know, about his *girls*. Heaven help us, I'm hardly in a position to complain about that sort of thing. It's just that he makes me feel like some . . . doddering nagging haggy old *wife*. And the worst thing is, though, I think a lot of it has to do, unconsciously, I mean, with revenge. I mean, I bet that what this is really about is Arthur."

"Arthur?" I said.

"Oh, you remember," she said. "That guy I met at that party John Paul and I went to last week. Oh, fabulous," she said to Mitchell, who was walking in with an immense load of pirogi. "But I really don't see how he can get so upset about a thing like Arthur. The guy was boring, he was stupid, and he wasn't particularly attractive, either. In fact, I really don't know why I did it. Just to assert myself, I suppose. Have some pirogi, Charlie." She held one out to me, speared on a plastic fork.

"No, thanks," I said.

"Really?" Cinder said. "Hmm. Mitchell?"

"*No food*," Mitchell said.

"Wow. Well, what are we going to do with all this shit?"

She looked helplessly at the pirogi. "Anyhow, I don't mind that John Paul likes women. I know he likes women."

"Likes women," I felt, was an inexact description. Something happened, even I could see, between John Paul and women, that didn't have all that much to do with what he thought about them. One evening recently, while he and Cinder and I were standing around in the kitchen talking, he rested his hand on my arm, high up, where a slave bracelet goes. Later, in my room, when I got undressed for bed, I looked at the place in a mirror, before I remembered what had caused it to burn like that.

"Oh, get real," Cinder said to a roach that was sauntering across the pirogi. "God. This place is such an ashtray."

"Oh—are you open?" said a girl in a very short skirt, hesitating at the door.

"Definitely," Cinder said. "Come in. Look around. Have some pirogi."

"Well, I don't think I will, really." The girl looked at the plate sidelong. "I'm on a diet. Goodness," she said, drawing nearer, "they're awfully pale. What exactly are they?"

"An acquired taste," Mitchell said, lying back and shutting his eyes again.

The girl looked from one of us to another.

"Well, I suppose all tastes must be acquired, really, musn't they?" I said nervously. "It's a confusing term. To me, at least."

"I've never encountered a taste I haven't acquired in about one microsecond," Cinder said, staring flatly at the girl, who shifted under the scrutiny. "Besides, why are you on a diet? You don't need to lose any weight, does she, Mitchell?"

The girl looked over at Mitchell. He unlidded his green, stranger's eyes and stared at her for a moment before the suggestion of a smile appeared on his face. She began to smile then, too, but bit her lip instead and looked down.

"Everything's half price today," Cinder said.

"Great," the girl said neutrally. She glanced at Mitchell again and then turned her back to us and moved the hangers along the rack with a rhythmic precision. Why were we watching her like that, I wondered. I felt terribly uneasy.

"That peacock-blue one would look really sensational on you," Cinder said.

"Really?" the girl said. "This one?"

"Are you kidding?" Cinder said. "With those legs of yours? The light in the dressing room's broken, but you can just slip it on over there."

"See? That's great," Cinder said. Next to the brilliant blue of the dress, the girl's legs gave off a candied gleam, as if they had never been exposed to the light before.

"It is good," the girl said, watching herself approach the mirror. "But it's very—I don't know if I could really carry it off."

"What you need is something like these with it," Cinder said, putting one of her own earrings to the girl's ear.

"Hmm," the girl agreed to the mirror, with which she had established a private understanding.

"You know what, Cinder," Mitchell said. "You should wear that color yourself." The reflection of Cinder's face floated behind the mirrored girl.

"I really like this dress," the girl said. "It's really good. The only trouble is, I'm looking for something to wear to dinner with my boyfriend's parents."

"I used to have a boyfriend," Cinder said. "Up until about an hour ago."

"Really?" the girl said. "You just broke up with some guy?"

"Broke up," Cinder said. "Fantastic." She related her story to the girl with as much relish as if it were the first time she'd told it. "He says he doesn't even care about me," Cinder said.

"He said he didn't care about you?" I asked.

"Well, that's what he meant," Cinder said.

"But maybe he meant something else," I said.

"I know what he meant, Charlotte. I know the guy. When you're in love with someone, you know what they're saying to you."

"That's terrible," the girl said, looking at Cinder round-eyed. "That happened to *me* once."

"So you understand," Cinder said.

"Oh, God," the girl said. "I really do."

Cinder stepped back and looked at her for a long moment. "I'd really like you to get that dress," she said finally. "You'd be a fantastic advertisement for my stuff. But let's face it. I mean, your boyfriend's parents! They'd have you out the back door in a couple of seconds, bound and gagged."

"Well," the girl said, looking into the mirror.

"Look." Cinder turned to me. "Would you wear that dress to your boyfriend's parents', Charlie?"

"What about you?" the girl said to Mitchell. "How would you react if I showed up in this dress?"

"I'd run amok," Mitchell said, lying immobile on the couch, his eyes closed. "I'd go totally out of control."

"See, I might as well, though," the girl said, examining the mirror again. "Jeff wouldn't care. Actually, his parents are fairly nauseating people anyway. In fact, his sister just cracked up. She tried to stab her husband with her nail scissors, and they had her put away. Anyhow, if I don't use it for dinner I can always wear it someplace else."

"Oh, shit, though," Cinder said. "I just remembered. That's the one with the crooked seam."

"Where?" the girl said. "I don't see it."

"Well, I wouldn't want anybody wearing it around. Listen, come back next week. I'll be making up some more, and I've got this incredible bronzy-brown that would be really good on you."

"Well, I really like this blue, though," the girl said.

"Yeah, but I'm out of that, unfortunately," Cinder said.

"What a sweet kid," Cinder said after the girl left. "And wasn't she pretty? I really hope she doesn't get hurt."

"Sweet!" Mitchell said, and snorted. "No!" he shrieked, twisting, as Cinder leapt onto the couch to tickle him. "Much too stoned!"

"You are such a cynic!" Cinder said. "Isn't he, Charlie?"

"Yes," I said. "Cinder—how did you know that girl would look good in that dress?" I asked.

"Well, that's interesting," she said, releasing Mitchell to devote her full attention to this question. "See, I always know. I'm always right about how people look, and how they're going to look in different things. That is, if they're worth looking at in the first place. And the horrible truth is, I can do that because I'm such a jealous person!"

"What do you mean?" I said.

"No, it's true," she said. "Really. My jealousy is a tool for looking at other people, and now John Paul is my special, sort of, lens. I look at other women through his eyes, and I know what it is in them that he would find attractive. It's awful. I'm completely subjugated to his vision."

"But, Cinder," I said. "It's a wonderful talent!"

"It's not a talent, Charlotte," she said, "it's an *affliction*." She looked furious.

"Cinder," I said after a moment. "Could we—do me up sometime? Make me look—I don't know, like that girl?"

"Oh, you don't want to look like that girl, Charlie, honey. Mitchell's right. She was a boring little thing. You don't want to look like everybody else anyhow. You've got your own looks."

"I know," I said. "But could we fix them?"

"You've got incredible potential, you know, Charlie," Cinder said. "I could spend hours on you. Sure, O.K., we'll do the whole thing—clothes, face, hair—"

"Don't do anything to her hair." Mitchell's voice floated into our conversation with an otherworldly pallor. "It's soft."

"Soft, yeah, but it's got to get cut or something," Cinder said.

"Like Big Bird," Mitchell added faintly.

"He's asleep," Cinder said.

"Cinder," I said, "could I try on that blue dress?"

"Oh, let's not get into it today, Charlie," she said. "I'm so destroyed. You must be exhausted yourself—I've kept you for hours. Mitchell, would you take me out to get drunk and disgusting? Then maybe you could take advantage of me, if you could stand it." Mitchell's eyes remained closed. "Oh, never mind," Cinder said. "That was a joke."

"Well, goodbye." I stood up. "See you at home later."

"They need any extra roaches at your office?" Cinder asked. At our feet, the plate of pirogi swarmed.

When I got back to the office, I just sat and sat and my mind kept wandering back to the store. Why was I so sad? After all, Cinder had said I was more interesting than that gleaming girl.

"Hands off!" a voice said suddenly from behind me.

"Oh, hi, Mr. Bunder," I said, noticing that my hands were in my hair. Well, it *was* soft.

"You look to be, say, in orbit." As Mr. Bunder sat down on a corner of my desk, the fabric of his trousers pulled against his thigh. It looked extremely uncomfortable, but I couldn't stop staring at it.

"Not concentrating, I guess," I said.

"Listen." He leaned in toward me. "Want to get something to drink?"

"Right now?" I asked. He had a pinkish, stippled look, as if he'd just gotten something to drink.

We settled down side by side in a booth near the bar. "So you're worried about your roommate, huh," he said.

"Yes," I said. "Well, not exactly." How hard it was to figure out how to say anything to anyone! "Well, actually, though," I said, "she does get these terrible headaches, but I think they're from tension in her back. She's upset about a man she's been going out with."

"Well, maybe I'll come over and check it out. I give a bad back rub." Mr. Bunder poked me on the arm. "But seriously," he said. "There are a lot of hard-noses out there. They get some poor little girl going—it gives them a big boost in the ego department. Then they see something maybe a bit better. Some knockout just sitting at the bar licking her chops. Beautiful women going begging in this city. Dime a dozen." He kept looking around the room. I wondered if I was sitting too far away from him and he was feeling insulted. On the other hand, perhaps I was sitting too close to him and he was feeling embarrassed.

"I'll get us a couple more of these," he said. "You like the olives, huh?" He held his olive in front of my mouth and I ate it, like a seal. For a moment, I was terribly hungry, but then I thought of the roach-capped pirogi, and I lost my appetite.

"So what brought you to New York?" he asked.

"Well . . ." I said. What had brought me to New York? "I split up with someone in Buffalo."

"Busted marriage, huh?" Mr. Bunder said. "Too bad."

"Oh, no. It wasn't a marriage. We were just trying it out." I searched my mind for something that would be interesting to Mr. Bunder. "He was an assistant professor." Mr. Bunder blinked. "Well, not that that has anything to do with it," I said. "But we weren't very compatible."

"Guess not," Mr. Bunder said. He sighed, looking around, and tapped with his glass on the table.

"Have you ever been married?" I asked, to be polite.

"Have I?" Mr. Bunder said. "Yeah. I have. I'm married right now." I wondered if I should leave. Mr. Bunder didn't seem to be having a very good time.

"You know," he said, perking up. "You look a little like that what's-her-name—Meryl Streep. You know that? Around the—the—mouth, or something. Olive! Olive!" He held his olive in front of me, but I was committed just then to pushing a little globule of water on the table from one side of my glass around to the other without breaking it up.

"What's the matter?" he said. "Need another drink?"

"No, thank you, I'm already drunk," I said, surprised. "I'm sweating."

"Terrific," Mr. Bunder said. "Well, maybe you want to go sweat at home. Check up on that little roommate of yours. I'll get you into a taxi before you fall over."

"Thank you, Mr. Bunder," I said outside.

"Call me Dickie, would you?" he said. "When you girls say 'Mr. Bunder,' I think you're talking to my father."

I had trouble getting past Mr. Bunder to climb into the taxi he'd hailed for me. Or perhaps he was planning to get into it, too. "Did you want to share this someplace?" I asked.

"Thanks, honey," he said, "but I think I'll hang around here for a while. See if any of the ladies at the bar is interested in an evening of fudge packing."

It had been nice of Mr. Bunder to ask me to join him. He must have seen that I was lonely, too. I felt sorry for him as I watched him go back into the restaurant by himself. He looked so pink and tender in his bristly little suit, and from behind he seemed to move choppily, as if propelled by warring impulses, like a truffle hound going back to work after a noon break.

"Where have you been, Charles?" Cinder said to me. "I've been desperate."

"I was having a drink with Mr. Bunder," I said.

"Mr. Bunder!" she said. "Do people still name their kids Mister? Oh, right. He's one of those cowpats you work for, isn't he?"

"Yes," I said. "Well, I mean . . . . Oh—Cinder, does 'fudge packing' mean something?"

"What? How should I know?" she said. "Christ, where do you hear this vile shit? Anyhow, listen. I really need your help. If you'd come half an hour later, you probably would have found me in a pool of blood with a machete between my ribs." She looked at me blankly for a moment. "Between my ribs? Is that what people say? It sounds wrong. 'Between my ribs,' 'among my ribs'—doesn't 'between my ribs' make it sound like you've only got two ribs? It's like people say 'between my teeth'—'I've got something caught between my teeth'—and it sounds like they've only got two teeth. I think you should say, 'I've got something caught *among* my teeth.' Well, no, that doesn't work, either, does it, because you can really only get something caught—oh, weird—*between two teeth!*"

"Cinder," I said, "what happened?"

"What?" she said. "Oh."

It seemed she had called John Paul back, and he'd agreed to come over, but then she'd remembered she already had a date with someone else.

"Oh," I said, and looked at her. "So why don't you call John Paul and say you made a mistake—tell him you can't see him tonight?"

"Charlotte," Cinder said. "We're talking John Paul here."

"Well . . ." I said. "What about the other guy? Could you call him?"

"Hmm. I didn't think of that," she said. "But anyhow I don't know how to reach him. I don't even know his name."

"You don't know his name?"

"He's just some guy I met on the street," she said. "Some Puerto Rican or something."

As we looked at each other, concentrating hard, the doorbell rang.

I crouched next to Cinder at the door, where she was peering through a crack. She plucked me back, but I'd seen a very young man, dark and graceful, in a crisp shirt. "Shit," Cinder whispered.

"How many years before someone is older than someone else?" I wrote on a little pad of paper we kept for lists.

"4 if yr a man 2 if yr a wman," Cinder wrote back. "But so wht?"

We sat absolutely still under Robert's photographed happiness while the footsteps outside the door continued back and forth and the doorbell rang again, and then, as Cinder and I stared at each other in horror, a second set of footsteps mounted the stairs. But it was Mitchell who spoke, not John Paul, and Cinder and I both let out our breath.

"Hey," Mitchell said. "Something I can help you with?"

"I'm a friend of Cinder's," the stranger said. "I was supposed to see her tonight, but she doesn't seem to be home."

"That's weird," Mitchell said, as Cinder muffled a gasp behind her hands. "She said she'd be in all evening."

"Well, if you see her," the other voice said, "tell her Hector was here."

I peeked out and watched the men walk together toward the stairs. How nice men were with each other, how frail and trusting, I was thinking, and just then an explosion of hilarity escaped from behind Cinder's hands, and the two men halted and turned back toward the door in perfect synchronization. "What was that?" Hector said.

After a moment of utter motionlessness on both sides of the door, the two men began to discuss the possibilities of marauders, gas leaks, and overdoses, and Mitchell decided to climb over the roof and down the fire escape into Cinder's room. "If I don't open the door for you in about fifteen minutes," he said to Hector, "just chop it down, I guess, or something."

Cinder and I scrambled silently back to her room. "This is a catastrophe," she said.

"Yes," I said. "It is."

"Mitchell is so sweet, isn't he, though," she said, "to go up over the roof like that. It's pretty hard. He did it once before, when I flushed my keys down the toilet at some ridiculous party."

"How did you do that?" I asked.

"Well," she said. "I mean, it wasn't on purpose. But he's the sort of person that would do that sort of thing."

"I don't think he'd climb over any roofs for me," I said.

"Mitchell isn't nice to you?" she said. "God. If I ever saw him not being nice to you, I'd beat him senseless. Oh, I mean, I know he can be sort of a snot sometimes," she said, "like a lot of those really great-looking men. It's not like women, you know. We're brought up to be able to handle being beautiful, but those really beautiful guys are brought up like hothouse flowers, and they're not taught what to do with all that stuff. They just get superaware of all that potential for, you know, damage, and they get sort of wooden. A lot of them can't even speak to a woman who isn't absolutely gorgeous herself. It's sort of like rich people, or people who are famous— they like their friends to be rich or famous, too, so that everyone understands everyone else on a certain level and no one has to worry about anyone else's motives."

Usually I enjoyed learning things from Cinder, but today everything she said made me feel worse. It wasn't fair of her, I thought, to call Mr. Bunder a cowpat without knowing him. Of course, she would have called him a cowpat even if she did know him. Robert would have called him a cowpat, too. Well, except that Robert would think that cowpat was a stupid thing to call someone. And actually, come to think of it, Robert wouldn't like Cinder one bit, either. And Cinder wouldn't like Robert. Well, Mr. Bunder was always nice to me.

"And men like Mitchell just worry and worry, you know?" Cinder was saying. "They're afraid they'll either be contaminated or unmasked if they get too near a woman who isn't beautiful. They're afraid their own beauty is all they have, and that it isn't really worth anything anyhow, and that it misrepresents their real inner disgustingness, and that they're going to lose it—all that stuff. Thank God John Paul isn't like that! He just loves being beautiful. He thinks he *deserves* to be beautiful, and it's like he's got this big present for anyone who happens to be around—drunks on the corner, women with baby carriages, the grocer."

The little claim John Paul had staked on my arm asserted itself again, just as, with a huge thud, Mitchell climbed in the window. "Oh, don't get up," he said. "I was just passing by."

"I'm really sorry, Mitchell," Cinder said. "I'll explain all of this later, but right now please, please get out there immediately and grab that kid before he does something really dumb."

"When is John Paul supposed to get here?" I asked when Cinder had dispatched Mitchell.

"Pretty soon. Now, to be precise. But he's always late," she said. "Actually, he probably won't come at all."

"Oh, I'm sure he will," I said. I would have liked to put an arm around Cinder, as she so easily did with me when I talked about Robert, but I could only sit there next to her with my hands in my lap.

"You know," she said, "I think I've just figured out why men treat me so badly. It's karma. I really think it is."

I could figure out a few things about men myself, I thought. I could figure out, for instance, that men who said you looked a little like Meryl Streep meant that they didn't find you attractive but they thought someone else might. And I could figure out that men who said you looked like Big Bird or a dinosaur skeleton didn't think anyone would find you attractive.

"You're lucky that you're so nice," Cinder said. "Men are going to treat you really well in your next life."

"You know what?" I said after a moment. "I think Mitchell and Hector are in the kitchen."

"Jesus," Cinder said. "You're right! What on earth is Mitchell doing, that maniac!"

"Does he know that John Paul's supposed to come over?" I asked.

"Good point. I guess I didn't get a chance to mention it." She sucked air in through her teeth. "Well, Charles," she said. "It's up to you now."

"No!" I said. "What do you mean? I can't!"

"You've got to, Charlotte," Cinder said.

I shut Cinder's door carefully behind me and explained to the two men who were sitting comfortably at the table drinking beer that Cinder needed to be left utterly alone. "She says she feels like—like—there's a machete in her head."

"Probably a brain tumor," Mitchell said, taking a sip of his beer.

"Should we call a doctor?" Hector said to me. He looked more solid at close range than he had out in the hall. He must have been twenty or twenty-one. "Or take her to the hospital?"

"No," I said. "I mean, this happens all the time. The only thing to do is let her rest."

"Well, I guess so. Listen—" Hector said. He wrote something on a piece of paper and handed it to me. "Here's my phone number. Could you ask her please to give me a call sometime when she's feeling better?"

Downstairs, Mitchell nodded and walked off, leaving me to go in the opposite direction with Hector. I wanted to say good night to Hector, but we were in the middle of the block, so if I did say good night I would have to continue with him afterward, which would seem peculiar, or else I would have to turn and go back in the direction from which we'd just come, which would seem . . . well, also peculiar. So I decided I would say good night at the corner.

At the corner, Hector turned to me. "Want to get something to eat?"

Something to eat! I was just walking with him to get him out of the apartment! "I guess not," I said. I turned to face him. "Thanks anyway . . . I really am hungry."

"Well," Hector said, "come on, then. There's a good place a couple of blocks away."

What was it that Puerto Ricans ate, I wondered as I walked along beside Hector, but the restaurant we entered was Italian, with pictures of harbors and flowers and entertainers overlapping on the walls, and cloths and glass-stoppered bottles of dark wine on the tables, around which sat large men and handsome, glistening women, all talking and laughing. It seemed, in fact, as if each table were a little boat, bobbing along on the hubbub of pleasure.

Hector and I were seated at our own table, and Hector got us outfitted with glasses for the wine, and a huge platter of vegetables—a whole fried harvest—and I felt that we ourselves had pulled anchor and were setting off like the others into that open expanse.

But then I was staring straight at a gold chain Hector wore. How had I come to be here with this person, I wondered. Yet the links lay flat along his neck, as sleek and secure as a stripe on some strange animal. "I'm sorry about Cinder," I said.

Hector glanced away from me. "Everyone gets headaches at one time or another."

What did he mean? "Actually," I said, "I have a headache myself now. It must be because I got drunk this afternoon."

"This afternoon?" Hector said.

"It was a mistake," I said.

"Oh," he said. "So was that Cinder's boyfriend?"

"Oh, heavens, no," I said. "Mitchell's just a friend. Actually, I never really thought about it before, but I suppose he is really quite attracted to Cinder. But you know what?" The words were forming themselves before I had a chance to think about them. "I don't think he's interested in women. I mean, in being involved with them." Why had I said such a thing? Hector would want to talk about Cinder, not Mitchell.

"I had a cousin like that," Hector said. "He liked girls pretty well, but he didn't want any girlfriends. He didn't like other boys, like a lot of boys do. But he wore drag all the time. Pretty dresses, silk underwear, you know? He was very nice. Everybody liked him, but he was about the strangest one in my family."

The waiter moved our vegetables over to make room for vast dishes of spaghetti and sausage.

"What happened to him?" I asked. "Your cousin."

"Oh, he's O.K.," Hector said. "He grew out of it. It was just a teenage thing for him. But he still doesn't go out much with girls. Hey, this stuff is good, isn't it? He teaches physical education in Pittsburgh now."

We took a long time with our spaghetti, while Hector told me more about his family. It sounded as if they were fond of each other. And he told me about an information-theory class he was taking. "Are you studying?" he asked me.

"I'm finished now. I'm a lot older than you." I looked straight at Hector. I wanted to make sure he understood that I wasn't trying to make him think that I was his age, that the fact that he was a lot younger than I was was of no interest to me. It was Robert, after all, I wasn't good enough for.

"Dessert and coffee?" the waiter asked before Hector could respond. "Or have you lost your appetite?"

"That's right." Hector gestured toward my plate as the waiter cleared it away. "You did pretty good, for a girl."

When we were finished, Hector asked, "So do you like to go dancing?"

For an instant, Robert commandeered the air in front of me. He sat with his feet on his desk, leaning back and smiling. "Flattered?" he asked.

"Oh, no!" I said.

"Too bad," Hector said. "I know a good place uptown."

"No." I got to my feet quickly. "I didn't mean I didn't want to go dancing—I meant I didn't not want to go dancing." I was breathing hard as I looked at him, as if I'd run to catch up with him.

"That's what you meant, huh?" he said. "Far out." But he grinned as he stood, and he stretched, letting one arm fall around me in a comradely manner.

Oh, it felt good to dance. I hadn't gone dancing since Robert and I had started being unhappy. Hector knew a lot of people in the place we'd come to, and we stopped and talked with them. They spoke to Hector in Spanish, but when Hector put a defending hand on my shoulder and answered in English everyone else switched into English, too, except for a tiny dark star of a girl who continued in Spanish with Hector in a husky baby voice. "Her cousin in Queens has a '62 Corvette that I want," Hector told me. "And she says he's thinking about selling it to me."

He bought us Cokes and finished his own in one motion, while I watched his head tilt back and his throat work. "You don't do drugs?" I said.

"I stay away from that stuff, mostly." He looked very serious. "It seems like you can do a lot of things behind it, but that's an illusion, see. I had a good friend, a heavy user, who died. Everyone thought he was a very happy guy. You see people, you talk to them—their faces say one thing, you never know what's inside." For a moment, he seemed almost incandescent, but then he smiled impatiently toward the room, laying aside his trustful seriousness. "Anyhow," he said, "I like to keep in shape." The gold around his neck winked, and I looked away quickly.

"Excuse me," I said. "I'll be back in a minute." I fought through the dancers and sat down near the wall. When I closed my eyes, I felt private for a moment, but when I opened them I was looking straight into the whole, huge crowd, right to where Hector was standing, listening attentively to the tiny dark girl. He looked dignified and brotherly as she smiled up at him, but then, suddenly, he flared into a laugh of pure appreciation.

In the ladies' room, I held a wet paper towel against my forehead while a herd of girls jostled and giggled around me. Keep in shape, I thought. What had that meant! Had I been expected to admire him? Who was Hector, anyway? What on earth did he think I was doing there with him? Did he think I was attracted to him? And why had I chattered on with him so during dinner? He was just some kid my roommate had picked up on the street! I was wearing, the mirror reminded me, the same nasty office dress I'd been wearing when I sat next to Mr. Bunder light-years earlier in the day. Hector belonged with that girl who was flirting with him, or with Cinder, not with me, and I knew that just as much as he could ever know that, and if he had wanted to prove something to, or because of, Cinder, he had certainly picked the wrong person to prove it with.

When I got to the exit I glanced back and saw Hector in the throng, struggling toward me. And although because of the music I couldn't hear him, I could see that he was calling my name. I stood in the cool air outside and closed the door slowly against the throbbing room, watching, like a scientist watching the demise of an experiment, as Hector's expression changed from surprise to consternation to . . . what? Was he enraged? Affronted? Relieved?

On the subway, I thought how if Hector had been there with me, if we had been heading downtown together, tired out from dancing, we would have looked aligned. His restful, measuring regard as he leaned back against the wall of the car would have been matched by mine, and our arms would have been close enough so that I could feel the dissipating heat from his against my much paler, thinner one.

There was a group of girls balancing at one of the car's center poles. They were slight and black-haired, like the girl Hector had been talking to, and like her they had long, brilliant nails. Their wrists were marvelously fragile, and their feet, in shiny leather, were like little hooves. I had never asked to compete with such girls, I thought, fuming.

I wanted to be alone when I got back to the apartment, but Mitchell was in the kitchen, pushing something around on a little hand mirror with a straw, and Cinder was lying on the floor in the peacock-blue dress.

"The dress with the bad seam!" I said.

"Madame wishes another snootful?" Mitchell asked, offering Cinder the mirror.

"Christ, no." Cinder turned over and groaned. "What is that stuff, anyhow?"

"Drug du jour," Mitchell said. "It was on sale."

"Oh, Mitchell, Jesus," she said. Mitchell had been right. She looked even better in that dress than the girl in the store had.

"Charlie," she said, turning to me. I could see that she had been crying. "Listen. Let me ask you something. Do men always tell you that you're really great in bed? That you're the best?"

Only an instant escaped before I knew what to answer. "Always," I said. "They always say that."

"They are so sick," she said. "What a bunch of sickos."

"Guess you had a bad time with John Paul," I said, even though I really didn't want to hear about it.

"That about sums it up," she said. "See that stuff on the floor? That used to be my gorgeous ceramic bowl. I really wish you'd been here, Charlie. I needed you."

"I was needed by you elsewhere," I said. "Remember Hector?"

"Hector?" she said. "What were you doing with Hector?"

"What was I doing with Hector?" I said. "How should I know what I was doing with Hector! I was doing you a favor, that's what I was doing with Hector!"

"Charlie," Cinder said. "What's the matter? Are you mad at me?"

"I'm not mad at you," I said. "Just don't call me that name, please. It's a man's name. My name is Charlotte."

"Come on," Cinder said. "Let's have it. Tell Cinder why you've got a hair across your ass."

"I do not have a hair across my ass," I said. "Whatever that means. I do not have a hair across my ass in any way. It's just that I got Hector out of here so you could see John Paul and then you don't even say, 'Thank you, Charlotte. I really appreciate that.'"

"Thank you, Charlotte. I really appreciate that," Cinder said. "Charlie—Sorry. Charlotte. Listen. You're my best friend. What point would there be in my saying, 'Oh, thank you,

Charlotte,' every time you did anything for me? You do thousands of things for me."

"Well," I said.

"Just like I do thousands of things for you. I mean, you know that I do things for you because I care about you and because I want to, not because I feel like I have to or because I want you to owe me anything. So you don't have to say, 'Thank you, Cinder, for letting me come live with you when I had no place else to go . . . Thank you, Cinder, for dragging me around with you everywhere and introducing me to all your friends.' I know you feel gratitude toward me, just like I feel gratitude toward you. But that's not the point."

"Well, I know," I said. What point? "But still."

"And anyhow," she said, "I did ask you to get that guy out of the apartment, but I didn't ask you to spend the rest of your life with him. What did you do, anyhow?"

"We had dinner," I said.

"Dinner! How hilarious!"

"I don't see why," I said. "People eat dinner every night. Besides, I had to do something with him. And then"—oh, so what, I thought—"we went dancing."

"Oh, unbelievable!" Cinder said. "I can just see it. One of those places full of little Latino girls in pressed jeans and heels, boys covered with jewelry . . ."

"That's—" I said. "That's—" I tried to seize the sensation that rippled under my hand, of gold against Hector's skin as he drank his Coke and laughed with the girl, but the sensation dried, leaving me with only the empty image.

"One of those places where everyone does this super-structured dancing, one of those places with putrid airwave rock . . ." Cinder said.

"One of those places where everyone's bilingual," I said. "Besides, you were going to go out with him yourself."

"Go out with him, yeah, but not, like, necessarily into public. I mean, God, Charlie—Charlotte—you were so nice to him!"

"Actually," I said, and a thought froze me where I stood, "he was nice to me." I looked at Cinder in horror, seeing the distress on Hector's face as I'd shut the door against him and the roomful of dancers. "He was nice to me, and I just left him there."

"Well," Cinder said. "He'll live."

"I might have hurt his feelings," I said. "It was a mean thing to do."

"Well, it wasn't really mean," Cinder said. "Besides, you're right. It was me he asked out, not you."

My brain started to revolve inside my skull, tumbling its inventory. "I'm going to call him and apologize," I said, rummaging through my pocket for the piece of paper with his number on it.

"God," Cinder said, looking at me. "He gave you his number?"

"To tell you the truth—" I said. And then I couldn't say anything else for several seconds. "He gave me his number for you. He wanted you to call him."

"Charlotte," Cinder said, rolling over. "You liked him."

"He's a perfectly nice man," I snapped. "I neither liked nor disliked him."

"Man?" Cinder said. "He's probably just barely gone through some puberty rite where he had to spear a sow or something."

"Don't be ridiculous," I said. "He's studying computer engineering. And you know what, Cinder? You're a racist—"

"Racist!" she said. "Now, where is *that* coming from?"

"That's right," I said, "you think you can say these idiotic things about him because he's a Puerto Rican. You don't take him seriously because he's a Puerto Rican—"

"It is not because he's a Puerto Rican!" she said.

"Not because he's a Puerto Rican," Mitchell echoed, and Cinder and I swiveled at the sound of his voice. "Not because he's a Puerto Rican. Because he's *like* a Puerto Rican. He's a Cuban."

"Cuban!" Cinder and I said in unison.

"At least, that's what he told me," Mitchell said. "When we were waiting for Cinder." Mitchell's eyes moved from Cinder to me and back again while we stared at him. His face looked white and slippery, like a bathroom tile. "Hector," he said finally. "You mean the guy who was here before. The Cuban."

"The Cuban!" Cinder whooped. "That's right—the Cuban, Charlie! Who's the racist now, huh?"

"Why don't you get off the floor?" I said. "You're getting stuff all over that dress."

"Come on, Charlotte," Cinder said, but she stood up, and for an instant she looked terribly uncertain. "I really don't see why you're getting so crazy about this. This is just *funny*."

Funny, I thought. It was funny.

But it wasn't that funny. "There isn't a thing wrong with that dress, is there?" I said. "Besides—" I took a breath. "Hector didn't think I looked like a dinosaur skeleton—"

"Dinosaur skeleton?" Cinder said. "What on earth are you talking about, Charlotte? Why would anybody think you look like a dinosaur skeleton? I really don't know what your problem is. You act like everyone's trying to kill you. You sit there with your mouth open and your finger in your nose like you don't know anything and you can't understand anything and you can't do anything and you want me to tell you what's going on all the time. But that's not what you want at all. You don't really care what I think. You don't care what Mitchell thinks. You just like to make people think you're completely pathetic, and then everyone feels absolutely horrible so you don't really have to pay any attention to anybody. You're like one of those things that hang upside down from trees pretending to be dead so no one will shoot it! You're an awful friend!"

I stared at Cinder.

Good heavens, yes.

But it was too late for me to do anything about being a bad friend. I stared and stared at Cinder's unhappy little face, and then I grabbed my suitcase from the closet and started sweeping things into it from the shelves. Oh, and Mr. Bunder! Hector! Cinder was right. I flooded with shame.

"Charlotte—" Cinder said, but there was nothing else I needed to know, and I scooped my stuff off the shelves and threw it into my suitcase as if I'd been visited by a power. "Charlotte—I'm sorry. I just meant you have a low self-opinion. You should try to be more positive about yourself."

"You'd better see if Mitchell's all right," I said, glancing around to see if there was anything I'd forgotten. "I don't think he is."

"Mitchell," Cinder said, "are you all right?"

"I just don't feel like talking right now," Mitchell said.

"Oh, great," Cinder said. "What a great evening. One friend crashing around like Joan Crawford, and the other fried to a fucking crisp. Come on, Charlotte. Just let's calm down and put your stuff away. John Paul will probably show up any minute to apologize, and he hates a mess."

And, Lord—I'd almost forgotten my photograph of Robert. What was it doing up there anyway—as if he were the president of some company? I yanked it from the wall with both hands, and it tore in half. "Oh, Charlotte," Cinder said. But, to my surprise, I didn't care. Robert had never looked like that picture anyhow. That was how I'd wanted him to look, but he hadn't looked like that.

"O.K., everyone," Cinder said. "Let's just be like normal people now, O.K.? Let's just relax and have a beer or something. Beer, Mitchell?" she asked, holding a bottle out to him, but he seemed to be listening for a distant signal.

"Charlotte," she said. "Beer?" But I, too, was busy elsewhere, and I didn't turn when she said, "Shit. Well, cheers," to see her tilt back the bottle herself, trying to make it look as if everything were completely under control. Well, she could try to make it look like that, she could try to make anything look like anything she wanted, but right then I just wanted everything to look like itself, whatever it might be. And I remember so clearly that moment, standing there astride my suitcase, with a part of that photograph of Robert in each hand, my legs trembling and my heart racing with a dark exultation, as if I'd just, in the grace of an instant, been thrown wide of some mortal danger.

WHAT IT WAS LIKE, SEEING CHRIS

While I sit with all the other patients in the waiting room, I always think that I will ask Dr. Wald what exactly is happening to my eyes, but when I go into his examining room alone it is dark, with a circle of light on the wall, and the doctor is standing with his back to me arranging silver instruments on a cloth. The big chair is empty for me to go sit in, and each time then I feel as if I have gone into a dream straight from being awake, the way you do sometimes at night, and I go to the chair without saying anything.

The doctor prepares to look at my eyes through a machine. I put my forehead and chin against the metal bands and look into the tiny ring of blue light while the doctor dabs quickly at my eye with something, but my head starts to feel numb, and I have to lift it back. "Sorry," I say. I shake my head and put it back against the metal. Then I stare into the blue light and try to hold my head still and to convince myself that there is no needle coming toward my eye, that my eye is not anesthetized.

"Breathe," Dr. Wald says. "Breathe." But my head always goes numb again, and I pull away, and Dr. Wald has to wait for me to resettle myself against the machine. "Nervous today, Laurel?" he asks, not interested.

One Saturday after I had started going to Dr. Wald, Maureen and I walked around outside our old school. We dangled on the little swings with our knees bunched while the dry leaves blew around us, and Maureen told me she was sleeping with Kevin. Kevin is a sophomore, and to me he had seemed much older than we were when we'd begun high school in September. "What is it like?" I asked.

"Fine." Maureen shrugged. "Who do you like these days, anyhow? I notice you haven't been talking much about Dougie."

"No one," I said. Maureen stopped her swing and looked at me with one eyebrow raised, so I told her—although I was sorry as soon as I opened my mouth—that I'd met someone in the city.

"In the city?" she said. Naturally she was annoyed. "How did you get to meet someone in the city?"

It was just by accident, I told her, because of going to the eye doctor, and anyway it was not some big thing. That was what I told Maureen, but I remembered the first time I had seen Chris as surely as if it were a stone I could hold in my hand.

It was right after my first appointment with Dr. Wald. I had taken the train into the city after school, and when the doctor was finished with me I was supposed to take a taxi to my sister Penelope's dancing school, which was on the east side of the Park, and do homework there until Penelope's class was over and Mother picked us up. Friends of my parents ask me if I want to be a dancer, too, but they are being polite.

Across the street from the doctor's office, I saw a place called Jake's. I stared through the window at the long shining bar and mirrors and round tables, and it seemed to me I would never be inside a place like that, but then I thought how much I hated sitting outside Penelope's class and how much I hated the doctor's office, and I opened the door and walked right in.

I sat down at a table near the wall, and I ordered a Coke. I looked around at all the people with their glasses of colored liquids, and I thought how happy they were—vivid and free and sort of the same, as if they were playing.

I watched the bartender as he gestured and talked. He was really putting on a show telling a story to some people I could only see from the back. There was a man with shiny, straight hair that shifted like a curtain when he laughed, and a man with curly blond hair, and between them a girl in a fluffy sweater. The men—or boys (I couldn't tell, and still don't know)—wore shirts with seams on the back that curved up from their belts to their shoulders. I watched their shirts, and I watched in the mirror behind the bar as their beautiful goldish faces settled from laughing. I looked at them in the mirror, and I particularly noticed the one with the shiny hair, and I watched his eyes get like crescents, as if he were listening to another story, but then I saw he was smiling. He was smiling into the mirror in front of him, and in the mirror I was just staring, staring at him, and he was smiling back into the mirror at me.

The next week I went back to Dr. Wald for some tests, and when I was finished, although I'd planned to go do homework at Penelope's dancing school, I went straight to Jake's instead. The same two men were at the bar, but a different girl was with them. I pretended not to notice them as I went to the table I had sat at before.

I had a Coke, and when I went up to the bar to pay, the one with the shiny hair turned right around in front of me.

"Clothes-abuse squad," he said, prizing my wadded-up coat out of my arms. He shook it out and smiled at me. "I'm Chris," he said, "and this is Mark." His friend turned to me like a soldier who has been waiting, but the girl with them only glanced at me and turned to talk to someone else.

Chris helped me into my coat, and then he buttoned it up, as if I were a little child. "Who are you?" he said.

"Laurel," I said.

Chris nodded slowly. "Laurel," he said. And when he said that, I felt a shock on my face and hands and front as if I had pitched against flat water.

"So you are going out with this guy, or what?" Maureen asked me.

"Maureen," I said. "He's just a person I met." Maureen looked at me again, but I just looked back at her. We twisted our swings up and let ourselves twirl out.

"So what's the matter with your eyes?" Maureen said. "Can't you just wear glasses?"

"Well, the doctor said he couldn't tell exactly what was wrong yet," I said. "He says he wants to keep me under observation, because there might be something happening to my retina." But I realized then that I didn't understand what that meant at all, and I also realized that I was really, but really, scared.

Maureen and I wandered over to the school building and looked in the window of the fourth-grade room, and I thought how strange it was that I used to fit in those miniature chairs, and that a few years later Penelope did, and that my little brother, Paul, fit in them now. There was a sickly old turtle in an aquarium on the sill just like the one we'd had. I wondered if it was the same one. I think they're sort of prehistoric, and some of them live to be a hundred or two hundred years old.

"I bet your mother is completely hysterical," Maureen said.

I smiled. Maureen thinks it's hilarious the way my mother expects everything in her life (*her* life) to be perfect. "I had to bring her with me last week," I said.

"Ick," Maureen said sympathetically, and I remembered how awful it had been, sitting and waiting next to Mother. Whenever Mother moved—to cross her legs or smooth out her skirt or pick up a magazine—the clean smell of her perfume came over to me. Mother's perfume made a nice little space for her there in the stale office. We didn't talk at all, and it seemed like a long time before an Asian woman took me into a small white room and turned off the light. The woman had a serious face, like an angel, and she wore a white hospital coat over her clothes. She didn't seem to speak much English. She sat me down in front of something which looked like a map of planets drawn in white on black, hanging on the wall.

The woman moved a wand across the map, and the end of the wand glimmered. "You say when you see light," she told me. In the silence I made myself say "Now" over and over as I saw the light blinking here and there upon the planet map. Finally the woman turned on the light in the room and smiled at me. She rolled up the map and put it with the wand into a cupboard.

"Where are you from?" I asked her, to shake off the sound of my voice saying "Now."

She hesitated, and I felt sick, because I thought I had said something rude, but finally the meaning of the question seemed to reach her. "Japanese," she said. She put the back of her hand against my hair. "Very pretty," she said. "Very pretty."

Then Dr. Wald looked at my eyes, and after that Mother and I were brought into his consulting room. We waited, facing the huge desk, and eventually the doctor walked in. There was just a tiny moment when he saw Mother, but then he sat right down and explained, in a sincere, televisionish voice I had never heard him use before, that he wanted to see me once a month. He told my mother there might or might not be "cause for concern," and he spoke right to her, with a little frown as she looked down at her clasped hands. Men always get important like that when they're talking to her, and she and the doctor both looked extra serious, as if they were reminding themselves that it was me they were talking about, not each other. While Mother scheduled me for the last week of each month (on Thursday because of Penelope's class), the cross-looking receptionist seemed to be figuring out how much Mother's clothes cost.

When Mother and I parked in front of Penelope's dancing school, Penelope was just coming out with some of the other girls. They were in jeans, but they all had their hair still pulled up tightly on top of their heads, and Penelope had the floaty, peaceful look she gets after class. Mother smiled at her and waved, but then she looked suddenly at me. "Poor Laurel," she said. Tears had come into her eyes, and answering tears sprang into my own, but mine were tears of unexpected rage. I saw how pleased Mother was, thinking that we were having that moment together, but what I was thinking, as we looked at each other, was that even though I hadn't been able to go to Jake's that afternoon because of her, at least now I would be able to go back once a month and see Chris.

"And all week," I told Maureen, "Mother has been saying I got it from my father's family, and my father says it's glaucoma in his family and his genes have nothing to do with retinas."

"Really?" Maureen asked. "Is something wrong with your dad?"

Maureen is always talking about my father and saying how "attractive" he is. If she only knew the way he talks about her! When she comes over, he sits down and tells her jokes. A few weeks ago when she came by for me, he took her outside in back to show her something and I had to wait a long time. But when she isn't at our house, he acts as if she's just some stranger. Once he said to me that she was cheap.

Of course, there was no reason for me to think that Chris would be at Jake's the next time I went to the doctor's, but he was. He and Mark were at the bar as if they'd never moved. I went to my little table, and while I drank my Coke I wondered whether Chris could have noticed that I was there. Then I realized that he might not remember me at all.

I was stalling with the ice in the bottom of my glass when Chris sat down next to me. I hadn't even seen him leave the bar. He asked me a lot of things—all about my family and where I lived, and how I came to be at Jake's.

"I go to a doctor right near here," I told him.

"Psychiatrist?" he asked.

All I said was no, but I felt my face stain red.

"I'm twenty-seven," he said. "Doesn't that seem strange to you?"

"Well, some people are," I said.

I was hoping Chris would assume I was much older than I was. People usually did, because I was tall. And it was usually a problem, because they were disappointed in me for not acting older (even if they knew exactly how old I was, like my teachers). But what Chris said was, "I'm much, much older than you. Probably almost twice as old." And I understood that he wanted me to see that he knew perfectly well how old I was. He wanted me to see it, and he wanted me to think it was strange.

When I had to leave, Chris walked me to the bar to say hello to Mark, who was talking to a girl.

"Look," the girl said. She held a lock of my hair up to Mark's, and you couldn't tell whose pale curl was whose. Mark's eyes, so close, also looked just like mine, I saw.

"We could be brother and sister," Mark said, but his voice sounded like a recording of a voice, and for a moment I forgot how things are divided up, and I thought Mark must be having trouble with his eyes, too.

From then on, I always went straight to Jake's after leaving the doctor, and when I passed by the bar I could never help glancing into the mirror to see Chris's face. I would just sit at my table and drink my Coke and listen for his laugh, and when I heard it I felt completely still, the way you do when you have a fever and someone puts his hand on your forehead. And sometimes Chris would come sit with me and talk.

At home and at school, I thought about all the different girls who hung around with Chris and Mark. I thought about them one by one, as if they were little figurines I could take down from a glass case to inspect. I thought about how they looked, and I thought about the girls at school and about Penelope, and I looked in the mirror.

I looked in the mirror over at Maureen's house while Maureen put on nail polish, and I tried to make myself see my sister. We are both pale and long, but Penelope is beautiful, as everyone has always pointed out, and I, I saw, just looked unsettled.

"You could use some makeup," Maureen said, shaking her hands dry, "but you look fine. You're lucky that you're tall. It means you'll be able to wear clothes."

I love to go over to Maureen's house. Maureen is an only child, and her father lives in California. Her mother is away a lot, too, and when she is, Carolina, the maid, stays over. Carolina was there that night, and she let us order in pizza for dinner.

"Maureen is my girl. She is my girl," Carolina said after dinner, putting her arms around Maureen. Maureen almost always has some big expression on her face, but when Carolina does that she just goes blank.

Later I asked Maureen about Chris. I was afraid of talking about him because it seemed as if he might dissolve if I did, but I needed Maureen's advice badly. I told her it was just like French class, where there were two words for "you." Sometimes when Chris said "you" to me I would turn red, as if he had used some special word. And I could hardly say "you" to him. It seemed amazing to me sometimes when I was talking to Chris that a person could just walk up to another person and say "you."

"Does that mean something about him?" I asked. "Or is it just about me?"

"It's just you," Maureen said. "It doesn't count. It's just like when you sit down on a bus next to a stranger and you know that your knee is touching his but you pretend it isn't."

Of course Maureen was almost sure to be right. Why wouldn't she be? Still, I kept thinking that it was just possible that she might be wrong, and the next time I saw Chris something happened to make me think she was.

My vision had fuzzed up a lot during that week, and when Dr. Wald looked at my eyes he didn't get up. "Any trouble lately with that sensation of haziness?" he asked.

I got scorching hot when he said that, and I felt like lying. "Not really," I said. "Yes, a bit."

He put some drops in my eyes and sent me to the waiting room, where I looked at bust exercises in *Redbook* till the drops started to work and the print melted on the page. I had never noticed before how practically no one in the waiting room was even pretending to read. One woman had bandages over her eyes, and most people were just staring and blinking. A little boy was halfheartedly moving a stiff plastic horse on the floor in front of him, but he wasn't even looking at it.

The doctor examined my eyes with the light so bright it made the back of my head sting. "Good," he said. "I'll see you in—what is it?—a month."

I was out on the street before I realized that I still couldn't see. My vision was like a piece of loosely woven cloth that was pulling apart. In the street everything seemed to be moving off, and all the lights looked like huge haloed globes, bobbing and then dipping suddenly into the pocketed air. The noises were one big pool of sound—horns and brakes and people yelling—and to cross the street I had to plunge into a mob of people and rush along wherever it was they were going.

When I finally got through to Jake's my legs were trembling badly, and I just went right up to Chris at the bar, where he was listening to his friend Sherman tell a story. Without even glancing at me, Chris put his hand around my wrist, and I just stood there next to him, with my wrist in his hand, and I listened, too.

Sherman was telling how he and his band had been playing at some club the night before and during a break, when he'd been sitting with his girlfriend, Candy, a man had come up to their table. "He's completely destroyed," Sherman said, "and Candy and I are not exactly on top of things ourselves. But the guy keeps waving this ring, and the basic idea seems to be that it's his wife's wedding ring. He's come home earlier and his wife isn't there, but the ring is, and he's sure his wife's out screwing around. So the guy keeps telling me about it over and over, and I can't get him to shut up, but finally he notices Candy and he says, 'That your old lady?' 'Yeah,' I tell him. 'Good-looking broad,' the guy says, and he hands me the ring. 'Keep it,' the guy says. 'It's for you—not for this bitch with you.'"

One of the girls at the bar reached over and touched the flashing ring that was on a chain around Sherman's neck. "Pretty," she said. "Don't you want it, Candy?" But the girl she had spoken to remained perched on her barstool, with her legs crossed, smiling down at her drink.

"So what did you think of that?" Chris said as he walked me over to my table and sat down with me. I didn't say anything. "Sherman can be sort of disgusting. But it's not an important thing," Chris said.

The story had made me think about the kids at school—that we don't know yet what our lives are really going to be like. It made me feel that anything might be a thing that's important, and I started to cry, because I had never noticed that I was always lonely in my life until just then, when Chris had understood how much the story had upset me, and had said something to make me feel better.

Chris dipped a napkin into a glass of water and mopped off my face, but I was clutching a pencil in my pocket so hard I broke it, and that started me crying again.

"Hey," Chris said. "Look. It's not dead." He grabbed another napkin and scribbled on it with each half of the pencil. "It's fine, see? Look. That's just how they reproduce. Don't they teach you anything at school? Here," he said. "We'll just tuck them under this, and we'll have two very happy little pencils."

And then, after a while, when I was laughing and talking, all at once he stood up. "I'm sorry to have to leave you like this," he said, "but I promised Mark I'd help him with something." And I saw that Mark and a girl were standing at the bar, looking at us. "Ready," Chris called over to them. "Honey," he said, and a waitress materialized next to him. "Get this lady something to drink and put it on my tab. Thanks," he said. And then he walked out, with Mark and the girl.

But the strange thing was that I don't think Mark had actually been waiting for Chris. I don't think Chris had promised Mark anything. I think Mark and the girl had only been looking at us to look, because I could see that they were surprised when Chris called over to them, and also the three of them stood talking on the sidewalk before they went on together. And right then was when I thought for a minute that Maureen had been wrong about me and Chris. It was not when Chris held my wrist, and not when Chris understood how upset I was, and not when Chris dried off my tears, but it was when Chris left, that I thought Maureen was wrong.

My grades were getting a lot worse, and my father decided to help me with my homework every night after dinner. "All right," he would say, standing behind my chair and leaning over me. "Think. If you want to make an equation out of this question, how do you have to start? We've talked about how to do this, Laurel." But I hated his standing behind me like that so much all I could do was try to send out rays from my back that would make him stand farther away. Too bad I wasn't Maureen. She would have loved it.

For me, every day pointed forward or backward to the last Thursday of each month, but those Thursdays came and went without anything really changing, either at the doctor's or at Jake's, until finally in the spring. Everyone else in my class had spent most of a whole year getting excited or upset about classes and parties and exams and sports, but all those things were one thing to me—a nasty fog that was all around me while I waited.

And then came a Thursday when Chris put his arm around me as soon as I walked into Jake's. "I have to do an errand," he said. "Want a Coke first?"

"I'm supposed to be at my sister's class by six," I said. In case he hadn't been asking me to go with him, I would just seem to be saying something factual.

"I'll get you there," Chris said. He stood in back of me and put both arms around my shoulders, and I could feel exactly where he was touching me. Chris's friends had neutral expressions on their faces as if nothing was happening, and I tried to look as if nothing was happening, too.

As we were going out the door, a girl coming in grabbed Chris. "Are you leaving?" she said.

"Yeh," Chris told her.

"Well, when can I talk to you?" she asked.

"I'll be around later, honey," Chris said, but he just kept walking. "Christ, what a bimbo," he said to me, shaking his head, and I felt ashamed for no reason.

When Chris drove his fast little bright car it seemed like

part of him, and there I was, inside it, too. I felt that we were inside a shell together, and we could see everything that was outside it, and we drove and drove and Chris turned the music loud. And suddenly Chris said, "I'd really like to see you a lot more. It's too bad you can't come into the city more often." I didn't know what to say, but I gathered that he didn't expect me to say anything.

We parked in a part of the city where the buildings were huge and squat. Chris rang a bell and we ran up flights of wooden stairs to where a man in white slacks and an unbuttoned shirt was waiting.

"Joel, this is Laurel," Chris said.

"Hello, Laurel," Joel said. He seemed to think there was something funny about my name, and he looked at me the way I've noticed grown men often do, as if I couldn't see them back perfectly well.

Inside, Chris and Joel went through a door, leaving me in an enormous room with white sofas and floating mobiles. The room was immaculate except for a silky purple-and-gold kimono lying on the floor. I picked up the kimono and rubbed it against my cheek and put it on over my clothes. Then I went and looked out the window at the city stretching on and on. In a building across the street, figures moved slowly behind dirty glass. They were making things, I suppose.

After a while Chris and Joel burst back into the room. Chris's eyes were shiny, and he was grinning like crazy.

"Hey," Joel said, grabbing the edges of the kimono I was wearing. "That thing looks better on her than on me."

"What wouldn't?" Chris said. Joel stepped back as Chris put his arms around me from behind again.

"I resent that, I resent that! But I don't deny it!" Joel said.

Chris was kissing my neck and my ears, and both he and Joel were giggling.

I wondered what would happen if Chris and I were late and Mother saw me drive up in Chris's car, but we darted around in the traffic and shot along the avenues and pulled up near Penelope's dancing school with ten minutes to spare. Then, instead of saying anything, Chris just sat there with one hand still on the wheel and the other on the shift, and he didn't even look at me. When I just experimentally touched his sleeve and he still didn't move, I more or less flung myself on top of him and started crying into his shirt. I was in his lap, all tangled up, and I was kissing him and kissing him, and my hands were moving by themselves.

Suddenly I thought of all the people outside the car walking their bouncy little dogs, and I thought how my mother might pull up at any second, and I sat up fast and opened my eyes. Everything looked slightly different from the way it had been looking inside my head—a bit smaller and farther away—and I realized that Chris had been sitting absolutely still, and he was staring straight ahead.

"Goodbye," I said, but Chris still didn't move or even look at me. I couldn't understand what had happened to Chris.

"Wait," Chris said, still without looking at me. "Here's my phone number." He shook himself and wrote it out slowly.

At the corner I looked back and saw that Chris was still there, leaning back and staring out the windshield.

"Why did he give me his phone number, do you think?" I asked Maureen. We were at a party in Peter Klingeman's basement.

"I guess he wants you to call him," Maureen said. I know

she didn't really feel like talking. Kevin was standing there, with his hand under her shirt, and she was sort of jumpy. "Frankly, Laurel, he sounds a bit weird to me, if you don't mind my saying," Maureen said. I felt ashamed again. I wanted to talk to Maureen more, but Kevin was pulling her off to the Klingemans' TV room.

Then Dougie Pfeiffer sat down next to me. "I think Maureen and Kevin have a really good relationship," he said.

I was wondering how I ever could have had a crush on him in eighth grade when I realized it was my turn to say something. "Did you ever notice," I said, "how some people say 'in eighth grade' and other people say 'in *the* eighth grade'?"

"Laurel," Dougie said, and he grabbed me, shoving his tongue into my mouth. Then he took his tongue back out and let me go. "God, I'm sorry, Laurel," he said.

I didn't really care what he did with his tongue. I thought how his body, under his clothes, was just sort of an outline, like a kid's drawing, and I thought of the long zipper on Chris's leather jacket, and a little rip I noticed once in his jeans, and the weave of the shirt that I'd cried on.

I carried Chris's phone number around with me everywhere, and finally I asked my mother if I could go into the city after school on Thursday and then meet her at Penelope's class.

"No," Mother said.

"Why not?" I said.

"We needn't discuss this, Laurel," my mother said.

"You let me go in to see Dr. Wald," I said.

"Don't," Mother said. "Anyhow, you can't just . . . wander around in New York."

"I have to do some shopping," I said idiotically.

Mother started to say something, but then she stopped, and she looked at me as if she couldn't quite remember who I was. "Oh, who cares?" she said, not especially to me.

There was a permanent little line between Mother's eyebrows, I noticed, and suddenly I felt I was seeing her through a window. I went up to my room and cried and cried, but later I couldn't get to sleep, thinking about Chris.

I called him Thursday.

"What time is it?" he said with his blistery laugh. "I just woke up." He told me he had gone to a party the night before and when he came out his car had been stolen. He was stoned, and he thought the sensible thing was to walk over to Mark's place, which is miles from his, but on the way he found his car parked out on the street. "I should've reported it, but I figured, hey, what a great opportunity, so I just stole it back."

Chris didn't mention anything about our seeing each other.

"I've got to come into the city today to do some stuff," I said.

"Yeah," Chris said. "I've got a lot to do today myself."

Well, that was that, obviously, unless I did something drastic. "I thought I'd stop in and say hi, if you're going to be around," I said. My heart was jumping so much it almost knocked me down.

"Great," Chris said. "That's really sweet." But his voice sounded muted, and I wasn't at all surprised when I got to Jake's and he wasn't there. I was on my third Coke when Chris walked in, but a girl wearing lots of bracelets waylaid him at the bar, and he sat down with her.

I didn't dare finish my Coke or ask for my check. All I could do was stay put and do whatever Chris made me do. Finally the girl at the bar left, giving Chris a big, meaty kiss, and he wandered over and sat down with me.

"God. Did you see that girl who was sitting with me?" he said. "That girl is so crazy. There's nothing she won't put in her mouth. I was at some party a few weeks ago, and I walk in through this door, 'cause I'm looking for the john, and there's Beverly, lying on the floor stark naked. So you know what she does?"

"No," I said.

"She says, 'Excuse me,' and instead of putting something on she reaches up and turns out the light. Now, that's thinkin', huh?" He laughed. "Have you finished all those things you had to do?" he asked me.

"Yes," I said.

"That's great," Chris said. "I'm really running around like a chicken today. Honey," he said to a waitress, "put that on my tab, will you?" He pointed at my watery Coke.

"Sandra was looking for you," the waitress said. "Did she find you?"

"Yeah, thanks," Chris said. He gave me a kiss on the cheek, which was the first time he had kissed me at all, except at Joel's, and he left.

I knew I had made some kind of mistake, but I couldn't figure out what it was. I would only be able to figure it out from Chris, but it would be two weeks until I saw him again. Every night, I looked out the window at the red glow of the city beyond all the quiet little houses and yards, and every night after I got into bed I felt it draw nearer and nearer, hovering just beyond my closed eyes, with Chris inside it. While I slept, it receded again; but by morning, when I woke up and put on my school clothes, I had come one day closer.

After my next appointment with Dr. Wald, Chris wasn't at Jake's. For the first time since I had gone to Jake's, Chris didn't come at all.

On the way home it was all I could do not to cry in front of Mother and Penelope. And I wondered what I was going to do from that afternoon on.

"And how was Dr. Wald today?" my father said when we sat down for dinner.

"I didn't ask," I said.

My father paused to acknowledge my little joke.

"What I meant," he said, "was how is my lovely daughter?"

I knew he was trying to say something nice, but he could have picked something sincere for once. I hated the way he had taken off his jacket and opened up his collar and rolled up his sleeves, and I thought I would be sick if he stood behind my chair later. "Penelope is your lovely daughter," I said, and threw my silverware onto the table.

From upstairs I listened. I knew that Penelope would have frozen, the way she does when someone says in front of me how pretty she is, but no one said anything about me that I could hear.

Later, Penelope and Paul and I made up a story together, the way we had when we were younger. Paul fell asleep suddenly in the middle with little tears in the corners of his eyes, and I tucked Penelope into bed. When I smoothed out the covers, a shadow of relief crossed her face.

That Saturday, Mother took me shopping in the city without Penelope or Paul. "I thought we should get you a present," Mother said. "Something pretty." She smiled at me in a strange, stiff way.

"Thank you," I said. I felt good that we were driving together, but I was sad, too, that Mother was trying to bring me into the clean, bright, fancy, daytime part of New York that Penelope's dancing school was in, because when would she accept that there was no place there for me? I wondered if Mother wanted to say something to me, but we just drove silently, except for once, when Mother pointed out a lady in a big, white, flossy fur coat.

At Bonwit's, Mother picked out an expensive dress for me. "What do you think?" she said when I tried it on.

I was glad that Mother had chosen it, because it was very pretty, and it was white, and it was expensive, but in the mirror I just looked skinny and dazed. "I like it," I said. "But don't you think it looks wrong on me?"

"Well, it seems fine to me, but it's up to you," Mother said. "You can have it if you want."

"But look, Mother," I said. "Look. Do you think it's all right?"

"If you don't like it, don't get it," she said. "It's your present."

At home after dinner I tried the white dress on again and stared at myself in the mirror, and I thought maybe it looked a little better.

I went down to the living room, where Mother was stretched out on the sofa with her feet on my father's lap. When I walked in he started to get up, but Mother didn't move. "My God," my father said. "It's Lucia."

My mother giggled. "Wedding scene or mad scene?" she said.

Upstairs I folded the dress back into the box for Bonwit's to pick up. At night I watched bright dancing patterns in the dark and I dreaded going back to Dr. Wald.

The doctor didn't seem to notice anything unusual at my next appointment. I still had to face walking the short distance to Jake's, though. I practically fell over from relief when I saw

Chris at the bar, and he reached out as I went by and reeled me in, smiling. He was talking to Mark and some other friends, and he stood me with my back to him and rubbed my shoulders and temples. I tried to smile hello to Mark, who was staring at me with his pale eyes, but he just kept staring, listening to Chris. I closed my eyes and leaned back against Chris, who folded his arms around me. When Chris finished his story, everyone laughed except me. Chris blew a little stream of air into my hair, ruffling it up. "Want to take a ride?" he said.

We drove for a while, fast, circling the city, and Chris slammed tapes into the tape deck. Then we parked and Chris turned and looked at me.

"What do you want to do?" Chris asked me.

"Now?" I said, but he just looked at me, and I didn't know what he meant. "Nothing," I said.

"Have I seemed preoccupied to you lately, honey?" he asked.

"I guess maybe a little," I said, even though I hadn't really ever thought about how he seemed. He just seemed like himself. But he told me that yes, he had been preoccupied. He had borrowed some money to start an audio business, but he had to help out a cousin, too. I couldn't make any sense of what he was talking about, and I didn't really care, either. I was thinking that now he had finally called me "honey." It made me so happy, so happy, even though "honey" was what he called everyone, and I had been the only Laurel.

Chris talked and talked, and I watched his mouth as the words came out. "I know you wonder what's going on with me," he said. "What it is is I worry that you're so young. I'm a difficult person. There are a lot of strange things about me. I'm really crazy about you, you know. I'm really crazy about you, but I can't ask you to see me."

"Why don't I come in and stay over with you a week from Friday," I said. "Can I?"

Chris blinked. "Terrific, honey," he said cautiously. "That's a date."

I arranged it with Maureen that I would say I was staying at her house. "Don't wear underwear," Maureen told me. "That really turns guys on."

Chris and I met at Jake's, but we didn't stay there long. We drove all over the city, stopping at different places. Chris knew people everywhere, and we would sit down at the bar and talk to them. We went to an apartment with some of the people we ran into, where everyone lay around listening to tapes. And once we went to a club and watched crowds of people change like waves with the music, under flashing lights.

Chris didn't touch me, not once, not even accidentally, all during that time.

Sometime between things we stopped for food. I couldn't eat, but Chris seemed starving. He ate his cheeseburger and French fries, and then he ate mine. And then he had a big piece of pecan pie.

Late, very late, we climbed into the car again, but there was nothing left to do. "Home?" Chris said without turning to me.

Chris's apartment seemed so strange, and maybe that was just because it was real. But I had surely never been inside such a small, plain place to live before, and Chris hardly seemed to own anything. There were a few books on a shelf, and a little kitchen off in the corner, with a pot on the stove. It was up several flights of dark stairs, in a brick building, and it must have been on the edge of the city, because I could see water out the window, and ribbons of highway elevated on huge concrete pillars, and dark piers.

Chris's bed, which was tightly made with the sheet turned back over the blanket, looked very narrow. All the music we had been hearing all night was rocketing around in my brain, and I felt jittery and a bit sick. Chris passed a joint to me, and he lay down with his hands over his eyes. I sat down on the edge of the bed next to him and waited, but he didn't move. "Remember when I asked you a while ago what you wanted to do and you said 'Nothing'?" Chris asked me.

"But that was—" I started to say, and then the funny sound of Chris's voice caught up with me, and all the noise in my head shut off.

"I remember," Chris said. Then a long time went by.

"Why did you come here, Laurel?" Chris said.

When I didn't answer, he said, "Why? Why did you come here? You're old enough now to think about what you're doing." And I remembered I had never been alone with him before, except in his car.

"Yes," I said into the dead air. Whatever I'd been waiting for all that time had vanished. "It's all right."

"It's all right?" Chris said furiously. "Well, good. It's all right, then." He was still lying on his back with his hands over his eyes, and neither of us moved. I thought I might shatter.

Sometime in the night Chris spoke again. "Why are you angry?" he said. His voice was blurred, as if he'd been asleep. I wanted to tell him I wasn't angry, but it seemed wrong, and I was afraid of what would happen if I did. I put my arms around him and started kissing him. He didn't move a muscle, but I kept right on. I knew it was my only chance, and I thought that if I stopped I would have to leave. "Don't be angry," he said.

Sometime in the night I sprang awake. Chris was holding my wrists behind my back with one hand and unbuttoning my shirt with the other, and his body felt very tense. "Don't!" I said, before I understood.

"'Don't!'" echoed Chris, letting go of me. He said it just the way I had, sounding just as frightened. He fell asleep immediately then, sprawled out, but I couldn't sleep anymore, and later, when Chris spoke suddenly into the dark, I felt I'd been expecting him to. "Your parents are going to worry," he said deliberately, as if he were reading.

"No," I said. I wondered how long he had been awake. "They think I'm at Maureen's." And then I realized how foolish it was for me to have said that.

"They'll worry," he said. "They will worry. They'll be very frightened."

And then I was so frightened myself that the room bulged and there was a sound in my ears like ball bearings rolling around wildly. I put my hands against my hot face, and my skin felt to me as if it belonged to a stranger. It felt like a marvel—brand-new and slightly moist—and I wondered if anyone else would ever touch it and feel what I had felt.

"Look—" Chris said. He sounded blurry again, and helpless and sad. "Look—see how bad I am for you, Laurel? See how I make you cry?" Then he put his arms around me, and we lay there on top of the bed for a long, long time, and sometimes we kissed each other. My shirtsleeve was twisted and it hurt against my arm, but I didn't move.

When the night red began finally to bleach out of the sky, I touched Chris's wrist. "I have to go now," I said. That wasn't true, of course. My parents would expect me to stay at Maureen's till at least noon. "I have to be home when it gets light."

"Do you?" Chris said, but his eyes were closed.

I stood up and buttoned my shirt.

"I'll take you to the train," Chris said.

At first he didn't move, but finally he stood up, too. "I need some coffee," he said. And when he looked at me my heart sank. He was smiling. He looked as if he wanted to start it up—start it all again.

I went into the bathroom, so I wouldn't be looking at Chris. There was a tub and a sink and a toilet. Chris uses them, I thought, as if that would explain something to me, but the thought was like a sealed package. Stuck in the corner of the mirror over the sink was a picture of a man's face torn from a magazine. It was a handsome face, but I didn't like it.

"That's a guy I went to high school with," Chris said from behind me. "He's a very successful actor now."

"That's nice," I said, and waited as long as I could. "Look— it's almost light."

And in the instant that Chris glanced at the window, where in fact the faintest dawn was showing, I stepped over to the door and opened it.

In the car, Chris seemed the way he usually did. "I'm sorry I'm so tired, honey," he said. "I've been having a rough time lately. We'll get together another time, when I'm not so hassled."

"Yes," I said. "Good." I don't think he really remembered the things we had said in the dark.

When we stopped at the station, Chris put his arm across me, but instead of opening the door he just held the handle. "You think I'm really weird, don't you?" he said, and smiled at me.

"I think you're tired," I said, making myself smile back. And Chris released the handle and let me out.

I took the train through the dawn and walked from the

station, pausing carefully if it looked as though someone was awake inside a house I was passing. Once a dog barked, and I stood absolutely still for minutes.

I threw chunks from the lawn at Maureen's window, so Carolina wouldn't wake up, but I was afraid the whole town would be out by the time Maureen heard.

Maureen came down the back way and got me. We each put on one of her bathrobes, and we made a pot of coffee, which is something I'm not allowed to drink.

"What happened?" Maureen asked.

"I don't know," I said.

"What do you mean, you don't know?" Maureen said. "You were there."

Even though my face was in my hands, I could tell Maureen was staring at me. "Well," she said after a while. "Hey. Want to play some Clue?" She got the Clue board down from her room, and we played about ten games.

The next week I really did stay over at Maureen's.

"Again?" my mother said. "We must do something for Mrs. MacIntyre. She's been so nice to you."

Dougie and Kevin showed up together after Maureen and Carolina and I had eaten a barbecued chicken from the deli and Carolina had gone to her room to watch the little TV that Mrs. MacIntyre had put there. I figured it was no accident that Dougie had shown up with Kevin. It had to be a brainstorm of Maureen's, and I thought, Well, so what. So after Maureen and Kevin went up to Maureen's room I went into the den with Dougie. We pretty much knew from classes and books and stuff what to do, so we did it. The thing that surprised me most was that you always read in books about "stained sheets," "stained sheets," and I never knew what that meant, but I guess I thought it would be pretty interesting. But the little stuff on the sheet just looked completely innocuous, like Elmer's glue, and it seemed that it might even dry clear like Elmer's glue. At any rate, it didn't seem like anything that Carolina would have to absolutely kill herself about when she did the laundry.

We went back into the living room to wait, and I sat while Dougie walked around poking at things on the shelves. "Look," Dougie said, "Clue." But I just shrugged, and after a while Maureen and Kevin came downstairs looking pretty pleased with themselves.

I sat while Dr. Wald finished at the machine, and I waited for him to say something, but he didn't.

"Am I going to go blind?" I asked him finally, after all those months.

"What?" he said. Then he remembered to look at me and smile. "Oh, no, no. We won't let it come to that."

I knew what I would find at Jake's, but I had to go anyway, just to finish. "Have you seen Chris?" I asked one of the waitresses. "Or Mark?"

"They haven't been around for a while," she said. "Sheila," she called over to another waitress, "where's Chris these days?"

"Don't ask me," Sheila said sourly, and both of them stared at me.

I could feel my blood traveling in its slow loop, carrying a heavy proudness through every part of my body. I had known Chris could injure me, and I had never cared how much he could injure me, but it had never occurred to me until this moment that I could do anything to him.

Outside, it was hot. There were big bins of things for sale on the sidewalk, and horns were honking, and the sun was yellow and syrupy. I noticed two people who must have been mother and daughter, even though you couldn't really tell how old either of them was. One of them was sort of crippled, and the other was very peculiar looking, and they were all dressed up in stiff, cheap party dresses. They looked so pathetic with their sweaty, eager faces and ugly dresses that I felt like crying. But then I thought that they might be happy, much happier than I was, and that I just felt sorry for them because I thought I was better than they were. And I realized that I wasn't really different from them anyhow—that every person just had one body or another, and some of them looked right and worked right and some of them didn't—and I thought maybe it was myself I was feeling sorry for, because of Chris, or maybe because it was obvious even to me, a total stranger, how much that mother loved her homely daughter in that awful dress.

When Mother and Penelope and I got back home, I walked over to Maureen's house, but I decided not to stop. I walked by the playground and looked in at the fourth-grade room and the turtle that was still lumbering around its dingy aquarium, and it came into my mind how even Paul was older now than the kids who would be sitting in those tiny chairs in the fall, and I thought about all the millions and billions of people in the world, all getting older, all trapped in things that had already happened to them.

When I was a kid, I used to wonder (I bet everyone did) whether there was somebody somewhere on the earth, or even in the universe, or ever had been in all of time, who had

had exactly the same experience that I was having at that moment, and I hoped so badly that there was. But I realized then that that could never occur, because every moment is all the things that have happened before and all the things that are going to happen, and every moment is just the way all those things look at one point on their way along a line. And I thought how maybe once there was, say, a princess who lost her mother's ring in a forest, and how in some other galaxy a strange creature might fall, screaming, on the shore of a red lake, and how right that second there could be a man standing at a window overlooking a busy street, aiming a loaded revolver, but how it was just me, there, after Chris, staring at that turtle in the fourth-grade room and wondering if it would die before I stopped being able to see it.

RAFE'S COAT

One sparkly evening not long after my husband and I had started divorce proceedings, Rafe stopped by for a drink before taking me out to dinner. In his hand was a spray of flowers, and on his face was an expression of inward alertness, and both of these things I suspected to be accoutrements of love.

"Marvelous new coat," I said. "Alpaca, yes?"

"Yup," Rafe said, dropping it onto a chair with an uncharacteristic lack of attention. "England last week. Well, then!" He looked around brightly in the manner of someone who, having discharged some weighty task, is ready to start afresh.

Heavens, he was behaving oddly. I waited for him to say something enlightening, or to say anything at all, for that matter, which he failed to do, so I sat him down and poured him a drink and waited some more.

"Incredibly strange out there," was his eventual contribution. "Dark and crowded."

"England," I said, mystified. "England has become dark and crowded."

"Yes?" Rafe said. "Oh, actually, I'd been thinking of Sixty-seventh Street."

Hmm. Obviously I would have to give Rafe quite a bit of encouragement if I wanted to hear about the girlfriend whom, by now, I was absolutely certain he'd acquired. And I did want to. I always enjoyed hearing about, and meeting, his woman of the moment. Rafe, like a hawk, swooped down upon the shiniest thing in sight, and his girls were always exotics of one sort or another, if only, as they often were, exotics ordinaire; but whatever their background, race, or interests, they were all amusing, marvelous looking, unpredictable, and none of them seemed ever to require sleep.

Unfortunately, these flashing lights of Rafe's life tended to burn out rather quickly, no matter how in thrall Rafe was initially. And this was the inevitable consequence, I believed, of the discrepancy between his age and theirs. It was not that I necessarily felt that Rafe should be seeing people of our own age (we were both thirty-three, as it happened). In fact, it would have seemed inappropriate. Rafe, at any age, would simply not be suited for the sobriety of adulthood. Still, the years do pass, and there were Rafe's girls, trailing along a decade or so behind him. They could hardly be blamed if they hadn't accrued enough substance (of the sort that only time can provide) to allow Rafe to stretch out his dealings with them beyond a month or two.

"So. I give up, Rafael," I said. "Tell me. Who is the lucky girl you're in love with tonight?"

"Tonight!" he said, and damned if he didn't look wounded.

Now, Rafe was my friend. It was Rafe who had accompanied me to parties and openings and weekends when John, my husband, was too busy (as he usually was) or not interested enough (and he rarely was), and it was Rafe who pulled me out of any mental mudwallow I might strand myself in, and it was Rafe I was counting on to amuse me now, while John and I parceled out our holdings and made our adieus and slogged through whatever contractual and emotional dreariness was necessitated by going on with life; and if Rafe was going to mature, this was certainly a very poor moment for him to have chosen to do it.

"As it happens," Rafe confessed unnecessarily, "I have started seeing someone."

"Really," I said.

"She's simply wonderful," he said with the fatuous solemnity of a man on the witness stand.

"Good!" I said. I did hope she was wonderful, even though I deplored the dent she seemed to have put in Rafe's sense of humor. "What does she do?"

"Well . . ." Rafe deliberated. "She's an actress."

"Poor thing," I said after some moments had elapsed during which Rafe executed several groupings of resolute nods. "It's such a difficult way to make a living."

Another nod-group. "It is. Yes it is. That's an Ansel Adams, isn't it? Is it new?"

"Darling. I've just moved it from the dining room."

"Oh, yes, of course." Rafe stared at it blankly. "Well, it's sensational in here, isn't it?"

"So, tell me," I said. "Is your friend in some sort of company or repertory situation? Or does she trot about in the summers being Juliet and My Sister Eileen and so on? Or must she spend every minute subjecting herself to scrutiny and rejection?"

"Well, she's done quite a bit of all of those things, yes. Not at the moment, but that's certainly the idea. Yes."

"Oh, dear," I said. "She doesn't have to work in a restaurant, does she? How awful!"

"Oh, not at all," Rafe said. "No. She's doing very well." He scanned the walls for material.

"I'm glad you like the Ansel Adams, Rafe," I said.

"As a matter of fact," he said, "she has a job on a soap opera."

"Well!" I said. "Isn't that splendid! And it will certainly tide her over until she finds something she wants." Oh, why did Rafe always do this? Girl after girl. He was like some noble hound who daily fetched home the *New York Post* instead of the *Times*.

"What's the matter with that?" Rafe said.

"Nothing," I said. "With what?"

"She's just exactly as much an actress as—oh, God, I don't know—Lady Macbeth would be, in one of those new-wave festivals you're so fond of."

"Just exactly," I said.

"It's honest work," he said.

"Heavens, Rafe," I said. "Did I say it wasn't?" These propositions of his were hardly sturdy enough to rebut.

"I'm quite impressed, really," Rafe said. My goodness, Rafe was bristly! Apparently he was quite embarrassed by this girl. "She's very young, for one thing, and she took herself straight to New York from absolutely nowhere, and immediately she got herself a job in a demanding, lucrative, competitive field."

Field! "Well, you won't get me to say I think it isn't impressive," I said, making it clear that this was to be the end of the discussion. "Can I give you another drink?"

"Please," he said. The sound of pouring gave us something sensible to listen to for a moment.

"So, then," I said. "What's the name of this show she's on?"

"Well," Rafe said, "it's called, as I remember, something on the order of, er, 'This Brief Candle.'" He focused furiously over my ear.

Well, stuffiness is often an early adjunct of infatuation,

and I was perfectly willing to let Rafe have his say. If he wanted to tell me that this girl should be knighted—or can-onized or bronzed—for getting herself a job on a soap opera, that was fine. What was so irritating was that every time Rafe thought I might open my mouth, he leapt to the attack, and by the time we got into a taxi, I would have been happier getting into a bullring with a bunch of picadors.

Fortunately, the restaurant Rafe had chosen turned out to be wonderfully soothing. It was luxurious and private, and at the sight of the cloakroom, with its rows of expensive, empty coats that called up a world in which generous, broad-shouldered men, and women in marvelous dresses (much like the one I myself happened to be wearing) inclined toward each other on banquettes, I was pierced by a feeling so keen and unalloyed it might have been called—I don't know what it might have been called. It felt like—well, grief . . . actually.

During dinner, Rafe and I stayed on neutral territory—a piece of recent legislation, Marty Harnishveiger's renova-tions, an exceptionally pointless East Side murder, and my husband and marriage.

"One really oughtn't be able to describe one's marriage as neutral territory, do you think?" I asked Rafe.

"Considering the minefields that most of our friends' marriages are," he said, "neutral territory might be the pref-erable alternative."

"I suppose," I said. "But 'preferable alternative' hardly seems, in itself, the answer to one's prayers. At least all those minefield marriages around us must have something in them to make them explosive."

"Probably incompatibility," Rafe pointed out. "On the other hand, I never really did understand why you married John."

"He's not so bad," I said. I reminded Rafe that John was in many ways an exemplary husband. "He's highly respected, he has marvelous taste, he's very good looking in a harmless sort of way, he's rich to begin with and makes good money on top of that . . ."

"No, I know," Rafe said. "I didn't mean to insult him. He's a very nice guy, after all. And I have to say you looked terrific together. It's just that—well, you never seemed to have much fun with him."

"Fun?" I said. "How do you expect the poor guy to be fun? He's not even alive."

Rafe looked suddenly stricken, as if he'd realized he might have left his wallet somewhere. I wondered what he was thinking about, but I didn't want to pry, so I went on. "Have you heard he's been seeing Marcia Meaver? They're probably sitting around together right this minute, wowing each other with forbidden tales of investment banking."

"She's quite nice, though," Rafe said after a moment. "I've met her."

"Oh, I suppose she is," I said. "I didn't mean to be nasty."

"I know," Rafe said. "I know you didn't."

We ordered brandies and leaned back against the leather, considering. I was just getting bored when Rafe hunched forward, peering into his glass.

"What?" I said.

"Nothing," he said. "Ah, well. I guess it just doesn't do, does it, to marry someone on the strength of their credentials."

"Oh, good point, Rafe," I said. "How ever did you think of it?"

"Sorry," he said.

"You're really crazy about this girl, aren't you?" I said.

Then, oddly enough, Rafe just laughed, and his sunny self shone out from behind his strange mood. "I know," he said, "I know. I always say, 'This time it's different, this time it's different,' but you know what? Each time, poor girls, it *is* different." And Rafe looked so pleased with himself and his girls, so confident of my approval—his smile was so heedless, so winning, so *his*—that, well, I was simply forced to smile back.

Smile or no, though, this girl had obviously had an effect on Rafe, and it occurred to me that it would be interesting to tune in on her show to see if I could pick her out from among her fellow soap girls. So the next morning I picked up a *TV Guide* on my way home from exercise class and scanned it for "This Brief Candle." I always did my work in the afternoons (we members of the grants committee of the foundation worked separately until after we had made our initial recommendations to the panel), and I had a lunch date at one, so I was pleased to find that the show aired at eleven.

When I turned on the set, a few cats wavered into view and discussed cat food, and then, after an awe-inspiring chord or two, an hour in the lives of the characters of "This Brief Candle" was revealed to the world. During this hour, a girl I later came to know as Ellie confided to her mother that she suspected her boyfriend of cheating on an exam in order to get into medical school to please his father. Then Colleen, apparently a school counselor of some sort, made a phone call to a person who seemed to be the father—no, the stepfather—of another person, named Stevie. She wished to talk to him, she said, about Stevie's performance. Ominous music suggested that Stevie's performance was either remarkably poor or a mere pretext for Colleen to see Stevie's stepfather. Perhaps Stevie and Ellie's boyfriend were one and the same person!

No, surely this Stevie fellow must be far too young. But, on the other hand—

Well, no time to mull that over: two men, Hank and Brent, I gathered, were parking a car outside a house and hoping that they would not arouse the suspicions of Eric, who, it seemed, was someone inside the house; Eric could not be made nervous, they told each other between heavy, charged silences, if they were ever going to get inside and break into his safe for those papers.

Oop! An office materialized, containing a devastatingly attractive silver-haired gentleman. Eric? Ellie's father? Stevie's stepfather? Aha! Not Ellie's father, because Ellie's *mother* walked in and said, "Forgive me for coming here like this, Mr. Armstrong, but I must speak to you right away about the plans for the new power plant." And surely Ellie's mother would not go around calling this man "Mr. Armstrong" if he were Ellie's father. Although she might, come to think of it, under certain circumstances, because, for instance, I couldn't help noticing that Mr. Armstrong's secretary was sitting right there with a very funny look on her face. (But wait: *plans* are something that could fit in a *safe*! And maybe Mr. Armstrong's secretary looked like that because she was in cahoots with Hank or Brent. Or Eric, for that matter.) "Come in here, Cordelia, where we can talk privately," said Mr. Armstrong, escorting Ellie's mother into an interior office. ("Cordelia," when *she* called *him* "Mr. Armstrong"? Oh, *sure*.) "Hold my calls, please, Tracy," he said to his secretary. "Certainly, Mr. Armstrong," Tracy said, the funny look solidifying on her face. No, clearly it was something about Mr. Armstrong, not some old *safe*, that had caused Tracy to look like that.

Here was someone named Carolyn being kissed passionately by a man in a suit. "Oh, Shad, Shad," she said. Shad? Why *Shad*? "Chad, my darling," Carolyn continued, wisely abandoning her attempt to kiss him while saying her lines. "Carolyn, Carolyn," said Chad, I suppose it was (although, come to think of it, I'd never heard of anyone called Chad, either). "Chad," said Carolyn. "Carolyn," said Chad. "Lydia!" said both Chad and Carolyn, breaking apart, as the camera drew back to reveal a woman standing in a doorway. "Well. My dear little sister," said this new woman, coolly. "And good old Chad. Aren't you going to welcome me home, you two? I've come back. And this time I've come back to stay."

"So!" I said when I got through to Rafe at his office. "I just saw 'This Brief Candle'—what's your crush's name?"

"Heather Goldberg," he said.

"What?" I said. "Oh. Her *nom*, not her name."

"How should I know?" Rafe said. "I can't watch that stuff—I'm employed."

"Well, how might I identify her?"

"She's the pretty one," he said.

I snorted. They were all pretty, of course, in a uniform fashion, like an assortment of chocolates whose ornamentations seem meaningless to nonaficionados.

"Why don't you bring her by for a drink this evening?" I said.

"Can't," Rafe said.

"Come on," I said. "I promise to put away the magnifying glass, the scales, the calipers . . ."

"Not by the hairs on my chinny-chin-chin," Rafe said. "Just kidding, of course—I'd love to. But anyway, you'll meet her at Cookie's next Thursday."

"Cookie's!" I said. "Oh, God, that's right. I'm dreading it." I hate parties. Particularly Cookie's parties, but Louise

Dietz had just published a volume of photographs of investi-
gative reporters at home, which was the ostensible raison d'être
of this do, so I had to put in an appearance at least.

"Whoop—my other line," Rafe said. "Want to hold?"

"No, darling. I'm frantic. Thursday, then." I hung up and
looked around. It had been nice with the TV on. All those
other people seeing exactly the same thing as oneself, at the
same time—one knew exactly where one was, somehow. It
seemed a flawless form of having company. But it was over so
suddenly.

I had things to do before lunch, but time was standing
completely still, as it does occasionally at that hour. Then
one's day will pass unexpectedly into a giant, permeable block
of sunshine that converts surfaces into hypnotic sheets of light
and drenches one's belongings in a false, puzzling specialness.
I hated it—it was terrible. I simply stood in front of the TV,
wrenched out of the ordinary smooth flow of entire minutes,
and I remembered being home from school as a child, pin-
ioned to my bed by the measles or whatever, while the world
blazed beyond me in that noon glare.

When I got to Cookie's on Thursday, Rafe and Heather
had not yet arrived. In fact, no one much had yet arrived,
so I wandered about the shrubbery in Cookie's living room
looking for a hospitable encampment. Eventually I distinguished Marcia Meaver's name in a stream of syllables that
issued from some source not far from me. Naturally, my curiosity was aroused. What was there to be mentioned about
Marcia Meaver? Except, of course, that she was going out with
my husband. Which, I must admit, did annoy me. It's one
thing, after all, when one's husband takes up with a fascinating woman or a woman of great beauty. But Marcia Meaver!
I felt I would have to rethink those years of my marriage—

John's standards were not, I realized, all that one might have supposed them to be.

I followed the voice I'd overheard, and it led me to a rather clammy blond boy. As I stood at his shoulder, listening, I came to understand that this boy worked under Buddy Katsukoru at the museum, and it was to Buddy that he was now praising himself, fulsomely and with riveting dullness, for having convinced Marcia to make to the museum a tax-deductible gift of some gowns.

"I will remember this," I said. "I've been giving my old clothes to the Salvation Army."

"Schiaparelli," the boy said dimly, without even turning to glance at me.

"Good grief!" Cookie trumpeted from behind us, incidentally saving the boy from the heartbreak of my response. "It's Lydia!"

"Heather, actually," said a girl's voice, and I turned and saw Rafe, and—and—and I couldn't figure out *what* I saw for a moment; but sure enough, if you were to exchange, paper-doll fashion, this girl's dashing suede for one of those demure TV-tart dresses, her calm regard for the shiftings of a tense, hectoring flirt, if you were to paint sharp black lines around this girl's eyes, what I saw, I realized, would in fact be Lydia, the femme fatale, as I'd supposed, of "This Brief Candle."

How interesting. I was eager to take Heather aside and let her share with me her feelings about exploring on a daily basis some dingy side of her personality, but Cookie cut in like a sheepdog and led her off. "Come tell me, dear," Cookie shouted tactlessly, "what it's like to be a bitch!"

"Imagine Cookie needing to ask," I heard the blond boy say as he and Buddy floated toward the bar. Well! Isn't that just absolutely Mr. Guest for you, though! Trashing the hostess the instant she's out of earshot! Cookie might not be the sweetest person in the world, it was true, but she would never do something cheap like that herself!

"So how's the whiz biz?" Rafe asked as he and I settled ourselves into the sofa. "Find any geniuses crawling around under that pile of grant proposals?"

"Not yet," I said. "Oh, it is slow work, no question."

"Oh, by the way," Rafe said, "Heather and I finally got to that performance piece for which you people so thoughtfully provided the funding. The one with the four-hundred-piece glass-harmonica orchestra, where the mechanical whale rolls over for a few hours. *Beached*, isn't it called? It was really great, I have to tell you, we really enjoyed it."

"I'm sorry you didn't care for it, Rafe. And if what you saw had been in fact what you describe, I would hardly blame you. But whether you personally did or did not care for it, the piece you refer to certainly must be considered an important piece. What *are* those—nachos? No thank you, Rafe. Really—a major piece."

"You know," Rafe said. "All these years, I've really wanted to ask you, how do you decide whether something really is a major piece or whether it's a major piece of crap? I mean, seriously, how do you decide whether something is good or not?"

"Well, seriously, Rafe, I decide in the same way that I decide whether Bergdorf's is a good place to shop. I decide in the same way that I decide on which wall to put the Ansel Adams that you so admire. I decide these things by decision-making processes."

"Ah, silly me," Rafe said.

"Really, Rafe. I can't imagine what it is about Cookie's soirée that's inspired you to disburden yourself, finally, of this canker of doubt you say you've harbored for so long. But if you must really hear right now how I can tell whether something is good, I'll explain it to you. The explanation is that I have been trained to do just that. Oh, of course I do have a certain natural eye—and ear—as, obviously, do you. But what you so clearly find to be a sort of sanctified caprice on my part, concerning my funding recommendations, is actually considered, systematic judgment. I'm not saying I could describe its sequence to you, but I have a solid background in the fine arts, as you know. I studied English and art history in school, and I've worked for years in art-related fields. And therefore, I'm qualified to make the judgments I make in the same way that . . . that, well, Mike Dundy over there is qualified to design the cars he designs."

"I take your point," Rafe said.

"Good," I said.

"But it does not suffice to answer my question," he said. "You see, if you were to drive around in a car of Mike's design, and the engine fell out, everyone could agree that there was a flaw in that design."

"Rafe," I said—I simply couldn't believe this! In all the time we'd known each other, Rafe had never indicated any distaste for my profession—"I am not saying that my work is a science. It cannot be. I am not saying that I'm infallible. All I'm saying is this: I'm not a profoundly gifted person myself. I'm a person whose small but very specific gifts and whose very specific training suit me for this task—the task of being able to seek out, with great care and a certain . . . actual precision, and to reward, others who *are* profoundly gifted."

"And here I thought it was all glamour and prestige. There's quite a lot of kicking and biting for those jobs, I understand, among folks who don't rightly appreciate the gravity of the trust, or the backbreaking labor involved in carrying it out."

"Well, I didn't have to kick or bite anyone for my job. I was merely appointed. And you know perfectly well that 'glamorous' is the last thing I find it! Trudging across that great tundra of manuscripts! Of course, you do learn how to, well . . ."

"Skim," Rafe said.

"Certainly not!" I said. "Just to—to read for the worthwhile bits. And I admit that it's very gratifying when you do stumble across something good. And once in a while, you do. You really do. You see, *that's* the thrill of the job for me, when that happens, and you know that *here's* someone who's going to be an important voice. Rafe, I'm sure this sounds pompous to you, but sometimes I'm reading the Arts and Leisure section or whatever, and there will be an article about someone we've encouraged—did you see, by the way, that there were three whole pages on Stanley Zifkin's studio in this issue of *Architectural Digest*?—Anyhow, I see these things, and I feel a sense of, well . . ."

"Ownership," Rafe said. "The sixth sense."

"You're very jolly tonight, aren't you?" I said.

"I'm a jolly good fellow. Ah, there," he said. Heather, having been released at last by Cookie, was coming toward us.

"What's happening in the real world?" Rafe asked her.

"Oh, just taking in the sights. All these people. It's so funny. Parties always make me think how funny it is that everything's all divided up into these different packages. A package of Cookie, a package of you, a package of me. When you see people all together, milling around like this, it seems so, sort of, arbitrary."

"It doesn't seem arbitrary to me at all," I said. "Cookie's

Cookie, and I'm not, thank heaven. Anyhow, what do you mean, 'everything'? What's this 'everything' that's divided into me and Cookie?"

Heather shrugged. "Oh, I don't know. Just everything. And what else is funny is that at every single party I've ever been to, every single person I speak to says how much they hate parties."

Rafe nodded. "Hatred of parties. The sentiment that unites all humanity."

"But we're all here," Heather said.

"That's right," Rafe told her. "It's a job that has to be done. Going to parties is the social analogue of carrying out the garbage."

"Well, anyhow," Heather said, "everyone seems to be having fun. Cookie's nice, isn't she?"

"No," I said. "I mean, she is, really, if you look deep enough. She can be very vicious, but underneath she's a fine person, really. She has principles at least, which is more than can be said for a lot of rich people." Something was tugging at my attention. "Jesus," I said. "Look at Geoffrey Berman's jacket! It's *hairy*. One of his research assistants must have grown it for him in a bottle."

"They're certainly crazy about him, aren't they?" Rafe said absently. Obviously, he was paying no attention at all to what I was saying.

"So—um, what does Cookie . . . apply her principles to?" Heather asked.

Rafe laughed.

"Well, I don't know," I said. "They're just something one *has*."

"Yes?" Heather said. "It sounds so . . . inert, sort of. Like a stack of fish on a plate."

"Fish on a plate!" I said. God, I was hungry. "Do you suppose there's anything edible within reach?"

We threaded our way around a nest of journalists who were disclosing to each other their coastal preferences, and reached the buffet table just in time to catch the gratifying sight of Buddy's friend spilling enchilada sauce on Cookie's Aubusson. Really, Cookie had never served more annoying food. Last year it had been julienned Asiatic unidentifiables; the year before that it was all reheated morels en croûte étouffés avec canard aux fraises poivrées kind of thing; and this year, Spam, it seemed, was more or less our lot. "And with her money," I said. "I really don't know what I'd do if I had Cookie's money."

"You could buy Cookie's sofa," Heather said. "That's what I'd do."

"Really?" I said. "That's odd. I can't really say I'm mad for it."

Heather wasn't listening, though. She and Rafe had become absorbed by the engineering problems of feeding each other tacos. Well, that was certainly something they weren't going to get any help with from me. Besides, there was no point in trying to have a rational conversation with Rafe when he was in one of his playmate-of-the-month moods. I wandered off and eventually found myself talking to Jules Racklin, whom I'd met here and there but never really talked to and who turned out to be a very interesting man. Very intelligent. *Very* interesting.

The day after that party, I happened to turn on the TV at eleven o'clock, and having so recently seen Heather, I do have to say that I was pretty mesmerized by Lydia. The plot of the show didn't seem to have progressed to any great degree since the episode I had seen previously, and at the appearance of each familiar figure, I felt a slight sensation of agreeable reinforcement, of knowing my way around.

I had tuned in while Eric was speaking on the phone. And while I had never actually seen Eric before, I was able to identify him by inference from the conversation I had heard between—um, let's see—Brent and . . . yes, Hank. As he talked, Eric moved a painting on the wall, exposing a safe at which he looked gloatingly for a moment. Then he replaced the painting, hung up the phone, and left his house, never noticing—the foolish fellow—that Brent and Hank were sitting in a car parked right across the street. Carolyn and Chad then drank cocktails and had an agonizing discussion (which I suspected was one of many) about whether they did or did not want to start a family. Carolyn appeared to acquiesce to Chad's insistence that it would be better to wait, but I saw right through her. She felt hurt, I could tell, and disappointed. Then Colleen appeared to be developing, in a supermarket, a rather modern crush on Ellie's mother, who herself, to judge from what followed, was somewhat more interested in Mr. Armstrong. Suddenly there was a woman from another universe holding a box of soap called Vision. What had happened? Ah, one episode of "This Brief Candle" had been concluded, of course. I turned off the set (I had a thousand things to do), and the little light in the center danced furiously, brighter and brighter, into oblivion.

Now. Right. The first thing was to call and thank Cookie. Cookie and I had the requisite little jaw about what a delightful evening, etc. (actually, it had turned out rather nicely, due to that nice Jules Racklin), and when I'd heaped upon Cookie what I hoped were sufficient thanks, I felt I might as well hit her up for a couple of grand for the foundation. Not that it would do any good, but you never knew. She might have some good ideas for sources, anyhow. Cookie always had on hand the scrap of information one needed, if one could bear to pick through the refuse to get it.

"Heavens, dear," she said, when I suggested a donation. "I'd be thrilled to, as you know or you wouldn't have asked, but I just don't have that sort of money lying around at the moment." My God. Poor Cookie had probably spent her last pesos on taco chips for the party. "Why don't you call Nina Morisette? That dame is absolutely loaded, I'm telling you, darling. To her, that kind of money is like two cents. And I mean *two cents*."

"Nina's such a tightwad, though," I said. "When you talk to her you'd think she was starving."

"Oh, I know, dear," Cookie said. "She is a witch, isn't she? But her familiar—what's his name? Garvin Something, Something Garvin—is the one to talk to. He's a complete fool, I promise you, and he can get her to give to any ridiculous thing."

"By the way," I said, feeling that the time had come to change the subject, "wasn't it nice to meet Rafe's girlfriend?"

"Wasn't it," Cookie agreed. "Such a sweet child. They all are, though, aren't they? I do wonder how he can tell all those sweet children apart. Ah, me. Then again, I suppose one might as well ask how anyone can tell us sour wrecks apart!"

"Ahaha," I agreed politely while Cookie ratified her little witticism with raucous baying.

"I talked to her for some time," Cookie continued when she'd recovered, "and she really did seem sweet, you know. It's amazing how evil she is on that TV show of hers."

"Yes, what is that girl up to?" I asked. "Lydia—isn't that her name?"

"Oh, well!" Cookie said. "It's quite exciting, really, because the girl who used to play Lydia got fired, so right before she left, the writers or producers or whoever had her seduce her sister Carolyn's fiancée, Jad, and then go off somewhere to make unseen trouble for a while, while the audience could forget what she looked like. In the meantime, Carolyn and Jad got married, and then Lydia (who's Heather now, of course) came back and started vamping Jad again like crazy. And that's just what she's doing for fun! She's also gotten herself involved with a fellow named Brent, just to spite Brent's girlfriend, Colleen, who really is a bit lame, when you get right down to it, and as a favor to Brent (at least that's what Brent thinks—it's really so she'll have power over him) Lydia's seducing this man Eric to get some blueprints from him that Brent can use to blackmail Mr. Armstrong!"

"Oh, no!" I said. "Is *that* who Eric was talking to on the phone just now? *Lydia*?" A silence descended on the other end of the phone like a gavel.

"I can't imagine," Cookie said.

"But weren't you watching?" I asked foolishly.

"Dear, that show is just something I stumble upon once a century or so," Cookie said, gingerly depositing my question in the toilet.

Damn. Cookie was actually embarrassed. And I would have to pay, for sure. "Well, anyway, dear," she said, "I'm glad you enjoyed yourself last night. I thought you must be enjoying yourself when I saw you there with Jules. He really is a scorcher, isn't he? Best-looking man I ever saw."

"Very pleasant," I said thinly. "Anyway, Cookie dear . . ."

"Oh, he's a dish, all right. I just knew how much you'd enjoy him. When he walked in alone, I got down on my knees and I thanked God that Pia Dougherty hadn't been able to make it. Naturally, I'd had to invite her, too, but, fortunately, it seems she's out getting photographed with some goats in Kashmir for somebody's spring collection. Oh, I don't know—I really just don't. Everyone talks about how gorgeous she is, but I really don't see it, do you? I mean, it's really *him*, isn't it? He's the really stunning one."

"Oh, the time!" I said. "Just look! I must hang up and run." I hung up and sat. Pia Dougherty, huh. Maybe Buddy would give me a good write-off if I donated my phone to the museum.

I must admit I wasn't having just the greatest time with men. I was finding that you have to get to know someone a bit in order to become interested in getting to know him at all, and that was such a bore! The same questions, the same little conversations, over and over: Were you close to your father? Just think—so, you, too, as a child, were afraid of getting hit by the baseball! Tell me, do you really believe that it's possible to rid oneself of unconscious concerns over fuel costs when discussing our Middle Eastern policies? And so on and so forth— just like having to slog through those statistics courses in college before being allowed to register for Abnormal Personality. I did go out now and again, of course, but in a perfunctory, frog-kissing sort of spirit, and a frog, in my experience, is a frog to the finish.

My own love life, at that time, then, provided me with no information to sort through—nothing to think about or try to get in order. It was as useful to the production of conversation as disappearing ink is to the production of literature, and so I began to tap, for all it was worth, that skill which one develops during adolescence, of turning to account the love lives of one's friends. And since among my friends Rafe had always tended to have the most multiform and highly colored love life, I looked forward most to seeing him.

Sadly, though, he had become quite uncooperative since he'd taken up with Heather. He rarely put in an appearance, and when he did, he just sat around lumpishly and quaffed down great quantities of my expensive Scotch.

"How are you these days, Rafe?" I would say.

"Fine," he would say, with a remote, childish formality. "Just fine."

"Yes? How's everything going?" I would say.

"Oh, fine, thanks. Very well."

"Good . . . And how's Heather?"

"Oh, she's quite well. Just fine. Say, you don't have any more of that Scotch, do you? It's awfully good."

One evening he came over in a state of overt grumpiness. It seemed that he and Heather had had tickets to something, but Heather had been required on the spur of the moment to learn a huge new set of lines. "One of the guys in the show was in an accident today," Rafe said, "so they have to do something about it."

"What can they do?" I said. "Either he was in an accident or he wasn't, I'd think."

"What I mean," Rafe said, "is that they'll have to write him out of the story for a week or so. And then they'll have to think of some reason why he's in a cast from head to toe. It's going to be pretty conspicuous, after all."

"Oh.—Yes.—I see. How awful. And rather eerie, for that matter. Will they think up some accident for him to have had in the script, do you suppose?"

"I don't know," Rafe said. "It seems logical."

"You know," I said, "a few weeks ago I happened to see the show, and this man whose name is Mr. Armstrong had this terrible cold. And somebody else said he'd gotten it from kissing his secretary, Tracy. And, you know, maybe the week before the actress that plays Tracy really had had a cold, come to think of it. But in any case the writers couldn't have manufactured that guy's runny nose."

"Yup. Part of the credit for that cold just has to go to the ultimate scriptwriter, doesn't it?" Rafe yawned, bored by his own cliché. "Hey, speaking of the determining hand, you're just about winding up this year's work, right?"

"Yes," I said. The panel was reviewing each other's recommendations all that month. "We don't start up again for a while. But to tell you the truth," I confessed, "I've been thinking about getting into publishing instead of going on with the foundation."

"Oh," Rafe said.

"'Oh'? Is that all? I thought you'd be pleased."

"Why?" Rafe said. "That is, I have no objection, but why did you think I'd be pleased, particularly?"

"I thought you disapproved of what I do."

"I don't," Rafe said. "I don't think I disapprove of it."

"I'm glad to hear that," I said. "In any case, I feel I've done my turn for society. I feel that now it's time for me to become involved in something for myself. I want to get somewhere—to use my abilities to . . . to . . . *build*, in some way. Don't you think that's important?"

"Well," Rafe said. "It seems to me that what's important is how you feel about your work while you're doing it."

"What?" I said. "I feel fine about my work while I'm doing it, whatever that means. And while I'm not doing it."

"That's good," Rafe said, without conviction.

"I feel just fine about my work," I said. "I really don't know what we're talking about."

"I'm not sure myself," he said. "But there's something about the way Heather . . . I mean, I've noticed, watching Heather, that, well, what she does doesn't make her feel important."

"I should think not," I said.

"No, but I mean, it doesn't make her feel *un*important either. I mean, I've noticed, watching Heather, that because she distinguishes between herself and her work, in some way, that—"

"Really?" I said. I really couldn't take one more instant of this. "Do tell me. How interesting. Let's see. You've noticed, you've noticed—that it's better to be on a soap opera than to subsidize art. No—you've noticed that it doesn't matter whether you're Eva Braun or Florence Nightingale as long as you *feel good about it*."

"You will be astonished to learn," Rafe said, "that that is not what I mean. I don't really mean that *you're* important, at all, in your work. I mean that it's the work itself that—oh, obviously, of course . . . I don't know. I've just been watching how, if it's really your work that's important to you, rather than some idea of yourself doing the work—that is, if your approach to your work is one of genuine interest in the work rather than yourself—then it will necessarily follow that the work will itself respond somehow, with a genuine—"

"Genuine!" I said. "Genuine! That's a pretty loaded word you're tossing around there! Look, Rafael, *everything* is genuine, if you're going to start giving me this kind of stuff! I've already told you that my work is important to me. I don't know why you insist on thinking it isn't. See, that's genuine Glenlivet you're drinking out of genuine Baccarat. You're sitting in a genuine Eames genuine chair. I don't know what you're talking about! Do you think I should go out and get myself killed in some war to prove I'm serious? Do you think I should get a job on a soap opera? What do you think? The Spanish Civil War is over! The entire Abraham Lincoln Brigade is dead! I really don't know what we're talking about! That's a genuine TV set over there on which a genuine simulacrum of a genuine version of your girlfriend is genuinely conjured up—and furthermore, my genuine body has the same damn genuine molecular structure as her body's damn genuine molecular structure!"

Heavens! What had gotten into me? What had the Abraham Lincoln Brigade or Heather's molecular structure to do with publishing? It was just that Rafe's murky attitudinizing really had gotten to me. It really had. He had really changed since he'd started seeing that girl.

"I'm sorry," I said. "I'm very sorry to say these things to you, but, really, Rafe, you used to be so charming."

"It seems so long ago, now, doesn't it?" he said sadly, swirling the ice cubes around in his drink.

It was a long, long time before I saw Rafe again. Several months, probably, elapsed before, one afternoon, he called.

"Can I take you to dinner?" he said.

"What, tonight?"

"Well, are you free?"

I was delighted he had called, actually. I was sorry I'd jumped on him that evening when he'd obviously just been confused and troubled; and when we met, at a very pretty Italian restaurant in my neighborhood, neither of us mentioned how long it had been since we'd seen each other.

Rafe ordered a bottle of Cliquot. "To the free peoples of the world," he said, lifting his glass.

"What's the matter?" I said. "Is Heather giving you a hard time?"

"Oh, we just haven't seen too much of each other for a while."

"You finally got tired of each other, huh?" I said.

"No. We just don't like each other. Jesus, that's not true." He raked his hands through his hair, which, in view of the horror he had of disarranging it, indicated profound anguish.

"Poor Rafe," I said, but with measured commiseration. I was waiting to hear more before deciding whether it was sympathy that was required or (had I been that sort of person) an "I told you so."

"She wanted to get married, you see. Have children." My God, what a thought. Rafe surrounded by weensy Rafe replicas. "In fact, she gave me something like an ultimatum. Oh, God. I'm too old to settle down. I've really got to start running around again."

"It does seem to suit you, Rafe."

"I just couldn't. She's a wonderful girl, but I couldn't. Particularly the children part, you know? I do want children of course, eventually, but just not right now. And just the fact that she says to me, 'Look, I really want children, I want them now, I think that if we're to continue we should get married,' and I don't have any response at all, except sheer terror—well, that indicates to me that it's wrong, you know? No matter how I think I feel about her, that proves that it's just wrong." How glossy his hair looked in the candlelight while he shoved it around like that! "Don't you think that's true?" he said.

"Well," I said slowly—I felt I was looking at us both from a great height—"I suppose it must be."

"See, that's what I mean," he said. "Here, have some of my zucchini. How do *you* feel about children, anyway? I've always wondered whether you were disappointed about not having any."

"I might still have some one of these days. I'm only your age, remember?"

"Sure," he said. "Of course. But how do you feel about them now?"

"Oh, I don't know, really," I said. "They are dear, but to tell you the truth, Rafe, I sometimes find them—I don't know—off-putting. I mean, those tiny faces all lit up with some entirely groundless joy, and then something happens and they just crumple all up like old Christmas wrappings. All that anguish, all that drama! I mean, it's quite cute and whatnot, but who can understand it? Of course, they're so sweet— absolutely adorable—and yet I can't help feeling that they're, well . . . *oddities*. Almost a bit creepy, somehow."

"I know," Rafe said, sounding faintly surprised. "That's sort of how I feel, really."

I looked across at him, sitting there lost in his fleecy sadness, and I wondered if Heather knew what she'd given away. Perhaps she really was looking for something more ordinary than life with Rafe, or perhaps, having been dazzled by him, as doubtless she had been, she feared that there was nothing to rely on beneath his sophistication and glamour. But that was the thing about Rafe, I knew. Underneath the alpaca and wool, underneath the—well, no matter—*fundamentally*, I mean, he was as good a man as you could ever hope to find.

"She really is a marvelous girl," Rafe said, as if in verification of his own opinion (although by then, of course, it didn't really matter if his opinion was correct or not). "She has a quality I've never really encountered in anyone else. A sort of directness, or clarity, that gives her courage. Like some magic sword."

It occurred to me that this quality Rafe so touchingly considered her to have was perhaps her quality (and it truly was a very attractive one) of youthful, vigorous ignorance concerning life's more serious sides. "Poor Rafe," I said. Poor Rafe.

"So. I've missed you," he said. "Tell me what you've been up to. Any luck with the job hunting?"

"To tell you the truth," I said, "I've decided to do some traveling before I tie myself down again. Some friends have asked me to come visit them on Patmos for a while, and I thought, oh, why not? I've been dying to get out of my place, anyway, so I'm packing everything up and I'm getting a subtenant."

"You're leaving?" Rafe said, looking up, and we looked right smack into each other's face.

I was just getting to sleep that night when the phone rang. It was Rafe. "Hello there," I said. "What's on your mind?"

"I was wrong," he said. "I had to call you. I misinterpreted the meaning of my own feelings." Had I been asleep, perhaps, when the phone rang? "I realized after we talked tonight," he said, "that I was wrong. If I turn away from this, I'm turning away from . . . from everything. I know that, and I'm going to ask Heather to marry me."

"I see," I said. I had a headache. I must have been asleep when the phone rang.

"That fear that I mentioned to you—it's just nothing, do you see? It's just something like—like that law in physics—you know?—that the strength of the reaction is equal to the . . . to the . . . the whatever. Remember that law? Isn't there some kind of law like that?"

"I don't know." My *head*. "I got a C in physics."

"Whatever," he said. "What I mean is that the reason I've been so frightened is because it's so important to me, the possibility of a life with Heather—a real life. It's a gift, I've realized. No, not a gift—an invitation, a test. If I'm able to accept it, do you see, for that reason alone I'm good enough to be given it."

"I see," I said. He sounded actually feverish.

"And, really, I actually do love her," he said.

"Well, then," I said. "That's what counts."

"I wanted to call you right away," he said. "Because we were talking. You know."

"I'm glad," I said.

"So," he said.

"So," I said. "Well, good night, Rafe, dear. Thank you for calling."

God damn it. I hated being awakened at night. I could never get back to sleep. Maybe I'd go make myself some warm milk. No one else was going to do it, anyhow, that was for sure.

I took out the milk, and my one pot and one cup that weren't packed yet, and very sensibly I poured, instead of milk into the pot, Scotch into the cup, thereby saving myself some dishwashing, and wandered into the living room, which was piled high with cartons prepared for storage.

A gift, huh? An invitation, a test? What on earth had happened to Rafe's brains in the few hours since I'd seen him? Jesus, I felt terrible, though. And if the truth be told, in fact, the shaming truth, another thing that I actually seemed to feel was (oh, God!) *lonely*! As if I were being excluded from this "real life," this . . . this "everything" that Rafe imagined he was being invited to share in! How amazing! I'm really not the sort of person who feels jealous of someone else's happiness (even supposing this folly of Rafe's were to be considered happiness). I'm not the sort of person who feels that one loses by another's gain. I'm the sort of person who takes pleasure in a friend's pleasure. Oh, I know there are people who believe the realm of human activity to be an exchange, as it were, where for every good thing acquired, some good thing has to be given back. "Here are my teeth," for instance, such people believe you would say when they fell out. "Now may I have that harvest table that's in the window of Pierre Deux?" These people believe that there is some system that ensures that you cannot have yards of eyelashes in addition to a talent for entertaining, unless the news vendor on the corner falls down a flight of steps and has to be hospitalized. And people of this opinion, naturally enough, quail when another person, even a friend as close as Rafe, threatens to bite into the world's short supply of happiness. But I am not of this opinion; I do not believe these things, and even if I did, I would be prepared nonetheless to be happy for Rafe. Even if he was making an awful mistake.

But then, the problem remained of why people did lose their teeth. Why didn't I have yards of eyelashes? Why would a news vendor have to fall down a flight of steps? Why would anyone have to be a news vendor at all? Obviously, if one were to understand all this, one would have to read some horrible math text about the laws of chance and probability. Anyhow, my head was still killing me.

How inhospitable my own living room seemed! Just all those cartons, and a huge, gilt, good-for-nothing mirror, exactly as empty as the room, and a few oddments I was leaving for the comfort of my subtenant, including a hideous Bristol vase that John had given to me early on in our marriage. He'd said the color reminded him of his childhood. Yuck. I'd offered it back to him, naturally, when he moved out, but he'd wanted it to stay with me. John was a loyal old boy, no doubt about that—loyal to the vase, loyal to his childhood—and now, from what I heard, he was being loyal to Marcia Meaver.

I slept, finally, for a few hours, after it had already become light, and got up just in time to catch the final segment of that day's "This Brief Candle." I turned on the set, and there was Heather (well, Lydia) right in my living room with her sister Carolyn and Carolyn's husband, Jad.

"Chad, darling," Carolyn said. (So it *was* Chad! I *swear* it was Chad.) "That was Hank on the phone. Something peculiar has happened at Mr. Armstrong's office. I must go right away."

"Well," Chad said to Lydia after the door slammed. He cleared his throat. "Guess I'll just go into my workroom and try to get a few things done." He smiled in a sickened, hopeless attempt at heartiness.

"Why don't you?" Lydia said, never taking her eyes off him for a second. "Why don't you, Chad? But first, my darling brother-in-law, I'd like you to sit down. Because you and I have a little matter to discuss. One that isn't going to be getting any littler, if you see what I mean. So we can't put it off much longer." Close-up of Lydia's face, inscrutably triumphant.

I stared and stared at the screen, but all there was to see, suddenly, was a batch of brats hell-bent on wrecking their clothes. I turned off the TV and sat, exhausted, while the little white light in the center boiled brighter and brighter until it was gone, and then, on some overpowering and incomprehensible impulse, I went to the phone and I called Cookie. Her line was busy, and even though it stayed busy for a good half hour, I just kept standing there, for some reason, dialing her number.

"Hello, dear!" she said, when I finally got through. "How marvelous to hear your voice! It's been weeks!"

"Hasn't it," I agreed. "Well, except for the Schillers' the other night."

"But that hardly counts, does it, dear?" Cookie said. "One feels one must creep about in disguise there, doesn't one, like an Arab."

"One does indeed," I said. Did Arabs creep about in disguise?

"It's torture, isn't it, how one daren't say a word at the Schillers', or one is sure to read some horrible twisted version of it in some publication the next morning. But on the other hand, of course, one must keep one's own ears open because of all that information flying around. I suppose it's rather what the agora must have been."

"I suppose so," I said. The agora? Arabs? Was Cookie taking some sort of course? An alphabetical survey of everything? I myself couldn't remember for the life of me what the agora had been.

"Each time I go to the Schillers' I come home utterly destroyed," she said. "And each time, I swear I'm never going to go again. But how can one turn one's back on such a spectacle?"

"This one looked relatively sedate to me," I said.

"Sedate!" Cookie roared. "Oh. You missed the bit when Marjorie went to get her coat and found Rupert Fallodin making *advances* to Alison."

"So what?" I said. "Some married people find each other attractive."

"I know that, dear," Cookie said with dignity. "But Rupert

has been seeing Marjorie for months, you know, and it was quite a shock to her. And when she came downstairs she made a few remarks about him. At the top of her lungs, to be precise. It was extraordinary! Some very unusual habits Rupert has, it seems. Of course, Marjorie had polished off about a quart of Scotch by that time. I mean, so had I, naturally, but so had she." Cookie barked happily. "Oh, it was a very steamy evening. Did you see Melissa Hober? She was tagging along behind Constance Ripp like an anthropologist tags along behind his Indian. Once, Constance stopped short, and Melissa almost broke that incredible chin of hers against Constance's skull!"

"It's hard to imagine Melissa tagging along behind anyone," I said.

"Oh, she can accommodate just about any degree of self-abasement if she thinks it'll get her published, you know. Constance is taking over as the poetry editor of *Life and Times*, you see, and evidently Melissa knows that Constance has an unfailing weakness for a pretty face, which is something Melissa obviously imagines herself to be in possession of."

"Constance?" I asked, amazed. "Is Constance gay?" How could Constance be gay? I was the sort of person who was usually very perceptive about other people, and it had never occurred to me that Constance was gay!

"Is Constance gay!" Cookie hooted. "Does a pope shit in the woods? Oh, dear! I never would have said a thing if I'd thought for a moment that there was one living soul who didn't know. Well, I'm sure it isn't really a secret, even though Constance does put on that ridiculous act. But what did you think Honoria della Playa was—the au pair girl?"

"Constance had an affair with Honoria della Playa?" I said.

"Oh! My mouth!" Cookie said. "But naturally I assumed you knew all about that."

Oh, Cookie was having a splendid day with me. But I really didn't have time for it. What was I doing on the phone, anyhow?! Here I was, participating in Cookie's juvenile, pointless gossip, when I had to get all this stuff into storage! I really had to hang up immediately. Immediately. "Well, darling—" I said.

"Oh! By the way," Cookie interrupted, "how's Rafe these days? I haven't seen him for absolutely ages."

"I haven't seen much of him myself, actually," I said. "I don't suppose you happen to have heard anything about him, have you?"

"Well, strange that you ask," Cookie said. "Isn't that strange. Amanda Krotnick called just now—right before you did, as it happens—and she was saying that she hasn't seen Rafe in a blue moon, either."

Amanda Krotnick. Amanda Krotnick. Oh, yes—her husband used to play squash with John.

"And Amanda told me that she's been following Rafe's girlfriend on TV, just out of a friendly interest in Rafe." (What? Oh, yes, I suppose Rafe had mentioned her to me. I think she used to go to gallery openings with him and that sort of thing once in a while, when I didn't feel like it or was tied up with John or something.) "And Amanda said that she thinks Heather's TV alter ego, Lydia, you know, is pregnant by her sister's husband, Jad. Isn't that something? You see (this is according to Amanda, of course), it really puts Jad in a very peculiar position, because apparently Lydia plans to go ahead and have the baby, and sooner or later, naturally, she's going to begin to show."

I sat down right on a carton. "The things they do on

those soap operas!" I said. "Imagine, if that's what people did with their time!"

"Well, I certainly don't have the time for them," Cookie said. "And I don't know how Amanda finds the time, either."

I hadn't meant that watching soap operas was an astonishing thing to do with one's time, although, of course, it was. I had meant that it would be astonishing if people spent their time the way people on the soap operas spend their time. But I didn't give a damn what I'd meant.

"So, what brings you to the phone, dear? What can I do for you?" Cookie said.

"Oh—" I said. "I was just calling. To say goodbye, really. I'm leaving soon, you know."

"Heavens! That's right!" she said. "We must get together before. Lunch next week?"

"Perfect," I said. "Lunch."

"Marvelous," Cookie said. "We'll call each other. Goodbye, dear."

Oh, God. How awful, that mirrored view of cardboard cartons. The reflection of pure desolation. At least I wasn't looking too awfully terrible myself, I noticed. Not too horrible, considering life and so forth. Somehow I'd managed to change remarkably little over the years.

All right—on with all the things to be done. What were they? Maybe I'd call Rafe.

"Hello," said a voice that belonged to Rafe himself, and I didn't have time to remember why I'd called. I'd been expecting a secretary to answer.

"Oh, Rafe," I said. "I just called to say . . . to say that I hope you got some sleep last night."

"I didn't," he said. My God, he sounded awful.

"That's too bad," I said, and neither of us seemed to have anything else to say. "Anyway."

"I'm going straight home when I finish up here today to get some sleep," he said. "But if you're not all booked up tomorrow evening, why don't I come by? I'll bring a picnic."

Rafe arrived the next night laden down with paper bags. "Assiette de eats," he said. He put the bags in the kitchen and hung up his coat. "What sensational flowers!"

"Aren't they," I said. "Oh, Rafe—squab! And grapes— and—good heavens!—*mauve* paper plates!"

"I had my reasons," he said. "I calculated that they would be an excellent foil for the—yes, *perfect*—pesto."

"Oh, and radicchio-and-fennel salad! My absolute favorite. You always find such good things, Rafe."

"It's my flair for life," he said with an odd look on his face.

"It's true, Rafe. That's one of the things I've always loved about you," I said, but the odd look hovered for a moment.

I opened a bottle of nice wine that I'd picked up and poured us paper cupfuls of it, and we made ourselves at home with our picnic, among the cartons.

"I got a new secretary today," Rafe said. "I found her in a club the other night. She's a cute kid, but the trouble with interviewing someone in a club is that you can't hear what they're saying to you. I guess I'll have to spend this week showing her how to answer the phone."

"Rafe," I said. How good it was to be sitting around together.

"What is this?" he said, reaching over. "China silk?" I sat very still while he rubbed my collar.

"Nice," he said, but by the time he sat back, I could see his thoughts were on something else.

"What is it, Rafe?" I asked.

"Nothing," he said. "Not a thing, not a thing."

"You know," he said after a moment. "I never meant you to think, that time, that I was saying that you were self-absorbed, or something of that sort."

"Oh, I know," I said. When had he said I was self-absorbed? "I don't think of myself as a particularly self-absorbed person, so it wouldn't really have struck home in any case." How strange. So Rafe had accused me of being self-absorbed.

"Anyhow," Rafe said, "I wanted to make sure you knew I never meant anything like that."

"Rafe, darling," I said, "would you mind getting me a glass of water?" I seemed to have gone through quite a bit of wine without really noticing. "Thanks."

"It's strange, you know," Rafe said. "I always thought Heather and I were having these conversations. And that I was listening to her. And even learning things from her. But I don't think she was ever actually saying anything in partic-ular, or even *being* anything in particular. I just sort of con-cocted it all by myself. I was really just staring at her, because she's so pretty."

I went to the kitchen and got us a bottle of Cognac. "No sense wasting this on the subtenant."

"I'm sorry about calling so late the other night," Rafe said.

"Why not?" I said. "We're friends." I certainly wished he'd get around to telling me what was going on between him and Heather. "Anyhow, I guess everything's resolved itself, in one way or another."

"Oh, yes," he said. "It was just one of those night things

that happen when you're by yourself sometimes. And it just evaporated."

"Yes," I said. I poured us both some more Cognac. "I guess you just figured it out on your own."

"Well, actually," he said, "I did call her. And we talked. We had a nice talk. We agreed that we were just never suited to each other, but that we'd always consider each other friends. Anyhow, she's gotten all mixed up with some guy. Evidently she thinks it's serious."

We drank and sat in the dim light and talked, and then it was very late, somehow, and Rafe was getting his coat. Rafe was putting on his lovely soft coat, and he was going to go.

"Well, good night," he said. "Thanks again."

"Rafe," I said suddenly, to my own astonishment, "why do you suppose you and I never had an affair?" Oh, was I going to be hung over in the morning!

"Well," he said, pausing at the door, "for one thing, you were a married lady."

"I know," I said. "But for another thing?"

"Oh, I just don't think it would have worked, do you?" he said. "We're too much alike, really, aren't we? We'd climb into bed and I'd say, 'Great sheets—where'd you get them?' Or I'd take off my clothes and you'd say, 'Oh, fabulous—underwear with bison.' That sort of thing. We just wouldn't really have been able to concentrate."

"Underwear with bison?" I said. "Really?" Rafe smiled. "Rafe," I said. "We're actually not alike anymore, though, are we? You've changed."

"Now, now," he said. "Don't do that." He licked a little tear from my cheek. "Yum." And he gave me a little kiss on the forehead.

I leaned against the door as it closed behind him. Oh,

Jesus. I was actually dizzy! I must really have gotten myself loaded. In any case, it was truly late, and sooner or later I was going to have to stand myself upright without benefit of the door and take myself off to bed. Which would entail turning around. Turning around to the sight of those cartons, that vase, the empty mirror, the nothing, nothing, nothing at all that had come of my life in New York. And what was it I was planning to get for myself on Patmos, then? What? Rocks, sheep, a stack of fish on a plate, that's what! And I turned, and stood, and looked, supporting myself against the door, for what felt like hours.

At least, that was what I remembered, in a bunched-up sort of way, when I woke up the next morning, somehow not hung over at all.

Rafe and I never managed to get in touch with each other before I left—I suppose I was just too busy getting ready. Oddly enough, though, I did run into Heather just about the day before I left, when the sort of impulse that later compels one not to jeer at people who turn to their horoscopes in the paper led me to Saks. It was she who recognized me first, even though I had been staring straight at the beautiful face I should have known so well.

"I hear you're going off on adventures," she said, taking my hand in a way that made me feel strangely at ease. "Are you excited?"

"I suppose so," I said. "Yes." I felt a bit dazed looking at her. She really was lovely. Very . . . vivid, in some way. "How did you hear I was leaving? From Rafe?"

"Yes," she said. "He called a week or so ago. I was glad. We'd just let things get bad, and I hate to leave things bad, or even just unresolved, with someone I've cared about. Don't you?"

"Well, yes," I said. "I suppose I must."

"So he came over and we talked. Really conversed, I mean, for a change. Instead of just fighting, or falling into bed, or any of those things you do with people when you're breaking up with them. It was nice. I was really glad he called. I couldn't have just called him, you know, even though I wanted to give him my news. It would have sounded like I was giving him a last chance, almost—that sort of thing, don't you think? But it really was all over between us quite a while ago."

"News?" I said. "Last chance?"

"Oh," she said, and stopped. "That is, I'm going to get married, you see."

"Really," I said. "How wonderful."

"Yes," she said. "In fact, Neil's supposed to meet me here any minute. You know, I feel I know you so well, even though we only met once. Rafe talked about you so often, though, I almost feel that we've . . . shared something."

"I feel the same way," I said.

"Oh, look," she said. "There's Neil now. I can introduce you."

It took me a moment to place the man who had walked up to us and was putting his arm around Heather. He certainly didn't look much like Brent, that drip in the car that Lydia was doing something or other with, although that, I saw, was who (in a manner of speaking, of course) he was. In person he seemed like a nice young man, and he was obviously very much in love, as, obviously, was Heather herself.

"Well, I've got to get myself upstairs and look for some new clothes," she said.

"Yes," I said faintly. She would be needing some.

"Nice to meet you," Neil said, as he and Heather washed away from me in the crowd.

What a marvelous-looking baby it was going to be, with parents like Heather and Brent—Neil, rather. Or Lydia, to think of it another way, and Neil, or Brent. Or Rafe. As a matter of fact. Come to think of it.

So many faces, so many faces. People were pouring in and out of the doors, swarming between the counters, rising in swatches on the escalators. So many faces just right there, and any face possible from all the branchings of history for that baby. The faces around me swam and blended, and for an instant I was almost too dizzy to stand, but then I saw Heather's face, quite, of course, itself, and all the other faces consolidated properly again upon their discrete owners, as Heather waved back to me from the escalator and smiled. And even though I had dozens of things to do, *dozens* of things, I stopped to wave back and watch as, brighter and brighter, a dwindling dot in the stream of shoppers, Heather was borne away to some other floor.

A LESSON IN TRAVELING LIGHT

During the best time, when it was still warm in the afternoons and the sky was especially blue and the smell of spoiling apples rose up from the ground, Lee and I drove down from the high meadows with our stuff in the van, looking for someplace to live.

The night before we left, we went down the road to say goodbye to Tom and Johanna. Johanna looked like glass, but Tom was flushed and in a violent good humor. He passed the bottle of Jack Daniel's back and forth to Lee and slapped him on the back and talked a mile a minute about different places he had lived and people he had met and bets he had won and whatnot, so I figured he and Johanna had been fighting before we got there.

"Done a lot of traveling?" Tom asked me.

"No," I said. He knew I hadn't.

"Well, you'll enjoy it," he said. "You'll enjoy it."

Tom was making an effort, I suppose, because I was leaving.

"Hey," he said to Lee, having completed his effort, "are you going to see Miles?"

"I guess we might," Lee said. "Yeah, actually, we could."

"Who's Miles?" I said.

"Is he still with that girl?" Tom said. "The one who—"

"No," Lee interrupted, laughing. "He's back with Natalie."

"Really?" said Johanna. "Listen, if you do see him, tell him I still wear the parka he left at our place that day." Tom stared at her, but she smiled.

"Who's Miles?" I said.

"Someone who used to live around here. Before I brought you back up the mountain with me," Lee said, turning to face me. His eyes, when he's been thinking about something else, are like a blaze in an empty warehouse, and I caught my breath.

After dinner Lee and I walked back to our place, and as the house came into view I tried to fix it in my memory. It already looked skeletal, though, like something dead on a beach.

"That's what it is," Lee said. "Old bones. A carapace. You're creating pain for yourself by trying to make it something more."

I looked again, letting it be bones, and felt light. I wanted to leave behind with the house the old bones of my needs and opinions. I wanted to be unencumbered, a warrior like Lee. When we'd met, Lee had said to me, "I feel like I have to take care of you."

"That's good," I had said.

"No it isn't," he had said.

I wondered if he ever thought about places he had lived, other faces, old girlfriends. Once in a while he seemed bowed down with a weight of shelved memories. Having freight in storage, though, is what you trade to travel light, I sometimes thought, and at those moments I thought it was as much for him as for me that I wanted Lee so badly to stay with me.

The first night of driving we stopped in Pennsylvania.

"We're very close to Miles and Natalie's," Lee said. "It would be logical to stop by there tomorrow."

"Where do they live?" I said.

Lee took out a big U.S. road map. "They're over here, in Baltimore."

"That's so far," I said, following his finger.

"In a sense," he said. "But on the other hand, look at, say, Pittsburgh." His finger alighted inches from where we were. "Or Columbus."

"Or Louisville!" I said. "Look how far that is—to Louisville!"

"You think that's far?" Lee said. "Well, listen to this— ready? Poplar Bluff!"

"Tulsa!" I said. "Wait—Oklahoma City!"

We both started to shout.

"Cheyenne!"

"Flagstaff!"

"Needles, Barstow, Bishop!"

"Eureka!" we both yelled at once.

We sat back and eyed the map. "That was some trip," Lee said.

"Are we going to do that?" I said.

Lee shrugged. "We'll go as far as we want," he said.

After all that, it looked on the map like practically no distance to Baltimore, but by the time we reached it I was sick of sitting in the van, and I hoped Natalie and Miles were the sort of people who would think of making us something to eat.

"What if they don't like me?" I said when we parked.

"Why wouldn't they like you?" Lee said.

I didn't know. I didn't know them.

"They'll like you," Lee said. "They're friends of mine."

Their place turned out to be a whole floor of a building divided up by curves of glass bricks. Darkness eddied around us and compressed the light near its sources, and the sounds our shoes made on the wood floor came back to us from a distance.

Natalie must have been just about my age, but there might be an infinite number of ways to be twenty, I saw, shocked. She sat us down on leather sofas the size of whales and brought us things to drink on a little tray, and she wore a single huge red earring. It was clear that she and Miles and Lee had talked together a lot before. There were dense, equidistant silences, and when one of them said something, it was like a stone landing in a still pond. I watched Natalie's earring while a comma of her black hair sliced it into changing shapes. After a while Miles and Lee stood up. They were going to see some building in another part of the city. "Anything we need, babe?" Miles asked Natalie.

"Pick up a couple of bottles of wine," she said. "Oh, yeah, and some glue for this." She opened her fist to disclose a second red earring in pieces in her palm.

"What's the matter?" I heard Lee say, and he was speaking to me.

Natalie and I moved over to the kitchen to make dinner, and she asked me how long Lee and I had been together.

"He's so fabulous," she said. "Are you thinking of getting married?"

"Not really," I said. We'd discussed it once when we'd gotten together. "It seems fairly pointless. Is there anything I can do?"

"Here," she said, handing me a knife and an onion. "Miles and I got married. His parents made us. They said they'd cut Miles off if we didn't."

"Is it different?" I said.

"Sort of," she said. "It's turned out to be an O.K. thing, actually. We used to, when we had a problem or something, just talk about it to the point where we didn't have to deal with it anymore. But now I guess we try to fix it. Does Lee still hate watercress?"

"No," I said. Watercress? I thought.

"It's very good," Natalie said, "but I still wouldn't be surprised if it ended tomorrow."

"Natalie," I said, "would you pierce my ears?"

"Sure," she said. "Just let me finish this stuff first." She took back from me the knife and the onion, which was still whole because I hadn't known what to do with it.

When Lee and Miles got back, I put the ice cube I was holding against my earlobe into the sink, and we all sat down for dinner.

"Nice," Lee said, holding his glass. Lee and I had always drunk wine out of the same glasses we drank everything else out of, and it was not the kind of wine you'd have anything to say about, so Lee with his graceful raised glass was an odd sight. So odd a sight, in fact, that it seemed to lift the table slightly, causing it to hover in the vibrating dimness.

"It is odd, isn't it," I said, feeling oddness billow, "that this is the way we make our bodies live."

Miles lifted his eyebrows.

"I mean," I said, forgetting what I did mean as I noticed that Lee had picked the watercress out of his salad, "I mean that it's odd to sit like this, in body holders around a disk, and move little heaps of matter from smaller disks to our mouths on little metal shovels. It seems like an odd way to make our bodies live."

I looked around at the others.

"Seems odd to me," Miles said. "I usually lie on the floor with my chin in a trough, sucking rocks."

"*Miles*," Natalie said, and giggled.

That night the clean, clean sheets wouldn't get warm, so I climbed out of bed and put on Lee's jacket and sat down to watch Lee sleep. He shifted pleasurably, and in the moonlight he looked as comfortable and dangerous as a lion. I watched him and waited for day, when he would get up, and I would give him back his jacket, and we could leave this place where he drank wine from a wineglass and strangers knew him so well.

In the morning Natalie and Miles asked if we wanted to stay, but Lee said we couldn't. We had planned to start out by the end of summer, he told them, and we were late.

Outside we saw how the light was already thin and banded across the highway, and we drove fast into sunset and winter. We were quiet mostly, and when we spoke, it was softly, like TV cowboys expecting an ambush.

That evening we bought some medicine at a drugstore because my ear had swollen up and I had a fever. I lay my head back into sliding dreams and woke into free-fall.

"Hey," Lee said, smoothing my hair back from my face. "You're asleep. You know that?" He scooped me over into his lap, and I nuzzled into his foggy gray T-shirt. "So look, killer," he said. "You want to stay here or you want to come in back with me?"

The next day my fever was gone and my ear was better.

For a while we were still where the expressways are thick coils and headlights and brake lights interweave at night in splendor. In the dark we would pull off to sleep in the corner of a truck stop or in a lot by a small highway, and in the morning, heat or cold, intensified by our metal shell, would wake us tangled in our blankets, and we would make love while fuel trucks roared past, rattling the van. Then we would look out the window to see where we were and drive off to find a diner or a Howard Johnson's.

We were spending more money than we had expected to, and Lee said that his friend Carlos, who lived in St. Louis, might be able to find him a few days' work. Lee looked through some scraps of paper and found Carlos's address, but when we got there, a group of people standing on the front steps told us that Carlos had moved. The group looked like a legation, with representatives of the different sizes and ages of humans, that was waiting to impart some terrible piece of information to a certain traveler. One of them gave us a new address for Carlos, which was near Nashville. Lee had never mentioned Carlos, so I assumed they weren't very close friends; but expectation had whetted Lee's appetite to see him, it seemed, because we left the group waiting on the steps and turned south.

Lee and Carlos were all smiles to see each other.

"What kind of money are you looking to make?" Carlos asked when we had settled ourselves in the living room.

"Nothing much," Lee said. "Just a little contingency fund. I'm clean these days."

"Well, listen," Carlos said. "Why don't you take the store for a week or two. I had to fire the guy I had managing it, and I've been dealing with it myself, but this would be an opportunity for me to look into some other stuff I've had my eye on." Carlos opened beers for himself and Lee. "Could I get you something?" he asked me, frowning.

"I'd like some beer, too," I said.

"Here," he said. "Wait. I'll get you a glass."

"Get back to Miami much?" Lee said.

"Too crowded these days, if you know what I mean," Carlos said. "Besides, I've pretty much stopped doing anything I can't handle locally. This is just where I live now, for whatever reason. And I've got my business. I don't know. It's a basis, you know? Something to continue from." He looked away from Lee and sighed.

During the days, when Lee and Carlos were out, I sat in back watching the sooty light travel from one side of the yard to the other. Sometimes a little boy played in an adjoining yard, jabbing with a stick at the clumps of grass there, which were stiff and gray with dirt. He was gray with dirt himself, and gray under the dirt. His nose ran, and the blue appliqué bear on the front of his overalls looked stunned.

I wondered what that boy had in mind for himself— whether his attack on the grass was some sort of self-devised preparation for an adulthood of authority and usefulness or whether he pictured himself forever on that bit of dirt, heading toward death in bear overalls of graduated size. I took to going in when I saw him and watching TV.

The night before we left Carlos's, Lee and I were awake late. We didn't have much to say, and after a while I noticed I was hungry.

"What? After that meal I made?" Lee said. "All right, let's go out."

Carlos was still awake, too, sitting in the living room with headphones on.

"Great," he said. "There's an all-night diner with sensational burgers."

"Burgers," Lee said. "You still eat that shit?"

Going into the diner, Lee and Carlos were a phalanx in themselves with their jackets and jeans and boots and belts, and I was proud to have been hungry. I ordered warrior food, and soon the waitress rendered up to me a plate of lacy-edged eggs with a hummock of potatoes and butter-stained toast, and to Lee and Carlos huge, aromatic burgers.

"Are you going to see Kathryn?" Carlos asked.

"I don't know," Lee said. "It depends."

"I'd like to see her myself, come to think of it. She's a

fantastic woman," Carlos said, balancing a French-fry beam on a French-fry house he was making. "She always was the best. You know, it's been great having you guys stay, but it makes me realize how much I miss other people around here. Maybe I should go out to the coast or something. Or at least establish some sort of nonridiculous romance."

"What about Sarah?" Lee said.

"Sarah," Carlos said. "Jesus." He turned to me. "Has Lee told you all about this marvel of technology?"

"No," I said.

"Well, I mean, listen, man," Carlos said, shaking his head. "She's a hot-looking lady, no question about it, but when I said 'nonridiculous' I had in mind someone you wouldn't be afraid to run into in the living room." He shook his head again and started drumming his knife on the table. "She sure is one hot-looking lady, though. Well, you know her."

"We have to get up really early," I said.

"That's O.K.," Lee said, but Carlos stood up. He looked exhausted.

"Yeah, sorry," he said. "Let's pull the plug on it."

Over the next few days I thought of Carlos often. His face had been shadowed when we said goodbye, so I couldn't recall it, and I thought how if I had been his girlfriend instead of Lee's I would have stayed there with him in that living room that seemed to just suck up light and would have heard from the inside the door slam and the van's motor start.

Lee and I drove back east a bit, to have a look at the Smokies. We parked the van in a campground under a bruise-colored sunset and set off on foot to pick up some food to cook outside on a fire. There were bugs, though, even though it was chilly, and the rutted clay road slipped and smacked underfoot, so we stopped at a Bar-B-Que place, where doughy families shouted at each other under throbbing fluorescent lights.

I had a headache. "It's incredible," I said, "how fast every place you go gets to be home. We've only just parked at that campground, but it's already home. And yesterday Carlos's place seemed like home. Now that seems like years ago."

"That's why it's good to travel," Lee said. "It reminds you what life really is. Finished?" he said. "Let's go."

"Let's," I said. "Let's go home." I inserted my finger under the canopy of his T-shirt sleeve, but he didn't notice particularly.

In time we came to a part of the country where mounds of what Lee said were uranium tailings winked in the sunlight, and moonlight made grand the barbed-wire lace around testing sites, Lee said they were, and subterranean missiles. It was quite flat, but I felt that we were crossing it vertically instead of horizontally. I felt I was on ropes behind Lee, struggling up a sheer rock face, my footing too unsure to allow me to look anywhere except at the cliff I clung to.

"What is it you're afraid of?" Lee said.

I told him I didn't know.

"Think about it," he said. "There's nothing in your mind that isn't yours."

I wondered if I should go back. I could call Tom and Johanna, I thought, but at the same instant I realized that they weren't really friends of mine. I didn't know Johanna very well, actually, and Tom and I, in fact, disliked each other. I had gone to bed with him one day months earlier when I went over to borrow a vise grip. He had seemed to want to, and I suppose I thought I would be less uncomfortable around him if I did. That was a mistake, as it turned out. I stayed at least as uncomfortable as before, and the only thing he said afterward was that I had a better body than he'd expected. It was a long time before I realized that what he'd wanted was to have slept with Lee's girlfriend.

When I'd returned home that afternoon carrying the vise grip that Tom remembered to hand to me when I left, I felt as if it had been Lee who had spent the afternoon rolling around with Johanna, not me with Tom, and my chest was splitting from jealousy. I couldn't keep my hands off Lee, which annoyed him—he was trying to do something to an old motorcycle that had been sitting around in the yard.

"Lee," I said, "are you attracted to Johanna?"

"What kind of question is that?" he said, sorting through the parts spread out on the dirt.

"A question question," I said.

"Everyone's attracted to everyone else," he said.

I wasn't. I wasn't attracted to Tom, for instance.

"Why do you think she stays with Tom?" I said.

"He's all right," Lee said.

"He's horrible, Lee," I said. "And he's mean. He's vain."

"You're too hard on people," Lee said. "Tom's all tied up, that's all. He's frightened."

"It's usual to be frightened," I said.

"Well, Tom can't handle it," Lee said. "He's afraid he has no resources to fall back on."

"Poor guy," I said. "He can fall back on mine. So are you attracted to Johanna?"

"Don't," Lee said, standing up and wiping his hands on an oily cloth. "O.K.? Don't get shabby, please." He had gone inside then, without looking at me.

Now home was wherever Lee and I were, and I had to

control my fear by climbing toward that moment when Lee would haul me up to level ground and we would slip off our ropes and stare around us at whatever was the terrain on which we found ourselves.

We started to have trouble with the van and decided to stop, because Lee knew someone we could stay with near Denver while he fixed it. We pulled up outside a small apartment building and rang a bell marked Dr. Peel Prayerwheel.

"What's his real name?" I asked Lee.

"That is," Lee said.

"Parents had some unusual opinions, huh?" I said.

"He found it for himself," Lee said.

Peel had a nervous voice that rushed in a fluty stream from his large body. His hair was long except on the top of his head, where there was none, and elaborate shaded tattoos covered his arms and neck and probably everything under his T-shirt.

We stood in the middle of the kitchen. "We'll put your things in the other room," Peel said, "and I'll bring my cot in here. That's best, that's best."

"We don't want to inconvenience you, Peel," Lee said.

"No, no," he said. "I'm only too happy to see you and your old lady in my house. All the times I came to you. When I was in the hospital. Anything I can do for you. I really mean it. You know that, buddy."

"He took me in," Peel said, turning to me. "He was like family." Peel kept standing there, blinking at the floor, but he couldn't seem to decide what else to say.

While Lee looked around town for parts or worked on the van, Peel and I mostly sat at the kitchen table and drank huge amounts of tea.

"Maybe you'd like a beer," he said one afternoon.

"Sure," I said.

"Right away. Right away," he said, pulling on his jacket.

"Oh—not if we have to go out," I said.

"You're sure?" he said. "Really? Because we can, if you want."

"Not unless you want one," I said.

"No, no," he said. "Never drink alcohol. Uncontrolled substance. Jumps right out of the bottle, whoomp! . . . Well, no real harm done, just an ugly moment . . ." He blushed then, for some reason, very dark.

When Lee came home, Peel and I would open up cans of soup and packages of saltines. "Used to cook like a bastard," Peel said. "But that's behind me now. Behind me."

One morning when we got up, Peel was standing in the middle of the kitchen.

"Good morning, Peel," I said.

"Good morning," he said. "Good morning." He stood there, looking at the floor.

"Do you want some tea?" I said.

"No, thank you," he said. Then he looked at Lee.

"Well, buddy," he said. "I got a check from my mother this morning."

"Was that good or bad?" I asked Lee later. Lee shrugged. "How does he usually live?" I said.

"Disability," Lee said. "He was in the army."

At night I felt so lonely I woke Lee up, but when we made love I kept thinking of Peel standing in the kitchen looking at the floor.

One morning I had a final cup of tea with Peel while Lee went to get gas.

"Thank you, Peel," I said. "You've been very kind."

"Not kind," Peel said. "It doesn't bear scrutiny. I had some problems, see, and your old man looked out for me. He and Annie, they used to take me in. He's a fine man. And he's lucky to have you. I can see that, little buddy. He's very lucky in that."

I reached over and touched one of Peel's tattoos, a naked girl with devil horns and huge angel wings.

"That's my lady," Peel said. "Do you like her? That's the lady that flies on my arm."

A day or two later Lee and I parked and sat in back eating sandwiches. Then Lee studied maps while I experimented along his spine, making my mouth into a shape that could be placed over each vertebra in turn.

"Cut that out," Lee said. "Unless you want to lose an hour or two."

"I don't mind," I said.

"Oh, there," Lee said. "We're just outside of Cedar City."

I looked over Lee's shoulder. "Hey, Las Vegas," I said. "I had a friend in school who got married and moved there."

"Do you want to visit her?" Lee said.

"Not really," I said.

"It isn't too far," he said. "And we can always use a shower and a bit of floor space."

"No," I said.

"Why not?" Lee said. "If she was your friend."

I didn't say anything.

Lee sighed. "What's the matter?" He turned and put his arms around me. "Speak to me."

"We'll never be alone," I said into his T-shirt.

"We're alone right now," Lee said.

"No," I said. "We're always going to stay with your friends."

"It's just temporary," Lee said. "Until we find a place we want to be for ourselves. Anyhow, she isn't *my* friend—she's *your* friend."

"Used to be," I said. Then I said, "Besides, if we stayed with her she'd be your friend."

"Sure," Lee said. "My friend and your friend. The people we've stayed with are your friends now, too."

"Not," I said, letting slow tears soak into his T-shirt.

"Well, they would be if you wanted to think of them as friends," Lee said. His voice was tense with the effort of patience. "You're the one who's shutting them out."

"Someone isn't your friend just because they happen to be standing next to you," I said.

Lee lifted his arms from around me. He sighed and leaned his head back, putting his hands against his eyes.

"I'm sorry you're so unhappy," he said.

"You're sorry I'm a problem," I said.

"You're not a problem," he said.

"Well, then I should be," I said. "You don't even care enough about me for me to be a problem."

"You know," Lee said, "sometimes I think I care about you more than you care about me."

"Sure," I said. "If caring about someone means you don't want anything from them. In fact, you know what?" I said, but I had no idea myself what I was going to say next, so it was just whatever came out with the torrent of sobs I'd unstoppered. "We've called all your friends because you don't want to be with me, and you want people I know to help you not be with me, too, but we won't even call my parents and they're only less than a day away because then I might turn out to be real and then you'd have to figure out what to do with me instead of waiting for me to evaporate because you're tired of me and we're going to keep going from one friend of yours to another and making other people into friends of yours and then they'll all help you think of some way to leave me so you can go back to Annie whoever she is or grind me into a paste just like come to think of it you probably did to Annie anyhow."

"Oh, Jesus," Lee said. "What is going on?"

I leaned my head against his arm and let myself cry loudly and wetly.

"All right," Lee said, folding his arms around me again. "O.K.

"Come on," Lee said after a while. "We'll find a phone and call your parents."

I was still blinking tears when we pulled into an immense parking lot at the horizon of which was a supermarket, also immense, that served no visible town. It had become evening, and the supermarket and the smaller stores attached to it were all closed, even though there were lights inside them.

"There," Lee said. "There's a phone, way over there." He reached for the shift, but I jumped out.

"I'll walk," I said.

There was a shallow ring of mountains all around, dark against the greenish sky, and night was filling up the basin we were in. The glass phone booth, so solitary in the parking lot, looked like a tiny, primitive spaceship.

I rarely spoke to my parents, and I had never seen the mobile home where they'd now lived for years. It couldn't be possible, I thought, that I had only to dial this phone to speak to them. Why would the people who were my parents be living at the other end of that phone call?

When I sat down inside the phone booth and closed the door, a light went on. Perhaps when I lifted the receiver instructions would issue from it. How surprised Lee would be to see the little glass compartment tremble, then lift from the ground and arc above the mountains. I picked up the receiver, unleashing only the dial tone, and dialed my parents' number.

My mother was out playing cards, my father told me.

"Why aren't you with her?" I said. "I thought you liked to play, too."

"You thought wrong," my father said. "And anyway," he said, "I can't stand the scum she's scooped up in this place."

"Well," I said, "I guess you've probably found friends of your own there."

"Friends," my father said. "Poor SOBs could only make it as far as a trailer park, you'd think they were living in Rolls-Royces."

"Well," I said.

"They're nosy, too," my father said. "These people are so nosy it isn't funny."

"Sorry to hear it," I said.

"It's nothing to me," my father said. "I don't go out, anyhow. My leg's too bad."

A tide shrank in my chest.

"Hear anything from Mike and Philly?" I said.

"Yeah—Philly's doing quite well, as a matter of fact," my father said. "Quite well. Spoke to him just the other week. He's managing some kind of club, apparently."

"Probably a whorehouse," I said, not into the phone.

"What?" my father said.

I didn't say anything.

"What?" he said again.

"That's great," I said. "What about Mike?"

"Mike," my father said. "He left Sharon again. That clown. Sharon called and said would we take the kids for a while. Of course we would have if we could. I don't think she's too great for those kids, anyhow."

A Greyhound bus had appeared in the parking lot, and a man carrying a small suitcase climbed out. I wondered where he could possibly be going. He walked into the darkness, and then the bus was gone in darkness, too.

"What about you?" my father said. "What're you up to? Still got that boyfriend?"

"Yes," I said. I glanced over at the van. It looked miniature in front of the vast supermarket window, itself miniature against the line of mountains in the sky. "In fact," I said, "we were thinking of coming to visit you."

"Jesus," said my father. "Don't tell me this one's going to marry you. Hey," he said suspiciously, "where're you calling from?"

It was almost totally dark, and cold lights were scattered in the hills. People probably lived up there, I thought, in little ranch-style houses where tricycles, wheels in the air, and broken toys lay on frail patches of lawn like weapons on a deserted battlefield.

"I said, where are you calling from?" my father said again.

"Home," I said. "I have to get off now, though."

As soon as I hung up, the phone started to ring. It would be the operator asking for more money. It was still ringing when I climbed into the van, but I could hardly hear it from there.

Lee and I sat side by side for a moment. "It's peaceful here," I said.

"Yeah," Lee said.

"No one was home," I said.

"All right," Lee said—there were different reasons he might have let me say that, I thought—"let's go on."

That night I apologized.

"It's all right," Lee said.

"No," I said. "And I really do like your friends. I liked staying with them."

"We won't do it anymore," Lee said.

"We can't stay at motels," I said. "And it's nice to get out of the van every once in a while."

Lee didn't say anything.

"Besides," I said. "We don't even know where we're going."

I wondered if Lee had fallen asleep. "What about your friend Kathryn"—I said it softly, in case he had—"that Carlos mentioned? Would you like to see her?"

"Well," Lee said finally, "she doesn't live that far from here."

As soon as we climbed out of the van in front of Kathryn's house, a girl flew out of the door, landing in Lee's arms. They laughed and kissed each other and laughed again.

"Maggie," Lee said, "what are you doing here?"

"Fact is, Lee," she said, "Buzzy's partner got sent up, so I'm staying here awhile case anybody's looking for anybody."

"Yeah?" Lee said. "Is Buzzy here?"

"He's up in Portland," she said. "He said it would be better if we went in different directions just till this cools off. I guess he's got a honey up there."

Lee shook his head, looking at her.

"Never mind, baby," she said. "I'll win, you know that. I always win." Lee laughed again.

Inside, Kathryn put out her hands and Lee held them. Then she looked at me. "You're cold," she said. "Stand by the fire, and I'll get you something to put on."

"I'm O.K.," I said. "Anyhow, I've got things in the van." But she took a huge, flossy blanket from the back of the sofa and wound it slowly around and around me.

"You look like a princess!" Maggie said. "Doesn't she?

Look, Lee—she looks like a princess that's—what are those stories?—under a dark enchantment." Kathryn stood back and looked.

We drank big hot glasses of applejack and cinnamon, and the firelight splashed shadows across us. Kathryn and Maggie and Lee talked, their words scattering and shifting with the fire.

Numbness inched into my body, and my mind struggled to make sense of what my ears heard. Maggie had left the room—I grasped that—and Lee and Kathryn were talking about Carlos.

"I miss him. You know that, Lee?" Kathryn was saying. "I think about a lot of people, but I miss Carlos."

"You should call him," I tried to say, but my sleeping voice couldn't.

"Well," Lee said.

"Wait," I wanted my voice to say. I knew I wouldn't be able to listen much longer. "He talked about you . . ."

"I don't know," Lee said. "I found myself feeling sorry for him. It was pretty bad. I hated to feel that way, but it seems like he hasn't grown. He just hasn't grown, and the thing is, he's lost his nerve."

"Kathryn," I wanted to say, and couldn't, and couldn't, "Carlos wants to see you."

I slid helplessly into sleep, and it must have taken me some time to struggle back to the surface, because when I'd managed to, Lee was saying, "Yeah, she is. She's very nice. We're having some problems now, though. And I don't know if I can help her anymore."

I heard it as a large globe floating near me, just out of reach. I tried to hold it, to turn it this way and that, but it bobbed away on the surface as I slipped under again.

I woke in a bed in another room, bound and sweating in the blanket, and I could hear Lee's and Kathryn's voices as a murmur. I flung the blanket away and pushed myself out of my clothes as sleep swallowed me once more.

In the morning I awoke puffed and gluey from unshed tears. I wrapped the blanket around myself and followed voices and the smell of coffee into the kitchen where Maggie and Kathryn and Lee were eating pancakes.

"That's one sensational blanket," Maggie said. "This morning it makes you look like Cinderella."

I dropped the blanket. "Now it makes me look like Lady Godiva," I said, not smiling. Kathryn's laugh flashed in the room like jewelry.

When I came back to the kitchen, dressed, the others were having seconds. "Oh, God," Maggie said. "Remember those apple pancakes you used to make, Lee? Those were the best."

"I haven't made those in a long time," Lee said. "Maybe I'll do that one of these mornings."

"If we're going to be staying for a while, I want to go get some things from town," I said, standing back up.

"Relax," Lee said. "We'll drive in later."

Kathryn and Maggie gave us a list of stuff they needed, and we set out.

"Kathryn's very beautiful," I said. "Maggie is too."

"Yeah," Lee said.

"You and Kathryn seem like good friends," I said.

"We're old friends," Lee said. "Your feelings never change about old friends."

"Like Carlos," I said. "Hey, why is Maggie's boyfriend giving her a hard time?"

"He's an asshole," Lee said.

"Kathryn doesn't have a boyfriend," I said.

"No," Lee said.

"She must get lonely up there," I said.

"I don't think so," Lee said. "Besides, people come to her a lot."

"Yes," I said.

"Like Maggie," he said. "People who need something."

We parked in the shopping center lot and went to the supermarket and the hardware store and the drugstore, and Lee climbed back into the van.

"You go on ahead," I said. "There's some other stuff I need to do."

"It's a long walk back," Lee said.

"I know," I said.

"You're sure you know the way?" he said.

"Yes," I said.

"It's cold," he said.

"I know," I said.

"All right," he said, "if that's what you want."

I felt a lot better. I felt pretty good. I looked around the parking lot and saw people whose arms were full of packages or who held children by the hand. I watched the van glide out onto the road, and I saw it accelerate up along the curve of the days ahead. Soon, I saw, Lee would pull up in front of Kathryn's house; soon he would step through the door and she would turn; and soon—not that afternoon, of course, but soon enough—I would be standing again in this parking lot, ticket in hand, waiting to board the bus that would appear so startlingly in front of me, as if from nowhere.

DAYS

I had never known what I was like until I stopped smoking, by which time there was hell to pay for it. When the haze cleared over the charred landscape, the person I had always assumed to be behind the smoke was revealed to be a tinny weights-and-balances apparatus, rapidly disassembling on contact with oxygen.

THE FIRST TWO WEEKS

I lie on the floor and howl with grief. A friend tells me, "During the third week it will occur to you that you're insane, and you'll think, Well, now I'm insane. What difference does it make whether I smoke or not? This is a trick to get you to smoke."

THE THIRD WEEK

I am insane, but I am determined to wait it out.

Today I bump into someone crossing the street. I begin an apology, but when he tells me to watch where I am going in a tone I consider unnecessarily condemning, I seize him by the lapels. For an instant we look at each other. Then I release him back into the surge of pedestrians and continue on, stiff with fear.

I have gained twenty pounds. I weep unstintingly for the victims of tragedy I see around me on subways, in restaurants, and on the street, but the victims look at me oddly and move away. I find that I have elaborate opinions about things I have never previously given a thought to, and that it is imperative that everyone within earshot understand exactly what I mean, and why, in detail, I mean it.

Everything makes me angry, unless it makes me sad. I cannot tell how long anything takes.

SPRING

The smoke-free air is a flat, abrasive surface that I must inch my way along, but I am subject to sudden seizures of pellucid hatred which impel me out the door during dinner or in the early hours of the morning, or, when I am too helpless to move, into weak, furious storms of tears. Although I am demanding and insatiable, everything I want is sucked dry of flavor and color and warmth by the time I get it, like packaged foods in an employee cafeteria. When I wake up in the morning, my jaws ache.

FRIENDS

My attachments to people are chaotic and unreliable. I can't tell whether I am behaving oddly or not. Sometimes I feel that people think I am but don't mention it, and this makes me angry when I think they're right. I am angrier, however, when I think they're wrong.

Sometimes I explode at a surprised acquaintance. I am afraid that I may say the final thing to someone, but these episodes occur so quickly that no one seems to comprehend what has happened. There is a feeling only of a slight break in continuity, as if a roomful of people had received an extraterrestrial visit that was posthypnotically expunged.

SUMMER

I have always not been able to do things, but I can't rely on this as a principle now. Unfortunately, it is now possible to find out what I am not able to do only by observing myself in action. If I start to shake or fume, whatever it is that I'm doing is something I don't do. I feel that I am a zoologist trying to discover the natural environment of an unknown animal found in a pet store. I wish this were the task of someone else, but the biological setup of our planet requires a rather strict one-to-one relationship between each corporeal entity and the consciousness with which it is accustomed to associate, and it seems that I am stuck. I will just have to keep trying various things, according to no principles whatsoever.

I TAKE A VACATION

I go spend several weeks in a huge house with many people where I seem unable to go outside into the sunlight. Instead I lie in bed in my dark, chilly room, drinking glass after glass of vodka. Once in a while I break an emptied bottle on the wall or the floor.

Occasionally I feel called upon to say something. "Well, I don't know," I say when I encounter someone in the kitchen, where I sit for hours late at night staring and crying. "I'm feeling a little weird lately." This seems to take care of the matter.

One day someone takes me to swim, which is something I have not done voluntarily for as long as I can remember, in the warm, curving pool of a nearby motel, which hums with fluorescent light.

I was once told that catatonics seem to enjoy swimming, and I can see why. The water registers one's presence and confers meaning to one's motor impulses, yet there is no threat in water, as there always is in air, of sudden, shattering injuries, inflicted or received.

I think I might like to try going swimming again, if I can find someplace to do it in the city.

Kathy tells me that she goes swimming at the YMCA, and she points out that there's no reason I shouldn't try it. She is an extremely judicious person. If she doesn't see any reason not to try it, I probably don't have to think through the whole thing to see if I do. Next Tuesday she will bring me as her guest.

I find that often between opening my eyes in the morning and putting on my final piece of clothing, three or four hours will elapse. Sometimes I am on my way out the door when something happens—the phone rings, or I notice that there are dishes in the sink, or I remember that I should get a load of laundry together, or I catch an unnerving glimpse of myself in the mirror, or I realize that I have errands that lie in opposite directions and that none of them is really important enough to take precedence over the others, or important enough to do at all, when it comes down to it, and that I don't have enough money to do all, or maybe even any, of them, and I probably never will, and even if I should, so what—and there I am for the rest of the day.

People quite often ask me what I do with my time. I don't know what to tell them. Actually, I don't know what they are getting at. What it really is that I don't know is why they want to make me feel the way they are obviously going to make me feel when they ask me this.

WEDNESDAY

Kathy took me to swim at the Y with her yesterday.

IN THE Y

The Y is this whole thing. In it there are floors and floors and floors, all equipped for different kinds of amusements. On the third floor alone, besides the locker room for women and the showers and the sauna, and the clothes dryer, and the lounge with a TV, there is a meeting room, the Mini-Gym, and the Martial Arts Room.

THE ROOF

On top of the Y there is a roof with brightly colored plastic chairs shaped like long, narrow hands, which hold people tenderly under the sun.

THE TRACK

There is a track on the eighth floor—a thin band around the edge of a room on which people in sneakers run slowly around to music that sounds as if it is coming from a cranked-up toy.

THE BASKETBALL COURT

There is nothing in the middle of the track—just a huge hole bounded by a railing, under which there is the seventh-floor basketball court. From the side of the track, Kathy and I watch long lines of people doing sloppy-looking exercises on the court below.

THE POOL

The tiny, cold pool is on another floor altogether, which seems mostly to have something to do with men. The pool has its own showers, and it has a man, too, who sits in a little glass booth. The pool feels unbearably cold, but Kathy convinces me that it's necessary to suspend one's evaluation of the temperature until after half a length.

KATHY

I ask Kathy how she can remember where everything is. She says, "Well, someone once asked my mother how she remembered all of our names, and I mean, that really just wasn't one of her problems with us."

But in fact Kathy can also, when the elevator stops in front of us, tell whether it's on its way up or down.

THE LOCKER ROOM

The best thing, I think, is the locker room. At its portals is Bess, who lights up in a smile upon seeing Kathy. Dusty sunlight streams down on her through the wire meshing on the windows.

In the locker room itself, everything is very quiet, and the lockers are arranged in rows, like a cornfield, so you don't have to stand in the middle of a bare room, all fat. There are large lockers to use while you're in the building and small lockers, not big enough for real clothes, to use when you're not. This is to save space (and it really does; I figured it out).

There are women combing their hair by dryers on the wall and talking quietly by their lockers. Somewhere a voice says, "Well, the trouble with anesthesiology is, everyone you work with is asleep."

THE SAUNA

The sauna is like a little tropical hut.

MONDAY

Kathy calls to ask if I want to go to the Y tomorrow. I'd like to, and probably I'll be able to, especially because she wants to meet there, so I won't be able to call her at the last minute and cancel.

SMOKING

It used to be that I never got angry. That is, I would start to feel angry, but the moment I opened my mouth to voice my feelings a cigarette would be inserted into it, and instead of expelling a stream of words I would inhale a stream of smoke. Only then would I exhale, casting a velvety mist over everything in the vicinity. How I long to do that again!

TUESDAY

We do get to the Y today, just as planned.

In the lobby we decide we are going to swim, sauna, and exercise. Many showers and changes of costume are entailed by this program, and when we try to determine the most expeditious way to proceed, I feel helpless and defeated. Kathy suggests we take each thing as we come to it, and I feel much better.

We hang our jeans and T-shirts on hooks in the large locker. We put our shoes on the bottom and line up the soap, shampoo, and our pocketbooks on the top shelf. The locker is like a small apartment, and we are keeping it nice. We have both more or less mooshed our underwear into our jeans, but everything is still at a manageable stage. It takes a lot of concentration to remember, between taking things off and putting things on, and putting in the large locker and on oneself the things that one has brought, and putting in the large locker and on oneself the things that have been in the small locker, exactly where each thing should go. But when we are finally ready to go up to the pool, I feel that I have a solid foundation on which to build.

Upstairs, without seeming to notice us particularly, the swimmers adjust their lines more narrowly, and we climb in. I swim back and forth, twice on my side, and twice with a kickboard.

It takes a lot of effort to keep your head from getting wet when you swim, so that in itself is probably very good exercise.

Downstairs, I can't help noticing that people shower at dramatically different tempi. No one in the shower seems disturbed by this, however, so I assume there is no normative manner in which to shower, and proceed in my own way. No one says anything about it, either encouraging or derogatory.

SPENDING TIME

I like the women who are here in the locker room in this long afternoon, and I wonder about their lives. A picture comes into

my mind and grows. In this picture I am still here in the locker
room, but it is winter now, and the light is falling. I have a career, in this picture. I am a banker, or an account executive,
whatever that is, or I work for a foundation. Every day after
work, I go to the Y and I swim back and forth in the pool or
stretch and bend in the tiny dark gym. There are other women
in the locker room, these women perhaps, and others. Their
lives are less substantial than mine, and they dress quickly and
simply, leaving before I do, to go home to small apartments. I
shower and dry myself and take from my locker a long silk slip
and a gown. I put on a necklace and earrings of dark pearls,
fine pale stockings, and shiny shoes with very high heels. I take
from my locker a long fur stole and wrap myself up in it. I walk
down the stairs—moonlight throws the shadow of the wire
cage across my gloved hand on the railing, and my shiny shoes
resonate on the linoleum. As I leave the building, the last few
others are hurrying off along the slushy sidewalk or unchaining
bicycles from the rack in front of the building. I am left alone
now on the wide front steps where I am waiting.

I wish it were winter now.

Ellen calls and asks what I'm doing with myself. When I say I
don't really know, she says, "Well, I mean, you get up, and
then what do you do?"

Sometimes it seems to me that there is a growing number
of women, and that I am not among them.

I joined the Y today. It will turn out to be a big, horrible
waste of money, but I just wanted to be at the Y, which is cool
and dim and echoing. It is automatically reassuring to be in

that building filled with people of different colors and backgrounds and ages. The web of commonality is a safety net, in case anybody might be falling. Falling . . .

For days I have not been able to get out of the apartment. About the point at which it is borne in on me that it is going to be impossible to leave, I begin to get angry. I feel as if years of rage have condensed around the sides of my brain and are dripping down into it, forming pools in which all its other contents are becoming sodden and useless.

Today I go to the Y and I change and shower and swim and shower and ride a bicycle that doesn't move in the Mini-Gym, and shower and sauna and shower and change, and now I have done all these things alone.

Oh, I see how Kathy can tell whether the elevator is going up or down. There is a little arrow that lights up when the door opens, either red, pointing down, or green, pointing up.

Today was my sixth time at the Y. I know Kathy so well, but I didn't know this about her: she has a whole life at the Y that she shares with scores and scores of people who don't know her at all. I like to come to the Y with Kathy and be part of things, but I like to come alone, too. I feel that I am cultivating a silent area of my life.

I think I'm swimming a bit better. I can do five lengths now, and I can swim on my back and on each of my sides. I still can't quite put my head in the water, though. The water is always cold at first, but I think about how short half a length is, and then I can do it.

Ellen calls again, to see if I am feeling O.K., which I am until she calls. I tell her that I'm swimming a lot these days. She says, "I didn't know you could swim. How much do you do?"

People will go so far to make each other feel bad. But I don't feel bad. After all, I do go swimming.

The Y is a secret that everybody knows! I see people there that I know from all sorts of other places, and I see people from the Y all over the neighborhood. Sometimes in a store I will see that a person behind the counter or one shopping in the next aisle is really a pleasant seal from the pool.

In the locker room today I run into Jennifer, a woman I know a bit from somewhere else. She tells me that swimming is the best exercise there is! What a nice person.

The pool is so cold today I can't even do my half a length to get warm. I stand there and stand there in the shallow end, but I just can't do it.

Downstairs I tell Bess, "Just couldn't swim today. Just too cold."

"Ummmm hmmmm," she says equably.

I get to the Y again today, but I just can't face the idea of getting into, or failing to get into, the pool. I can't face going back home, though, either, so I settle on the Mini-Gym, which is very soothing. It has the ghostly atmosphere of a schoolroom during vacation.

Today a man does sit-ups facing the windows. A woman, also facing the windows, bends in half exactly as the man's fingers reach his toes. Another woman opposite the first stretches her arms in an arc above her head. I choose a central latitude, perpendicular to the others. I lie on my side and begin to raise a leg to the silent count.

I have just realized something really terrifying—*I don't swim!* I feel sick. What did I think I was doing, going swimming? I wasn't going swimming! I can't swim! I can't even put my head in the water!

This can't go on, my just coming to the Y to do exercises. It is a *known fact* that no one can do exercises regularly. Every single magazine article about it says they're just too boring to do regularly. Also, it only takes half an hour. One change of clothes, one shower, and then I have to go home.

Late at night I think of the terrible things I've put my friends through in the past months. I begin to think of the things I've always put my parents through, and I know this means big trouble. I get out of bed in a sweat of fear and call my friends, crying stormily, and cry more because I've awakened them.

THURSDAY

At the Y today, chunks of a conversation that had been going on around me in the shower suddenly reassemble—feet, minutes, miles, and pacing—to reveal, whole in my auditory memory, a conversation about running.

ALSO THURSDAY

THAT I CANNOT SWIM DOES NOT NECESSARILY MEAN I CANNOT RUN. This thought breaks over me with repeating fresh force, like peals of hallucinatorily echoing thunder.

FRIDAY

Now that I have been sensitized, I realize that for months I have been surrounded by a continuous susurrus about running.

SATURDAY

Not only is running not cold, but I won't drown if I should stop suddenly. I think on Monday I'll just give it a whirl.

MONDAY

I can't get out of the apartment. The hours stretch and telescope. I find myself standing over the kitchen table, which I had approached for some reason earlier. I break out of position only to find that some minutes have elapsed during which I have been staring into the mirror. At what, I wonder. I remember that I had meant to get something from the table, but I seem to be sitting in the other room, where a dull awareness of things to be done impinges on me. Outside the window, the day, in nervous jumps, dies.

TUESDAY

This morning I am propelled to the Y. I don't know exactly how I am going to pitch into my goal of running once I get there, but it can't be all that impossible. I clearly remember the track that Kathy showed me the first day she brought me, and what it was was a track, is all, with people running around it.

Besides, I could always sound out the friendly guard, whose name, I have learned, is Surf—or Serf, it could be. Oh—it could be Cerf, come to think of it. I change into my gym clothes and a pair of socks borrowed from a sock-wearing friend and my old but unloved blue sneakers and wander out into the hall, where I do in fact find Surf.

Am I going to grab him by the shoulders, cover his hands with kisses, and implore him to tell me what I should do? No. I casually mention that I am going to do some running today.

"Have you ever run before?" he asks. I look at him closely, but the face that looks back is a neutral one. I tell him that I haven't. "Well, don't do too much," he says. "About four laps today. You've got to go easy at first."

Good. Without having aroused his suspicion (what do I mean? suspicion of what?) I have gotten the information I need, which is that, despite the supercharged atmosphere of conversations about it, there is no particular trick to running, unless, of course, there is something so obvious that Surf wouldn't have thought to tell me, or so embarrassing that he couldn't bring himself to tell me, or so ineffable that he wasn't able to tell me.

I take the elevator to the eighth floor, which is where the track is, I know, even though I haven't seen it since my first day.

THE TRACK

Now that I am about to set foot on it, I find the track a great deal more interesting than I did when I last saw it. There is a tiny, enticing stairway on the far side of the track. A sign pointing down to it says, TO THE PHYSICAL OFFICE. What sort of office could that be?

On the track are some people I have seen in the locker room, the pool, or the Mini-Gym, and some entirely new people, including a few leathery men who look too old even to walk. All of these people are running slowly around the track, and I study them to see if there's anything I can pick up about what they're doing, but the basic move seems to be just what one would think—one foot down, then the other in front of it, the first again in front, and so on.

Then suddenly I myself step out onto the track, easing myself into the light traffic. It becomes almost instantly clear that the slowness with which the others had appeared to run is illusory. They are running fast, very fast indeed. My legs are moving as fast as I can move them, I lean out ahead of my feet, my mind empty of everything except the sounds of feet and breath, but everyone on the track is streaking by me. The track itself, which only minutes earlier appeared to be a tiny oval, now seems immense. It takes a long, long time to round the ends, and the straight goes on forever. I notice also that there is a bunchy, horizontal cast to my forward progress in comparison to that of my trackmates.

It occurs to me that the four laps suggested by Surf are an unrealistic goal, and I downward revise to three.

Downstairs Jennifer is at her locker, and while I'm working up the energy to open mine, I tell her that I'm running now, instead of swimming.

"Terrific," she says warmly. "How much do you do?"

"Three laps," I tell her. We look at each other in consternation. Then I think to add that today was my first day, and we are less embarrassed.

WEDNESDAY

My legs hurt incredibly. I lie in bed while the hours parade by me, icy and knowing, like competitors in a beauty contest.

THURSDAY

At the Y I run three laps, I walk five laps, and then I run two more laps!

On the way home, I treat myself, on impulse, to a pair of socks, all my own, and appropriate in appearance. I just go into a store and ask for tube socks.

I have always wondered, up until this moment, whenever I have heard them mentioned, what tube socks are. Now I realize that not only do I, like everyone else, know exactly what tube socks are but also that they are exactly what I want. (How could I ever have pretended to myself that I don't know what tube socks are?! Nobody can't know what tube socks are! They're SOCK TUBES, and they are the only sort of socks that make any sense, because you just stick your foot into one any old way and leave it there, and the sock, not your foot, has to adjust. The feelings of confusion produced by the term "tube sock" are not, I realize, due to the nature of the tube sock itself but rather to the term's implication that all socks are not tube socks and the attendant question of why they are not.) The pair I pick out has elegant bands of navy and dark red near the tops.

It seems that my commitment to my socks was warranted. It is now several weeks since I bought them, and I have still been going to the track. Not every day, of course, but what I would call several times a week. I only fear that my impulses to run are a mistake, like my impulses, for instance, to sew, which, upon examination, invariably turn out to be impulses of some other kind—impulses, perhaps, to own a certain garment, or impulses to be *able* to sew, or impulses to be the sort of person who likes to sew, or whatever, but not primary sewing impulses.

In an attempt to eliminate possible hypocrisy from my approach, I have taken to testing myself as I stand at the edge of the track. I say to myself in a voice of profound compassion, a voice that it would be rude to ignore and one that it is difficult not to answer in the way it obviously hopes to be answered, "Well. That certainly does look difficult. If we don't want to do it today, we truly needn't. We can just come back tomor-

row! We don't always have to feel like running—sometimes
we're just too tired, or too busy, or too weak. It doesn't mean
we won't run again ever; it just means we won't run today."
But I recognize behind the seductive insinuations a familiar
enemy who wishes to swindle me out of my little bit of fun.

On the track my mind fills to the top with running.

FALL

Today I walk into the Y shivering. The guards at the elevator,
who always greet me now, say, "What'sa matter? You cold?" I
nod yes. They look at each other and giggle. "You need a
man," one of them ventures. "That's right!" the other chimes
in. "You need a man!" They roar with laughter and punch
each other on the arm. "You need"—they lean on each other,
weak with hilarity—"you need a man like *us*!" they shout as
the elevator door closes, shutting me in with five men whose
grim gazes never waver from the truncated scene.

People have stopped giving me advice right on the track, so I
must look more comfortable. People often ask me how long
I've been running and how far I can run and tell me that the
first two miles are the hardest, but that's different. I can run
fifteen laps now, sometimes, which is a far cry from three,
and I can almost keep up with the slowest of the tiny, ancient
men who scuttle along the inside railing of the track.

What hasn't stopped is something far more humiliating
than unsolicited advice. When I finish my exercises, I walk,
instead of taking the elevator, up the many flights to the
track. This is seriously difficult, and I do it largely for the

beneficial effect it must therefore have on my willpower. Almost every third time I make this journey (thus, about once a week) some huge bozo thunders by and says something like: "Think you're going to make it? Haw, haw" or "What have *you* been up to? Haw, haw." I used to just nod and smile weakly. "Haw, haw," I would agree as each bozo would thud off, but now I feel that I have matured beyond this exchange.

Today as I am clambering up the stairs an immense pink man in tiny white shorts careens up behind me. "You sure look beat!" he roars happily. I am ready to enter into a discussion of *his* looks, but he is gone. I feel the familiar sensation of burning rubber right below my follicles, indicating that quite soon I will be overwhelmed by fury or sorrow and the rest of my day will be spent in raging immobility. I sit down on the steps. I won't be able to run now, but I don't dare go home, either. This man has just happened by, and I am about to have been *upset* by him.

Life's blows are so swift. One is just living along (walking up some stairs, for example), and at just any moment one could contract a viral inflammation of the brain, or a loved one could be getting squashed by a car, or a carton of lead statuettes could fall on one's foot. Had I done one more round of exercises, I never even would have encountered this man who has revealed, with one careless stroke, the ruin that is my life.

A STRANGE LACK OF CONSEQUENCES

It turns out that I was all right after I met that man yesterday. Something was his fault (at least, nothing was my fault). But it didn't turn out to be his fault that I couldn't run, because I *could* run. I ran, I saunaed, I showered, I got dressed, and I went home.

One thing that's quite nice about this running is that you just keep doing what you have just been doing, without having to stop to think about it.

I RISK CONSCIOUS FEELINGS OF DESIRE

I can no longer deny myself awareness of the fact that while I wear plain navy-blue sneakers—carried over, probably, from my horrible camp days, which, like everything else, scarred me for life—everyone else has highly evolved, stripy, elegant sneakers in the colors of toys designed in Italy for rich kids.

In the sauna today someone tells me that you begin to lose weight after you begin to run two miles a day. "Of course," she adds, "you have to stop eating, too."

Well, I'll cross that bridge when I come to it. Not that I'm running every day, either.

I CONVERSE LIKE OTHERS

I am beginning to have conversations about running, just as other people do. But I can't quite get the hang of it. When people say to me, smiling, "You don't mean *you* run," I think it must be true that in some real sense I don't. It angers me that I must be so assertive on such shaky grounds to make people believe that I run, and that then when they believe me, they don't care.

I AM A SELF-RELIANT PERSON

I develop a routine of stopping about halfway through my run and either walking around the track or shaking myself up on a shake-up machine I've watched other people use. I can run more this way, and the second stint is easier.

Kathy says she would like to use the machine, too, but she thinks it may be embarrassing. I am immediately embarrassed, but then I remember that it cannot precisely be said to be myself who is embarrassed. I go and use the machine.

Today I overhear a conversation between a man and a woman I know. "Oh, hey," she says. "I got those Adidas you told me to."

"The green ones?" he asks. "Fantastic."

My God. For years I have understood Adidas to be an airline. I undergo a sudden perceptual intensification, as if I were a special instrument being trained onto its proper task by expert operators. I pull up a chair and sit down. My acquaintances smile and sparkle and toss their beautiful hair. The woman is saying, "You're right about running outside. It's a whole other thing, really fantastic." Their eyes shine, their teeth flash.

"I run too!" I say suddenly.

"You?" They turn and gaze at me. "In those?" They point at my black boots with their high, spiky heels, and they laugh. I pull my feet under me and look at the floor.

Something like a pain is accruing around my left heel. If it keeps up, I may go see if the PHYSICAL OFFICE might pertain to it.

My pain is still there. If it is there again the next time I run, I'll go to the PHYSICAL OFFICE.

Sure enough, my pain is there again. I'll go to the PHYSICAL OFFICE the next time I run, if I still have it.

Today my heel hurts so much that after a few laps I have to stop. After standing at the edge of the track for a bit, I bolster myself up and follow the arrow to the PHYSICAL OFFICE.

BREAKTHROUGH

The PHYSICAL OFFICE turns out to be a small greenish room. A grinning man welcomes me, and we nod to each other many times, and then I explain that I've done something to my heel. The man prods it. "I don't know," he ventures. "Seems like you've done something to your heel."

I agree this must be it. "What should I do?" I ask. "I really can't run."

"It's probably a good idea not to run for a few days," the man tells me.

"Do you think I should get running shoes?" I ask.

The man looks reflectively off into the distance. "You know," he says, "you could probably use a pair of running shoes."

"Well, thanks a lot, then," I tell him airily. We nod and smile and wave.

Suddenly I know just what I want, what to do about it, and where to go to do it. I have sometimes passed a place, it suddenly occurs to me, called Runners World, which has in its window a line of glowing shoes.

I GET HELP

I go looking for Runners World, and there it is, to my surprise, right where I expect it to be. Several people are in the store, all talking about running, and I sit and listen to them with interest for some time until a man leaning on the counter asks if I would like some help. He seems to be the ideal man, intelligent, handsome, and concerned, so I tell him yes, I would. I explain that I think I may need shoes. He asks me where I run and how much.

"Then this is the shoe for you," he says. "The SL 72." He hands me a pair of boxy, royal-blue shoes with white stripes and deeply ridged soles. I had hoped for something more streamlined, with slanting, aerodynamic stripes rather than these neat, horizontal ones, in a less wholesome color; but if this is the shoe for me, this is the shoe for me.

And when I put them on, my feet are more comfortable than they have ever been before. The man who has selected these shoes for me alone tells me that he is a running coach at the Y.

"Do you run in the morning?" he asks. "Lots of girls run in the morning."

I feel that there is nothing I can't say to this man. I lean up to him and ask softly, "What's the difference between running inside and running outside?"

"Colder outside," he says, and hands me my shoes, all tucked up into their box.

My shoes live in my locker along with my tank suit, goggles, and swimming cap (which, who knows, I might want to use sometime), my yoga pants, my T-shirt, my soap and shampoo and skin cream, and several pairs of tube socks.

I can run more easily and quickly, and my feet don't hurt.

Jennifer is in the locker room today when I go in, and I show her my shoes. "Hey, wow," she says. She reaches into her locker. "Look!" she says, holding out to me an identical pair.

WINTER

I see Ellen today, and before she gets a chance to ask what I'm up to, I tell her that I'm running a lot lately. She is delighted to hear it. It seems that she, too, after getting home from the office, reading to the kids, clearing up after the dinner guests, studying for her orals, and knocking off an article or two for some little journal, likes to get in a few miles.

Yesterday I asked the woman in the laundry around the corner why I always get less underwear back than I put in. It has taken me years to ask this question. The woman tells me that naturally I always get the same amount of underwear back that I put in and turns back to her work, looking both insulted and smug. I stand and stare at her, unable to think of anything to say, while tears of hatred run off my face.

I spend the rest of the day walking in short bursts and stopping in phone booths, where I stand for five or ten minutes. There is no one I can bear to call. I think the woman in the laundry may be right. Even if she is wrong, it is unlikely to be her fault, really, that my underwear is disappearing. Even if she takes pleasure in depleting my raggy stock of underwear for some reason, it hardly matters. But then, why am I so angry?

In the locker room I overhear a woman telling some friends that she has picked a fight with her boyfriend this morning, saying brutal and humiliating things to him and getting him to say brutal and humiliating things to her. After she throws him out of the apartment, she slashes every one of her paintings.

At this her friends gasp. "Oh, no!" they say, with a horror that to me is obviously utterly formal and hollow. "How terrible!"

"No it isn't," the woman says. "They were bad paintings. They were all shallow and vain and cowardly."

Oh, how I wish I could paint! My paintings, too, would be shallow and vain and cowardly, and I would go home right now and slash them to ribbons.

The locker room is full of ex-smokers, doing prodigious amounts of exercise, talking torrentially at uncontrolled volume, gaining weight at a fantastic clip, lying in the sauna till they're faint, crying, drinking quantities of carrot juice, and bearing in, over the weeks, a bright rainbow of shoes.

Kathy is back in town after months away, and I get to take her to the Y on my guest pass, and we use my locker. "Hi," "Hi, Kath," "Howrya doin'?" people say, glad to see her but not at all surprised, because everyone comes and goes. Kathy has returned to find me a good person to go running with.

RUNNING

Sometimes it's quite easy to run. I step out on the track, and I run around and around and around, and once in a while, a spring is released in my body after a mile or so, and I am flooded with power. Sweat springs to my surface, and I speed along with no effort, as in a dream of flying. I try to forget these episodes as soon as they're over; I feel that running on the basis of hoping for another one would be like believing in God in order to pray for a Mercedes.

Sometimes it's very difficult to run, and boring, too. Each lap seems endless, and my legs feel stiff and weighted. It's even difficult on these days to remember how many laps I've done. On these bad days, I sometimes feel so tired that just going home is a major endeavor. People in the street seem to sense my fatigue and say wounding things about me. These people should be more careful. People look so solid, I look so solid, walking along; but hit suddenly with something heavy, people could just topple over or gust into the air like old, empty cardboard boxes.

On extremely good days, I step smartly out the door to

go home, and people in the street move over to include me in their numbers, or even nod approvingly as I walk along exhibiting human health. On such days the winter seems mild and pleasant.

AN UNPLEASANT ENCOUNTER

Today I get to the Y much later than I've ever been there, and everything is completely different. The basketball court below the track is thronging with tiny little girls in bright leotards shimmering on balance beams and bouncing into the air on trampolines, like bright kernels of popcorn. The track is very crowded, and the people on it look serious and fast. A lawyer I know is among those running, and I feel self-conscious. There is an implicit pressure in the growing dark at the windows, so unlike the pale, tranquil wash I am used to there.

After I run a mile, I take a breather by the side of the track, and a man standing near me says, "You weren't out there very long." I can't tell what this man is up to, but I can tell it's not right. "How much did you do?" he asks.

"'Bout a mile," I tell him.

"That's not very much," he says, in the whining, punitive tone of an adult bent on forcing a child to admit to a wrongdoing. "How long have you been running?"

When I was about thirteen, a man sitting next to me on a train put his hand more or less up my skirt. He just sat there then, perfectly happy, and I just sat there, afraid of hurting his feelings in case he hadn't noticed where his hand was, or had a good reason for having put it there, or something, until the stop before mine, when I said, "Oh, I'm sorry, I have to get out soon." Ever since then I have made an effort to evaluate dispassionately my rights and needs against those of others; but it's not so easy, as we all know, and I often err to the advantage of one party or the other.

I decide to give the man next to me the benefit of the doubt, and I tell him how long I've been running. "Oh?" he says. "That's funny. You should be used to it by now." And he steps out on the track again.

I step out, too, to run, but I find that I can't, and lock into a standstill at the inside of the track, although stopping on the track is, for good reason, absolutely forbidden. My visual field—a wheel of thundering men encircling a space through which little red and blue and green girls are flying—tilts and spins, as in a film.

The man passes me once, twice, three times. He knows that I am there, but he won't look at me. The fourth time he goes by, my hand shoots out and grabs his arm. I glimpse the lawyer I know looking surprised, but not surprised enough for me. "What did you mean, I should be used to it?" I ask the man in my grasp. My hands are shaking. "Oh, not really anything," he says. His tone is careful. "You must have meant something"—I speak slowly, with admirable self-control— "and I wonder what it was you did mean."

"I'll tell you," he says. "I want to finish running first, and then I'll talk to you." He breaks away. I wait. I keep waiting, and the man keeps running. He's obviously quite tired, but he's too alarmed to stop. When he gets a bit blue around the edges, I thread my way off the track, stand for a minute out of sight on the stairwell, and then peek back out, catching the eye of my man, who is now walking, to show him that he need not think I'm gone. He starts to run again. Satisfied, I go down to the locker room.

At a locker near mine, a blond woman with a nice atmosphere whom I have often seen on the track is changing her clothes. I tell her what has just happened to me.

"What a drip," she says. "Most people here aren't like that at all. I bet you felt like picking him up by his feet and smashing his head on the track," she says in her pleasant voice, pulling up her socks.

"Gee, I feel awful," I say, and sniffle.

"Me too," she says. "I think I'm coming down with a cold." We go downstairs together and out into the benign evening.

MY DREAM

This is a dream I frequently have: I glance down at my hand. The posture I have denied it for so long, the gesture it has so often hopelessly initiated, is suddenly deliciously completed. I am holding a lit cigarette! I am now able, I reason in my dream, to display the scope of my will. I can either inhale from this cigarette in my hand or not, as I freely choose. I freely choose to inhale, and the fantasy instantly collapses; the entire mendacious simulacrum shivers and falls at my feet, leaving me—a slave who will have to smoke now, forever—in the barren waking world where it is easy to recognize the dreadful thing I had briefly mistaken for choice. Then I wake truly, empty-handed in the merciful morning.

SPRING

I do three miles! At the end of my second mile, and then at the end of my second and a half, rather than feeling I am at the end of my capacity, I feel as though I have established a new relationship with my legs, and I don't want to stop, ever. But I do at the end of three miles, anyhow, because I don't want to hurt myself or to become a different sort of person without giving the matter proper thought.

I call up Kathy and tell her. "Hey, Kath, I ran three miles!" "Hey, wow, that's really great!" she tells me. I try to describe the sensation I had of sudden ease and endless availability of energy. "I think that's what they mean by a second wind," Kathy says. "That's why it's possible for a person like you or me to run three or six or twenty-six miles, because you can get it over and over again."

"Sometime I'd like to try for five miles," I tell Kathy. "Why not?" she says, excited by the idea. "They say the first three miles are the hardest."

The days are becoming brighter and longer. The air and the city have expanded in the warmth, and there is room to walk around. In different parts of the city, clusters of silvery buildings gleam, their surfaces reflecting clear sky and sailing clouds, and men and women stride among them, their clothing billowing like pennants. In the bright sunshine, stores spring up, windows full of gaudy running shoes. What a bore.

TUESDAY

On my way to the Y I notice how hot it is. Far too hot to run. I turn around and go home, where I have things to do.

WEDNESDAY

It is even hotter today.

THURSDAY

I run today, but after a mile I am ready to die of boredom and exhaustion.

During the past few weeks I've felt so impatient at the Y. I find that somehow I can hardly run, it is too hot to sauna, the conversations I overhear are dull and trivial, and the exercise apparatuses look dingy and foolish.

The man who gave me a hard time on the track has established residency in my mind. I discover that just as he exercises power over me, I can exercise power over him. This man in my mind may have a low opinion of me, but I can have a low opinion of him, too, if I so choose. I can have a low opinion of his low opinion of me as well. Also, I notice, I can have a high opinion of his low opinion of me, an opinion that according to this very schema is worthless. I amuse myself by raising and lowering him in my estimation and by combining in various ways, and then distinguishing between, him, his opinion of me, me, and my opinion of him.

It seems that an opinion of someone is not a serious matter.

———

The sun penetrates through the sky to my skin, and I blink in the light like a bear coming out of hibernation. I feel that I have been dreaming watchfully in this hibernation, my sleeping brain accounting for many passing years, and that I have awakened suddenly, shedding the strain of my dreams, to find that less time has elapsed than has been mourned in my sleep.

Years have passed, it is true, but not many, many years.

Halfway to the Y I remember that I haven't brought my towel. I turn around and go back to the apartment. After I lock the door again, go downstairs, and proceed three or four blocks toward the Y, I remember that once again I have forgotten my towel. I can rent one at the Y, but the one I rent would not be *my* towel, which had figured (in its own small way, to be sure) in my plans for the day. I turn around, go home, hang up some clothes I had left on a chair, make the bed so I won't get in it, and leave, locking the door and heading for the Y, forgetting, it occurs to me some few blocks later, my towel.

Clearly I am not supposed to go to the Y today. But then, what am I supposed to do? I stop to think, causing a pileup on the corner.

Back at home I sit down on the neatly made bed. I put my hands over my ears and shut my eyes to clear my mental field. A little directive asserts itself. It is appearing as neatly as if it were being typed out on a fortune-cookie slip. I AM HUNGRY, it tells me, and, by gum, I *am* hungry. Today, instead of going to the Y, I will take myself out to lunch.

I allow my new skills to lead me to a restaurant. I notice with some surprise that the restaurant I have chosen is a pretentious vegetarian restaurant, crowded and uncomfortable. I consult myself and reveal that I would like soup du jour and a house salad. The soup, which I already know to be over-priced, turns out to be terrible as well. I eat it with great relish. My salad arrives, a wilting pile of vegetable parings garnished with American cheese.

"Chopsticks?" asks the waitress. I do a quick internal scan. "Yes, please." I top off my lunch with a cup of lukewarm coffee, pay the shocking check, and ease myself out of my small torture chair, sighing with satisfaction.

At home I again ask myself what I would like to do, and again my answer arrives. I want, it appears, to write letters. Perhaps there's been some mistake, I think. But I decide to try, and I find it is true: I do want to write letters.

It is amazing to be able to find out what I want to do at any given moment, out of what seems to be nothing, out of not knowing at all. It is secretly and individually thrilling, like being able to open my fist and release into the air a flock of white doves.

My new insight has stood the test of time. Three days have passed, and it has not faded. I call Kathy and tell her that I've discovered the point of life.

"Gosh!" she says. "What is it?" Kathy is always up for some-thing new.

I tell Kathy about the point of life being to have a good time. "Gee," says Kathy, rolling this around on her brain. "That's very interesting. But you know," she adds gently, "I'm not really sure that I really like having a good time, exactly."

Naturally I have anticipated this objection. No one likes to have a good time, but this is due to a misconception as to what a good time is, or faux fun, I explain grandly. "The thing is," I tell Kathy, "you're the only person who can tell what it is to have a good time, and since you're the only person who can have your own good time, whatever it is that a good time is, is what a good time is! So you can just know what it is and have it!"

"Gosh," says Kathy. "Maybe so. I'm going to think about that." She is feeling pretty good herself, having landed a terrific new job, which she tells me all about.

I keep expecting to wear out my new divinatory gift with gluttony, like someone who catches an enchanted fish and makes more than the allotted number of wishes, winding up with a pudding on his or her nose, or living in the pigsty, or whatnot; but it seems, on the contrary, to grow more and more reliable, and with ever-increasing frequency and rapidity I think of what I would like to do and I do it.

The days just clutter up with things I feel like doing and then do. One after another, I fill up and dispatch dayfuls of things.

SUMMER

I haven't been to the Y for months, and I almost forgot about it, but this evening I pass it by on my way to dinner. It is fairly late, and many people are leaving the building, walking down the front steps alone or in twos and threes, unchaining their bicycles from the racks in front, and dispersing into the evening. I am quite a distance away, but I feel as though I can see them clearly. Their faces are calm, and they seem invigorated, as if they have been running. The evening sky is domed above the large, lit building, and more and more men and women stream through the doors, radiating outward toward the next thing they are to do, each headed, it looks from where I stand, dead on target.

TRANSACTIONS IN A FOREIGN CURRENCY

I had lit a fire in my fireplace, and I'd poured out two coffees and two brandies, and I was settling down on the sofa next to a man who had taken me out to dinner when Ivan called after more than six months. I turned with the receiver to the wall as I absorbed the fact of Ivan's voice, and when I glanced back at the man on my sofa, he seemed like a scrap of paper, or the handle from a broken cup, or a single rubber band—a thing that has become dislodged from its rightful place and intrudes on one's consciousness two or three or many times before one understands that it is just a thing best thrown away.

"Still in Montreal?" I said into the phone.

"Yeah," Ivan said. "I'm going to stay for a while."

"What's it like?" I said.

"Cold," he said.

"It's cold in New York, too," I was able to answer.

"Well, when can you get here?" he said. "We'll warm each other up."

I'd begun to think that this time there would be no end to the waiting, but here he was, here was Ivan, dropping down into my life again and severing the fine threads I'd spun out toward the rest of the world.

"I can't just leave," I said. "I have a job, you know."

"They'll give you a few weeks, won't they?" he said. "Over Christmas?"

"A few weeks," I said, but when he was silent I was sorry I'd said it.

"We'll talk it all over when you get up here," he said finally. "I know it's hard. It's hard for me, too."

I turned slightly, to face the window. The little plant that sat on the sill was almost leafless, I noticed, and paint was peeling slightly from the ceiling above it. How had I made myself believe this apartment was my home? This apartment was nothing.

"O.K.," I said. "I'll come."

I replaced the receiver, but the man on the sofa just sat and moved his spoon back and forth in his cup of coffee with a little chiming sound.

"An old friend," I said.

"So I assumed," he said.

"Well," I said, but then I couldn't even remember why that man was there. "I think I'd better say good night."

The man stood. "Going on a trip?"

"Soon," I said.

"Well, give me a call when you get back," he said. "If you want to."

"I'm not sure that I'll be coming back," I said.

"Uh-huh, uh-huh," he said, nodding, as if I were telling him a long story. "Well, then, good luck."

I flew up early one morning, leaving my apartment while it was still dark outside. I had packed, and flooded my plant with water in a hypocritical gesture that would delay, but not prevent, its death, and then I'd sat waiting for the clock face to arrive at the configuration that meant it was time I could reasonably go.

The airport was shaded and still in the pause before dawn, and the scattering of people there seemed to have lived for days in flight's distended light or dark; for them, this stop was no more situated in space than a dream is.

How many planes and buses and trains I had taken, over the years, to see Ivan! And how inevitable it always felt, as if I were being conveyed to him by some law of the universe made physical.

We'd met when I was nineteen, in Atlanta, where I was working for a photographic agency. He lived with his wife, Linda, who had grown up there, and their one-year-old, Gary. But he traveled frequently, and when he would call and ask me to go with him or meet him for a weekend somewhere—well, Ivan was one of those men, and just standing next to him I felt as if I were standing in the sun, and it never occurred to me to hesitate or to ask any questions.

And Ivan warmed with me. After their early marriage, Linda had grown increasingly fearful and demanding, he told me, and years of trying to work things out with her had imposed on him the cautious reserve of an unwilling guardian. It was a habit he seemed eager to discard.

After a time, there was a divorce, and Ivan moved about from place to place, visiting and taking photographs, and I got a job in New York. But he would call, and I would lock the door of whatever apartment I was living in and go to him in strange cities, leaving each before I could break through the transparent covering behind which it lay, mysterious and inert. And I always felt the same when I saw Ivan—like an animal raised in captivity that, after years of caged, puzzled solitude, is instantly recalled by the touch of a similar creature to the natural blazing consciousness of its species.

The last time we were together, though, we had lain on a slope overlooking a sunny lake, and a stem trembled in my hand while I explained, slowly and quietly, that it would not do any longer. I was twenty-eight now, I said, and he would have to make some sort of decision about me.

"Are you talking about a decision that can be made honestly?" He held my chin up and looked into my eyes.

"That is what a decision is," I said. "If the next step is self-evident, we don't call it a decision."

"I don't want to be unfair," he said, finally. And I came to assume, because I hadn't heard from him since, that the decision had been made.

Soft winter light was rolling up onto the earth as the plane landed, and the long corridors of the airport reflected a mild, dark glow.

An official opened my suitcase and turned over a stack of my underpants. SOMETHING TO DECLARE . . . NOTHING TO DECLARE, I saw on signs overhead, and strange words below each message. Oh, yes—part of this city was English-speaking, part French-speaking. A sorry-looking Christmas wreath hung over the lobby, and I thought of something Ivan had said after one of his frequent trips to see Gary and Linda in Atlanta: "I can't really have much sympathy for her. When she senses I'm not as worried about her as she'd like me to be, she takes a slight, semiaccidental overdose of something or gets herself into a little car crash."

"She loves you that much?" I asked.

"It isn't love," he said. "For all her dependence, she doesn't love me."

"But," I said, "is that what she thinks? Does she think she loves you that much?"

He stood up and stretched, and for a moment I thought that he hadn't registered my question. "Yeah," he said. "That's what she thinks."

Near the airport exit, there was a currency-exchange bureau, and I understood that I would need new money. The man behind the cage counted out the variegated, colorful Canadian bills in front of me. "Ah," he said, noticing my expression—he spoke with a faint but unfamiliar accent—"an unaccustomed medium of exchange, yes?"

I was directed by strangers to a little bus that took me across a plain to the city, a stony outcropping perched at the cold top of the world. There were solitary houses, heavy in the shallow film of light, and rows of low buildings, and many churches. I found a taxi and circumvented the question of language by handing the driver a piece of paper with Ivan's address on it, and I was brought in silence to a dark, muscular Victorian house that loomed from a brick street in a close row with others of its kind.

Ivan came downstairs bringing the morning gold with him and let me in. His skin and hair were wheat and honey colors, and he smelled as if he had been sleeping in a sunny field. "Ivan," I said, taking pleasure in speaking his name. As he held me, I felt ebbing from me a terrible pain that I had been unaware of until that moment. "I'm so tired."

"Want to wake up, or want to go to sleep?" he said.

"Sleep," I said, but for whole minutes I couldn't bring myself to move.

Upstairs, the morning light, gathering strength, made the melting frost on the bedroom window glow. I slept as if I hadn't slept for a week, and then awoke, groping hurriedly through my life to place myself. Understanding, I looked out the window through the city night shine of frost: I was in Montreal with Ivan, and I had missed the day.

I stood in the doorway of the living room for a moment, looking. Ivan was there, sharing a bottle of wine with two women. One of them was striking and willowy, with a spill of light curls, and the other was small and dark and fragile-looking. When had Ivan become so much older?

The small woman was studying a photograph, and her shiny hair fell across her pretty little pointy face. "No, it is wonderful, Ivan," she was saying. She spoke precisely, as if picking her way through the words, with the same accent I had heard at the airport. "It is a portrait of an entire class. A class that votes against its own interests. It is . . . a *photograph* of false consciousness."

"Well, it's a damn good print, anyway," the other woman said. "Lovely work, Ivan."

"We're playing Thematic Apperception Test," Ivan said, and the dark girl blushed and primly lowered her eyes. "We've had responses from Quebec and England. Let's hear from our U.S. representative." He handed me the photograph. "What do you see?"

Two women who, to judge from this view, were middle-aged, overweight, and poor stood gazing into a shop window at a display of tawdry lingerie. High up in the window was a reflection of mounded clouds and trees in full leaf. I did not feel like discussing the picture.

"Hello," the small girl said, intercepting my gaze as I looked up. "I am Micheline, and this is my friend Fiona."

Fiona reached lazily over to shake hands. "Hello," I said, allowing our attention to flow away from the photograph. "Do you live here, Fiona, or in England?"

"Oh, let's see," she said. "Where do I live? Well, it's been quite some time since I've even seen England. I've been in Montreal for a while, and before that I was in L.A."

"Really," I said. "What were you doing there?"

"What one does," she said. "I was working in film."

"The industry!" Micheline said. A hectic flush beat momentarily under her white skin, as if she'd been startled by her own exclamation. "There is much money to be made there, but at what personal expense!"

"Fiona has a gallery here," Ivan said.

"No money, no personal expense." Fiona smiled.

"It is excellent," Micheline said. "Fiona exhibits the most important new photographs in Canada. Soon she will have a show of Ivan's work."

"Wonderful," I said, but none of the others added anything. "We're rather on display here, Ivan," I said. "Are you planning to do something about curtains?"

Ivan smiled. "No." Ivan's rare smile always stopped me cold, and I smiled back as we looked at each other.

"It is not important," Micheline said, reclaiming the conversation. "The whole world is a window."

"Horseshit," Fiona said good-naturedly, and yawned.

"Yes, but that is true, Fiona," Micheline said. "Privacy is a—what is that?—*debased* form of dignity. It is dignity's . . . atrophied corpse."

"How good your English has become," Fiona said, smiling, but Ivan had nodded approvingly.

"The rigorous Northern temperament," Fiona said to me. "Sometimes I long for just a weekend in Los Angeles again."

"Not me!" Micheline said. She kicked her feet impatiently.

"Have you lived there as well?" I asked.

"No," she said. "But I am sure. Beaches, hotels, drinks with little hats—"

"That's Hawaii, I think," I said.

"Perhaps," Micheline said, looking sideways at me out of her doll's face.

"So what about it?" Ivan said. "Have you two decided to stay for dinner?"

"No," Micheline said, jumping to her feet. "Come, Fiona." She held out her hand to Fiona, blushing deeply. "We must go."

"All right." Fiona yawned and stood. "But let's have a rain check, Ivan. Micheline raves about your cooking. Maybe we'll come back over the weekend for Micheline's things. Sorry to have left them so long. We've been a while sorting things out."

"No problem," Ivan said. "Plenty of closet space."

At the door, Micheline was piling on layers and layers of clothing and stamping like a little pony in anticipation of the snow.

"Tell me about them," I said to Ivan after dinner, as we lay on the sofa, our feet touching. "Who are they?"

"What do you mean, 'who'?" he said. "You met them."

"Come on, Ivan," I said. "All I meant was that I'd like to know more about your friends. How did you meet them? That sort of thing."

"Actually," he said, "I hardly know Fiona. Micheline just brought her over once before."

"Micheline's so extreme," I said, smiling.

"She's very young," Ivan said.

"I used to be young," I said. "But I was never that extreme, was I?"

"She's a purist," Ivan said. "She's a very serious person."

"She seemed a bit of a silly person to me," I said. "Have she and Fiona been together long?"

"Just a month or so," he said.

"Micheline doesn't seem as if she's really used to being with another woman, somehow," I said. Ivan glanced at a page of newspaper lying on the floor below him. Some headline had caught his eye apparently. "She was sort of defiant," I said. "Or nervous. As if she were making a statement about being gay."

"On the contrary," Ivan said. "She considers that to be an absolutely fraudulent opposition of categories—gay, straight. Utterly fraudulent."

"Do you?" I said.

"What is this?" Ivan said. "Are you preparing your case against me? Yes, *The People of the United States of America versus Ivan Augustine Olmstead*. I know."

"How long did she live here?" I said.

"Three months," he said, and then neither of us said anything or moved for about fifteen minutes.

"Ivan," I said. "I didn't call you. You wanted me to come up here."

He looked at me. "I'm sorry," he said. "But we're both very tense."

"Of course I'm tense," I said. "I don't hear from you for six months, then out of the blue you summon me for some kind of audience, and I don't know what you're going to say. I don't know whether you want some kind of future with me, or whether we're having our last encounter, or what."

"Look," he said. He sat upright on the sofa. "I don't know how to say this to you. Because, for some reason, it seems very foreign to you, to your way of thinking. But it's not out of the blue for me at all, you see. Because you're always with me. But you seem to want to feel rejected."

"I don't want to feel rejected," I said. "But if I've been rejected I'd just as soon know it."

"You haven't been rejected," he said. "You can't be rejected. You're a part of me. But instead of enjoying what happens between us, you always worry about what *has* happened between us, or what *will* happen between us."

"Yes," I said. "Because there is no such thing as an independent present. How can I not worry each time I see you that it will be the last?"

"You act as if I had all the power between us," he said. "You have just as much power as I do. But I can't give it to you. You have to claim it."

"If that were true," I said, "we'd be living together at least half the time."

"And if we were living together," he said, "would you feel that you had to go to work with me or stay with me in the darkroom to see whether my feelings about you changed minute by minute? It's not the quantity of time we spend together that makes us more close or less close. People are to each other what they are."

"But that can change," I said. "People's interests are at odds sometimes."

"Not really," he said. "Not fundamentally. And you would understand that if you weren't so interested in defending your isolating, competitive view of things."

"What on earth are you talking about, Ivan? Are you really saying that there's no conflict between people?"

"What I'm saying is that it's absurd for people to be obsessed with their own little roles. People's situations are just a fraction of their existence—the difference between those situations is superficial, it's arbitrary. In actuality, we're all part of one giant human organism, and one part can't survive at the expense of another part. Would you take off your sock and put it on your hand because you were cold? Look— does the universe care whether it's you or Louis Pasteur that's Louis Pasteur? No. From that point of view, we're all the same."

"Well, Ivan," I said, "if we're all the same, why drag me up here? Why not just keep Micheline around? Or call in a neighbor?"

He looked at me, and he sighed. "Maybe you're right," he said. "Maybe I just don't care about you in the way that you need. I just don't know. I don't want to falsify my feelings."

But when I saw how exhausted he looked, and miserable, loneliness froze my anger, and I was ashamed that I'd allowed myself to become childish. "Never mind," I said. I wished that he would touch me. "Never mind. We'll figure it out."

It was not until the second week that I regained my balance and Ivan let down his guard, and we were able to talk without hidden purposes and we remembered how it felt to be happy together. Still, it seemed to me as if I were remembering every moment of happiness even as it occurred, and, remembering, mourning its death.

One day, Ivan was already dressed and sitting in the kitchen by the time I woke up. "Linda called this morning," he said. "She let the phone ring about a hundred times before I got it. I'm amazed you slept through it."

I poured myself a cup of coffee and sat down.

"I wonder why people do that," he said. "It's annoying, and it's pointless."

"It wasn't pointless in this case," I said. "You woke up."

"Want some toast?" Ivan asked. "Eggs?"

"No, thanks," I said. I hardly ever ate breakfast. "So, is she all right?"

"Fine," he said. "I guess."

"Well, that's good," I said.

"Remember that apartment I had in Washington?" he said. "I loved that place. It was the only place I ever lived where I could get the paper delivered."

"How's Gary?" I said.

"Well, I don't know," Ivan said. "According to Linda, he's got some kind of flu or something. She's gotten it into her head that it's psychosomatic, because this is the first time since he was born that I haven't come home for Christmas."

"Home," I said.

"Well," Ivan said. "Gary's home."

"Maybe you should go," I said.

"He'll have to adjust sometime," Ivan said. "This is just Linda's way of manipulating the situation."

I shrugged. "It's up to you." I wondered, really for the first time, what Ivan's son looked like. "Do you have a picture of Gary?"

"Somewhere, I think," Ivan said.

"I'd like to see one," I said.

"Sure," he said. "You mean now?"

"Well, I'd like to," I said.

Steam rose from my coffee and faded into the bright room. Outside the window, light snow began to fall. In a few minutes Ivan came back with a wallet-sized snapshot.

"How did you get into this picture?" I said.

He took it from me and peered at it. "Oh. Some friends of Linda's were over that day. They took it."

"So that's Linda," I said. For nine years I'd been imagining the wrong woman—someone tired and aggrieved—but the woman in the photograph was finely chiseled, like Ivan. Even in her jeans she appeared aristocratic, and her expression was somewhat set, as if she had just disposed of some slight inconvenience. She and Ivan could have been brother and sister. The little boy between them, however, looked clumsy and bereft. His head was large and round and wobbly-looking, and the camera had caught him turning, his mouth open in alarm, as if he had fallen through space into the photograph. A current of fury flowed through me, leaving me as depleted as the child in the picture looked. "What if he *is* sick?" I said.

"Kids get sick all the time," Ivan said.

"You could fly down Christmas Eve and come back the twenty-sixth or twenty-seventh."

"Flying on Christmas Eve's impossible anyhow," he said.

"Well, you could go down tomorrow."

"What about you?" he said.

"What about me?" I said.

"If I can even still get reservations," he said.

"Call and see," I said. "I'll call." Linda had probably never, in awe of Ivan's honey-colored elegance that was so like her own, hesitated to touch him as I sometimes did. As I did right now.

The next day, Ivan bought some toys, much more cheerful and robust than the child they were for, and then I watched him pack. And then we went out to the airport together.

I took the little airport bus back alone, and I felt I had been equipped by a mysterious agency: I knew without asking how to transport myself into a foreign city, my pockets were filled with its money, and in my hand I had a set of keys to an apartment there. The snow still fell lightly, detaching itself piece by piece from the white sky, absorbing all the sound. And the figures past which we rode looked almost immobile in their heavy clothing, and not quite formed, as if they were bodies waiting to be inhabited by displaced souls. In the dark quiet of the bus, I let myself drift. Cities, the cities where I visited Ivan, were repositories of these bodies waiting to be animated, I thought sleepily, but how did a soul manage to incarnate itself in one?

All night long I slept easily, borne away on the movements of my new, unfettered life, but I awoke to a jarring silence. Ivan had taken the clock.

I looked around. It was probably quite late. The sun was already high, and the frost patterns, which seemed always on the verge of meaning, were being sucked back to the edges of the window as I stared. In the kitchen I sat and watched the light pooling in rich winter tints across the linoleum, and eventually the pink-and-pewter evening came, and frost patterns encroached on the windows again. How quickly the day had disappeared. The day had sat at the kitchen window, but the earth had simply rolled away from under it.

It was light again when I woke. I thought suddenly of the little plant on my windowsill in New York. It would be dead by now. I felt nauseated, but then I remembered I hadn't eaten the day before.

There was nothing in the refrigerator, but in the freezer compartment I found a roll of chocolate-chip-cookie dough. How unlike Ivan to have such a thing—what circumstances had prompted him to buy it? Ah—I saw Micheline and Ivan with a shopping cart, laughing: the purists' night off.

I searched through the pots and pans—what a lot of clatter—but there was a cookie sheet. Good. I turned on the oven and sawed through the frozen dough. Soon the kitchen was filling with warmth. But an assaultive odor underlay it, and when I opened the oven door, I found the remains of a leg of lamb from earlier in the week that we'd forgotten to put away. The bone stood out, almost translucent, and the porous sheared face of meat was still red in the center. "Get rid of all this old stuff," I heard myself say out loud in a strange, cheerful voice, and I jabbed a large fork into it. But I had to sit for several minutes breathing deeply with my head lowered before I managed to dump the lamb into the garbage can along with the tray of dough bits and get myself back into bed, where I stayed for the rest of the day.

The next afternoon, it seemed to me that I was ready to go out of the apartment. I took a hot bath, cleansing myself carefully. Then I looked through my clothing, taking it out and putting it away, piece by piece. None of the things I'd brought with me seemed right. Steam poured from the radiators, but the veil of warmth hardly softened the little pointed particles of cold in the room.

The hall closet was full of women's clothes, and there I found everything I needed. I supposed it all belonged to Micheline, but everything felt roomy enough, even though she looked so small. I selected a voluminous skirt, a turtleneck jersey, and a long, heavy sweater. There was a pair of boots as well—beautiful boots, fine-grained and sleek. If they belonged to Micheline, they must have been a gift. Surely she never would have chosen them for herself.

The woman who stood in the mirror was well assembled, but the face, above the heavy, dark clothing, was indistinct in the brilliant sunlight. I made up my eyes heavily, and then my mouth with a red lipstick that was sitting on Ivan's bureau, and checked back with the mirror. Much better. Then I found a jacket that probably belonged to Ivan, and a large shawl, which I arranged around my head and shoulders.

Outside, everything was outlined in a fluid brilliance, and underfoot the snow emitted an occasional dry shriek. The air was as thin as if it might break, fracturing the landscape along which I walked: broad, flat-roofed buildings with blind windows, low upon the endless sky. There were other figures against the landscape, all bundled up like myself against the cold, and although the city was still unfathomable, I could recall no other place, and the rudiments of a past seemed to be hidden here for me somewhere, beyond my memory.

I entered a door and was plunged into noise and activity. I was in a supermarket arranged like a hallucination, with aisles shooting out in unexpected directions, and familiar and unfamiliar items perched side by side. If only I had made a list! I held my cart tightly, trusting the bright packages to draw me along correctly and guide me in my selections.

The checkout girl rang up my purchases: eggs (oh, I'd forgotten butter; well, no matter, the eggs could always be boiled, or used in something); a replacement roll of frozen cookie dough; a box of spaghetti; a jar of pickled okra from Texas; a package of mint tea; foil; soap powder; cleanser; violet toilet paper (an item I'd never seen before); and a bottle of aspirin. The girl took my money, glancing at me.

Several doors along, I stopped at a little shop filled with pastries. There were trays of jam tarts and buns, and plates piled up with little chocolate diamond shapes, and pyramids of caramelized spheres, and shelves of croissants and tortes and cookies, and the most wonderful aroma surged around me. "Madame?" said a woman in white behind the counter.

I looked up at her, over a shelf of frosted cakes that held

messages coded in French. On one of them a tiny bride and groom were borne down upon by shining sugar swans, and my heart fluttered high up against my chest like a routed moth. I spoke, though, resolutely in English: "Everything looks so good." Surely that was an appropriate thing to say—surely people said that. "Wait." I pointed at a tray of evergreen-shaped cookies covered with green sugar crystals. Tiny bright candies had been placed on them at intervals to simulate ornaments. "There."

"Very good," the woman said. "The children like these very much."

"Good," I said. What had she meant? "I'll take a dozen."

"Did you have a pleasant Christmas?" she asked me, nestling my cookies into a box.

"Yes," I said, perhaps too loudly, but she didn't seem to notice the fire that roared over me. "And you?"

"Very good," she said. "I was with my sister. All the children were home. But now today it feels so quiet." She smiled, and I understood that her communication had been completed, and we both inclined our heads slightly as I left.

"Hello," I said uncertainly to the butcher in the meat market next door. It occurred to me that I ought to stop and get something nourishing.

"What can I do for you?" the butcher asked in easy English.

"Actually," I said dodging a swift memory of the leg of lamb in Ivan's garbage can, "I'd like something for supper." Ah! I had to smile—what the woman in the bakery had been telling me was how it felt to be a person when one's sister and some children were around.

"Something in particular?" the butcher asked. "If I'm not being too nosy?"

"Please," I said across a wall of nausea. "Sausages." That had been good thinking—at least they would be in casings.

"Sausages," he said. "How many sausages?"

"Not so many," I said, trying not to think too concretely about the iridescent hunks of meat all around me.

"Let's see," he said. "Should we say . . . for two?"

"Good," I said. Fortunately there was a chair to wait in. "Did you have a pleasant Christmas?" I asked.

"Excellent," the butcher said. "Goose. And yours?"

"Oh, excellent," I said. I supposed from his silence that that had been insufficient, so I continued. "It feels so quiet today, though. All the children have gone back."

"Oh, I know that quiet," the butcher said. "When they go."

"They're not exactly my children, of course," I said. "They're my sister's. Stepsister's, I mean. My sister would be too young a person to have children old enough to go back anywhere. You know," I said, "I have a friend who believes that in a sense it doesn't matter whether I'm a person with a stepsister who has children or whether someone else is."

The butcher looked at me. "Interesting point," he said. "That's five seventy-eight with tax."

"I know it sounds peculiar," I said, counting out the price. "But this friend really believes that, assuming there's a person with a stepsister, it just doesn't ultimately matter—to the universe, for instance—whether that person happens to be me or whether that person happens to be someone else. And I was thinking—does it actually matter to you whether that person is me or that person is someone else?"

"To me . . . does it matter to me . . . ." The butcher handed me my package. "Well, to me, sweetheart, you *are* someone else."

"Well." I laughed uneasily. "No. But do you mean—wait—I'm not sure I understand. That is, did you mean that I might as well be the person with the stepsister? That it's an error to identify oneself as the occupant of a specific situation?" The butcher looked at me again. "I mean, how would you describe the difference between the place you occupy in the world and the place I occupy?"

"Well"—his eyes narrowed thoughtfully—"I'm standing over here, I see you standing over there, like that."

"Oh—" I said.

"So," he said. "Got everything? Know where you are?"

"Thanks," I said. "Yes."

"You're all set, then," he said. "Enjoy the sausages."

Back at the apartment, I unpacked my purchases and put them away. Strange, that I missed Ivan so much more when we were together than when we were apart.

I was dozing when I heard noises in the kitchen. I went to investigate and found a man with black hair and pale, pale skin standing near the table and holding the bakery box to his ear as if it were a seashell.

"Sorry," he said, putting it down. "The door was open. Where's Ivan?"

"Gone," I said.

"Oh," he said. "Be back soon?"

"No," I said. Well, I was up. I put on the kettle.

"Sit down," he said. "Relax. I don't bite." He laughed—the sound of breaking dishes. "Name's Eugene." He held out a hand to me. "Mind if I sit for a minute, too? Foot's killing me."

He pulled up a chair across from me and sat, his long-lashed eyes cast down.

"What's the matter with your foot?" I said after a while.

"Well, I'm not exactly sure. Doctor told me it was a calcium spur. Doesn't bother me much, except just occasionally." He fell silent for a minute. "Maybe I should see the guy again, though. Sometimes things . . . become *exacerbated*, I guess is how you'd put it. Turn into other things, almost."

I nodded, willing him toward the door. I wanted to sleep. I wanted to have a meal.

"I was walking around, though," he said, "and I thought I'd drop in to see Ivan."

"I'm going to have a cup of tea," I said. "Do you want one?"

"He doesn't have any herb tea, does he?" Eugene said. "It's good for the nerves. Soothing." He was wearing heavy motorcycle boots, I saw, that were soaking wet. No wonder his feet hurt. "Yeah, Ivan owes me some money," he said. "Thought I'd drop by and see if he had it on him by some chance."

I put the teapot and cups on the table. I wondered how soon I could get Eugene to go.

"Where're you from?" Eugene said. "You're not from here, are you?"

"New York," I said. I also wanted to get out of these clothes. They were becoming terribly uncomfortable.

"Yeah, that's what I thought. I thought so." He laughed miserably again. "Good old rotten apple."

"Don't like it much, huh?" I said.

"Oh, I like it all right," Eugene said. "I love it. I was born and raised there. Whole family's there. Yeah, I miss it a lot. From time to time." He sipped delicately at his tea, still looking down. Then he tossed his thick black hair back from his face, as if he were aware of my stare.

"Aren't you cold?" I asked suddenly. "Walking around like that?" I reached over to his leather jacket.

"Oh, I'm fine, thank you, dear," he said. "I enjoy this. Of course I've got a scarf on, too. Neck's a very sensitive part of the body. Courting disaster to expose the neck to the elements. But this is my kind of weather. I'd live outside if I could." He lifted his eyes to me. They were pale and shallow, and they caught the light strangely, like pieces of bottle glass under water. "Candy?" he said, taking a little vial from his pocket and shaking some of its powdery contents out onto the table.

"No, thanks," I said.

"Mind if I do?" He drew a wad of currency from another pocket and peeled off a large bill.

"That's pretty," I said, watching him roll it into a tight brown tube stippled with green and red. "I've never seen that one before."

"Pretty," he said. "You bet it's pretty. It's a cento. Still play money to me, though. A lot better than that stingy little monochrome crap back home, huh?"

Eugene tipped some more from the vial onto the table.

"So why don't you go back?" I said. "If you like it so much."

"Go back." He sniffed loudly, eyes closed. "You know, I don't feel this stuff the way a woman does. They say it's a woman's drug. I don't get that feeling at the back of my head, like you can." His light eyes rested on my face. "Well, I can't go back. Not unless they extradite me."

"For what?" Maybe I could just ask Eugene to go. Or maybe I could grab his teacup and smash it on the floor.

"Shot a guy," he said.

"Yes?" I tucked my feet under me. This annoying skirt! I hated the feeling of wool next to my skin.

"Now, don't get all nervous," Eugene said. "It was completely justified. Guy tried to hurt me. I'd do it again, too. Fact, I said so to the judge. My lawyer kept telling me, 'Shut up, maniac, shut up.' And he told the judge, 'Your Honor, you can see yourself my client's as crazy as a lab rat.' How do you like that? So I said, 'Listen, Judge. What would you do if some cocksucker pulled a knife on you? I may be crazy, but I'm no fool.'" Eugene leaned back and put his hands against his eyes.

I poured myself some more tea. It felt thick going down. I hadn't even had water, I remembered, for some time. "Would you like another cup?" I asked.

"Yeah," Eugene said. "Thanks."

"You know Ivan a long time?" he asked.

"Nine years," I said.

"Nine years. A lot of bonds can be forged in nine years. So how come I never met you? Ivan and I hang out."

"Oh, God, I don't know," I said. "It's an on-and-off type of thing. We're thrashing it out together now."

"You're thrashing it out together," he said. "You're thrashing it out together, but I only see one of you."

"Right," I said. "So how did you get to Canada, anyhow?"

"Oh. They put me in the hospital," he said. "But I've got friends. Here," he said. "Look." He emptied a pocket onto the table. There was a key chain, and an earring, and something that I presumed was a switchblade, and a bundle of papers—business cards and phone numbers and all sorts of miscellany—that he started to read out to me. "Jesus," he said, noticing me inspecting his knife. "You'll take your whole arm off that way. Do it like this." He demonstrated, flashing the blade out, then he folded it up and put it back in his pocket. "Here—look at this one." He handed me a card covered with a meaningless mass of dots. "Now hold it up to the light." He grabbed it back and placed it over a lamp near me. The dots became a couple engaged in fellatio. "Isn't that something?"

"Yes," I said. "I think you should go now, though. I have to do some things." His face was changing and changing in front of me. He receded, rippling.

"Wait—" he said. "You don't look good. Have you been eating right?"

"I'm all right," I said. "I don't care. Please leave."

"You're in bad shape, lady," he said. "You're not well. Sure you don't want any of this?" He offered me the vial. "Pick you right up. Then we'll fix you some more tea or something. Get some vitamins into you."

"No, no. It's just these clothes," I said, plucking at them. "I've got to get out of these clothes." He was beautiful, I saw. He was beautiful. He sparkled with beauty; it streamed from him in glistening sheets, as if he were emerging from a lake of it. I kicked at Micheline's boots, but Eugene was already kneeling, and he drew them off, and the thick stockings, too, and my legs appeared, very long, almost shining in the growing dark, from beneath them.

"Got 'em," he said, standing.

"Yes," I said, holding my arms up. "Now get this one," and he pulled the sweater over my head.

"Sh-h-h," he said, folding the sweater neatly. "It's O.K." But I was rattling inside my body like a Halloween skeleton as he carried me to Ivan's bed and wrapped a blanket around me.

"Look how white," I said. "Look how white your skin is."

"When I was in the jungle it was like leather," he said.

"Year and a half, shoe leather. Sh-h-h," he said again, as I flinched at a noise. "It's just this." And I understood that it was just his knife, inside his pocket, that had made the noise when he'd dropped his clothes on the floor. "You like that, huh?" he said, holding the knife out for me.

Again and again and again I made the blade flash out, severing air from air, while Eugene waited. "That's enough now," he said. "First things first. You can play with that later."

When we finished making love, the moon was a perfect circle high in the black window. "How about that?" Eugene said. "Nature." We leaned against each other and looked at it. "You got any food here, by the way?" he asked. "I'm famished."

By the time I'd located a robe—a warm, stripy thing in Ivan's closet—Eugene was rummaging through the icebox. "You got special plans for this?" he said, holding up the violet toilet paper that apparently I'd refrigerated.

"Let's see . . ." I said. "There're some sausages."

"Sausages," he said. "Suckers are delicious, but they'll kill you. Preservatives, saturated fats. Loaded with PCBs, too."

"Really?" I said.

"Don't you know that?" he said. "What are you smiling about? You think I'm kidding? Listen, Americans eat too much animal protein anyhow. Fiber's where it's at." He nodded at me, his eyebrows raised. "What else you got?"

"There's some pickled okra," I said.

"Ivan's into some heavy shit here, huh?" he said.

"Well . . ." It was true that I hadn't shopped very efficiently. "Oh, there are these." I undid the bakery box.

"Holy Christ," Eugene said. "How do you like that—little Christmas trees. Isn't that something!" He arranged them into a forest on the table and walked his fingers among them. "Here we come a-wassailing among the leaves so green," he sang, and it sounded like something he didn't often do.

> "Here we come awandering
>   so fair to be seen.
> Love and joy come to you,
>   and to you your wassail too,
> And God bless you and send you
>   a happy New Year,
> And God send you a happy New Year."

"What's the matter?" he said. "You don't like Christmas carols?" So I did harmony as he sang another verse:

> "We are not daily beggars
>   that beg from door to door,
> But we are neighbors' children
>   whom you have seen before.
> Love and joy come to you,
>   and to you your wassail too,
> And God bless you and send you
>   a happy New Year,
> And God send you a happy New Year."

Eugene clapped. Then he made an obscene face and stuck a cookie into his mouth. "Oh, lady," he said, holding the cookie out for me to finish. "These are fuckin' *scrumptious*."

That was true. They were awfully good, and we munched on them quietly in the moonlit kitchen.

"So what about you and Ivan?" Eugene asked.

"I don't know," I said. "I'm starving with Ivan, but my life away from him—my own life—I've just let it dry up. Turn into old bits and pieces."

"Well, honey," Eugene said, "that's not right. It's your life."

"But nothing changes or develops," I said. "Ivan just can't seem to decide what he wants."

"No?" Eugene looked away tactfully, and I laughed out loud in surprise.

"That's true," I said. "I guess he decided a long time ago." I stared down at the table, into our diminished cookie forest, and I felt Eugene staring at me. "Well, I didn't want to be the one to end it, you know?" I said. "But time does change things, even if you can't see it happen, and eventually someone has to be the one to say, 'Well, now things have changed.' Anyhow, it's not his fault. He's given me what he could."

Eugene nodded. "Ivan's a solitary kind of guy. I respect him."

"Yes," I said. "But I wish things were different."

"I understand, dear." Eugene patted my hand. "I hear you."

"What about you?" I said. "Do you have a girlfriend?"

"Who, me?" he said. "No, I'm just an old whore. I've got a wife down in the States. Couldn't live with her anymore, though." He sighed and looked around. "Sixteen years. So what else you got to eat here? I'm still hungry."

"Well," I said. "There's a roll of cookie dough in the freezer, but it's Ivan's, really."

"We should eat it, then." Eugene laughed. "Serve the arrogant bastard right." I looked at him. "Don't mind me, honey," he said. "You know I'm crazy."

I woke up once in the night, with Eugene snoring loudly next to me, and when I butted my head gently into his shoulder to quiet him down he wrapped his marvelous white arms around me. "Thought I forgot about you, huh?" he said distinctly, and started to snore again.

Sunlight forced my eyes open hours later. "Shit," said a voice near me. "What time is it?" The sun had bleached out Eugene's luminous beauty. With his pallor and coarse black hair, he looked like a phantom that one registers peripherally on the streets. "I've got a business appointment at noon," he said, pulling on his jeans. "Think it's noon?"

"I don't know," I said. It felt pleasantly early. "No clock."

"I better hit the road," he said. "Shit."

"Here," I said, holding out his knife.

"Yeah, thanks." He pocketed it and looked at me. "You be O.K. now, lady? Going to take care of yourself for a change?"

"Yes," I said. "By the way, how much does Ivan owe you?"

"Huh?" he said. "Hey, there's my jacket. Right on the floor. Very nice."

"Because he mentioned it before he left," I said.

"Yeah?" Eugene said. "Well, it doesn't matter. I'll come back for it, like—when? When's that sucker going to get back?"

"No," I said. There was really no point in waiting for Ivan. I wanted to conclude this business myself right now. "He forgot to tell me how much it was, but he left me plenty to cover."

Eugene looked down at his boots. "Two bills."

I put on the robe and counted out two hundred dollars from my purse. It was almost all I had left of the lively cash. "And he said thanks," I said.

I stood at the open door until Eugene went through it. "Yeah, well," he said. "Thanks yourself."

At the landing he turned back to me. "Have a good one," he called up.

I went back inside and put some eggs on to boil. Then I twirled slowly, making the stripes on the robe flare.

How on earth had I forgotten butter? The eggs were good, though. I enjoyed them.

After breakfast I rooted around and found a pail and sponges. It made me sad that Ivan had let the apartment get so filthy. He used to enjoy taking care of things. Then I sat down with a mystery I found on a shelf, and by the time Ivan walked in, late in the afternoon, I'd almost finished it.

"Looks great in here," he said after he kissed me.

"I did some cleaning," I said.

"That's great," he said. I thought of my own apartment. There would be a lot to do when I got home. "Jesus. Am I exhausted! That was some trip."

"How's Gary?" I said.

"Well, he was running a little fever when I got there, but he's fine now," Ivan said.

"Good," I said. "Did he like his presents?"

"Uh-huh." Ivan smiled. "Particularly that game that the marble rolls around in. He and I both got pretty good at it after the first few hundred hours."

"I liked that one, too," I said.

"He's a good kid," Ivan said. "He really is. I just hope Linda doesn't make him into some kind of nervous wreck."

"How's she doing?" I asked.

"Well, she's all right, I think. She's trying to get a life

together for herself at least. She's getting a degree in dance therapy."

"That's good," I said.

"She'll be O.K. if she can just get over her dependency," he said. "I'll be interested to see how she does with this new thing."

He would be monitoring her closely, I knew. What a tight family they had established, Ivan and Linda—not much room for anyone else. Of course, Gary and I had our own small parts in it. I'd probably been quite important in fencing out, oh, Micheline, for instance, just as Gary had been indispensable in fencing me out.

"Hey," Ivan said. "Who's been sitting in my chair?" He bent down and picked up a scarf.

"Someone named Eugene stopped by," I said. "He said you owed him money."

"Jesus. That's right," Ivan said. "Well, I'll get around to it in the next day or so."

"I took care of it myself," I said.

"Really? Well, thanks. That's great. I'll reimburse you. Sorry you had to deal with him, though."

"I liked him," I said.

"You did?" Ivan said.

"You like him enough to do business with him," I said.

"Yeah, I know I should be more compassionate," Ivan said. "It's just that he's so hard to take."

"Is any of that stuff true that he says?" I asked. "That he shot some guy? That he lived in the jungle?"

"Shot some guy? I don't know. He has a pretty extensive fantasy life. But he fought in the war, yeah."

"Oh," I said. "I see. Jungle—Vietnam."

"I keep forgetting," Ivan said. "You're really just a baby."

"That must have been awful," I said.

"Well, he could have gotten out of it if he didn't want to do it," Ivan said.

"He probably thought it was a good thing to do," I said. "Besides, people can't arrange their lives exactly the way they'd like to."

"I disagree," Ivan said. "People only like to think they can't."

"You know," I said, trying to recall the events of the day before, "I was having some sort of conversation with a butcher about that yesterday."

"A butcher?" Ivan said.

"Yes," I said. "And, as I remember, he was saying something to the effect that people are only free to the extent that they recognize the boundaries of their lives."

"Sounds pretty grim," Ivan said. "And pretty futile."

"Not exactly futile," I said. "At least, I think his point was that if I know that over here is where I'm standing, well, that's what gives rise to the consciousness that over there is where you're standing, and automatically I get a map, a compass. So my situation—no matter how bad it is—is my source of power."

"Well," Ivan said. "That's a very dangerous way of thinking, because it's just that point of view that can be used to rationalize a lot of selfishness and oppression and greed. I'll bet you were talking to that thief over by St. Lawrence who weighs his thumb, right?"

"Well, maybe I'm misrepresenting him," I said. "He was pretty enigmatic."

Ivan looked at me and smiled, but I could hardly bear the sweetness of it, so I turned away from him and went to the window.

How handsome he was! How I wished I could contain

the golden, wounding hope of him. But it had begun to diverge from me—oh, who knew how long before—and I could feel myself already reforming: empty, light.

"So how are you?" Ivan said, joining me at the window.

"All right," I said. "It's good not to be waiting for you."

"I'm sorry I missed Christmas here," he said. "Montreal's a nice place for Christmas. Next year, what do you say we try to do it right?"

He put his arm around me, and I leaned against his shoulder while we looked out at the place where I'd been walking the day before. The evening had arrived at the moment when everything is all the same soft color of a shadow, and the city seemed to be floating close, very close, outside the window. How familiar it was, as if I'd entered and explored it over years. Well, it had been a short time, really, but it would certainly be part of me, this city, long after I'd forgotten the names of the streets and the colors of the light, long after I'd forgotten the feel of Ivan's shirt against my cheek, and the darkening sight separated from me now by a sheet of glass I could almost reach out to shatter.

BROKEN GLASS

As I exited through the terminal gate I thought, for an instant, that the plane had set me down in the exact spot from which it had lifted me up hours earlier, that I was distant only by some uniform tickings of the clock from the things I'd fled: the daily drive home from work past the hospital towers, the sight of the newspaper I'd combed every evening for articles that could penetrate the caul of pain and drugs in which my mother lay, the sounds of my own language, through which the furious chattering in my brain seemed to erupt with terrible force. Airports, train stations, hospitals—one looks much like another, whether it marks the beginning of a journey or the end; and when I reminded myself that I'd just flown several thousand miles, it was borne in upon me that my mother was going to be as dead here, now, as she had been in Chicago this morning.

Lovers and family members called to one another in the crowded lobby and embraced, and I was claimed by Ray, as he insisted on being called, the real-estate agent who had located a place for me in the town I'd chosen almost at random from a huge and uninformative guidebook. When I held out my hand to him, something like alarm flickered in his face. Had he expected some other sort of woman? No matter; I didn't want to know. We had about an hour's drive ahead of us, and I was determined to avoid the sort of intimate, confessional conversation that strangers are said to have. I had not gone into the circumstances of my trip in my letter or over the phone—I preferred to be considered simply a vacationer.

In the car I sat as far from Ray's damp heartiness as possible, and I looked out the window while he talked. I'd never been far from Chicago, and I'd chosen to come to Latin America because of its unfamiliarity to my imagination. All the alluring places that during my mother's lifetime I'd yearned to see belonged sealed now, I felt, in a completed past where they would remain contemporaneous with my mother.

The colors of the landscape that flowed around me were soft and dense, but the light itself was a rippling gold, and the clumps of trees and the sandy slopes and hollows seemed like moving islands tilting toward, then away from us in the fragile ocean of air. Eventually, we descended into a plateau ringed by mountains, and the disorienting glitter of the air melted in the low warmth, and soon distinguishable ahead of us against the tawny dryness was a tumble of feathery green and blossoms. Ray nodded. "Been a prime piece of real estate for something like a thousand years," he said soberly.

We drove downward into a maze of cobbled streets bordered by high rosy walls, and we slowed to avoid a woman with several children who was crossing our path. On the woman's head was a bundle—wrapped in plastic, I saw, as a pickup truck veered around us, raising a wake of brilliant dust. In the back of the truck was a crowd of men whose copper-colored faces and black hair shone above their work shirts. I glanced at the rather spongy person beside me. "Oh, you won't be bored," he said. "We have a wonderful group down here. Very fine people from all walks of life. Tennis, golf, sites of historical interest, pools. Perfect climate, of course—anything you want. To tell you the truth, we think we're pretty clever. Not that we'd ever say so to our friends back home." He smiled playfully, buoyed up for a moment by his own wit, and I turned away, mortified, as if I had seen something disastrously personal.

We parked high up on one side of the town. I followed Ray through a large wooden gate and was astonished to see the lush garden that lay beyond the wall, just off the dry, dusty street. "You're upstairs over the garage," Ray said, leading me through the garden and across a slate patio to a white house with a tiled roof. "But we have to get the keys from Norman."

The front of the house was glass, and although the sun was too strong for me to see clearly into the unlit interior, I had the impression for an instant that a man, in something that looked like a bathrobe, hovered in back. "Mr. Egan. Mr. Egan," Ray called, and as a woman came to the door the man I thought I'd seen became shadows. "Oh, hello, Dolores," Ray said.

"Mr. Egan is not available," the woman said, smiling at me. The words had a fresh, odd sound in her accent, as if their meaning were not quite set. "I will take you upstairs."

"That won't be necessary, thank you, Dolores," Ray said. "Just let me have the keys and we'll manage."

Ray led me up a flight of whitewashed steps on the outside of the house to the door of what turned out to be a small apartment. "You needn't worry much about tipping, by the way," he said. "They don't expect it. Just meals and that sort of thing. Well—kitchen, closet, bathroom. Oh, bed—well, obviously. Water's generally potable, but you might boil to be on the safe side. We think it's a nice little place. Norman's wife used to use it as a sort of studio, I believe. I understand that she used to paint." He paused, and something seemed to strike him. "Nice fellow, Norman. Of course, we can all use the extra income."

"Is she still living?" I asked.

"Pardon me?" Ray said.

"Mr. Egan's wife," I said. "Did she die?"

"I see." Ray nodded, as if I'd made some sort of point. "Not at all, not at all. Well, looks like Norman's left you some provisions, but there are plenty of restaurants in town. Food's quite safe as a rule. Have to watch out a bit for the men, of course, but nothing actually dangerous, I mean." He held the keys out to me and then put them down on the table. "So," he said, and looked at me, his arms at his sides.

"Thank you," I said. "I'm sure everything will be fine."

So he left, and I stood still to let the sound of his voice drain away into the heavy, bright, humming afternoon. Then I opened my suitcase and put my things in the closet and arranged my jars of lotions and creams on the bureau.

What to do? At work I would have been finishing for the day, organizing my files for the next morning. And soon, at the hospital, the patients would be receiving little paper cups holding pills, like the cups of candies at a children's birthday party.

I went and sat on the small balcony that overlooked the garden. The air lapped against my skin with an unfamiliar silkiness, and scalloped rings of mountains surrounded me like ripples. Here and there, I could see softly rounded churches, with spires and crosses. My mother had been ill for so long that all time had flowed toward her death, and I feared that all time would flow backward to it as well. I had become thirty-four waiting for my own span to be placed over that fulcrum—an irrevocable placement.

Down below me a small white rabbit nosed out among

the plants and zigzagged out of sight. Its pink eyes and the pink lining of its ears looked particularly sensitive to pain.

I noticed that my nice traveling skirt was already wrinkled and ingrained with dust, and a wave of sorrow engulfed me, as though I'd betrayed something placed in my care. This was only the strain, I understood, of the last weeks—the extra hours at the hospital, the extra hours at work to justify the time off I knew I would be taking, the funeral arrangements, the ordeal, especially, of sorting through my mother's papers and disposing of all the little things my mother had acquired over the years for one purpose or another, now also dead.

How thorough my preparations had been! My mother herself, though, had been utterly unprepared. For close to twenty-five years her life had consisted of little more than the miseries of a slow degenerative illness, but as her future declined in value and her suffering increased, her fear increased also. She had feared death greatly, and life clung to her like a burning robe.

I thought with sudden fury of the doctor who stood with me in the hospital corridor only a few days ago. He had been unprepared as well, and he looked helpless, like a little boy all dressed up in a doctor suit. Yet he must have known for a long, long time that sooner or later he would have to face someone the way he faced me that day, and say those things.

That night my sleep was shallow and unpleasant, and when I woke I had the queasy sensation of having been brought up short, as when one steps from a boat onto fixed ground, and that was how I remembered that I was finished for good with trips to the hospital.

Just as it occurred to me that I would have to plunge into an unknown universe merely in order to obtain some coffee a man with a trim silver beard appeared at my door. "Good

morning, good morning. I'm Norman, your evil landlord,"
he said, holding out to me an armload of roses.

"Thank you," I said. The flowers, still richly furled and
heavy with droplets of water, were a living, modulated, faintly
sickening salmon color.

"Vase under the sink," Norman said. I judged him to be
in his late fifties, and he would have been quite good-looking,
I thought, except that his face seemed to have been stamped
by a habit of geniality and then left unattended. Despite his
jaunty white clothes, he seemed uncomfortable.

"My wife would have done a real arrangement for you,"
he said. "She has quite a flair for it. Gardening, too."

"Did Mrs. Egan do the garden here?" I asked.

"Sandra," he said. "Well, she doesn't do too much now.
We have the boy handle it." Norman wandered over to the
window and peered out, shading his eyes. "I suppose one gets
tired of things." I remained standing, anxious to get on with
my day.

"It's a shame," Norman said, turning to me. "Used to be,
when we first moved in here, you could see the mountain from
this window every day of the year. Sacred, you know. Of
course, this whole area was considered special—conquered over
and over again by different tribes till the Spanish came and
grabbed it up. Cities right on top of other cities down there.
But—it's fascinating—every one of those peoples used the same
big pyramid up on the mountain to worship in their own way.
Splendid ruins—Sandra and I used to take picnics . . ."

I squinted out the window. "Oh, you can't see anything
today." Norman dismissed with a little wave the blue sky and
dazzling sun. "All kinds of industry now mucking things up.
People coming in from the country—crowding, pollution,
that sort of thing." He sighed. "Anyhow, nice to know you've

got a view, eh? Whether you can see it or not. Well . . ." He put forth a mild, formalized version of a chuckle. "But we still love it. And, please—if you need anything, I hope you'll ask. There are always so many little things one doesn't quite know what to do about. One expects things to be one way, but then they turn out to be—not to be just exactly the way one expects."

"Yes," I said, from the depths of a sudden fatigue. "Perhaps you'd know where I might be able to buy some coffee."

"Coffee," he said. "Well—coffee. They'd have it in town, of course. Dolores handles that sort of thing for us. Oh, yes," he said, misunderstanding my look of surprise, "we're very lucky with Dolores. Down here we don't like to be very, *very* formal"—he winked at me—"but Dolores came to us very young. Husband disappeared—you know the way they do— and Sandra taught her everything."

"Really," I said.

"Well, we were in the restaurant business, you see. We had lovely establishments. New Orleans, Dallas, Cincinnati, Fort Lauderdale—all over. And in every one of those places we had a wonderful, cultivated clientele. Sandra and I always personally oversaw everything. Oh," he said. "I brought something else for you." He handed me a little book. "This might prove useful. And remember, don't feel shy. If you have questions, or you need something, you just come right downstairs and ask."

"I don't suppose I'll be bothering you often," I said, taking the opportunity to discourage further visits from him. "I'm really just here to—"

"Of course," he said. "You're young and adventurous. You didn't come here to hang around with a couple of old—a couple of old . . . people."

Young and adventurous, I thought irritably, as we went out together; young and adventurous. But as I closed the door behind us, I glanced back into the room, and I felt as if I'd been slapped. With the jars of cream out on the bureau, it was true that the place looked like a girl's first apartment, like the apartments my college roommates had gotten for themselves when we graduated and I'd moved back in with my mother.

When I opened the front gate, the town I'd driven through only the day before took me by surprise, as if my imagination had perversely reconstructed a fleeting hallucination. The concave whorl of tangled streets lay below me in a glaze of sun, and I wound downward, baffled by the high walls. How quiet all the people around me were! They spoke in low voices, and averted their heavy-lashed eyes as I passed by. Even the children made hardly any noise. Trucks and motorcycles and an occasional flustered chicken provided all the sound.

At the base of the town, I found a small square, and although I was anxious to do a few errands and get my bearings, its lacy little white iron benches looked so ceremonial and expectant that I felt obliged to sit down for a moment. I chose a spot in the shade of a broad-leafed tree and surveyed the odd patch of a park around me. Paved walks threaded through it, and it was dotted with tiny tiled fountains. Heavy prismatic beams seemed to converge on it from many different suns, giving everything an exaggerated dimensionality in which it was impossible to judge distances, and in the very center was a band shell, confected from curls of iron and pearly glass, whose dome rose above the leaves of nearby trees. Around the edges of the square, people who looked like dolls in costumes, with black yarn hair, sold things: painted toys, hardware, bursting red fruits, clothing, hideous stuffed dogs, or masks—a fantastic, impossible catalogue of items. Aromas of ripe—overripe—fruit, and dust, and some kind of peppery cooking oil swirled lazily around me.

It was hot. I looked at my watch and was dismayed to find that it had stopped. What ought I to do? I thought, standing hurriedly. But I forced myself to sit back down and relax. I opened the little book that Norman had given me—a compilation of phrases in English and translation which the author seemed to consider indispensable to travelers:

> *This dress is too long (too short).*
> *" " is made to fit badly.*
> *It is badly made.*
> *That is more than I can pay for this dress*
> *(basket) (rug) (bowl).*
> *No, thank you, I do not want it.*
> *Good. That is a fair price.*

"Is it something unpleasant that you read?" I heard, and I looked up to see a man standing over me. He seemed so close, in my alarm, that every detail of the medal lying on his exposed chest looked immense: the hair around it and the skin, glistening with sweat, appeared magnified.

"No," I said to the large white teeth above me. I snapped the book shut and walked off on trembling legs.

Soon I had gotten myself back under control, and I paused to see where I was. Next to me an opening in the street wall gave onto something that appeared to be a sort of general store. Inside, past dusty cases of beer stacked along the buckling aqua-colored wall, I found coffee and other things I needed.

At the counter, two almond-eyed little girls painstakingly picked what I hoped was the correct amount of coins from a heap I put in front of them. Supervising this proceeding was a large woman in long, ruffled skirts, who grinned at me. I was painfully aware of being the absurd tourist, and I stared at the woman, who only grinned with greater gusto.

It took me quite some time to find my way back to the square, where I stood looking helplessly at the streets that twisted up in a funnel around me. Eventually I managed to identify my route back, but at its mouth a row of women now sat, wrapped in shawls, and as I approached they stretched out their hands without glancing at me. There was no way to avoid them. I divided my change into equal portions and distributed it among the women, being very careful not to touch them.

The first thing I saw when I opened the door to my apartment was my heartless line of creams and lotions on the bureau. I quickly put the jars into the medicine chest, and then I examined the packages and cans of food that Norman had provided. Later I lay down to read. But instead of holding the book, I was rising up to where I saw myself asleep. I dreamed of a cool, dark sleep that was ruptured almost immediately by noisy intruders who disputed and harangued for hour after hour in many guises and landscapes. Several times during the night they drove me into the solitude of wakefulness, at the boundaries of which they waited, shrieking and bobbing, until I was weak enough to be captured again.

In the morning I woke to see my few purchases of the day before on the bureau, where I'd left them. How odd this light made everything look—the coffee, the sugar, the soap—like menacing little idols. And later, when I opened the gate onto the street, I once again experienced a little shock, as if the town, simmering below me in the dusty gold, had just materialized to greet me.

I was determined to get a good start on the day, so I headed right down to the square, where I remembered having seen a news kiosk. Most of the publications for sale turned out to be comic books devoted to slaughter and tragedy, but there were several magazines with interesting pictures. I paid the older of the two boys who worked at the kiosk, while the other, who must have been around seven, stared at me, his face an upturned circle with a point at the chin.

In the heat of the afternoon, when shutters rolled down over the shop doorways, I inspected the restaurants and cafés that faced the square, but they were filled with roughly clothed men, drunk even at that hour, and foreigners speaking English or German at an arrogant volume. Sorrowful vendors circulated among the tables, and there were flies.

Persisting, I discovered a restaurant in a little courtyard that looked clean and quiet. After I settled at a table near a blossom-clogged fountain, I realized that the restaurant was part of a hotel, whose guests—small, ancient people in dressing gowns—spoke a language I did not recognize. I managed to order something from a young waiter, who encouraged my clumsy efforts with unwelcome enthusiasm, but when my meal came, steaming and covered with an assaultive spicy sauce, I could feel that the expression on my face replicated the one I had so often seen on my mother's when she confronted her tray of trembling sickroom substances. I watched, humiliated, as the wizened diners around me ate hugely, with evident enjoyment, and I reminded myself that if I were in Chicago I would have no trouble obtaining a nice, crisp salad and a refreshing glass of iced tea.

Norman was on his terrace when I returned, chatting with a man and woman who seemed to be about my age. The three of them sipped from frosty glasses, and a small boy squatted nearby, barking menacingly at a baleful setter. "Stop that, please, John-John," the man said.

"Oh, he's all right," Norman said, smiling at me in greeting. "Mister's used to children, aren't you, Mister?" The dog yawned with pleasure as Norman scratched his ear. "Mister and that old bunny rabbit belong to the people next door, but they like to come visiting."

"Excuse us," the man said as the boy sprinted off in tight circles, spluttering like a balloon releasing its air. "I'm Simon Peter Murchison, and this is my wife, Annette. And that dignified personage now disporting himself in the compost is our firstborn, John-John."

"Would you believe it?" Annette said. "We bought that little shirt in Florence for him."

"Don't be in a rush, now," Norman said. "Won't you sit down and have a drink with us, please? Dolores—" he called.

"Where has our son picked up these *habits*?" Annette smiled, inviting me to marvel with her.

"Yes, we've been all over since he was born," Simon Peter explained loftily.

"For pleasure?" I asked.

"For a pittance." He chuckled in the direction of his drink. "University salary."

"How nice to have a field that takes you around," I said obediently, as I craned to read his watch.

"History of Ecclesiastical Architecture in Colonial Countries," Simon Peter said. We all glanced up at the silhouettes of crosses that stood out on the peaks around us, black against the shining sky.

"These are so delicious, Norman," Annette said, accepting a fresh drink from Dolores. "What do you put in them?"

"Oh, just about any kind of fruit you can think of. And then just about any kind of alcohol you can think of." Norman winked at me.

"Are you teaching here now?" I asked Simon Peter.

"I've picked up a semester," he said. "But essentially we're based in Europe for the moment."

Annette turned to me. "Do you know Europe?"

"No," I said.

"You should," she said. "You should try it. The things that are good here? They're even better there. Of course, prices have really soared since we first went. But now here, even with the devaluations, prices are a completely different thing than they used to be. We're priced right out now, on Simon Peter's salary." She cast a sour glance at the house. "You've certainly found yourself a bargain."

"I've just come for a short time. Besides," I said deliberately, "I inherited a small amount of money."

"There," she said. "You see?"

"Anyhow, we're glad to have you with us," Norman said.

"It seems like a wonderful place for children," I said.

"In many ways, yes," Simon Peter said with a vague judiciousness. "In many ways I suppose it is. At least they're happy enough."

"These children here can afford to be happy," Annette said. "They're spoiled rotten."

"Well, anyway," Norman said.

"No, it's a shame," Annette said. "I know these people. My parents came here every winter until I was twelve. These people are sweet, kind people; I grew up with them. They don't want to hurt anyone—they're Indians. But they're so irresponsible. They keep having children and having children—

they just can't be taught to stop. And there isn't enough food, there isn't enough money, and so they starve. And now these people have become dishonest. You used to be able to leave them to take care of your house while you were gone, with all your silver or anything. Now they'll steal your wallet right on the street."

"They're a fine people, really," Norman said to me. "For the most part. And the little ones are darling."

"John-John," Simon Peter called warningly to his son, who towered over a plant from behind which the rabbit peeked out, twitching.

"No, I love these people, Norman," Annette said. "But you can't trust them anymore. Well, everyone has to eat, of course. I understand that. But they breed like——" Annette glanced with annoyance toward the shrubbery, where John-John now crouched holding a rock—"like I don't know whats."

"Well," Simon Peter said, "the climate's still perfect."

"Have you been up to the mountain yet?" Annette gestured toward the empty sky.

"I've really just arrived," I said.

"We'll go while you're here," she said. "There are some very good market towns up there. You can still get the most marvelous textiles and ceramics for practically nothing."

"How nice," I said. "Well . . ." I felt I had spent enough time on these witless marauders. "I really must be going upstairs now." As I stood, I realized how potent Norman's drink had been.

"Will anyone stay for some supper?" Norman asked.

"Don't you wish Mommy would let you?" Annette said to John-John. "Thank you, Norman. We wish we could."

"Well, please come back soon," Norman said. "Sandra will be dying to see you both."

"Hush now, honey," Annette said to John-John. "We're saying good night."

"She's due in at the end of the week," Norman said. We all looked at John-John as he tugged at Annette's hand and loosed a descending wordless whine. "Sandra."

"Well, isn't that wonderful, Norman," Simon Peter said, frowning.

So this was what was meant by "traveling," by "taking a vacation"—these unnavigable currents, this sudden immersion in the lives of utter strangers, their thin, dreadful lives.

That night sleep came for me like a great ship sliding between the dark sky and the dark water, and it bore me off to a territory that I recognized with horror, as I lost consciousness, from the night before. My dreams coiled and merged until I could no longer sustain sleep and woke exhausted, tossed by a shrill crowd onto the bed where I found myself.

The air was faintly sparkly, and a freshness drifted in through the open windows. While I lay there, trying to emerge into full consciousness, a memory permeated me like a single low vibrating tone: My mother stood in the water, smiling at me. She would have been just slightly older than I was now. I wore a bathing suit the shade of vanilla ice cream, with the most special little candy-colored blobs—special, delicious colors. My mother held out her hand to coax me out farther. The cool sand where I stood became wet and wet again with a mild pulse of water. The sand gave beneath my feet each time a wave pulled back, then smoothed mysteriously before each return. I took my mother's hand and walked into the water to where the sand became round stones. I looked at my divided legs, and at the stones that wobbled when I moved, in the clear, different thing. My mother was happy. When had I ever seen her so happy? Where could we have been? I clung to her hand and edged in farther.

When I woke again, the sun was a yellow rayed circle over the garden.

For about a week I saw nothing of Norman, and the curtains of the main house were drawn. But Dolores continued to come and go, smiling her luminous smile, and a gardener appeared several times to redistribute mounds of dirt with an aggressive air of weariness and expertise which was surely intended for Norman's eyes. And so, as there seemed no need to inquire after Norman, I did not. In the mornings I hurried down to the news kiosk and then had my juice and coffee in the hotel restaurant while I looked at my magazines. I walked, then visited the dilapidated little museum in town, and after a midday meal I would join a busload of rapacious tourists to visit one of the nearby villages where Indians made textiles or worked copper, or I went to the square to read about the history of the area. Afterward, I shopped for the small evening meal I would assemble back at the apartment. I had no time to spare.

Then one morning, as I came downstairs, I saw Norman climbing out of his car with a load of parcels. He looked cheerful in his crisp white clothes, and he gave me a friendly wave as he headed toward the house.

"What have you brought me?" a woman called out to him from the doorway. "Treats," she said. "Good. And look—an American girl. He's wonderful," she said to me. "He does everything he can to keep me from—to keep me amused. You *are* an American girl, aren't you? You do understand what I'm saying?"

"This is our little tenant, Sandra," Norman said.

"Well, at least he didn't bring me the Van Kirks," the woman continued. "Or the Murchisons. Or, God forbid, the Geldzahlers."

"Oh, now, Sandra," Norman chuckled hesitantly toward me.

"But they'll be over soon enough. And besides," Sandra said, "we love them. They're our friends. Now"—she smiled formally at me—"are you going to stay and at least have a—a glass of juice with us, or are you one of those busy, busy people who have to rush off somewhere all the time?"

"Nowhere to rush to here," Norman said.

"I'll stay for a moment," I said reluctantly, "but I do have errands." What if the hotel stopped serving breakfast at a particular time?

"Dolores—" Sandra looked around and then left the room.

"So . . ." Norman said, sitting down.

I could leave my magazines until after breakfast, of course, but I hadn't brought anything with me to read. Furthermore, I'd planned to go to the museum right after breakfast, and the kiosk wasn't on the way.

"How nice," I said to Norman, "that your wife has arrived."

"Looks well, doesn't she?" he said vaguely.

"Tell me," Sandra said as she came back into the room, "do you play bridge? Or golf?" She was tall and athletic-looking, and her bright sundress suited her, but she had the hardened flesh of someone who has lain too long around a swimming pool.

"I'm not much for games," I said.

"Good," she said, pushing back her wiry bronze hair. She seemed exasperated by her own sensuous, slightly ramshackle vitality, and I felt grateful to have my orderly body. "Norman just plays to bore himself nerveless." Norman, who had been fussing with some small pieces of wood, smiled up at his wife cautiously, but she avoided looking at him. "He used to make such fun of them. Thank you, Dolores." She smiled brightly at Dolores, who set a glass of juice in front of each of us. "Alas. You must come and entertain me while he plays with his . . . *cronies*." She turned to Norman suddenly. "What have you got there?" she asked.

"Oh," he said, opening his hand to reveal a little dog he'd assembled from the pieces of wood. "One of these silly things. Cute, aren't they? Japanese." He and Sandra gazed at the little figure in his palm, perplexed and abstracted.

"What pretty glasses," I said, picking up my juice.

"Yes," Sandra said. She reeled her attention back from Norman's hand. "Those. Yes, they are quite pretty, aren't they? They're local work. It's a shame they don't make them any longer."

"Well, we've got ours," Norman said with a jolly lift of an eyebrow. "We got them years ago, and we still have them."

"Like everything else we got years ago," Sandra said crossly. She took a sip of her juice and set the glass down, pushing it away from her on the table. "They used to do such lovely work in this area," she said to me. "Norman and I used to bring carloads and carloads back home with us. Oh, those trips!" She looked at Norman for an instant. When she looked away again, she held out her hand, and he clasped it. I was decades away from them in the long silence.

"Would you like something instead of the juice, darling?" Norman said.

"Would I like something instead of the juice." Sandra looked at him and withdrew her hand from his.

"No, I just—" he said, and stopped. He set the little wooden dog on the table and watched it as if it were going to perform a trick.

"Well," Sandra said, seeming to remember me. "But I hope you're having a lovely, lovely time."

"She is," Norman said.

"We always do, ourselves," Sandra said. "Wonderful climate, wonderful friends—pool, sun, tennis . . ."

"And they're a happy people," Norman said.

My day, of course, was pretty well ruined. To salvage something of it I took an unfamiliar street into the square; although every street looked alike, and the walls, their colors softened by an aged, powdery bloom, hid most of what lay beyond them, each doorway and gate opened onto a little scene as precise and mystifying as a stage set, and today I walked slowly, to look. Here and there I could see part of a garden littered with fallen flowers, or the twisted trunk of a tree whose branches arched above the walls. I passed a shop where paper goods were displayed as proudly and elaborately as if they were precious rarities, and a tiny restaurant, consisting of several cheerfully painted tables and a stove, on which sat a stewpot. A jewel-colored parrot presided from his perch. Nearby in a roofed space, a woman leaned back against a polished sports car, resting, her eyes closed. She wore a little uniform with a starched pinafore, and she fanned herself slowly with a large stiff leaf. Stretching out behind her, on and on, I could see a slope covered with tiny shacks. Lines of washing crisscrossed it, and children played there. Several ponies—real ponies they were, of course—stood, flicking their tails. When the maid opened her long obsidian eyes I was unsettled, as if something potent were being released through them. But she didn't seem to see me. Perhaps I was invisible in the strong light.

Later I wandered through an outdoor market I hadn't come across before. I was attracted to an array of miniatures spread out on a blanket, and I picked one up to admire it. It was a tiny scene exactly like the one I stood in front of at that moment: a woman wearing a shawl around her head and shoulders and a long skirt sat behind a display of her wares just like the woman who looked up at me now. But the miniature woman sold tiny foodstuffs—the smallest imaginable carrots and scallions and tomatoes and bottles of milk. I was charmed by the little tableau; but when I tilted it to inspect the toy woman's face, I saw that it was a skull, its mouth open in greedy bliss. Seeing my expression, the living woman in front of me broke into peals of laughter, and my hand seemed frozen to the nasty toy. I was shaking when I reached the news kiosk. Both boys looked at me with concern, and I was glad that it was not possible for us to communicate with one another.

Upstairs that night I took myself by surprise in the mirror. An American girl—no wonder Norman and Sandra insisted that I was young. I'd seen a small-featured face, unusually composed, and an almost aggressively fresh pink-and-white complexion that seemed to have been acted upon by neither internal nor external weather. I had always assumed that life would start for me at about the age I had reached now; it was the age at which my mother considered hers to have started, the age at which she had married for the first and only time, had conceived her first and only child. But soon after that late, small budding of her life she had been left with only a wedding ring, a settlement, a disease, and a daughter, of course—a daughter who was now thirty-four years old.

After Sandra's arrival there was a great deal more activity downstairs. Sandra and Norman were often out sunbathing, or sitting on the terrace, where Dolores brought them elaborate little meals. In the evenings, they frequently had gatherings. The guests, often people who hardly would have spoken to one another in the United States, were bound together here by the conviction, based on the spending power of their dollars, of their own merit, and necessarily, therefore, the merit of their companions. They reinforced this conviction by continuous complaints about the town (and it was true that nothing ever happened on time, nothing was ever properly done, there were endless, inexplicable shortages of goods—it was a world of exasperating shrugs and smiles), and all conversations on these evenings were suspended in a medium of expatriate complicity, where no one had ever suffered any past indignity or disappointment, where no one, in fact, seemed to have any antecedents whatsoever. No one ever asked me anything about my own life. Any sharp-edged remnant of life "back at home" that might mar the smooth afternoons was washed away in the evenings' floods of alcohol. The morning sun burned off the hangovers. There was only one beautiful day and then another, and life being squandered.

During these parties of Sandra and Norman's I would go upstairs as soon as possible. But the loud voices and laughter seemed amplified in my little apartment, and after an hour or two I would feel weak with grief and rage, as one does when one is ill. When I managed to avoid an event of this sort altogether, Dolores would appear at my door with an invitation for me to join the company, and on those evenings that I sent her downstairs with excuses she would return with a tray of party food, decorated with flowers or paper constructions or carved miniatures. Usually I put the food into the refrigerator and saved it for several days before I threw it out, but once, as soon as I'd shut the door behind Dolores, even though I was terribly hungry I threw it wrathfully into the garbage.

When there were no parties I sat inside with the lights dimmed, fearing the exhausting importunities that would surely ensue from downstairs if I were to be seen on my balcony.

One evening, to escape from Norman and Sandra I went to the square. And as I approached I was amazed to find myself in the company of the entire town. The street walls exhaled the retained heat of the day, and a sudden scent of honey was released into the air as people filed in from all directions, arm in arm, and perched on the embellished benches or the rims of the tiled fountains, or strolled along the little paths. The sky flowed pink to green, and across it birds convened in wide streaks, screaming, and settled, with the dark, down into the trees.

I found a spot for myself on a bench between two elderly women. Although the sheen of daylight hung over the sky high across from me, here under the canopy of trees and birds it was truly night. The steady, intricate play of the fountains wove up all the sounds, and small lamps spilled light onto the glossy leaves. All around the square the cafés filled with customers.

No one bothered me. No one spoke to me. I watched the children tumbling about, playing tag up and down the little paths or kicking large, bright, slow balls to one another. Two little girls in identical starched and ruffled dresses bought a balloon from a boy hardly older than themselves. Expertly he disengaged their choice from the massive cluster that bobbed above him. A group of little girls, with ribbons in their silky black hair, tottered, still rubbery with infancy, under a stream of translucent spheres that bloomed from the wand of a vendor of bubble liquid. Little boys ran up a flight of shallow stone steps and slid down its broad border over and over. Teenagers sat entwined, kissing or reading comics, and older couples meandered hand in hand. Some vendors had spread out cloths to display their goods, and others sold sweets from carts, or glowing drinks made of crushed fruit. Musicians played— some in groups, others singly—without reference to each other, and then a band appeared in the little bonbon of a band shell, the brass of their instruments flashing more brightly than the sound. The porous night absorbed noises rapidly here, and activity streamed silently around one, like the sort of dream that binds the body and absorbs the voice as one struggles to break into the waking world.

After that, I often fled to the square in the evenings. It was like being part of a little music box. Every night the fig- ures assumed their positions—the birds, the boys and girls, the parents, the grandparents, the couples, the vendors, and the musicians all took their places at the same time, and the men who sold bubble-making liquid sent their streams of bubbles tirelessly into the air while the tiniest children twirled, en- chanted, beneath them.

Later the town would pitch and boil as I slept. Faces I'd hardly noticed in the square rose up around me and spoke urgently, but I could not understand the words. The flowery walls that lined the streets split open in the pale brilliance of my dreams, revealing broad veins of cardboard shacks where bodies tossed and groaned in their own sleep. Women sat wrapped in their shawls; they reached out, but when I put change into their open palms they threw it on the ground, shrieking. I was ill; I lay in bed, dreaming, with my hands on the covers, unable to move or call out. My mother stood with her back to me, moonlight sluicing down on her. She poured transparent juice from a pitcher into a glass, but it made no sound. She turned and walked toward me, grinning in pain, making a balloon dance on a string. Inside the balloon was a baby. Its face swam toward the surface, hugely distorted. My mother jerked on the string, grinning, making the balloon dance. I saw it was falling, I saw it was plummeting down toward the slate ground, suddenly a great distance away; but a roaring silence masked its impact.

I always awoke into the quiet before dawn with my heart pounding. I would pour myself a glass of water and swallow it slowly to regulate my breathing as I walked back and forth in my room. The moonlight that streamed into my dreams had given way to a softer dark, but how bright the stars were still—like tiny holes in a skin that hid a pure light beyond. Often I hardly knew where I was, as I drank my water and walked, so altered had the world been by my sleep. And all around me dream images of my mother—forgotten images from all the ages at which I'd known her—slipped into shadows. I myself was no age in my dreams, the age one is to oneself. Exhaustion would topple me back into the life of my sleep, which seemed to be flowing on independently of me, just like the life my body entered in the mornings. And after several more hours I could feel myself working free again, but just as I sped up toward a sunlit surface the picture would spin and I would wake plunging downward into a daytime world as protean as my dreams.

In the afternoons, when the sun had baked the town into opaque, reliable shapes, I sat in the square and refreshed myself by reading about the history of the peoples who had occupied the area. Throughout the history of the military struggles, the vanquished had absorbed, to some degree, the victor, and had ultimately asserted at least some subtle ascendancy. And although the stately cities thought to be buried beneath me in layers were as invisible as the mountain where the remains of the pyramid still stood, pockets of ancient languages and customs had survived intact among the people who pursued their

quiet activities around me in the square. It seemed remarkable
to me that these people were adrift at the margins of a history
now generated elsewhere, and yet were the living descendants
not only of the ultimate, fierce Spanish conquerors but also of
the glamorous nations that had ruled here when this had been
the center of civilization. I read about them all—the succession of vivid, vanished empires that ended during the reign of
a bellicose, death-obsessed people, who had been technologi-
cally and martially accomplished but otherwise less refined
than their predecessors. These final Indian rulers used the
pyramid as an altar for human sacrifice, and I could not bring
myself to visit the ruins. I wondered if Norman or Annette
ever imagined the blood that had flowed down stone steps
over his picnic spot, her marketplace.

One night when I came up the hill from the square I found
Norman and Sandra on the patio with a young couple utterly
unlike the reddened, tuberous creatures who were usually to
be found there. "Come here," Sandra called. "I want you to
meet Marcus and Eileen." The woman's skirt flounced out
from her tiny waist, and her toylike high-heeled shoes were
dazzlingly white and free of dust. "They're our neighbors."

"Yes, I am Marcos," the man said, standing. "And my wife,
Elena."

"Now, where did I get 'Eileen' from?" Sandra said.

"For whom can I get something to drink?" Norman said,
clapping his hands together.

"It's Dolores's night off," Sandra said. "God knows what
she does."

"What is it you are drinking, Norman?" Elena asked, reaching out a slender arm.

"Water." Norman smiled sheepishly.

"Yes, certainly, but let me taste," Elena said. Her long red nails gleamed against the glass.

"A little water," Norman said as Elena took a delicate sip.

"A little water with a big gin," Marcos said.

"Yes, give me one of those, please, Norman," Elena said.

"And for me, too, please," Marcos said.

"Nothing for me, thank you," I said.

"Oh, come on," Sandra said.

"No, really," I said. "Thank you."

"These two live right next door," Sandra said, indicating the hedge through which Mister and the rabbit made their frequent appearances. "And *this* one"—she tucked my arm under hers—"lives upstairs. She came all the way from— from—America"—Sandra landed with relief on the word— "and now she's right here in this garden. She *hates* us, isn't that right?" Sandra winked at Elena. "We're bad neighbors and she hates us."

"You must forgive me, please," Elena said to me. "I do not speak very well English. Marcos, my husband, he speak it very well."

"You speak English like a princess," Sandra said. "Just like a princess. Isn't it odd, you know, how you can live right next door to people and never see them at all?" Marcos smiled, allowing a dark radiance to flow briefly out to Sandra.

"Here we are," Norman said. "Three waters, one water, and a nothing."

"Norman and I were just telling these lovely people about some of our other friends right here in town," Sandra said. "Now. You don't know Dr. and Mrs. Rafaelson, you said. Skipper and Lillian."

"Unfortunately, we do not," Marcos said with finality.

"Let's see," Sandra continued. "The Van Kirks, the Geldzahlers, the Murchisons—Oh! You must know the Dawsons. They do a lot of charity work at the church."

Elena's black hair seemed to flex and breathe as she smoothed it back. "I do not think so, do we, Marcos?" Marcos took a sip of his drink and shook his head without looking up. I feared I was to be condemned along with the other invaders from the U.S. without getting my own trial.

"Well, we're all very fortunate to be able to live in a town with such fine people," Norman said.

Mister squeezed through the shrubbery and seated himself between his owners. He looked up adoringly at Marcos, his tail beating on the ground, and Marcos raised his glass slightly in salute. "Poop on Mister," Sandra said as Elena bent down to stroke his fur.

"Poop on Mister," Norman said. "Mister Poops. We love Mister," he explained to me.

"Mister is a very good dog," Elena said. "To get Mister we have to go to the place where—how do you say, that place—"

"Pound," Sandra said. "Kennel."

"The place where they make the dog that have the history, the good family . . ."

"Dog breeder," Norman said.

"Yes, and now if Mister have good children they are worth very much in U.S. dollars."

"Oh, yes," Norman said. "Lovely things, setters. Sandra and I have had many fine animals ourselves."

"But we don't try, we don't try to have him, how do you say that thing?"

"That's a thing we don't say." Sandra nudged me. "We don't say it."

"Bred," Norman said, nodding.

"Yes, bred," Elena said. "We don't care about this thing."

"No, who cares?" Sandra said. "Dirty old dogs. Oh, Mister knows I love him."

"Yes, if they are healthy, the children, this is what we care," Elena said.

"Look." Marcos rested a finger lazily on my wrist. "Do you see?" And I could just make out, in the direction he indicated, the outline of a peak—flat, like a shadow cast from some original behind us—that rose above the others.

"The mountain," I said, pleased. "This is the first time I've seen it."

"It does not like to be seen often," Marcos said.

"No?" I responded reluctantly to his coyness. "Why not?"

"It is consecrated ground," he said, tracing a pattern on his frosty glass. "Young girls used to be sacrificed there." Perhaps he hoped to shock me, but of course I was already familiar with the facts. "Their blood was dedicated to the gods who made the sun rise."

"I know," I said. "Those poor girls."

Marcos shrugged. "Those poor gods," he said. "Compelled to make the sun rise, the days go around in their circle."

"Compelled?" I said. "I would have thought that gods could do as they liked."

"Oh, no." Marcos lifted his eyes to me. I was annoyed by the degree to which he and his wife made their good looks a public concern, but I was not able to look away. "There are advantages, I am sure, to being a god, but that is not one of them. After all, prayer forces gods to respond, does it not?"

"I suppose one could think of it that way," I said. "I don't happen to."

"No?" Marcos said. "But the rain, the revelation, the vision, the growth of crops, the investiture of wisdom or power—

even salvation—these things have always been granted if the preparation is correct."

"Nevertheless," I said, becoming crude in my irritation, "it seems rather wasteful, doesn't it? All those girls hacked to bits to make the sun come up, when it seems to come up all by itself these days."

"Perhaps it does." Marcos smiled. Against my will I imagined him dressing in front of the mirror, buttoning his shirt (as far as he had buttoned it) over his muscular chest while his eyes narrowed with satisfaction. "Or perhaps we benefit from the unselfish labors of our predecessors. Here the past lives on in us. Do you not see it when you look at me? The raised basalt knife, the bound virgin, the living heart plucked from the breast—"

"Please," I said. "That's quite enough. Besides, everyone has a history. I suppose you're saying that I am a . . . that I'm a . . ." But I was too addled by his gruesome joking to think of an analogy.

"Yes," he said. "You see? You do not know what you are. You come from a corner of America that eradicated its original population. For you the past is something that is terminated, because your own past is an erasure. What a sad thing, I think! You cannot look back and see your present, you cannot look inward and see your future—"

"That may be so," I said evenly, though I could feel myself flushing with rage—surely it was the presence of Sandra and Norman that had provoked this platitudinous sermonizing. "But I should think you would be grateful to have that particular chapter of your history shelved. Some people consider it barbaric, you know. Besides, it seems to me that you're making great claims for an area that itself no longer has an indigenous culture. The people here now come from all over."

"From all over," Marcos agreed, delighted. "Bringing with them civilized customs, yes? They come from wherever one can be indicted for tax evasion. Or war crimes. Or fraud. They come for the climate." He looked at me. "And for what have you come?"

"The climate," I said, tears stinging from behind my eyes as he laughed.

"I have upset you," he said. "But I am only playing." A spoiled, stuffy look came over him as he became bored with tormenting me. "My family, of course, is pure Spanish."

"Such a relief," I said, "to learn that it is your practice also to usher in the sunrise without all that . . . 'preparation,' I believe, is what you called it."

"Oh, I do not think we are suited for that now, in any case—that preparation," he said. "Because at the final moment all of it must be discarded."

Now that I was utterly beside myself, Marcos seemed to have forgotten me entirely, and he spoke as if he were musing in private. "I'm afraid I don't quite follow you," I said stiffly.

"Yes," he said. "Selecting the sacrifice, bending one's being to the desired thing, achieving the proper conditions for prayer—at the final moment this labor and struggle fall away like torn cloth, and the petitioner must face his goal unprotected. I do not think we, now, would be able to endure that."

"Endure what, you two?" Sandra said, turning to us. "What don't you think we could endure?" She gestured vaguely. "We can endure this. Anyhow—" She took both my hands as I stood up to go, and she looked into my face searchingly. "The main thing is, Are You Having Fun?"

"Yes," I said. "Of course."

"Good." She released me and shook her head slowly. "Because that's the main thing."

Now Marcos began to appear in my dreams. He was a jeering, insistent, impinging presence, but once, just before I awoke, he repented and took me, for comfort, into his arms. I showered immediately upon getting out of bed, but the feeling of him clung to me maddeningly throughout the day.

One morning soon afterward I was on my way out when Norman and Sandra called to me from the patio. "If it isn't just the lady we were talking about!" Sandra said. "Come have breakfast with Mr. and Mrs. Useless. Dolores——" she called, pointing at me.

"Of course, we don't want to keep you if you have things to do," Norman said, as I hesitated.

"Oh, she doesn't have anything to *do*," Sandra said.

"No, the reason we hoped to see you this morning," Norman said, "is that some very old, very dear friends of ours, Gerald and Helen Moffat, have just come in from Minneapolis, and we're having a little party for them this evening. We thought maybe we'd forgotten to tell you."

"Are you from Minneapolis?" I asked.

"No," Norman said. "Our friends are."

"Norman," Sandra said, "have you spoken to Skipper and Lillian again?"

"Well," Norman said, "they'll do their damnedest to make it, but apparently Skipper hasn't been feeling too well. Nothing serious. But," Norman said to me, "there will be plenty of lovely people, and you're a lovely person, and we know you'll enjoy the others."

"Thank you," I said. First my morning, and now my evening. "I'll certainly come, unless——"

"Now, where——" Sandra twisted around in her chair. "Oh,

there," she said as Dolores appeared with a glass of juice and a plate of bacon and eggs for me.

Norman broke off a gardenia from a plant near him and put it on my plate. "Don't we do everything beeyoutifully?" Sandra said.

"Beeyoutifully, beeyoutifully," Norman chanted.

"And will the Moffats be staying with you?" I asked.

"No, no," Norman said. "They keep a lovely place here in town. Right out where our old place was. Just the other side of the golf club."

"Golf club," Sandra said. "Golf club, golf club. Who knows what anybody's talking about, with golf *clubs* and *golf* clubs? Anyhow, it sounds like some kind of expression, doesn't it?" I looked at her politely. " 'Those people live just the other side of a golf club.' It would mean, for instance, a tiny bit, but not too much. Just beyond the pale, kind of." She laughed and clapped her hands together. "You would say, 'Oh, those two? They're lovely people, but they've gone just the other side of the golf club.' "

"Oh, yes," I said.

"Dolores," Sandra said, "we're *waiting* for our coffee."

Norman turned to pinch back the gardenia plant. "They have a marvelous pool," he said. "Just let us know if you want to use it. They'd be delighted."

"Is that to make it flower?" I asked him.

"Yes," Norman said. "I don't know. These silly things just flower in this climate no matter what you do." He got up to inspect some plants that made a border along the hedge. "That darned rabbit did a lot of damage, Sandra," he said plaintively. "We're going to have to get the boy to replace these."

"Well, anyhow," I reassured him, "I haven't seen it around lately."

"I'll bet you're dying for your coffee," Sandra said. "I know I am."

"Where do you suppose it went?" I asked. "The rabbit."

Sandra made a face and brushed some crumbs from the table. "Just look at this mess," she said.

Norman straightened up and sighed. "He had to take it out," he said, looking at the ground. "I don't know why."

As Norman wandered farther along, poking at the plants, Sandra spoke rapidly to me in a low voice. "I think those people next door ate the rabbit," she said. "But I don't want to say that to Norman. He'd have a fit. He loves rabbits. That rabbit was such a pest, though, wasn't it, eating all those plants. But it was cute. We don't have them at home. Well, we do, I suppose, we could, but people eat them here." She watched absently as Dolores approached, but then continued, enraged, "Oh, well, why not, after all? People have to eat." As Dolores poured our coffee, Sandra looked at me and raised an eyebrow. "Thank you, Dolores," she said with exaggerated graciousness.

I was embarrassed, but Dolores seemed oblivious of the sudden savage rudeness that Sandra would occasionally unleash. "We eat cows," I said.

"You don't happen to have anything like—a Valium, do you?" Sandra asked. "Or upstairs?"

"I don't," I said. "No."

"Well, good for you. Who needs that stuff? Yes," she said after a moment, "that's true. We do eat cows. And chickies. And piggie-wigs. But they're all revolting."

We sat and looked at Norman as he peered about among the plants. "This coffee is delicious," I said.

"Oh! If you want delicious—" Sandra said, jumping to her feet. She went inside and came back with a bottle. "Just try it," she said.

"What is it?" I asked. I looked from Sandra to Norman, who had returned to stand above me.

"Don't feel you have to, if you're not in the mood," he said.

"Oh, Norman. It's practically the national *drink*," Sandra said.

"But if she doesn't want to—" Norman said.

Sandra opened the bottle, and we all listened while she poured some into my coffee. "It's just for her. To try."

I took a sip. "Lovely, isn't it?" I said, although I found it strong and peculiar.

Sandra watched me as I drank, her chin resting on the backs of her clasped hands. "Yes," she said.

She shook herself, as if from sleep, and poured from the bottle into Norman's cup and then into her own. "Sandra—" Norman said. But she didn't look at him, and the three of us drank, our eyes lowered.

"Well . . ." Norman sighed. He raised himself up and shambled back to the border plants.

"He can't sit still," Sandra said. "It worries me."

Norman shook his head once again over the plants and then turned back to us, shading his eyes from the sun. "Can I give you a ride somewhere?" he asked me. "I've got to go down to the golf club for a quick game."

"You see?" Sandra called gleefully. "Well, stay this side!"

"I'm going into town," I said. "I don't think it's on your way."

"Got to drive anyhow," Norman said. "Just jump into the car, hippity-hop."

That evening the party glimmered below me with candles and lanterns. My room was like part of the evening, and as the rich murmur rose up to me I watched Dolores and a boy, who were both dressed in white with local weavings over their clothes, as they circulated, carrying trays among the guests. When I shut the door behind me to go downstairs, I could feel my apartment swell with dreams poised to overtake me on my return.

I made a quick circle through the garden—naturally, Marcos and Elena were not there—and I noticed Simon Peter heading in my direction. I turned away just in time and found myself facing a snub-nosed woman in a ruffled dress, with sticky-looking yellow-brown rolls of hair like varnished wood shavings. "You don't have a drink!" she said. "Well, I hope you can hold out for about an hour. The best thing to do is just to go in and pour yourself something, but it makes Norman so miserable if he sees. How long ago was it they moved from the big house? Nine years? Ten years? Still, I suppose it's a difficult adjustment. Sandra looks quite well, though, doesn't she?"

"Yes," I said.

"Sometimes it's worse when she's just come out of the clinic," the woman said. "It's hard to remember, isn't it, that she was the one who really ran the show all those years when Norman was such a souse. Oh, she was just as capable as anything! Of course, he was always just . . . *sweet*, wasn't he? A *gentle* man, Bob always says."

How dare she, I thought. How dare this stranger tell her friends' secrets to me. But as I thought it I realized that Sandra and Norman had already offered me this information about themselves, and I looked down to avoid the reflection in this woman's face of my own brutality and cowardice.

"Such a pity about this weather," the woman said. "All this haze. Or smog, whatever it is. We never used to have this." She patted her careful permanent. "Oh, I see that you're admiring my sash," she said. "Guatemalan. Old, the girl said, and she seemed honest. I think she was German."

"I'm sure," I said, looking around for Norman and Sandra. I would say good night and then leave.

"Excuse me?" the woman said.

"Pardon me?" I said. "Yes, it must be."

"Well, at least I was told it was," the woman said. "They still do marvelous things, of course, but I wouldn't recommend it. Bob and I were horribly disappointed ourselves last year. We had a wonderful view of the lake, but otherwise it was impossible. And the meals! Well, I'm sorry to have to tell you that it really wasn't food at all."

"Perhaps I will go inside and get myself something," I said, but at that moment the boy appeared with a tray of frothy drinks. He was very young, really a child, and he was absolutely radiant. He seemed delighted with his tray and his uniform.

"Uh-uh," the woman said loudly as the boy started to move off. "Hold still there." As the woman drained her glass and exchanged it for a full one, I realized that the boy looked exactly like Dolores—he must have been her son.

"Hello, hello," Norman said. He was crossing past us on the lawn, and he held firmly by the elbow a woman who walked unsteadily in high-heeled sandals. "All set up, I see. Good."

"Muriel," said the woman with Norman. "No one *told* me you were here yet."

"Just," said the woman I was talking to. "Barely a week."

"Marvelous," the other woman called back over her shoulder as she and Norman continued on their way. "And how's Bob?"

"Well, you know." Muriel leaned across me to answer her retreating friend. "He's been out on the course all day." Both women laughed and waved. "Actually," Muriel said to me, "he just can't stand to come to their parties any longer. He was so close to Norman, after all, and since they lost the Fort Lauderdale place Bob has hardly had the heart to see them. But I feel we just have to come out for Gerald and Helen, don't you? You know"—she paused and turned on me a look of blind radar—"I don't remember you from Fort Lauderdale—"

"Isn't this lovely," said Sandra, arriving in a whirl of skirts. She put a bare, somewhat slack arm around Muriel. "Everyone all together."

"Just a moment, dear," Muriel said, reaching over with a piece of Kleenex to wipe a bit of lipstick off Sandra's tooth. "There. I was just telling your young friend here about your beautiful, beautiful place in Fort Lauderdale."

"We had such fun, didn't we?" Sandra said.

"Where do you two know each other from?" Muriel said.

"Oh, she's my darling," Sandra said. "Isn't she cute? But she's so busy. Full of important things to do." She crinkled her nose and put it against mine for a moment. "I hate you when you're busy," she said. She turned to Muriel. "Where's Bob?" she said. "I haven't seen Bob all evening."

"He was miserable not to be able to make it," Muriel said. "But he was simply exhausted. He spent the entire day on the course with Dr. Skip."

I realized that I'd never seen Sandra's face in repose before. She focused dispassionately on Muriel as Muriel carefully picked a fallen blossom off her dress, and when Muriel looked up again Sandra was still gazing at her. "He gets tired," Muriel said, glancing at me to enlist my support. "He's not as young as he used to be." But I was looking at her in just the way that Sandra had looked at her, and Sandra herself turned and walked off.

"There!" Muriel said. "Well, I suppose I've done something now, but that's just the kind of thing——" An expression of dull triumph spread across her face. "She blames us. She blames Norman. But what else can Norman do? He's the only one with the authority to commit her."

But over on the patio something was happening. Just as Norman reached down to take a drink from Dolores's son, Sandra strode up. Norman seemed unable to move as he watched Sandra grip the child's shoulder and with her free hand take a drink from the tray, lifting it high above her head. The child stared, his huge eyes gleaming with fear, and the glass seemed to hesitate where Sandra released it, twinkling lazily in the air, before it shattered on the slate. The sound seemed a signal for the party to resume, more noisily than before, and the entire event was swallowed in the cleft of silence that closed behind us while Sandra raised the glasses one by one from the boy's tray and let them drop.

As I crossed the lawn, a pulpy hand grabbed mine. "You're not going to be all upset now, are you?" a voice said. The voice and hand belonged to a large man in Bermuda shorts. "It's over and done with," he said. "Tomorrow no one will even remember." I snatched my hand away and continued across the lawn.

I found Sandra in the living room leaning on Dolores, who comforted her as if she were a child. Her crying sounded like a small, intermittent cough. Norman stood several feet away, looking up at the moon. His face was wet with tears, I saw, and, like the face that looked back at him from the moon, it was indistinct, as if it were being slowly worn away. There was nothing I could do here.

Near the gate, Dolores's son was kicking listlessly at the wall. We pretended not to notice each other as I went out.

By the time I got to the square it was nearly empty. Four men still stood at equidistant points around the band shell conjuring streams of bubbles from their bottles of colored liquid, but the other vendors and the crowds had disappeared, and the last remaining people must have assumed, as I sat down on a bench, that I was waiting for something.

Had Sandra and Norman ever been aware of the life they were making for themselves? Probably not. It seemed that one simply ate any fruit at hand, scattering the seeds about carelessly and then years later found oneself walled in by the growth. I cast my mind back into my own past, straining to see any crossroad, any telling choice, that would indicate the destination toward which I was moving, but there was only the gentle clacking of the broad leaves above me and a slight scent of roses eddying through the night air.

If only I could be lifted up and borne off to someplace further along in time, to where the hours would move forward in a benign, steady procession and I would spend the modest coinage of daily life among pleasant people. I closed my eyes wearily for a moment, and when I opened them, a piece of chiffon seemed to wind around me, a billowing thing that had belonged to my mother's mother. I pored over it, studying the thrilling colors that were unfaded by previous exposure to memory. I held it up, filtering a cold afternoon light through its ravishing thinness. The patterns were larger, and the threads and the dark interstices between them, and then it was gone and the night was around me again. Yet I'd seen that forgotten scarf as perfectly as if some globe underfoot had rotated thirty years back, placing me right next to it.

And now there was another rotation, and I was crouching in the alley, where garbage cans clustered like mushrooms, and the brick apartment buildings rose up and up, casting a private weather around me. Most of the windows were dark and vacant, but in some, white shades were pulled halfway down. One cord and ring turned aimlessly, ominously, in a ghostly breath of air. I watched and watched until a tightening circle of darkness closed around it.

I sat shivering and miserable at the edge of a community pool where my mother sent me to swim on Saturdays. Lights, reflected from under the water, rippled on the dark walls and ceiling, and the tile room echoed with loose booming sounds. Chlorine stank, and burned in my nose and eyes.

During recess I leaned against the fence as classmates played tetherball—an awful game, dogged and pointless. Sharon, a bossy fat girl, came over and stood next to me. She had never talked to me before, but now she asked me to go skating after school. I looked at her uneasily. Had she felt sorry for me? As I stalled, I saw anxiety erode her self-assurance, and her purpose became clear—she thought I'd be easily acquired: "Sharon is making friends now," her relieved parents would be able to say. Well, I did not have to be her life raft. "No, thank you," I said. My strength had returned. "I have to get back to my mother."

In the university library I talked with a man from one of my classes. I was stricken with a fear that he was going to ask me to have coffee, and while I waited, trying to concentrate on what he was saying, his face became less and less familiar. Suddenly he checked his watch and turned away, leaving me confused.

My friend Pamela and I sat in our favorite café after an early Sunday supper, studying our check. We opened our purses, and each of us carefully counted out what she owed. The headlights of the cars that drove past were sulfurous yellow in a cold autumn drizzle. Time to go—the office tomorrow.

Well. Yes. That had been only last month. I blinked at the shapes of the foliage becoming visible against the velvety night. What random, uneventful memories. In any case, it must be terribly late, and I ought to be asleep, but as I rose to go, there was the sudden rush of entering a tunnel, and I sat with my mother, holding one of her hands. I traced with my finger the huge, adult bones, the fascinating veins that crossed it like mysterious rivers; I fitted my attention exactly to the ridgings of her knuckles, the wedding ring, her pale, flat nails. "Your hand is so beautiful," I said.

"My hand is hideous," she said, withdrawing it. "I have hideous hands. They're old." Later, in private, I cried until I felt sore. How old had I been then? Not more than seven, I suppose, but how well I knew those hands when I saw them lying, truly old, as frail as paper on the hospital coverlet. The light from the window fell across them, and across my mother's sleeping face, her skin soft, like a worn cloth, as I stood in the doorway wondering if I should make some small noise to see if she was ready to wake. But light was coming through the walls of the hospital room, and they faded, and my mother faded, into the sparkling dawn.

Heavens. Vanished. How quickly the long night had turned to morning. How little there was behind me. I got up from the hard bench, stamping slightly to bring the blood back into my feet. Colors began to pulse into the day, and a terror took hold of me at being out here in the open as, deeper and surer with every beat, colors filled up the leaves and the flowers and the steep walled streets and the circle of mountains all around me, and the sky, too, where a round yellow sun was rising.

People were appearing in the square, quietly preparing for business, and I saw that there was a row of women already sitting cross-legged on the sidewalk, waiting for change. As I quickly distributed mine among them, one of the women said something to me. How thin she was, that woman—there was practically nothing left of her. At the correct moment she would need only to shrug off her ragged shawl in order to ascend from the sidewalk, weightless.

When I passed the news kiosk, only the little boy was there. My terror intensified; where was the boy's brother? I wanted badly to ask, but of course I was not able to, and as the child waved to me I caught a sudden glimpse of what those gods of Marcos's would see if they were to look down now at their former venue: a dying beggar; a little boy beginning his working life in earnest; a community of refugees from failure, ravaged by their pursuit of some deadly specter of pleasure; a lonely woman moving into middle age. We would be a pretty sight, I thought, rocketing along our separate courses—tiny shooting stars burning out in space. But they were not going to look down, those gods. They had been released, and now they were free behind the screen of smog and pollution that protected them from the clamor of their new, unskilled petitioners, and as the day carried the people around me toward whichever of the positions they were to assume that night in the square, I would have to search unaided through my raucous sleep for the dream in which my mother would take my hand and step into the moving current.

All around me the tin shutters were rolling up, and the streets grew crowded and noisy with traffic, and people with bundles of goods poured down into town like cataracts of melting streams, and in what seemed to be no time I'd been flung upon this tide back at the gate, breathless and disheveled. But as I headed for the refuge of my apartment, a gleaming from among the stale litter of ashtrays and dishes drew me over to the patio. Oh, so many of the beautiful glasses—a little heap, I thought, of something over and done with. How sorry Sandra was going to be when she woke up!

I bent over the flashing splinters, and when I raised my eyes again I saw to my surprise that the living-room curtains were open and that Norman and Sandra were already awake. I peered cautiously into the dim interior, and I watched, shading my eyes, as they moved slowly about, making an ineffectual attempt to neaten up after the party. When they came to the door to answer my knock, I was shocked to see how old they were in this morning light, and seedy in their worn robes, like people just come from a hospital. They looked at me bewildered, as if they couldn't quite place me—and, goodness knows, I had never come to them before—but I wasn't able to explain myself or to speak at all. And as we stood and stared at each other, I saw on their faces the record, which was changing right in front of me, of countless challenges met and usually lost, and then, understanding what they must do, they composed themselves and invited me in.

UNDER THE
82ND AIRBORNE

For Wall, of course

A CAUTIONARY TALE

"Stop that, Stuart," Patty said as Stuart struggled with the suitcases, which were way too heavy for him, she thought. (Almost everything was way too heavy for Stuart.) "Just put those down. Besides," Patty said, "where will you go? You don't have anyplace to go." But Stuart took her hand and held it for a moment against his closed eyes, and despite the many occasions when Patty had wanted him to go, and the several occasions when she had tried to make him go, despite the fact that he was at his most enragingly pathetic, for once she could think of nothing, nothing at all that he could be trying to shame her into or shame her out of, and so it occurred to her that this time he really would leave—that he was simply saying goodbye. All along, Patty had been unaware that time is as adhesive as love, and that the more time you spend with someone the greater the likelihood of finding yourself with a permanent sort of thing to deal with that people casually refer to as "friendship," as if that were the end of the matter, when the truth is that even if "your friend" does something annoying, or if you and "your friend" decide that you hate each other, or if "your friend" moves away and you lose each other's address, you still have *a friendship*, and although it can change shape, look different in different lights, become an embarrassment or an encumbrance or a sorrow, it can't simply cease to have existed, no matter how far into the past it sinks, so attempts to disavow or destroy it will not merely constitute betrayals of friendship but, more practically, are bound to be fruitless, causing damage only to the humans involved rather than to that gummy jungle (friendship) in which those humans have entrapped themselves, so if sometime in the future you're not going to want to have been a particular person's friend, or if you're not going to want to have had the particular friendship you and that person can make with one another, then don't be friends with that person at all, don't talk to that person, don't go anywhere near that person, because as soon as you start to see something from that person's point of view (which, inevitably, will be as soon as you stand next to that person) common ground is sure to slide under your feet.

Poor Patty! It hadn't even been inclination or natural circumstances that led her to Stuart—it was Marcia. And perhaps if it hadn't been for Marcia, Patty and Stuart never would have carried their association further than their first encounter, which took place almost exactly a year before the sweltering night when Stuart packed his things and left.

Patty had been in Manhattan for several weeks, living in the ground-floor apartment that Marcia had sublet to her, but Patty had been too shy to go down the hall, as Marcia had instructed her, and knock on Stuart's door, so she didn't meet Stuart until one evening when, on her way out for an ice-cream cone, she found two men chatting above an immense body stretched out across the hall floor. Bodies! she thought. Chatting! Marcia had not prepared her for this.

"Relax," said one of the men, calling Patty's attention to the thunder that reverberated around them. "She's snoring. It's a vital sign. I'm Stuart, by the way, and this is Mr. Martinez, our superintendent, and that's Mrs. Jorgenson down there. I bet you're Marcia's friend."

"Nice to meet you," Patty said. "Should we call an ambulance?"

"Marty and I used to," Stuart said. "But it just makes her mad."

"She get so mad," Mr. Martinez said. "The mens come, they put Mrs. Jorgenson on hammock, she bounce up like Muhammad Ali."

"Maybe we should try to get her to her apartment," Patty said.

"You can try," Stuart said. "But she lives on Three, and she's even bigger when not all of her is on the floor."

"Is nice girl!" Mr. Martinez announced happily, pointing at Patty.

In fact, Patty had been ready to abandon Mrs. Jorgenson and go about her business, but Mr. Martinez's praise revitalized her concern. "There must be something we could do," she said.

"Not really," Stuart said. "She just does this for a while, and then she goes back upstairs. But she could probably use a blanket." So Patty went back into Marcia's apartment and got her Hudson Bay blanket, which the two men gently tucked around Mrs. Jorgenson.

"Nice young girl come to make home," Mr. Martinez declaimed accusingly to the hallway, "but what she see? Is Mrs. Jorgenson and floor." He turned grieving eyes to Patty and made a tiny gallant bow. "You need something, miss, you come to Marty."

"Well," Stuart said. He moved slightly, buffering Patty against the dismal spectacle of Mrs. Jorgenson. "I was just looking for a girl to make cookies with anyhow."

"So Marcia was right," Stuart said as he set the cookie ingredients out on his counter. "She told me you were nice. 'Caring,' actually, is the word she used, which I have to say is a word that makes me fundamentally throw up. You know, I watched you dragging in all those cartons, and I figured you had to be you. I've been waiting for you to come say hello. I thought maybe you were avoiding me."

Patty was puzzled by Stuart's probing pause. "Of course not," she said.

"Well, here we are, anyway. Yeah, Marcia talked and talked about you. Patty this, Patty that."

"Really?" Patty said. Certainly Marcia could talk and talk, she thought, but it wasn't usually by way of praise for her female friends. "Marcia and I used to be in the same dormitory. She was a few years ahead of me."

"I know," Stuart said. "You'd be surprised the things I know about Marcia. We're very tight. In fact, there was serious consideration put into my going out to Austin with her while she set up her practice."

"Oh?" Patty said. She wasn't sure why she'd expected Stuart to be glamorous, although, now that she thought about it, Marcia's descriptions of him had been studded with words like "artistic" and "unpredictable." Well, he might be artistic and unpredictable, but he didn't seem glamorous enough even for Marcia, whose tolerance had been widely remarked upon at school. But perhaps Marcia and Stuart's relationship had professional roots. "Are you involved in therapy, too?" Patty asked.

"Therapy," Stuart said. "All right. Let's get it over with. Let's just concede that therapy's the most revolting expression of the hydra-headed pragmatism of our times." Patty picked uneasily at the chocolate chips while Stuart pressed forward with the tedious sifting. "Of course, Marcia always thinks what she wants," he said, "but, between you and me, that's actually why I let her go out West alone. Total misappropriation and subversion of the insights of a few geniuses."

"But therapy can be very helpful to people," Patty protested.

"Yeah, to would-be thieves and assassins crippled by restrictive superegos," Stuart said.

"Well, I don't really know much about it." Patty felt she'd become lost on some twisting private path. "I studied graphic design."

"Uh-huh," Stuart said unreceptively.

"Actually, that's why I've come to New York," Patty said. But Stuart maintained a bristly silence as he spooned dough onto tins, so Patty glanced around for clues. "Are you . . ." She noticed stacks of paper and a typewriter. "Are you a writer?"

"In the sense that I sometimes write things," Stuart said. "Here. Or are you too mature to lick the bowl?"

"Well, what— Thanks," Patty said, accepting the bowl. "What sorts of things do you write?"

"A little of this, a little of that. Look, I really don't want to get into this thing of 'I do this' or 'I write that.' If you develop a stake in some rickety prefab construction of yourself, you have to keep shoring it up."

"But that's an unproductive way to think, isn't it?" Patty said. "I mean, people have different things to contribute. Everybody's part of a system."

"I agree," Stuart said. "And I'm the worthless part. I'll tell you something. I think that every really good system has a significant worthless sector. The rotting leftovers on which the healing penicillin mold grows. That's me. Except that now greed is shrinking the world—you know what I mean? Desire for personal gain is collapsing the entire range of human activity into, essentially, resale value. So at this moment in history there's no room for people like me, who don't contribute anything that's recognizably salable."

Patty hesitated. Was she being *criticized*? "But graphic design is something I *enjoy*," she said. "And I might be able to succeed at it."

"Ha!" Stuart said. "Maybe what you consider failure I consider the milieu of freedom."

"Look—" He was *smug*, Patty thought. "I understand that you think there's something wrong with my career choice, but I don't understand why."

"That's cute." Stuart leaned back and squinted at her. "That's sweet. You're *earnest*, you know that? You look like a Girl Scout, with your little face, and your little sneakers and stuff. But the problem is, you're going for the wrong merit badge. Yeah, Marcia warned me I was gonna have to take you in hand. And the first thing is, it's that *word* is what I'm saying; that word 'career'—it's a meaning substitute used to camouflage a trench. I mean, that's exactly what I'm saying: the more you identify yourself with a set of economic expediencies, the greater your interest in rationalizing indefensible practices. And that's why people whose jobs yield a large income or a lot of prestige are usually incapable of thinking through the simplest thing. In fact, in my opinion, abstract ability decreases in direct proportion to prestige and income."

"Stuart"—Patty was held in check by the tranquilizing aroma seeping from the oven—"that is absurd. That is absolutely ridiculous. Take me, for example. I don't have any job at all, but I don't think more clearly than anybody else."

"True," Stuart said. "But that's because you *want* a job. You've been corrupted by desire."

"Desire has absolutely nothing to do with me and jobs at this point." Exasperation empowered Patty to bound with unaccustomed agility across clumps of thorny concepts. "At this point, the relationship between 'me' and 'job' is 'need.' I need a job!"

"See?" Stuart nodded triumphantly, as if apprehending some brilliantly crafted but specious argument. "You've already found a way to construe this degraded appetite of yours as need."

"Then how do you suggest I pay the rent, please? I've been scraping and scrimping since December so I'd be able to get here and have some time to find a job—"

"Since December?" Stuart said.

"That's right." Patty was far too annoyed to remark Stuart's sudden attentiveness. "No movies, no dinners out, no—"

"You and Marcia planned this out in December?"

"What's the matter?" Patty said. "Is something the matter?"

"Listen," Stuart said. "I apologize. I don't know why I'm such an asshole. It just sort of comes over me from time to time." He looked around restlessly and tapped his foot. "Just standard-issue archaic bohemian bullshit."

"Wait—" Patty was stricken. "You have a right to your opinion."

"By the way," Stuart said. "Just what, exactly, is Marcia charging you for her miserable sty?"

"Well, I know it's a lot more than she pays for it herself," Patty admitted, "but it's still way under the open-market rate, because it's rent-stabilized. So even if she makes a big profit from me, it's still much cheaper than anything else I'd be able to get. It's the only way I could afford to come to New York and the only way Marcia could afford to leave." ("One hand washes the other," Marcia had remarked cheerfully when she explained this to Patty.)

"Yeah," Stuart said. "Marcia. I should have guessed. It was

Marcia who actually drafted the Hammurabi Code of Friendship, did you know that?"

Considering that he'd almost gone to Austin with Marcia, he was being kind of nasty about her, Patty thought. But she had to remember how quickly it had become understood in the dorm that when Marcia appeared at the door of one's room gripping a six-pack or offering the loan of her car, she had probably just slept with one's boyfriend.

"And you know what she's going to do next," Stuart continued ominously. "The instant this building goes co-op, she'll reclaim her apartment, buy it at the insider's price, and sell the tiny squalid treasure for a king's ransom."

Why was he talking about Marcia's apartment like that, Patty wondered. It was no more tiny, no more squalid than his own! (And it was true that while Marcia's apartment was now bare except for Patty's few things and Stuart's was cozy with layers of an accreted past, while Marcia's faced the air-shaft and Stuart's faced the garbage cans that lined the street, the two were virtually identical.) Besides, it was Stuart's problem if he was living like that at his age, Patty thought—he must be at least thirty-five. If Marcia could do better for herself, why should he hold it against her? "Well, it seems fair enough to me," Patty said.

"Oh, Jesus," Stuart said. "I suppose. No wonder I drive everyone nuts. No wonder everyone can't wait to get rid of me."

"Stuart—" Patty said. "Hey, you should try one of these cookies! And some of what you were saying is very interesting."

"Let's just drop it," Stuart said. "I'm an asshole."

"Oh, look"—Patty cast about—"you've got Sprouse's *Tented Desert*!" What luck to have recognized the title among all those books; as she remembered, her English Lit teacher had said it was fabulous. "Could I borrow it?"

"Sure," Stuart said listlessly. "Whatever you want."

"People say it's fabulous," Patty said.

"People who admire it," Stuart said.

Patty looked at him warily. "You don't think Sprouse is a good poet?"

"He's an O.K. poet." Stuart picked a crumb from the table and glanced around for someplace to deposit it. "A *small* poet."

But gradually Stuart's gloom cleared, and Patty found that she was grateful for his company: she'd been lonely. When she went back down the hall, there was no sign on the floor of Mrs. Jorgenson or her blanket, but as she passed the spot where they'd lain a psychic net seemed to be cast over Patty, and later, trying to sleep, she flopped about, struggling, unable to disengage her mind from the phantom form of supine Mrs. Jorgenson. How tender Mrs. Jorgenson's puffy ankle had looked, where it was exposed by her rolled-down stocking. From the shadowy crevasse there, demons now leapt to haunt Patty.

Patty had assumed, until this night, that she'd been drawn to New York by a lodestone buried at the core of her unexplored life. And images had seemed to shimmer out from the direction of its pull—images, for instance, of gleaming white drafting tables accoutred with complex systems of shallow drawers; a wineglass, held in a powerful, manicured (ringless) hand, which cast a bouncing patch of brightness on table linen; the balcony of a brownstone where a marvelous man lounged while he waited in the surging twilight for the woman inside to finish dressing.

But now, as Patty lay in bed, what she saw was herself—herself as Mrs. Jorgenson, distended and bleary from poverty's starchy diet; herself weeping into her gin at a darkened bar while some grimy bore expatiated incoherently into her ear; herself standing over the stove while she ate, straight from the pan, her scrambled eggs. Oh, *were* they scrambled eggs? Dear Lord, she prayed, *let* that stuff be scrambled eggs. And all around Patty's little bed circled the terror that perhaps those former shimmering lures had not been signs of some central imperative but were instead the snares of a mocking siren; that perhaps she was soon to be dashed, like Mrs. Jorgenson, against the rocks (so to speak) of the hall floor.

The weeks that followed were truly disheartening. By August, Patty had exhausted the heady sensation of exerting mastery over a new apartment, the temperature fluctuated between ninety-eight and a hundred and two degrees, and she had sat through numbers of futile interviews and sent out numbers of futile résumés. The city, in fact, appeared to be quite over-stocked with women, each more ornamental and accomplished than any nineteenth-century young lady, huge quantities of whom, Patty noticed with growing terror, were waitresses.

It would be a temporary necessity, she reasoned; she would have to support her job hunt by waiting on tables. And soon her days were occupied with getting rejected for two entire lines of work, one of which she had recently despised. So in the evenings she was glad when either Stuart or Mr. Martinez would open his door to her, expanding the city that seemed to have no room for her by day.

Often Stuart was eager to share his views and his casse-roles of vegetarian oddments with Patty. On other occasions, Mr. Martinez would hear her footsteps in the hall and invite her in. He would alternately extol and revile the United States while he and Patty sat together at his kitchen table eating slabs of a gelatinous confection with a plantlike undertaste and drinking a clear, stinging beverage that implied unregulated domestic production. Patty suspected it was this beverage, rather than his heavy accent, uneven grasp of English, or discursive approach to conversation, that made Mr. Martinez so difficult to understand, but after she'd had several glasses herself she could easily follow his tortuous Delphic outbursts. And she would watch, rapt, when he became agitated, either with despair or with gaiety, and swelled slightly, turning a deep translucent red, like a plastic bag filling with wine.

One evening Mr. Martinez, unsteady in his doorway, beckoned to Patty. "Miss, miss," he whispered. His apartment was dark except for the flickering of a few candles, and it was saturated with the fragrance of his arcane beverage. "Come, missy," Mr. Martinez said, drawing Patty over to a photograph that was propped up on a shelf between two candles.

She glanced at Mr. Martinez, but he only stared at the picture, breathing heavily and holding her hand in both of his. She peered back through the darkness and scaled herself down to enter the picture. Oh—there was a field, a great golden sweep of field distantly edged by tiny pointed mountains, and there were people sitting at a table in the foreground: an elderly couple, a young woman, and four or five children. They all had broad, appealing faces, like Mr. Martinez's, and black hair that gleamed in the sunlight. Sunlight poured down. The people smiled into the sunlight—dazzled, yielding smiles. Sunlight poured down on them and out from the picture into the dark room where Patty's hand, in Mr. Martinez's, was beginning to register discomfort.

"Mr. Martinez," she said, but he was transfixed, and tears ran down his face in rivulets. "What is it, Mr. Martinez? What is that picture?"

"But this is—" His eyebrows flew up, his arms dropped to his sides in helpless incredulity. "You do not know this? This is . . . *Colombia.*" He sat down at the kitchen table, and, laying his head upon his folded arms, he sobbed. "This is *my wife* . . ."

The next day Patty filled out yet another job application and waited in a line of girls that snaked up several flights of stairs. Clearly her chances were poor. But she didn't really care—she was back in the dark room where she'd stood the night before next to Mr. Martinez. She had remained with him for a time, patting him on the head, but the rhythm of his sobs did not alter, and eventually she tiptoed out, closing the door behind her.

After reaching the front of the line she entered a room, where a man sitting at a wide desk took her application and put it aside without glancing at it. "What do you want," he said, looking all the way up, then all the way back down, her, "days or nights?"

"Nights," she said.

"I don't have nights," he said.

"Days," she said.

He looked up, then down, her again. "I don't have days," he said, and turned away.

Maybe she'd had enough. The thing to do was to sit down, get a bite to eat, and think rationally about her next step. It had come as a jolt that life was something to be waged, rather than relied on. And yet, Patty reminded herself, everyone on earth must have the wherewithal for it. Even Mrs. Jorgenson had the presence of mind to exist; Mrs. Jorgenson, in fact, had so developed the knack of being herself that she could fall down on the floor and lie there snoring. Whereas if she, Patty, were to fall down on the floor, Patty thought resentfully, she would only have to pick herself up again, feeling foolish.

Just who were all these people in this city? And how did they survive? The stakes were so high, the margin of comfort so slim, and yet Patty was surrounded by people who had managed to find a place for themselves here. Look at Mr. Martinez. How incredible that he was in New York, Patty thought as she entered a restaurant that had just opened up near her apartment. Something was working in the depths of her brain, churning up disturbances that broke as they surfaced, like muddy bubbles rising from a swamp. Yes, how incredible that all of them were here: herself, Mrs. Jorgenson, Stuart, the girls waiting in the line today, Mr. Martinez, the bulky, bearded, pear-shaped man with tiny feet who stood near the jukebox now, in the otherwise unpopulated restaurant, staring at her. Here they all were, an entire—well . . . *confraternity*, sort of, of strangers, all brought together here by . . . by what? What was it they had in common? Was it something fundamental—something too profound to be grasped? Or was it something . . . *extrinsic*, manifest in, for example, er—she studied the bulky man, who was ambling toward her—frayed belt loops?

"Want something to eat?" the man asked. "Or did you just drop by to admire me?"

"Oops," Patty said, shifting her gaze to the menu he offered. "I'd like—" Right. Who cared why they were there? They were there because . . . because they were there. "O.K. A beer and a medium-rare Jarlsburger."

"I haven't got my liquor license yet," the man said. "And the meat hasn't been delivered today."

"Uh-huh," she said. "Well, how about orange juice and scrambled eggs with bacon?"

"Meat," the man said, poking his large haunch. "Have an omelette. You'll like the Chive 'n' Chèvre." He wandered off through a swinging door, from behind which awful metallic crashings began to issue, and returned to Patty's table at a rather faster rate. "He says I've wrecked his pans," the man announced cryptically just as a shockingly tall and starved-looking man burst through the swinging door.

"And what else, Arnold," the tall man raged, "is where's my check, huh? Where's my check? You promised! Can I have it? Are you going to give it to me? No? O.K. That's it." He paused on his way out to kick the jukebox.

Arnold watched the door close before sitting down at Patty's table. "Always in a hurry," he said. "I would have had it for him tomorrow." He regarded Patty, chin in hands. "Can you cook?"

"No," Patty said. "But I'm not really hungry."

"Too bad," Arnold said. "I need a cook."

"I can waitress," Patty said. "Do you need a waitress?"

"What don't I need?" Arnold rubbed his eyes. "Do you have a lot of experience?"

"Actually—" It was futility that kept Patty honest. "I don't have any experience."

"So what?" Arnold rubbed his eyes again. "I don't have any business."

That was not an idle boast, as it turned out. Arnold kept the restaurant open all night in hopes of compensating for his lack of a liquor license by scooping up, while his competitors slept, the restless wanderers disgorged from the bars at closing time. Thus far, however, Arnold's business had remained conceptual, and Patty had emerged virtually empty-handed every morning at six o'clock after a long night of staring toward the door. Occasionally, of course, someone would come in, causing both Patty and Buddy, the new cook, to panic from overexcitement and inexperience. Errors leapt from them like sparks from struck flint, and they would soon exhaust the self-conscious customer with nervous attentions.

Stuart reassured Patty over a celebratory sunrise supper he prepared for her during her first week of work. "Listen," he said. "By the time the place gets busy, you'll be an ace." As he reached over to pour her a glass of fancy fizzy grape juice that had set him back substantially, Patty noticed the tiny trucks emblazoned on his matted flannel pajamas.

"Stuart," she said fondly. "But you shouldn't be so proud of me—I can't even make enough to live on, you know."

"Well, you can't interpret that as a personal shortcoming," Stuart said. "It's just the fiscal structure of the city these days—Manhattan isn't going to just hand itself over for any little bag of beads now. All these rich bastards driving up the property values have kind of made it impossible for everyone else. I used to be able to scratch up a living with enough left over to do stuff—go to movies, eat out, spend the day observing humanity. Now you want to sit someplace for more than five minutes you got to slap down forty bucks for some kind of noodles with duck feet and grapefruit."

"I don't know." Patty was a bit irritated by Stuart's display of sourness just at the moment she was beginning to feel up to New York's idiosyncratic rigors and to adapt to the glare of its treasures. "Actually, I'm getting to like it."

"It's still New York," Stuart said. "But it's changed. You're practically a kid, so you don't know. Besides, you've just gotten here. And, believe me, you're lucky, because you're one of the last. No one except millionaires can afford to come here. Or stay, if they get here. Manhattan's just a playpen for rich people now, but it used to be paradise, Patty, I'm telling you—a haven for the dispossessed. People used to come here who couldn't go anyplace else on earth—stainless, great-souled, fucked-up fugitives, who woke up somewhere one morning and said, 'Hey, who are these people who call themselves my parents? These people are not my parents.' 'What is this place that's supposed to be my home? This is not my home.' This city was populated by a race of changelings, Patty, who kept things new, people who can't be replicated, who are really alive while they're alive—a dying race. And now it's being overrun by gangs of plundering plutocrats, the living dead, who clone themselves in bank vaults."

"Stuart—that is completely illogical. You want something that's always new but you don't want anything to change. And I think you're being horribly unfair to all businessmen and professionals on the basis of a few overeager examples."

"'Examples,'" Stuart said. "'Overeager.' 'Examples of a few overeager Storm Troopers.' Listen, I'm not talking about Ben and Jerry, I'm not talking about Jonas Salk, I'm not talking about responsible 'businessmen and professionals.' I'm talking about tunnel-visioned profiteers and parasites—and they're surrounding us right now, munching mâche with walnut oil. You think it takes Alaric or a fleet of nuclear submarines to destroy a city? I'm telling you, Patty—destruction is irreversible, I don't care what its source is. You're very casual about this because you don't remember anything."

"Of course I remember things, Stuart. I'm not an infant. And I'm not as ignorant as you think, either."

"You don't remember anything," Stuart insisted. "How could you? You don't remember Jean Seberg, you don't remember Joris-Karl Huysmans. I bet you don't even remember semiotics—"

"Everything changes, Stuart. It's not a tragedy if something changes—"

"As to particulars, not as to value! We were *proud* to be wretched refuse. We had bookstores. In the fall old men sat under the gray sky on benches littered with gold leaves and played chess. Girls wearing plaid skirts carried flutes and sheet music. Back then people thought about sex—"

"People still think about sex," Patty objected involuntarily.

"You call that sex?" Stuart said with bitter, preoccupied opacity. "And you could drink O.K. cheap wine at tables with checked cloths."

"So what! Who cares what kind of tablecloths were in fashion when you were my age? All I'm saying is that after two months of crawling through the streets I'm a waitress in a restaurant with no customers!"

"And you should be unbelievably Goddamned grateful," Stuart shouted, "to have been blessed with a job that won't cheapen your mind!"

But business remained slow, Arnold was no more forthcoming with his paychecks than formerly, and the paychecks that law obliged him to dispense to a waitress were close to meaningless anyway. The restaurant had acquired one steady customer, George, but George was too poor to leave much of a tip. Still, Patty was pleased to wait on someone who endured with unsatirical equanimity the storms of cutlery that rained from her hands. And Buddy was thrilled to have a subject of refined tastes on whom to perform culinary experiments (gratis, when Arnold wasn't around).

"Oh, my, Patty," George said one night. A slightly soiled gentility permeated his soft speech, and his elegant face changed constantly under fleeting shadows of emotion. He was certainly from America, but from what part or circumstances

Patty was unable to guess. Even George's age Patty couldn't pin down to the decade. "All this standing around must be very tiresome for you."

"It is, really," she admitted.

"*I* know." George brightened. "Why don't we play a game?"

"All right," she said.

"That's the spirit." George beamed expectantly. "Shall we play 'What Famous Monarch'?"

"O.K.," Patty said. "How do you play?"

"Ah," George said. "Well, for instance, I think of a certain famous monarch, and I think of something about that monarch, and then I say to you, 'What famous monarch blah-blah?,' for example, or 'What famous monarch blah-blah?'"

"Maybe you'd better go first," Patty said.

"Very well." George gathered himself into thought. "What famous monarch . . ." he said meditatively, "preferred being under a horse to being on one?"

Under a horse . . . under a horse . . . Patty ransacked her crated-up years of education. "Oh, George," she said with disgust. "Not Catherine the Great!"

"Well, that was an easy one," George said primly. "Just to show you how to play.

"Your turn," George said later, as Patty cleared his plate and wiped his table, scattering crumbs all over his trousers.

"Well . . ." Patty said. Besides, she didn't know anything *about* history. She didn't know anything *about* monarchs. Ah! (Hee-hee.) "O.K., what famous monarch is ahead of the times in a German museum?"

"Ahead of the times . . ." George looked pained. "Hmm.

"Well, I give up, Patty," he said some minutes later. "That's a toughie."

"Nefertiti!" she announced.

"What?" George said. "But Patty—that doesn't make any *sense*, dear. I mean—well, a *head*, after all. That is, naturally I could have mentioned any number of royal portraits. But 'ahead' of the *times*—I mean, *whose* times, exactly? Do you see? You see, it's a pun, dear, but it doesn't make any *sense*."

Patty slunk around cleaning tables and consolidating bottles of ketchup until George's good humor reasserted itself. "Speaking of ahead," he said, "what famous monarch became a head of a church because of a child?"

"Mary?" Patty ventured unhappily.

"Mary?" George said. "Which Mary? I'm afraid I don't understand."

"Well . . . the Virgin Mary?"

"Gracious, Patty, I really don't think you could call the Virgin Mary a *monarch*. Or the head of a church, exactly. I was referring to Henry VIII, of course."

"O.K.," she said. "So then what famous monarch lost her head over a child?"

"Anne Boleyn," George replied, giving Patty's hand a consolatory little squeeze.

Arnold's business eventually began to pick up, and Patty felt that she could repay some of Stuart's generosity. He was beginning to look a bit mangy, in fact, so she took to inviting him over for breakfast before she left for work in the evenings. Besides (she had to be honest), she was a terrible cook, and Stuart actually enjoyed cooking.

"Guess what," Stuart announced one night as he broke eggs into one of Patty's bowls. "Rand fired me today."

"What?" Patty said. Rand published a small magazine,

for which Stuart wrote about film. "I thought you and Rand were buddies. Doesn't he take you out drinking with him?"

"Yeah," Stuart said. "He's really upset about this, but apparently he and his wife had a big fight."

"So I don't get it," Patty said. "What's that got to do with it?"

"Well, I was trying to do him a favor," Stuart said. "I feel so sorry for him. His wife's absolutely nauseating, you know—and one thing is, she likes to have these parties to show off people she's met to people she's met, and she makes Rand bring someone from the staff each time. So last month I was the sacrifice. And she grabs me, and she's telling me that Devereaux is 'a genius,' 'the only American auteur,' and what do I think of him. And I try to be noncommittal, because I don't want to be forced to say, 'But lady, he's just one more crypto-fascist Hollywood cowboy.' So she tells me I've got to write about him. She's *met* him. He's 'a remarkable man.' So 'penetrating.' And then she turns that cash-register face to me and she says, 'He doesn't suffer fools gladly.' Well, that's something that gets to me, Patty. It just does. When someone looks at you like that and says, 'He doesn't suffer fools gladly,' what they mean is 'He doesn't suffer fools *like you* gladly,' or maybe only 'He doesn't, *like you*, suffer fools gladly,' but in any case it's definitely a challenge, don't you agree? Still, to be accommodating, I go to this screening of *Pulsepoint*, only it seems like Devereaux *does* suffer fools gladly. In fact, it seems like fools are Devereaux's favorite thing. So that's kind of what I wrote my piece about."

"Good going, Stuart." Patty sighed.

"And she sort of took it out on Rand, because I guess she'd planned this big party especially to invite Devereaux. Poor Rand. Here, I think this is done."

Patty was just about to start in on the plate of fragrant French toast Stuart had put in front of her when a small commotion erupted in the hallway. Stuart opened the door to inspect, and Patty, hovering behind him, saw Mrs. Jorgenson sprawled out in front of the mailboxes while a well-dressed man and woman bickered in undignified descant over her stately snores.

"Phyllis," the man was saying, "I really don't think this person ought to be lying here like this."

"We're going to be late," the woman said. "Why do you always have to be Mr. Nice Guy?"

"She wants a blanket," Patty said thickly from behind Stuart, and two sets of icy blue eyes stared up at her.

Mr. Nice Guy went upstairs to get a blanket, and Patty realized that he and the woman (who now stood next to her in uncomfortable silence) must be the art dealers who had recently moved into the apartment above Marcia's. Mr. Martinez, in whose view their arrival represented an influx of undesirables, had informed Patty that the couple had taken the apartment—small and shabby as it was—in anticipation of a move to co-op. "Now you will see," Mr. Martinez had predicted grimly, "they make takeover." And certainly the first sounds of renovation were already militating against Patty's daytime sleep.

For an instant Mrs. Jorgenson stopped snoring and opened her eyes, exposing a malevolent but impersonal irony—the expression of a tough old animal in a sprung trap. "Bugger," she said obliquely. As she resumed her snoring, Mr. Nice Guy returned, bearing a blanket, which he draped ineptly over her while his wife fidgeted with distaste.

Patty and Stuart went back to their breakfast, but the inky cold pressing in at the window had contracted the apartment; the chairs and table felt cramped and brittle.

"As you said, Patty." Stuart nodded morosely at his French toast. "Everything changes. It's not a tragedy."

Patty looked at Stuart closely. "Your apartment *is* rent-stabilized, isn't it?"

"Yeah," he said. "Of course, I'm due for an increase in November. But it is rent-stabilized."

"You're due for an increase? In November?"

"It hardly matters," he said. "I'm a couple months behind anyhow."

"You're *behind*?" Patty put down her fork.

"Well, Marty intercedes for me with Mr. Feltzer."

"But that can't go on forever, Stuart." Stuart was just *sitting* there, watching the butter and syrup congeal on his French toast. "Stuart!"

"I know. It's my own fault. You don't have to tell me, Patty. I ought to have done things differently."

"Now, just relax, Stuart. Let's think this out. There must be something—I mean, you can always—"

"See, Patty? I've made my own bed here. No one owes me a thing."

"But you could always . . ." What *could* he do, Patty thought. There would be no point in his looking for a cheaper apartment—people had to scheme and connive for apartments ten times the price of Stuart's. "Well, you could just for a while . . ."

"No, Patty," Stuart said, hollow-eyed. "You want your own life. You don't need me around."

"But actually, Stuart—" Oh, why *her*? Why *her*? "Actually, I think you'd better."

So Stuart set up his little bed in Marcia's kitchen and fitted his belongings in among Patty's. At first Patty felt as if she were in the eye of some oddly dissipating hurricane. Stuart was jumpy and he hankered after physical activity, but he was also frail and cursed with notably poor coordination. He would leave eagerly for a little run or to shoot baskets with the towering boys who hung around the lot on the corner, only to return almost immediately, fretful, winded, and streaming with sweat. It was Patty who opened stubborn jars, while Stuart, in an unbecoming agony of humiliation, shook out his cramping hand.

Still, he was clean and tidy, although one wouldn't have guessed it to look at him, and he good-naturedly performed the household chores, at which Patty was useless anyhow. The standard of Patty's meals rose, while their cost fell, and for a while Stuart had a run of luck with part-time jobs—he worked happily for a small press until it went out of business, and he received several checks when some of his writing was performed as "soundscapes" at a club, before he told the owners they were pretentious—so he was able to manage his share of the rent.

When Patty returned from work in the mornings, Stuart would wake up long enough to read her to sleep. If it had been an ordinary night at work, he would pick up whatever he himself was reading, and Patty would soon be bored into somnolence. But if it had been a busy night and Patty was wide awake, Stuart would read old, strange, majestic tales of princes turned into swans; swans believed to be second-rate ducklings; suitors who would be magically invested with insight that enabled them to choose the correct path, door, direction, or answer; nearly blameless girls imprisoned within evil trances; and soldiers or poor boys whose wits were to secure them brilliant futures. And as Stuart read, Patty would glide into sun-dappled dream forests where she encountered these creatures, known so well to her, though they were hidden temporarily, in their false conditions, from themselves.

But the independent unit created by two people is an unstable compound, a murky bog in which wayward growths flourish, and it was not long before Stuart decided that he and Patty ought to be sleeping together, a view he began to express (as Patty experienced it) with mosquito-like persistence.

"No," Patty said.

"Why not?" Stuart said.

"Because." Where were all those marvelous *men* she'd been promised by herself? Why did she have to discuss this with *Stuart*?

"So why because?"

Patty fixed him with a look intended to fracture his cheery insensitivity. "Because I'm not attracted to you, Stuart."

"You would become attracted to me if you were to sleep with me," he argued affably.

"But I'm not going to sleep with you," she said.

"Don't you see the beauty of it, Patty? It's sound in every way—politically, economically, aesthetically. You and I would be an entire ecology, generating and utilizing our own energies."

"I'm not here to . . . to provide physiological release for you," she said.

"Why not? I'm here to provide it for you. Listen, you're going to start suffering from pelvic distress one of these days. There could even be colonic or arterial consequences, you know."

It wasn't fair, Patty thought—Stuart obviously felt entitled to win every argument just because he knew more words than she did. She could only repeat herself stubbornly while he continued to whine and orate, disguising his little project in various rationales, until it seemed that one wolf, in different silly bonnets, was peeping out at her from behind a circle of trees.

"All right," she said to Stuart one night. It was miserably cold outside, but she was off work, and she just couldn't face the harangue that would flow unobstructed if she stayed in the apartment with Stuart. "All right. I've had it. This is it. Out."

"What?" Stuart said, having been halted in midsentence.

"Out." She reached for one of her own suitcases and started loading it with Stuart's neatly folded clothing.

"What are you doing?" he said, aghast.

"Out. Now. Out, out." She picked up the suitcase in one hand and shooed Stuart to the door with the other. "This is enough to get by on for a while. Let me know where you are and I'll send the rest on to you."

"You know," Stuart said as he trotted down the hall in front of her, "Marcia kept saying 'Oh, Patty is so *centered*. Patty is such a *woman*,' but actually, Patty, you're a very nervous person."

On the street Patty flagged down a taxi. "Take this guy to Port Authority," she said, giving the driver a ten. She shoved Stuart into the back seat next to his suitcase and ran along behind the taxi as it took off, flapping her skirt.

As she walked back down the hall, whimpering, Mr. Martinez peered out from his doorway. "The mens—the mens—" he said, his voice vibrant with commiseration. "They must do this thing. Do not cry, missy. He will come back."

But, back inside the apartment, Patty did cry. She cried and cried, from exhaustion, rage, loneliness, remorse, and relief. And when she'd finished she walked slowly to the phone and dialed the number Marcia had given her.

"Hello, Marcia," she said stonily. Patty was not sure why she had called, but she knew, with a weariness that must accompany the end of a lengthy and sordid police investigation, that it was necessary. "How are you?"

"Fine," Marcia said. "I'm feeling very good about myself."

"Splendid," Patty said.

"Good Lord, *you* sound awful," Marcia said brightly, and instantly sobered. "There isn't some problem about the apartment, is there?"

"Marcia," Patty said, becoming fully aware of her own suspicions as she voiced them, *"you promised me to Stuart."*

"I did not!" Marcia said. "Heavens, Patty, what can you mean?"

"He never even knew, the poor sucker, did he! For six months you plotted to palm him off on me, and he never even *knew.*"

"Calm down, Patty." Hah! At least Marcia sounded alarmed—undoubtedly she'd expected Patty to remain a credulous, pitiful schoolgirl forever. "I'm serious, Patty. You'd better learn how to deal with your feelings before you do something really self-destructive."

"And furthermore, Marcia"—the room swarmed with visions of pores, ducts, glands, nodes, hairs, and membranes—"he's *disgusting!*"

"He's only as disgusting as you are to yourself," Marcia said serenely. "Honestly, Patty—I simply thought you two would enjoy one another."

Even in the airshaft the weather was dismal, and Patty sat and watched a cruel sleet slide down the windowpane, until Stuart showed up, a few hours later, looking as if he'd been fished up from the Styx. Patty opened the door without a word, and without a word Stuart came in. He parked himself in front of the cold stove, his eyes fixed unseeingly on the filthy puddles forming around him.

Patty experienced a wrenching meld of triumph and defeat. If it had crossed Stuart's mind (and it certainly must have) to seek refuge with Marcia in Austin, he, too, would have had to face the grim truth that Patty had been lured to this apartment so that Marcia could (and with a clear conscience!) leave him behind. Well, Patty thought, she had been set up, but in point of dreadful fact she was fiercely glad to see Stuart.

Later, as they lay in their separate beds, Patty spoke gruffly into the dark. "Are you all right now, Stuart?"

He hesitated, but misery conquered pride. "I'm cold."

He snuffled, and when Patty climbed in with him and he turned his back to cuddle his bony shoulders against her, he was indeed shivering. "Want to read to me, Stuart?" she said.

"O.K.," he said, gladdening instantly and switching on his light. "Let's see. O.K., this is *Tristes Tropiques*. And right here Lévi-Strauss is propounding his interpretation of the face and body paintings of the Caduveo, some of the last living Brazilian Mbaya-Guaicuru:

> "But the remedy they failed to use on the social level, or which they refused to consider, could not elude them completely; it continued to haunt them in an insidious way. And since they could not become conscious of it and live it out in reality, they began to dream about it. Not in a direct form, which would have clashed with their prejudices, but in a transposed, and seemingly innocuous, form: in their art. If my analysis is correct, in the last resort the graphic art of the Caduveo women is to be interpreted, and its mysterious appeal and seemingly gratuitous complexity to be explained, as the phantasm of a society ardently and insatiably seeking a means of expressing

symbolically the institutions it might have, if its interests and
superstitions did not stand in the way. In this charming civili-
zation, the female beauties trace the outlines of the collective
dream with their makeup: their patterns are hieroglyphics de-
scribing an inaccessible golden age, which they extol in their
ornamentation, since they have no code in which to express it,
and whose mysteries they disclose as they reveal their nudity."

How happy Stuart seemed, Patty thought despairingly, to
be back from his banishment, to have the little glow of his
reading lamp around him. How happy he was with this damned
book—his constant companion these days.

By the time Patty woke, Stuart was out and about, but the
depression beside her in the bed was still warm. She thought of
her own cold bed in the next room, and without taking the
time to change or make coffee she climbed up to the third
floor and knocked on Mrs. Jorgenson's door. People had pushed
her around, she thought—people had taken advantage of her.
"Mrs. Jorgenson," she called. The peephole underwent a telling alteration as Patty stared into it, but all she could hear was a
peculiar sibilance, as of Dobermans running lightly through
crumpled newspaper. "Mrs. Jorgenson—listen, Mrs. Jorgenson.
This is Patty, from downstairs. It's winter, and I'm cold. You
have enough blankets now, Mrs. Jorgenson, and I want mine
back." She put her ear to the door, but there was only that continuous rustling sound. "That's my good Hudson Bay blanket,"
she called into the doorframe, "that my parents gave me when
I was little to take to camp. It's mine, Mrs. Jorgenson, and I
want it!"

"Whore!" Mrs. Jorgenson yelled from inside. *"Prostitute!"*

In December, Arnold acquired his liquor license, and business increased radically. By that time, practice had eroded Patty's gross incompetence, but no one would have been equipped for the onslaught of customers that poured through the doors all night long. Soon it became necessary for Arnold to hire reinforcements, and with other waitresses working on her shift Patty's job, now lucrative, became more or less bearable as well.

Most of the cooks, bartenders, and waitresses with whom Patty worked took the grueling terrors of restaurant life in good part. Together they would fear, face, endure, and fear afresh the Sisyphean ordeal of customers in exchange for the flexible schedule that allowed them to continue their dancing classes, their short runs Off Broadway, their studies of Indo-European, or the pursuit of voluptuous amusements.

Patty, who had intended to strike no such bargains with life, became increasingly impatient with the easygoing attitude of her co-workers, but there was one waitress, Donna, by whom Patty was deeply impressed. Donna was a tall, good-looking woman around Patty's age, who during the week supervised a direct-mail campaign for a knitwear empire and on the weekends moonlighted as a waitress. "But not for long," she told Patty. "And you'll get out of here soon, too."

"I hope so," Patty said. "But look at Buddy and Menlo and Sheila—they've been here almost as long as I have."

"Don't be so hard on yourself, Patty," Donna said. "Those guys are lifers."

Lifers. Yes, Patty thought, compared to Donna the rest of them were children, playing. And perhaps in twenty or thirty years they would still be clustered near the waitress stand, and she with them—wrinkled children, playing.

The customers, in contrast, seemed veritable incarnations of passing time. Someone would come in every night for a month and then disappear altogether. Romances would blossom and die, people and their involvements would develop in unpredictable directions.

"Isn't that the truth, Sugar?" said Ginger, a customer to whom Patty commented one evening on this phenomenon. Ginger was the gorgeous but moody prima of a troupe of huge male dancers engaged for a long run at a nearby theatre. They danced as women, and they came in often after work, sometimes in dashing rehearsal sweats, but more frequently in full flamboyant costume and makeup. Tonight, the yellow gossamer wings attached to Ginger's gown set off his pearly black skin and imperious, fantastical beauty. "Yes, things sure do move along in Manhattan. You drop by your favorite *boîte* one time, and you say, 'Where's Hank?' And they say, 'Hank?' And you say, 'Hank, you know, sweetheart, the guy who *sits* here every night?' And they just shrug, like they never heard of him. I go home and see my momma, Sugar, she's still chasin' the same chicken around the yard." Ginger allowed his slanting lids to dip for an instant in dismissal.

Almost the only one of the pioneer customers who still appeared with frequency was George. "Tell me, Patty," he said one night, "what famous monarch . . . gave forth a fatal dazzle?"

"I really don't know, George," Patty said testily. "I'll think about that while I wait on some of these other people."

Everything was going wrong that night. Toast was too dark, drinks were too light, customers temporized over the tiny menu while the second hand sped, but if Patty told them "Let me give you a moment," they would grab her wrist. "Don't move!" they'd say. "I know what I want. Um, Lois, you go first." Arnold cowered in the basement abusing substances and gloating over the books, even though the kitchen was running out of soup and potato skins and ribs. And it was near Christmas, so nobody was tipping and everyone was upset, and it was a long time before Patty got back to George. "I give up, George," she said.

"Spoilsport," he teased. "Just *guess*."

"I don't *know*, George. Oh, all right—Marie Antoinette."

"Marie Antoinette?" George looked stunned. "Marie Antoinette was a famous monarch, Patty, but she did not give forth a fatal dazzle. The famous monarch who did give forth a fatal dazzle was Louis Quatorze, the Sun King."

"What about the affair of the diamond necklace?" Patty demanded. This was *not* how she had imagined her adulthood. "What about that?"

George balanced his chin on a finger and thought. "Well," he said, "I suppose that counts. But do you know, Patty"—he improvised a rueful smile, and his tone was light, although vitality was draining rapidly from his face and voice—"I don't think you care about Louis Quatorze. I think you only care about female monarchs."

"Actually . . ." Patty said. All around her, people were demanding food, drink, clean spoons, napkins, the fulfillment of infantile fantasies, sweets, smiles, anything they could get away with. "Actually, I don't really care about any monarchs, to tell you the truth."

But when things calmed down, Patty returned to George's table penitent. "How're you doing here, George?" she asked.

"Fine, Patty," he said with awful self-possession. "Please tell Buddy it was delicious. Patty, do you know what George III's mother said to him?"

"No, George," she said. "What did she say?"

"She said, 'George, be a king.'" George gazed out over Patty's head at a distant empire. "'George, be a king.' . . ."

And when Patty returned to George's table later, she found only more change than he could afford, she knew, and on his plate a pile of little bones that suggested he'd curled up there and died.

One night at work Donna announced to Patty that she was quitting. "I've met this man, Fletcher. Some corporation has hired him to develop a magazine about the media, and I explained to him that he should put me in charge of circulation."

"That's great, Donna." Patty sighed.

"And it's just about time for you to start leading a real person's life yourself. Listen, Patty, keep in touch. You never know—something just might turn up at the magazine."

At least Patty had the opportunity, while she languished at the restaurant, to scrutinize the apparently inexhaustible parade of customers for information that would lead to her missing drafting table, her brownstone, her escort. It may seem that because there is not much room for certain kinds of elaboration in the act of ordering something at a restaurant little is expressed by it. But in fact the very restriction of the situation is the precondition of deep grooves through which individual personalities are extruded with great force. "You do *that*?" is what your waiter or waitress or bartender is thinking as you place your order. "You're like *that*?" And although you may assume that you are behaving pretty much as everyone before you has behaved in a similar situation, that is a serious misconception, one not shared by those who stand and face you.

Patty had no leisure for the random yield of disinterested

science, but as the months slid by she was able, through diligent observation, to harvest a crop of utilitarian specifics from the people who paused in front of her, in unwitting demonstration of the selves they had tended and grown in the extreme climates of the city. In spite of Stuart's alarmist denunciations, Patty persevered in maneuvering her appearance from undistinguished wholesomeness to the assertively stylish, with only several errors, such as the silk-wrapped nails, acquired at great expense, that felt like lobster claws extending from her fingers as they clicked against her tray.

Still, Patty was forced to note, while many of the customers were graced with beauty or wit or marvelous clothing, few seemed to have achieved a far-reaching or reliable measure of the success that she had assumed New York offered for the asking. Luck must be in scant supply these days. On the other hand, perhaps people came to this restaurant during some sort of interim stage, or limbo; certainly Patty never knew how people fared before they started coming to the restaurant or how they fared after they stopped. People seemed simply to appear and then to vanish. She hadn't seen George, for instance, since the night of the unpleasantness. Life had moved on for him. Or, as she once shamefacedly reflected, she had forced it to move on.

And then, at the beginning of summer, Ginger told Patty that he and his company were going to California. "I just hate to leave, Sugar. But, Lord—the overhead these days! It's just too steep for an artist. Here, don't you look so sad now. Take a load off your feet for a minute."

It was a slow night, and Patty let Ginger lift her onto his lap, where she nestled contemplatively against his papier-mâché breasts and admired the steely sheen of his arm, folded so gently around her. His arm was as smooth and hard as steel, too, as Patty's finger, trailing idly along it, discovered, but its surface was as welcoming as satin. And this surface— which seemed more lovely to Patty than skin, less perishable, just as precious—raised on her own a velvety nap as she shifted, straining for some position of perfect rest.

"Oh, look," Ginger said, while Patty let the back of her hand enjoy the delicious indentation from which the curve of Ginger's shoulder flared. "Look how sweet! Look at those tiny pink nails, that little milky face. And freckles." Patty closed her eyes to better appreciate Ginger playfully favoring one freckle, then another. "Long, long lashes." Ginger brushed his cheek against Patty's lashes, and when she opened her eyes again the eyes that gleamed back were feral and slanting. "Little flower mouth," he said, and Patty's mouth opened, too, as he arched, letting her glide it from his jeweled earlobe down his polished neck and along the sweep of his collarbone, but there was a quick explosion in her brain as "Waitress! Waitress!" someone called, and Patty scrambled trembling to her feet, scraping her shoulder against papier-mâché.

Patty had developed the habit of routinely clambering in with Stuart when she got home, for warmth and company, but that morning she prowled back and forth across the apartment. Stuart didn't wake up, so eventually Patty poured herself a glass of cranberry juice and drew up a chair across from his bed, where he lay in a little humid wad, wheezing, appearing to become more and more exhausted as he slept, like a shipwreck victim unconscious on a seaborne plank. How painful a sight it was! How painful it was to be reminded that Stuart's helplessness was something beyond a manipulative ruse! Patty and Stuart had laid to rest the question of sex (sex between the two of them, that is), and although Stuart raised it from time to time, he did so clearly in the spirit of commemorative iteration. It almost made Patty sad that he had come to be as un-interested, actually, in the prospect as she was herself. She sipped at her cranberry juice, watching him, thinking.

Her presence must have made itself felt, because Stuart wheezed mightily, thrashed, and flung himself into a sitting position. "Patty," he said.

"Stuart," she said, "what famous monarch gave forth a fatal dazzle?"

"Come here and give me a hug, Patty-Cake," he said. He moved over to make room and politely turned his back to her.

"Come on," she said. "Please guess what famous monarch gave forth a fatal dazzle."

"Well . . ." He sighed. "O.K. Jupiter, then."

"*Jupiter*," she said. "That's a stupid guess. Jupiter isn't even a monarch."

"Oh, yeah?" Stuart cleared his throat. "Well, listen to this, Miss Smarty:

"Oh, thou art fairer than the evening's air,
Clad in the beauty of a thousand stars.
Brighter art thou than flaming Jupiter.
When he appeared to hapless Semele:
More lovely than the monarch of the sky.
In wanton Arethusa's azure arms,
And none but thou shalt be my paramour."

When Stuart stopped, a spectral resonance hung in the room as if a cello had been playing.

"So?" Patty demanded, forcing back tears.

"So Jupiter's the *monarch* of the sky," Stuart said. "Get it? And he also fries Semele, which, in my opinion, is, like, an irrefutably fatal dazzle. Anyhow, what do you care?"

"It's just a game," Patty said miserably. "What Famous Monarch."

"Oh," Stuart said. "Trivial Pursuit for right-wing extremists. Anyhow, all monarchs give forth a fatal dazzle. Fatal dazzle is the sort of sine qua non of monarchy. The steady effulgence of enlightened self-government, for example—"

"Stuart," Patty interrupted, "I don't want to talk about this." Morning had arrived in the airshaft; a thousand stars had dimmed. Mr. Nice Guy and his wife would be waking just above Marcia's ceiling, and, above theirs, Mrs. Jorgenson. "I'm tired, Stuart. I'm lonely. I want a real boyfriend."

"Well, Patty," Stuart said softly. She could feel his laborious breathing behind the fragile arc of his rib cage. "I just can't help you there."

Customers generated themselves from air; where there had been one, now there were twenty. Patty rushed back and forth in terror, first for menus, then, thinking better of it, for knives and forks.

"Don't fret, Sugar," said a man, putting a calming arm around her. From the prodigality and exquisite subtlety of the painted designs that covered his body, Patty realized that this man was a chief.

"Take a load off your feet. We Brazilians tend to be hunting-and-gathering peoples." And the band was indeed now plucking burgers and drinks and platters of ribs from under the tables, from out of the waitress stands and light fixtures.

"I never thought of looking there!" Patty said, astonished, but the chief was moving off with his band as they continued their hunt into the forests of the ever-expanding restaurant. "Wait," she wheedled. "Please—I'll get your bread and butter . . ." But the wonderful painted people who had paused so briefly in her sleep on their way off the face of the earth were disappearing through the trees. "Please don't leave!" she cried loudly, waking herself up.

"I'm here for you, baby," Stuart murmured from out of his own dream.

Baby! Patty propped herself up on her elbow and stared at Stuart's pale, knotted face. Who in God's name could *Stuart* be calling *baby?*

"Stuart," she said that afternoon over coffee. "I think I've let myself get sidetracked somehow."

"Hey, are you wearing some different kind of eye makeup these days?" Stuart asked.

"No," Patty said. "Listen, Stuart. It's time for me to start doing something interesting."

"You are doing something interesting," he said.

"That's not what I mean, Stuart, as you know."

"If you're not careful," he said, shaking a finger, "your wish will come true and you'll wake up one morning shackled to some corporate cutthroat who cracks jokes about his interior designer."

"Slurp slurp," she said.

"Look, you're too poorly informed to be familiar with the behavioral and attitudinal alternatives that are history's legacy, but trust me, Patty. You're at a crossroads here. We're all soldiers in the battles between historical forces and you'd better look down at your uniform to see what side you're fighting for before you do something you'll be sorry about."

"Stuart, are you telling me that I ought to be a waitress for the rest of my life?"

"It's honest work," he said.

"Honest!" Patty said. "It's *funny*. TV and books and movies are full of *waitress* jokes. But it's extremely *hard work*!"

"What do you think work is?" Stuart said. "What do you think people have been doing all these millennia? What do you think less privileged people do? Not less intelligent, not less attractive, not less deserving—less *privileged*. Just because history has tossed a bouquet to your weensy little culture, you think actual work is an ignominy, a degradation—"

"You know"—Patty was *not* going to let Stuart outtalk her—"considering how . . . how *entranced* you are by the sanctity of toil, it's a wonder you never indulge in any yourself."

"I've tried," said Stuart, instantly in the right.

"I know." Patty held up her hand. "I take it back."

"I've tried waiting on tables, I've tried moving furniture . . ."

"I know," she said. "I know I know I know I know, never *mind*. Yaargh." He had tried. It was indisputable. He had tried waiting on tables, but, being Stuart, was confined to low-income jobs in dingy coffee shops or delis, where he was fired before his first shift was out, having kindled, to his own perplexity and the manager's fury, little feuds that sprang up like brushfires at the tables and in the kitchen. He had tried moving furniture—for three days he'd gone off in the mornings with fear in his eyes and returned in the evenings looking shocked and broken. On the fourth day his body had refused to raise him from bed and reproached him with racking pains. He would have tried, gladly, to drive a taxi, except that he couldn't drive and no instructor would let him learn, and when occasionally Patty had insisted that they travel by taxi, Stuart wedged himself back in his seat, peeking through his fingers and gasping in such a way as to provoke the driver into a murderous bumper-car rage. "But you know what, Stuart?" Patty bore down on her powers of expression. "It seems to me that if it's a foregone conclusion you're going to fail at a given undertaking you might examine your own motives to see whether there's something hypocritical about them."

"Hypocritical!" Stuart said furiously. "And you used to be *nice.*"

"*Caring*—a word that makes you throw up! I used to be caring."

"Nice. You used to be pretty nice. Nice. A little, pretty nice glob of unformed humanity who couldn't put two words together. Now, barely one year later, slimy sophistries drop from your lips like vipers and toads."

"Wait!" Patty said, standing. Because the most incredible thing had just occurred to her. If she was going to get on with her life, it was not only she who had to get a job—Stuart would have to be gotten a job as well! As things stood, he couldn't possibly afford an apartment of his own, and she couldn't just put him out on the street to starve. Even Marcia, after all, had left him provided for, and now it was Patty who had to help him, whether he wanted help or not. "That's not what I meant, Stuart," she said ingratiatingly. "I expressed myself poorly. I only meant why should you wait on tables or move furniture when there are so many other, better, things you're suited for?"

" 'Better.' " Stuart sniffed.

"Better paid, then, if you prefer."

"Patty," he said, "just what are all these things I'm so well suited for?"

"Well, I don't know, Stuart. How should I know? Why couldn't you . . . write copy, for example?"

"What is copy, actually?" Stuart said. "Is it anything like prose?"

"Or be a reviewer again, for some publication. Or get something done with some of your poems? After all, you're an artist, really."

"Yeah, and why don't I rack up a bunch of grants while I'm at it, and have my picture taken for magazines? '*Artist*'— you know what you think an artist is, Patty? You think an artist is some great-looking big guy in a T-shirt, with a bottle in one hand and a paintbrush in the other, who has five hundred thousand dollars zooming around the stock market, and a car like a big shiny penis."

"Stuart," Patty said patiently as she tried to inhibit a telltale blush, "please don't be revolting. The point is that I have complete respect for your convictions, no matter what they might be. It's just that I worry."

"Don't worry," he said.

"Well, I do worry. And I'll tell you one thing I'm especially worried about right now. The Nice Guys. Yesterday Mr. Martinez told me they want a duplex. And you know what that means. That means they're going to have to get someone out—either us or Mrs. Jorgenson. And Mrs. Jorgenson isn't going to go without making trouble. We're an illegal sublet, Stuart. We're not supposed to be here. Especially you. We could get Marcia evicted!"

Stuart sighed. "I'm sorry, Patty. I know you want me to leave."

"Oh, Stuart," she said guiltily. "I just want you to find something that will make you *happy*."

"But Patty." He looked at her. "I *am* happy."

Patty, however, had stumbled upon a decision lying in her path, and during the next few days she treated Stuart with the solicitude due to the condemned.

But when she called Donna, there was a bad moment. A minuscule silence preceded Donna's first words. "Oh. Patty," Donna said then. "Right."

So Patty judged it best to come straight to the point: she wanted to talk to Fletcher at the magazine. She was aching for an outlet for her talents. She had developed a feverish interest even in layout, which he could surely exploit. If there was nothing open in that line at the moment, perhaps she could meet him, in case something were to open up in the future. Or in case there was anything. Anything at all.

"Unfortunately, it's not the greatest timing," Donna said. "Everything's all sort of set up now."

"But if we could just meet," Patty said.

"I could give Fletcher your number," Donna said.

"And you know what?" Patty said. "My roommate's a writer. And he's had a lot of journalistic experience."

"Well," Donna said, "the problem is, Fletcher already has a lot of writers."

"I understand," Patty said. She took a deep breath to clarify her mind. "Anyhow, it might not work out with Stuart. He's like a lot of artists—very unpredictable, if you know what I mean. Kind of dangerous."

"Mmm . . ." Donna said. "Dangerous . . ."

And when Patty finished talking (talking and talking) Donna said, "Well, we might as well all have dinner one night when you're not working. At least we'd—at least we'd get a chance to, you know . . . meet."

"Patty," Stuart said. "Why do I have to do this?"

"You just have to, Stuart, you have to." Oh, God, Patty thought. If she weren't careful, Stuart's suspicious nature might lead him to the conclusion that she was trying to market them both. "Donna's asked me to do this, and I can't go alone, because she's just . . . finding her way around with this guy, who also happens to be her employer, and who, I understand, is a very serious and profound person, incidentally, so she wants to be with some people who are . . . pleasant. And . . . pleasant to be with. And, by the way," Patty said, to change the subject, "you're not planning to wear that shirt, are you?"

"What's the matter with my shirt?" he said. "I thought nerds were considered fashionable these days."

"Not actual nerds, Stuart. Just people who look like nerds."

"Patty," he said. "I really don't want to do this."

"Forget about the shirt, Stuart. However you're comfortable. I just don't want to walk in looking pathetic and desperate."

"Desperate about what?" Stuart asked shrewdly.

To pacify him, Patty agreed to forgo a taxi. They picked their way uncompanionably in the steaming evening through a cluster of shapeless creatures who sat at the subway entrance, surrounded by bags that appeared to be stuffed with filthy, discarded gifts, muttering to themselves in garbled fragments of some lost language. Mrs. Jorgenson would undoubtedly be joining them—assuming Patty could protect herself and Stuart—when the Nice Guys got their duplex. Well, Patty thought, good riddance.

Patty grew increasingly ill-tempered as she and Stuart sweltered underground, waiting for the shrieking train. And by the time they reached the restaurant her mascara was creeping downward and she was cross through and through.

So this is it, she thought, looking around at the mirrors and linen, at the graceful sprays of freesia. So this was where everyone had been while she'd been eating Stuart's barley-and-zucchini casseroles.

Donna was already at a table with Fletcher—a man, as it turned out, of unparalleled presentability. "Hel*lo*," Patty said.

"Well, well," said Donna, across whose face was written "I thought you said this guy was an *artist*." But Donna was not one to let the failings of others cloud her mood, Patty knew, and by the time drinks had been brought she was mollified.

Donna had buffed herself up to a high gloss in the months since Patty had seen her (nothing wrong with *her* mascara), and she was talking with Fletcher of matters entirely foreign to Patty. But strangely, Patty realized, Stuart could manage this conversational obstacle course strewn with technical matters peculiar to periodicals and the private lives of various people involved with them; Stuart knew how to join in.

Obviously, however, Stuart participated entirely without pleasure. It was for her sake, Patty thought, because of her injunctions, and therefore the situation was— Heavens! The situation was dangerous!

Just as Stuart began to fidget noticeably, a new waiter appeared, to deal out menus.

"Oh—" said Fletcher, evidently startled to have been faced with someone as handsome as himself. "The pasta's excellent, incidentally, but I'd avoid the fish."

Patty looked at him bleakly. Why were they all here? This wasn't an interview; it wasn't—it wasn't— She couldn't even think of what it was that this wasn't. She looked at the prices on the menu, and she looked at Donna and at Stuart and back at Fletcher. *Fletcher* didn't care what this was or wasn't; he was just having dinner!

Nerves had dismantled Patty's appetite, and the menu seemed to be written in Esperanto, so when the waiter returned Patty simply tagged along with Donna and Fletcher. "Fine," she said. "I'll also have the salade panachée and then the perciatelli all'amatriciana."

The waiter turned and stared at Stuart. "O.K.," Stuart said hopelessly. "What the hell."

"*Certainly*," said the waiter with deferential contempt.

"Who does that kid think he is?" Donna said as the waiter left. "He's a *waiter*."

Fletcher continued the line of thought he'd been pursuing with Donna as the waiter returned with their salads. "So my point is that Jay Resnick is doing a feature series on Saffi Sheinheld for *Dallas by Daylight*. And Saffi happens to be the senior vice-president of SunBelt, *Dallas*'s biggest account. Now, I would consider that ethically questionable."

Ethically questionable— That *fool*, Patty thought. There'd be no holding Stuart now. "Hey, Stuart"—she foraged wildly in her salad—"this purple thing is a *pepper*."

For a while Patty struggled to match the fun bits of her salad with his, and although Stuart suffered quietly, he looked like a rag doll that had been thrown over a cliff, and soon Patty felt that she, too, was teetering on the brink.

"Donna tells me you're in graphics," Fletcher said, flinging Patty a rope.

"Terrific field." Patty swung to safety. "So incredible, for example, how design, or even layout, can send these tiny, subtle signals. 'Buy me,' for example, or—"

"Visual appeal," Fletcher agreed, glancing up as the waiter arrived with their pasta. "Crucial." The waiter smirked.

"Is that *bacon*?" Stuart demanded, pointing at his plate.

"It's *only* a little pan*cetta*," the waiter said.

"I understand you're into film," Fletcher said obliviously to Stuart.

"'Into'?" Stuart said. "'Film'?"

"Look," Patty said, plunging into her salad and unearthing a greenish disk rimmed with hair. "I bet no one else has one of these!"

"Or have I misunderstood?" Fletcher said to Stuart as if Patty hadn't spoken.

"Kind of," Stuart said with an equability that made Patty's heart plunge. "What I really 'am,' see, is mentally ill."

"Yes?" Fletcher was guarded but ready to be amused.

"Yeah," Stuart said. "Mental illness. An exacting mistress. It doesn't leave me a lot of time for other things to be . . . 'into.' Like racquetball. Or parenting. Or leveraged buyouts."

Patty looked down at the table, struggling against an untimely smile, and then looked meekly back up at Fletcher. But Fletcher had been enveloped, during the silence, by a glacier. His disapproval gleamed faintly out from behind centuries of ice, which Donna's voice splintered like a hatchet. "I don't think that's very funny," Donna said. "A lot of people actually *are* mentally ill, you know."

"Patty—" Stuart yelped.

"All *right*, Stuart," Patty said, getting to her feet. "Stuart, you didn't eat any of that pancetta, did you? Stuart has a . . . a sensitivity to various additives used in pork products." She was sick of this; she didn't care how ridiculous she sounded; these people had never intended to help them. "And you can just never tell when it might— Listen, Stuart, we'd better get you home before you—Here, this should cover our share." Stuart in tow, she made her way clumsily to the door.

On the way back to Marcia's in a taxi, Stuart was oddly tranquil. And it was he who, after minutes of silence, spoke first. "I'm sorry if I put a crimp in whatever the hell you were trying to accomplish," he said quietly.

Contradictory responses raced through Patty's brain for expression, and clogged. "Give me a break, Stuart," she managed to say.

"I understand," Stuart said. "Your better judgment's been under a lot of pressure."

"Stuart—" Patty was gratified to find that indignation was the attitude forceful enough to distinguish itself from the mute tangle choking her. "Please don't talk to me as if I were a criminal. Don't talk to me as if I were a psychopath. I know the difference between right and wrong. It was wrong of me not to be more forthcoming with you. It was wrong of me to wreck a good opportunity through carelessness. It was wrong of me to waste all that money. I know that what I did was wrong, and I'm trying to apologize." But Stuart just hunched over and looked out the window, where the lights were streaming by. "Stuart—"

"Take it easy, Patty," he said. "I'm not angry."

"Then don't act like this," she said. "Just criticize me, please. Give me a lecture."

But Stuart only patted her hand as if she were an overtired child, and it was when they got back inside the apartment that he himself took his things from the closet and packed them up. "Where will you go?" Patty said. "You don't have anyplace to go." And when Stuart took her hand and held it for a moment against his closed eyes, she might have been touching a fallen leaf or petal, or the wing of a chloroformed butterfly.

After Stuart closed the door behind him it was very quiet. And then it kept on being very quiet. Patty had to force herself to stand up and go to the door.

Outside, the evening trembled with threats of a summer

storm, and the air was alive with residues of color. In the growing dark the sky was beginning to twinkle with a thousand little windows.

Mr. Martinez smiled up at Patty from the stoop, where he sat watching a bunch of spindly, raucous, big-eyed children as they danced in some sort of circle game, playing with a violent urgency, competing against the approaching storm for what was left of the evening. "Hello, miss!" Mr. Martinez said.

Patty smiled at him absently. How beautiful that restaurant tonight had been! And now, of all things, she was hungry. If Stuart hadn't left, they could at least have gone someplace for a cheap bite. Well, it hadn't been *her* fault that he'd left—it hadn't been her *fault*.

As Patty stood, lost in thought, she saw George walk by. "George!" she cried, clattering down the steps. "George!" She tapped him on the shoulder, but the creature that turned around was not George—oh, surely not George—but some awful ghoul with sunken cheeks and stained, broken teeth and eyes that burned as she shrank back. "Sorry," she breathed. "A mistake."

"Mistake!" he shrieked. "Sorry! Always sorry, sorry, sorry. Well, I do life, and I do death. Pass this block, blah-blah, blah-blah. Pass this block, we never see *you* again." A flash of lightning illuminated the awful creature as a contraption of bones in retreating white silhouette, and her own eye sockets flashed white, too, around her, before she blinked and looked back over her shoulder.

In an island of street light Mr. Martinez still sat blissfully watching the ring of dancing children. Everything was just as it had been a moment before: the little scene, the street, the building where Patty had lived for a year; everything was just the same, of course, yet it all looked slightly uncanny— looming and mutable—as if it were something she'd known only from photographs.

"Mr. Martinez," she tried to call, though Mr. Martinez himself seemed newly a stranger, and her voice, hoarse and ghostly, hardly carried back to her own ears. The smallest of the dancing children spun, and leapt into the center of the circle. Street light glanced off the child's tiny gold earring, and Mr. Martinez, with narrowed eyes, rocked back in delight, flinging his arms wide in a tap dancer's gesture of embrace. But for what? Just what was the guy so pleased about, anyway, Patty thought irately, but his arms stretched wider and wider, and he smiled as if he were smiling at the sun.

UNDER THE 82ND AIRBORNE

Two pallid eggs, possibly the final effort of some local chicken, quivered on the plate as the waitress set it in front of Caitlin. The waitress raised her canted black eyes, and behind her Caitlin saw Holly entering at the far end of the room, flanked by two men. Holly's hair was blond now, a terrible kitchen-ette color, but her face was Todd's exactly, or what Todd's had been at that age. Incredible: Caitlin and Todd had been as young as Holly was now; Holly was now so old—as old as Caitlin and Todd had been! And in the moment before Holly and the men reached her table Caitlin had all too much time to contemplate this stunt, a stunt that had taken twenty years to prepare.

Perhaps she'd been rash to make this trip; certainly she'd had something in mind other than this dingy place and Holly and her friends trooping in like judges. A restful gathering on the beach, something of *that* sort—coconuts filled with rum. A respite from New York, where life had begun to feel chaotic and shapeless, during which she could reconnoiter with all that now seemed to be left of her past—Holly.

For some time, things in New York had been going along just well enough to ignore. Then recently Neil had begun to complain—to formulate an exhaustive catalogue of com-plaints, each item of which Caitlin considered no more than a shabby justification for seeing other women. Which he was more than welcome to do, as it happened, although, in point of sheer fact, there was also the rent to be considered.

Caitlin temporized, spending more and more time at the bar where she worked, waiting for life with Neil to take an upward turn, or for something else to come along, but in the silence that followed Neil's noisy departure Caitlin's surroundings became audible—the daily din of the customers reliving, as she poured their drinks, the talismanic episodes of their pasts; the ghoulish whispering of her own future. And when she understood that there was no one waiting to replace Neil—no one at all—her life roared in her ear like an empty shell.

The problem was, she thought, she'd let herself lapse; she had not been on a stage for some time after Holly was born. When she took up work again she'd had a brief spate of good luck but then job offers became more and more infrequent. She grew out of the roles to which she'd been suited; she grew into no others. And the truth was, she realized, astonished, she hadn't performed for years now—it was probably years since she'd even auditioned.

In the course of one week she forced herself to attend two open casting calls where scores of people had waited in a large room, some of them women her own age, who were quite clearly too old for the part for which they, and she, were trying out. These women had dressed carefully, as she herself had, to appear nonchalant and young, and, sitting there, had looked at her with something like hatred. At the second audition the script rattled in Caitlin's hands, and the director, a boy in a fashionably floppy suit, stopped her after she'd read no more than half a page. Later someone told her that the calls were a union requirement—that both shows, in fact, had been cast before the calls took place.

When she returned to the apartment after the second audition she examined herself in the mirror. Her gray-blue eyes were still clear and wide, her pale-brown hair still gave off light. From a distance she could have been a girl, but tonight her face was disfigured by the meaningless history of a stranger. Surely her intended self was locked away somewhere, embryonic and protected. She searched the mirror, but the impostor on duty there stared bafflingly back.

She had a drink, and then another, straining through the tumult of her panic to understand what she was to do, and then it came to her that she must see Holly.

"What's the matter, Mama?" Holly said guardedly when Caitlin reached her on the phone.

"I'm glad to talk to you, too," Caitlin said, thrown as always upon hearing Holly's light, high, rapid voice, her slight Southern accent.

"It's after midnight," Holly said.

"It took me long enough to find you, you know," Caitlin said, although, strictly speaking, she happened to have Holly's new number, which Todd's sister Martha had included in one of her infrequent but vigorous letters of ill-concealed denunciation. "You didn't even tell me you'd moved."

"Did someone just dump you, Mama?" Holly said. "Is that it?"

Caitlin shrank inward. When Holly was a child she'd arrive every summer, a distrustful little stranger from Todd's world, with Todd's accent. More recently she and Caitlin had spent several weeks a year together. Not enough time, of course. But still, had it been Caitlin's fault? "You've got my number," she said. "Call when you have time."

"No, wait, Mama, don't," Holly said. "Don't. I'm sorry."

Holly was taking a break from school, she said; she'd been

planning to let Caitlin know. She'd moved in with her boy-friend, who was in business. He traveled a lot, south, to other countries. Daddy liked him—he was alert. He spoke some Spanish. Sometimes she went with him on his trips. She was fine, she said; happy.

"Are you happy?" Caitlin said. "You sound tense."

"I'm happy, Mama," Holly said. "I told you."

Caitlin let a moment elapse.

"Sorry," Holly said.

"Listen," Caitlin said. "How about this? Come visit—why not? We'll have a great time. We'll go around New York like tourists. And then you'll tell me all about your friend. I've been auditioning like a madwoman, and I need to relax, too."

"I don't need to relax," Holly said. "I'm relaxed. Besides, Mama— Listen, I'm sorry. But this is just not a good time—Brandon and I are going on a trip."

But she'd been *counting* on seeing Holly . . . "Well, then," she said. She held the phone in dazed confusion for a minute or so, trying to think of a way to disengage herself from the conversation before she cried, or said something she would regret. But then she heard herself asking, to her own surprise, "How's Todd?"

"Daddy?" Holly said. "Oh, Daddy's O.K. Business has been bad, though, lately," she added. "He seems sort of worn out."

Todd's busty secretaries, his little pocket Christmas calen-dars, his showroom of clownish plumbing fixtures—could Caitlin have despised them so much if they were not inde-structible? How terrible if they should turn out not to be. "I'm sure Linda's taking good care of him, though," she said.

"Yes . . ." Holly admitted uncertainly.

"Everyone gets older," Caitlin said. "You wouldn't believe it if you saw me."

"Mama—" Holly said. "Are you O.K., Mama?"

"Fine," Caitlin said. "Anyhow."

"Wait, Mama—" Holly said. "Please."

Caitlin waited while Holly readjusted the phone.

"Listen," Holly said. "Well, anyhow. So Brandon and I have to take this little trip now. Anyhow, otherwise—" Holly stopped. "I mean it would be really nice to see you. But I mean, we're not going to have any time on this trip. This is a business trip."

"Well, if that's the only problem," Caitlin said. "I'm a terrific traveler." Before Holly was born she'd spent quite a bit of time on the road, back and forth between California and New York. "No one has to take care of me—I love to go off on my own and explore."

After a minute Holly sighed. Then she spoke. "All right, Mama," she said. "O.K."

Within three days Caitlin had made all her New York arrangements, bought a plane ticket to the town whose name Holly had spelled out for her, and acquired, under Holly's instructions, a visa. But when she changed planes in Miami early one morning, she wondered if there was something she'd failed to take into account. "What does your friend do in that place?" Caitlin had asked Holly on the phone. "It's *business*, Mama," Holly had said. "Anyhow, what do you care? It'll be a vacation. It'll be warm." And Caitlin packed a suitcase full of festive, warm-weather clothing, new and borrowed. But the few other women waiting at the gate were prim and sour; aside from them, and some miserable-looking boys whose heads were practically shaved, and several thick-set athletic types incongruously bad-tempered in their color-ful, open Hawaiian shirts and cutoffs, the passengers were pale men with briefcases, who sat forward in their chairs, looking neither to the right nor to the left.

The silence at the gate grew more and more concentrated until a few minutes before the plane was to be boarded, when a portly woman in Bermuda shorts strode in. A little blue sailor cap bobbed on top of her iron-gray hair, and she gripped a small boy by the arm. "Guess what he's got in there!" the woman said. She released the child's arm to thump the knap-sack he was wearing. "He's got a Big Mac! Every time we come up, we stop at McDonald's last thing, so he can bring a burger or two down to his brother." The boy rubbed his arm and blinked resentfully. His face was small and peeled-looking, and there were bluish shadows beneath his eyes. "I hope you got yourself one," the woman said to Caitlin. "Be-cause you're not going to be having one for a while, I guess, are you?"

Caitlin offered the minimum smile and extracted a fash-ion magazine from her bag.

"Who are *you* with?" the woman said, settling heavily into one of the tiny seats near Caitlin.

"Excuse me?" Caitlin said.

"Excuse *me*, excuse *me*," the woman said, raising her hands as if to ward Caitlin off. "Well, I don't mind talking about my people then. Because we stick strictly to religious instruction. Of course, we're required to distribute a certain amount of aid as well, but out there in the countryside reli-gious instruction is the thing that really counts, isn't it?"

"Really," Caitlin said, casting a glance at her magazine.

"You bet your boots it is," the woman said. "Arms them

against temptation. Of course"—she chuckled—"I suppose arms arm them, too. But seriously, you've got to reach them first, don't you? Their hearts are good, you can take that from me—they're honest, and they're hardworking, despite what you hear. But they're gullible, you see; they're still Indians, when you get right down to it. And the Cubans and the Catholics come sidling along, telling them that God loves the poor. And we know where *that* leads, don't we? So we do what we can with shoes and rice—these people don't eat potatoes, you know. And leadership's planning a home for the widows and orphans, so they see that we intend the best for them. Not that there aren't risks." She raised a stern eyebrow and looked piercingly at Caitlin. "I hope you don't mind my asking," she said, "but is this your first time down?"

Caitlin looked up from her magazine, but the woman's features were like a pile of root vegetables screening her expression. "It is, actually," Caitlin said.

"Well," the woman said, relaxing her scrutiny, "you're all right in the city, aren't you? Fewer mosquitoes. You can get quite a decent hunk of meat, too, you know. And there are several clean English-language cinemas—I mean, if you can stand the blood."

On the plane Caitlin watched with relief as the woman in the sailor cap proceeded past her up the aisle, pulling the boy, from whose knapsack trailed a suggestion of grease. "Chin up!" the woman called, and the man in the next seat glanced at Caitlin.

"Completely insane," Caitlin explained, to put the man at his ease.

"Yes?" he said. He seemed doubtful.

"I couldn't believe my ears," Caitlin said. "Hamburgers. Indians. Subversives . . ."

"Tend to be a problem, I suppose," the man said. "They say not, of course, but one expects them to put a good face on it. Still, one never knows—in Guatemala things really are under control." He raised his eyebrows and nodded at Caitlin. "To tell you the truth, though," he confided anxiously, "this is my first time down here."

"Footloose little crowd," Caitlin said. "Aren't we?"

"Ha-ha," the man agreed. "You see, we've been doing quite a decent business in Guatemala and Salvador the last few years, and the office thought, Well, why not give it a whirl? All these places are so darn hungry for trade—terms are favorable, and there aren't so many silly restrictions as in some places I could mention."

Caitlin glanced across the aisle, but the situation there didn't look much more promising—there were only the ill-tempered men in cutoffs, who were already drinking from cans of beer they must have carried on with them.

"And things being what they are at the moment," the man continued, "there's a lot of disposable income clanking around down there, believe it or not. Not per-capita speaking, of course—per-capita speaking, still just about the poorest damn place in the hemisphere. Well, I mean except for Haiti."

Haiti—Caitlin had been in a play once, with wonderful costumes, about voodoo. "I always think Haiti's so fascinating," she said.

"Really?" The man looked somewhat alarmed. "Incidentally, what is it that brings you here?"

"My daughter." Caitlin smiled at him. "Isn't that amazing?"

"I'll say," the man said.

"Well, I was practically a child bride, of course," Caitlin said.

"Yes?" the man said. He appeared to be puzzled. "And is she at the Embassy, your daughter?"

"Embassy?" Caitlin looked at him. "What on earth for?"

"Oh, sorry," he said. "I just—no, I guess not." He glanced at her, inventorying her in a category she couldn't identify, and then receded into a private melancholy. Caitlin returned in irritation to her magazine, and the man bent over his open briefcase, shadowy preoccupations playing across the pale screen of his face. But when the stewardess came around he grew morosely cordial again. "Can I get you a drink?" he said.

"Thanks," Caitlin said. "Just a vodka tonic, please."

"Bourbon for me, dear," the man said to the stewardess. "Terrif."

"That's better," he said, turning to Caitlin a few minutes later. "You know, if you and your daughter would care to stop by for a drink, I'm at the—well, here." He took a business card from his wallet. "I'll write down the name of my hotel."

"Thank you," Caitlin said. Underneath the scrawled name of the hotel was printed "TechNil, Cleaning Products for the Home, Harvey Gumbiner, Vice-President in Charge of Distribution."

"And if the two of you are planning to be down here through the summer," Harvey said, "they'll probably be having their party at the Embassy on the Fourth. They do in most places, anyhow. Wonderful custom, in my opinion—usually the event of the year. Any U.S. citizen, of whatever stripe or persuasion, is welcome to attend. People come from every sector of the business community. Hot dogs, hamburgers—just like your own backyard. Corn flown in fresh . . ."

Caitlin adjusted her seat backward. No, it had been a good

idea, this trip; there would be new people, parties, interesting men . . .

"But don't misunderstand me," Harvey said hurriedly. "You do hear of the occasional embarrassment in these sensitive areas. Episodes, poor taste, so on. Seems odd, but that's human psychology, isn't it?" He frowned at his empty plastic cup. "*Our* money, *our* protection, but people seem to feel funny about that sort of thing. More blessed to give than to receive, I suppose. Well, another drink?"

"I shouldn't," Caitlin said, looking around for the stewardess.

The airport was a stark little affair outside of which a sad mob waited under the bloated sky. Inside, in the lines where papers were to be checked and stamped, luggage was to be inspected, and unconvincingly ornate money was to be issued, Caitlin's fellow passengers once again looked away from one another, tense and silent. Harvey disappeared quickly into the maw of the baggage-claim area, the disheveled beer drinkers were nowhere to be seen, and even the woman in the sailor cap seemed to have been seized with a seriousness of purpose. She went through her tasks quickly, with a cold efficiency, and when she passed by, her mouth set, neither she nor the boy with her seemed to recognize Caitlin. An official of some sort appeared, to speak to the cluster of furtive-looking boys from the plane, who were now standing right behind Caitlin. Their pale scalps glimmered like mushrooms through their short hair, and a damp fear came off them as they responded to the official's question, nodding soberly, their faces a shifting balance of expressions—resignation, eagerness, rage, and obedience— that canceled each other into an unstable blankness.

A mournful taxi-driver brought Caitlin, without commentary or questions, to the hotel where Holly had directed her. There Caitlin registered with a woman whose listlessness was almost overpowering. At least the woman spoke English, Caitlin thought—in fact, it seemed that almost everyone did.

Caitlin's room was an undeceiving simulation of luxury. Streaks of disinfectant testified to its cleanliness, and the faint stench of synthetics recalled best-forgotten mornings in motels. Caitlin followed a thunderous choking into the bathroom, where the toilet was paralyzed in a permanent flush. She washed her face with the fibrous soap that had been provided and inspected the other complimentary toiletries—tiny plastic packets, bonded shut, of shampoo and bath foam in violent, improbable colors.

She sat on the bed and looked out the window. The hills around the town were covered with vegetation, fecund but dying; the town appeared to be constructed of pale, decomposing, organic concrete. There were fingerprints on the bleary clouds. No sense unpacking—she'd move to a happier hotel later. She left her suitcase in the closet and went downstairs to the restaurant, where she was to meet Holly.

The restaurant was the color of dying vegetation. Most of the customers and all of the waitresses had heavy black hair and black, slightly slanting eyes that made their ordinary suits and dresses look to Caitlin like disguises. She ordered breakfast. Where was Holly?

It was twenty years ago that Caitlin had found herself pregnant. She'd been on tour, in a small revue that had become unexpectedly popular, and she'd met Todd in the bar of the hotel where she was staying with the other members of her company. His childish respectability, his crafty innocence were comical, but he was very good-looking, and Caitlin was slightly drunk, and the whole thing was irresistibly ridiculous, not only to her but also to the boys from her cast, who were with her in the bar, waiting. In the morning, Caitlin let herself be persuaded to spend the night with Todd again, and by the end of the week he took her breath away.

She swung back and forth across the gulf between her attraction to him and the stunning tedium of his conversation. At first the sensation was like a toy. The boys in the company came down with a group fever; Todd was, they agreed, delicious. The boys made up stories—uproarious, hyperbolic romances—in which Todd starred opposite Caitlin, the surrogate. All the boys, and Caitlin, too, would be weak with laughter by the time Todd appeared after the show to take her home, and then the boys would become pouty and sultry, throwing Todd into good-natured confusion. It didn't matter, Caitlin thought; the show would be moving soon.

But then she was pregnant. She would wake up in the morning and the fact would be waiting to claim her. During the day she would be blanketed by a dullness that was impossible to fight off—she couldn't grasp anything for more than a moment.

Of course, she could get rid of the baby—not much problem there—but then what was it she'd been planning for the whole rest of her life? The truth was, she thought alone in her hotel room, she couldn't count on having this sort of job forever. And each time she brought herself to consider her course of action, what presented itself in place of an answer was a question once again.

For whole minutes the world would be suspended, and she

would feel emptily cheerful, even happy; then she would remember what was happening inside her and a heavy fear would press her down. Days and days passed in this way, and then one day, among the shreds of feelings that rose and fell around her on harsh little gusts, a sort of hope appeared. Gradually, it grew in substance and weight, and one night she had a dream.

She dreamed that she was lying in her bed, exhausted and despairing, but then she noticed a wonderful piece of furniture against the wall, all covered with rosettes and cherubs. She got up from bed and opened it, and there, sparkling in the darkness, was the solution to her problems.

It was a ridiculous dream, but when she woke up it struck her with the force of an actual possibility that the means for her happiness was right inside her. When she told Todd she was pregnant, his face registered a self-satisfaction that made her sick with rage, and then immediately he began to plan.

For some time after they were married, Todd would plead with Caitlin to tell him what he'd done, but eventually he stopped, since it was clear that he'd done nothing. Later, he would beg Caitlin to stay, in a mounting voice and a mawkish, lofty, and fraudulent tone that drove her into venomous frenzies of threats. During several of these outbursts Holly had been in the room; she'd pushed at Caitlin's knees and shrieked as though Caitlin really were going to leave that very second. "Don't! Don't!" Holly would cry. "Mama, don't leeaave—" and then, for days afterward, the three of them would be shaken and fearful, shadowed by the horror of things that had almost been done.

When Holly was three and a half, Caitlin really did leave. Todd was courteous and formal—he had become a great deal more self-possessed since his days at the hotel bar—but his efficiency in the matter of Holly revealed a long-entrenched and fully assimilated hatred, of which Caitlin had been entirely unaware. He had little trouble insuring that Caitlin's access to Holly was legally limited; evidently he had been ready for some time.

Now, as the waitress moved away, Holly appeared—different in immeasurable tiny details from the person who existed in the custody of Caitlin's imagination—and gestured to one of the two men with her. "Mama, this is Brandon," she said in her rapid little uninflected voice. "My fiancé."

Although he looked hardly older than Holly, Brandon had a finished, knife-edged glint. His eyes were shockingly blue and expressionless, and his hair was a lucent, pure flax color, to which Holly had attempted, apparently, to match her own. *Fiancé?* Later, when they could really talk, she must tell Holly not to do this.

The other man, Lewis, must have been practically twice Holly's age. He was large and a bit soft-looking. His curly hair was greasy, and coarsened from the sun; a pitted nose stuck out between his mustache and his aviator sunglasses. He wore jeans, and a short-sleeved shirt under which Caitlin could see a faded, rose-colored T-shirt clinging sensually to his broad torso.

They sat down with Caitlin, and Lewis ordered breakfast for himself, Holly, and Brandon in Spanish. Holly's natural expression, Caitlin noticed, was still stubborn and slightly worried—even as a toddler she had been literal-minded and deliberate. But she had lost some of Todd's starchy look, and the tank top and shorts she was wearing suited her better than the ruffled things she'd favored as a child.

Brandon stretched out his long legs and looked appraisingly at Caitlin. But Holly blinked rapidly, then glared at her plate and rubbed at a splotch on it with her thumb.

"Well," Caitlin said.

"Glad you could take the time to come down here and join us all, ma'am," Brandon said to her quietly. He turned the blue beacon of his stare on Holly. "Aren't we, sweetheart?" he said, and she looked up at him, her mouth open.

Brandon looked oddly clean, as though he'd just showered off some identifying characteristics, and his brilliant, empty eyes could have belonged to an animal—some creature attuned only to the most minute signals of scent and sound. His accent was identical with Holly's, but his speech was alarmingly controlled. Fiancé! Well, of course it was all back in fashion now—table settings, shame, property agreements—but it seemed such a short time ago that no one had gotten married. No one, of course, except Todd.

Holly cleared her throat. "So, what about those auditions you've been doing, Mama? You find anything good?"

Caitlin pushed her hair back. "Nothing," she said. "Everything around is shit."

"An entertainer, huh?" Lewis said, poking his fork toward Caitlin. "You know, I admire entertainers. I always had a bit of a secret letch to be an entertainer myself. I played the drums when I was a kid, drove the whole neighborhood nuts. Then when I got back from Vietnam my buddies and I had a band. Gross National Product—" Caitlin could see him look at her behind his aviator glasses. "Maybe you remember it?"

"Not really," she said politely.

" 'Not really,' " he mimicked. "Surprise, surprise—no one fucking remembers. What do you want? We played exclusively scummy neighborhoods."

Holly and Brandon attended to their food with fastidious absorption, but there was a disturbance occurring in another part of the room. "*Buenas,*" someone was declaring loudly. Caitlin turned around to see a young man going from table to table, greeting the customers.

"*Buenas,*" he announced, stopping at their table. "How are you fine people today?" His accent was so slight as to seem just a crisping around the edges of words. "I'm Ricky." He extended to Caitlin a hand in a little black backless glove that snapped at the wrist. "Just down from Miami?"

"Miami?" she said. His clothing looked like a scout uniform from a pornographic movie; his bare, heavily muscled thigh was level with her face.

"I like Miami," he said. His hands settled lightly, one on Holly's shoulder, one on Brandon's. "People there are friendly, not like here. *This* place—bunch of crazy refugees trying to stab you in the ass all the time." He kneaded Holly's shoulder absently under the strap of her tank top. "You got a plane?" he said to Brandon. "Maybe I'll go up with you this weekend."

Holly had turned a bit pink, but Brandon was looking thoughtfully into the distance.

In the silence, Ricky seemed to notice his hand on Holly's shoulder. He lifted it and waved. "O.K., good people—see you at the club."

Brandon resumed eating and Holly continued to poke at her eggs as Caitlin looked from one to the other. "Friend of yours?" she said.

Brandon's look of extreme neutrality intensified. Neither he nor Holly looked up. "Because if you ask me," Caitlin said, "there's such a thing as just too stoned."

"Oh, we all know each other down here," Lewis said.

"Not like Guatemala. Here, everything's under control. A place for everyone, everyone in his place. Small operation, enough pie to go around; smoothly functioning system of checks and balances."

"Remember when we used to play that game, Mama?" Holly said suddenly. She turned to look at Caitlin. "Remember that? We played 'We're in Holly's room, in our house, in Durham, in North Carolina, in the United States of America, in the Western Hemisphere, on the planet Earth, in the solar system, in the universe . . .'"

Holly's room, with its new furniture and the glut of horrible bears from Todd's family. How could Holly remember that? She wouldn't even have been four. She had played soberly with her bears and teacups while Caitlin, in a reverie of scene-study classes and rehearsals, had brushed the light, sweet hair back from her face and the two of them had pursued, in the stale, fruity afternoon sunlight, the protean task of being mother and daughter. "I remember," Caitlin said.

"Well," Holly said. "Now we're in the restaurant, in our hotel, in Tegucigalpa, in Honduras, in whatever it is, in the Western Hemisphere, on the planet Earth, in the solar system, in the universe . . ."

"'Honduras' . . ." But where were the white sand and palm trees, vacationers spotting one another amid crowds of perspiring natives and trading private, approving glances? Well, of course, Caitlin knew, there were all kinds of other things going on now in this part of the world. "Just what exactly is this stuff we keep hearing about down here now?" she said, trying to construct something solid from fragments she'd heard on television.

"You might be thinking of the war, ma'am," Brandon said.

"Yes . . ." Caitlin tried to remember. "Well, there's a war here, of course."

"No, ma'am," he said.

Caitlin looked at him sharply. If only she'd been able to have Holly with her in New York more often! "Do you think you could find something else to call me?" she said.

"Mama—" Holly began, but Brandon touched her wrist, and she looked down at the table.

"Well," Lewis said, standing. "I'll just be off to freshen up a bit."

Brandon nodded to him, but Holly just stared at her plate, eyebrows furrowed. How helpless she looked! Caitlin reached over to her. "My baby," she said. "Your hair used to be such a lovely ash brown."

"Hash brown, Mama," Holly said. "Like yours."

"Honey?" Brandon said. He turned to Caitlin. "It's a hard thing—here she hasn't seen you in so long, and then you have to be going off again so soon."

"No I don't," Caitlin said.

"Yes you do," Holly said.

"You know what?" Caitlin said, rage distending the words. "Why don't we go to the beach right now, before some of us start to get mean?"

"What beach?" Holly said. "Besides, Brandon has to work this afternoon, and I have to help him."

"Now, sweetheart," Brandon said. "I've got to go out to Palmerola, load up all that stuff for Salvador. You don't want to hang around for that, do you?"

"Yes I do," Holly said to her plate in a particularly little voice.

"Well, I can go with you," Caitlin said.

"No you can't," Holly said.

Caitlin turned to her. "Enough," she said. "First you drag me to this terrible place, then you say I can't even come with you this afternoon."

"You can't," Holly said. "They won't let you. Besides, I didn't drag you anywhere. You invited yourself."

"I beg your pardon," Caitlin said.

"I'm sorry," Holly said. "I'm sorry."

"Well," Caitlin said. "I certainly did not invite myself."

"Well, you did," Holly said, "you certainly did. And now you're already complaining again, just like you always do. Just like you're some princess and I'm something that washed up one day on your—"

"Do we have to—" Caitlin said.

"You act like I come from a *pig*sty. You act like Daddy and I are I don't know whats. You're ashamed of me. Look— you can hardly even look at me."

"How can you say that! Do you think I would have stayed with your father for fifteen minutes if it hadn't been for you? If it weren't for you I wouldn't be able to recognize your father in a police lineup."

"That's *exactly* what I—"

"All *right*," Caitlin said. "If you don't want me here, I'll leave."

"So, good!" Holly said. "Leave! You think you can just show up somewhere and be all *charm*ing and—and *love*ly, and then whatever you've done won't matter, and someone will bail you out of whatever stupid slimehole you've fallen into. You think you can just walk away from anything and then by the time you turn around again everything will be just the way you want it to be. It makes me just want to throw *up*!"

"Honey?" Brandon said softly. "Sweetheart? We're in a *res*taurant." He turned to Caitlin. "She's overexcited."

"I can see that, Brandon," Caitlin said. "I'm her mother."

Brandon stood. "I'm just going to take her away now, and we'll give you a call later when we're feeling better."

"That's what *you* think," Holly said furiously. She stormed out of the room while Brandon held out his hand to Caitlin.

"Pleasure to meet you, ma'am," he said with opaque calm.

Jesus, Caitlin thought. How idiotic. Holly would be sorry later—she always was. But in the meantime . . . Oh, well. Out for adventures. She sighed and looked at the swamp on her plate; how on earth had the others managed to eat these miserable, depressing eggs?

The hilly streets were crowded. Puffs of dust and low, slowly roiling clouds veiled the chalky buildings and churches, and groups of black-haired schoolchildren in blue uniforms flowed around Caitlin, as yielding as a haze of gnats. Men and women passed with soft, despondent expressions; at first, Caitlin smiled cheerfully at them, but the smiles they returned were conciliatory and apologetic, as though hers were something to be evaded, or endured.

Those shorn boys on the plane had been soldiers, of course, Caitlin thought. But who were all these other Americans? Like the burly, red-faced boy who was drinking a beer as he walked. His bright red T-shirt came toward her. "FEED THE HOMELESS TO THE HUNGRY" it said. "Gramma's looking good," the boy himself said and belched into her ear as he lurched lightly against her.

She steadied herself at a low wall and rubbed her ankle, fuming. When she looked up she saw that she was in a stone plaza, where a knot of ragged people was forming around something. She joined the grimy crowd and saw at its center a man sitting on a blanket, surrounded by small heaps of dried plants, a large trunk, and jars of smoky liquid, inside of which indistinct shapes floated. Of course, Caitlin couldn't understand what he was saying, but his voice rose and fell, full of crescendos and exquisitely disturbing pauses, and his eyes glittered with irony as he gathered up all the vitality that had dissipated from his dusty audience and their torpor burned off in the air crackling around him.

The women in the crowd giggled and tilted their heads against one another's shoulders; the men squirmed and smiled sheepishly. Suddenly the man on the blanket went still. He stared, then lifted his arms high and plunged them into the trunk, from which he raised, as the women screamed and scattered, a great snake that seethed luxuriantly in his hands. Caitlin found herself clinging to a barefoot woman, who smiled to excuse herself, and then, as the crowd drew together again, the man on the blanket placed the twisting snake around his shoulders and reached into the trunk for a second time.

This time what he drew forth was a small white waxy-looking block. The crowd peered and craned. The man looked sternly back and silence fell. He passed his hand across the block, and as the crowd sighed like a flock of doves rising from a tree, the block began to foam.

In an instant the onlookers were rushing forward, drawing from their pockets bills as worn and dried out as they themselves were, which the man on the blanket collected, passing out bars of soap in a blur of speed.

And then it was over. The man had packed up his herbs and his snake and his trunk—the bottles and blanket, everything gone, leaving only a few dazzled lingerers and Caitlin, who was penetrated by a rich sorrow.

She took her compact out of her bag and looked in the mirror. *Oh*. Time to redo her makeup and sit down for a refreshing snack. She looked around. Hopeless. But up on the rim of town she saw a towering structure. Perhaps that was where all the cafés and nice shops were. To cheer herself up, she bought a clump of sticky candy from a little stand on the street to eat while she walked.

The steeply inclined streets curved up across little ravines choked with garbage, and, with every dip or turn as Caitlin drew nearer, the massive tower disappeared and then loomed again in the tinted, fumy air.

Up high the town was more prosperous. Houses were set back from the street behind dry gardens. Spectral cars slid by, their occupants invisible behind black glass, and muscular dogs strained at their tethers, baying as Caitlin passed, or snapping their teeth. She paused for a moment, breathless from the heat, and the garden beside her heaved—heavens, there was a man in camouflage clothing!—and she turned away quickly, to find herself right in front of the towering building. It was Harvey Gumbiner's hotel.

Beige light draped the vast lobby, masking clusters of people. "Praise the Lord," someone seemed to be saying, and something stirred in a deep chair. Pale men, like those on Caitlin's flight, spoke quietly, disclosing the contents of their briefcases to dark men in sunglasses. A group of backpackers with Bibles whispered in a corner. A breathtaking girl walked by dreamily with a blond man of about fifty, who looked permanently soaked in alcohol. He wound her long black hair around his hand. She whispered something to him, and he smiled, closing his eyes, her hair still coiled around his hand like a leash.

Caitlin found Harvey in the bar with a man named

Boyce—from the Embassy, Harvey explained. Boyce's eyes were inflamed, and he scratched at himself. "Allergies," he said unhappily and waved to a group of waitresses, who leaned against the bar, gazing out the window like convicts, or children. One disengaged herself, walking slowly, and shifting her weight from haunch to haunch. She stopped, swaying slightly, at their table, still looking out the window as though she were asleep.

"Is the rum here sensational?" Caitlin asked. The waitress smiled helplessly, then shrugged. "O.K.," Caitlin said. "What's to lose? Cuba libre, please. *Bless* you," she said to Boyce, who had choked.

When her drink arrived, she told Harvey and Boyce about the man with the amazing soap.

"That's impossible," Harvey said. "Soap that lathers without water?" He squinted at Caitlin. "How much did this 'soap' cost?"

"Two of those things," she said. "The red ones."

"Two lempiras!" Harvey said. "It cost two lempiras? That's damned expensive, you know—that's about a dollar."

"Seems reasonable." Boyce rubbed at his eyes. "If it doesn't require water. After all, they don't have water."

"Of course it requires water," Harvey said. "Soap requires water—I *know* soap. Obviously, it's some sort of trick. Two lempiras! You know, this is a very expensive country. I mean considering how damn poor it is. I stopped to buy some batteries this morning for my radio? And two batteries cost me thirteen lempiras! Now, I call that damned expensive."

"Well," Boyce said, waving his hand slightly, "what you see here in Tegucigalpa is a dual economy. The international community that's arrived with all the expansion confuses the picture; the wealthy Nicaraguan émigrés, the new-rich military——" He cleared his throat furiously. "Excuse me. No, what I mean is that the prices you're seeing confuse the picture, because those prices are for foreigners, not for Hondurans. Out in the smaller cities—Choluteca, for example—you don't see those prices."

Harvey frowned. "Still," he said. "I mean, look: two batteries for my radio cost me thirteen lempiras. Now, that simply has to affect the people in—what did you say? Choluteca."

"Well, *no,*" Boyce said. "Because my point is, the people in Choluteca *don't have radios.*"

"Ah. How do you do?" A well-dressed man had stopped at their table to address Boyce. "Excuse me, I shan't interrupt."

"Well," Boyce said. "Mr. Best." He looked away, but Harvey was already introducing himself and Caitlin. "O.K." Boyce sighed. "Might as well sit down."

"My, my," Mr. Best said. "I see that all our friends are arriving."

"*Oh* boy," Boyce said. "*That's* right—entire international press corps. Another couple of hours they'll be clogging the pool like lemmings."

Caitlin looked around and saw that men and women with large bags slung over their shoulders were filtering into the bar. "Why so many reporters?" she said.

Mr. Best smiled and motioned for drinks from a waitress who was idly stacking glasses in a pyramid at the bar.

"It seems, my dear," Harvey said, as the pyramid of glasses tumbled to the floor, causing convulsions of giggles among the waitresses, "that you and I have arrived on a rather tense day. The White House has announced that Nicaragua invaded Honduras last night."

"Oh, that's what it is," Caitlin said, trying to remember. "Honduras and Nicaragua are at war——"

"Well," Boyce said. The three men looked at Caitlin. "Not exactly."

Harvey glanced at Boyce, then turned to Caitlin and smiled. "You see, *we're* in Honduras. And Honduras is a democracy—everything is fine here. But next door in Nicaragua? Well, about nine years ago the dictator there—an extremely unattractive man—was overthrown—"

"By Communists," Boyce and Mr. Best said simultaneously.

"Yes," Harvey said. "And, of course, that's no good. So we give money to Nicaraguans who liked it better the other way—the Contras, they're called—to fight the new government. And we let the Contras encamp here in Honduras, where we can—"

"Excuse me," Mr. Best said. "One slight correction." He twinkled charmingly at Caitlin. "Honduras is a neutral country—the Contras are *not* here."

"No, the *point*," Boyce said loudly to Caitlin, "the point *is* that Honduras is a highly sensitive strategic area. Of course we have financial interests in the region—we've never attempted to deny that—but the point is that, *strategically* speaking, Honduras is money in the bank. And that's why the Soviets and the Cubans are stirring up these indigenous movements all over the place. Otherwise, *Jesus.* I mean, these people are pacific; they don't know what's going on—they're *farmers*, for heaven's sake. And that's the point, you see—that we're not just here because we go all gooey inside when we think about the relationship between free enterprise and democracy!"

Caitlin looked at him. She liked to travel. But this was not traveling.

"I can see that I haven't convinced you," Boyce said

gloomily. "I can see you think I'm overestimating the danger in order to justify intervention, or God knows what kind of things you've been reading. But that's not true, it's not *true*. Think of the proximity to the United States, think of Cuba, think of the Canal. When's the last time you really thought about the map? I want you to close your eyes and picture the map."

Caitlin took a sip of her drink, and in the reddish mist behind her eyelids tired, dusty figures—like the people in the stone plaza—scrambled across a confused surface. But then flat colors began to mass: the blue of North Carolina, sweet pink of New York, orange of California; little mountain ranges and lakes, little capitol buildings jogged up and down, waiting to be superimposed. They fanned out over the map, the map swung into the night, a light shone in North Carolina from Holly's room, where Holly sat alone, in her tiny rocker, cradling a bear, waiting. The rum came up Caitlin's straw again, washing it all away in a flood of gold as she opened her eyes to see Mr. Best watching her with a faint smile.

"'Mr. Best,'" she said slowly. He was dark, and very attractive. "Are you from Honduras?"

"I live much of the time in Tegucigalpa, but the import-export business requires an unfortunate amount of travel. It becomes a chore."

"Yes." She looked at him. "I'm an actress, so I know."

"Ah." Mr. Best raised his eyebrows. "An actress . . ."

"But just what brings you here?" Boyce said suddenly.

Really, Caitlin thought—from the moment she'd gotten to her plane people had behaved as though they'd never seen a tourist before. But she only glanced at Mr. Best and laughed. "My daughter's fiancé is in business here, and the two of them invited me down. So, of course, I drop everything I'm doing, I hop on a plane, and as soon as I get here they have to dash off to some other town. Pomarola, I think they said."

"Palmerola—" Boyce said.

"Palmerola," Harvey said, glancing at Boyce. "That's no town—that's the U.S. base, isn't it? Where the U.S. Army is?"

"*Honduran* base," Boyce said. "Where the *Honduran* Army is."

"Quite right." Mr. Best twinkled at Caitlin again. "The U.S. Army is not here."

"And just what," Boyce said, reddening, "does your daughter's fiancé do?"

The force of his interest confused Caitlin for a moment, but she composed herself in the calm emanating from Mr. Best and remembered the conversation at breakfast. "Oh, Brandon's quite the entrepreneur. He has his own plane and he flies around from country to country."

"Really," Mr. Best said thoughtfully. "A young man I ought to know. Let me give you my card; perhaps we could all meet for dinner one evening." Boyce stared in astonishment as Mr. Best extracted a card from his wallet, but when Caitlin reached over to take it Mr. Best frowned and replaced it. "Sorry," he said, selecting another, "that one was . . . incidentally—" He stood and turned to Boyce. "I believe I'm expecting something from you today?"

"Yes, yes, yes," Boyce said. He raked his hands through his hair. "Stop by the Embassy. See my secretary. . . . Oh, God," he said as Mr. Best left, "I'm so *tired*. Oh," he said sourly, as Lewis came through the entrance. "Hello, Lewis. Long time no see."

"'Long time no see,'" Lewis said. "Kinda catchy. Well, well, well, this appears to be a most congenial company."

Boyce picked petulantly at the label on his beer bottle, but Harvey held out his hand. "Harvey Gumbiner," he said.

"You're putting me on," Lewis said, drawing up a chair. "Hello, pretty lady." He patted Caitlin on the shoulder. Whatever "freshening up" meant to Lewis, it did not include changing his clothes.

"You two know one another," Boyce announced accusingly.

"So the joint's already jumpin', huh?" Lewis said.

Caitlin looked around. By now most of the chairs were occupied by journalists, and a small, good-looking dark girl with a camera over her shoulder pirouetted lazily by the window. "Attractive young people," Harvey said, looking at the girl. He picked up a handful of peanuts from a dish on the table and shoved them into his mouth.

"All waiting to watch the 82nd Airborne Division fall out of the sky," Lewis said.

"*What?*" Harvey said.

"Well, naturally," Boyce said sheepishly. "We could hardly not respond, could we? I mean 'Reds,' get it? '*Invading a democratic ally.*'"

"The *82nd Airborne!*" Harvey said, turning to Caitlin as though this were supposed to mean something to her. "Well, you and I certainly picked one hell of a day to show up."

"Relax," Lewis said. "There's no one here for them to fight with—this is a photo op."

"In fact," Boyce admonished, "this is a very important moment. Which requires documentation. Because when everyone back home sees this footage, of all these courageous paratroopers diving into the jungle, they're going to understand the danger; they'll see what an invasion means, and maybe then they'll get it through their heads why we're here. Why

I'm here, why I've been posted in this Goddamned cow town
for the last year and a half. Year and a *half*, mind you. No restaurants, no night life, white-trash hoodlums out at Palmerola *terror*izing the women. My *God*," he said to Caitlin. "I
mean, have you seen Guatemala *City*?"

"Cheer up," Lewis said. "A job's a job."

"What the hell is *this*—" Harvey interrupted. Caitlin followed his horrified gaze to where Ricky was goose-stepping
through the lobby in his khaki shorts and black gloves.

"Just Ricky," Lewis said. "On his way from the casino,
looks like."

"He's not *American*, I hope," Harvey said.

"We don't strictly have jurisdiction over him," Boyce said
stiffly to Harvey. "We don't strictly have jurisdiction over the
casino—"

"No, but if it *offends* you so painfully," Lewis said, "why
don't you just—"

"This is a free country," Boyce said shortly. "We intend
to keep it that way. Now, if you'll excuse us, Mr. Gumbiner
and I have a—"

Lewis picked up Boyce's beer bottle and waved it. "Be
our guests," he said. "Goodbye."

"That Boyce," he said as Boyce and Harvey disappeared
through the lobby. "You don't blame the laundromat 'cause
you've got dirty laundry, right? I mean, if you want clean
hands, stay out of the kitchen. Because people ought to stand
behind what they do. You should say, 'Well, look, these
things are what we do. Because we believe in certain things.
So we have to do certain things.'" There was something odd,
Caitlin thought, about his distant look, as though he were
peeking out from behind it to check her reaction. "Anyhow,"
Lewis said, abandoning whatever he'd been driving at, "I've

got to admit he's pretty cute. *Rotten* liar, isn't he? Poor guy, he's never going to get out of Tegucigalpa."

"He sure got out of here in a *hurry*," Caitlin said. *And* with Harvey, her fallback position for dinner.

"Hope it wasn't something I said." Lewis held up the beer bottle and nodded to a waitress.

"Hello, Lewis." One of the journalists sat down. "Sorry to interrupt."

"How sorry?" Lewis said pleasantly. " 'Cause I'm just curious."

The journalist closed his eyes and smiled briefly, turning his back to Caitlin. "Bingo," he said. "All kidding aside, though, I want to know something about this invasion."

"What's to know?" Lewis said, and winked at the waitress who was setting down his beer.

"I'd like to know, for example," the journalist said, "if there *was* one; I'd like to know, for example, if any Nicaraguans actually crossed the border."

"Got me," Lewis said. "No one knows where the border is. Yuk yuk. Of course there was an invasion, honey bunch—didn't you hear that on the news?"

"You know what, Lewis?" the journalist said. "Don't you ever worry that someone might mistake you for garbage and throw you to the sharks?"

"Look at me, pal," Lewis said, putting down his bottle. "What do I look like to you? Joint fucking Chiefs of Staff? If you want the story, why not go out and get it? Or better yet, why not just sit tight in Washington and listen while they tell it?"

"Thanks anyway, man." The journalist tipped his beer slightly and sauntered off, nodding self-consciously to the good-looking dark girl, who didn't see him.

"Rude little cliché-bound bastard," Lewis said. A muscle jumped in his arm. "I give the guy enough information to jam a memory bank, and look at the way he acts."

"So he's an asshole," Caitlin said. "That's his problem, not yours." She hadn't followed the conversation, but that much was clear. "And you were very open with him." She nodded. Then nodded again.

"Yeah." Lewis closed his eyes. "Well. Mutual respect, in a manner of speaking."

After a moment he opened his eyes again. "Look. Look at this spectacle; look at this mass of human waste. In a few hours, not forty kilometers away, the sky's going to be black with specks—the 82nd Airborne floating down, all the cameras in this room pointing up. Photographs of vines, photographs of specks, give the folks back home a look at what it means to live near Communism. What do you bet three-quarters of these jerk-offs were in Vietnam, photographing specks and vines? After a hard day's work, they're going to come back here, sit around the pool, talk about the old days. Sit around the pool here, Panama City, San Salvador, Managua, get all weepy about how they sat around the pool in Saigon, Vientiane, Phnom Penh, Bangkok. Hey, now they get to do it all again. Specks, vines, flames, buddies fallen in the line of duty yada yada, brings tears to the eyes." He paused and darkened. "You're thinking who am I to talk, right? Vines and specks, we all got a taste for it back then."

So . . . yes. So why *was* Holly here, exactly? "I hate this place," Caitlin said.

"So what are we waiting for?" Lewis said. "Fresh air! Countryside!" He motioned to the dreaming waitress for a check. "Come on, we're out of here."

Lewis's jeep clung like an animal to the road as it undulated away from town. Clay-colored earth covered with acres of shacks, made from what looked to Caitlin like garbage—cardboard, plastic, scraps of wood—gave way to sunlit valleys and grand, pine-covered hills. Caitlin gazed out the window, until Lewis switched on a tape and driving rock and roll obliterated the landscape. "Our sound," Lewis said. "But kids are still growing up on it. Isn't that wild? We were rebels, but we created this enduring institution. Now it's just one more thing that's always been there. But for me it always sounds like that time when it was just invented. Remember what it was like? Remember how loose and new everything was?"

Caitlin remembered. There was always something happening, and something good just about to happen—no end of things ahead. Someone always had money, night horrors were gone by morning, the nasty and boring bits melted away in rainbows. "We had fun," she said.

"Yeah," Lewis said. "We had fun. But you know what?" He frowned and switched off the tape. "For me, there was a certain parting of the ways from you guys. During the war they used to ship us over to Bangkok to chill out. And a lot of times, in the bars, we'd hear the new songs, we didn't know what was going on. The lyrics, I mean. What was everybody talking about? It was *our* home, right? I mean we were *representing* this place, we were fighting for its stuff, this was our generation. But evidently back at 'our home' there was this whole other life going on. So, I mean, who were *we* supposed to be?"

"Now look," Lewis said a few minutes later as they pulled off the highway onto a dirt road. "What do you see?"

"I give up," Caitlin said.

"That's right," Lewis said. "Nothing. You can zip up and down all day long and never know these villages are here."

And as he spoke, in fact, a little village was unfolding like paper flowers in a glass of water. First there was only the dusty road, and then there were oxen, with flowing horns and long Egyptian faces, and ribs that stood out, stretching their hides, yoked to a cart with great wooden wheels. A small boy sat astride one of the oxen, his ribs protruding, too, above his swollen belly. He sat and stared as the jeep passed, though Caitlin waved, and then the road was lined with painted walls, velvety in the sun, with openings that led into what must have been tiny homes or shops.

Lewis parked where the road stopped and the walls opened out onto a little village square waving with lilies, in the center of which sat a few wooden benches in the shade of an enormous tree, whose bluish bole shot up and up to a dense and massive dome of leaves floating, very green, against the deep, even sky. Tiny birds darted and chattered. In the heat, little yellow butterflies danced above the high grass, making the air around them flicker, but a chilly darkness was pouring down stone steps out of a church that faced the square. Doves, resting among the cracked angels on its immense wooden doors, ruffled up as Caitlin and Lewis passed through.

Phantom colors dropped from the high windows. A barefoot woman knelt, her hair streaming down her back, and far away, in the shaft of light that pierced the altar, Christ hung bleeding and serene in his perpetual agony. "Let's go," Caitlin whispered. "I want to go."

The heat was intense, but it didn't seem to bother Lewis. He guided Caitlin out behind the church to a lane where, inside tiny painted rooms, she could see some rough pieces of furniture, or a case or two of soft drinks and shelves that held a few cans or sacks of food. On one dirt floor huge and glossy avocados lay mounded like a heap of slumbering animals, and through another doorway Caitlin saw a circle of old men in coarse clothing playing oddly shaped stringed instruments. They sang in a fragile harmony, and a pale marine light came from their dark eyes as they listened intently to the notes their fingers released, their faces skeletal and papery. People disappeared inside as Caitlin and Lewis passed, and children hung back.

The lane branched off into mud paths. A stream glittered; beyond it low dwellings were nearly hidden by blossoms and vines that festooned them like hair ribbons. Caitlin looked around and saw no one. "Let's go," she said. "These people are strange."

"They're just paranoid," Lewis said. "Probably think we're looking for Communists."

"Why would they think that?" Caitlin restrained a childish giggle of apprehension.

"Why not?" Lewis said. "It's a good place, come to think of it. Look at these people—they're starving. Didn't you see their faces?"

As Caitlin looked again, a child burst from the wide silence and flashed across a field, all brown legs and bright tatters. Tiny points of fear sparkled across Caitlin's skin—she turned and ran herself.

Lewis caught up with her easily at the church. "Hey," he said, holding her by the wrist, "take it easy. I want to take your picture."

"Come on," Caitlin said. "Let's get out of here."

"I said I want to take your picture," Lewis said. "What's

the matter with you?" He turned her wrist until she fell back onto the stone steps. "Smile," he said, lifting a little camera she hadn't noticed him carrying.

She stood up, staring at Lewis in fury, and teetered for a second.

"Sorry," he said. "I get all excited to have English-speaking company.

"Look," he said, opening the car door for her. "Not bad, huh?" He handed Caitlin a little snapshot, newly extruded from his camera, in which she sat, an awkward smudge on stone steps, one hand grasping the other wrist.

She grasped her wrist as the road buckled and writhed beneath the jeep. She looked terrified in the picture, she looked ill. These people were starving—she wanted to talk to Holly. Could Holly have meant those awful things she'd said at breakfast? Where *was* Holly? Caitlin had come to see her. She wanted to see *Holly*. "I feel terrible," she told her.

"I didn't really hurt you"—but it was Lewis, answering lightly—"did I, sweetheart?"

"Lewis—" The heat was *phenomenal*; Caitlin wanted to reach under Lewis's shirt and dry her forehead on his soft, rosy T-shirt, but it was covered with dark, wet patches. "I don't feel good."

"You don't feel good?" Lewis glanced at her. "Listen, you didn't eat anything funny today, did you?"

"I didn't eat anything today," Caitlin said. "Just a bite of those shitty eggs at breakfast. And a piece of candy on the street."

"On the *street*?" Lewis said. "You *ate* something on the street?" And then Caitlin was sick all over his car.

"What, are you ignorant?" Lewis said later as he put her to bed in her hotel room. "You should never eat stuff on the street." The toilet, still flushing violently, crashed and thundered behind his voice. "Anyhow"—he poured a glass of water from a jug on the bureau—"take two of these little jobbies, and you'll be fine in a couple of hours."

"Lewis," she said. "Lewis . . ."

"I'll be checking on you later," he said from the doorway. "And I plan to see you as good as new. Now, you want me to send someone up about the toilet? 'Cause that thing is fucking barbaric."

Caitlin's eyes felt grainy and far too large. The room was grainy. It broke up into sizzling whorls of black and white dots; zigzags were breaking from her head. The sound of running water was supposed to be refreshing! Boyce said they didn't have water; so why didn't they take some of hers, whoever they were? Flowers and butterflies throbbed through the torrent—eyes glittered behind them. In the stone plaza, ragged throngs clamored for magic soap, its secret existence undetected by the imperial magnates who swarmed through the Miami airport, dangerously close. They weren't true, those things that Holly had said at breakfast, and the proof was that she was *here*. Why had she come, if not to see Holly, if not to see what had happened to all that time she'd had! And Holly was too harsh; things *could* be undone, with a little imagination—repositioned, seen in a different light. Except—except that she was so sick; because if she were sick and *dying*, then everything that had ever happened would stay forever, just the way it was right now.

Beyond the screen of Caitlin's illness Holly was sitting, dipped in some phosphorescent substance, happy, light. Caitlin struggled and thrashed, trying to call out to Holly, but it was Lewis once again who answered her. "Ready to get up?" he said.

"Did Holly leave?" Caitlin said.

"Holly?" Lewis said. "You've been asleep for hours."

"I have to talk to Holly," Caitlin said.

"They're not back yet," Lewis said. How had he gotten into her room again? He must have taken her key. "How about something to eat? We'll go down to the strip—check out *le tout* Tegoose."

"I'm not hungry," Caitlin said. "When is Holly going to be back? I want to wait for her."

"Forget it," Lewis said. "They won't be back. Not tonight. It's almost midnight now, and *no* one does these roads after dark. Anyhow, you should get out of here for a bit; get some air."

It was true. Caitlin felt weak and strange. The toilet still thundered, and this room that Holly had put her in was hot and sour and stinking.

In the floating pools of darkness by the elevator, two men in uniform lounged. "Relax, princess." Lewis guided her into the elevator, and the door shut her into safety. "Those guys weren't waiting for you." But they'd been carrying what must have been automatic rifles. Just like that man, Caitlin realized, she'd seen earlier in the garden near Harvey's hotel, though she hadn't taken it in at the time. Now he, and others she'd hardly noticed, began to march toward her, in their various uniforms, through her memory. They'd been by the side of the road, in shadow, now that she thought of it, yes they had, and in town, perched high above the thronging people, watching. On the way out Caitlin and Lewis passed by the restaurant, where waiters who looked like champions now circulated instead of the waitresses, sleek and unsmiling.

The streets were so steep and curving that now, in the dark, the little lights—the lights of street lamps and houses—appeared to be strung all up and down the air. "Yeah, it's pretty at night," Lewis said. "And pretty in the day when the sun's out—brightens it up like a little smile. Funny place to use as a control panel, though, isn't it? Wouldn't think to look at it that it's one of the premier cities in the U.S. Just like Chicago—except for this thing of location, I mean."

Lewis opened the door with a flourish onto his apartment—a single room one flight above a small, shuttered store. There was hardly any furniture—just a bed, a television, and a night table next to the bed which held a lamp, a carved box, an ashtray, and a fishbowl containing a little goldfish and an ugly ceramic castle. One of the walls, though, was layered like a child's bulletin board with clippings and photographs and insignia, including a Confederate flag and an Iron Cross. "Little TV?" Lewis said. He lifted his shirt to unstrap a holster and pistol, which he put down on the night table, and reached over to switch on the set.

It grew bright, and tiny men drifted across it in parachutes. Groups of them bloomed and bloomed, darkening the screen again, and then the scene was gone, replaced by the street where Caitlin had been walking earlier in the day. She saw the stone plaza in the background, and streaming by in the foreground children in school uniforms and crowds of men and women with their soft, defeated expressions. "But in downtown Tegucigalpa today," an announcer intoned sonorously, "it was business as usual for—"

"Enough?" Lewis said. He turned off the volume and sat down on the bed.

"Lewis—" Caitlin said. True, they hadn't been waiting for her, those guys by the elevator. But they had been waiting for someone. "Let me ask you something."

"Sure," he said. "Here, you pick." He handed her the carved box, which was filled with thick joints. "All export quality."

As she bent over him to accept a light, her glance fell on a snapshot pinned up among the things on the wall behind him. Although the figure in the snapshot seemed to be a man, the body was so mutilated that Caitlin could not be sure. Patches were torn from it, and the arms and legs were twisted, but the young face was shockingly intact.

"That was a union guy," Lewis said. "He stirred up a lot of big trouble in a lot of little towns. Hey, why the long look? Don't you understand what's going on? Don't you know what kind of world those people want us to live in?"

Caitlin handed him the joint and watched his eyes narrow with pleasure as he inhaled. They smoked for a while quietly, passing the joint back and forth, and Caitlin thought of her hotel room—the little room that had harbored her in her sickness. "Lewis—" she said.

"This is that guy's chain, in fact," he said, pulling at the neck of his T-shirt to reveal a silver chain. "You know, I never talked about this to anyone before, but I have this fantasy that the guy's got a wife somewhere—a widow. Very beautiful, very innocent, and she has this matching chain. And someday I'm going to see this beautiful Honduran girl somewhere with a bunch of little kids, wearing that chain, and wham—just like that I'll be married, have a family life of my own."

"What does Brandon do for a living?" she said.

"That what's been on your mind?" he said. "That what's been bothering you?"

She shrugged, watching him.

"Good," he said. "'Cause I was afraid you were getting bored with me."

"No," she said. Out the window the little lights burned merrily.

"Good," he said. "I'm glad to hear it. Well, you can relax. Brandon's strictly in transport. Well-regulated, high-paying, protected work. Mostly doesn't even know what his cargo is. Kids these days, very sensible—no romance in them at all. Butch—hey, Butch," he said, tapping the fishbowl. "Come say hello to my new friend. Isn't she pretty? Isn't my new friend Caitlin pretty? Ach," he said, turning away from the circling fish, "fuck you. To tell you the truth, Butch isn't particularly gregarious. You know, some people say that a fish is not a good pet because it's not an affectionate companion. But I say, hey—who are you to evaluate the affection of a fish? You look in the bowl, and you see what you see. Furthermore, that is one ridiculous way to approach the question of a pet. Because, for instance, what is a pet? A pet is another little consciousness to balance out the fact of your own, which can otherwise sometimes feel like—how can I put this?—like the whole bowl. So there a fish qualifies, right off the bat. Then you have to think, well, what are the specific features of a fish? And they are (a) a fish floats, which is a good quality in and of itself; (b) a fish does not have to be walked, which the same; and (c) a fish has a very wise, eternal type of nature. Whew." He took the little camera from his back pocket and stretched out on the bed with an arm over his eyes. "No high like a reefer high."

"No," Caitlin said. She accepted a fresh joint from him and sat down in the corner, leaning against the wall.

"Of course," Lewis said, "each fish as an individual is not eternal, which is the down side of fish. To give you an example: I was recently living in the Philippines. Got myself all set up with a fancy tank and a fish to match—a particularly beautiful and pleasing specimen, a sort of blue-and-yellow-banded disk with a flirty tail. Well, that fish swam up and down, around and around its little castle there, thinking its own private thoughts from one end of the day to the other. You could watch that thing for weeks on end and never move—no matter what you'd seen during the day, no matter what, that fish would put it all in perspective. It was a very beautiful being. But one evening I was having a little drink with some buddies, and one thing led to another and so on and so forth, and, what with this and that, by the time I got home, which was not for a couple of days, as it happened, when I walked in the door, there was that fish, lying on the surface, belly up."

"Maybe you should feed this one now," Caitlin said. The fish looked agitated; it was darting back and forth, bumping against the glass. "I think it's hungry." Or maybe it was suffocating—the bowl was filthy, with trailing bits of pale debris floating around in it.

For a moment Lewis seemed not to have heard, but then he lifted the ashtray from the night table and flung it against the wall. "Fucking fish," Caitlin heard him say through the noise of the impact, which was reverberating around and around her like a lasso about to snap tight.

Ten steps to the door, not more than ten. But the door itself was on the other side of the bed. Lewis lay back down, looking at Caitlin past the fish. "Hey," he said. "What are you doing down there on the floor?"

Those boys from the plane had looked so easily damaged, with their shorn heads, and dangerous, like a litter of newborn animals, squirming blindly, and clumsily exposing their tiny teeth and claws. "Do you have your orders?" the official at the airport had asked them softly, and they had nodded, pale and helpless.

"Come here," Lewis said. He reached over and unscrewed the bulb in the night-table lamp. The room flickered nervously in the greenish light from the TV, and the mounds of Lewis's reclining shape—his big legs, his broad torso and shoulders, the hair curling up from his forehead—looked to Caitlin like a landscape; perhaps little figures in parachutes were already beginning to choke the air beyond it, spreading out like spores all over the villages in the distance, the breathing hills and living valleys.

The day Caitlin had left, really left, Todd (by which time she was no longer welcome to stay) the sky had been as silken and pure as a banner. Holly had not cried at all that morning, or even seemed to understand.

When the taxi arrived to take her to the airport, though, Caitlin had cried. She'd knelt down beside Holly, holding Holly's little face in her hands, but Holly had hardly seemed to see her. "Can I go play with Patricia today, Daddy?" Holly had said, turning away as though Caitlin were invisible, as though Caitlin had simply ceased to exist. "Can I go play with Patricia?"

"Hey," Lewis said.

Caitlin started. She saw the fish darting and circling in the flickering light, bumping against the glass as though at any moment its cloudy little bowl could be a great fresh pond, strewn with leaves and flowers.

"Look," Lewis said, "I thought I told you to come here."

THE ROBBERY

From the bed where she lay with her feet propped up on a pillow, Jill could see out into her garden, now in its most lavish aspect, and beyond, over the hedge to the Binghams' lawn, on which their white house floated. It looked as pristine and enigmatic as a freshly ironed dress, but only two days before, someone had forced the lock on the door while the Binghams were out, and had raged through, appropriating some of their possessions and leaving others in ruins.

"We should have invited them tonight," Jill said.

"The Binghams?" Nicholas said. "We never invite the Binghams."

Nicholas, just out of the shower, was wrapped in the most beautiful, soft robe. As he walked by the window the last shining strokes of sunlight fractured around him as though he were an emissary from some wholly harmonious universe, and Jill was newly abashed by his perfection. But right behind him, across the lawn, the Binghams, previously so hale and confident, were falling at this very moment—turning and turning in bottomless space. Jill steadied herself, rubbing her cheek against Nick's robe as he sat down next to her. "It's just that I dropped over to see them after work today. They seemed so shaken. Really, we should make a gesture . . ."

"But we couldn't exactly invite them now, could we?"

Nick pinched a lock of Jill's yellow hair into a little switch and brushed at her face with it. "If you want, you can . . . *bring them a casserole.*"

Nick said it to amuse her, Jill knew, but occasionally she would be overcome by an actual little terror that he really did yearn for something beyond their enveloping domesticity, that he might simply disappear one day back into the city, the palace of steel and glass that rose above the lake, bright blowy evenings and nights dense with reflections and murmurs.

The city. As a child, Jill had driven in with her mother, to go to one of the stately old department stores, or to a matinee when the ballet came to town. She always wore one of her nicest dresses then, and Mary Janes with white knee socks. "Lock your door, Jill," her mother would say, and at that moment the earth seemed to become transparent, and they would drive toward its center, penetrating worlds and then worlds. When they reemerged on the surface, which was settled on a human scale with houses and shrubs and newly covered driveways, her mother would draw in her breath deeply, and the road would heal up behind them and become opaque. But later the hidden day would emit around Jill the troubling light of a dream, and she could see herself and her mother sitting across from one another in the wood-paneled restaurant that smelled deliciously of rolls; she could see how they'd watched from the red plush seats as tiny figures spun and trembled on the distant stage, how they'd driven without stopping past sidewalks that glittered with glass and heat where congregations of thin black people sat on stoops fanning themselves and staring with inturned concentration and then along lakeside boulevards where the very rich strolled in the breeze and mild sun.

"Don't go away," Jill said, reaching as Nick stood.

He smiled and disengaged himself. "So, who are we to-night?" he said, disappearing into the dressing room.

"No one exciting, I'm afraid," she said. "Bud and Amanda. Kitsy and Owen."

"No one exciting!" he said. "Had you not realized that Kitsy has ensnared Bud?"

"Nick, no." Jill frowned. "What makes you think such a thing?"

"A deep source," Nick said. "No, but after all—subtlety is hardly Kitsy's strong suit."

"What is it about me?" Jill said. "I never see these things."

"You," Nick said, "are not meant to see such things."

Jill surveyed her distant toes for a moment. "Poor old Owen. Poor Amanda. Anyhow," she said, "I don't believe it." Jill never believed the intermittent tales about Kitsy. She suspected that people made them up simply because Kitsy was so irresistibly unlikely a subject of the stormy infatuations and disappointments to which she was rumored to be susceptible. And Kitsy and *Bud*! No, impossible.

" 'Poor Amanda'?" Nick said. "Is that what I heard you say? 'Poor *Amanda*'? Poor Owen, yes. And poor Bud—obviously he's only obliged Kitsy in order to get some response from 'Poor Amanda.' But you watch—Poor Amanda won't even do Bud the courtesy of being jealous."

"Oh, dear. Well, in any case—" Jill sat up slowly, appearing in the mirror behind Nick. "I suppose I should go downstairs and see how things are going." Was it the light, or were there circles under her eyes?

Nick concentrated on the mirror, toweling his wet hair. "Amanda's problem is that she considers herself to be irresistible."

"Well, she is very beautiful," Jill said, letting herself lie back again into the square of sunlight that spilled over the pillow, "as even you must admit. And I think you're hard on her. She loves Bud, in her own way."

"I wouldn't absolutely count on that if I were you," Nick said, but he turned from the mirror to smile directly at her.

Jill really did like Amanda, and so, she was sure, did Nick. Nonetheless, it was partly for the pleasure of Nick's protests that she would praise Amanda, whom she had known ever since Amanda had arrived, the new girl in Jill's sixth-grade class, from California, the golden place where people's fathers went when they got divorced. Amanda, equipped with bright loops of hair and an amazing charm bracelet, had been immediately and steadily the center of attention, and even then, her calm, puzzled stare of displeasure had been a terrible thing.

"Oh, and Susan and Lyle are coming," Jill said. "Is that better, or worse?"

"That's good," Nick said, returning his attention to his hair. "I like them. And it's fun to be charming to Susan."

"Nick, that's wicked. You know it makes her uncomfortable."

"It doesn't," Nick said. "Why?"

"Because," Jill said, and stopped. It amused Nick, she knew, that she considered her Jewish friend exotic.

"Because why?" Nick said.

"Because she's—oh, you know Susan. I mean she's so . . . *intelligent*," Jill said, and was rewarded as Nick exploded in laughter and gathered her up.

"You're wonderful," he said. "Do you know that? You're perfect." And Jill tingled with a sheepish pride, like a child who has fortuitously performed some clever act. "By the way," Nick said, stepping back to study her, "how are you feeling?"

"Fine," she said. Although actually, she noticed, she was feeling rather queasy. "Much better."

There had been no need, after all, for Jill to check on anything in the kitchen, where Roo had everything completely in hand.

"Dressing—" Jill said. "Should I make some?"

"All done," Roo said.

"And the silver?" Jill said.

"Everything's done, Mrs. Douglas," Roo said.

Four years earlier, when Roo had come to work, Jill had asked to be called by her first name, but Roo had simply, magically, caused the suggestion to vanish. Although the small formality had come to appear to Jill an implicit and constant antagonism, at the time she had hardly noticed—she had been far too grateful to have someone in the house who could take care of things so marvelously well.

It was Amanda who had arranged it. Jill had been about to have Joshua, but she hadn't wanted to leave work, and she had interviewed, she told Amanda, full scores of half-wits and psychopaths. Then, one week before Joshua was due, Amanda called. "Lucky Jill," she said. "I've got something for you."

Subsequently, Amanda had not only become further involved with Roo but had involved herself with Roo's family as well. Amanda had helped out financially when Roo had her own baby, James, two years ago, and Amanda had helped Roo's sister May get into a nurse's training program. Moreover, Amanda successfully waged an ongoing campaign to shame the entire neighborhood into providing odd jobs for Roo's older brother, Dwayne, though he was too passive and defeated, Jill thought, to do a decent job of anything, even were he not taking drugs. And so, suppose she were to go completely insane and fire Roo because she couldn't stand the tension, Jill had several times reminded herself, the fact was she would have to answer to Amanda.

Happy shouts floated into the kitchen from the yard. Jill went to the window and saw Joshua and James working away with paper and crayons in the back yard, under the casual supervision of Katrina, who lay next to them, sunbathing. "It sounds like the boys are having fun," Jill said.

Roo relented and smiled.

"I think I'll go out and inspect," Jill said. She hoped Roo didn't think her own little smile was cowardly.

"Joshua is making a portrait," Katrina said, shading her eyes from the late glare and smiling up at Jill. She pulled up the straps of her inadequate bathing suit and sat up. Jill looked away for an instant. If she were that girl's mother, she thought, and then remembered that Katrina's mother was someone far away. "What is your picture, Joshua?" Katrina said.

"Mommy," Joshua said, without looking up. He was absorbed, or so it seemed, in his drawing, and Jill obligingly bent over to admire it: yellow crayon hair, round blue crayon eyes, pink crayon cheeks—it could have been a drawing of Nick's idea of her. "How pretty, darling." And what a dazzling little boy Joshua was; how exactly like Nick. "Thank you."

"This is a picture of you, Mommy," Joshua insisted with academic clarity.

"And what about James?" Jill bent down over James's squiggle-covered paper, and James looked up at her wide-eyed. He was so dark—much darker than Roo. "What is that, James?" she said.

"Mommy . . . ?" James said. He looked at Joshua, who did not respond.

Jill resisted a potent impulse to pick James up. Her new

baby would be—she was sure of it—much more approachable than Joshua, sweetly dependent, and cozy.

"That's mine——" Joshua yelled, grabbing for a crayon that James had casually reached for, and James started to wail as the crayon split in two.

"Joshua," Jill said. "You've frightened James."

"He broke it." Joshua's face was bare with outrage. "It was mine. I was using it, and he took it."

"It will work just as well like that," Jill said. "Look—poor James. He's frightened."

Joshua stared at her. "This is really not fair," he announced.

"Look, Joshua——" Katrina said. "Look at that little animal in the tree! What is that called? Look, look, look——" And Joshua did look while Katrina picked up James, who was now bellowing with sorrow.

It was too complex, Jill thought as she returned inside, it was too difficult. How could Joshua be expected to know how to behave or to feel? And James—surely it couldn't be good for James. Of course Jill wanted the boys to be together on an entirely equal basis, but there could be no pretending that their situation was identical—how could there be? With Roo *working* in the house? It would be transparently false of her to pretend such a thing, and therefore unsettling to both the boys.

Yet, even as it was, she felt that she seemed to be in the wrong about something, and that no matter what she did—since things would necessarily remain unsatisfactory in one way or another—it would still seem to be she who was in the wrong. But what more could she do? Every action, every thought, was fastidious. Yet it was as if they were engaged in some secret war, the terms of which were known only to

Roo. Well, she was just going to have to speak frankly, she decided, as she stepped into the kitchen. "Roo—" she said.

"Yes, Mrs. Douglas," Roo said, but the blood that was crashing in Jill's ears drowned out her thought.

"I don't know what I was about to say," she said. "Isn't that silly? Oh—in any case, I tried to think of anything I might need Dwayne for, but I'm afraid I don't have anything right now."

Roo didn't glance at Jill, though she must have known, Jill thought, that she was desperate to have something done about the garage. "Yes, Mrs. Douglas," Roo said.

"At least there isn't anything at the moment," Jill said.

Still, perhaps it was best that Roo understand that Jill did not intend to have Dwayne around her house again. After the last time, when he'd done the floors, Jill had been so concerned that she actually checked the silver, as absurd as that was, she realized when she calmed down. But he had been so high—"I'm sorry," Jill said.

"Dwayne's out in St. Louis now, anyhow," Roo said. "He's got something steady."

"Well, that's wonderful," Jill said. Wonderful, though if Roo had only bothered to mention it earlier, they could have avoided this dangerous exchange.

"Mother," Joshua said from right next to Jill.

"Hey, now," Roo said. "Where did you come from?"

"Mother, do I get to help you?" Joshua said.

"Aren't you going to say hello to Roo?" Jill reminded him.

"I want to help you," Joshua said.

"Don't whine, please," Jill said. "We're all finished. Look, Roo's even finished with the fruit salad."

"Roo?" Joshua said.

"Yes, baby." Roo ruffled his hair, and he smoothed it out automatically.

A year or so earlier Jill had been bringing a stained table-cloth down to the basement to be laundered, and there was Joshua, sobbing in Roo's arms, absolutely shrieking, really, with an extravagance that was unfamiliar to Jill, as Roo rocked him. When they saw Jill, Joshua stopped crying immediately, and Roo set him down. Joshua walked out then, right past Jill, and Roo turned back to her work as Jill stood, holding the tablecloth. The truth was that Jill had been riven by jealousy at the time. Of course she was ashamed of her jealousy later, and she had regretted that, after the episode, Joshua had become so formal, really rather distant with Roo. Still, even that formality was better than the actual rudeness Joshua was displaying this afternoon. Where could he be picking that up?

"Roo," Joshua said, "is James coming back again Tuesday?"

"Depends on whether May's working Tuesday," Roo said. "If May can't mind him for me, I'll have to bring him."

Joshua sighed theatrically and scuffed his feet.

"Joshua," Jill warned.

But Joshua overrode her. "He doesn't play right. He breaks things. He's too little."

"I know, baby," Roo said. "That's why you've got to be patient with him." But Joshua shook her hand from his shoulder, sighed again, and scuffed his way loudly to the screen door, which he allowed to slam behind him.

"I don't know what *that's* all about," Jill said, burning. "He adores James. He's always asking for James."

Altogether it was a relief when the doorbell rang. Owen and Kitsy were the first to arrive, and when Jill opened the door, Owen was already in the middle of a bow. "Goodness me—" he said. His voice was a graphitelike emollient, a granular medium in which the words spread out soothingly.

Jill laughed and kissed him. How innocent he made the world seem; he was so completely himself, rueful and mysterious, precariously balanced, like an underwater explorer. Behind thick, gogglelike glasses, his eyes swam in unstable magnification.

"Mosquito," Kitsy said, slapping.

"Uh-oh," Nick said. He put an arm around Kitsy and gave Owen a pleased, telegraphic nod. "Let's run for cover."

"Let us," Owen said, wandering inside. "Possibly the shelter of the bar . . ."

"What to drink?" Jill asked.

"They've got me on Scotch tonight," Owen said vaguely.

"Gin-tonic, please, darlin'," Kitsy said. "A healthy one. I've been doing battle with the tomatoes all day." Kitsy smoothed back her oat-colored hair as her attention traveled across the room, randomly encountering and dismissing objects. "I don't know how you do it all," she said. "And with a job. Jobs, tomatoes, Joshua . . ." Could it be true, Jill wondered, about Kitsy and Bud? Kitsy was so . . . like a parakeet on a perch—blinking and rounded over her prim little feet. But when the doorbell rang, Kitsy didn't move, though her eyes brightened and narrowed.

Bud and Amanda and Susan and Lyle arrived in a clump and were reabsorbed, after some initial milling, into configurations that left Jill with Bud and Susan. Bud looked controlled, Jill saw—possibly furious, and when, in another part of the room, Amanda laughed, he closed his eyes almost blissfully for an instant, before turning his attention, with surplus force, to Susan. "So where do you get all these wonderful garments, Susan?" he said, tugging at a tassel on the large shawl she wore.

"Oh—" Susan waved her hand and laughed, but Bud waited unyieldingly with a half-smile and lifted eyebrows. "All

right," Susan said. She cleared her throat. "Well, this particular
one's from Mexico. And it is lovely, thank you, Bud, isn't it?"
She turned to Jill, and her large eyes looked lost, and metallic.
"You know, when Lyle and I were back in March, we didn't
see anything of this caliber. Hardly any cotton at all, in fact.
Isn't that odd? It was my understanding that they grew it."

"Cash crop," Bud said. "Grow it for export."

"Oh, yes," Susan said dubiously. "Well, that doesn't sound
so good, does it?"

Clearly Bud was beginning to enjoy himself now, Jill saw,
that Susan was flustered. Really, he was rather attractive with
that little space between his teeth and his raffish, dark halo of
receding hair. "Hear you've been having the worst kind of
trouble with that painter you and Lyle have in your beach
house," he said.

"Gracious, this *drink*," Susan said. "Naughty Jill." But Bud
only looked down at his glass and swirled the ice patiently, so
Susan, patting at a fan-shaped ornament that was struggling
upward from her heavy hair, sighed and continued. "I'm afraid
it did turn into a bit of a melee," she said.

"What a shame," Bud said. "But very generous of you
and Lyle."

"Well, the man's an enormous talent," Susan said. To her
astonishment, Jill saw Kitsy direct a damp, shining glance in
their direction, but Bud shifted slightly, so that his back was
squarely to her. "And the dreadful truth is that Lyle and I
hardly ever use the place. So we thought, now isn't it criminal to waste it like this when there must be—oh, well . . ."
She laughed self-deprecatingly.

"Not a bad way to pick up a bargain," Bud said. He laughed
along with her, then made an elaborate display of sobering.
"Oh, Bud, how vulgar," he said in falsetto.

"Not that Lyle and I minded for ourselves," Susan said, reddening. "But the Foleys found trash all over their beach. And they actually had to call the police about the noise . . ." Bud clucked sympathetically.

Susan, having gained momentum, was now irrepressibly confidential. "We did manage to get him out finally," she said. "But there was quite a scene. He *pointed* his finger, and accused Lyle of 'artistic imperialism' if you can believe it."

"Artistic imperialism—" Jill laughed. "My!"

"Yes—" Lyle said, joining them. Towering over Bud, Lyle rocked mournfully back and forth on his toes, and pushed his floppy hair behind his ear in discomfiture. "It really was funny." Jill smiled at his baffled sorrow and put an affectionate hand on his arm. He was like a gigantic boy, with those glasses and that pink, open mouth.

"Mrs. Douglas—" Roo said. She stood just behind the entrance to the living room, holding James.

"Yes, Roo," Jill said. Roo had changed into very high heels and a white dress that Jill had kept in the closet for two years after Joshua was born, before coming to terms with the probability that she would never fit into it again. "Come in."

"I'm just saying the taxi's come," Roo said.

"Oh. Well, thank you, Roo." But she'd never—she'd never seen Roo actually wearing the dress. "Good night, then."

"Oh, Roo," Kitsy called. "Don't you look stunning." And there was a silence as Roo turned slightly to readjust James, exposing the fine articulation of her arms, and her narrow bare back. Where could she be going like that, Jill wondered. And with James—

"Hello, James," Amanda said, raising her glass slightly.

"And will I see you on Tuesday, then, Roo?" Jill asked senselessly.

"Yes, Mrs. Douglas," Roo said, her face scrupulously expressionless.

Jill sighed. If only there were still people in the world like the people who had worked for her parents—people made flexible and melodious by their hard lives; special, quiet people with gentle hands and outlandish, old-fashioned names. Jill remembered one woman in particular, Evaline, and her husband, Vernon, who had helped occasionally in the yard. Jill hadn't thought about them in years, she realized with surprise. How she had adored them! But then once—sometime, she did not remember when, sometime when she was a child—her mother had told her something: a story about a past that Vernon and Evaline had in common, things that had happened before they'd met, even before they'd been born.

And the story was (Jill's mother had been doing her nails, Jill remembered, when Jill had gotten her to tell it) that Vernon and Evaline each had a grandparent, or grandparents, who had been slaves, whose own parents had been taken to America—kidnapped away from their families, bound up in chains, and put on boats with other prisoners whose language they could not understand. And then they had been brought to America and sold.

Jill stood very still. She felt as though she knew what her mother was telling her, but did not know, at the same time, and she wanted her mother to tell her again, but for some reason she did not dare to say so. " 'Sold'?" she repeated very, very quietly.

"That's what I said, Jill." Her mother spread out her fingers and stared at her nails with a sorrowful, absent irony.

So, they'd been sold. And bought—just like the little lizard Jill's father had bought at the circus for her. "But you must never, never mention this to them," her mother said. "They would be terribly hurt."

Jill's throat was dry, and her skin prickled oddly. "Why, Mother?" she said.

"Because," her mother said. Then she looked at Jill, as though Jill had just come into the room, and stood up. "Because, Jill, it was their own people who did that to them." And after that, Jill had felt very shy with Vernon and Evaline.

"How she does it," Kitsy said, when the door closed behind Roo. "And that adorable little boy."

"You send her home in a taxi?" Bud said.

Jill laughed, and the memory of Evaline and Vernon and her mother dispersed. "Do you think we're rich like you? Just to the station."

"I was going to *say*," Bud said.

"I suppose she has to go all the way to the far side of the city," Kitsy said. "What a saint that girl is—but, oh, that dreadful brother!"

"The Utterly Worthless Dwayne," Nick said.

"Not utterly," Amanda said, and sat down. "Roo adores him." She crossed her legs and surveyed the little gold sandal dangling from her high-arched foot. "He practically brought her up, you know."

"Be that as it may"—Kitsy addressed Amanda's shoe— "things are otherwise now."

"Mmm," Amanda said. And in the pause Kitsy's comment flopped about like a stranded fish. "Incidentally," Amanda added, "he's doing something creative about his problem, finally."

"You don't mean to say he's hocked his needles?" Nick said, and Bud laughed shortly.

"How ashamed you'll be, Nicholas," Amanda said, "when

I tell you that he's joined a drug-rehabilitation program in St. Louis."

"A drug-rehabilitation program—" Jill frowned. "Are you sure? That's not what Roo—"

"Of course I'm sure." Amanda raised her eyebrows slightly. "I helped him get into it."

"Quite a triumph, Amanda," Nick said. "But it could be short-lived."

Amanda smiled faintly, but Jill was distressed: It was part of Nick's charm that he was contrary, absolutely intolerant of hypocrisy. But therefore—because he considered Amanda's activities to be merely adornments that issued from vanity rather than conviction—Amanda could provoke him into assuming and defending truly unattractive postures.

"After all," Nick said, "this is your little project, not his, isn't it, Amanda. A man like Dwayne is almost certain to drop out. Just look at the statistics."

"Nick," Jill said.

"He'll tear through a wad of state money," Nick said. "Or Bud's money, if that's what it is, and then he'll drop out, and we'll all be back where we started, except that his self-esteem, and Roo's hopes, will be shattered."

"I'm sorry to admit," Kitsy said, "that I think Nicholas has a point."

"Oh, my—" Owen's voice spread into the room. "Look at this tray, all undefended and just littered with shrimp."

"These *are* delicious, Jill," Lyle said. "Anyone else? Kitsy? Amanda? Bud?"

"No, thanks," Bud said. "So how's life in the futures, Lyle?"

"What?" Lyle said. He looked up, his mouth open. "Oh, picking up, Bud, thanks."

"The thing is, Amanda"—Nick leaned back in his

chair—"you're not doing anybody a favor. Dwayne is just pulling your strings."

Amanda made a little face at Nick and pushed her gleaming bracelets up her arms. "You do have to agree," she said, "that Dwayne would have had a very different life if it hadn't been for the war."

"Isn't it strange, Amanda," Nick said, "how everyone would have had a different life if it hadn't been for everything? Certainly I agree that men like Dwayne had a very hard time. Yes, it was easier for white kids to avoid the draft; yes, the men who did end up fighting were treated pretty badly—and by people who never had to confront the issue of what they themselves would have done if they'd been drafted. But you've got to remember, Amanda, that it's possible to have any number of responses to a problem, and I think that *you'll* agree with *me*: no one *has* to take drugs, and no one *has* to become a criminal. Now, I was as opposed to that war as anybody in this room. But in hindsight, we see—whether we like it or not—that, once there, we should have stayed there. Look what happened the minute we left. But here are Dwayne and his friends, behaving as if they're the only people in the world who ever had a difficult time. 'Oh, us poor black veterans—sacrificed to do the dirty work of the U.S. government . . .' Well, of course I'm sympathetic to their situation— it's unfortunate; no one would deny it, but the truth is that this position of theirs is untenable. And it's disingenuous. Because, in point of fact, it was those very men who stood to *gain* from being in the army. They picked up some valuable skills, they picked up a free education—"

For a moment Amanda's face was white, but then she laughed and shook back her hair. "You're really quite a Nazi, you know, Nick," she said.

"And don't you forget it, Fräulein," Nick said, smiling at her slowly.

"Frau, to you." Amanda smiled slowly back.

"Jill—" Owen glided in front of her, severing her attention from—from what? Jill felt a gust of irritation. "Now I have a serious question for you," he said.

Nick got out of his chair and walked to the window. He stared out, in the direction of the Binghams'.

"And that question," Owen said, "is this. Does Joshua plan to put in an appearance before dinner, or must I hunt him down?"

"I'm afraid I told him he had to stay upstairs," Jill said. "He was a horror this afternoon."

"Not Joshua," Kitsy said. "It's not possible."

"Alas, it is." Jill stopped for a moment, overcome. "In fact—well, as a matter of fact he was gruesome to poor little James. And absolutely rude to Roo."

"Roo-too-roo," Lyle said. "Roo-too-roo—"

"What are you saying, Jill?" Nick said, turning from the window as Lyle tossed a shrimp in the air and caught it in his very pink mouth.

"The truth is," Jill said, "I think Joshua sometimes resents sharing Roo." She didn't dare look at Nick. "And Katrina."

"He knows how to share," Nick said. "I've seen him share very generously with his friends."

"It must be hard for him in his own house, though," Kitsy said.

"Certainly," Bud said. "I know I wouldn't share Katrina with anyone."

"No one imagines you would, Bud," Amanda said, as Kitsy erupted in a volley of tiny coughs.

"Excuse me," she gasped. "Swallowed."

"This is something I don't enjoy hearing, Jill," Nick said.

"He was just tired today, honey," Jill said. "I don't think Katrina gave him his nap."

"Nick," Amanda said quietly, "you're making a scene over nothing."

Nick looked at her, then took a large swallow of his drink.

"In any case," Owen said, taking Jill's arm gently, "I'd quite like to see the little viper."

"He'll be thrilled, Owen," Jill said. "He was asking for you all afternoon." And at that moment, she felt so grateful to Owen that she might have been telling the truth.

Upstairs, Joshua welcomed Owen with a bonhomie and poise that caused Jill's eyes to brim. He presented Owen with a select offering of toys and stood back as Owen, sprawled out on the floor, affected to be defeated by the workings of first one, then another. "Don't be discouraged, Mr. Plesko," Joshua said. "These things take time."

Owen put down a little plastic hammer and sighed. He really did look sad, Jill thought.

"Does Mrs. Plesko like toys?" Joshua asked.

"Mrs. Plesko has a way with a toy," Owen said. "She's younger than I am, you know. By virtually hundreds of years."

"Do you think she'd like to come play, too?" Joshua asked hopefully.

"No more come-play tonight, Mr. Joshua," Katrina announced from the doorway.

"Katrina—" A bolt of candor cleared Owen's face as he struggled to his feet, and his eyes loomed up behind his glasses like fish.

Katrina lifted her light, springy hair from the back of her neck for a moment and smiled at Owen. "Joshua," she said. "It's time for our bath."

Owen's expression had resumed its unclear underwater shiftings, but Jill had seen enough. "Well, Katrina," Owen was saying, "it looks like you've been in the sun." He looked down at his shoes.

"This sun—" Katrina closed her eyes and leaned her head back. At the opening of her shirt, Jill saw, was a little triangle of skin that glistened as white as her teeth. "I could spend my whole life under this sun . . ."

Owen started to speak but looked down at his shoes again instead.

"So, Joshua." Katrina smiled. "Are we ready?"

But Joshua had gone oddly sullen. "I have to see my dad first," he said. "Tell my dad to come upstairs."

"He can't," Jill said sharply. But then she knelt and hugged Joshua so hard he squeaked. "I'm sorry, darling. Not right now." As they went downstairs together, neither Jill nor Owen spoke.

Everyone else had gone out into the garden, and Jill and Owen, drawn out behind them through the French doors, were able to disengage from their distressed intimacy. Jill paused on the terrace and watched as the others fanned out across the sloping lawn. They drifted alone or in twos among the spires of delphinium, and the peonies, whose huge blossoms shed a waxy glow and a lovely, tormenting fragrance. The colors of the lawn and the flowers intensified with the dark; the night was saturated with the concentrated colors of summer. Beyond the hedge, lights showed in the top story of the Binghams' house. Little clusters of sound sparkled in the air like fireflies—the chiming of glass, leaves clicking against one another, Amanda's tiny, shimmering laugh. Jill closed her eyes, and the sounds intermingled, into a distant surf. For a moment, Nick was behind her. His hand moved up her neck, then down. He let her hair glide through his fingers. When she opened her eyes, he was gone.

By the time they all sat down to dinner, they had become an ensemble; the night and the garden had uncoiled the skein of associations and habits, memories and dependencies that ran between them, dropping it over them in a loose net. Jill lifted her glass, and the amber sea in it moved—these were her friends.

Bud was asking Owen's advice about a lawsuit he was considering bringing against an account, Lyle was counseling Kitsy about London hotels, Nick was unusually animated—Susan *was*, in fact, enjoying the focus of his charm, Jill saw, as he embarked on a lengthy and involved anecdote; her large eyes misted with effort as she nodded, listening intently. "But how true!" she said earnestly when Nick completed his story and burst out laughing. Amanda twirled between her fingers a little flower she had broken off in the garden, smiling at it quizzically.

"Isn't that the Bingham house?" Lyle asked. "Right next door?"

A silence fell. "Yes . . ." Jill said.

"So terrible," Kitsy said.

"Just what exactly was it that happened?" Lyle asked.

"Well, it might not seem like much to you," Kitsy said. "But it was devastating for them."

"No," Lyle said, "all I meant was—"

"Of course they're insured," Kitsy said. "But it's their privacy, isn't it? And to have one's own home *invaded* like that! Those poor old people—they never did anyone any harm."

"I don't know," Bud said. "Spencer's a hard man on the golf course."

Kitsy cast a reproving glance at her fork. "You know what I mean, Bud," she said.

"Doesn't he make pesticides?" Susan said, and looked brightly around the table. "I mean, didn't Mr. Bingham manufacture pesticides?" she said.

"Well——" Nick stopped smiling. "Actually, there are new studies indicating that if pesticides aren't used, a plant will produce its own, much more toxic, sub——"

"That's so strange," Susan said. "Or really, there's nothing really strange about it, is there? And that's—I mean, Mr. Bingham manufactured pesticides and there's nothing strange about that, and someone broke into his house, and there's nothing strange about *that*, either. But don't you sometimes have the terribly vivid sensation that under this thing we refer to as 'life' is something that—how do I say this?—that there is this thing going on, and we *make* it, or it makes itself, possibly, and then there is this other thing that it looks like, or seems like, which is only sort of a top view of the first thing. A reflection, if you see what I mean. And usually those two things are exactly alike, or at least, reasonably alike. Or—well, I suppose you might say, they coincide, the bottom and the top. So, in any case, it's as though we decide what our lives are going to be like—we deal in futures, or we manufacture pesticides, or we take a trip to Europe, or whatever it *is*, and everything seems to be just the way we've planned it, because, in the vast majority of instances, it *is*. Exactly the way we've planned it. And so the thing that we think is going on is just like the thing that *is* going on, and everything is just the way we've decided it ought to be. But sometimes the . . . the thing on the top and the thing on the bottom are completely different—they've *diverged*, somehow, and we wouldn't even know that they'd diverged, except sometimes the thing on

the bottom just pops *out*, it pops out! *Into* the top thing. Because, suppose, for instance, that one of us—oh, goes to Venice, for example, and just falls into a canal. Well, I don't
suppose any of us would do that, but I mean people still *die*,
for example. Not that that's exactly—but, you see, things are
going on in some continuous way, somehow, and, in a sense—
Well, look. If you have a party, then people talk to other
people. Things happen between people. Or even just happen,
like somebody's baby has Down's syndrome, just to mention
a—well, happen. When there isn't anything to do about it,
nothing, nothing, nothing at all to do about it, because things
only happen in one direction—"

Susan stopped, and a laugh bounced slowly out of Owen,
like a rubber ball falling down steps.

"It's strange," Susan said, turning to him. "I don't know
what I mean . . ."

Susan was never much of a drinker, Jill thought. But in
fact she herself was expanding outward, and the few sips of
wine she'd had with dinner were causing everything to pass
over the convex surface of the evening in long, slow, luminous flashes. Nick, at the other end of the table, seemed to be
at the other end of a tunnel; the gentle sounds of conversation
rode at the margins of a darkness enclosing her.

There had been things—there was something about
Owen . . . She had been angry, if she wasn't mistaken, but the
anger had consumed itself, leaving an ashy void. And something had happened—oh, Nick and Amanda had had . . . was
it a quarrel? about Roo and her brother; and something had
happened with Roo—yes, Roo had been wearing Jill's *dress*,
of all things. And before that was when Joshua had been so
bad. And before that—oh, yes. Before that, she had visited
the Binghams. Of course; she had visited the Binghams, and

that must be why she felt so sad. And so ill, really—like an apple with a hidden soft spot spreading under the skin. It must be because of her visit to the Binghams that everything seemed so flat and bad—so stained.

Although Hattie and Spence Bingham lived right next door, they and their house seemed to belong to an earlier era, distant in space as well as in time. They were near eighty, Jill thought, though they'd never looked anything like it until today, when they had looked much, much older. Even their vitality, issuing, as it did, from an untroubled and unreflecting pleasure in success, seemed to sequester them in a more vigorous and brightly colored period.

Jill and Nick had attended several enormous parties or receptions held on the Binghams' lawn, which was glorious in the spring and summer with flowers and blossoming fruit trees. The Binghams were marvelous hosts. And once or twice a year Jill would stop over to have tea with Hattie. The heavy drapes in the living room were always open, allowing the light to fall in rich panels across the polished floor and the deep silence of the old furniture, and Hattie would serve Jill tea and slices of a dense buttery cake, as well as cookies so fragile they almost disappeared by themselves.

But this afternoon it had been Spencer who opened the door. "Well, Jill," he said. Without letting go of the doorknob, he glanced back into the dim hall.

"I've interrupted, haven't I?" Jill said. "I'll come back tomorrow."

"No, no," Spencer said, and displayed his cordial smile. "Come in, Jill. Hattie," he called, "we have a visitor." He dropped his voice. "She'll be glad."

"Well, invite Jill in, Spence," Hattie said, and then Jill saw that Hattie was having difficulty with the stairs, so there was nothing to do except wait through the painful descent. "A visitor is supposed to come in and visit. Come in, Jill, and sit down."

But when Jill did sit, in a generous upholstered chair near the fireplace, there was a silence.

"I can't stay long," Jill said. "I just dropped in to say how sorry I was to hear about—about the other night."

"Oh, yes," Spencer said, as if he were picking up a story in the middle. "Wednesday night. Well, we'd been over at the DeForests' for cocktails. They had a little do for that young man—the new head of cardiology over at Lakeview. And then we went into town for dinner. We usually do on Wednesdays, party or no party, so you see what a bad thing a habit is. Because this Wednesday, when we got back and opened our door—well, it was just like being somewhere else—it was like something that hadn't happened. I mean, if you were to go back outside and come in again, it wouldn't have happened."

"What Spence means," Hattie said, "is that we opened the door of our own house, and we didn't even know where we were—everything torn apart—drawers dumped out, furniture every which way, papers all over the place—private papers!"

"And the dolls, of course," Spencer said.

"*We* want some tea, don't we," Hattie said.

"Hattie," Spencer said. "Sit down, Hattie—don't bother with that—"

"Not for you, you tyrant, for our guest—"

"No, no," Jill said. "I really can't stay."

"Well, Spence has to have his tea," Hattie said. "Unless he's going out. Are you going out, Spence?" She turned to Jill. "He's just been sitting around like an old man. Why don't you call Bob Niederland, dear, and play some golf? Get outside and do something."

"Why should I do anything?" Spencer chuckled unhappily. "I'm an old man, and I like it right here."

"Well, we have to have *something*," Hattie said. "Otherwise, it isn't a party."

Spencer and Jill sat quietly as Hattie made her way toward the kitchen. "Her leg is bothering her, I think," Spencer said, frowning hopefully over at Jill. "Have you noticed?"

"Not at all," Jill said, embarrassed.

The Binghams had never seemed absorbed in their own problems before. In fact, they'd never seemed to have problems, or to think of themselves at all, beyond whatever satisfaction they took from being themselves. Certainly they had never referred to their bodies, to infirmities. "And as you can imagine," Spencer said after a time, "she's heartbroken about the dolls."

"I couldn't even find the tea," Hattie said, returning with juice and a plate of cookies that seemed to have come from a package. "Ruby and I worked all day to restore a modicum of order around this place, but I still can't find a thing. That darned thief—"

"Don't suppose he took the tea," Spencer said. He smiled at Jill. "Didn't have the style of a tea drinker."

"He got our Lacy, did you hear?" Hattie said. "He broke most of the others, or spoiled them, but he took the four or five really valuable ones, including Lacy."

"She was the first one we owned," Spencer explained to Jill. "We found her in Smoky Mountain country. The first time we went down there, the year we were married."

"Oh, the Smoky Mountains in those days . . ." Hattie said. "Well, we went back after the war once, and of course everything had changed. But in those days—well, you can't imagine—it was so remote, just those cloudy green hills and silent roads, dirt roads, with leafy little hidden enclaves here and there of those peculiar mountain people. You could hear the train whistle sometimes, from way up over the mountains, but that was as close as the world came. And they still spoke their own kind of English then, practically some sort of Elizabethan English—they were almost like an odd little race of animals. Anyhow, Spence and I were driving around up there, and we stopped in Asheville, to poke around some big barn of a place full of antiques. Junk, really—and I spotted Lacy. Can you imagine? She had a handmade lace dress and a lovely white wax face—so elegant and perfect it was almost eerie. Some poor mountain woman's dream of a lady, I suppose. And that's what started us. Afterward, we liked to look wherever we went, and eventually we found ourselves with a whole world, all sorts of nationalities, all sorts of periods. But we never looked for value. Who would have dreamed that dolls would become an item of value? Of course, everything does sooner or later, now. Isn't it funny? Old toasters and everything—all that ugly kitchen trash we hated so. But we never even thought of that. It was the feeling. You couldn't believe what people put into some of those little things—all the beauty and personality that anyone could imagine, that anyone could want in a human being . . ." Hattie sighed and looked past Jill out the window.

"And do you think that's what they broke in for?" Jill asked. "The dolls?"

"What?" Hattie said.

"Oh, there's no question about it," Spencer said. "We've been over it a hundred times, with each other and with the police. There's no question that there was someone involved who'd learned the value of the individual dolls."

"Oh—" Jill said. She put down her cookie, which was slightly stale, she noticed.

"They got Spence's Confederate rifle, too," Hattie said, suddenly indignant. "He was very fond of it."

"Picked up some loose cash, and a bit of silver," Spencer said. "But nothing much. Just enough to make it look like any old break-in. At least until we could collect our wits."

"There was stuff all over the place," Hattie said. "There was even—oh, lord . . ."

"Oh, now, it doesn't matter," Spencer said.

"He had even taken a drawer of my underthings and scattered them around," Hattie said. "You see, there was simply no need for all that violence."

"We know," Spencer said. "That's what we're saying."

"But the worst was the ones he *didn't* take," Hattie said to Jill. "Oh, you could hardly believe your eyes—little arms and legs all over the place—their bodies all twisted; sawdust, stuffing pulled out of them, porcelain faces smashed up, eyes just staring at the ceiling, or the floor, or wherever they'd been thrown. Hurled, really," Hattie said. "They were ours. We found them, we loved them, but now they're ruined, and I feel sorry that I ever brought them here. It's as though this was never our house, we just thought it was. All you could think was blood."

Through the Binghams' window Jill had looked at the hedge that hid her own house from view. Long shadows fell across the lawn, and a late, ciderlike light sliced through the room, charging a panel of tiny suspended dust particles between herself and the Binghams. Beyond it, Hattie and Spencer were insubstantial, wavering, as though they had just acquired a contagious susceptibility to old age. "I'm sorry about the tea, Jill dear," Hattie said.

"I notice that Jill keeps her own counsel," Owen was saying. "I'd give a penny, or more, for Jill's thoughts on this matter."

"I'm afraid I—" Jill ransacked the previous few moments for any words she might be able to retrieve. "Well, I'm afraid I really haven't any thoughts on the matter at all." She laughed.

That serene lawn. The china, and all that glowing old wood. What a flimsy fortress the Binghams' house had proved to be. This was what their lives had come down to—the husks of their bodies. The Binghams had valued themselves highly. They had accepted as their due many beautiful things. But the instant the robbery tore away the fragile illusion of their invulnerability, their merit no longer seemed secure, either. And what the world had rendered up to them, it was now clear that the Binghams kept on sufferance. What they had, Jill thought, what they were, could be tossed aside at any moment, just like the oldest of their possessions, their bodies.

"Susan tells me you have some night bloomers," Lyle was saying. "May I have a tour?"

"Heavens—" Jill said. Only she and Lyle were left at the table. "Thank you, Lyle—no, I'd better make coffee."

As Jill went through the swinging door into the kitchen, a shadow swelled on the wall, twisted, and broke in two.

"Jill." Nick spoke at her side. "Are you feeling all right?"

"—All right?" Jill said.

"Poor baby," Amanda said. "You were looking all green out there."

Jill looked at Amanda, and at Nick. "I'm fine," she said.

"You'll be fine," Nick said, and patted her rear end. "You know," he said to Amanda, "she wasn't sick for one minute with Joshua."

A hard presence stepped forth within Jill and faced her. Nick was selfish, this presence announced. He was arrogant; he was domineering and reckless; he overestimated his skill in all things, and underestimated the abilities of others; he drove too fast, he thought too little, he expected too much; he was careless, deceitful, and calculating. Jill had not told Amanda, she had not told anyone except Nick, that she was pregnant. "Did you make coffee?" she said.

"We were just going to," Nick said. "You didn't look up to it."

"I'm fine," she said. "I'll do it."

Jill waited until the swinging door had come to rest behind Nick and Amanda, and then she turned out the lights and sat down at the counter. Was she going to be sick, she wondered.

Out in the garden Owen was wandering among the high, pale blossoms. Shapes and lines were etched shockingly against the brilliant night, and even from where she sat, Jill could see the tense flare of petals, blades of grass arching with the weight of gathering condensation, and the creases of Owen's face, arranged, as always, into folds that might prefigure either bliss or grief. Owen bent down over a flower, his large padded backside catching the moonlight, and straightened up again as Amanda appeared on the terrace. Her arms were crossed against her chest, although the air was warm and still. She closed her eyes and tilted her face back. Her nails, her hair, and her thin gold bracelets shone. "Hello," Owen said, and the small sound was right next to Jill's ear.

Amanda opened her eyes. "Hello," she said. She and Owen smiled at one another tentatively, sadly, and then Amanda returned inside.

Alone again, Owen made a circuit of the garden. Really, Jill thought, she ought to feel pity for him. In all the time she had known him—except for that one instant upstairs tonight—even in the face of Kitsy's corrosive deficiencies, her inept, gnawing flirtations, his demeanor had never altered.

Owen stopped in the far corner of the yard, at Joshua's swing set. He pulled the swing back and released it, pausing to watch as it rocked back and forth, before he moved on. Jill turned on the light and made coffee.

When she returned to the living room, it seemed to Jill that something must have happened in her absence. Nick was again stationed at the window, gazing darkly out in the direction of the Binghams', Lyle was perched, none too steadily, on the piano bench, and Owen leaned against the open French doors, but attention seemed to be directed toward the center of the room, where Bud, speaking loudly, strode back and forth between the armchairs in which Susan and Amanda were seated, while Kitsy hovered at the periphery, as though she were unable to approach more closely. Bud's voice was poisonously reasonable, and although he addressed himself ostensibly to Susan, who watched him like a browbeaten jury, he looked steadily at Amanda, who sat, eyes closed and head back, swinging her foot.

"I'm just trying," Bud said, "to clarify what you were saying earlier, Susan, about product-liability law. That is—correct me if I'm wrong—but wasn't your point that we need those laws if we're to have any *viable* protection of the consumer, and yet, at the same time, you say, those laws are vulnerable to abuse and exploitation by unscrupulous people. Wasn't that your point?"

"I really—" Susan said.

"And all I'm saying," Bud said, "is that I'm in total agreement with you: it is no longer possible to rely on laws or institutions, because we now have a certain sort of individual who twists laws or institutions, and undermines them by using them for his or her own purposes. The rest of us can hardly be blamed if we're suspicious. Or are forced to behave cynically ourselves."

Amanda sighed.

"You laugh, my darling," Bud said. "But I'm serious."

"But are we saying—are we talking about something?" Susan said.

"Yes," Bud said, as Amanda said, "No."

"I'm a bit lost here, myself, Bud," Lyle said, turning around at the piano. "Could you define your terms?"

"You're a *deliberate* son of a bitch, aren't you, Lyle," Bud said pleasantly. "I'm simply speaking generally. About the misapplication of principles."

"But, Bud," Susan said. "It's hardly a *principle's* fault if someone—"

"How true," Owen said. "Now let us—"

"No, Lyle," Kitsy said, claiming a central position on the arm of Susan's chair. "I think that what Bud is talking about is a climate, a climate in which people invoke principles in order to pursue their own selfish—"

"Why not let Bud persecute his own wife, Kitsy?" Nick said.

"That's right," Bud said. "Why not let me persecute my own wife. I think I was doing a damned good job of it."

Amanda smiled, but Kitsy flinched as though she'd been slapped. "Do whatever you want to your own wife. I really don't give a shit."

"Would anybody like to tell me what this is about?" Jill said.

"Nothing," Nick and Amanda said in unison.

"We're talking about a climate, Jill"—Kitsy's face was clenched with anger—"of selfishness, of turning things to our own advantage. Of taking things that belong to other people or pretending not to notice if someone else does. These are things—"

"'Things,'" Susan said. "Does anything feel dizzy?"

"—and these are things we're all involved in," Kitsy said. "All of us. Collusion. Because take the thing we've all been thinking about all evening—the Binghams. My point is, for instance, that we're all involved with the Binghams."

"The Binghams!" Nick turned from the window with a laugh of surprise. "We're all involved with the *Binghams*?"

"Heaven knows what you're involved with," Kitsy said. "I wouldn't know." She looked at Amanda. "But one thing I do know, Nicholas, is that every one of us understands exactly who broke into the Binghams' house, and not one of us is willing to say or to do anything about it because of what some people call—"

"The plot thickens—" Lyle pounded on the piano. "*We know who broke into the Binghams'.*"

"And just who is it," Amanda said, "that we all know to have broken into the Binghams', Kitsy?"

"'Who'?" Kitsy said. "Dwayne, obviously."

"Who's Dwayne?" Lyle said, lifting his palms comically.

"Dwayne!" Susan said gaily to Lyle, as everyone else looked at Amanda. "The brother of that girl who works here, isn't that right?"

"What on earth gives you the idea that it was Dwayne?" Amanda said, recovering. But Jill had to sit down. Of course it was Dwayne, she thought. Kitsy was right. She'd only pretended to herself because of Amanda that she didn't know. But now— "Would you mind telling me *how* we all know it was Dwayne?" Amanda said.

"'*How*,'" Kitsy said. "What do you mean, 'how'? Who

else could it be? He knows the house, he's worked there. He always needs money—everyone knows what a drug addict will do for money. It had to be Dwayne. But we're trying to protect a whole group of people, even though we know perfectly well—"

"'*Group* of people'—" Amanda said. She stopped and stared at Kitsy.

"I am now going to play chopsticks," Lyle announced.

"Shut up, Lyle," Susan said gently and with unexpected lucidity.

"—Listen to yourself, Kitsy," Amanda said. "Just listen to what you're saying—"

"And you," Kitsy said. "Listen to what *you're* saying. You're saying that such people shouldn't even have the dignity of being held accountable for their own failure to adjust to society. But that's pa—"

"Do you think it was Dwayne who stole Bunny Wheeler's Majolica vases?" Amanda said. "Do you think it was Dwayne who stole that Soutine from the Art Institute?"

"—that's *patronizing*. It's not fair to *them*. Other immigrant groups have made something of themselves. Other immigrant groups haven't depended on us for help. Even if they've come from tragic situations, even if they've lost everything—" Kitsy gestured toward Susan. "Like the Jews—"

"Well, now," Lyle said. "Let's not—"

"Look at the Jews," Kitsy said. "Look at the Asians—*they've* suffered, *they've* been persecuted, *they've* been slaughtered. But *their* children play the violin. They get into Harvard. They carry out the garbage. Other immigrant groups—"

"Just one small point," Owen said, "is, immigrants are people who *decide* to go somewhere. People who pack a suitcase, buy a ticket—"

"Oh, I know it sounds ridiculous when I put it like that," Kitsy said.

"It certainly does, Kitsy," Bud said. "Amanda—"

"I know how it sounds, *thank* you, Bud," Kitsy said furiously, but as she turned to Owen, Jill saw, her expression was shockingly piteous. "And that's what I used to think, too. You know, that they'd been slaves and so on, so they couldn't be expected et cetera, et cetera—"

"But that's not even my—" Owen said.

"And, Owen, darling"—Kitsy sprang toward him, gesticulating with her glass—"the terrible thing is that you're so good and kind yourself that you don't see the terrible things that happen to people, the terrible things that people do to one another—" As she leaned against him, tears spilled from her closed eyes.

"There, there," Owen said, but his arms hung at his sides.

"I'm sorry that you're unhappy, Kitsy," Amanda said. "I'm sorry if I've said anything or done anything to cause you unhappiness. But I'm afraid I have to clear the record, because the fact is that it was not Dwayne who robbed the Binghams."

"I'd be the last to doubt your word, sweetheart," Bud said. He was breathing shallowly, Jill saw, just as she was, herself. "But just how are we to believe you?"

"Yes," Jill said, or didn't say. She saw Amanda's fluctuating color, her shining gold bracelets, as though through a fever. "How?"

"Since you must know," Amanda said. "Since it's been decided that it's absolutely everybody's business, the fact is, I checked. At Dwayne's program. Dwayne was there—in St. Louis. He was at a meeting that night—"

Jill's hand tingled, and for a moment all she heard was a breeze outside, riffling the leaves, but then there was an up-

roar. Kitsy was speaking loudly, and Owen turned away toward the garden. Lyle pounded on the piano, Susan, for some
reason, was crying, and Bud and Nick were laughing. Nick
whooped with laughter. "Amanda," he said, flinging his arms
around Amanda while she stood, furiously still, "you're perfect, do you hear me? Perfect," he was saying, as the room
waved around Jill, gelatinous with Nick's laughter. But Bud
had stopped laughing, Jill saw. He was staring at Nick and
Amanda, and it was only Nick who was laughing.

No, Susan was laughing, too, Jill realized. Susan was not
crying—she was laughing. She was splayed out over her chair,
laughing without pleasure or comprehension. "What's going
on?" she managed to say, through fresh inundations of laughter. "Why is everybody laughing?"

"Well, that really was the worst, wasn't it," Nick said later,
with satisfaction. There had been kisses, and tears, and poorly
balanced hugs, and everyone had gotten out the door, though
whether anybody had gotten home or not, Jill didn't care. She
turned away as Nick unbuttoned his shirt—she had already
changed in the dressing room.

"Tomorrow will be spectacular," Nick said. "Everyone
on the phone all day apologizing. If anyone even remembers
what happened—"

Jill waited until the words came of their own accord.
"What did happen?"

"Nothing." He laughed. "You sound like Susan. Nothing
happened. Just one of those tectonic upheavals between old
friends."

"Nothing matters," she said. "Does it, Nick?"

"Well, this doesn't matter," he said. Her stare seemed

simply not to reach him. She turned to the mirror and slowly combed her hair.

"You know—" He climbed into bed. "We're not going to need this blanket tonight. The thing is, though, I really do feel sorry for Owen. Not a day goes by that Kitsy doesn't make a spectacle of herself in one way or another."

"You mean that she deserves to be humiliated because she's not attractive. You think that only women like Amanda ought to be able to have affairs."

"Darling—" Nick turned to her and held out his hand. "What's the matter? You're not feeling well, are you."

"The truth is," Jill said, "that Kitsy's in a miserable position."

"She's damned fortunate," Nick said. "Owen puts up with her completely."

"Yes," Jill said. "It's like a sentence of penal servitude."

"I really don't know what you're talking about, Jill." Nick dropped his hand. "At any rate, it's over."

"Besides," Jill said. "You should have seen him with Katrina tonight. It was disgusting."

"Oh, for God's sake." Nick sighed. "Well, I suppose we're going to have to be more careful of you from now on."

In the mirror, Jill watched him close his eyes and turn.

"Would you get the lights?" he said. "Or do you want to read?"

"No." She switched off the lights. "Go to sleep."

She sat down in the chair with her feet up and her arms around her knees, watching as the night settled into the room. She saw Nick's eyes gleam for a moment in the darkness. "Look at the moon," he said, his voice thickening with sleep. "What a moon . . ."

"Nick—" Jill said.

"What, sweetheart?"

"When the baby comes, I want to stop working."

"Stop working? I thought you liked your job, Jill."

"It's only a part-time job, honey. We spend more on help than I make."

"That doesn't matter. I can afford it. If you want to work, you should work."

"But it isn't really *for* anything, Nick. It's just an office job. It isn't really very interesting. I'm not particularly good at it, I don't do anybody any good—"

"Do you want to be one of those women who just sit around the house all day?"

"Why are we married if you're so disappointed in me?" Jill said. "Did you marry me just so you could be disappointed in me?"

"This is ridiculous," Nick said. "You're exhausted. As far as I'm concerned, if you want to work, that's fine, and if you want to stay home, that's fine, too. But I don't want to discuss this any more tonight. I'm going to sleep, and I think you should, too."

"I want to stay home," Jill said. "I want to take care of my home and my children. I don't want all these strangers in my house anymore."

But Nick lay still. He looked like marble, the sheet looked like carved marble in the pearly indigo of the room. "Nick—" Jill said. His lashes fluttered, his eyes gleamed again for an instant. He spoke indistinctly and turned.

Jill settled back in her chair, her face tilted toward the window. Cool waves of darkness slid in from outside; there was a brief, plangent rush of leaves. Below, in the garden, flowers were tossing about, sighing and giving off their tender light from generous blossoms, thick, pale stems. The grass was

wet and tangled, and through it a little path led out from the
far corner of the yard, past the swings, and out behind the
Binghams' house. It went along behind all the houses on
the block—the tidy, sleeping houses—and picked up on the
next block, and then the block after that, and then the block
where the new houses were being built, and the smell of wood
and wet concrete wound through the air. When the path
faded out, Jill found herself in a meadow, where she had never
been before. Or perhaps she had—yes, she had been there, but
now it looked strange, with sticky shafts of milkweed and
patches of rough, sour grass pushing up from the mud. Next
to her, a layer of chemical suds floated on a ditch. Though it
was only twilight, Jill could see the red glare from where the
city curved out in the distance, the fierce glare from the steel
mills. Jill picked her way among huge spools of wire and
pieces of track that lay about the burned-looking ground, and
sooner or later she found a little house where she'd seen Evaline once, a long, long time ago, in a Sunday dress and a hat
with wooden cherries on it. There were a few chicks in the
yard, and some tires, and a half-buried old washing machine;
and she must have skirted the city, because now she could
even see the metal lozenges of the mills at its far side. I'd better
hurry and go inside, she thought; because the greenish wedge
of twilight was pressing down quickly upon her and the little
house.

In the bare wooden room that was the house, many people
were waiting. Jill wandered around and around among them,
but they paid no attention to her whatsoever, which was odd,
Jill thought, because, of all those people—old people sitting
and fanning themselves anxiously, and babies who sat, distracted
and silent, on the floor—she herself was the only white one.
But evidently the people there were concentrating on some-

thing, waiting for something that was going to happen, and they had no time for Jill, none at all. And just as she was growing beside herself with impatience, she saw a woman stirring something on the stove from which came rich, dark tendrils of aromas, streaked with traces of something that was familiar, although Jill couldn't place it.

"Don't be rude," said a voice in Jill's ear. "You know what this is."

That's disgustingly unfair, Jill thought, and I'm going to leave; I never wanted to be here in the first place. But she could not make her way through the crowded vigil—even though morning was soaking into her sleep, and she could feel Nick pick her up and carry her to the bed, she could not fight her way through.

She was just starting to struggle in earnest when she saw the two boys—Roo's James and her Joshua. They had gotten hold of some marvelous toy, a translucent sphere inside which tiny figures whirled and orbited, and Jill watched as the thing spun, lofting into the air. She caught her breath as James tensed, his tiny face pointed with effort, but before James could catch it, Joshua reached out. "It's mine—" Joshua called, and, as the fragile thing bounced from the tips of Joshua's fingers, Jill, too, reached and cried out, just managing to wake, her hair damp and clinging to her forehead, before James was able to open his mouth.

PRESENTS

The waves go on and on—there is no farther shore; a boat here and there in the dark water, a cluster of fronds, an occasional sunset. Cheryl closes her eyes, and the warm night-blue water rushes out around her. "Think it's really like that?" she asks. Cheryl's voice is arresting—low, and with a city accent that gives each word the finality of a bead dropping into place along a string; sometimes strangers to whom she speaks pause before responding, and look, if they haven't looked before. "Think it's really that blue?"

"Blue?" Carter glances down at his shirt. "Nothing's this blue. Not even this. It's the lights in here—make everything vibrate." He tips the little glass bottle in his hand and spills a neat white line from it onto his forearm, which he extends to Cheryl with balletic solemnity.

"You know what?" Cheryl says when her attention returns to Carter's shirt. "It's sort of . . . not beautiful, isn't it? Sort of—"

"Don't insult my shirt," Carter says. "Are you insulting my shirt? That's not nice; it was a gift. I wonder why people wear these things, come to think of it. They're ugly, they're stale, they're not even funny, but you can't get rid of them. They disappear for a few years, then, wham, they're back again, worse than before. Fact, I'm going to make a stand. I'll never accept another one from anybody, I don't care who tries to give me one." He taps another line neatly out from the bottle onto his forearm and inhales it, all in one fluid sequence. "Don't let anyone tell you I've lost my talent," he says.

Cheryl, leaning against the sink, smiles. "So what is it like?" she asks. "You been there?"

"Huh?" Carter says. "Ah." He presses his fingers against the corners of his eyes. "Yeah. I did a film there. It was like a film set. It was like a hotel room."

When Cheryl and Carter return from the men's room, Danny is waiting at the table, with a fresh round of drinks, in exactly the same position they'd left him. His soft dark hair, his soft white skin, his muscular roundness, his stillness—he is dark and still enough to absorb all the clatter around him.

When did Danny and Carter last see each other? Cheryl tries to figure it out. It must have been five or six years ago that Carter moved out to the Coast—long before Cheryl started going out with Danny—when she was just a child and would stop in here with her mother, Judith, for a hamburger and a soda before going back up the block to do her homework or go to sleep while Judith stayed on at the bar. Cheryl might well have seen Carter here in those days, but he would have been just one among many people who hung out at Danny's table.

Danny, of course, is delighted by Carter's unexpected appearance tonight. He has often spoken of Carter to Cheryl—their friendship, to him, is a living thing. But Carter, who seemed comfortable enough downstairs in the men's room with Cheryl, is formal here at the table, and querulously passive, as if he were being forced to wait for some event that would reveal to him exactly why, after all these years, he has taken the trouble to look Danny up.

"Put quite a dent in this," Carter says, handing the little bottle back to Danny.

"That's what it's for," Danny says. "You don't even need to ask—it's always here."

" 'Here'!" Cheryl says as Danny pats his pocket, surprising herself with her own disloyalty, but Carter only glances over at her as if taken unawares by some unidentified disturbance.

"In fact"—Danny frowns slightly—"let me lay a little of this on you."

"No," Carter says. "Thanks. This is—this is just old times' sake."

"Well, that's good, right?" Danny says. "I took a break recently myself."

"I work much better now," Carter says. "Nothing to distort my concentration."

Danny nods, smoothing things over. Or, Cheryl wonders, has he really not noticed the cruelty of Carter's remark. "They keep you pretty busy out there, I guess," he says.

"It's not too bad," Carter says. "Nothing too much for a while, though. Everything's shit this year."

"Well," Danny says, "we're always glad to see your work here. Cheryl and me. Everyone."

Carter's look, as it sweeps across the room possibly assessing conditions for departure, provokes a rustle of self-conscious laughter from girls at nearby tables.

"Carter made a movie in Hawaii," Cheryl interposes.

"Hawaii," Danny says. "Interesting. That's interesting. I wasn't aware of that."

"It was a while back," Carter says.

"You were doing a series just now, right?" Danny asks.

"Right," Carter says.

"I haven't seen that for a while," Danny says.

Carter smiles as if yielding to a barbed witticism. "The network said it was too specialized for the viewing public. Meaning the sponsors couldn't follow the plot, so they took it off the air."

"That's what I thought," Danny agrees. "That's what I thought. You know, I never saw that movie—I thought I'd seen all your movies."

"What movie?" Carter says. "Oh. Well, you might not have known. It was supposed to be—well, actually, it was supposed to be Hawaii, in fact, through some error of efficiency. Course they had to chop down the palm trees so there'd be room for the fake palm trees. But otherwise it was a good idea for a location. An exciting concept."

Danny laughs obligingly, but Carter's irritability threatens to overflow and swamp the conversation.

"At least you've got the shirt," Cheryl says.

Carter looks at her blankly, then down at his shirt. "Right," he says. "Girl on the crew gave it to me," he explains to Danny. "So I wear it from time to time, out of respect for her memory."

"Holy shit," Danny says. "She died?"

"Out of respect for her memory," Carter insists. "Because I can't remember her. Hair, I think. Or makeup. Except maybe I got it for myself, come to think of it, to remember myself by, because the thing about that movie was, my performance had the exact level of distinction and authenticity illustrated by this shirt."

Danny looks perturbed. "I don't like to miss any of your work," he says.

"You would have liked to have missed this."

"It was probably a lot better than you think," Danny says.

"You probably just think that because of some personal situation or whatever. Anyhow, I'll try to rent it."

A silence falls between the two men, in which Cheryl feels ensnared, implicated.

"Anybody need to make a trip to the powder room?" Danny asks finally.

"Thanks." Carter pushes his glass away. "But I've got to sleep. I'm seeing those guys tomorrow."

"Look at that," Danny says, turning to watch as Cheryl takes a sip of her drink, a frozen Margarita. "The things girls drink—green things, pink things. The things they do. I love it. Paint, curls, things that shine . . ."

Carter looks at Cheryl. It is the first time, she thinks, that he has really looked at her. "Yes, indeed," he says.

"If it's sleeping, don't worry," Danny says. "I've got something for later that'll help with that."

Carter withdraws his look from Cheryl, erasing her. "Right," he says, accepting the little bottle from Danny. "Anybody care to join me?"

"I'm O.K. for the moment," Danny says. Cheryl looks down at her drink.

"I hate to see the guy so unhappy," Danny says, watching solicitously as Carter disappears toward the men's room. "He's seeing those guys tomorrow, I guess. Well, he's a good man."

"Excuse me a minute," Cheryl says. The tentative, probing note in Danny's voice is making her uneasy. "I want to say hi to Roy."

Although the tables are nearly full, the population at the bar is sparse, and Roy is killing time polishing glasses. "Would you look at this shit, please?" he says, holding a smudged glass up for Cheryl's inspection. "Day-shift assholes."

Roy takes a personal pride in the ruin that is the world,

and there are times when each of its details provides him with a welcome occasion for disgust. But Cheryl is perfectly at home with these moods of his; he has been more or less living with Judith for nearly seven years. "Could I have a soda, please, Roy?" she asks.

"Knock it back, Princess," Roy says, handing her a Coke.

Cheryl simply doesn't like the taste of alcohol, although on nights like this when she's getting high she has to drink it to take the edge off. But it suits Roy to theorize, with infuriating magnanimity, that Cheryl's reluctance to drink inevitably stems from some of the scenes Cheryl witnessed between Judith and his predecessors—real drinkers, problem drinkers, "walking slime" Roy has called them, and Judith and Cheryl agree—who beat Judith in unassuageable furies, as if she were losing her looks to spite them. Which she would have, she's told Cheryl, if she had been in charge of the matter herself.

When Roy and Judith are annoyed with Cheryl they accuse her of squeamishness, coldness, high-minded snottiness; they affect to believe that her habitual prudence is a matter of principle rather than temperament; they ridicule her roughly and coarsely, as though to present proof, by contrast, of the defects they attribute to her.

At such times Danny, for his part, seems slightly gratified, as if these allegations were a guarantee of Cheryl's quality. It is the silken coolness of Cheryl's face and hair that he praises; he praises her reserve. He declares that he would marry her on the spot, but this appears to be an axiom, which requires no response. He does not make it necessary for her to examine her feelings about him—as he is the first to point out, she is very young.

"So, Carter back to stay?" Roy asks.

Cheryl shrugs. "He's looking into a few projects," she says, trying out Carter's word. "He might do a play."

"Ho," Roy says. "Greasepaint. Footlights. Very tony. He's looking kind of nervous. He got stagefright already?"

"He's not nervous," Cheryl says.

"He looks nervous. He looks like shit. And no wonder. He hasn't made a decent picture since *Apple Pie*, you realize that? I understand he's got himself a bit of a reputation these days. Fooling around, making demands, and so forth. Very high-handed."

"Guess they keep you pretty well informed about him, Roy."

"Hey. You read things. You hear things."

Evidently Roy is determined to bully her tonight. Cheryl has spent the last few days at Danny's, and it must be that in her absence Judith has been singing her praises, or the praises of some father of Cheryl's that Judith has invented for the purpose of torturing Roy. Well, good. Cheryl wishes her mother were around right now. For once, Judith's rash mockery, her raucous slatternly astuteness would be a pleasurable danger—a relief from Roy's goading prissiness and the indecipherable pressures emanating from Danny. "Is Mother coming in tonight?" she asks.

"I expect she'll show up in due course," Roy says. "To get a load on. At least, she didn't give me reason to presume she had alternative plans. Naturally she would of been here already if she'd known who you and Danny were entertaining."

Judith always snorts at the mention of Carter. Nothing personal—merely that she's bound to be skeptical in regard to the sudden celebrity of a familiar face.

"He come in to score tonight?" Roy asks.

"He came in to see Danny," Cheryl says.

"Uh-huh," Roy says.

"He's clean."

"He's clean," Roy says. "He just likes to hang out in the can 'cause he feels insecure in public. Ah, time was he'd come in, he and his buddies from acting class, the picture of innocence, slumming. Fresh-faced silly-ass kids putting away the beer and shooters, thinking up things to deplore. Seems like no time at all before he's over at Danny's table."

Cheryl sighs. What does she care?

"Speaking of which," Roy says, "you tell that boyfriend of yours I want a word with him. Guess he's forgotten me in all the excitement."

"Take it easy, Roy. If Danny said he'd do something for you he'll do it."

"And you watch yourself, my girl," says Roy, smug and fatherly now that he's managed to exasperate her. "It's a known fact this guy's a demon with women."

"Grab your stuff, sweetheart," Danny tells Cheryl when she returns to the table. "We're going up to Carter's for a bit."

Cheryl hesitates. But Danny seems at ease, perfectly in control, and he is waiting. "You have to be up in the morning?" she asks Carter.

"No, no." Carter speaks with an automatic, beleaguered graciousness. "Be nice if you drop by. It's still early."

"It's *early*," Danny says, putting an arm around her. "We won't stay long."

They stop at the bar on their way out, and Roy extends an enormous hairy arm, spreading a wide but transparent smile over cold appraisal. "Great to see you back again," he says.

"Great, yeah, great to see you," Carter says, abashed.

"Going to stick around for a while?" Roy says.

"Depends on whether a few things work out," Carter says.

"Well, best of luck to you." Roy's smile becomes still wider and more punishing as Carter becomes more uncomfortable. "Don't be a stranger, now." Cheryl can just hear Roy telling Judith later how arrogant Carter has become. She can just see the two of them shaking their heads over it, over life. But why should Carter remember Roy, anyway?

"Here you go," Danny says, handing Roy an issue of *New York*.

"I read this one already," Roy says obtusely.

"Page 38," Danny says. "A terrific article. I saved it for you."

Roy's puzzled frown transmutes into a huge and genuine grin. "My man," he says, and at this moment he and Danny could be father and son, united in the intricate execution of some athletic feat. Danny can always bring out the best in Roy, and sometimes when Cheryl sees them together she is reminded of the time, when she was eleven or so, that Judith discovered Roy behind the bar here and brought him back home with her. What a surprise he'd been—good-looking and boyish. Engaging, genial. Roy: a miracle.

"If my mother comes in—" Cheryl says.

"What, tell her what?" Roy says peevishly.

"Oh, fuck off, Roy," Cheryl says.

"The guy's practically family," Danny explains to Carter on the way uptown. "He lives with Cheryl's old lady—remember? Judith?"

Carter shakes his head. He appears not to be concentrating.

"She's one terrific lady," Danny says. "Very talented. She

was Miss New York State one year. You should see some of those old pictures of her. Gorgeous. Looks just like Cheryl in a funny bathing suit. Same eyes, same legs, same hair."

There was a time when people frequently asked if Cheryl and Judith were sisters, but now Judith's kitten face is pouchy with alcoholic malice and sentimentality.

"She's quite a character, quite a lady," Danny says. "She used to be a dead ringer for Cheryl."

"Is that right?" Carter says.

Although Judith is not quite forty, what people now say is "She must have been a good-looking woman at one time."

"Dead ringer," Cheryl says, again disloyal. And when Carter directs to her a slow smile, rich with bitter complicity, she is as shocked and shamed and thrilled as if she herself had voiced some declaration.

As soon as Danny empties a gram bottle onto Carter's shiny dark coffee table, it is Cheryl who digs in, using the tiny gold spoon Danny had given her as sort of a joke shortly after they started going out. "Like getting pinned," he'd said. "You know about that? Like those old-time beach-party movies." Danny loves movies, particularly ones—his *friends*—that date from his early childhood.

Cheryl feels steadier right away, and decides to strike off on her own and explore. It seems that this is a hotel, or something like a hotel. There had been a uniformed man in the elevator, and there were many elevators, or several at least, and downstairs in the lobby other uniformed men, and, distantly, in a dim gilded recess, something like a desk, Cheryl now realizes, and beyond that a huge set of double doors, glassy but dark, possibly leading to a restaurant where there would be heavy white cloths on the tables, and waiters in white jackets.

Cheryl goes from Carter's living room back to his small foyer and chooses one of several doors. Although the building seems old and solid, the rooms in this apartment have an almost abstract regularity, and they flow from one to another—chambers and chambers, Cheryl thinks—in a random manner, as if the phenomena of daily life eluded categorization. The furniture, also stripped of the burdens of particularity, is unused-looking, and here and there is a clean glass ashtray holding a matchbook.

Eventually Cheryl comes across a room where there is an enormous bed, and she stretches out upon it, taking care to keep her shoes from touching the stiff, glossy spread. There are a number of doors in this room, too, and large mirrors on three of the walls. But the wall to Cheryl's left is almost entirely glass.

She is in the sky here, and rolled out beneath her, a spectacular toy, is the Park. At its borders the shadowy towers of toy buildings, flecked with gold windows, rise into the night. And inside the Park pale light from globy lamps coats the branches and trunks of trees in a soft gleam. It is still early enough in the year so that no leaves hide the shapes of these trees. A little car glides through them soundlessly, along a curving drive. There are no sounds here whatsoever, behind the heavy glass, and no motion of air.

What sorts of trees are those, below her, Cheryl wonders. What shapes will their leaves be? Cheryl imagines that she herself is here to make these decisions. She imagines the toy people below looking up expectantly, searching the windows for her face—the giant serious face of the child who is to arrange their toy lives.

Cheryl stands, causing a phalanx of Cheryls, not children at all, to rise in the mirrors. The bedspread retains no impression of her body, and, more strangely, the first door she opens leads directly back into the living room, where Carter and Danny are.

Danny is happily going through a stack of movie cassettes, most of which feature Carter, and Carter has evidently called down for drinks. Danny locates *The Timekeeper*, his favorite of Carter's movies, and puts it on the machine. Harsh splinters of light are flung out into the room, and Danny watches, rapt, as Carter appears onscreen and proceeds, with fever-pitch caution, to break into a safe. The corporeal Carter, however, perches nervously on the arm of the sofa where Danny and Cheryl sit, and from time to time he springs up to range back and forth as if he were tethered to the screen, until a room-service waiter arrives with drinks, releasing him.

The waiter pauses for a moment, watching a tiny wind-whipped Carter climbing down a fire escape, before he sets the drinks down on the coffee table. "That was a terrific film, Mr. Hall."

"Thank you," Carter says. He signs the check and hands the waiter a large tip. "Thanks."

"Thank you, sir," the waiter says, lingering by the sofa. "I admire your work tremendously."

"Oh—" Carter looks around, but as Danny is resolutely staring at the screen, he is forced to assume the role of host. "Please," he says, handing the waiter a book of matches from the ashtray on the coffee table. "Help yourself."

"Don't mind if I do." The waiter produces a beautiful professional smile. Perhaps he, too, is an actor. Deftly and authoritatively he scoops a small portion from the white mound on the coffee table onto the matchbook cover, lifting it to his right nostril, and inhales quickly. Cheryl thinks of him downstairs in the restaurant she has imagined there, tossing salads and carving roasts on a silver trolley. Is this something she has ever seen in real life, she wonders. The waiter repeats the operation, using his left nostril.

"Outstanding," he says. His eyes rest briefly on Cheryl and Danny, who are motionless on the sofa, staring at the screen. Then he puts the matchbook down on the coffee table in front of them with a little click. "Well, thank you, sir," he says to Carter.

"Thank you," Carter says. "Thanks very much." He closes the door behind the waiter and returns to stand behind the sofa.

"Look at that," Danny says to Cheryl, pointing at the screen with proprietary pleasure.

The waiter has left a bottle of Finnish vodka on ice, and a large bottle of soda, and three setups, and although Carter has also requisitioned a frozen Margarita, Cheryl decides in favor of vodka-and-soda. This is one evening she intends to stay high, and it may take a fair amount of alcohol to maintain her current fine equilibrium. She doesn't want to throw a whole lot of sugar on top of that.

"Look," Danny says. "We're coming up to the part on the bridge."

"I can't watch this," Carter says. But what he can't seem to do is turn away.

"How the hell do you do that?" Danny asks as Carter appears, shirtless in a slushy rain, running along a bridge. "You look like you were *dying* of fear."

"I was dying of fear," Carter says. "I was fucking dying of fear. We were all fucking dying of fear. It was probably the coldest day of the last twenty years, the bridge was iced over, no one could agree how to set up the shot. Everybody was slipping around like fish—we almost lost the camera operator a few times."

"Very dedicated guy, huh?" Danny says respectfully.

"On top of that, we all had some kind of flu, but we couldn't slow down—we were already four days behind schedule because the first director turned out to be a bit of a junkie and got himself fired and replaced with this kid who'd never done a feature before, although of course when this came out he was red hot until his second one came out. Now he can't get a job in the mailroom. So there's some bondsman standing around waiting to grab the film if this kid falls one more second behind, and the producer's there, too, and they're watching each other and the director like ferrets and trading antibiotics, and alternating trips to the bathroom to throw up, and everything is one, two takes, and meanwhile—" But Carter's sentence is fractured by a volley of bullets as well as a loud buzzing. "Excuse me," he says. He looks irritated, but Cheryl thinks there's a note of satisfaction in his voice. "House phone."

Carter disappears into the foyer and returns a minute or so later with a tall woman whose hair is just a bit longer and lighter than Cheryl's. So exaggerated are the slenderness and curvature of this woman's lines that she seems to be on the other side of some distorting lens.

"My, my," the woman says. She drops her jacket on the sofa near Danny. "Home movies."

Carter shrugs, but he walks wearily to the set and turns it off.

"Hey," Danny protests, in a jokey, affectionate manner.

Carter pushes his hair back with both hands. "Suzannah, Danny, Cheryl," he says.

"Pleased to meet you," Danny says.

"You were going to call me, Carter," Suzannah says.

"I forgot," Carter says.

Danny is the first to recover, and he undertakes the task of setting things right. "Help yourself," he says to Suzannah, indicating the mound on the coffee table.

Suzannah seems to have been waiting for this offer. "No, thank you," she says quickly and coldly. She stares at some point embedded in space, but an awful disorder atomizes the room again, and she shifts ground, sitting down next to Cheryl. "I had a brutal day," Suzannah says confidingly to her. "I've simply got to sleep—I have to look halfway decent tomorrow."

Cheryl is happy to fall in with Suzannah's childish amiability. "Are you a model?" she asks.

"I'm an actress," Suzannah says, no longer amiable.

Carter laughs softly, and Suzannah stands up. "How did the audition go?" Carter asks.

"Very well, thanks," Suzannah says. She walks over to the TV and starts the tape again. "I won't keep you. I just came by to pick up a few things."

"Absolutely." Carter's voice is enmeshed in the flickering of the movie. "Go right ahead." Pointedly he picks up the matchbook and hunkers down by the coffee table.

Suzannah pauses at the door to the bedroom. "I thought you had a meeting in the morning," she says.

"I do," Carter says.

"We should go," Cheryl says to Danny.

"Don't leave," Carter says, putting his hand out to Cheryl. His eyes shadow as he looks up at her. Then once again he bends over the table, but this time Suzannah doesn't look—she has gone into the bedroom.

"Can we go back?" Danny says. "We missed a lot on the bridge." He rewinds the tape himself, then sits down again, with his hands behind his head. "Ah," he says as Carter materializes in front of them shirtless and half crazed with panic.

Carter watches with intense concentration from the arm of the sofa, but before his image even reaches the bridge he gets up to replay the beginning of the scene. Danny seems not to mind Carter's intervention, even when Carter stops the tape to stare at a frame, which he does several times. In fact, Danny only nods, as if Carter had carried out an impulse of his own. Danny seems to be growing more and more at home here, at the same time that Carter seems to be growing more and more distressed, held in thrall by the figure on the screen.

In the bedroom Suzannah, with unnecessary energy and commotion, is taking from a closet and a bureau drawer items of clothing which she then folds and puts into a Bloomingdale's bag. Cheryl watches from the doorway, but the mirrors have caught the dense, subtle colors of the Park, and on top of them, in serially reflected planes, the dark bed floats irresistibly. Suzannah continues to stride back and forth as Cheryl enters and lies down on the bed, her hair fanning out. If one of them leaves, Cheryl thinks, there will still be an infinite number of people in the mirrors. But "if two of us leave," she comments aimlessly, aloud, "there won't be any people at all."

"What is the matter with you?" Suzannah says, and slams the bureau drawer. "You're really out there, aren't you?"

"I just wondered if you wanted to talk," Cheryl says, although she hadn't particularly. She feels good, she feels fantastically good. She hadn't particularly wondered anything.

"Well, no, actually, I don't want to talk, thank you." An infinity of Suzannahs toss their hair. "Now that you mention it, I don't want to talk. I'm sure you want to talk, but I haven't just put a month's income up my nose, and I don't actually want to talk."

How often, particularly before the advent of Roy, would Judith dramatize herself in just this way, overstating the indignity of her situation so as to justify to herself her own lack of generosity or affection, forcing the tolerance of those around her in order to elicit a response that would validate her accusations of cruelty or thoughtlessness, defending, at her own expense, the territory to which her appearance entitled her until age shrank the margins of that territory, leaving her stranded (as who could know better than Cheryl) within the confines of her own devalued body?

The brawls that Cheryl has seen! Brawls that Judith's memory seasons to a satirical palatability, so that her persecuting demands and the grudging male objects of them reappear anecdotally, amusing and typological, like shifty cartoon mice armed with bottles and planks, saber-toothed cartoon cats stalking them. Cheryl is enraged by this miniaturization, and she herself has no such power over the past. For her, it rises up with the force of experience and subsides dizzyingly, leaching out all colors, severing gravitational pull, setting everything flying. Recognizable terrain falls away beneath her at these times with a roar, an unstable bluff.

It crosses Cheryl's mind that she is a coward. And certainly she has endured the coward's punishment, waiting, always waiting, while Judith piles on the provocations, for the inevitable rotation toward catastrophe. The two of them, Cheryl and Judith, scamper into Cheryl's focus as an awful comedy act: the panicked child, clutching at every flimsy scrap of junk as the rubble rains down, and the mother, dabbing at a last tear, ready to go out dancing.

Really ridiculous, Cheryl thinks. And in the suppleness

of her mood the awful sensations attenuate and slip off. But Suzannah's helpless brutality, treacherously familiar, compels Cheryl's vigilance. "Carter seems like a very emotional person," she commiserates cautiously.

"An emotional person," Suzannah responds with scorching gentility. "An emotional person. Gosh, I appreciate your pointing that out. I don't think anyone has ever—has ever *had* that insight. But you know what, see—all those emotions, those fancy little emotions of his, what they are is little circus tricks. Because that's what Carter is—a fancy little circus animal. And when he gets bored with one trick he tries a new trick, and he practices it until everyone applauds. And when everyone applauds he's sick of that trick, and he drops it. But if he gets scared—well! Three *months* he's been back here straightening himself out, one decent offer and it all falls apart." She wipes with her palm at the teary film glistening on her face, as if a fly had alighted there. "He got tired years ago of the bit he and I worked up together, but he still calls me in from time to time, whenever he's planning to degrade himself in some especially terrific way and he doesn't have a big enough audience." She gives her shopping bag an efficient little shake to settle the contents. "A good enough audience."

Yes, Cheryl thinks, gazing out at her Park as Suzannah cries. Her heady languor is opening out into a great, clear field. It is easy to understand that Carter would become bored with Suzannah. Even Suzannah's flaring beauty leaves no place to rest. Still, as Cheryl understands all too well from Judith's noisy love affairs, self-serving anguish of this sort requires cooperation, and at one time Carter must have fanned the flame. Circumstances sometimes arise in which it is made clear that Danny has no interest in, or talent for, this particular sort of romance, and at these moments Cheryl almost floats with relief. Maybe she's not in love with Danny, she thinks, but she does value him at his worth. He is always polite, always respectful, never intrusive or careless; he believes in behaving correctly and (except for certain terrible occasions to which she has only heard allusions) does not lose control of himself; he is responsible for his actions; and he is amazingly generous. Cheryl knows he helps out Roy from time to time, for instance, and Judith, too, although certainly neither is ever able to pay him back.

Suzannah blows her nose. "O.K.," she says in a tiny, docile voice. "Ready."

Suzannah does not look at anyone as she retrieves her jacket from the living-room sofa, and she knots her scarf with elaborate concentration.

"I'll go down with you," Danny offers. "Sorry, honey," he says to Cheryl. "I got a call. I'll be back in a little while."

"You could give me a lift home," Cheryl says.

"Well, it's the wrong direction," Danny says. "Why not wait for me here? This is a very impatient guy."

"Stick around," Carter says, reaching for Cheryl's hand again. "How come everybody's leaving?"

"O.K., sweetheart?" Danny says, giving Cheryl a little kiss on the cheek. He turns to Suzannah. "If you're going uptown I can drop you."

Suzannah looks at Carter. "No, thank you," she says.

As soon as Danny and Suzannah are out the door, Carter returns to watching himself on tape with complete absorption. Great, Cheryl thinks. Maybe she'll just take a taxi home. Or go back to the bar and hang out with Judith and Roy. This is a frequent source of annoyance; Danny is obliged to carry his beeper everywhere. Even worse, some of his clients consider themselves entitled to a social occasion. Danny of course is sympathetic to this and sensitive to his clients' needs, but Cheryl hopes this particular errand will be a brief one. There is a quick savage rift in her bright frame of mind: naturally Danny, who sincerely loves to be surrounded by people, never would have questioned whether Carter truly wanted her to stay, never would have suspected that he was simply profiting by her presence to dispatch Suzannah.

"Come here," Carter says without turning around. "I want you to watch something." And Cheryl, rocked by an unruly gratitude, sits down in the bleaching glare from the screen, next to him.

Carter fills their glasses again, and they refresh themselves, he by means of the matchbook and she by means of her little gold spoon, and then Carter plays once again the scene on the bridge. "Here," he says after they've watched it several times, "I'll show you something else." He makes several selections from the pile of cassettes on the floor and proceeds to play moments from them. Each scene that he shows features himself, usually in a state of extreme but suppressed tension or elation, and Cheryl marvels at the difference between the man she is sitting next to and the man she is watching; on-screen Carter seems smoothed out—hard and lustrous, his complications forced back into an invisible core that radiates alarmingly into all of his actions. The real Carter, with his exhausted boy's face, his clearly shifting uncertainties, is more interesting to Cheryl.

"You can't see what goes into it, can you?" he says.

She looks at him, waiting.

"I mean you can't see it," he says, gesturing toward the screen. "I can't see it, either. I can't see it any more than you can. They take what I do and they pour it into this huge machine, and the incredible thing is it usually comes out just the way they want it. And that's terrific, I suppose, that's just great, I'm not saying it isn't. I'm proud of it, I'm proud that I can do it. It's difficult, it's scary as hell, hardly anyone can do it very well. I'm amazed every time it works. But the thing I want to say is, the *reason* I'm proud is not because it's a good thing to do, it's just because I can do it, don't you think? I'll tell you what I think. I think that people like to do what they're able to do. People love to do what they're able to do. That's what nature is, right? The expression of itself."

What he means, Cheryl thinks, is— Wait, no, it's obvious. But obvious the way air is obvious, and in fact the air in the room is massing and separating—part breaks off, soaring. Above her, beating dark, then bright, the shadowed undersides, bright top sides, there: she can stabilize it, it melts brightly back . . .

"So of course," Carter is saying, "everyone is grateful to anyone who lets them do what they're able to do. I'm grateful to those people out there for letting me do what I can do. And the confusing part is, those people are grateful to me, but only because I can generate a lot of money for them, and that's a talent that they recognize. They've got a very pragmatic approach to talent. 'Look, look,' they say. 'That looks like *money*. Oops, no, that's a bottle cap. There, hey, *that* looks like money. Oh, whoops, it's a candy wrapper.' And they just throw out anything, they have absolutely no interest in anything, that they don't know just what to do with, that isn't already money. So they're pretty grateful to me. But I'll tell you something else, which is . . . They don't like me! They used to like me, they used to be very interested in my opinions. About the script, about the camera angles, about the caterers, you name it. But at the moment I am persona non grata. Particularly in the editing room, let me tell you—persona non grata. And the reason is, I'm just not so grateful to them as I used to be. Because, wonderful, wonderful, they let me do what I can do, but look what it ends up as. It ends up as *nothing*. And it's the same for all of us—the actors, the directors, the editors, the cinematographers, the designers. We can all do these amazing things, these incredible things, and people let us do them because it all generates money. But look at the final products: not worth spending two hours watching, let alone months and months making. Certainly not worth squandering all that ability on. Ridiculous, hollow, hypocritical, cynical, corrupt trash. And I'm grateful to do it. But the thing is, I'm trying to exert some control finally, trying to hold out for something decent. But, see, there isn't anything decent, so you get into these habits of rationalizing: 'Oh, it's not really so bad, you know; it doesn't actually *glorify* violence, it *depicts* violence.' 'It isn't *actually* pointless, it's a *parody* of pointlessness.'"

"Maybe—" But what? Cheryl's attention has been a bright ribbon threading through this billowing newness. "Maybe you should—"

"I don't know why I'm talking about this," Carter interrupts. "I don't know why I'm saying these things to you. What do you care? You probably *watch* all this shit."

What? Cheryl freezes.

"You probably think it's all fantastic—"

"As a matter of fact," Cheryl says—normally she might not find it worth it to protest, but she feels good; she'll be generous, help him and herself out of this—"I don't happen to think about it at all. You think it's big news those movies are stupid? You think you're the only person that ever noticed?"

"I'm sorry," Carter says. "I'm sorry. You're right, I'm sorry."

"Everybody knows they're stupid. Nobody but you cares, is all."

"You're right. Listen, I'm mortified. I apologize, O.K.? I've got a terrible attitude, I know." He holds up a little peace offering on the matchbook. "It's just that I'm so used to people who take it absolutely seriously—I'm so used to dealing with these very aggressive, very combative people, who act as if this moronic shit was the most important stuff in the world. I don't know any people like you. I'm completely out of touch with the real world."

"You think I'm the real world?" Cheryl says. "Jesus."

"Yeah," Carter says. "Anyhow, the only living inhabitant."

Cheryl shakes her head and smiles provisionally.

"What a smile," Carter says. "And this play—I've sort of said I'll do it, but I don't know. I haven't actually signed anything. I'm supposed to do that tomorrow. Tomorrow, Christ—what time is it? Today. And there are a lot of good reasons to do it. Because, for one thing, it would be something to do. And for another thing, it's O.K. I mean, there's nothing actually criminal about the script. Also, I haven't been near a stage for years, and it's a completely different set of techniques. Very interesting. Working in real time. With other performers. Everybody spinning a web of concentration. Doing the same thing over and over and making it better." He lies down with his head in Cheryl's lap. "Different techniques." He grins. "Shouting."

"Um," she agrees contentedly.

"What do you know about it?" he says as Cheryl smooths his hair back from his face. "Don't stop, that feels good. And at least there's a real script, you know? Some sort of a text. Even if it's complete shit from beginning to end, at least it's *something*—it was written by an actual human being, not by a million monkeys at a story conference, with everybody else, like me, throwing in their ax to get ground. 'Oh, I don't think that's right for my *character*. *My* character wouldn't do that; my character's a *saint*. He might rob the bank, but he wouldn't shoot the poor old guard, he'd shoot the shitty *cop*, who beats his wife.' Hey," he complains, as Cheryl neglects his hair in order to scoop up a little spoonful from the coffee table. "Me, too, at least. Not that this play's Ibsen, you understand. The guy's a novelist is the problem, not a playwright, but this is his first play, so everybody's falling all over themselves about it. Especially him, you know? All these guys have a play up their sleeve, they all think they can write a play. But it's a special thing, a special set of skills. Not to denigrate this guy—he's an excellent writer. Excellent. But he just can't write for the stage, when you get down to it. He can't write for actors. All very static, very ponderous. Guy doesn't have a clue. So it could be . . . see, you know what—" He raises his glass, looking through it quizzically, with one eye shut, as if it were a prism. Then he drains what remains inside it. "Kind of thirsty," he says, casting his eyes sideways comically at Cheryl. "No. Thing I meant to say is, there are two sides to every issue. Got that?"

"O.K.," she concedes.

"Wait," he says, peering at his glass again and rotating it. "There's one side to every issue, except it's wraparound. Well, anyhow, never mind, my *point* is, there are a lot of reasons not to do this play, am I right? I mean it's the actors that are left holding the bag, particularly on a stage. No camera, for one thing. And you can't just waltz out onto the stage and play an idea. An idea! Because that's what you look like—print, believe me. But the producers are *crawling*. I'm the only person for this role, I've got to do it, I'm perfect, it was written for me, it would be great for me to do stage work. But the truth is, I'm gonna tell you the truth, which I didn't understand until this second. The truth is, it wouldn't be great for me. It wouldn't be great for me at all, it would be great for them; it would be great for the box office. Unless maybe I can do a little bargaining—talk to them about rewrites, because unless they do something about my part the thing it would be for me is catastrophic, because, see, the entire universe is waiting for me to make the wrong move. 'Did he—could he—oh, no, look, I think maybe he—yes, he—oh, *too bad*, he *sucks!*' So I can't afford to, you know, afford to take something just because it's respectable."

Carter falls silent, while Cheryl drifts along on these considerations.

"You know that girl you met before," Carter says.

"Suzannah," Cheryl says carefully.

"Yeah, Suzannah. She practically had me talked into this thing. She always thinks I should accept offers, just because they're there. Routine challenges. See, that's what she'd do. Course she doesn't have the opportunity to do it, 'cause nobody offers her anything. But that doesn't stop her from having opinions about the way I should conduct myself on every point. Protocol for every possible contingency. What it is is she can't take the strain of constant fluctuation. Which is what life is."

"Maybe that's just how you feel right now," Cheryl says.

Carter sighs. "No," he says, into the sofa.

Cheryl is only briefly ashamed at having caused Carter to dispense with Suzannah this way. After all, Suzannah had been so determined to treat her and Danny like, as if they were—Cheryl doesn't want to think what. To treat them as she had treated them, despite the obvious fact that they were invited guests, friends of Carter's.

"What about you?" Carter says. "Here I am talking and talking. Tell me about you."

But Cheryl's life—a toy life, she thinks—has taken place far below, on an edge of the city which cannot even be seen from up here. "Nothing to tell," she says.

"Come on, no holding out. Tell me—I don't know, tell me about . . . oh, life with Mom, the beauty queen."

Cheryl pauses. She is not equipped! Danny is always far too protective, far too private, to air his concerns. And Judith's exhaustive catalogues of her own calamitous life are vehicles, weapons, ornaments, decoys—anything but confidences. Whereas Carter, she feels, has been so wholehearted, so candid, so sure of her understanding and participation. She longs to offer him an exchange of equivalent value and substance. But how can she present Judith, as a stranger, for inspection? What sound relic can she possibly reclaim from the churning chaos of her own history? She needs some likeness of Judith that she can pull out and hand over, one that will bear up, converting scrutiny to admiration. She concentrates, framing an approximation of Judith, fans it out in aspects, and reaches back, passing over the recurrent scenes, the vanity and pitiable hopes, the violent, precarious gaiety, the carping remorse—far back to when Judith was young and people were eager to give her things, to keep her happy. "It was wonderful when I was little," Cheryl says. She hears her own voice, dropping the words one by one into the huge room. "My mother made everything into an adventure. Everything was special for her. She loved to have fun, she loved to get presents. Everyone always said that she was the child, really, and I was the grownup. It was sort of a joke. I was a very finicky little girl. Sort of disapproving."

"Disapproving, huh?" Carter says fondly.

"And my mother was absolutely wild. She'd laugh and laugh at me about it." Cheryl is halted suddenly, choked by old horror as Judith twists free, shattering the suffocating confections in which Cheryl has attempted to convey her to Carter, and she is shouting, hoarse and frantic, from the next room, and some man is there shouting, too. And Cheryl keeps watching frozen from the doorway until—so quickly that she sees it happen over and over again—Judith folds inward, as Cheryl's own legs buckle, onto her knees, and covers her mouth with her hands. *No more!* But the blood seeps out through Judith's fingers, and then it is Carter, instead of Judith, that Cheryl finds herself guarding through the clearing screen of blood. She turns away, sickened. What is it that he wants? "It's easy to hurt a person who's like that," she finishes, closing down the commotion. "It's easy to disappoint them."

"Disappoint them," Carter says. "Yeah, I know the sort of person. I've got limited patience for that myself. It's always *their* expectations, *their* ideas about everything, that they impose on you. Like that girl Suzannah. And you're supposed to feel guilty about disappointing them."

Something winds off from Cheryl in a slow coil and slides out of reach. What has happened?

"What's the matter?" Carter says. "I know what it is. You always take care of people, don't you, I bet. And no one takes care of you. You haven't even had anything to eat tonight, you know that? Going to waste away, leading this life. What do you want, a salad? Chef's salad?" Carter picks up the phone. "Steak? How about some chicken? High-caliber protein, very healthy. Too boring, huh? Speak to me, they got a lot of stuff down there. Shark? Roast pig? Your own personalized roast pig, little apple in its mouth? You tell me, they got everything."

Wonderful—the waiter arriving with a silver trolley, covered dishes, the waiter in his white jacket, looking at her, the dealer's girlfriend. Cheryl shakes her head, shaking him away. "I'm not hungry," she says. "Please don't call down."

"O.K., O.K.," Carter says. "No calling down, we won't call down. I don't know what you got against it. Your pig, though. Come on, tell you what—let's check out the archives."

The kitchen is vast and spotless. A frying pan, an insubstantial-looking pot, and a spatula stand out in the dim light with an accusing and vaguely ludicrous purity. "Anyone ever been in here before?" Cheryl says. "It looks like a . . . it looks like . . ."

"Right," Carter says. "It looks like a museum. On the moon, for after it's all over. Kitchen Division of the Moon Museum of Humans. No, hey, I use this place all the time. Look, all sorts of stuff. Cornflakes; milk for cornflakes; orange juice, except it's museum property, probably about a thousand years old; capers. What's this?" He takes a paper bag from the bottom shelf of the refrigerator and peers into it. "Pastrami on rye," he comments, returning the bag to the shelf.

"Keeping that for hard times ahead?" Cheryl says.

"What hard times? No hard times ahead. I'm keeping it for . . . I'm keeping it for a keepsake. Can't just throw a magnificent thing like that into the garbage."

Carter picks up the box of cornflakes and inspects it closely. "Not so fast," he says, holding the box over his head as Cheryl reaches for it. "You don't think I know what I'm doing, do you? Listen, I make these things all the time. All us great chefs are men." He takes two heavy bowls from a cupboard and pours cornflakes into them, finishing with a sommelier's flourish and a glance of sly triumph at Cheryl.

"That's really something." She smiles, waiting for Carter to hand her the carton of milk and the bowl filled with packets of sugar, but he is lost in contemplation of a cornflake.

"These things are absolutely incredible," he says, "you know that? These things are insufficiently appreciated. If they cost a hundred dollars a box, rich people would line up for them."

Cheryl draws over to admire the cornflake in Carter's palm, and it does seem an impossible thing, all suspended froth. "How do they make these things, anyway?" she asks. "What are they?"

" 'What are they?' " Carter says magisterially as he puts an arm around Cheryl. "What are they? They are . . . a mystery." The two of them sway slightly, considering the magnitude of things, and Cheryl traces, with slightly drunken precision, the outline of an island on his shirt, that happy sea.

"You like my shirt," he says. "You like my shirt so much I'm going to give it to you."

"You can't give it to me," she says.

"I'm about to experience an anxiety surge. I'm developing severe feelings of competition in regard to my own shirt. I've got to give it to you."

"You can't give it to me," Cheryl says. "It's your souvenir."

"Souvenir," Carter says. "If there's one thing I don't need, it's a souvenir. Come on, I want to show you."

In the bedroom Carter plants himself in front of the closets with a piratical stance. "Booty," he says, flinging open the door from behind which Suzannah had earlier removed her things. "What about this suit? This was when I was a mobster. Look at those lapels. Could carve a tusk with them, huh? Now, this thing—this was from a duel. Fight over some lady. She was a tart, though, as it turned out." He pauses to raise an admonitory eyebrow at Cheryl. "Fatigues, satin jacket—well, that one wasn't wardrobe, we all got that, from my last movie, still sitting on a shelf somewhere."

Carter continues to ransack the closets, piling costumes

and objects on the bed in mirrored splendor. "Powdered wig, motorcycle helmet, pith helmet, space helmet, five-pound jar of Gummi Bears from an A.D., little model Chrysler Building. Yeah, I been in a lot of different time zones, a lot of different incarnations. Oops," he says, remembering, "I was gonna give you my shirt. Turn around. I'm very self-conscious about my chest. I don't want you to see my chest."

"I've seen your chest," Cheryl points out. "I saw your chest about two hundred times tonight. Everybody in the world's seen your chest."

"Ha—" Carter wags a finger. "You're trying to confuse me, trick me into exposing myself. Think I don't know the difference between . . . whoops, the difference between—"

"You win," Cheryl says. She could use a little pick-me-up in any case. "I'll wait for you out there." And she is surprised, upon entering the living room, to see her little gold spoon lying on the coffee table, because she never leaves it out. Never.

In a moment Carter appears, wrapped in a huge black cape. Vampire? Swordsman? And he hands Cheryl the shirt folded small and bright, like a little flag. In return Cheryl holds out for him her spoon, containing almost all that remains of what Danny had deposited on the coffee table.

Silent in the gauzy first light, they sprawl on the sofa, feet to feet. Cheryl is feeling a little ragged. She is usually regulated by Danny's rather sparing intake, she realizes, although she has suspected on recent occasions that Danny is involved with greater quantities than he lets on.

"You're a lovely kid," Carter says. "Lovely kid. Actors always need new life." He sighs. "I'm beginning to be afraid of things, you know? I don't know how that happened to me. When I was your age I used to see people acting out of fear—I never thought it would happen to me. I thought, I'll never get like that. These days I'm so scared I can hardly walk across the room. Sometimes you see people, their life just hasn't worked out. Ever worry that you're going to be one of those people?"

"Sure," Cheryl says. But what does he mean, worked out? She reaches over, pressing at the residue of white on the coffee table, and licks her finger.

"You can really scarf that up, can't you?" Carter says. "You're a real little vacuum cleaner."

"I'm just keeping you company," Cheryl says, stung.

"*You're* keeping *me* company," Carter says. "That's pretty funny. Hey, don't look at me like that. I'm just being honest. It's for your own good. End up on the trash heap, you go on like this."

His foot is jiggling wildly, Cheryl notices. "Want a drink?" she asks. "Or I might have some Valium."

"Shit," Carter says, as tears gather in his eyes. "I'm so fucking sick of being confused."

Cheryl sighs. Danny could have left them one more tiny little eighth or so if he was going to be away this long. He'd certainly know they'd be needing some by now.

"Sorry," Carter says. "I'm sorry, but you don't know what it's like to be frightened. Really frightened, I mean. You're too young to know what that's like. But me, everything I do is motivated by fear now. At least Suzannah's got that part right. I can't even work anymore. I don't have the heart to work. I'm afraid to do this play, I'm afraid to do a movie—"

God, he is *tireless*, Cheryl thinks. And she just isn't interested in some whole new . . . "Do you want her to come back?" she says reluctantly. New *exercise*.

"What—Suzannah?" Carter says. "Where's that drink you were going to make me? Truth is, though, at one time she was a very good friend to me. We took acting class together years ago, and this'll probably seem pretty strange to you but I didn't know anyone like her. All I knew was these very snooty, very convoluted prep-school kids. And at first she seemed so fresh to me, so clear. Course, all it is is, like a lot of good-looking women, she's got a stake in appearances. And that's why she'll never be a good actress, she'll just be one more dime-a-dozen model. Until they turn her out to pasture."

Out to pasture.

"What's the matter?" Carter says, sitting up to look at her. "You don't like me now. You have to like me. I made you like me."

Cheryl hands him his drink without looking at him.

"You forgot the lime," he says, but she still won't look at him. "You're fired, you forgot the lime. Hey." He tugs gently at a lock of her hair, and she closes her eyes. "O.K." He shrugs. "You don't want to play anymore. I don't know why everybody's always so pissed off at me."

"She'll come back," Cheryl says. "If you want her to."

"Not this time," Carter says an instant before the house phone rings, and Cheryl thinks she detects once again a muted triumph as Carter goes to answer it. "Well, there's the man, I guess," he says. "Certainly took his time, didn't he?"

Danny is breathless and apologetic.

"Shouldn't have left me alone with your girlfriend," Carter says. "We're in love, except of course she won't speak to me."

"I am really sorry," Danny is saying. "Listen, I really didn't expect this. I got very hung up by this guy, and there was absolutely nothing I could do. I mean, he's a very good friend. My broker, actually. But he's had some big problems lately, and he really needed to talk. By the way, if you're looking for a broker, this is definitely a guy to consider. He is very, very sharp. And a very fine person."

Still, Cheryl thinks. At least he means it. He does mean it.

"Hey, sweetheart," Danny says, "you're not mad 'cause I had to work, are you?"

Cheryl glances involuntarily at Carter, who looks quickly away. Surely he couldn't think Danny stayed away intentionally—*how dare he?* "We have to go," she says. "I'm tired, and Carter has a big day ahead of him. Meetings, decisions . . ."

"Right, that's right," Danny says. "Oh, yeah, wait—I promised you something to help you sleep, didn't I?"

"I can't sleep," Carter complains. "I've got to talk to those guys."

"Sleep first," Danny orders soothingly. "It'll do you good. These little green ones are for that, and here's something to get you back up again. Help you with your ordeal."

Carter makes no acknowledgment of the few capsules and the new little glass bottle Danny places on the coffee table.

"Oh, wow," Danny says to Cheryl, seeing her gold spoon lying there. "Don't forget this."

"Or this." Carter doesn't look at her, but he stands to hold out the garish folded shirt, and when Cheryl makes no move to take it from him he tucks it directly into her purse. "What do I owe you?" he asks Danny quietly. "For this stuff?"

"Please," Danny says. "Absolutely not. Not this time. Say, that's some— What do you call that thing—a cloak?"

"What a character," Danny says as the doorman holds the door open onto the bright, noisy street. How loud everything is out here! "Literally gave you the shirt off his back, huh? If he decides to stick around, we'll probably be seeing a lot of him. Look, I got a parking space right here. Is that luck, or what?" His face is an impenetrable mask of sweetness, well disposed and as satisfied as if he'd just rolled the evening up and tucked it back into his pocket. He reminds her of someone, Cheryl thinks. Oh, yes: he reminds her of Danny.

Cheryl climbs into the car next to him. A ride home, why not? She is fantastically tired, truly exhausted, and it won't be much fun, later, to wake up. She closes her eyes, and Danny bobs up in the pitching dimness and away. All her surroundings are coming loose, peeling off as the dimness balloons— her antecedents, chunks of her life crumple like Danny and blow past. There is nothing she recognizes, no one even to wave to! What a pity—she smiles slightly, and an instant before she is engulfed by a blissful wave of fatigue she opens her eyes and sees the man who was Danny smiling, too—what a pity that she so eagerly handed Judith over, in a version as diminutive and harmless as Judith ever rendered herself, to serve the transient purposes of a stranger. It would have been so simple just to let Judith out, all ravenous and fractured and appalling, to make some splendid uproar in commemoration of this departure. She thinks her mother might have done that, for her, with pleasure.

THE CUSTODIAN

For years after Isobel left town (was sent from town, to live with an aunt in San Francisco) Lynnie would sometimes see her at a distance, crossing a street or turning a corner. But just as Lynnie started after her Isobel would vanish, having been replaced by a substitute, some long-legged stranger with pale, floaty hair. And while Lynnie might have been just as happy, by and large, not to see Isobel, at those moments she was felled by a terrible sorrow, as though somewhere a messenger searching for her had been waylaid, or was lost.

It was sixteen years after Lynnie had watched Isobel disappearing from view in the back seat of her father's car when Lynnie really did see her again. And then, although Isobel walked right into Lynnie's shop, several long, chaotic moments elapsed before Lynnie understood who Isobel was. "Isobel," she said, and, as the well-dressed customer browsing meditatively among the shelves and cases of expensive food turned to look full at Lynnie, the face that Lynnie had known so well—a girl's face that drew everything toward it and returned nothing—came forward in the woman's.

"Oh," Isobel said. "It's you. But Mother wrote me you were living in Boston. Or did I make that up?"

"You didn't make it up," Lynnie said.

"Well, then," Isobel said, and hesitated. "You're back."

"That about sums it up," Lynnie said. She let her hand bounce lightly against the counter, twice. "I hear you're still in San Francisco," she said, relenting—they were adults now.

"Mmm," Isobel said. "Yes." She frowned.

Lynnie cleared her throat. "And someone told me you have a baby."

"Oh, yes," Isobel said. "Two. And a husband, of course. All that sort of thing." She and Lynnie smiled at one another—an odd, formal equilibrium.

"And you," Isobel said, disengaging. "What are you doing these days?"

"This—" Lynnie gestured. "Of course, I have help now."

"Heavens," Isobel remarked unheatedly.

"'Heavens,'" Lynnie said. "I know." But either more of a reaction from Isobel or less would have been just as infuriating. "Heavens" or "How nice" was all that anyone had said when Lynnie retreated from Boston and managed, through effort born of near-panic, to open the store. All her life Lynnie had been assumed to be inadequate to any but the simplest endeavor; then, from the moment the store opened, that was something no one remembered. No one but her, Lynnie thought; she remembered it perfectly.

"Isn't it funny?" Isobel was saying. "I drove by yesterday, and I thought, How nice that there's a place like that up here now. I'll have to stop in and get something for Mother, to cheer her up."

"I'm sorry about your father," Lynnie said.

"Yes," Isobel said. "God. I was just at the hospital. They say the operation was successful, but I don't know what that's supposed to mean. It seemed they might mean successful in the sense that he didn't die during it." Her flat green glance found Lynnie, then moved away.

"Hard to think of him . . . in a hospital," Lynnie said. "He always seemed so—" He'd seemed so big.

"Strong," Isobel said. "Yes, he's strong all right. He and I are still on the most horrible terms, if you can believe it. It's simply idiotic. I suppose he has to keep it up to justify himself. All these years! You know, this is the first time I've been back, Lynnie—he came out for my wedding, and Mother's made him come with her twice to see the boys, but I haven't been back once. Not once. And there I was today—obviously I'd decided to get here before he died. But did he say anything—like he was glad I'd come? Of course not. Lynnie, he's riddled with tumors, he can't weigh more than a hundred pounds, but he behaved as though he were still sitting in that huge chair of his, telling me what I'd done to him."

Lynnie shook her head. How easily Isobel was talking about these things.

"So," Isobel said.

"Well," Lynnie said.

"Yes," Isobel said.

"I'll wrap up some things for your mother if you want," Lynnie said. "I've got a new pâté I think she'll like. And her favorite crackers have come in."

"Lovely," Isobel said. "Thanks." She pushed back a curving lock of hair and scanned the shelves as though waiting for some information to appear on them. "So Mother comes into your store."

"Oh, yes," Lynnie said.

"Funny," Isobel said. Isobel looked like anyone else now, Lynnie understood with a little shock. Very pretty, but like anyone else. Only her hair, with its own marvelous life, was still extraordinary. "How's your mother, by the way?" Isobel said.

"All right," Lynnie said, and glanced at her. "So far."

"That's good," Isobel said opaquely.

"And at least she's not such a terror anymore," Lynnie said. "She's living up north with Frank now."

"Frank . . ." Isobel said.

"Frank," Lynnie said. She reached up to the roll of thick waxed paper and tore a piece off thunderously. "My brother. The little one."

"Oh, yes," Isobel said. "Of course. You know, this feels so peculiar—being here, seeing you. The whole place stopped for me, really, when I went away."

"I'm sure," Lynnie said, flushing. "Well, we still exist. Our lives keep going on. I have the store, and people come into it. Your mother comes in. Cissy Haddad comes in. Ross comes in, Claire comes in. All six of their children come in. . . ."

"Six—" Isobel stared at Lynnie; her laugh was just a breath. "Well, I guess that means they stayed together, anyway."

"Mostly," Lynnie said. But Isobel only waited, and looked at her. "There was a while there, a few years ago, when he moved in with an ex-student of his. Claire got in the van with the four youngest—Emily and Bo were already at school— and took off. It didn't last too long, of course, the thing with the girl, and of course Claire came back. After that they sold the stone house. To a broker, I heard."

"Oh," Isobel said. Absently she picked up an apple from a mound on the counter and looked into its glossy surface as though it were a mirror.

"They're renovating a farmhouse now," Lynnie said. "It's much smaller."

"Too bad," Isobel said, putting down the apple.

"Yes."

"Was she pretty?" Isobel asked.

"Who?" Lynnie said. "Ross's girl? Not especially."

"Ah," Isobel said, and Lynnie looked away, ashamed of herself.

Isobel started to speak but didn't. She scanned the shelves again vaguely, then smiled over at Lynnie. "You know what else is funny?" she said. "When I woke up this morning, I looked across the street. And I saw this woman going out the door of your old house, and just for an instant I thought, There's Lynnie. And then I thought, No, it can't be—that person's all grown up."

For a long time after Isobel had left town, Lynnie would do what she could to avoid running into Ross or Claire; and eventually when she saw them it would seem to her not only that her feeling about them had undergone an alteration but that they themselves were different in some way. Over the years it became all too clear that this was true: their shine had been tarnished by a slight fussiness—they had come to seem like people who were anxious about being rained on.

Newcomers might have been astonished to learn that there was a time when people had paused in their dealings with one another to look as Ross walked down the street with Claire or the children. Recent arrivals to the town— additions to the faculty of the college, the businessmen and bankers who were now able to live in country homes and still work in their city offices from computer terminals—what was it they saw when Ross and Claire passed by? Fossil forms, Lynnie thought. Museum reproductions. It was the Claire and Ross of years ago who were vivid, living. A residual radiance clung to objects they'd handled and places where they'd spent time. The current Ross and Claire were lightless, their own aftermath.

Once in a while, though—it happened sometimes when she encountered one of them unexpectedly—Lynnie would see them as they had been. For an instant their sleeping power would flash, but then their dimmed present selves might greet Lynnie, with casual and distant politeness, and a breathtaking pain would cauterize the exquisitely reworked wound.

It is summer when Lynnie and Isobel first come upon Ross and Claire. Lynnie and Isobel live across the street from one another, but Isobel is older and has better things to do with her time than see Lynnie. And because Lynnie's mother works at the plant for unpredictable stretches, on unpredictable shifts, Lynnie frequently must look after her younger brothers. Still, when Lynnie is free, she is often able to persuade Isobel to do something, particularly in the summers, when Isobel is bored brainless.

They take bicycle expeditions then, during those long summers, often along the old highway. The highway is silent, lined with birchwoods, and has several alluring and mysterious features—among them a dark, green wooden restaurant with screened windows, and a motel, slightly shabby, where there are always, puzzlingly, several cars parked. Leading from the highway is a wealth of dirt roads, on one of which Lynnie and Isobel find a wonderful house.

The house is stone, and stands empty on a hill. Clouds float by it, making great black shadows swing over the sloping meadows below with their cows and barns and wildflowers. Inside, in the spreading coolness, the light flows as variously clear and shaded as water. Trees seem to crowd in the dim recesses. The house is just there, enclosing part of the world: the huge fireplace could be the site of gatherings that take place once every hundred, or once every thousand, years. The girls walk carefully when they visit, fearful of churning up the delicate maze of silence.

For several summers, the house has been theirs, but one day, the summer that Lynnie is twelve and Isobel is just turning fourteen, there is a van parked in front. Lynnie and Isobel wheel their bicycles stealthily into the woods across the road and walk as close as they dare, crouching down opposite the house, well hidden, to watch.

Three men and a woman carry bundles and cartons into the house. Bundles and cartons and large pieces of furniture sit outside, where two small children tumble around among them, their wisps of voices floating high into the birdcalls and branches above Lynnie and Isobel. The woman is slight, like a child herself, with a shiny braid of black hair down her back, and there is no question about which of the men she, the furniture, and the children belong to.

Lynnie squints, and seems to draw closer, hovering just too far off to see his face. Then, for just a fraction of a second, she penetrates the distance.

The sun moves behind Lynnie and Isobel, and the man to whom everything belongs waves the others inside, hoisting up the smaller child as he follows. Just as Lynnie and Isobel reach cautiously for their bicycles, the man looks out again, shading his eyes. They freeze, and for a moment he stands there peering out toward them.

Neither Lynnie nor Isobel suggests going on—to town, or to the gorge, or anywhere. They ride back the way they've come, and, without discussion, go upstairs to Isobel's room.

Isobel lies down across her flounced bed while Lynnie wanders around absently examining Isobel's things, which she knows so well: Isobel's books, her stuffed animals, her china figurines.

"Do you think we're the first people to see them?" Lynnie says.

"The first people *ever*?" Isobel says, flopping over onto her side.

Lynnie stares out Isobel's window at her own house. She doesn't know what to do when Isobel's in a bad mood. She should just leave, she thinks.

From here, her house looks as though it were about to slide to the ground. A large aluminum cannister clings to its side like a devouring space monster. "Do you want to go back out and do something?" she asks.

"What would we do?" Isobel says, into her pillow. "There's nothing to do. There's not one single thing to do here. And now would you mind sitting down, please, Lynnie? Because you happen to be driving me insane."

As she leaves Isobel's, Lynnie pauses before crossing the street to watch her brothers playing in front of the house. They look weak and bony, but the two older boys fight savagely. A plastic gun lies near them on the ground. Frank, as usual, is playing by himself, but he is just as banged up as they are. His skin is patchy and chapped—summer and winter he breathes through his mouth, and even this temperate sun is strong enough to singe the life out of his fine, almost white hair. She looks just like him, Lynnie thinks. Except chunky. "Chunky" is the word people use.

Inside, Lynnie's mother is stationed in front of the TV. At any hour Lynnie's mother might be found staring at the television, and beyond it, through the front window, as though something of importance were due to happen out on the street. The television is almost always on, and when men friends come to visit, Lynnie's mother turns up the volume, so that other noises bleed alarmingly through the insistent rectangle of synthetic sound.

Lynnie brings a paper napkin from the kitchen and inserts it between her mother's glass of beer and the table. "May I inquire . . . ?" her mother says.

"Isobel's mother says you should never leave a glass on the furniture," Lynnie says. "It makes a ring."

Lynnie's mother looks at her, then lifts the glass and crumples the napkin. "Thank you," she says, turning back to her program. "I'll remember that." A thin wave of laughter comes from the TV screen, and little shapes jump and throb there, but Lynnie is thinking about the people from the stone house.

Lynnie's mother can be annoyed when she knows that Lynnie has been playing with Isobel; Isobel's father works for the same company Lynnie's mother works for, but not in the plant. He works in the office, behind a big desk. Whenever Lynnie is downstairs in Isobel's house and Isobel's father walks in, Lynnie scuttles as though she might be trodden underfoot. In fact, Isobel's father hardly notices her; perhaps he doesn't even know from one of her visits to the next that she is the same little girl. But he booms down at Isobel, scrutinizing her from his great height, and sometimes even lifts her way up over his head.

Isobel's mother is tall and smells good and dresses in neat wool. Sometimes when she sees Lynnie hesitating at the foot of the drive she opens the door, with a bright, special smile. "Lynnie, dear," she says, "would you like to come in and see Isobel? Or have a snack?" But sometimes, when Lynnie and

Isobel are playing, Isobel's mother calls Isobel away for a whispered conference, from which Isobel returns to say that Lynnie has to go now, for this reason or that.

When Lynnie looks out the window of the room she shares with Frank, she can see Isobel's large, arched window, and if the light is just right she can see Isobel's bed, too, with its white flounces, and a heavenly blue haze into which, at this distance, the flowers of Isobel's wallpaper melt.

One day, doing errands for her mother in town, Lynnie sees the woman from the stone house coming out of the bakery with the children, each of whom carefully holds a large, icing-covered cookie. The woman bends down and picks up one of the children, smiling—unaware, Lynnie observes, that people are noticing her.

Lynnie sees the woman several times, and then one day she sees the man.

She has anticipated his face exactly. But when he smiles at her, the little frown line between his eyes stays. And the marvelousness of this surprise causes a sensation across the entire surface of her skin, like the rippling of leaves that demonstrates a subtle shift of air.

When Lynnie sees Isobel she can't help talking about the people from the stone house. She describes variations in their clothing or demeanor, compiling a detailed body of knowledge while Isobel lies on her bed, her eyes closed. "Should we give them names?" Lynnie says one afternoon.

"No," Isobel says.

But Lynnie can't stop. "Why not?" she says, after a moment.

" 'Why not?' " Isobel says.

"Don't, Isobel," Lynnie pleads.

" 'Don't, Isobel,' " Isobel says, making her hands into a tube to speak through. Her voice is hollow and terrifying.

Lynnie breathes heavily through her mouth. "Why not?" she says.

"Why *not*," Isobel says, sitting up and sighing, "is because they already have names."

"I know," Lynnie says, mystified.

"Their names," Isobel says, "are Ross and Claire."

Lynnie stares at her.

"They had dinner at Cissy Haddad's house one night," Isobel says. "Ross is going to be teaching medieval literature at the college. He's in Cissy's father's department."

" 'Department'?" Lynnie says.

"Yes," Isobel says.

Lynnie frowns. "How do you know?" she asks. How *long* has Isobel known?

Isobel shrugs. "I'm just telling you what Cissy said." She looks at Lynnie. "I think Cissy has a crush on him."

"What else did Cissy say?" Lynnie asks unhappily.

"Nothing," Isobel says. "Oh. Except that he's thirty-five and Claire's only twenty-three. She used to be one of his students."

"One of his students?" Lynnie says.

" 'One of his——' " Isobel begins, and then flops down on the bed again. "Oh, Lynnie."

One day Lynnie sees Cissy Haddad in the drugstore. Lynnie hurries to select the items on her mother's list, then waits until Cissy goes to the counter. "Hi," she says, getting into line behind Cissy. She feels herself turning red.

"Oh, hi, Lynnie," Cissy says, and smiles wonderfully. "Are you having a fun summer?"

"Yes," Lynnie says.

"What're you doing?" Cissy says.

"Just mostly looking after my brothers," Lynnie says. She feels bewildered by Cissy's dazzling smile, her pretty sundress. "And riding around and things with Isobel."

"That's good," Cissy says. And then, instead of saying something useful about Isobel, which might lead to Ross and Claire, she asks, "Are you coming to high school this year? I can't remember."

"No," Lynnie says. "Isobel is."

Cissy peers into Lynnie's basket of embarrassing purchases.

"What are you getting?" she asks.

"Things for my mother," Lynnie says, squirming. "What about you?"

"Oh," Cissy says. "Just lipstick."

One fall day when Lynnie gets home from school, her mother summons her over the noise from the TV. "You got a phone call," she says shortly. "The lady wants you to call her back." And Lynnie knows, while her mother is still speaking, whom the call was from.

Lynnie dials, and the soft, dark shadow of Claire's voice answers. She is looking for someone to help with the children on a regular basis, she explains, several afternoons a week. She got Lynnie's name from Tom Haddad's daughter. She knows that Lynnie is very young, but this is nothing difficult—just playing with the children upstairs or outside so that she can have a couple of hours to paint. "I thought I would be able to do so much here," she says, as though Lynnie were an old friend, someone her own age, "but there's never enough time, is there?"

"I'll need you just as much with the boys," Lynnie's mother says later. "And you'd better remember your homework."

"I will," Lynnie says, though, actually, beyond a certain point, it scarcely matters; however hard she tries, she lags far behind in school, and her teachers no longer try to stifle their exclamations of impatience. "I'll do my homework." And her mother makes no further objections; Lynnie will be earning money.

Claire leads Lynnie around in the house that used to be Lynnie and Isobel's. Now it is all filled up with the lives of these people.

Everywhere there is a regal disorder of books, and in the biggest room downstairs, with its immense fireplace, there are sofas and, at one end, a vast table. A thicket of canvases and brushes has sprung up in a corner, and Lynnie sees pictures of the table on whose surface objects are tensely balanced, and sketch after sketch of Ross and the children. "What do you think?" Claire says, and it is a moment before Lynnie realizes what Claire is asking her.

"I like them," Lynnie says. But in fact they frighten her—the figures seem caught, glowing in a webby dimness.

In the kitchen huge pots and pans flash, and a great loaf of brown bread lies out on a counter. Claire opens the door to Ross's study; stacks and stacks of paper, more books than Lynnie has ever seen breed from its light-shot core.

Upstairs Bo and Emily are engrossed in a sprawling project of blocks. Emily explains the dreamlike construction to

Lynnie, gracefully accepting Bo's effortful elaborations, and when Lynnie leaves both children reach up to her with their tanned little arms.

Twice a week Lynnie goes to the stone house. Bo and Emily have big, bright, smooth wooden toys, some of which were made by Ross. Lynnie strokes the toys; she runs her hand over them like a blind person; she runs her hand over the pictures in Bo and Emily's beautiful storybooks. But then Claire counts out Lynnie's money, and Lynnie is to go. And at the first sight of her own house she is slightly sickened, as upon disembarkation—not by the firm ground underfoot but by a ghostly rocking of water.

When Claire finishes painting for the afternoon, she calls Lynnie and Bo and Emily into the kitchen. For a while, although Bo and Emily chatter and nuzzle against her, Claire seems hardly to know where she is. But gradually she returns, and makes for herself and Lynnie a dense, sweet coffee in a little copper pot, which must be brought to the boil three times. They drink it from identical tiny cups, and Lynnie marvels, looking at Claire, that she herself is there.

Some afternoons Ross is around. He announces that he will be in his study, working, but sooner or later he always appears in the kitchen, and talks about things he is reading for his book.

"What do you think, Lynnie?" he asks once. He has just proposed an idea for a new chapter, to which Claire's response was merely "Possible."

Lynnie can feel herself blush. "I don't know," she says.

Amusement begins to spread from behind his eyes. "Do you think it's a good idea?" he asks.

"Yes," she says, wary.

"Why?" he says.

"Because you just said it was," Lynnie says, turning a deeper red.

He laughs happily and gives Lynnie a little hug. "You see?" he says to Claire.

When the snow lies in great drifts around the stone house, students begin to come, too, and sit around the kitchen. They drink beer, and the girls exclaim over Bo and Emily while the boys shyly answer Claire's gentle questions and Lynnie holds her coffee cup tightly in misery. Now and again, as he talks to them, Ross touches the students lightly on the wrist or shoulder.

Late one Saturday afternoon, Lynnie is washing dishes in her own house when her mother walks in with several large grocery bags. "I was just in town," she announces unnecessarily, and grins an odd, questioning grin at Lynnie. "Now, who do you think I saw there?"

"I don't know who you saw," Lynnie says, reaching for a dishcloth.

"The man you work for," her mother says.

"How do you know who he is?" Lynnie says.

"Everybody knows who he is," her mother says. "He was in the stationery store. I just went in to get some tape, but I stuck around to watch. Muriel Furman was waiting on him. She almost went into a trance. That poor thing." Lynnie's mother shakes her head and begins to unload groceries. "Homeliest white woman I ever saw."

"Mother," Lynnie says. She stares unhappily out the little window over the sink.

"I've seen the wife around a few times, too," Lynnie's mother says. "She's a pretty girl, but I wish her luck with him."

Lynnie has not been to Isobel's house once this year. Isobel comes and goes with Cissy Haddad and other high-school friends. From across the street Lynnie can sometimes see their shapes behind the film of Isobel's window. At night, when Isobel's light is on and her window is transparent, Lynnie watches Isobel moving back and forth until the curtain closes.

One afternoon as Lynnie is arriving home, she almost walks into Isobel. "Wake up, Lynnie," Isobel says. And then, "Want to come over?"

"Lynnie, dear," Isobel's mother says as Lynnie and Isobel go upstairs. "How *nice* to see you."

It has been so long since Lynnie has been in Isobel's room that Isobel's things—the flouncy bed and the china figurines and the stuffed animals she used to see so often—have a new, melancholy luster. "How's high school?" she asks.

"It's hard," Isobel says. "You won't believe it."

But Lynnie will. She does. Almost every day she remembers that that is where she is going next fall—to the immense, tentacled building that looks like a factory. She has reason to suspect that she will be divided from most of her classmates there, and put into the classes for people who won't be going on to college—the stupid people—with all the meanest teachers. No one has threatened her with this, but everybody knows how it works. Everybody knows what goes on in that building.

Lynnie picks up a stuffed turtle and strokes its furry shell.

"How's school?" Isobel asks. "How's old Miss Fisher?"

"She doesn't like me," Lynnie says. "Miss Fish Face."

"Oh, well," Isobel says. "So what? Soon you'll never have to see her again." She looks at Lynnie and smiles. "What else have you been up to?"

Lynnie feels slightly weak because of what she is about to tell Isobel. She has been saving it up, she realizes, a long time. "Well," she says slowly, "I've been babysitting for the kids at the stone house."

"Have you?" Isobel says, but as she says it Lynnie understands that Isobel already knew, and although Isobel is waiting, Lynnie cannot speak.

"You know what—" Isobel says after a moment. "Lynnie, what are you doing to that poor turtle? But do you know what Cissy's father said about that man, Ross? Cissy's father said he's an arrogant son of a bitch." She looks at Lynnie, hugging her pillow expectantly. "I heard him."

Lynnie and Claire and three students watch as Ross describes various arguments concerning a matter that has come up in class. The students look at him with hazy, hopeful smiles. But not Lynnie—she is ashamed to have heard what Isobel said to her.

Ross glances down at her unhappy face. "Apparently Lynnie disagrees," he says, stroking a strand of her pale, flossy hair behind her ear. "Apparently Lynnie feels that Heineman fails to account for the Church's influence over the emerging class of tradesmen."

The students laugh, understanding his various points, and Ross smiles at Lynnie. But Lynnie is ashamed again—doubly ashamed—and leans for comfort into the treacherous hand that still strokes her hair.

Lynnie has two Rosses who blend together and diverge unpredictably. Many mornings begin drowsily encircled in the fleecy protection of one, but sometimes, as Lynnie continues to wake, the one is assumed into the other. He strokes Lynnie's hair, inflicting injury and healing it in this one motion, and she opens her eyes to see her own room, and Frank curled up in the other bed, breathing laboriously, susceptible himself to the devious assaults of dreams.

In the fall, Lynnie is put, as she had feared, into the classes for the slowest students. Had anyone entertained hopes for her, this would have been the end of them.

A few of her old schoolmates are confined to her classes, but most have sailed into classes from which they will sail out again into college, then marriage and careers. She sees them only in the halls and the lunchroom and on the athletic fields. Every day they look taller, more powerful, more like strangers.

Most of those in her classes really are strangers. But in some ways they are as familiar as cousins met for the first time. Their clothes, for instance, are not right, and they are the worst students from all the elementary schools in the area. The boys are rough or sly or helpless, or all three, like her brothers, and the girls are ungainly and bland-looking. They stand in clumps in the halls, watching girls like Isobel and

Cissy Haddad with a beleaguered envy, and trading accounts of the shocking things such girls have been known to do.

Oddly, Isobel is friendlier to Lynnie at school, in full view of everyone, than she is out of school, despite Lynnie's stigma. "Hi, Lynnie," she calls out with a dewy showpiece of a smile, not too different from her mother's.

"Hi," Lynnie answers, facing a squadron of Isobel's friends.

One afternoon as Lynnie approaches her house a silence reaches for her like a suction. Her brothers are not outside, and the television is not on. No one is in the kitchen or up-stairs. She sits without moving while the winter sky goes dark. Across the street Isobel turns on the light in her room and sits down at her little desk. After a while she leaves, turn-ing off the light, but Lynnie continues to stare at the blank window. By the time Lynnie hears her mother's car, her arms and legs feel stiff. She waits for a moment before going down-stairs to be told what has happened.

Frank is in the hospital with a ruptured appendix, her mother says; her face has a terrible jellylike look. If she could see her own face, Lynnie wonders, would it look like that?

There will be no more going to the stone house; she will be needed at home, her mother is saying, staring at Lynnie as though Lynnie were shrinking into a past of no meaning—the way a dying person might look at an enemy.

The next day, Lynnie seeks out Isobel in the lunchroom. "A ruptured appendix," Isobel says. "That's really dangerous, you know."

"My mother says Frank is going to be all right," Lynnie says doggedly.

"Poor Lynnie," Isobel says. "So what are you going to do if Ross and Claire hire someone else?"

Lynnie puts her head down on the lunch table and closes her eyes. The sweet, unpleasant smell of the lunchroom rises up, and the din of the students, talking and laughing, folds around her.

"Poor Lynnie," Isobel says again.

Later that week, Lynnie brings Isobel to the stone house. Claire makes coffee, and when she brings out a third tiny china cup, Lynnie is unable to hear anything for several seconds.

Ross comes in, whistling, and lets the door slam behind him. "What's this?" he asks, indicating Isobel. "Invader or captive?"

"Friendly native," Claire says. "Isobel's going to be our new Lynnie."

"What's the matter with our old Lynnie?" Ross says. He looks at Isobel for a moment. "Our old Lynnie's fine with me."

"Oh, Ross." Claire sighs. "I told you. Lynnie's brother is sick."

"Hmm," Ross says.

"He's in the hospital, Ross," Claire says.

"Oh, God," Ross says. "Yes, I'm sorry to hear that, Lynnie."

"First day of the new semester," Claire says to Lynnie. "He's always disgusting the first day. How are your new students, my love?"

"Unspeakable," Ross says.

"Truly," Claire says. She smiles at Isobel.

"Worse than ever," Ross says, taking a beer from the

refrigerator. "There isn't *one*. Well, one, maybe. A possibility. A real savage, but she has an interesting quality. Potential, at least."

"I used to have potential," Claire says, "but look at me now."

Ross raises his beer to her. "Look at you now," he says.

Ross holds the door as Lynnie and Isobel leave. "I've seen you in town," he says to Isobel. "You're older than I thought."

She glances up at him and then turns back to Claire. "Goodbye," she says. "See you soon."

"See you soon," Claire says, coming to join them at the door. "I do appreciate this. I'm going to have another baby, and I want to get in as much painting as I can first."

"You're going to have another baby?" Lynnie says, staring.

"We're going to have hundreds of babies," Ross says, putting his arms around Claire from behind. "We're going to have hundreds and hundreds of babies."

Afterward, Lynnie would become heavy and slow whenever she even thought of the time when Frank was sick. Their room was desolate while he was in the hospital; when he returned she felt how cramped it had always been before. Frank was testy all the time then, and cried easily. Her family deserved their troubles, she thought. Other people looked down on them, looked down and looked down, and then when they got tired of it they went back to their own business. But her family—and she—were the same whether anyone was looking or not.

Isobel's mother stops Lynnie on the sidewalk to ask after Frank. The special, kind voice she uses makes Lynnie's skin jump now. How could she ever have thought she adored Isobel's mother, Lynnie wonders, shuddering with an old, sugared hatred.

At night Lynnie can see Isobel in her room, brushing her hair, or sometimes, even, curled up against her big white pillows, reading. Has Isobel seen Ross and Claire that day? Lynnie always wonders. Did they talk about anything in particular? What did they do?

At school, Isobel sends her display of cheery waves and smiles in Lynnie's direction, and it is as though Ross and Claire had never existed. But once in a while she and Isobel meet on the sidewalk, and then they stop to talk in their ordinary way, without any smiles or fuss at all. "Claire's in a good mood," Isobel tells Lynnie one afternoon. "She loves being pregnant."

Pregnant. What a word. "How's Ross?" Lynnie says.

"He's all right." Isobel shrugs. "He's got an assistant now, some student of his. Mary Katherine. She's always around."

Lynnie feels herself beginning to blush. "Don't you like him?"

"I like him." Isobel shrugs again. "He lends me books."

"Oh." Lynnie looks at Isobel wonderingly. "What books?" she says without thinking.

"Just books he tells me to read," Isobel says.

"Oh," Lynnie says.

It is spring when Lynnie returns to the stone house. She is hugged and exclaimed over, and Emily and Bo perform for her, but she looks around as though it were she who had just come out of a long illness. The big, smooth toys, the wonderful picture books no longer inspire her longing, or even her interest.

"We've missed you," Claire says. Lynnie rests her head against the window frame, and the pale hills outside wobble.

But Claire has asked Isobel to sit for a portrait, so Isobel is at the stone house all the time now. The house is full of people— Lynnie upstairs with Emily and Bo, and Ross in his study with Mary Katherine, and Isobel and Claire in the big room among Claire's canvases.

In the afternoons they all gather in the kitchen. Sometimes Mary Katherine's boyfriend, Derek, joins them and watches Mary Katherine with large, mournful eyes while she smokes cigarette after cigarette and talks cleverly with Ross about his work. "Doesn't he drive you crazy?" Mary Katherine says once to Claire. "He's so opinionated."

"Is he?" Claire says, smiling.

"Oh, Claire," Mary Katherine says. "I wish I were like you. You're *serene*. And you can *do* everything. You can paint, you can cook . . ."

"Claire can do everything," Ross says. "Claire can paint, Claire can cook, Claire can fix a carburetor . . ."

"What a useful person to be married to," Mary Katherine says.

Claire laughs, but Derek looks up at Mary Katherine unhappily.

"*I* can't do anything," Mary Katherine says. "I'm hopeless. Aren't I, Ross?"

"Hopeless," Ross says, and Lynnie's eyes cloud mysteriously. "Truly hopeless."

Now and again Ross asks Isobel's opinion about something he has given her to read. She looks straight ahead as she answers, as though she were remembering, and Ross nods soberly. Once Lynnie sees Ross look at Mary Katherine during Isobel's recitation. For a moment Mary Katherine looks back at him from narrow gray eyes, then makes her red mouth into an O from which blossoms a series of wavering smoke rings.

One day in April, when several students have dropped by, the temperature plummets and the sky turns into a white, billowing cloth that hides the trees and farmhouses. "We'd better go now," one of the students says, "or we'll be snowed in forever."

"Can you give me and Lynnie a lift?" Isobel asks. "We're on bikes."

"Stay for the show," Ross says to her. "It's going to be sensational up here."

"Coming?" the student says to Isobel. "Staying? Well, O.K., then." Lynnie sees the student raise her eyebrows to Mary Katherine before, holding her coat closed, she goes out with her friends into the blowing wildness.

"We should go, too," Derek says to Mary Katherine.

"Why?" Mary Katherine says. "We've got four-wheel drive."

"Stick around," Ross says. "If you feel like it." Mary Katherine stares at him for a moment, but he goes to the door, squinting into the swarming snow where the students are disappearing. Behind him a silence has fallen.

"Yes," Claire says suddenly. "Everybody stay. There's plenty of food—we could live for months. Besides, I want to celebrate. I finished Isobel today."

Isobel frowns. "You finished?"

"With your part, at least," Claire says. "The rest I can do on my own. So you're liberated. And we should have a magnificent ceremonial dinner, don't you think, everybody? For the snow." She stands, her hands together as though she has just clapped, looking at each of them in turn. Claire has a fever, Lynnie thinks.

"Why not?" Mary Katherine says. She closes her eyes. "We can give you two a ride home later, Isobel."

Bo and Emily are put to bed, and Lynnie, Isobel, Ross, Claire, Mary Katherine, and Derek set about making dinner. Although night has come, the kitchen glimmers with the snow's busy whiteness.

Ross opens a bottle of wine and everyone except Claire drinks. "This is delicious!" Lynnie says, dazed with happiness, and the others smile at her, as though she has said something original and charming.

Even when they must chop and measure, no one turns on the lights. Claire finds candles, and Lynnie holds her glass up near a flame. A clear patch of red shivers on the wall. "Feel," Claire says, taking Lynnie's hand and putting it against her hard, round stomach, and Lynnie feels the baby kick.

"Why are we whispering?" Ross whispers, and then laughs. Claire moves vaporously within the globe of smeary candlelight.

Claire and Derek make a fire in the huge fireplace while Ross gets out the heavy, deep-colored Mexican dishes and opens another bottle of wine. "Ross," Claire says. But Ross fills the glasses again.

Lynnie wanders out into the big room to look at Claire's portrait of Isobel. Isobel stares back from the painting, not at her. At what? Staring out, Isobel recedes, drowning, into the darkness behind her.

What a meal they have produced! Chickens and platters of vegetables and a marvelously silly-looking peaked and scroll-rimmed pie. They sit at the big table eating quietly and appreciatively while the fire snaps and breathes. Outside, the brilliant white earth curves against a black sky, and black shadows of the snow-laden trees and telephone wires lie across it; there is light everywhere—a great, white moon, and stars flung out, winking.

Derek leans back in his chair, closing his eyes and letting one arm fall around Mary Katherine's chair. She casts a ruminating, regretful glance over him; when she looks away again it is as though he has been covered with a sheet.

Isobel gets up from the table and stretches. A silence falls around her like petals. She goes to the rug in front of the fire and lies down, her hair fanning out around her. Lynnie follows groggily and curls up on one of the sofas.

"That was perfect," Claire says. "Ideal. And now I'm going upstairs." She burns feverishly for a moment as she pauses in the doorway, but then subsides into her usual smoky softness.

"Good night," Lynnie calls, and for full seconds after Claire has disappeared from view the others stare at the tingling darkness where she was.

Ross pushes his chair back from the table and walks over to the rug where Isobel lies. "Who's for a walk?" he says, looking down at her.

Mary Katherine stubs out a cigarette. "Come on," Ross says, prodding Isobel with his foot. Isobel looks at his foot, then away.

Ross is standing just inches from Lynnie; she can feel his outline—a little extra density of air.

"Derek," Mary Katherine says softly. "It's time to go. Lynnie? Isobel?"

"I can run the girls home later," Ross says.

"Right," Mary Katherine says after a moment. She goes to the closet for her coat.

"Come on, you two," Ross says. "Up. Isobel? This is not going to last—" He gestures toward the window. "It's tonight only. Out of the cave, lazy little bears. Into the refreshing night."

Ross reaches a hand down to Isobel. She considers it, then looks up at him. "I hate to be refreshed," she says, still looking at him, and shifts slightly on the rug.

"I don't believe this," Mary Katherine says quietly.

Lynnie sits up. The stars move back, then forward. The snow flashes, pitching her almost off balance. "Wait, wait," Isobel says, scrambling to her feet as Mary Katherine goes to the door. "We're coming."

In the car Derek makes a joke, but no one laughs. Next to Lynnie, Isobel sits in a burnished silence. Branches support a canopy of snow over them as they drive out onto the old highway. Three cars are parked in front of the motel. They are covered with snow; no tire tracks are visible. All the motel windows are dark except one, where a faint aureole escapes from behind the curtain. Isobel breathes—just a feather of a sigh—and leans back against the seat.

Lynnie wakes up roughly, crying out as though she were being dragged through a screen of sleep into the day. Frank is no longer in his bed, and the room is bright. Lynnie sits up, shivering, exhausted from the night, and sees that the sun is already turning the snow to a glaze.

"You got in late enough," Lynnie's mother says when Lynnie comes downstairs.

"I tried not to wake you," Lynnie says.

"I can imagine," her mother says. "You were knocking things over left and right. I suppose those people gave you plenty to drink."

"I wasn't drunk, Mother," Lynnie says.

"No," her mother says. "Good. Well, I don't want you staying late with those people again. You can leave that sort of thing to Isobel. She looked fairly steady on her feet last night going up the drive."

Lynnie looks at her mother.

"I wonder what Isobel's parents think," Lynnie's mother says.

"Isobel's parents trust her, Mother," Lynnie says.

"Well that's *their* problem, isn't it?" her mother says.

Isobel has stopped coming to the stone house, and her portrait leans against the wall, untouched since she left. But one day, at the beginning of summer, she goes along with Lynnie to see the new baby.

"He's strange, isn't he?" Claire says as Isobel picks him up. "They're always so strange at the beginning—much easier to believe a stork brings them. Did a stork bring you, Willie? A stork?"

Through the window they can see Ross outside, working, and Lynnie listens to the rhythmic striking of his spade and the earth sliding off it in a little pile of sound. "We're planting a lilac," she hears Claire say. Claire's voice slides, silvery, through the gold day, and Ross looks up, shading his eyes.

The sun melts into the sky. Lynnie hears Claire and Isobel talking behind the chinking of the spade, but then once, when there should be the spade, there is no sound, and Lynnie looks up to see Ross taking off his shirt. When had Claire and Isobel stopped talking?

Isobel stands up, transferring Willie to Lynnie.

"Don't go," Claire commands quietly.

"No . . ." Isobel says. Her voice is sleepy, puzzled, and she sits back down.

The room is silent again, but then the door bangs and Ross comes in, holding his crumpled shirt. "Hello, everyone," he says, going to the sink to slap cold water against his face. "Hello, Isobel." He tosses back dripping hair.

"Hello," Isobel says.

Lynnie looks up at Claire, but Claire's eyes are half closed as she gazes down at her long, graceful hands lying on the table. "Yes," Claire says, although no one has spoken.

"Ross," Isobel says, standing, "I brought back your book." She hands Ross a small, faded book with gold on the edges of the pages.

He takes the book and looks at it for a moment, at the shape of it in his hand. "Ah," he says. "Maybe I'll find something else for you one of these days."

"Mm," Isobel says, pushing her hair back.

Willie makes a little smacking sound, and the others look at him.

"When's good to drop things by?" Ross says.

"Anytime," Isobel says. "Sometime." She pivots childishly on one foot. "Saturdays are all right."

Claire puts her hands against her eyes, against her fore-head. "Would anybody like iced tea?" she asks.

"Not I," Isobel says. "I have to go."

The students have left town for the summer—even Derek. At least, Lynnie has not seen him since the night it snowed. And Mary Katherine herself is hardly in evidence. She comes over once in a while, but when she finishes her work, instead of sitting around the kitchen, she leaves.

Lynnie might be alone in the house, except for Bo and Emily. Claire is so quiet now, sealed off in a life with Willie, that sometimes Lynnie doesn't realize that she is standing right there. And when Lynnie and the children are outside, the children seem to disappear into the net of gold light. They seem far away from her—little motes—and barely au-dible; the quiet from the house muffles their voices.

Ross is frequently out, doing one thing and another, and his smiles for Lynnie have become terribly kind—self-deprecating and sudden, as though she had become, over-night, fragile or precious. Now that Isobel has finally gone away, Ross and Claire seem to have gone with her; her ab-sence is a vacuum into which they have disappeared. Day af-ter day, nothing changes. Day after day, the sky sheds gold, and nothing changes. The house is saturated with absences.

Now Lynnie sees Isobel only as she streaks by in the little green car she has been given for her sixteenth birthday, or from the window in her room at night before she draws the curtain. One Saturday afternoon when Lynnie is outside with her brothers, Ross pulls up across the street. He waves to

Lynnie as he walks up Isobel's drive and knocks on the door. Lynnie watches as Isobel opens the door and accepts a book he holds out to her. Ross disappears inside. A few minutes later he reemerges, waves again to Lynnie, and drives off.

These days Lynnie's mother is more irritable than usual. There have been rumors of layoffs at the plant. Once, when Lynnie is watching TV with her, they see Isobel's father drive up across the street. "Look at that fat bastard," Lynnie's mother says. "Now, there's a man who knows how to run a tight ship."

Even years and years later, just the thought of the school building could still call up Lynnie's dread, from that summer, of going back to school. Still, there is some relief in finally having to do it, and by the third or fourth day Lynnie finds she is comforted by the distant roaring of the corridors, and the familiar faces that at last sight were the faces of strangers.

One afternoon the first week, she sees Cissy Haddad looking in her direction, and she waves shyly. But then she realizes that Cissy is staring at something else. She turns around and there is Isobel, looking back at Cissy. Nothing reflects from Isobel's flat green eyes.

"Isobel—" Lynnie says.

"Hello, Lynnie," Isobel says slowly, and only then seems to see her. Lynnie turns back in confusion to Cissy, but Cissy is gone.

"Do you want a ride?" Isobel asks, looking straight ahead. "I've got my car."

"How was your summer?" Isobel asks on the way home.

"All right," Lynnie says. The sky is a deep, open blue

again. Soon the leaves will change. "I was sorry you weren't around the stone house."

"Thank you, Lynnie," Isobel says seriously, and Lynnie remembers the way Cissy had been staring at Isobel. "That means a lot to me."

Lynnie's mother looks up when Lynnie comes into the house. "Hanging around with Isobel again?" she says. "I thought she'd dropped you."

Lynnie stands up very straight. "Isobel's my friend," she says.

"Isobel is not your friend," her mother says. "I want you to understand that."

On Saturday, Lynnie goes back to her room after breakfast, and lies down in her unmade bed. Outside it is muggy and hot. She has homework to do, and chores, but she can't force herself to get up. The sounds of the television, and of her brothers playing outside, wash over her.

A car door slams, and Lynnie gets up to look out the window—maybe Isobel is going somewhere and will want company.

But it is not Isobel. It is Ross. Lynnie watches as Ross goes up Isobel's front walk and knocks on the door. The sound of brass on brass echoes up to Lynnie's room.

Isobel's car is in the driveway, but her mother's and father's are gone. Lynnie watches as Isobel appears at the front door and lets Ross in, and then as dim shapes spread in Isobel's room.

Lynnie returns to her bed and lies there. The room bears down on her, and the noise; one of her brothers is crying. She turns violently into the pillow, clenched and stiff, and for a while she tries to cry, but every effort is false, and unsatisfactory. At certain moments she can feel her heart beating rapidly.

Later, when she gets up again, Ross's car is gone. She turns back to the roiling ocean of sheets on her own bed, and reaches out, anticipating a wave rising to her, but it is enragingly inert. She grabs the unresisting top sheet and tries to hurl it to the floor, but it folds around her before it falls, slack and disgusting. The bottom sheet comes loose more satisfyingly, tearing away from the mattress and streaming into her arms like clouds, but a tiny sound bores into the clamor in her ears, and she wheels around to see Frank standing in the doorway with his hand on the knob. He looks at her, breathing uncomfortably through his mouth, before he turns away, closing the door behind him.

That night Lynnie's mother sits in front of the television in the dark, like a priestess. The cold, pale light flattens out her face, and craterlike shadows collect around her eyes, her mouth, in the hollows of her cheeks. "And what do you think of your employer visiting Isobel?" she says.

Across the street, Isobel's window blazes. "He lends Isobel books," Lynnie says.

"I see," her mother says. "Quite the little scholar."

The next day, Lynnie rides her bicycle to the stone house to say that she will not be working there any longer. Pedaling with all her strength, she is not even aware of reaching the edge of town, though afterward she can see every branch of the birchwoods along the old highway as it flashes by, every cinder block of the motel, even the paint peeling from its sign.

Claire stands in the doorway while Lynnie talks loudly, trying to make herself heard through the static engulfing her.

She has too much homework, she tries to explain; she is
sorry, but her mother needs her. Her bicycle lies where she
dropped it in her frenzy to get to the door, one wheel still
spinning, and while she talks she sees dim forms shifting behind Isobel's window, a brief tumbling of entwined bodies on
the damp leaves under the birches, the sad, washed light inside the old motel, where a plain chest of drawers with a mirror above it stands against the wall. In the mirror is a double
bed with a blue cover on which Ross lies, staring up at the
ceiling.

"Yes . . ." Claire is saying, and she materializes in front of
Lynnie. "I understand . . ." From inside, behind Claire, comes
the sound of Ross whistling.

It is the following week that Isobel leaves. Lynnie watches
from her window as Isobel and her mother and father load up
her father's car and get into it. They are taking a trip, Lynnie
thinks; they are just taking a trip, but still she runs down the
stairs as fast as she can, and then, as the car pulls out into
the street, Isobel twists around in the back seat. Her face is
waxy with an unhealthy glow, and her hair ripples out around
her. Lynnie raises her hand, perhaps imperceptibly, but in any
case Isobel only looks.

So nothing has to be explained to Lynnie the next day or
the next or the next, when Isobel does not appear at school.
And she is not puzzled by the groups of girls who huddle in
the corridor whispering, or by Cissy Haddad's strange, tight
greetings, or by the rumor, which begins to circulate almost
immediately, of an anonymous letter to Isobel's parents.

And when, one day soon after Isobel's departure, Isobel's
mother passes her on the sidewalk with nothing beyond a

rapid glance of distaste, Lynnie sees in an instant what Isobel's mother must always have seen: an impassive, solid, limp-haired child, an inconveniently frequent visitor, breathing noisily, hungry for a smile—a negligible girl, utterly unlike her own daughter. And then Lynnie sees Isobel, vanishing brightly all over again as she looks back from her father's car, pressing into Lynnie's safekeeping everything that should have vanished along with her.

HOLY WEEK

SUNDAY

Everything as promised: Costumes, clouds of incense—processions already begun; town tingly with anticipation. Somber, shabby brass bands. Figures of Christ, the Virgin Mother—primitive, elegant—on wooden float-type-things (*anda*, word McGee used). Men in purple satin churning around them. From wooden-shuttered hotel window can see people crossing square with armloads of palm. Truly pleased Zwicker decided to send me. (Shd. make up for Feb. issue/Twin Cities!)

Square in middle of town, town little dish set in ring of mountains, high under the sun. Air glimmery, uncertain; clouds draping mountains, colors diffusing into soft sky. Soft sun. Walls like cloud banks, pretty colors fading, wearing down to stone. Decay subtle, various. Ruins of earthquake (1770s? Check). Shattered arches, pediments, columns—huge. Grasses taking root in the tumbled stone, sprouting tiny white flowers. Churches: lush stone vines, stone fruit. In square, stone fountain with stone shells and mermaids.

Crowds lining the streets—tourists, Indians. Mostly Ladinos (McGee explained: mixed race, Span.+Indian). Indians impenetrable as they watch Jesus pass by, ribs showing through white plaster skin, trickling red plaster blood; they watch so intently, holding their babies up to look. Unnerving, the way they watch, way they walk, gliding along in those fantastical clothes of theirs. Silent emissaries from a vanished world, stranded in ours—gliding through the streets with baskets of flowers on their heads, through the square, through these new centuries of ruins. Squat on their heels at the corners selling hallucinatory textiles or tiny orchid trees, letting the happy tourists haggle. Barefoot, dirt-poor, dressed like royalty—incredible. Only thing: poor judgment to have brought Sarah?

Had awful morning in capital, waiting to hook up with McGees. Awful city. Diesel fumes up your nose. Big black puffs of dirt—soot, or something. Hang there in the air, then whisk over and deposit themselves on your face and clothes. Sarah and I sat in big hotel, shiny and gloomy, full of dark, heavy-faced men in suits and sunglasses. Many mustaches. Daughters in prom dresses, limp sons. Some Americans, too. Prob. business—don't look like tourists. Hotel bar very dark, suit/mustache people gazing over their drinks at Vietnam movie showing on enormous screen. Movie mesmerizingly vile—machine guns, gore, etc., Vietnamese girl, U.S. soldiers in camouflage swarming all over her.

Sarah glowering at screen, running her hands impatiently through her hair, making it fluff up like little yellow chick feathers. Offered to go for walk with her. She said, "Thanks, Dennis. Out there?"

Vietnamese girl ripped down middle. Sarah (very loud): *Shit.* Men glancing at us through currents of black and greenish air. What to do? Had warned Sarah not to drink Margaritas until she got used to the altitude.

Two clean, hardy U.S. types, mid-sixties approx. abruptly confronting us. McGees, of course. "I'll bet you're our man," Mrs. (Dot) said. "The Desk told us you'd be in here."

Clearly Zwicker had not mentioned Sarah. Husband (Clifford) produced expression of aggressive blandness, Dot underwent violently shuttling succession of reactions. How well I've come to know the looks! Might as well be back in Cedar Rapids.

Sarah stared, affronted, as Dot nodded with pity at her tiny skirt, patted her arm. "*Lovely* to meet you," Dot said.

"So," McGee said. We all stood, looked at the screen. A bomb exploded over a small village. McGee snorted, shook his head. Said, "All set, everyone? Luggage up front?"

Filthy little eateries by the side of the road. Harsh dust, like grains of concrete, all over everything. Leaves, trees, caked with harsh, pale dirt. Buildings rotting, people streaming along—so many, so poor—bellying out into the road in the clouds of black exhaust, receding behind us, big, glossy cars shooting past them. Buses swaying on the sharp curves, top-heavy with cargo, clinging passengers.

Tried to monitor conversation in back between Sarah and Dot. Truth is, was very nervous about what Sarah might say, in her mood. Now, this is the *actual* problem about being involved with someone twenty-odd years younger. A trade-off, in my opinion. On the one hand, the intensity, the clarity (generally) of Sarah's reactions. On the other, her impatience, stubbornness, unwillingness to see the other point of view. Fundamentally youth's refusal to acknowledge the subtlety, complexity of a situation; at worst, adds up to a sort of insensitivity.

Still, Dot admittedly hard to take. Could hear her enumerating, at some length, flaws in local postal system. Glanced back, saw Sarah in glaze of boredom, rousing herself to nod sanctimoniously. Frowned warningly, and she shot me electrifying little smile.

McGee pleasant enough. Seemed to enjoy driving. Said he'd been delighted to meet Zwicker when he was up in the

States in the fall: *delighted*. Told McGee how highly Zwicker had spoken of him; said that it was entirely due to him that Zwicker was so eager to get piece on town for supplement (true). McGee offered to help in any way he could. Asked what sort of thing I was after—hotels, restaurants, Easter celebrations? All of it, told him, though supplement particularly interested in food.

He nodded. Said, "We'll see to it." Said he would be more than happy to take me around to restaurants, introduce me to important local grower (could give me interesting regional recipes). Said it would mean a lot, good press coverage in the States. Said tourist revenues had fallen off catastrophically in past decade.

Stark landscape; droopy gray sky. Pines. Long, dark, sad hills. Billboards (all Span., of course) advertising herbicides, pesticides, fungicides, etc. Another: Cement Is Progress. Ant-like figure in valley, tiny beyond billboards, giant load of wood on his bent back. Just like ant with giant leaf, or some other impossible burden.

The sight was timeless, stonily beautiful—solitary peasant in the field. The man's life curved out behind him in a pure, solid arc. Tried to imagine how it felt to have such a life—I mounted the arc, swooped up, then down along it. *Atomized* on contact with the man at the bottom; shards of my life flew all over the car—son, ex, house in Claremont. Dorm all those years ago in Princeton, bank where I worked for so long, new office at the supplement. Waking in my sunny Cedar Rapids bedroom, sometimes Sarah next to me. Other women I've been involved with, movies I've seen, opinions I've held—a burst sackful of items flying all over the car.

Glanced back at Sarah again to reincorporate myself, but her clear eyes were directed out the window, and her piratical earring gleamed—a signal! Meaning? Sarah's earring, my son, my office—all *signals*, incoherent fragments, of which I ought to be the unifying principle; encoded dispatches from my own life! Too loud, too bright to decipher—the urgent, jagged flashing: a messenger shouting across a chasm. A knife lying on the counter. A ditch by the side of the road . . .

MONDAY

Was in strange state yesterday. Better now. Odd how that happens—everything completely inscrutable, intractable, portentous; then everything completely fine. Like having two abutting brains, one of them utter chaos; sickening sensation of slipping through some membrane. Perhaps triggered yesterday by psychobiological response to unfamiliar foods? Pollens?

In any case, over. Hotel first-rate, good night's sleep. Dinner, just Sarah and I, at ex-convent (Santo Tomás, daily except Tues. Spectacular. Must write up, despite food). This morning breakfast in hotel courtyard—flowers, darting hummingbird; fruit, rolls, coffee. Impossible not to feel happy. Sarah clearly blissful. Stretching, reaching over to run her finger along my wrist. Waiter (Ricardo) utterly charmed by her. Had to smile at his expression when she ordered third portion of fruit and rolls.

How could I have doubted, yesterday, it was right to bring her? Of course it was. I think. (Joke.) Ah, so hard to sort out, me and Sarah. What can we really have with one another, ultimately? Occurs to me sometimes that, for all her wildness, restlessness, she wants something more from me than I (obviously) can give.

Have to remind myself always she's at an odd point in life. Hard to remember the terror—a sort of swampiness, feeling of wandering around in a swamp, while some awful *fait accompli* is preparing to drop on top of you.

Looked up and saw her watching me—eyes elongated, sparkling. "You're thinking, Dennis."

"Not really," I said. That look of hers! "I was wondering why you picked me up that night at the Three Chimneys, actually."

"I did that?" Sarah said. "Whoops. Well, gosh, Dennis—I must have thought you'd be fun."

A bit of pineapple lodged in my throat.

"Cheer up, Dennis," Sarah said as I coughed. "A lot of men would be thrilled to be considered a sex object, you know."

"Oh—now, actually, Sarah," I said. "To be serious for a moment, I know the McGees aren't the world's most fascinating people, but it's by their good offices, really, that we're here."

"Yup," Sarah said, patting her stomach as she glanced at it fondly. "Your point?"

"Well," I said, "the fact is, there are certain ways in which everyone is sensitive. For instance, everyone can tell when they're being mocked."

Sarah burped daintily and looked pleased with herself. "Almost everyone," she said.

Sarah gone out for a walk. Can just see from window her tiny bright skirt disappearing around corner. Processions continue. Men in purple satin (Jerusalemites, McGee says) carrying *andas*. Takes dozens to carry each one. Sweat streaming down their faces. Occasionally one stumbles on the cobblestones, slight panic in his eyes. Forcefully primitive representations of Adam and Eve, the world; funny little artificial flowers and flamingos, Christ with loaves, fishes. Tourists darting about with cameras.

Extraordinary activity taking place right outside window. People with immense baskets of flowers, using stencils to make a big rectangular picture with the petals, right on the street. Birds, butterflies, a basket of flowers, all made out of flower petals, appearing on the cobblestones outside. Such a poor country, such impassioned profligacy!

Town even more crowded than yesterday. Young Scandinavians, Americans, Germans, tall and vain, lounging in the square, stretching out bare, tanned legs, trading information, chatting up the Indians, selling each other drugs; Europeans on the balconies of posh vacation homes, drinking from glasses of wine or iced tea as the incense drifts up past them.

Amazing sight on the porticoes of the municipal building across from square—huge families spreading out blankets, starting up little fires in front of the Cathedral to cook corn, stockpots. Children running up and down, playing on the steps, lifting one another to drink from the disease-bearing fountain in the square. Confusing, people like these. Hard to tell who's Indian, who's Ladino. McGee explains many Indians want to pass (status thing, I presume—should have asked). You cut your hair, stop wearing that amazing clothing, speak Span rather than own languages (of which there turn out to be 22!!!!), and bing! Just like that, you're Ladino.

Sarah glorious in knot of Indian children. No question they are cute—what eyes, what smiles! Those ragged, princely

little outfits, runny noses . . . Like nesting dolls in series—
each taking care of an even tinier child. They play with Sarah's hair, combing it, fascinated, with her comb (which trust
she will wash).

Hotel Flor. *Daily 7:00 a.m.—9:30 p.m. After a morning of
browsing through town, the Flor is a delightful stop for the
weary traveler. A large sala to the rear of the hotel, with its
peaceful garden well-hidden from the bustling street, is an ideal
spot for a refreshing meal. A "typical plate" is available at
lunch or dinner, which includes beef accompanied by guaca-
mole, succulent fried plantains, silken black beans, and
chirmol—the favored regional sauce, sparkling with lightly
cooked tomatoes, green onions, and cilantro. Or, for the homesick, the menu offers baked chicken, and a satisfying array of
steaks.*

*Others might prefer to settle into one of the generous chairs
ranged along the leafy courtyard just within the high hotel
walls, to linger over a snack and a frosty drink while listening
to the music of a live marimba band, intermingled with the
calls of the brilliant red, green, and blue parrots, permanent
residents of the huge, gnarled trees in the center of the courtyard. Etc., etc. Mention rooms? Large, airy, clean; waitresses
in native dress.*

Tried to persuade Sarah to order chicken (always safe),
though her *plato típico* turned out to be O.K., I think. Guaca-
mole looked delicious, but warned Sarah off it when I saw
little bits of uncooked green stuff—herbs? chives?—peeking
out. Had drinks there later with McGees, though, in courtyard, and they said guac. sure to be safe in a place like the
Flor. Watched them polish off two orders of chips slathered

with it. Sarah had some, too. Can't blame me if she gets sick! McGees have been down here so long they must have all kinds of protective antibodies.

Was glad I'd had talk with Sarah in morning about the McGees—she was charming with them over drinks. Serious, respectful, asking them how long they've been living down here, etc. Dot explained they still kept home in Virginia, to be near son, daughter-in-law. Had come down frequently for work during seventies and eighties, she said. Fell in love with town. Sarah managing very creditable rendition of rapt attention.

Marimba band started up jarringly. Odd sight—musicians in ceremonial (McGee said) clothing, staring straight ahead, the little mallets bouncing all over the keyboards. Played "I Love Paris." Eerie, uninflected instrument—bit nerve-racking after a time. Band angry about something?

Sarah asked McGee what his job had been. Tactfully avoided word "retirement." McGee said he had been in government for forty years. "Yes"—he said; looked like he was savoring the memory of a marvelous wine—"I was with the Department of Agriculture."

Something squawked, causing Dot to heave like a wave. "Oh, look," she said, subsiding. "Aren't they fun?"

Loutish parrot fussing in the tree above us. Sarah got up to talk to it. "Say something, bird," she said. "Something interesting, please."

Her yellow hair was right next to the bird's red plumage. Its crazy little eyes were rolling around like beads in a dish. "Be careful," I said. "They can take your finger off just like that."

Sarah sighed. Sat back down. Was looking incredibly pretty. Noticed that the courtyard, strangely, was rather lugubrious.

All that shade! Marimbas playing "Happy Birthday" over and over—aimless, serpentine version.

Noticed Sarah goggling in the direction of hotel gate. Turned, myself, to chilling vista: line of soldiers marching past, rifles held out at the ready. It took me a long, choppy instant to understand that I was looking at young boys—they were practically children, but their boots and uniforms had transformed them into something toylike and fathomless, and their eyes were hard with rage. "Is there some kind of trouble here in town?" I said to McGee, when I could speak.

"Not at all," McGee said. "Simply routine."

"You know, they just don't get the point down here," Dot said. " 'Happy Birthday' has a *point*. It must have been a request."

McGee chuckled at Sarah, who was still wide-eyed and greenish. "Not to worry," he said. "Just a symbolic prelude to negotiations." Told us that the town is a national showpiece, so army stays away, for the most part. Evidently, though, have been rumors since Feb. about guerrillas in the surrounding villages. But, McGee said, no actual fighting.

Sarah and I had gotten guidebooks, of course, before leaving, and I had tried to tell her whatever I knew about the region. Not easy to remember what's happening where, though. Who we support and why. All these countries! Veritable stew of armies, guerrilla groups, death squads, wobbly emerging democracies, etc. "A strong military, isn't it?" I said.

Then—oh, so much. So much. How to remember? Careful—get down *just as happened*.

"Well, the reports of abuse tend to be sensationalized in the States," McGee said. "Although it's true these boys can make a mighty nuisance of themselves. Foreigners are perfectly safe, of course, but the tourists don't like the look of it one bit," he added, just as I overheard Dot asking Sarah if she liked to shop.

"Do I like to shop," Sarah said musingly. "Well, now, there's a—"

"What are you two saying over here?" I asked hurriedly.

"Girl talk," Dot said, with a smile to Sarah of pained forgiveness. "I was asking your young friend if she liked to shop. Because, seriously, for those of us who do enjoy such things, this is the town for it. If I were you, in fact, I'd do some collecting now, while it's still possible. Because they're beginning to use synthetic pigments and machines. And even here in town the people don't know what the old things are worth."

Sarah opened her mouth, but I preempted her. "Sarah will have to budget her shopping time," I said. "We won't always be able to count on her company—she's brought along a lot of reading for her thesis."

"Thesis," Dot said. She and McGee exchanged some minute eyebrow work as Sarah made a quick face at me. "I'm impressed."

"Well, well," McGee said. "What field?"

"Art history," I said. "Sarah plans to write about Van Meegeren, the forger."

McGee picked an insect from his drink. "A subject well worth pursuing, I'm sure," he said.

Sarah tilted her head modestly, as though McGee had conferred a great honor. "Let me ask you, Cliff," she said. "Is this army one of the ones we like, or one of the ones we don't like?"

"'We?'" McGee said. Sarah's expression! Poor, unsuspecting McGee. "The United States? Nothing's ever that simple, is it?"

Sarah smiled at him. "Well," she said.

"Oh, *no*—" I said. "That is, do you believe it? They're playing 'My Funny Valentine.'"

"You have to remember, dear," Dot said to Sarah, "the function of the army is to protect people. The army protects the people who own farms from the guerrillas. The army protects the president."

Sarah nodded. "Except in the case of a military coup, I guess," she said sympathetically.

"I de*test* 'My Funny Valentine,'" I said.

But Dot was gurgling delightedly. "*You*," she said, and shook her finger at Sarah.

"Unfortunately—" McGee frowned. "The army is necessary whether we like it or not. This place is teetering on the brink."

Sarah was gazing at McGee with a terrifyingly detached interest.

"Tired?" I said to her. "Time for a nap?"

"Brink of what?" Sarah said.

McGee looked away impatiently. "'*Brink of what?*' she says."

"Well, I could use a nap," I said. "If nobody else could."

"Listen to me, dear," Dot said. She leaned forward and looked into Sarah's eyes. "We may not love the army, but you should understand that everyone hates the guerrillas, now. Even the people they claim to represent. There was a time, of course, when those people put their trust in the guerrillas, but now it's clear to everybody that the guerrillas only cause misery for innocent people."

"Misery how?" Sarah said. "Innocent of what?"

"Sarah," I said.

"After all," Dot said. "There are bound to be—"

"Well, now," McGee said. He gestured around the courtyard full of laughing foreigners. "Every place has its problems. All right, then?" He smiled at Sarah. "Enough said."

"No, Cliff," Dot said. "I think everybody here should understand that where people are behaving suspiciously—if there's any reason for the army to suspect that a village or a family has been tainted—there are bound to be reprisals."

"Naturally. Everyone understands that." McGee turned to Sarah. "Dorothy's only . . ."

"I'm just—" Dot began.

"Dot's only *saying*," McGee said, "that people here have to be more cautious about their affiliations than we at home do."

"For God's sake," I said, much more loudly than I'd intended, just as the marimbas stopped, "what *is* all that screaming?"

Sarah and the McGees turned; stared at me from under a dome of silence while the parrot screeched and cackled hellishly on its dark branch.

El Sombrerito. *Lunch and dinner, Mon.–Sat. Clean, Amer.-owned. Wide variety of steaks, roast chicken. Desserts baked on premises. Pleasant ambiance, rotating shows of local art (paintings, macramé, etc.). Mango mousse a standout—luxurious, satiny, etc.*

TUESDAY

La Marquesa. *Breakfast, lunch, and dinner, Mon.–Sat. Moderately priced. Dramatic view of volcano, mountains.*

Courtyard, waitresses in native dress. Eggs, pancakes, steaks.
Ice creams (not rec.).
   Must look into Sabor de China and Giuseppe's.

Sarah and the hotel maid fascinated with one another, despite the fact that they can't talk to each other at all. María a round, humorous-looking girl. Indian, I surmise (despite maid's uniform) from the long hair, the measuring, satirical expression, the lofty, graceful, telltale walk (saw her in street yesterday carrying trays of toilet paper stacked on her head). Also, Spanish seems not much better than mine. Surely not her first language. She and I communicate with one another by shouting (Procession this morning?!? Yes!?! Nice??! Good!!!).

Since Sarah speaks no Spanish whatsoever, she and María have managed with a much more dignified vocabulary of gestures and smiles. But this morning, as María was changing our bed, Sarah enlisted me as interpreter. "Come on, Dennis. Ask her something."

"What thing?" I said.

"I don't know," Sarah said. "Ask where she lives."

"Don't you think that's prying?" I said.

"No." Sarah looked at me. "Why would that be prying?"

"Well, it isn't, really," I said. "But, after all. She may not want to talk about her private life with strangers. Tourists. She may feel sensitive about that sort of thing. She might very well feel she was being patronized. After all, she's not just a curiosity—she's as real as you or I."

Sarah made a loud snoring sound, which caused María to shake with laughter.

So, after a few garbled exchanges, I was able to tell Sarah that María lived in one of the villages outside town with her husband, her mother, and her children, about an hour's walk away.

"An hour's walk!" Sarah said. "That's a big commute. Do you think she really walks?"

"*¿Qué dice?*" María said.

When I told her what Sarah had said, more or less, she leaned toward me, widened her eyes theatrically, and lowered her voice. "I don't really walk!" she confessed. "I *run.*"

"You run?" I asked her. (Wanted to say, Why on earth, something like that, indicating amazement, but couldn't think how. Surely not literally *on earth*.) "Why?" I said.

She lowered her voice even further. "*Cafetales!*" she said, and launched into a confidential torrent of chatter.

"What's she talking about?" Sarah asked.

"I don't know," I said.

"But what's she *saying*?" Sarah said.

"I don't *know*," I said. "Her Spanish is peculiar. All I can tell is she's saying something about someone *being* somewhere. In the coffee plantations she goes through to get here. I don't *know*."

Just then María took it into her head to ask if Sarah and I had any children. "*¿Qué?*" I said. "No."

"No, what?" Sarah said.

"No, nothing. No, you and I don't have any children."

Sarah laughed. "Relax, Dennis," she said. "Ask her how many children she has."

But María seemed to have anticipated the question. "Tell the señora," she was already saying, solemnly and proudly, "I have seven children. Four of them are living and three of them are dead."

Rest of morning very nice. Sarah hauled me right back into the bed María had just made. Then the market for about an hour with the McGees, after which they dropped us off for lunch at La Mariposa, introduced us to owner. Place very agreeable, will be able to write up nicely. (Daily except Sun.,

12 p.m.–10 p.m.) Gardens, fountain. Very popular with Americans, like ladies at table nearby wearing outfits made from native textiles. "Have you ever *seen* anything so beautiful," they kept saying to one another.

Perhaps can find tactful way to suggest house wine less than ideal. Also meat. (Sarah's baked chicken might have been nice, but somewhat raw, alas.)

Sarah began very funny imitation of the beauty-loving ladies at the table near us. Had to shush her—probably friends of the McGees. Owner cruised by to talk with us for a few minutes. Said how hard things are for restaurants now, prices increasing geometrically, value of currency plummeting, everything grown for export. Told us that price of black beans ("the traditional food of our poor") has almost doubled in recent months. Sarah: "So, what are your poor eating now?"

Couldn't help smiling. Owner smiled, too—with hatred. "I really wouldn't know," he said.

Actually, town might be most beautiful thing I've ever seen myself. Gets more beautiful as eye adjusts. So high, so pale, so strange. Flowers astonishing—graceful rococo shapes, sinuous, pendant, like ornamentations on the churches. Every hour of the day, in every changing tint of air, new details coming forward. The ancient stillness. All the different ancientnesses—Spain, Rome, themselves so new compared to the Indians. All converging right here in the square. Concentrated in the processions, in every dark eye.

Sarah, for all her snootiness to Dot about shopping, can't resist stopping at every corner and every market. Our room now draped with astounding textiles, bits of Indian clothing—

crammed with flowers and little orchid trees. (María shakes her head, amused, all indulgence with Sarah.)

Early this evening processions of costumed children all over the place. Sarah enthralled. Flower-petal pictures appearing everywhere—*alfombras* (carpets) McGee tells me they're called. Put down only to be trampled within hours by the processions—celebration of the suffering of Christ.

Saw a man lifting a mesh sack of mangoes about twice his size. Bent way backward over it, slipped its strap around his forehead, then drew himself forward so that the mangoes rested on his back, as though he were a cart. Sarah stopped in her tracks and stared.

I put a comforting arm around her, tried to move her along. Think it must be particularly humiliating to be stared at if you're doing uncongenial work. "It certainly does look awful to us," I said. "But it must be different for people who do it every day."

"Sure," Sarah said. "The difference is that they do it every day."

I held Sarah away from me and looked at her. "Sarah?" I said. "Are you angry at me?"

"No," she said tentatively.

The group of ladies from the table near us at lunch walked by and waved as though we were all old friends. One called over to us: "How are you enjoying it? Gorgeous, aren't they, the processions?" Shaded her eyes, flashed a toothy smile. "*Thought*-provoking!"

Sarah waved absently, then frowned and nestled against me. I stroked her hair, and the perfume of incense and flowers rose up around us. "Dennis," she said meditatively, "don't you like me?"

"Don't I like you?" I said. I held her away from me and

studied her, but she was serious. "What do you mean? I adore you."

I smiled and gave her a squeeze, but it was a few moments before she spoke. "So then, listen, Dennis. Why did you have to trot out my—my *credentials* for the McGees?"

"I thought you'd be pleased," I said, amazed. Explained that I'd only been trying to provide her with an excuse not to see them. "Besides," I said. "Why shouldn't I be proud of you?"

She drew away from me. "Dennis, who are these people to demand respectability from me? I don't *like* these people. These people are idiots."

Felt oddly stricken. Can't really blame Sarah—that's how she feels. But, still, McGees are clearly doing their best to be hospitable, pleasant. "Of course, the McGees might not be our favorite people," I said. "But why should they be?" Tucked an unruly label back inside Sarah's T-shirt. "And, after all, they're perfectly harmless."

Sarah stared sadly into the lively crowds.

"Besides," I said. "They're getting on." I stooped over, quavered. "I'll be like that soon myself, I suppose."

Sarah frowned again, then laughed. "Oh, *Dennis*," she said, but her hand crept over and curled into mine, like a pliant little animal.

Buen Pastor. *Lunch, dinner, Tues.–Sun. Of the many beautiful restaurants in town, perhaps the loveliest is* Buen Pastor. *Enjoy a cocktail of platonic perfection outside in the moonlit garden. Or, if the evening is cool, in the bar, where a fire may be roaring at the massive colonial hearth. There are likely also to be fires in each of the several beautifully propor-tioned dining rooms. It has to be said that the menu, though worthy, is not particularly inspired, but each of its few items is carefully prepared (the steak* au poivre *is sure to please) and the wine list is adequate. The staff is happy to assist you in your selections (all speak English here), and despite the luxury of the surroundings, a memorable evening with cocktails, wine, and a full meal for two will put hardly a dent in your wallet. The atmosphere is relaxed, intimate, and romantic.*

WEDNESDAY

"Relaxed, intimate, and romantic!" was the first thing I heard this morning— Woke up to see Sarah reading the notes about *Buen Pastor* I'd started to slam together last night when we got in from dinner, which I'd imprudently left right in the typewriter. (No more of that, you can be sure! From now on, everything gets put away immediately. Locked up.) Sarah laughed incredulously. "You call that place relaxed, intimate, and romantic?"

"For God's sake," I said. "That's just a draft! I hadn't even finished."

"Well, when you get around to 'revising your draft,'" Sarah said, "you might mention that the first thing you see when you get to the door is some kind of *butler* with a machine gun."

"Submachine gun," I said. "Machine guns are larger."

"Oh, well, then," Sarah said.

"Besides," I said. I rubbed my eyes. "I can't just put that into my piece, can I, Sarah?"

"Why can't you?" she said. She sat down next to me on the bed. "Dennis."

"Because," I said. "Sarah, please. I'm supposed to be writing about people's *vacations*."

Sarah stuffed a corner of the pillow into her mouth.

"I'm sorry," I said. Couldn't suppress a sigh. "I wasn't aware, last night, that the guard upset you."

"Naturally he upset me," Sarah said. "I assumed he upset you, too."

"Of course he did," I said. "Naturally he upset me." (Naturally I was upset when I went to give my name to the maître d' and saw that thing pointing at me. But it isn't as though restaurants at home don't have their own security systems.) "Sarah—" I took her hand. "What's happened? Has something happened? Have you been having an awful time here?"

Gloomy, theatrical pause. "The truth is, Dennis," she said, "I've been having a terrific time."

That sound ominously familiar; that muted, baffled, fragile tone designed to censure. Can't understand it—some sort of curse hovering over me that makes women sad? The women who are attracted to me are active, capable women. Women with interesting and demanding careers. Women, sometimes, with reasonably happy marriages, families. (Which, granted, can have its drawbacks, but one expects it, at least, to ensure a certain degree of stability.) Yet how rapidly these self-sufficient women become capricious and sulky. Absolutely unglued. Even the perky, adventurous wives who come my way (unsolicited, unsolicited!) simply *transform* themselves. And these women, who, I think it's fair to say, engage me for nothing more than, to use Sarah's (rather crude) word, *fun*—these same women—invariably begin to accuse me, in the most amorphous terms, of some unsubstantiated crime. It's a strange thing. It is. All these women, showing up on my doorstep, demanding my attention and affection. And then, when I've given them every bit of attention and affection I've got, insisting that I've failed them in some way. "Self-absorption," one of them said. "Shallowness of feeling," said another. As though I were some kind of broken *vending* machine!

Margaret S.? Who actually claimed I was "rejecting" at the very moment *she* was leaving *me?* Even Cynthia—my own wife—so happy when I married her, so confident; the way she became self-pitying and tremulous in front of my very eyes! Implored her to tell me what was the matter. Huge error. The matter was me, naturally; I was not really interested in her. Not *interested*! And the way, when I pointed out the irrefutable demonstrations of my interest, she would become incoherent: "Not that, not that! You know that's not what I'm talking about."

"Sarah," I said, "when we were in San Francisco you told me you loved traveling. That's what you said. You said you *loved traveling.*"

"When we were in San Francisco," Sarah said, "and I told you I loved traveling, we were in San Francisco."

"Well, but travel is travel," I said. "One sees new things."

"'New things!'" Sarah said. "Guys in uniforms with automatics?"

"Now, that's not fair," I said gently. Waited for a moment so she would hear the whining tone of her own voice, see the roomful of her happy purchases, see out the wooden-shuttered window, where a jaunty little halo of cloud sat over the peak of a volcano, and women padded silently by with their black-eyed babies bundled on their backs.

"I'm sorry, Dennis," she said. Clambered over into my lap. Twined herself around me. "I just feel so strange. I don't know what's going on. The thing is, I really *am* having a terrific time."

Faint sounds of a brass band and the fragrance of incense were beginning to filter into our room with the buttery sunlight. Persecuting loveliness. Rubbed the tender edge of Sarah's ear. Pointed out that the restaurant was something like an airport, if you thought about it: protection irrelevant to most of the travelers.

"Well, I *know*," Sarah said. "But who's all the protection *from*, here? I mean, look, Dennis, who is the enemy?"

Snuggled her against me. Reminded her that we've all read about such things; pointed out that we're overreacting, she and I, simply because we're *here*.

Made me think: How tempting it is to put oneself into the drama—"It's awful; *I've* seen it." Unattractive, self-aggrandizing impulse. Reminded Sarah of the morning we were having breakfast at her place and Karen stormed in, ranting about factory farming, and we kept saying, "We know, Karen, we know, it's really awful." Lifted Sarah's chin and was rewarded with a reluctant smile. "But Karen couldn't stop talking, remember? Because she had just *seen* it the day before. So, to her, it seemed just incredibly *real*?"

"The thing is," I said, "we could go around sniffling all the time, but terrible things are going to happen whether we sniffle or not. Yes, the lives some people lead are horrifying, but if you accept the idea that it's better for some people to be fortunate than for no people to be fortunate, then it's preposterous to make yourself miserable just because *you* happen to be one of those fortunate people. I mean, here we are, in an amazingly beautiful place, witnessing possibly the most lavish Easter celebration in the whole of the New World. Wouldn't it be morally reprehensible not to enjoy it?"

Sarah sighed. "I know," she said. "You're right."

"We could reject that out of principle," I said. "But what would the principle *be*?"

"All right, Dennis." Sarah jumped up and fluffed her hair. "I already said I agree."

Came back to the room later, tempers restored by breakfast. María there, putting a jug of fresh water on the table. Said, "Procession now?! Nice!!"

"Tell me something, Dennis," Sarah said when María left. "*Do* you ever think about having another child?"

"Of course not," I said. "I mean, I think about it, of course, but I don't think about actually doing it."

"Take it easy," Sarah said. "I was just wondering."

"I already have one perfectly good child," I said. "An adult, now, actually, almost. It doesn't make sense to start all over at my age. For someone your age—well, that's a different story. You *should* have children."

"I didn't say I wanted children," Sarah said crossly.

"You have every right to want children," I said. Looked at her closely—a bit puffy? Due for her period any minute now, I think. "You're one of those women who can do it all, you know. Career, family—"

"Hey," Sarah said. "I didn't say I wanted *children*. I was just asking how you feel."

"I know," I said. "Goodness." I was just *saying* how I feel. Especially hot today; was noticing it very suddenly—room darkened swoopingly. Put my head in my hands, then Sarah was speaking: "Listen, Dennis—are machine guns, like, a *lot* bigger than submachine guns?"

"Some of them," I said. The fact is, David is much more vivid to me as I imagine him now, playing basketball with his friends, strolling away from the house in Claremont on his way to a movie, spinning along in his rattly little car, than he seems when he's sitting across from me in some padded restaurant, waiting patiently for our visit to be over. "Why?"

"Because I think maybe that's one out there."

"Good Lord," I said. Sat up to look out the window and saw a wooden platform coming down the street. It looked amazingly like one of the *andas*, except that it was accompanied by a convoy of soldiers in uniform instead of townspeople in purple satin, and in place of Christ or the Virgin Mary, it displayed a mounted machine gun. "Yup, that's what it is, all right," I told Sarah.

The soldiers—the hard-eyed, ravenous-looking boys— surged up beyond the window, and in their midst the lordly, searching weapon reigned. A plunging shame weakened my hands and my knees as though at any second that instrument of terrible destruction might swing around toward me, discovering the foolish incidentalness of my body, its humiliatingly provisional life. No one on the street appeared to notice the entourage. A path cleared apparently by casual occurrence; only sign of anything out of the ordinary: a barely perceptible slowing, a thickening of motion as it passed.

Sarah and I stood at the window, watched until the entire retinue, with its platform and its sickening gleam of metal, turned the corner. Within an instant nothing left but the soft bustle of the street.

I put my arm around Sarah, and the small intimacy conducted away my panic. Tried to reassure her: "If there were anything out of the ordinary occurring, someone would tell us."

"Someone did tell us," Sarah said.

"Who?" I said.

"María," she said.

"The maid?" I said. "I mean someone who actually knows."

"Like who?" Sarah said.

"Like a journalist, for example."

Sarah stared at me. "Dennis," she said. "*You're* a journalist."

"All right, Sarah," I said. "Please."

Does Sarah know how cruel she is sometimes? Obviously there's no way in the world I'd be doing something of this sort if the bank hadn't gone the way banks tend to go these days. "But you know what I mean. Obviously I'm not saying María doesn't know what's happening to her. Obviously she does know what's happening to her. All I'm saying is that she has no way of *understanding* it. In context, that is. If I were you, I really wouldn't worry about María. She has quite a little flair for drama, but the truth is that her attention is on the Easter celebrations. Festivities. Frivolous matters"—I smiled and pushed a strand of hair from Sarah's eyes—"just like ours is."

"Dennis," Sarah said. "The *maid* is afraid to come to *work*. There's a mounted *machine* gun rolling down the street."

"I am not disputing that," I said. "Obviously. It's only that—Sarah, tell me something frankly. Are you embarrassed by what I do?"

"Embarrassed!" Sarah said, and actually blushed. "By what you do? Of course not, Dennis."

"Look, Sarah," I said. "This travel/restaurant business is every bit as much a joke to me as it is to you. And I would certainly never dream of calling myself a *journalist*—"

"Well, of course you're a—"

"I would never dream of calling myself a journalist *at this point*," I said. "But it's an easy target, isn't it? It's easy to be snobbish about this, just because it doesn't seem 'important' in some superficial way. And who knows, it's not impossible, that in a few years I could be—well, I could hardly hope for anything like the foreign desk, I suppose. But I won't be *anywhere* if I'm not reasonably—and, besides, it's only fair to Zwicker, who, quite frankly, took *pity* on me, no matter what you might think of his half-witted—"

"No, you owe him a lot, Dennis," Sarah said.

"No, I owe Zwicker a lot. He's giving me a rather decent salary, he's given me a job that some people might consider cushy, even prestigious, so the fact is that—"

"No, it's terrific, Dennis. Look. He sent you to San Francisco, he's going to send you to London. And we would never in a million years be here if it weren't for—"

Etc., etc., as I remember. But somewhere around that ridiculous point I slightly crumpled up a bit. Heat, and actually I don't think either of us is exactly used to the altitude yet, either. And then Sarah was really very sweet for a long, long time. And afterward she seemed quite pleased. But the strange thing about sex (tho. maybe it's different for a woman) is that if you start off feeling a little bad sometimes, sometimes when it's over, you can really feel awful.

> El Lomito Borracho. *12:00 p.m.–9:30 p.m. This cheerful steak house with its whitewashed walls and posters of Indians draws a young crowd, mostly Germans. The sirloin with grilled onions is probably your best bet here, but be sure to ask for your meat—as anywhere in the region—bien asada (well done).*

THURSDAY

> Café Bougainvillea. *Hours subject to change. Juices, coffee, milk shakes, cakes. Pleasant. Hygiene questionable.*

Town at fever pitch today and yesterday. Air sharp and bright—mountains entirely revealed, like a crown tossed around us. Crowds larger, aboil. More people arriving by foot or bus to camp across from the square with their little bundles of possessions, blankets. Flowers furiously blooming. *Alfombras* spread out for the boot. Chilling roll of drums, sepulchral brass, sun flashing in the air like swords. This morning Christ in scarlet robes, rocking down the streets in an ocean of incense; swarms of purple-gowned Jerusalemites. Sweat pouring from the faces of men bearing the *andas*. McGee bobbing in and out of the crowd, snapping pictures.

"Do you see those men in shackles, walking next to the cross?" Dot said. "Those are the thieves. Do you see? The amazing thing is, they use real criminals. Just petty thieves, probably, or poor drunks. But this afternoon, when the procession goes by the square, the whole town will sing an anthem about forgiveness, and one of the thieves will be untied and released into the crowd, just the way they did it in Jerusalem."

"That's beautiful," Sarah said.

"Yes . . ." Dot said, frowning. "Oh, it's a lovely holiday. The painted eggs, the mystery of spring, the little candies hidden on the lawn for the children. And here! My goodness. The flowers, the processions . . ."

Sarah inscrutable; peering out at the procession, working away absently at a ragged nail with her teeth.

"It's just that they take it all so *literally*," Dot said. She sighed. "Like this business with the thief. I mean, this is something that happened almost two thousand years ago—do you see what I mean? It's a *holiday*. But they are so literal-minded. You'll see. On Saturday, Sunday—nothing. No processions, no *alfombras* . . . They're not interested in the

Resurrection at all, really. Today and tomorrow are the big days. The Crucifixion is the part of it they relate to." She nodded admonishingly at Sarah. "*Martyrdom*. You see, they pick so at the story—the Crucifixion, the poor, the rich. That sort of thing. The imperial authorities. The soldiers."

The crowd was jostling around us, Dot serenely accustomed to it—burbling on, unfazed. "We used to go out to the little villages. Santa Catarina and so on. But no more. They've taken the wonder right out of it, haven't they? Of course, they *are* very poor—no one would deny them that. Still, it's just tempting fate, isn't it? To glorify it the way they do?

"When Cliff was still with the Department of Agriculture we had a place out by the lake, and we would go to the celebrations there. The people are mostly seasonal labor on the plantations, so, as you might imagine, it's been a fertile area for guerrilla activity; and now, of course, the people bring politics into simply *everything*.

"And the priests can be just as bad. There was one, just about ten years ago, in the village across the lake from us. An American, if you please. Who should have known better. It's a terrible story, really. It makes me *sick* to tell it—I'm sorry the whole thing came up. You see, it was what he allowed them to do, some of these people in his parish. He let them dress up the figures of the saints—the figures of Christ, even—as Indians." Dot nodded as she looked from Sarah to me. "Well, not just *Indians*—actually as guerrillas, do you see? With the little masks and so forth? And they did it right in that great big church of theirs, which is practically the only real building in that town. Father Tobin thought he could get away with it, I suppose, because he was American. But he might have stopped to think how he was endangering his

parishioners. What sort of priest is that, I ask you? His parishioners were disappearing by the score."

The pavement swiped briefly up at me, and I reached out
to steady myself against Dot's arm. "No hat?" Dot said. She
gave me a penetrating look, and steered us through the crowd
to a shady spot. "Reckless creature. Anyhow, it made us just
as mad as anything. But of course I'm not Catholic myself, so
to my mind the whole *thing* is a bit—there, look! Execution-
ers!"

Group filed by dressed in black, black conical hats, but
faces eerily covered by flaps of white fabric with holes cut out
for the eyes. Saw a Pontius Pilate—pointed him out to Sarah:
"Do you see the sign he's carrying? It says, 'I wash my hands
of the blood of this innocent man.'"

"This is just the sort of thing I mean," Dot said.

"What's what sort of thing?" Sarah said. But Dot was
gazing out with displeasure.

Felt unaccountably nervous—started chattering at Sarah:
"Well, it's complex, isn't it? Because the thing is that the local
people said to Pilate, 'Look. You've got to get rid of this fellow Jesus. He's got this whole mob of crazy hillbillies behind
him, and they're saying his claims supersede the claims of
Rome.' And *Pilate* said, 'Well, I don't happen to think Jesus is
guilty of anything, but I can't stop you from doing whatever
you want to him, can I? Because I can't intervene in local affairs.' So who knows who was using who? After all, you
could say that it was very much in Pilate's interest, as well as
the interest of the local authorities, that Jesus be killed, because, after all, Jesus was certainly fomenting unrest in Pilate's province."

Sarah turned to me. "So you mean the guy with the
sign—"

"Well, *no*," I said. "I'm just trying to point out various ironies of the situation . . . And it's interesting to remember that that's where those phrases come from. You know: 'I wash my hands of it.' 'My hands are clean.' And so on. They come from the Bible."

"As do so many," Dot said vaguely. "Oh, there he is—" She waved as McGee appeared from the crowd, coughing from incense. "I thought we were going to have to send out the Romans! Did you get some good ones?"

"Indeed I did," McGee said. "Ought to have some beauties."

"Clifford left the lens cap on last year," Dot explained.

"By the way," Sarah said to her. "What happened to the priest?"

"Excuse me?" Dot said.

"The priest in the village near the lake," Sarah said.

"Well," Dot said. "Do you mean— I mean, no one knows, exactly, do they? That is, they came in a van, as usual. But the windows were smoked glass, of course, and they weren't wearing uniforms. The van slid up behind him, they say. Just the way those vans do. I'm afraid they got him just outside the church." Dot shook her head. "You can still see the bullet holes. And it took quite some time to scrub down the wall and the street, we were told . . . Well. But no one recognized them. No one knows who they were."

FRIDAY

Sabor de China and Giuseppe's both awful. Best to skip.

Last night, after all the wooden shutters were closed and the town was quiet, Sarah and I went out. Above the encircling mountains the sky was bright with stars; down on the ground the night was pouring back and forth, glistening over the cobblestones and churches. Sarah and I walked around for a bit, then sat down in the square next to a pale-trunked palm.

Was terribly aware how quickly it would be over, sitting with her there in the fragrant night. Thought of her ten years hence: a dinner party, high over some sparkling city, Sarah in a wonderful little dress, more beautiful, even, than now. Gazing out the window, next to someone—a colleague, an admirer . . .

Could feel the future forming in embryo—the sort of longing that sleeps watchfully in one's body through time and separation. Could imagine so clearly—Sarah at this future party, confiding to this admirer: Her first involvement with a mature man, her introduction to so much that was new . . . No, she and I won't have meant *nothing* to each other . . .

The shine of her hair like a little light around her as she absorbed the night, breathing it into her memory for that moment in the future. Raised her hand and stroked it, spreading out the fingers; kissed her palm. Asked what she was thinking.

"I'm thinking, Thank God we're rid of the McGees for once." She laughed.

I looked down at her hand.

"What's the matter, Dennis?" she said.

Said I was sorry about the McGees. Sorrow, in fact, had fallen over me like a gentle net. "They really are idiots."

"Well, they're not *idiots*," Sarah said.

I looked at her. "That was *your* word," I said.

"Yes? Well, I was wrong, then," Sarah said. "Wasn't I."

Across from us the people in the shelter of the porticoed municipal building slept, cradling the town in the mesh of their breathing.

"*'Tainted,'*" Sarah said. "I mean, *Jesus.*"

Noticed that the people in front of the municipal building were stirring, rousing themselves in a dreamlike way, rolling back the blanket of sleep, sitting up—first one or two, then several more, shaking others gently by the shoulder until, soon, they were all awake, getting to their feet, smoothing out their rumpled clothing.

In moments they were in the square with us, talking in low, eager voices. Some were speaking Spanish, some were speaking languages I'd never heard. Were paying no attention to us at all; leaned over the basin of the fountain to splash themselves or their babies with water, or to reach up with tin cups for its less polluted streams.

But then—as unexpectedly as they'd appeared in the square, they filed out again. Absolutely weird. Sarah and I paused a moment, then followed. Soon we were in a part of town we'd never seen before. Lanterns swaying from stone arches, heavy shutters swinging open as we passed by—behind them women in black staring out at us from candlelit rooms or patios.

Crowd led us to a churchyard dense with people, tiny stands selling food, wooden toys, shiny whirling things. No tourists, no wealthy Ladinos, none of the Europeans who keep houses here in town. All the people ragged and thin— surroundings incredibly festive, but their faces, as they milled about, were serious. Abstracted.

The sky was scattered with stars, balloons, plumes of incense. Above a long flight of wide, shallow steps a scrolled church (such delicate adornments! carved fruit, carved vines) floated like a dove, pale pink in the moonlight. Candles alight everywhere, flickering, converging into a flickering river at the huge, open church doors.

Tantalizing aromas: food frying in vats or simmering in huge kettles or roasting on sticks over fires. Sarah pulling me from one culinary spectacle to another in an agony of cupidity. "Look, Dennis—can you believe it? There's real food in this country!"

"Don't even think of it," I said.

"Please," she said. People were eating patiently, without greed, as though they were preparing themselves for something. Men were so thin it was hard not to watch them as they ate—so frail. Several had what looked like a band of hair shaved from the top of their heads—worn away from hauling loads by a strap, I suppose. Sarah hovered longingly by a woman frying huge disks of tortilla, then using them to scoop up a bright, chunky sauce. "I can't stand it!"

"Out of the question," I said. At our feet a flock of tiny children chewed solemnly at the dirty treat. "Do you imagine I'd let you do something like that to yourself? But listen. The minute we get home I'm taking you to the Red Fox Inn for a decent meal."

"Do you promise?" Sarah said as the crowd carried us with them into the floating church. Was just making me swear it, but then she gasped and took my arm.

We were at the front of the crowd—the entire floor between us and the altar was a picture, a picture carpet, made of flower petals, like the *alfombras*, but vast: Jesus, all of flowers, white-robed on a mountaintop with waves of power radiating from his raised hands. And beneath him, pouring out toward us, becoming us, a flower multitude—the poor, the mourning, the meek, the hungry, the pure in heart, the persecuted . . .

Behind us, people were pushing their way forward. I glanced back and saw that the crowd was not flowerlike at all, but thin and dry as tinder, their eyes alight with a fanatical, incendiary ecstasy of poverty.

My God. Who *were* these people? Their legs were ulcerated, their feet were bare and thickened, their backs were bent from hauling wood or fruit or coffee, but what act of madness might they not be capable of? The guerrillas in the neighboring villages dozing tensely under the dark trees, the children who work the raging fields, the maids, the porters, the farmers, curled up on their beds or straw mats, alert in their sleep, dreaming their dangerous dreams. People who can't afford a newspaper. People in whose languages no paper will ever be printed, people who couldn't read one if one *were* printed in their languages—these people who don't even know there's a world out there, it's these people who could burn the world to the ground. Stunted and sloe-eyed, with the delicate, slanting planes of their faces, their brilliant clothing, their ancient, outlandish languages, they seem like strange, magical creatures. But, no! These people have lives that go from one end of the day to the other. They eat or go hungry. They have conversations behind closed doors—

As Sarah and I were thrust out the side door we saw a small knot of soldiers dispersing in the courtyard below us, blending into the crowd. My hands felt weak again, and damp. *Tainted*, I thought; *tainted*. Next to me Sarah picked up a wobbly child who was steadying himself against her knees, and nuzzled his soft, black baby hair, through which I could absolutely *see* the columns of lice tramping. But when I opened my mouth to warn Sarah I could hardly croak.

The baby waved his new little hands for balance—his new little enemy hands. His swimming black baby eyes reflected for an instant, in exquisite miniature, the thousand or so candles, the floating church, the thick, blest, kindled crowd. Which of the reflected men could that baby hope soon to be? Which of the frail old enemy men?

A little girl tugged urgently at Sarah's skirt and held out her arms to claim her brother as a noise manifested itself at a distance. The noise came toward us slowly, solid and tidal, but separated, as it approached, and we were engulfed in shouts, hoofbeats, chanting, as lanterns and torchlight wavered through smoke and incense.

Facing us, at the head of the mob, two Roman centurions reined in their huge horses to a nervous, hobbled trot. Around them surged the Jerusalemites in their purple satin and Roman foot soldiers holding lances, as well as hundreds of town dwellers in ordinary clothing.

A trumpet sounded, and the edgy crowd fell silent. The sky gleamed black, the moon was streaking through the clouds. Sarah's pale face narrowed and flashed like a coin, and I had the sensation that if I concentrated I would be able to remember all the events that were to follow—every detail . . .

And, yes, one of the centurions was already holding out a scroll: *Jesus of Nazareth was condemned to die by crucifixion!* The pronouncement rang out against the stone of the church like something being forged; its echo pulsed in a cataract of silence.

SATURDAY

Hotel Buena Vista. *Breakfast, lunch, and dinner daily. The Buena Vista offers probably the best lunch deal in town. Help yourself to the unlimited buffet, complete with tortillas made fresh in front of your eyes by Indian women in full dress, take a swim, and if you've happened to come on the right day, view a fashion show around the pool, all for about the price of a hamburger and fries back home. Exotic birds wander the grounds, and caged parrots enliven the scene, as well. The fare is standard, but the steaks are flame-grilled, and tasty.*

Clouds below us, plane not too crowded. Sarah sitting with a book on her lap, gazing out the window, at nothing.

This morning, as we were leaving, it was just as Dot had said it would be. No *alfombras*, no processions, tourists thinning out. No trace whatsoever of the pilgrims in front of the municipal building. Just women in black, privately lamenting Mary's murdered child. But yesterday—Friday—processions were volatile, grief-stricken, unrelenting: Christ in black, prepared for his death, then Christ on the cross, broken.

Felt v. peculiar—ill-tempered, rattled—all yesterday morning. Suppose from my disorientation of Thurs. night+looming lunch with McGees.

And then—the *Buena Vista* itself! *¡Dios!* Curvy Ladino girls modeling hideous clothing around the pool, children streaking between them, landing in the water with loud splashes, bloodcurdling shrieks. Indian women making tortillas, watching with expressionless sentry eyes. Well-to-do visitors from the capital dispatching slender, olive-skinned sons to the parking lot with little plates of rice and beans for the maids. A species of splotchy, knobby tourists (Evangelicals, apparently; McGee says they get a big price break at the *Buena Vista*) sunning themselves in plastic lounge chairs, laughing loudly and nervily, as though they'd just hoodwinked their way out of prison.

Sarah struggled with her little sink stopper of a steak for a few minutes, then got up and ambled around the lawn, looking unusually pensive. When she sat back down, she started telling the McGees about something she'd seen a few days ago. Had she mentioned it to me? Don't think so. Said she'd seen three big guys grab a boy as he walked out of a store—nobody was paying attention except for one lady, who was yelling. Then the men bundled the boy up, put him on a truck. "I didn't really think much about it at the time," Sarah said. "It was like a tape playing too fast to make any sense of." She looked from Dot to Cliff. "I suppose I just assumed it was a kid getting picked up for a robbery . . ."

"Oh, Lord," Dot said with a sigh.

"Now, Dorothy," McGee said.

"No, Cliff." Dot's voice trembled slightly. "I don't care. Their poor mothers. You know"—she turned to Sarah—"after the boys are trained, they're sent to other parts of the country, because it does work out better if they don't speak the language, doesn't it? Oh, I know that it's all necessary, but it's terribly hard for the families. Their families love them. Their families need them to work." She turned back to McGee. "I think it's disgusting, Clifford, frankly."

McGee lifted his hand for peace. "I never said—" he began, but just at that moment a tall man of thirty-five or so approached. His thatchy hair and matching mustache were the color of dirty Lucite. A large, chipped tooth might have given his smile an agreeable, beaverlike goofiness except for an impression he gave of the veiled, inexhaustible rage you see in certain ex-alcoholics. "Excuse me," he said. "Do you happen to be Clifford McGee?"

"I am he," McGee said judiciously, extending his hand.

"My name's Curtis Finley," the man said. "I work with

your old outfit, and you were pointed out to me once at the Camino."

"So, they've got you down here, do they?" McGee said. "Have a seat. We're just—what is it they say?—*improving the shining hours*."

Sarah stood up suddenly, then flopped back down into her chair. Finley glanced at her. "Thank you, sir," he said to McGee. "Yes, I've been here for a bit, now. I'm on my way to supervise a project up north."

"Really," McGee said. "A lot going on up there. You'll have to come by when you get back, let me know how things went. I like to keep up."

"I imagine you do, sir," Finley said. "They still talk about you at the office." The two men smiled at each other, and a faint smell of sweat imprinted itself on the air.

Dot nodded toward Sarah, who was splayed out glumly in her chair. "*This* young lady saw a recruitment the other day," Dot said.

"Dorothy," McGee said, as Finley looked sharply at him.

"Those cretins," Finley said. He turned to me and Sarah, showing his teeth to indicate friendliness. "So, what brings you folks down here?"

"Dennis is a journalist," Sarah said. She drew herself together and smiled primly.

Finley looked away from her legs. "Recruitments are very unusual here in town," he told me. "And technically against the law. In fact, as I understand it, something's being done about them now."

"I'm not really a *journalist*," I assured him hurriedly. "I'm just doing food. Hotels, Easter celebrations in a general sort of way . . ."

"I see . . ." Finley said.

"Actually," I said, "I'm a banker."

"Oh." Finley looked at McGee.

"No," Dot said. "You see, Dennis is doing the most marvelous thing—he's writing a nationally syndicated article about Holy Week. Isn't that wonderful?"

Finley frowned. "Oh." He showed his teeth again. "Well, how are you enjoying it? Beautiful town, isn't it?"

McGee shifted in his chair. "We're taking these two to the de Leóns' tonight, for dinner," he said. "They're old friends, and the cook does wonderful things with regional produce."

"Oh, yes." Finley looked at me with vague bitterness. "Interesting fellow, de León. Never met him personally. Good morning, isn't he?"

"Pardon?" I said.

"Good morning," McGee said. "You've seen them in the supermarkets. Oranges, grapefruits. Even some bananas with the little sticker that says—"

"Oh, yes," I said. "Of course. Good Morning!"

"Yes," McGee said. "that's de León. Good Morning! Oranges, Good Morning! Grapefruits. Coffee's his main thing, but he's all over the place now, really."

"Had some trouble with a son, I remember hearing," Finley said.

McGee nodded. "A bad patch. Over now."

"Kid had one wicked case of red-ass, as I heard it," Finley said. He turned to Sarah. "If you'll pardon me."

"Excuse me?" Sarah said with a misty smile. "Sorry, I wasn't really . . . Oh, Mr. Finley, do you happen to know what this pretty vine is?" She pointed to an arborlike construction above us.

"Curtis," Finley said. He peered overhead, then looked at Sarah. "Vine?"

"I think," Dot said, squinting distantly, "that the rain is going to come early this year. Last night I saw lightning from over by the coast."

McGee smiled comfortably. "Same family as the Japanese wisteria," he said.

Later Sarah hunched over in the big chair in our room, hugging her knees while I walked back and forth.

"Just because a fellow doesn't happen to recognize one particular plant," I said, "does not mean he's some kind of *impostor*."

Sarah sighed noisily.

"Well, after all," I said. "But, besides. I think one has to ask oneself what, in all honesty, are the alternatives."

"What on earth are you saying, Dennis?" Sarah said.

Mustn't let Sarah force me into positions—her willful naïveté, threat of shrillness. Always have to remember to relax, keep perspective. Allow her to relax. Tried to point out calmly that, whatever one thinks of this method or that, people's goals tend to be—on a certain basic level—the same. "We all want life to improve for everyone; we're all struggling, in our own ways, to make things better. Yes, even people who differ from us can be sincere, Sarah—I mean, unless you're talking about a few greed-maddened dictators. Psychopaths, like Hitler, or Idi Amin. Sociopaths, I guess, is what the word is now. Is that what they say in your classes, 'sociopaths'?"

Sarah gazed down at her sandaled toes and wiggled them.

"But it's funny," I said, perching next to her on the arm of the chair. "Isn't it? The way terminology can change like that. It must reflect a wholesale shift in the way moral reasoning, or whatever, is perceived to work. I think it's so interesting, that, don't you? They used to say 'psychopaths' when I was young."

Sarah wiggled her toes again. "Isn't it wonderful," she leaned down to say to them, "the way that bogus agronomists are crawling all over the place, struggling to improve life for everyone?

"Oh, yes, Sarah," she answered herself in a crumply little voice. "Deeply heartwarming. But that word 'agronomist'—I think the word you want is 'agriculturalist,' interestingly. You know, when I was just a *little* toe—"

"Oh, Sarah," I said.

"Ex*cuse* me, Dennis." Sarah looked at me icily. "I was talking to my *foot*."

For the rest of the afternoon, we were very, very cautious with one another. Was dreading dinner. But Sarah was on her good behavior, or a variant of it. Was weirdly tractable, polite. Just as well, especially because the de Leóns turned out to be exactly what one would have expected—exactly what one would have feared.

The Sra. steely in linen and small gold earrings. The Sr. somewhat more appealing. Handsome, very Spanish, melancholy. Obvious habit of power; cordiality engineered to infinitesimal degrees of correctness. Daughter, Gabriela, petite like mother. Pure, unclouded face, whispery clothing—quite taken with Sarah; many limpid smiles. Missed the States, she said, her friends from boarding school in Connecticut. Threatened "So much to talk about." All three excellent English.

Maids, passing out hors d'oeuvres and cocktails—rum+Good Morning! fruit juices. Gigantic house, huge collection of antique Indian textiles, pre-Columbian artifacts, splendid colonial furnishings, etc. Evening inexplicably slippery at first—odd tides of dusk from the series of enclosed patios and gardens flowing around the bulky forms inside. Everyone floating a bit, like particles dislodging themselves from something underwater, which was my mind.

Found Sarah in a hallway, staring at a row of photographs. From behind, I watched her examining the face of a beautiful young man, pale, black-haired, who was staring into the camera with an expression of sardonic resignation.

"That's my son, Rubén," said Sra. de León, who had come up quietly next to me. "We're very proud of him. He's living in Paris, now. He's been a great help to his father in the last few years." She gave Sarah a frosty, slightly challenging smile.

Eventually we were all moored around the table. Dinner excellent. Amazed by quality. Sadly, though, was unhungry in the extreme. Throughout parade of courses McGees and de Leóns conversing with the informal amiability of old friends: an archaeological site just uncovered nearby, then lurid local gossip—a nun from the U.S. who claimed to have been abducted from a convent in town and tortured. Though eventually, de León told us, the Embassy revealed that the cigarette burns all over the nun's back had been inflicted by a lesbian lover.

"It's always in small places that the most incredible things happen, isn't it?" Dot said. "New York City can't compete with this story."

De León turned to Sarah with a brief burst of male charm. "This government is a collection of amateurs," he said obscurely.

"Vicente is sentimental about the old days," Sra. de León said. "When less was required of us."

"I will not walk around my own property armed," Sr. de León said, his warmth disappearing in the frozen wastes of his wife's smile.

There was a small silence as Sra. de León looked at her napkin with an amused, measured loathing. "Ah," she said, as maids brought in trays of dessert and coffee. "Here we are."

The McGees appeared to be accustomed to the climatic shiftings between the de Leóns. "Vicente"—McGee waved his fork—"Angélica has outdone herself tonight."

"A triumph," I said, gently pedaling Sarah's foot. "And I never would have dreamed it was possible to do something like this with a banana."

"Oh, nor I," Sarah said, withdrawing her foot.

"Very simple," Sr. de León said. "Just caramelize lightly, add a little orange, a little rum, and flame." He handed me a small stack of cards; turned out he had had all the recipes from dinner typed up.

Gabriela laughed. "Daddy is so shy, isn't he," she said.

"Yes, ha," I agreed. Consommé with Tomato, Avocado, and Cilantro, I read. Sole with Good Morning! Grapefruit. Carrots with Zest of Good Morning! Orange. Volcano Salad. Good Morning! Bananas with Juice of Good Morning! Oranges and Rum. Dark Roast Good Morning! Coffee and Cardamom Chewies. "I hardly know how to thank you," I said. "These will really *make* my article—"

"It is my great pleasure," de León said.

"And it will be nice to have some decent press up there for a change," Gabriela said.

"Gaby," Sra. de León chided.

"No, but it's true," Gabriela said. She turned to Sarah. "You know, it happens all the time. Some reporter, who knows nothing about this country, who doesn't care anything about it, who only cares about making a reputation for himself, comes down and says he wants to write an objective story about life here. And the next thing you know, you open up some magazine and read the most fantastic stuff. As if the country were one big concentration camp—as if all we ever did was bomb the villages."

Sarah put down her fork.

"I *know*," Gabriela said. "Never one word about the *wonderful* things—"

"Gaby," Sra. de León said, and put down her own fork, "why don't you show our new friends the garden."

It was a great relief to leave the table. Gabriela led us through the pungent floral riot, and cut some elegant little lilies for Sarah. Sarah thanked her; asked how far the plantation extended. Gabriela looked puzzled for a moment, then laughed. Explained that we weren't on the plantation at all— that it was hours and hours away, over terrible roads. Said, "Of course, these days if we were to go we would use helicopters, and it would only take minutes. But we never do anymore. Even Daddy hardly goes."

Sarah silent, considering. Then asked who was it, that being the case, who saw to the planting, harvesting, etc.

Gabriela mercifully innocent—entirely impervious to offense potential of Sarah's question.

"Oh, we have what amounts to a rather large village living up there," Gabriela said. "And some very reliable overseers. But we always used to go out at harvest time ourselves, anyway."

Frankly, was very touched by her regretful tone. "You enjoyed it," I observed.

"Oh, yes," she said. "I loved it. We all did. We loved to watch the harvest, to ride around the countryside on our horses . . . Well, it was a long time ago, when we could do that—that was back when our Indians still had their own little plots of land up north, and we had them brought down on trucks for the harvest, big trucks, from their tiny villages. And they were all from different villages, so they wore different colors and patterns in their clothes, and they spoke all sorts of different languages. They were so strange, so beautiful. I used to love to listen to them, and to watch them. To watch them harvesting the coffee . . ."

"Harvesting coffee," I said. "You know, I never think of coffee as a legume, but, of course—*coffee beans!*"

Gabriela smiled and shook her hair. In the moonlight she had a newborn look. "Coffee isn't really a bean at all," she said. "It's a berry. It's very nice to look at—it turns bright red. But it's a nuisance to pick. You really have to watch what you're doing or you can strip the plant. Still, at least, it's not heavy, as long as you're not hauling the sacks. So it's one thing that small children can learn to do. Fortunately for the families."

Sarah started to speak, and stopped.

"It was so beautiful," Gabriela said. "I wish I could show it to you as it was then . . ." She sighed. "You have to forgive me for talking and talking like this. But there are so few people who would understand what it's like for me. People here can't really understand because most have never lived in the States or Europe, and my friends in the States can't understand, because they've never been here."

"Do go on," I said. I glanced reprimandingly at Sarah.

"Oh, I don't know . . ." Gabriela smiled faintly, as though she were watching something across the garden. "Well, it's been so long since I've been back, hasn't it. I was about twelve, I suppose, the last time. That's right—because my brother, Rubén, who's in Paris now, was sixteen. It's incredible to think about that time, really. It was very confusing. It was very hard, particularly for my parents, because it was just when things were at their worst in this country, and the guerrilla movement really had some strength. And Rubén had picked up some funny ideas. He was just at that age, you know, when children are very susceptible. And I suppose some older boys had gotten hold of him because our family, well"—she smiled sadly—"because our family is very well known. And Rubén began to go around saying things he couldn't possibly even have understood—talking about giving land away, 'returning it,' was how he put it. And ruinous increases in wages. Things that would absolutely destroy his own family. And Mommy and Daddy tried to reason with him. They were very patient—they kept telling him, Rubén, you know, certain people own the land. They have legal title to it. You can't just snatch it away from them, can you? And if we're to drink coffee, if we're to eat fruit, someone is going to have to pick it. And it's a tragedy, of course, that you can't just pay the laborers anything you'd like, but it's a fact. It's simply a fact. Because what do you think would happen to the world if we did? And a banana cost ten dollars? Or a cup of coffee cost twenty dollars? But Rubén would always just slam out of the house. So it was a very hard time for us all. And of course that was the period when the workers had to be watched very, very closely, because, you can imagine—if it was possible to contaminate Rubén, imagine how much easier it would be with a poor, uneducated Indian."

Gabriela reached out to touch a pink rambling rose. "So," she said, "we were all up for the harvest one year, and there was a morning when I woke up very, very early. Before the sun rose. I woke up to this delicious smell, this absolutely delicious smell, of roasting coffee. And I thought, well, now it's time to get up. And then about one thousand things happened in my mind all at once, because I realized it wasn't time to get up—it wasn't time to get up at all, and something was happening that couldn't possibly be happening. And so, before I even knew what I was doing or why, I rushed over to my window. And the window was black and red—black with night and red with fire, wave after wave of fire in the black sky. And the whole storehouse, all our coffee, was up in flames."

"Oh—" Sarah said. She sat down on the rim of an old fountain from which cascaded tiny weightless white flowers.

"Yes," Gabriela said. She seated herself next to Sarah and drew me down beside her. "It was terrible. And after that I never really went back. Mommy and Daddy felt it would be too dangerous, and of course it wasn't nearly as pleasant, because security was tightened up a lot, too. The army came— there are still hundreds of soldiers living there, in fact." She laughed. "Daddy doesn't like that at all. He says it's more of a—what do you call it?—protection racket, than protection, and that the army is bleeding us worse than the workers. But what can you do, after all? And there are guard towers now, and the landing strips, and those awful, you know, *fences*. So it's not so nice anymore.

"But Rubén went back once again with my father. And instead of bringing him to his senses, it all just seemed to make him worse—angrier and wilder and more unhappy. My parents wanted him to go away to school. To Harvard, or perhaps to Oxford. But he wanted to stay in the country, and it turned out to be a very bad thing for everyone that he did. Because then he really became involved with all these crazy student groups. It was so sad. They were so young—they thought they were idealists, but, really, they were just being used. Rubén had been such a sweet boy, such a wonderful brother, but he became very hard. It was just this hard, awful propaganda all the time."

Gabriela frowned at a petal she was smoothing between her fingers. "He said terrible things. He said that we were thieves, you know, and so on. And it's not as though any of us are thrilled with the way things are, of course, but after all—it is people like our parents who generate the entire economy here." She sighed. "He said that people were starving. Heavens! You have to be *stupid* to starve in this climate, don't you?" She turned to Sarah for confirmation and smiled gently. "The fruit simply drops off the trees.

"Anyhow, during the next year, several of our workers and some of the other students—friends of Rubén's—got killed and were found by the side of one road or another. So, even though none of them were from important families, we were all terrified for Rubén. And in fact it was late that same year that the first letter arrived."

Inside, in the soft light, we could see Gabriela's parents and the McGees sipping their coffee and chatting contentedly. I closed my eyes and raised my face to the tiny white flowers above us, as though they were a spray of cool water.

"And the letter stated it all in no uncertain terms— They knew who he was, they knew *where* he was, and so forth. Well, my father got on the phone right away, and started sending my brother to see important people. My father had friends in the police, and friends in the army. And he even had several friends in the Embassy—your embassy here—so we thought we could take care of it quickly enough. But every day went by, and everyone my brother talked to said they didn't know anything about it—they couldn't find out who was sending the letters. And one day Rubén went to see a colonel in the army, whom Rubén and I had known since we were *babies*—my father is the *god*father of one of this man's children. And Rubén came back from that meeting looking like a corpse."

A little leaf spiraled down through the air and landed on Gabriela's dress. She picked it off and looked at it affectionately before she let it flutter away. "Because the Colonel said, you know, right away, that of course he'd help, and he made a phone call while Rubén was sitting right there in his office. The Colonel explained the situation over the phone to whoever it was he'd called, and then he just sat there on the phone, listening, for about twenty minutes, Rubén told us later. And when he hung up, Rubén asked what the other person had said, and the Colonel said, 'Nothing.'"

Gabriela stopped speaking for a moment, and as she resumed, Sarah's cold hand rested briefly on mine. "So the Colonel stood up to walk Rubén to the door, and at the door he burst into tears. And he said, 'I'm sorry. I can't help you. But now, listen to me, please—there's something I have to say to you.' He put his hands on Rubén's shoulders and looked into his eyes, and said, 'When you leave your house, be sure to tell somebody where you're going. Always walk in the direction of traffic'"—Gabriela leaned up for a moment, as I had, into the cool spray of white flowers—"'and be very, very careful when you cross the street.'"

This morning particularly blue and bright. Ricardo's greeting, María's smile, the roses, the hummingbirds—everything bright, large, standing out in the blue air as though I'd been far away for a long time. Woke up famished. Couldn't eat enough. Melon, grapefruit, pineapple, banana—I ate and ate. Thought of all that fantastic food last night, just sitting in front of me. Laughed slightly. "Horrible, wasn't it?" I said to Sarah. "Thank God we'll never have to do that again." My fork scraped startlingly against my plate. "Sarah?" I said.

Saw she hadn't touched her fruit or her juice or her coffee. I speared a piece of banana and held it out to her. "No?" I said. Waved it temptingly. "All right, but you'll be starving by the time we get to the airport."

She looked at me, then slammed her napkin down onto the table and stalked off.

Made an embarrassed farewell to Ricardo, hurried to our room, where I found Sarah sitting, staring at me accusingly from the unmade bed—the geological record of the aeons of our horrible night, our tense, mid-sleep lovemaking during which the ghouls from Gabriela's wild story rubbed their wicked little numbing dream hands and waited.

"Oh, for heaven's sake," I said, as it dawned on me. "All right. I apologize, Sarah, all right? I'm a brute. I'm insensitive. I'm a white male." Sarah folded her arms. "But frankly, my dear, it *is* a common expression. A manner of speaking. I rather imagine you've used it yourself upon occasion—"

Sarah interrupted. "But guess what, Dennis? I'm the person who's never going to *be* starving. Because that's the person I am, as it turns out. I'm the same person as Dot, Dennis, the same person as Gabriela—"

"Oh, come, now," I said.

"'*Oh, come now,*'" Sarah said. She kicked savagely at the mattress. "Because don't you get it? I mean this is a *war*, Dennis. We're soldiers, *and that's our uniform*." She started to cry with a thin, infuriating animal anguish. "See, I don't understand why I didn't *know* that. I don't understand why I haven't read about all this in the newspaper."

"In the newspaper!" I said. "You don't understand why you haven't read about this in the *newspaper*? About what, please, Sarah—why you haven't read about what?" Felt I was wading through a dark, cold river. An ashy river clogged with garbage and bones. "You don't know why you haven't read about who you *are*? In the newspaper? Do you consider that a front-page story? Sarah, listen to me. What are you trying to do to me? Are you trying to spoil all the *good* things? Yes, I suppose I should rush off to Zwicker and say, 'Stop the presses, chief, there are some problems out there—rich people make more money than poor people. Life is unfair and people suffer.' God knows, Sarah—it's not as though I don't agree with you, but think about it for a moment, please; use your head. You don't read about yourself in the newspaper because that's not what a newspaper is for. And you don't read in the newspaper about the things that go on here, because *the things that go on here aren't news*."

God, it was awful. Mortifying. Sarah sobbing, me ranting—was *profoundly* mortified by my outburst. Got blue in the face apologizing, while Sarah sniffled and hiccuped and packed her beautiful textiles, sneaking beleaguered glances over her shoulder at me as though I had forced her at gunpoint to buy them. Made me feel literally like the Gestapo.

Thankfully, by the time we got to the airport she seemed to have exhausted herself—was just sleepy and absentminded, like a child after a tantrum.

On the plane Sarah stared at her closed book as a thin shield of cloud glided beneath us, but I peered across her out the window to watch the little country beneath us vanish.

Oh, the ravages of traveling. Poor Sarah. Unfamiliar rules, disturbance of one's biological rhythms. Whole populations of new microbes . . . The plane went blood-dark for an instant; pale skin boiling up into sticky black welts, slow lines of black-windowed vans patrolling the pale mountains . . .

Hadn't even occurred to me before—I'm *sick*! Bet we both are. Bet we've both picked up some sort of parasite. Damn, damn! Well, God knows I tried to be careful.

Oh, so much to do this week. Doctor. Work up a piece for Zwicker, of course. Unpack. Phone calls. Stacks of mail, naturally—naturally most of it catalogues. It's funny, I always intend to throw them right out, but when it comes down to it I can never resist leafing through, to see all the idiotic junk—programmable toasters, telephones disguised as footballs—that someone has spent time dreaming up and someone will spend money to buy. Shook my head and forced a chuckle, but Sarah continued to look out the window. "Hey," I said, tugging playfully at her sleeve. "I promised I'd take you to the Red Fox Inn tonight, remember?"

"The Red Fox Inn?" Sarah looked at me, then a veil dropped over her expression, and she turned back to the window.

All right. Yes, the planet is littered with bodies. No one's going to dispute *that*—and the bodies are surrounded by clues. But what those clues mean, and where they point—well, that's something else altogether, isn't it?

Took Sarah's unresisting hand, and for a moment feared I was going to burst into loud, raucous weeping. Strange airplane light showing the fatigue behind her closed eyes; showing the age, deep within her, boring its way to her surface.

But will it improve, the world, if Sarah and I stay in and subsist on a diet of microwaved potatoes? Because I really don't think so. I really don't think—and this is something I'll say to Sarah when she's herself again, I suppose—that by the standards of any sane person it could be considered a crime to go to a restaurant. To go someplace nice. After all. Our little comforts— The velvet murmur, the dimming of the street as the door closes, the enfolding calm of the other diners . . . that incredible moment when the waiter steps up, smiling, to put your plate before you . . .

IN THE STATION

Sounds stretch out in the station—footsteps, crackling announcements, rag ends of instructions and goodbyes echo and balloon, tangle in a mass that hangs high up under the sooty vaulting of transoms and girders. Far below, where a thin scurf of yellow electric light drifts among the newsstands and plaintive groups of benches, Dee Dee clutched her ticket and inspected rows of shiny candy bars and magazines. In the distance the station dissolves into a watery daylight where points of darkness appear, and swell, hissing, into trains.

Dee Dee reached, then hesitated, as though she were choosing cards from a gypsy's pack. "Pardon," a man said shortly, jostling her as he plucked a newspaper from in front of her. The train, she remembered; the important thing was getting on the train.

But where were Carl and Márta? Just a moment ago they had been walking toward the gate. She looked frantically at the flow of people—the line was already beginning to form: unhealthy-looking English families, ladies in twos, the occasional pampered businessman of the sort Dee Dee had seen in the restaurants, and, because it was summer, throngs of students, Americans especially, talking and lounging theatrically. Everyone wore the resolute, slightly exaggerated expressions of people beginning a journey, as though, fearing irremediable dislocation, they were determined to stamp themselves upon their own futures.

The line collected, and swayed with an absent fretfulness as Dee Dee searched it for Carl and Márta. Ah—there they were, standing a little off to one side. And something was wrong: Márta shook her short, dark hair; her hands flew up. Carl shied as if she were bombarding him, in her pretty accent, with little pellets.

Dee Dee started forward, then stopped. As though signaled by her panic, Carl and Márta turned. Dee Dee smiled uncertainly and waved with her bag of new magazines and candy. For a moment they simply looked at her.

She went light with dread—she was a scrap of something blowing away from them, tumbling away in Márta's somber, lashy gaze. Carl's hair gleamed like stiff filaments of silk. Then he raised his hand in a false little wave of reassurance, and Dee Dee was standing in place again.

Carl and Márta turned back to each other. "Carl," Márta said, and Carl looked at her with terror, as though, Márta thought, she were some beast poised to destroy him.

How enraging. How *enraging*; was he trying to make her say something terrible to him? Well, she just might; if Dee Dee didn't show up soon to stop her, heaven only knew what she might say.

Márta had been in a vicious mood since waking. She'd opened her eyes onto the freezing damp the English affected to consider summer, only to discover that her flatmate, Judit, had drunk the last of the coffee. "No more at all?" Márta demanded, ransacking the cupboard.

"Not unless you remembered to pick some up," Judit said,

unmoved. "It was on your list. Oh, by the way, István called this morning."

Márta shut the cupboard doors with wonderful composure. "Why didn't you tell me?" she said.

"You were asleep," Judit said. "Remember?"

Márta sat. She ran her hands through her hair and listened to Judit's spoon tinkle in her coffee cup. What a day for István to call. "What did he want?" she asked.

"István?" Judit shrugged. "I could hardly interrogate him, could I?"

The instant Judit disappeared into the bathroom to deplete the hot-water supply Márta dialed István. A courtesy; just to tell him she would be away for several weeks. With Carl. But István was out, of course. Or in—behind the sunny, mendacious message on his machine. Márta's heart blackened; in with some girl, doubtless. Márta hung up without leaving a message.

She'd hurried to the station, but Carl and Dee Dee had not arrived yet. How grim it was, dirty and glum—and, with all the rushing strangers, treacherously neutralizing; she could hardly remember who she herself was. So István had decided he wanted to see her again. Too late; too bad, for him.

The air around her was stale with discarded hopes, angers, attitudes no longer useful to those who were traveling. She huddled on a bench to wait, beset by tales, half-heard in her childhood, of cold, of deportations, of police—events that filtered down like ineradicable pollutants from filthy times.

When she saw Carl and Dee Dee coming toward her she merely looked at them, her chin lifted. While Dee Dee hung back, goggling and dawdling like a child, Carl greeted Márta with a crisp little kiss on each cheek. She was not charmed. Did he not see how she felt? Did he not care?

She watched him as they waited in line for tickets. That limpid, meditative look of his! It was like a steel door, behind which he crouched, hiding.

He handed Dee Dee her ticket. "Is there anything you want before we get on the train?" he said. "It won't be so easy to find things in English, remember."

Dee Dee looked at him and put her hand over her mouth, then shambled off to a newsstand, leaving Márta to go to the train with Carl.

Something was bothering Carl. That, at least, was obvious. Márta looked at him, but his studied air of reverie enforced her silence. Still, the trip had been his idea; he had wanted her to come along. At least, he had pretended to. "Carl," she said.

"Yes!" He turned to her with the transparently fraudulent expansiveness of someone forced to replace a tempting book on a shelf. "What is it?"

She stared at him, searching his face. He *didn't* want to go. *Carl did not want to take this trip.* It was true; Márta was certain—she had the curse of being right. "Tell me, Carl, please," she said, "why we are doing this."

He flinched. "What do you mean?" he said, and then they both turned as though they'd been prodded from behind. Far down the station, Dee Dee stood in her bulky yellow slicker, a lost little lump, looking at them.

Márta had met Carl some weeks earlier at a party she'd attended with István and Judit. István was being suspiciously attentive and delightful; many attractive women were present. István loved parties. He rose to the occasion of being admired, and his paintings were beginning to sell.

Márta had been talking to István when a woman of fifty

or so approached. She wore large pieces of ocher-smeared abalone on a thong around her neck and was known to collect paintings. "I don't believe we've met," she said to Márta in a voice like an electric drill, and turned her back.

Her adornments, she was explaining to István, had once served as the currency of some now-impoverished coastal tribe. Márta began to drift away. István plucked at her sleeve, smiling merrily. She looked at him. He shrugged, and turned back to the woman.

In the hot, lively room, Carl was conspicuous for his satiny blond melancholy. Márta placed herself on the arm of a sofa not far from him and gazed out the window at the brooding houses across the street.

Carl drifted next to her and spoke easily, as though they shared some delicate and slightly sorrowful information. Was István watching? If so, certainly he would be jealous. Márta concentrated on sparkling empathetically up at Carl, but then understood that Carl was expecting her to respond to something. To what? she wondered. She made a modestly self-disparaging gesture. It served; Carl began to talk again.

He was truly handsome, she realized. Her sparkle lapsed as she stared. Carl lowered his eyes; his smile was clearly involuntary.

"Do you know many people here?" Márta asked stubbornly through her blush. Over Carl's shoulder, she saw István talking to a girl. The girl was as fragile and responsive-looking as a fawn. She had lovely, trustful eyes, and István was talking to her with the earnest concern that Márta recognized as the hallmark of his most gluttonous moments. Poison squirted into her veins. "Excuse me," she said to Carl. "I have a simply splitting migraine."

Carl brought her to her flat. She was pale and silent. She

had let István treat her too badly for too long; he expected her
to put up with anything. And tonight, as she had peeked back
into the party on her way out with Carl, István had glanced at
her with cold dismissal.

Carl settled her on the sofa. He wrapped a blanket around
her feet, found aspirin and a glass of water, and stood back
uncomfortably. How cramped and shabby the flat looked! In
Carl's impeccable Occidental presence Márta saw it clearly.
When she looked up at Carl he brushed away the tiny tears
that hung ornamentally from her lashes. "You must rest," he
said.

Could she have bored him? "No, no," she complained.
"Sit and talk to me." And he settled gingerly in a straight-
backed chair. She hoped Judit would come in.

But by the time Judit returned, Márta was alone, still
curled up on the sofa with the blanket around her feet, reading a novel to nurse a frail feeling of well-being.

Judit glowered. Judit and István had known each other
from childhood in Budapest, and Judit took István's side in
everything. Márta had heard, from others of course, how for
years Judit had tagged along after István, defended him, run
errands for him; how she'd been ignored by him, except when
he was sick or bored or wanted to meet one of her friends.
"He isn't going to call you again," Judit said.

Márta looked up from her book, raising her eyebrows in
pleasant inquiry. "István?" she said.

Judit snorted.

Poor Judit. All those girls, and never Judit. And it never
would be Judit.

But despite Judit's pronouncement, István did call. He
called the very next day. Judit handed the phone silently over
to Márta and left the room with a look of gratified persecution.

"Did you get home all right last night?" István said. His voice was silvery with sarcasm.

"Yes, thank you," Márta said. "I was accompanied."

"I am aware of that," István said.

"I felt ill," Márta said. "When I got home I had to lie down."

In the silence she felt a little giddy—István was supposed to have been apologizing by now. "I didn't like to interrupt you," she said. "You were having such a good time."

"I know what this is about," he said. "This is about nothing. I don't even know that girl. I only wanted her to meet you—that's why I was talking to her."

"What girl?" Márta said.

"Don't be ridiculous," István said. "She's only just arrived. You would be able to help her so much if you would only think of someone besides yourself for a change."

"How can you even—" Márta began.

"If only you would dare to be a little kind to someone. A little friendly. Eva has no job yet, she has no friends here—"

Márta stared at the phone in incredulity. What about *her*? She had arrived alone and almost penniless only eight months before. The only reason she had survived was that she had taken the trouble to plan, painstakingly, from Budapest, so that she would not have to exploit other women's escorts at parties. And for all her trouble, what did she have? What she had was, yes—a jealous flatmate, a shiftless roué of a lover, and a dull job in the store of a Hungarian goldsmith. Hardly enough to be tossed out in handfuls to passing girls. She hung up loudly and waited, but the phone was silent.

No matter, she thought, her eyes stinging.

But the days went by and István still didn't call. So then,

when Carl did, relief transformed her terror into a tremulous elation.

Carl took Márta to dinner in a pretty French restaurant. The china was thin, milkily luminous in the candlelight, gold-rimmed. On their table were a few flowers so exquisite they seemed about to perish with a little cry. And all around them from the other tables was a soothing rustle, like that of foliage, or money.

Outside, too, was the London Márta had come to but had never before entered. The great green floating parks, the pantherlike cars, the lofty ivory-colored crescents and terraces, the darkly shining shop windows, behind which salesgirls who looked like whippets showed one jewel-like dress, then another, to customers with excellent shoes and handbags.

Márta had begun to think that London might close her inescapably into the brittle émigré life she dreaded, some contemporary version of the lives of relatives she'd heard about in Paris and New York, great-aunts and distant elderly cousins whose apartments were like satellites crammed with dried old bits of uprooted finery. They drank streams of tarry coffee in tiny cups, they ate those few local pastries to which they could resign themselves, as they waited to be orbited back to prewar Budapest.

But, no— Deliverance was everywhere. Márta closed her eyes in thanks, then directed at Carl a smile of gratitude so forceful it almost knocked over a passing waiter.

The smile Carl returned was somewhat puzzled. Indeed, he seemed not to be saying anything much of interest. His firm, he was telling Márta, manufactured machine tools. It was based in Stuttgart but exported goods all over Europe, the United States, and Canada. He would prefer to be on the theoretical rather than the applied end of things, but—he shrugged—this was not bad for now. He enjoyed the irregular schedule, the travel, the flexibility . . . He picked up the saltcellar and examined it, frowning.

"And how is it that you're working for a German company?" Márta asked.

"Why not?" He glanced at her. "After all, I am German . . . Of course it's rather . . . That is, technically I did grow up there"—he hesitated—"as I think I was saying to you the other evening . . ."

The other evening! At the party? At her flat? She'd had so much on her mind! "My father and stepmother . . ." Carl coughed. "But I spent all that time here, of course—school, university. Those holidays at Andrew's . . . Actually, people do tend to take me for English."

"How wonderful it must be," Márta said, throwing a hasty cover over her confusion, "to be as much at home one place as the other."

Carl laughed sadly. "'As much at home.' Indeed . . ."

"But to travel, as well," she added encouragingly. Perhaps he didn't appreciate his own good fortune; she herself would love to travel, to be able to travel, to be able just to delve into this new, this real, London. Not to have to worry, always, about money.

"Yes," Carl was saying. "It's good, isn't it, traveling. Sometimes you get a feeling that things could change. Or open up. You thought it was an endless dark tunnel, but then . . ." He picked up the saltcellar again.

"But yes," Márta said. "Oh, I would like so much to see things the way you have seen them. Places that you can see so easily. France, Italy— Perhaps even this summer I will take a little time from my job . . ."

"Yes?" Carl said quietly.

A couple brushed by on their way to a table, glancing at Márta and Carl with interest, admiration. Márta smiled at Carl, and his eyes, as he smiled back, were moist. Oh, how could she have expended so much longing on someone like István, who had such a low opinion of her?

In the morning the London she opened her eyes onto was Carl's—the blue sky, the serene green-and-ivory city. But all that week Carl didn't call. That week and the next and the next. What on earth could have happened? Dinner had seemed so . . . *special.* A special, private atmosphere had embraced them. But perhaps, she thought, it embraced Carl and everyone—the person from whom he bought his toothpaste, the parking-lot attendant . . . Still, when he'd put her in a taxi to go home and kissed her caressingly on the cheek, she had the sensation of dissolving beautifully, like some sugary confection.

Perhaps he was working—he could have been called away unexpectedly.

Or perhaps he'd spent the evening with her out of pity. For the hideous foreigner.

The mirror told her one story, then another, while from one day to the next the lovely façade of Carl's London wore slowly away. Behind it, the dirty brick industrial city squatted, waiting to entrap Márta.

"By the way," Judit said one evening. "I happened to see István today."

"Yes?" Márta said, turning away to steady herself.

"He was with that girl from the party," Judit said. "They were talking together so seriously."

At work, Márta flirted recklessly with the men who came in to buy necklaces or rings for women. The men were sickeningly receptive. She smiled as she put their jewels into boxes, and amused herself by seeing them stuffed into hateful pink hunting coats, sailing off big nervous horses, and hurtling clumsily through the air.

At the end of the third week Carl did call. And Márta was astonished to find, at that moment, that she wasn't angry. On the contrary, she experienced, as she held the phone, a bridal gravity, as though the entire period of Carl's silence had been a preparation of some kind.

When Carl came to pick her up, he, too, was subdued, almost quizzical. He stood in the doorway, his hands in his pockets, looking at her. New calm began to emanate from her like light. Ah, yes. Clearly something had altered and intensified between them since they'd seen one another.

That evening's restaurant was sleek and Italian. Márta sipped her wine with contentment, beautiful again, safe again in London. Carl leaned back languidly while she talked; he seemed to take in what she was saying through his eyes, rather than his ears. Freed by his attention, she talked easily. Her life seemed to her to be pleasurable, and of interest. "Will you stop back for a drink?" she asked, and blushed.

Judit was in the sitting room when they came in. As Carl took her hand Judit's sullen expression transmuted into one of canine grief. "Please excuse me," she said, standing. "I must sleep."

Carl had gone to the window, where he stood looking out.

"Yes," he said after Judit's door closed behind her. "Well." He glanced delicately in the direction of Judit's room. "Am I staying?" he asked.

He was sculptural, fastidious, ritualistic, consecratory. His silky hair slid through Márta's fingers. Oh, those blind combustions with István! Márta cried out briefly in regret and then forgot István altogether. In the morning when she woke, Carl's

eyes were already open. He lay on his back with his hands behind his head. "Birds," he observed, and ran his thumb lightly
along her collarbone. She listened: Yes, birds! How marvelous.

She lay wrapped in the sheet, watching as Carl dressed.
Already he seemed far away. "My sister will be arriving on
Thursday," he said, adjusting his shirt. "It's been a very long
time since I've seen her. Would you come meet her? I'd like
that so much."

Carl's sister. Márta saw her perfectly. A tall girl in a fluid
dress, pale blond and lovely. She and Carl strolled together, re-
united, through sun-splashed green. A flock of pigeons lofted
before them. Márta shivered—a little familiar chill of exclu-
sion. "How splendid," she said. "I long to meet your sister."

A few evenings later Márta found her way to the address
Carl had given her on the phone. It was a large white house
that faced a silent square. Not a breath of air disturbed the
shrubbery. Behind the door, maple and silver glimmered.
The walls were covered with something dark and precious.
Carl led Márta up a flight of stairs and into the recesses of the
house, where there was a smallish kitchen. A tall girl with
long, lion-colored hair turned to Márta, resting a red nail
against her mouth.

Márta stepped forward as though magnetized, her legs
trembling slightly. She felt terribly unhappy. "You're very
pretty," she was dismayed to hear herself saying reproachfully.

The girl swept her hair back as though it were a burden.
"You are, too," she said in a swooping English drawl. Her
eyes narrowed and gleamed as she smiled. "Very pretty . . ."

"Márta," Carl said, "Jane. And this is my sister, Dee Dee."
Márta swiveled in the direction Carl indicated: a girl of indeterminate age—fourteen or fifteen possibly, Márta guessed—
sat at the table, scowling through a fringe of preposterously

black hair. Márta started to speak, and stopped. No one could say this girl was pretty.

"The poor child's been sleeping," Jane said. "She just got in this morning, and she's disorientated."

"I'm tired," Dee Dee corrected inattentively. "Sort of. Not every minute." The flat American assertions were like a series of little shoves. "Where are you from?" she said to Márta. "You have an accent."

"An accent," Márta said faintly. How could this girl be Carl's sister? "Really."

"Oh, yeah," Dee Dee said. "I get it. Well, I'm from Long Island."

" 'Long Island.' " Márta inclined her head. Whatever that might be.

"Would you like some tea?" Carl asked.

"No," Dee Dee said. "Yes. But I want some food."

"Thank you," Márta said. Where was she? She sat down across from Dee Dee and rubbed her forehead.

Jane reached into the refrigerator and held out at arm's length a white cardboard carton. "Disgusting," she said, and tossed it into the garbage. "Poor pet. Oh, why is there never anything to eat around here?"

"I'm *starving*," Dee Dee said. She sighed noisily and put her head down on the table in an apparent access of self-consciousness.

"Andrew will be here soon," Carl said. He spoke gently. "And then we'll go."

"Someplace fun, I hope," Jane said. "I'm going up to change."

"Jane—?" Dee Dee said.

"Yes, sweet," Jane said vaguely. "I'll be down soon."

Out the window a rain began to fall, as fine as dust. In the silence, Dee Dee slurped her tea.

"Hello," a man said from the doorway of the kitchen. He directed an odd little smile at Carl. "Hello, love," he said to Dee Dee. His handsomeness was like a thrown gauntlet. "You've had some sleep, I trust."

"Uh huh," Dee Dee said. She smiled, then frowned. Her glance swept the sink, the man's face, the ceiling. She opened her mouth and pretended to yawn.

"Andrew," Carl said. "I'd like you to meet Márta."

"Ah, yes." Andrew turned to Márta as though he hadn't seen her before. "So very pleased to meet you." Irony, conspicuously absent from his greeting to Dee Dee, leaked now into his smile.

"Hello," Márta said. They looked at one another for a minute before Andrew turned away. "Good," he said. "Well, is everybody ready? Where's Jane? Jane the drain?"

The restaurant was a solid block of noise, around which chrome and glass flashed harshly. At the bar, women pulsating with jewelry and men in suits as voluptuous and dark as storm clouds snagged one another on heated, gloating, scornful glances. Several turned to look, Márta noted by means of the mirror, as she passed by. No, to look, more likely, at Jane—Jane in her bare green reptilian dress. Márta smoothed down her little skirt and sniffed.

At the table Andrew handed Dee Dee the wine list. "Preferences?" he said.

Dee Dee looked at him dubiously.

"I forgot," he said. "Americans only drink champagne. Champagne it is, then."

How long was it exactly, Márta wondered as she sipped at her champagne, since Carl had seen this sister of his? She looked at the two of them. There was no resemblance. Well, actually, though, there was the faintest resemblance— subterranean, impossible to pinpoint. And at the moment, in fact, Carl looked just Dee Dee's age. No, younger than Dee Dee. Lost. His elegance had reduced into the elegance of a privileged and neglected child. "Are you here on holiday?" Márta leaned over to shout at Dee Dee.

"Holiday?" Dee Dee shouted back. "Oh, vacation. Well, that's one way to look at it, I suppose. I mean, I don't have to be back at school until September, but basically Mother's just dumped me on Carl." Carl raised a languid hand in demurral, but Dee Dee was in full swing. "She wants to romp around with her new boyfriend in private. Actually, she just got furious because I pointed out a few facts. Like the fact that she's old enough to be Kevin's—well, I don't know how old he is exactly, but probably about a quarter of her age. And the fact that she kicked my father out of the house, but I mean who actually *paid* for it, if you see what I mean. Not that my father's the most—but on the other hand, she married him, I didn't. And he does have his good points. Like, for example, he's not a gigolo."

Carl was gazing dreamily toward the larval roiling at the bar. "Strange," he said. "I always think of her as very young. Of course, I can't picture her with any precision—to me she's just a sort of princess with the face smudged out."

"You don't—" Márta began, not loudly enough. Talking here was like pitching something over a fence. "You don't remember your mother?"

"Well, she wasn't my mother for very long," Carl said absently.

"Yeah, but that's exactly what she looks like anyhow," Dee Dee said. "A princess with the face smudged out. *Nightmare on Elm Street Part Seventy*. When she and her friends are sitting around there are so many face lifts that if someone tells a joke there's this tearing sound. Her hair still looks exactly like yours, Carl. Isn't that amazing, har har? And you should see the house. Thank God I've only got one more year before college. Brass everywhere. Little marble stuff. Chandeliers. It looks like a whorehouse."

The waiter loomed over them threateningly. "Partridge for me," Jane said.

"Yes, yes," Márta said hurriedly. "For me, too." If Jane were just to reach out and swat her, Márta thought as Carl and Andrew conferred over Dee Dee's order, she would be sent sprawling.

A silence rocked unsteadily in the wake of the departing waiter. Everyone frowned, except Dee Dee, who smiled. Smirked, Márta thought. And why not? She had succeeded in stupefying all of them.

Americans seemed to feel the need to talk, Márta had observed before. And yet theirs was a country into which the concept of conversation seemed never to have penetrated. Dee Dee! So charmless, so graceless, yet she evidently considered it perfectly appropriate to crawl out to the center of the stage and wave her rattle, as though she were of special interest simply by virtue of her parents' shortcomings; astounding to think that she actually must be near seventeen! She spoke of the ordinary confusion of her private life with respect, even awe, as though she were describing the play of monumental cosmic forces. But *obviously* life was grotesque—there was no personal credit to be extracted from that, Márta thought; if life progressed in a natural fashion she herself would be alone somewhere now with Carl.

The waiter refilled Dee Dee's glass for the third—Márta counted—time. Madman. Soon he would be hauled off in chains, to prison, where he belonged.

Jane was delicately picking her partridge to pieces with her fingers, working away at the little bones with her teeth.

On Márta's own plate a carcass lay horrifyingly mauled. Besides, so what if Dee Dee's mother had had a little tuck here or there—obviously she could afford it! Did Dee Dee consider herself entitled to some shrunken old saint in a babushka? Surely no one was supposed to believe *Dee Dee's* hair had come into the world black like a telephone.

The swelling foreignness of the evening, the noise—Márta was shrinking into a darkness from which she could only peer out at the giant shining creatures who sat so distantly around the table. The huge seesaw sounds they made could not be folded into her tiny ears. She saw Andrew lean over to Jane and say something. She saw Dee Dee watch with adoring round-eyed humility as Andrew and Jane looked at each other and laughed. Far away next to her, Carl nodded pleasantly. Why didn't he help her?

"Carl, Carl!" Dee Dee called, and Márta could hear again. Dee Dee was pointing at a plate passing overhead, on which a squat glossy hummock lolled under a quivering sauce. "Can I have that for desert?"

"Of course," Carl said. "Whatever you like." He and Jane and Andrew gazed at Dee Dee with a tender, elegiac indulgence, as though she were an event that had taken place on earth many years earlier, before some great catastrophe.

"You know what?" Dee Dee said happily.

Recalled, the others looked at her with a false brightness.

Evidently she had nothing to say.

"You know what?" she began again, and achieved traction. "Carl, do you know how Mother met Kevin? He works at an auction house, and she went to cruise an escritoire, but she came home with him."

Jane tipped a little bird bone in tribute. "Good for her."

"Yeah," Dee Dee said. "That's true, but—" She stopped, and turned the dark color that precedes tears. "But what if he doesn't . . . I mean, what if he only . . ."

"How well I know the type," Andrew said as Dee Dee fell into a despondent silence. "Jane, isn't that your friend Blaisdell over there?"

"Where?" Jane said. "My God."

In the far reaches of the room, a party of red-faced young men—rich simpletons, Márta calculated, barely out of public school—looked up as a woman announced herself with the aid of a toy trumpet. One of the men was wearing a paper hat. They all pounded on the table as the woman, singing "Happy Birthday," proceeded to take off her drum majorette's outfit.

It was all just barely audible. Carl appeared to be paying no attention, though Dee Dee watched with interest, and Jane was regarding the spectacle with sparkling, narrowed eyes. "Excuse me," she said.

Jane reached the table just as the woman with the toy trumpet refastened a final button and hurried off. Jane sat down and draped an arm around the man in the paper hat. He, and the others too, stared at her with the joyful, wondering incomprehension of men who are about to pass out.

Andrew leaned across Dee Dee to Carl. "See the one in the hat? Guess who took Jane to Paris a couple of weeks ago when you and I were in the South of France."

"Really," Carl said.

"You were just in the South of France," Márta observed.

For an instant the room was a tableau. Every face, every object frozen, haloed with a warning brightness.

"Just for old times' sake, really," Andrew said. "We only

stayed a few days, because Carl became incredibly shirty over something."

Carl pushed his plate away. "Not at all," he said.

"No?" Andrew said. "Well, good. I can't think why you would have done." He turned to Márta. "Has Carl told you about Cubby and Kaye?"

Márta looked at Andrew. The South of France. During the whole time Carl hadn't called, when she might reasonably have assumed he was working, he had been in the South of France.

"Well, but after all," Andrew said, "there's nothing to tell. Evidently they were friends of my father's—from Kenya, possibly, but no one really remembers. It's all lost in the mists of time and brain damage. They're English classics, Kaye and Cubby. Titled, demented—generations of primordial aristo-cratic inbreeding."

Dee Dee listed suddenly against Andrew's arm. He brushed her hair away from her forehead. "We used to go to their place from time to time on holiday. Carl and I. Especially if my mother was off someplace. The idea was, we'd be getting looked after." He looked at Carl. "Which was indeed the case—we long ago came to the conclusion that the servants were wardens in disguise."

Carl raised his eyes to Andrew, then looked down with a faint, self-mocking smile.

"Dee Dee—" Márta said. Dee Dee's head was sliding along Andrew's arm. "Dee Dee, do you want to go?"

"No," Dee Dee said.

Andrew resettled her against his shoulder. "But Carl hadn't been for years and years," he said. "And Cubby was forever saying, 'Wasn't there some other little chap?' or 'Where's dear, dear Carl?' or however it all happened to come up in his mind at that particular moment. So he and Kaye were simply over the moon when I told them Carl had gotten in touch with me and was going to be staying at my place for the summer."

"Did I get in touch with you?" Carl said mildly.

"Oh," Andrew said. "That's right. You ran into me. By chance. And then you got in touch with me."

Into the sudden hollow of silence at the table, Dee Dee inserted a little hiccup.

"I think," Márta addressed Carl, "that it's time to take your sister home."

"Jane?" Dee Dee sat up. "Where's Jane?"

"It's all right, ducks," Andrew said. "Jane's found a friend."

Outside, it was still drizzling. "Will you come with us?" Carl said to Márta as he opened the taxi door for Dee Dee.

"No," Márta said. "*Thank* you."

By the time she reached her flat she had to fight the clamor pressing in on her just to get the key into the lock. Carl had looked at her as he said good night with a trace of surprise. Oh, that innocent face! In fact, he was so slippery that he had made her not be able to understand why she was angry herself. Which was worse behavior in its way than István's.

Judit sat at the kitchen table eating, directly from its deli wrapping, a cheese-and-pickle sandwich on limp English bread. "Up so late?" Márta spoke insouciantly in English.

Judit sighed. "I was just getting some work done. Have a nice evening?"

"Lovely," Márta said. "Carl took me to the most marvelous place. Do you ever wonder why London is such a quiet city? It is because everyone who lives here is inside this restaurant. On the street, it is all chauffeurs waiting."

"How pleasant," Judit said.

"Very," Márta said. "We had a great deal of champagne because Carl's baby sister has come to stay with him. And Carl's friend Andrew brought with him the most beautiful girl, Jane."

"So," Judit said. "Your life is glamour and more glamour." She wadded up the deli wrappings; they landed in the garbage with a deadly little plop.

In the morning when Márta awoke, anger lay next to her like a cover that had slipped off during the night. She felt around for it and readjusted it over herself.

What a hateful evening. How remote Carl had been, how abstracted. But how handsome! Oh, the world of difference between the banquet he seemed to offer and the crumbs that fell her way. Why, with all their talk of traveling that evening in the French restaurant had Carl not even mentioned that he was going to the South of France? What a shrew he made her feel.

Poor Dee Dee. That poor little pit pony! Alone, a foreigner—all she had was Carl! Márta imagined herself—in a little suit, perhaps—showing Dee Dee around London; really, Dee Dee was rather cute, if you managed to think about her in the right way. Márta eyed the phone. There were swans in a park somewhere, she understood—she could show them to Dee Dee. Take her shopping. Explain to her peculiar English customs, like tea . . . How well, she wondered, did Dee Dee actually know Carl?

Dee Dee was late, of course, and the restaurant Márta had designated—one whose name had echoed, potently English, all the way to Márta in Budapest—was crowded with Saturday shoppers. Their faces looked ashen and fatigued against the prettily colored walls and carpets, and the uniformed hostess eyed Márta with suspicion. Márta cleared her throat. "Yes, I'm waiting for my—" Her what?

"Excuse me?" the hostess said. "Of course. Well, there aren't any tables at the moment anyhow. You can see for yourself. More and more crowded all the time now. Where do they all come from? Days when you hardly hear a word of English spoken." She lifted one foot, then the other, as though she were accustomed to perpetual pain. "I don't know if you've noticed the change. Perhaps you don't remember. It's only in the last few years that London has become so"—she cocked her head conspiratorially to indicate the roomful of tea drinkers—"*cosmopolitan*."

"Hi," Dee Dee said from near Márta's shoulder. In her yellow slicker she looked like a huge bathtub toy.

"You'll have to keep your coats," the hostess observed morosely. "The cloakroom's closed for renovations."

"That's okay," Dee Dee said. She rubbed at her nose with her wrist.

"Well, management doesn't care for it," the hostess said. "It lowers the tone."

Márta burned with self-consciousness as she poured out the tea. It was all so primitive and complicated. At the tables all around them women in tweeds or chadors and men in pinstripes dealt with the fussy pots and tongs and strainers with the ease of tycoons handling ticker tape. And what about this pot of plain hot water, Márta wondered. Was she supposed to be *doing* something with it? No matter. Dee Dee appeared not to notice her awkwardness. In fact, for all Dee Dee appeared to be noticing, Márta could have taken her to the filthy corner caf. There was no sign of life from Dee Dee at all. Not even self-pitying monologues, let alone meaningful discourse about Carl. No, Dee Dee was quietly absorbed in stacking up the expensive little cakes that tasted like Kleenex filled with toothpaste, and eating them mechanically, one after the other.

Dee Dee's eyes were fixed on Márta's plate, where a little cake sat inscrutably, bitten. She was trying to think of something to say. It was difficult, though—especially since Márta had been frowning since they'd sat down. Dee Dee felt cold and rubbery. What if Márta hated her? What would happen then?

After her mother had announced to her that she was to be sent to Carl for the summer, Dee Dee had been racked by rapid alterations between joy and misery, hope and panic. She had seen Carl only once. When she was a child, probably around four. Where had they been? She, Carl, their mother, of course . . . It was a big house. The floor shone, there were flowers in huge vases, several women—tall, broad-shouldered, with long, whooshing skirts; a fat man with dark hair. Someone said, would the baby like to see the pony? Carl took her hand. *She was the baby.* Carl led her outside, the house darkened behind them. In a grassy little enclosure a white creature pranced and curvetted. Dee Dee stared straight ahead. *Was she feeling her own hand holding Carl's, or was she feeling Carl's hand holding hers?*

Dee Dee carried the memory privately, a picture in a locket. She never asked her mother about it. At the worst times, she allowed herself to take it out and contemplate it. The angelically serious boy stayed older than she was; he was ahead of her, drawing her along as though she were secured to him by some unseverable attachment. As indeed she was.

When Dee Dee descended the stairs the morning of her

departure for London, her mother had looked at her narrowly. "You've simply got to lose five pounds," she said. "Ten would be better. You can get away with things as a child that you can't at your age, you know."

All right. All right. If Carl was ashamed of her, if he didn't want her around, Dee Dee would take off on her own somehow. She had with her a reasonable amount of money—her mother and her father had been separately, guiltily openhanded, and at an early age she had cultivated the prudent habit of skimming small amounts from her mother's unguarded cash against unforeseeable eventualities. There were times, during the savage quarrels between her parents, between herself and her mother, when, her face stiff from the strain of shame or tears or fury, she imagined herself liberated—cast out, fugitive, all the trashy screen of words left behind; words and the trashy names of things and accusations and expectations. The rocking of the darkened carriage, the purifying monotony of hooves, of tracks. Looking out at the flowing night, clean, unknown, dignified, new. Dependent on no one, loved by no one . . .

But when Carl greeted her at Heathrow there was no sign of recoil. He kissed her on both cheeks and picked up her bag. She had recognized him immediately; he was just as he ought to have been.

Early in the evening Dee Dee had awoken in her new room. The walls were covered with something green, like ribbon. Silver-framed photographs were scattered on a polished dressing table. Standing in the doorway was a woman with long, blondish hair. "Hello," Dee Dee said.

"Hello," the woman said.

Where was Carl? Where was Andrew? "I'm Carl's sister," Dee Dee said.

"Right." The woman shook out her hair. "Carl said." She sat down on the foot of Dee Dee's bed and yawned. "I'm Jane," she said. "Here for long?"

Jane was wearing a kimono and her feet were bare. "I don't know," Dee Dee said.

"Mm," Jane said. She reached for one of the silver-framed photographs. "I suppose not . . ."

Dee Dee crawled out from under the covers and peered over Jane's shoulder. The photographs were all of people from some other time. They looked not real at all—implausible, approximate, costumed. "Who are they?" Dee Dee said.

"Andrew's posh relations, I should think," Jane said. "This must be his mum—looks enough like him, doesn't it?"

She handed Dee Dee the photograph. It was true; as Dee Dee saw Andrew's face within the woman's, the opaque surface of dated style melted. The woman's skin warmed, her curls had just sprung back from a breeze. A starry, dangerous blur of excitement hung in front of her eyes like a little veil, and her beauty rose from the black-and-white paper like steam, so evanescent it suggested imminent fatality—a car, a boat, a wild animal . . . Dee Dee handed the photograph back to Jane.

"What?" Jane said, glancing at her.

"I don't know," Dee Dee said. *London*. Only a few days earlier she had been talking to her mother, and they had started to quarrel, and her mother had said, "All right, I've had it. I'm sending you to Carl." Dee Dee looked at Jane in amazement. "I was just there," she said, "and now I'm *here*. Mother and I were just *talking*, and now I'm here . . ."

Jane stood up. "Well," she said. "That's the way it works, isn't it. Anyway"—she smiled kindly from the doorway as Dee Dee pulled on her jeans—"Carl's pleased."

Dee Dee stared soberly into the silver-framed mirror and carefully combed her hair.

That's the way it works. She wandered out to the stairway. *Carl's pleased.*

It was pitch-dark when Dee Dee next woke up. What had awakened her? There was the familiar unevenness in the air of recent disturbance.

But where was she? She felt around for a light—oh, yes. Andrew's house. She felt a bit strange. From dinner maybe. She remembered: she'd drunk a lot of wine. It had been very noisy. Jane had been there, and Carl, and Carl's friend Márta, and Andrew. How nervous she'd been! She'd talked a lot. But what had she said? And how had she gotten upstairs?

She listened carefully into the lush undergrowth of silence. At first she could make no sense of it, but then she heard something from downstairs. She got up, as she had so often at home, and crept out to the landing. All the closed doors around her! More frightening than the faint light from below.

Dee Dee edged herself down the stairs, halfway to the next landing. Legs extended on the sofa into her view. Andrew's—those were his socks. "I'm sorry," someone said quietly. Carl. He sounded far away. "Really," he said. "I really am."

"Must we discuss it?" Andrew said.

Dee Dee strained into the silence.

"What?" Andrew said. "Did you say something?"

Dee Dee could feel Carl sigh. "No," he said.

"But *I* said, must we discuss it?" Andrew said.

Carl cleared his throat. "No," he said. "I'm sorry."

"What?" Andrew said. "You're what?"

"Don't," Carl said. "Please."

"Don't *what*," Andrew said. "Please *what*. Oh, God. Why are you *here*?"

"I don't know," Carl said. "I'm sorry."

"Don't be sorry," Andrew said. "Just tell me why you're here."

"I thought it would be—" Carl said. "I don't know."

"You don't know," Andrew said. "Of course you know."

"I wanted to be—I thought we'd be able—"

"You see," Andrew said. "Oh, how idiotic. You see, this is what you say now. This is what you always say. But then it's *you* who always—"

"I know," Carl said. "I'm sorry. But not anymore."

Darkness boiled up around Dee Dee. After a minute Andrew spoke again. "Then why are you here?" he said. His voice twisted like a wilting flower. "Why are you here?"

The next evening Dee Dee was waiting on the sofa when Carl returned.

"Where is everyone?" Carl said.

"Jane never came back," Dee Dee said. "I guess. And Andrew wanted me to tell you he was going somewhere with Timothy."

"Ah," Carl said. "Hm. Well, in that case." He looked around at the walls as though he were trying to remember something. "Takeaway all right?"

Dee Dee stretched out on the sofa, her empty plate balanced on her stomach. Carl sat in a high, straight-backed armchair; he appeared to be sitting in a bell jar of light. The boy who had hovered by her, always available in moments of extreme need, who had led her from one year to the next—had that boy become this man? "Carl—" Dee Dee said.

"I was thinking," he said. "You know, it's idiotic, your being here in Europe and just lying around the house."

"It's only Friday," Dee Dee said. Where was *Carl*? "I only just got here yesterday."

"I ought to take some time off," Carl said. "Or arrange with my firm to go someplace."

"Go someplace?" Dee Dee sat up. "I mean—"

"Someplace else," Carl said. "After all, why should you stay in London? It's so—well, and also it's . . ."

Dee Dee ran her hand over the velvety covering of the sofa. It was only last night that Andrew had lain in this very spot.

"And you know," Carl said. "It occurs to me. What did you think of Márta?"

Carefully, Dee Dee felt her way toward the answer. "I liked Márta," she said. She looked at Carl gravely. "I felt very comfortable with her."

"Because I was thinking," Carl said. "Maybe Márta should come with us."

The restaurant was emptying out. There were only a few remaining parties of ladies, and, at the next table, a hunted-looking man whose pinstriped shoulders carried a dusting of white. Márta's little frown intensified, and Dee Dee's heart began to beat rapidly; what had she done now? Oh, no—and what had happened to that bitten little cake on Márta's plate? She had some impression that she herself had . . .

"So you say Carl is planning some sort of trip," Márta said. She turned her teacup in her hands.

"Well," Dee Dee said. Had Carl expected *her* to ask Márta? "I mean . . ."

"He really ought to let us know, don't you think?" Márta said crossly. "That brother of yours really ought to let us know when he is sending us on trips."

"Didn't he call you today?" Dee Dee said timidly. "I'm sure he tried to call you today."

Márta looked at her blankly. She seemed to be concentrating, as though she were identifying some faint piece of music.

"Márta?" Dee Dee said.

"Shh," Márta said. She leaned toward Dee Dee, lowering her eyes. "Do you think that man is attractive?"

"What man?" Dee Dee said. The only man she could see was the one at the next table.

"Don't look," Márta said. "He is very aware of us." Márta gazed in unearthly majesty at her teacup, and a hush consumed the room as a marmorial glow lit her face, her arms, her throat. But then she burst out laughing, causing a renewed murmur of conversations and teacups. "Oh, what a ridiculous country this is!" she said. "'The cloakroom is closed for renovations—'" She imitated the hostess's pruny expression. "The cloakroom! Closed for renovations!" She burst out laughing again and smiled over at Dee Dee with a merriment that seemed entirely unwarranted.

"I had a nice time today," Dee Dee said that night to Carl. They were in a room on the second floor that held a great number of books. "With Márta."

"Good," Carl said. He peered at a horse print on the wall in front of him.

"Have you had a chance to—I mean, I'm glad you're going to ask her to come on our trip," Dee Dee said.

"You know," Carl said, "I spent a lot of time in this room when I was your age."

"Excuse me—" A boy a few years younger than Carl leaned around the door. "I can't find a corkscrew."

"There's one in the drawer to the right of the sink," Carl said.

"Oh," the boy said. "Well, I couldn't find it."

Carl shrugged. "Sorry."

"The thing is," the boy said, "I can't find Andrew, either."

Carl sighed and pushed back his hair. "Andrew went out," he said.

"Oh," the boy said. "Well, when you see him, tell him Christopher and Angelica and I waited."

Carl nodded.

"Thanks," the boy said. He looked at Carl uncertainly and then withdrew. Carl put his head in his hands.

That miraculous hair of his—so like their mother's. "Carl?" Dee Dee said after a moment. "Could we take a train?"

"A train?" Carl lifted his head. "If you like." He sighed. "Well, I suppose I'd better call Márta, hadn't I, before it's too late."

"Carl?" Dee Dee said. "It isn't too late . . ."

"Yes," Carl said. "I mean, it's already after ten."

From high under the grimy glass, two pigeons swooped over Dee Dee as she hurried along. On their way—who could guess from where to where? The line where Carl and Márta stood arguing tensed and rippled as Dee Dee approached, like the tail of a nervous animal; the train would be boarding any minute.

"What is the matter?" Dee Dee heard Carl say. "Why are you angry?"

"Why ask me?" Márta said. "When you know very well."

"Know what?" Carl said. "I don't know. What have I done?"

"Done," Márta said. "You haven't 'done' anything."

"Then why—"

"It's what you *think*."

"I see," Carl said. "And now you know what I'm thinking."

"I happen to," Márta said.

"Very good," Carl said. "But you could be wrong."

"I happen to know," Márta said. "And I happen also to be right."

"Yes?" Carl said. "Good. So what is it that I'm thinking?"

"You know what you're thinking," Márta said. "Why should I tell you? You're thinking that you don't want to go."

"I'm thinking that I don't want to go!" Carl said. "On this trip? Of course I want to go. This trip was my idea—why wouldn't I want to go?"

"I don't *know*—" Márta said. "I don't know why not. You tell *me* why not."

For a moment the line paused in its progress, then continued around Carl and Márta into the open doors of the train. "Márta," Carl said. "We have to get on the train now. Where's Dee Dee? Oh, there you are."

"You get on the train," Márta said. "You get on the train since that's *what you want*. But what am I going to do?" Her eyes shone, furious and teary, and a freezing little laugh hung in the air. "Now I've taken time off from my job, I have no money. You don't care whether I live or die—"

"Oh, please," Carl said. "Márta—Márta, please. We have to go now."

"We?" Márta said. "Yes? Why should I go somewhere with you when you don't know the difference between me and a . . . *suitcase*. I will stay here, where at least there are certain people who do want to see me."

Carl looked at her. His face closed over. "Oh, what is the point?" he said. "Why should I say anything? No one ever believes me. I'm sorry, Dee Dee—" He put his hand on Dee Dee's shoulder. "We'll have to work this out before we—"

But Dee Dee slipped out from under his hand. Hugging her bag of magazines and candy bars against her chest, she mounted the steps of the train.

Carl's and Márta's shocked faces glowed as she fled along a corridor. The train breathed and shuddered. From the other side of its metal membrane Dee Dee could feel all the last sad leave-takings, torn away, fluttering idly upward in the station like slips of burning paper, floating as the dead words curled into the faint edge of flame, darkening into ash . . .

She opened the heavy door onto one of the compartments. She felt in her pocket for her ticket, and took a seat. She was alone. Would Carl and Márta be looking for her, pacing up and down beside the train? Or would they still be arguing, each trying to get the other to say what they needed to hear? But perhaps, in fact, Carl had already capitulated, and Márta, victorious, was already abandoned. In which case Carl—well, Carl could go on his way back to Andrew's house.

The door of Dee Dee's compartment opened; the train slid into motion. A stooped, elderly man appeared. He stood briefly, balancing, then took a seat across from her. In the gauzy dimness he looked to her impersonal, unformed—like a mound of clay on a sculptor's table. Yes, she thought; that's how she would look to him.

The carriage swayed, the train roared into a tunnel. How was she going to take care of herself, Dee Dee wondered. Still, how does anyone? *From far away Carl had accompanied her.* In darkness Dee Dee gazes out the dark window—faint lights bobbing in the silver frame. Any moment, she knows, day will pour in, extinguishing the lights, molding onto her face and the face of her traveling companion the masks of themselves: a man made ordinary by evasions and fears, a girl who won't engage our sympathy or hopes. But just for the moment, aren't they free? What rare, dear beings are hidden here now by these shadows?

ALL AROUND ATLANTIS

For my brother, David

and our father, George

and in memory of our mother, Ruth

THE GIRL WHO LEFT HER SOCK
ON THE FLOOR

Jessica dangled a sock between her thumb and forefinger, studied it, and let it drop. "There are times," she said, "one wearies of rooming with a pig."

Pig. Francie checked to see what page she was on and slammed *World History* shut. "Why not go over to the nice, clean library?" she said. "You could go to the nice, clean library, and you could think nice, clean thoughts. I'll just root around here in the homework." She pulled her blanket up and turned to the window, her eyes stinging.

Faint, constant crumblings and tricklings . . . Outside, spring was sneaking up under the cradle of snow in the valley, behind the lacy gray air that veiled everything except the girl, identifiable as hardly more than the red dot of her jacket, who was winding up the hill toward the dorm.

Jessica sighed noisily and dumped a stack of clothing into a drawer. "I will get to that stuff, please, Jessica," Francie said, "if you'll just kindly leave it."

Jessica gazed sorrowfully at Francie's ear, then bent down to retrieve a dust-festooned sweatshirt from beneath Francie's bed.

"You know," Francie said, "there are people in the world— not many, but a few—to whom the most important thing is not whether there happens to be a sock on the floor. There are people in the world who are not afraid to face reality, to face the fact that the floor is the natural place for a sock, that the floor is where a sock just naturally goes when it's off. But do we fearless few have a voice? No. No, these are words which must never be spoken—true, Jessica? This is a thought which must never be thought."

It was Cynthia in the red jacket, the secretary, Francie saw now—not one of the students. Cynthia wasn't much older than the seniors, but she lived in town and never came to meals. "Right, Jessica?" Francie said.

There was some little oddness about seeing Cynthia outside the office—as if something were leaking somewhere.

"Jessica?" Francie said. "Oh, well. *'But the poor, saintly girl had gone deaf as a post. The end.'*"

Jessica's voice sliced between Francie and the window. "Look, Francie, I don't want to trivialize your pain or anything, but I'm getting kind of bored over here. Besides which, I am not your personal maid."

"Oink oink," Francie said. "Grunt, grunt. *'Actually, not the end, really, at all, because God performed a miracle, and the beautiful deaf girl could hear again, though everything from that moment on sounded to her as the gruntings of pigs.'*"

"*As* the gruntings of pigs?" Jessica demanded. "Sounded *as* gruntings?"

"Oink oink," Francie said. She opened *World History* to page 359 again. "An Artist's Conception of the Storming of the Bastille." Well, and who were "Editors Clarke & Melton," for that matter, to be in charge of what was going on? To decide which, out of all the things that went on, were *things that had happened*? Yeah, "World History: The Journey of Two Editors and Their Jobs." Why not a picture of people trapped in their snooty boarding school with their snooty roommates?

"Anyhow, guess what, next year we both get to pick new roommates."

"If we're both still here," Jessica said. "Besides, that's then—"

"What does *that* mean?" Francie said.

"You don't have to shout at me all the time," Jessica said. "Besides, as I was saying, that's then and this is now. And if I were you, I'd stop calling Mr. Klemper 'Sex Machine.' Sooner or later someone's going to—"

But just then the door opened, and the girl, Cynthia, was standing there in her red jacket. "Frances McIntyre?" Cynthia said. She stared at Francie and Jessica as though she had forgotten which one Francie was. And Francie and Jessica stared back as though they had forgotten, too. "Frances McIntyre, Mrs. Peck wants to see you in the Administration Building."

Jessica watched, flushed and round-eyed, as Francie put on her motorcycle jacket and work boots. "You're going to freeze like that, Francie," Jessica said, and then Cynthia held the door open.

"Francie—" Jessica said. "Francie, do you want me to go with you?"

Francie had paused on the threshold. She didn't turn around, and she couldn't speak. She shook her head.

What had she done? What had been seen or heard or said? Had someone already told Mr. Klemper? Was it cutting lacrosse? Had she been reported smoking again in back of the Science Building? Because if she had she was out. Out. Out. End. The end of her fancy scholarship, the end of her education, the end of her freedom, the end of her future. No, the beginning of a new future, her real future, the one that had been lying in wait for her all along, whose snuffly breathing she could hear in the dark. She'd live out her days as a checkout girl, choking on the toxic vapors of household cleaners and rotting baked goods, trudging home in the cold to rot, herself, in the scornful silence of her bulky, furious mother. Her mother, who had slaved to give ungrateful Francie this squandered opportunity. Her mother, who wouldn't tolerate a sock on the floor for as long as one instant.

Mrs. Peck's bleached blue eyes stared at Francie as Francie stood in front of her, shivering, each second becoming more vividly aware that her jacket, her little, filmy dress, her boots, her new nose ring all trod on the boundaries of the dress code. "Do sit down, please, Frances," Mrs. Peck said.

Mrs. Peck was wearing, of course, a well-made and proudly unflattering suit. On the walls around her were decorative, framed what-were-they-called, Francie thought— Wise Sayings. "I have something very, very sad, I'm afraid, to tell you, Frances," Mrs. Peck began.

Out, she was *out*. Francie's blood howled like a storm at sea; her heart pitched and tossed.

But Mrs. Peck's voice—what Mrs. Peck's voice seemed to be saying, was that Francie's mother was dead.

"What?" Francie said. The howling stopped abruptly, as though a door had been shut. "My mother's in the hospital. My mother broke her hip."

Mrs. Peck bowed her head slightly, over her folded hands. "EVERYTHING MUST BE TAKEN SERIOUSLY, NOTHING TRAG-ICALLY," the wall announced over her shoulder. "FORTUNE AND HUMOR GOVERN THE WORLD."

"My mother has a broken hip," Francie insisted. "Nobody dies from a broken fucking *hip*."

Mrs. Peck's eyes closed for a moment. "There was an embolism," she said. "Apparently, this is not unheard of. Patients who greatly exceed an ideal weight . . . That is, a Miss Healy called from the hospital. Do you remember Miss Healy? A student nurse, I believe. I understand you met each other when you went to visit your mother several weeks ago. Your mother must have tried to get up sometime during the night. And most probably—" Mrs. Peck frowned at a piece of paper and put on her glasses. "Yes. Most probably, according to Miss Healy, your mother wished to go to the toilet. Evidently, she would have fallen back against her pillow. The staff wouldn't have discovered her death until morning."

Bits of things were falling around Francie. "'Wouldn't have'?" she plucked from the air.

"This is, of course, a reconstruction," Mrs. Peck said. "Miss Healy came on duty this afternoon. Your mother wasn't there, and Miss Healy became concerned that perhaps no one had thought to notify you. A thoughtful young woman. I had the impression she was acting outside official channels, but . . ."

"But *all's well that ends well*," Francie said.

Mrs. Peck's eyes rested distantly on Francie. "I wonder," she said. "It might be possible, under the terms of your scholarship, to arrange for some therapy when you return." Her gaze wandered up the chattering wall. "A hospital must be a terribly difficult thing to administer," she remarked to it graciously. "I have absolutely no one to bring you to Albany, Frances, I'm afraid. I'll have to call someone in your family to come for you."

Francie gasped. "You can't!" she said.

Mrs. Peck frowned. She appeared to be embarrassed. "Ah," she said, no doubt picturing, Francie thought, some abyss of mortifying circumstances. "In that case . . ." she said. "Yes. I'll have Mr. Klemper cancel French tomorrow, and he—"

"Why can't I take the morning bus?" Francie said. "I've

taken that bus a thousand times." She was going red, she knew; one more second and she'd cry. "Don't cancel French," she said. "I always take that bus. *Please*."

Mrs. Peck's glance strayed up the wall again, and hesitated. "HONI SOIT QUI MAL Y PENSE," Francie read.

Mrs. Peck took off her glasses and rubbed the bridge of her nose. "Miss Healy," she mused. "Such an unsuitable name for a nurse, isn't it. People must often make foolish remarks."

How could it be true? How could Francie be on the bus now, when she should be at school? The sky hadn't changed since yesterday, the trees and fields out the window hadn't changed; Francie could imagine her mother just as clearly as she'd ever been able to, so how could it be true?

And yet her mother would have been dead while she herself had been asleep, dreaming. Of what? Of what? Of Mr. Davis, probably. Not of her mother, not dreaming of a little wad of blood coalescing like a pearl in her mother's body, preparing to wedge itself into her mother's heart.

If you were to break, for example, your hip, there would be the pain, the proof, telling you all the time it was true: *that's then and this is now.* But this thing—each second it had to be true all over again; she was getting hurled against each second. *Now.* And *now again—thwack!* Maybe one of these seconds she'd smash right through and find herself in the clear place where her mother was alive, scowling, criticizing . . .

Out the window, snow was draining away from the patched fields of the small farms, the small, failing farms. Rusted machinery glowed against the sky in fragile tangles. Her mother would have been dead while Francie got up and took her shower and worried about being late to breakfast and was late to breakfast and went to biology and then to German and then dozed through English and then ate lunch and then hid in the dorm instead of playing lacrosse and then quarreled with Jessica about a sock. At some moment in the night her mother had gone from being completely alive to being completely dead.

The passengers were scraggy and exhausted-looking, like a committee assigned to the bus aeons earlier to puzzle out just this sort of thing—part of a rotating team whose members were picked up and dropped off at stations looping the planet. How different they were from the team of sleek girls at school, who already knew everything they needed to know. Which team was Francie on? Ha-ha. She glanced at the man across the aisle, who nodded commiseratingly between bites of the vile-smelling food he lifted from a plastic-foam container on his lap.

All those hours during which her life (along with her mother) had gone from being one thing to being another, it had held its shape, like a car window Francie once saw hit by a rock. The rock hit, a web of tiny, glittering lines fanned out, and only a minute or so later had the window tinkled to the street in splinters.

The dazzling, razor-edged splinters had tinkled around Francie yesterday afternoon in Mrs. Peck's voice. "Your family." "Have someone in your family come for you." Well, fine, but where on earth had Mrs. Peck got the idea there *was* anyone in Francie's family?

From Francie's mother, doubtless, the world's leading expert in giving people ideas without having to say a single word. "A proud woman" was an observation people tended to make, vague and flustered after encountering her. But what did that mean, "proud"? Proud of her poverty. Proud of her poor education. Proud of her unfashionable size. Proud of bringing up her Difficult Daughter, Without an Iota of Help. So what was the difference, when you got right down to it, between pride and shame?

Francie had a memory, one of her few from early childhood, that never altered or dimmed, however often it sprang out: herself in the building stairwell with Mrs. Dougherty, making Mrs. Dougherty laugh. She could still feel her feet fly up as her mother grabbed her and pulled her inside, still hear the door slam. She could still see (and yet this was something she could never have seen, really) skinny Mrs. Dougherty cackling alone in the hall. *"How could you embarrass me like that?"* her mother said. The wave of shock and outrage and humiliation engulfed Francie again with each remembering; she felt her mother's fierce grip on her arm. Francie was an embarrassment. What on earth could she have been doing in the hall? An *embarrassment*. Well, *so be it.*

On the day she had brought Francie all the way from Albany to be interviewed at school, Francie's mother—wearing gloves!—had a private conversation with Mrs. Peck. Francie sat in the outer office and waited. Cynthia had been typing demurely, and occasionally other girls would come through—perfect girls, beautiful and beautifully behaved and sly. Francie could just picture their mothers. When she eventually did see some—Jessica's tall, chestnut-haired mother among them—it turned out that her imagination had not exaggerated.

Waiting in the outer office, Francie feared (Francie hoped) she was to be turned ignominiously away. Instead, she was confronted by Mrs. Peck's withering smile of welcome; Mrs. Peck was gluttonous for Francie's test scores. That Francie and her mother looked, each in her own way, so entirely *unsuitable* appeared to increase, rather than diminish, their desirability.

When her mother and Mrs. Peck emerged from the office together that afternoon, a blaze of triumph and contempt crackled behind the veneer of patently suspect humility on her mother's face. Mrs. Peck, on the other hand, looked as if she'd been bonked on the head with a plank.

Surely it was during that conference that Francie's family had been born. Her mother's gift (the automatic nuancing of the unspoken) and Mrs. Peck's mandate (to heap distinction upon herself) had intertwined to generate little tendrils of plausible realities. Which were now generating tendrils of their own: an imaginary church with imaginary relatives—*suitable* relatives— wavering behind viscous organ music and bearing with simple dignity their imaginary grief. Oh, her poor mother! Her poor mother! What possible business was it of Mrs. Peck's *when* her mother had wanted to go to the toilet for the last time?

Several companionable tears made their way down Francie's face, turning from hot to cold. The sensation consoled her as long as it lasted. When she opened her eyes, she saw the frayed outskirts of town.

Francie climbed the stairs cautiously, lest creakings draw the still gregarious Mrs. Dougherty to her peephole. She paused with her key in the lock before contaminating irreversibly the silence, her mother's special silence, which, she thought, a person had to shout to be heard over. Francie leaned her head against the door's cool plane, listening, then turned the key. The lock's tumbling sounded like a gunshot.

A little colorless sunlight had forced its way around the neighboring buildings and lay, exhausted, across the floor. A fine coating of city grime sealed the sills in front of the closed windows like insulation. Her mother's bed was tightly made;

the bedspread was as mute as the surface of a lake into which a clue had been dropped long before.

The only disorder in the kitchen was a cup Francie had left in the sink when she'd come to see her mother in the hospital three weeks earlier, still full of dark liquid in which velvety spots had begun to blossom. Francie sat down at the table. The night she'd finally dared to ask her mother what had happened to her father they'd been in here, just finishing the dishes. Francie remembered: her mother was holding a white dish towel; she started to speak.

Too late, then, for Francie to retract the question—a question that had been clogging her mouth ever since the day, years before, when Corkie Patterson had pummeled into her the concept that every single person on earth had a father. As Francie clutched the wet counter her mother spoke of the sound—the terrible fused sound of brakes and the impact—the crowds out the window, which at first hid everything, the siren circling down on their block like a hawk. She did not use the word "blood," but when she finished her story and left the room without so much as a glance for Francie, Francie lifted her dripping fingers and stared at them.

After that, Francie's mother was even more unyielding, as though she were ashamed of her husband's death, or ashamed to have spoken of it. And Francie's father evaporated without a trace. Francie had only cryptic fragments from before that night in the kitchen with which to assemble the story: her parents married at eighteen, she'd figured out. Had they loved each other? The undiminishing vigor of her mother's resentment toward absolutely everything was warming, in its way—there must have been love to produce all that hatred.

The bathroom, too, was clean—spotless, actually, except for a tiny smudge on the mirror. A fingerprint. Hers? Her mother's? She peered past it, into her own face. Had he even known there was to be a baby? Just think—things that you did went on and on, turning into situations, for example. Into people . . .

As little as Francie knew about him, it would be infinitely more than he could have known about her. There were no pictures, but if she were to subtract her mother's eyes . . . In just a few years, she would see changes in her face that her father had not lived to see in his.

"In a few years!" Bad enough she had to deal with "in a few minutes." *When you return*, Mrs. Peck had said. Well, sure, a person couldn't just stay at school, probably, when her mother died. But what on earth was she supposed to do here?

Her mother would have told her. Francie snatched open a drawer and out flew the fact of her mother's slippery, pink-ish heap of underwear. Her mother's toothbrush sat next to the mirror in a glass. In the mirror, past the fingerprint, her mother's eyes lay across her own reflection like a mask.

The hospital floated in the middle of a vast ocean of construction, or maybe it was demolition; a nation in itself, of which all humans were, at every moment, potential citizens. The inevitable false move, and it was wham, onto the gurney, with workers grabbing smocks and gloves to plunge into the cavity of you, and the lights that burned all night. Outside this building you lived as though nothing were happening to you that you didn't know about. But here, there was simply no pretending.

Cynthia had come up the hill, Mrs. Peck had sent Francie home, and now here she was—completely lost; she'd come in the wrong entrance. People passed, in small groups,

not touching or speaking. The proliferating corridors and ro-
tundas bloomed with soft noises—chiming, and disembodied
announcements, and the muted tapping of canes and rubber
shoes and walkers. The ceilings and floors were the same color
and had the same brightness; metal winked, signaling between
wheelchairs and bedrails. Francie tried to suppress the notion,
which had popped up from somewhere like a groundhog, that
her mother was still alive, lost here somewhere herself.

Two unfamiliar nurses sat at a desk at the mouth of the
wing where Section E, Room 418, was. In their crisp little white
hats they appeared to be exempt from error. They looked up
as Francie approached, and their faces were blank and tired, as
if they knew Francie through and through—as if they knew
everything there was to know about this girl in the short, filmy
dress and motorcycle jacket and electric-green socks, who
was coming toward them with so much difficulty, as if the air
were filled with invisible restraints.

But, as it turned out, when Francie tried to explain herself,
using (presumably) key, she thought, words, like "Kathryn
McIntyre," and "Room 418," and "dead," even then neither
of the nurses seemed to understand. "Did you want to speak
to a doctor?" one of them said.

A tiny, hot beading of sweat sprang out all over Francie.
From the moment she was born people had been happy to tell
her what to do, down to the most minute detail; Eds. Clarke
& Melton knew just what was happening; there were admo-
nitions and exhortations plastered all over the walls—this is
how to behave, this is what to think, this is how to think it,
that's then, this is now, this is where to put your sock—but no
one had ever said one little thing that would get her through
any five given minutes of her life!

She stared at the nurse who had spoken: *Say it*, Francie

willed her, but the nurse instead turned her attention to a form attached to a clipboard. "Is Miss Healy around?" Francie asked after a minute.

The fact was, Francie would not have recognized Miss Healy; she'd hardly noticed the broad-faced, slightly clumsy-looking girl who'd been changing the water in a vase of flowers as Francie had listened to her mother describe, with somber gloating, the damage to her body, the shock of finding herself on the ice with her pork chop and canned peaches and so forth strewn around her, the pitiable little trickle of milk she had watched flow from the ruined carton into the filthy slush before she understood that she couldn't move.

"She never complained," Miss Healy was saying, in a melancholy, slightly adenoidal voice. "She was such a pleasant person. You could tell the terrible pain she was in, but she never said a word." Miss Healy directed her mournful recital toward Francie's elbow, as if she were in danger of being derailed by Francie's face. "And when the people from her office brought candy and flowers? She was just so *polite*. Even though you could see those things were not what she wanted."

Oh, great. Who but her mother could get someone to say that her pain was obvious but that she never complained? Who but her mother could get someone to say she was polite even though everyone could tell she didn't want their gifts? No doubt about it, the body they'd carted off almost a day and a half ago from Room 418 had been her mother's—Miss Healy had just laid waste, in her squelchy voice, to *that* last wisp of hope.

"The thing is," Francie said, "what am I supposed to do?"

"To do?" Miss Healy said. Her look of suffering was momentarily whisked away. "I mean, unfortunately, your mother's dead."

"No, I know," Francie said. "I get that part. I just don't know what to *do*."

Miss Healy looked at her. Clearly Francie was turning out to be, unlike her mother, *not a pleasant person*. "Well, you'll want to grieve, of course," Miss Healy said, as if she were remembering a point from a legal document. "Everyone needs closure." She frowned, then unexpectedly addressed, after all, Francie's problem. "I'll call downstairs so you can see her."

Fading smells of bodies clung to the air like plaintive ghosts, their last friendly overtures vanquished by the stronger smells of disinfectants. An indecipherable muttering came from other ghosts, sequestered in a TV suspended from the ceiling. Outside the window huge, predatory machines prowled among mounds of trash.

Miss Healy returned. "Mrs. McIntyre isn't downstairs. I'm really sorry—I guess they've sent her on."

They? On? If only there were someone around to take over. Anyone. Jessica, even. At least Jessica would be able to ask some sensible question. "On . . ." Francie began uncertainly, and Jessica gave her a little shove. "On where?"

"Oh," Miss Healy said. "Well, I mean, does your family use any in particular?"

Francie stared: Where would Jessica even begin with that one?

"Does your family have a particular one they like," Miss Healy explained. "Mortuary."

"It's just me and mother," Francie said.

Miss Healy nodded, as if this confirmed her point. "Uh-huh. So they'd have sent her on to whatever place was specified by the next of kin."

Francie felt Jessica start to giggle. "It's just me and mother," Francie said again.

"Just whoever your mother put down on the AN37-53," Miss Healy said. "Not literally the next of kin necessarily—she couldn't have used you, for instance, because you're a minor. But just, if there's no spouse, people might put down someone at their office, say. Or she might have used that nice friend of hers who came to visit once, Mrs. Dougherty."

Yargh. It wasn't enough that her mother had died—no, they had to toss her out, into that huge, melted mob, *the dead*, who couldn't speak for themselves, who were too indistinguishable to be remembered, who could be used to prove anything, who could be represented any way at all! "My mother *hates* everyone at her office," Francie said. "My mother *hates* Mrs. Dougherty. Mother calls Mrs. Dougherty that buggy Irish slut."

Miss Healy drew back. "Well, I guess your mom wasn't expecting to *die*, exactly, when she filled out that form," she said, and then recovered herself. "There, now. I'll call down again. Even *this* crazy morgue has files, I guess."

Out the window a wrecking ball swung toward a solitary wall. Miss Healy hesitated. She seemed to be waiting for something. "I called that lady at the school," she said. She stood looking at Francie, and Francie realized that she and Miss Healy must be almost the same age. "I just didn't figure there'd be some other way you'd know."

"How did mother get all the way out here?" Francie asked the man who greeted her.

The man's little smile intensified the ruefulness of his expression. "We get a lot of folks out this way," he said. "You might be surprised."

"That's what I meant," Francie said. "I meant I was surprised."

The man jumped slightly, as if Francie had gummed him on the ankle, and then smiled ruefully again. "Serving all faiths," he explained, gesturing at a sign on the wall. *"Serving all faiths,"* Francie read. *"Owned and operated by Luther and Theodore T. Ade. When you're in need, call for Ade."* "Also," the man added, "competitive pricing. But mainly, first in the phone book."

He disappeared behind a door, and Francie jogged from foot to foot to warm herself—it had been a long walk from the last stop on the bus line. She looked around. Not much to see: a counter holding some file folders, a calendar and a mirror on the wall, several chairs, and a round table on which lay a dog-eared copy of *Consumer Reports*. So this was where her mother had got to—nowhere at all.

"Won't be another minute." The man was back in the room. "Teddy T.'s just doing the finishing touches."

Finishing touches? Francie blanched—she'd almost forgotten what this place was. "You're not using lipstick, are you?" she managed to say. "Mother hated it."

The man glanced rapidly at the mirror and then back at Francie.

"Lipstick," Francie said. "On her."

"'On her . . .'" the man said. As he stared at Francie, the room lost its color and flattened; swarming black dots began to absorb the table and the counter and the mirror. "I'm very sorry if that's what you had in mind, Miss, ah . . ." dots streamed out of the dot man to say. The riffling of file folders amplified into a deafening splash of dots, and then Francie heard, "I'm very, very sorry, because those were definitely not the instructions. I've got the fax right here—from your dad, right? Yup, Mr. McIntyre."

Francie's vision and hearing cleared before her muscles got a grip on themselves. She was on the floor, splayed out, confusingly, as her mother must have been on the ice, and the man was kneeling next to her, holding a glass of water, although, also confusingly, her hair and clothing were drenched—sweat, she noted, amazed.

"O.K. now?" the man asked. Next to him was a cardboard box, about two feet square, tied up with twine.

Francie nodded.

"Happens," the man said, sympathetically.

Francie finished the water slowly and carefully while the man fetched a little wooden handle and affixed it to the twine around the box. Things had gone far beyond misrepresentation now.

"And here's the irony," the man said. "We deliver."

All night long, Francie fell, plummeting through the air. When she finally managed to pry herself awake with the help of the pale wands of light along the blinds, she found herself sprawled forcefully back on her mattress, aching, as if she'd been hurled from a great height. On the kitchen floor was the cardboard box. Francie hefted it experimentally—yesterday it had been intolerably heavy; this morning it was intolerably light.

O.K., first in the phone book, true enough. ("See display ad, page 182.") "Hi," Francie said when the man answered. "This is Francie McIntyre. The girl who fainted yesterday? Could you—" For an instant, Miss Healy stood in front of her again, looking helpless. "First of all," Francie said. "I mean, thanks for the water. But second of all, could you give me my father's address, please? And, I guess, his name."

Kevin McIntyre—not all that amazing, once you got your head around the notion that he happened to be alive. And he lived on a street called West Tenth, in New York City. Francie looked out the window to the place where there had been for some years now a silently shrieking crowd and a puddle of blood, into which long, splotty raindrops were now falling. Strange—it was raining into the puddle, but at the level of the window it was snowing.

In the closet she found an old plastic slicker. She took it from the hanger and wrapped it around the cardboard box, securing it roughly with tape. Yes, everything had to be *just right*. But the only thing she'd actually *said* to Francie in all these sixteen years was a lie.

Francie looked around at the bluish stillness. "Hello hello," she called. Was that her voice? Was that her mother's silence, fading? What had become of everything that had gone on here? "Hello hello," she said. "Hello hello hello hello . . ."

The bus ticket cost Francie eighteen dollars. Which left not all that much of the seventy-three and a bit that she'd saved up, fortunately, to get her back to school and, in fact, Francie thought, to last for the rest of her life. "But, hey," Jessica returned just long enough to point out, "you'll be getting free therapy."

Francie put her box on the overhead rack and scrambled to a window seat. *West Tenth Street.* West of what? The tenth of how many? How on earth was she going to find her way around? If only her mother had let her go last year when Jessica invited her to spend Thanksgiving in New York with her family. But Francie's mother had been able to picture Jessica's mother just as easily as Francie had been able to. "Out of the question," she'd said.

". . . if *there's no spouse* . . ." So, her mother must have used his name on that form! They must never have got a divorce.

Could he be a bigamist? Some people were. And he might think Francie was coming to blackmail him. He might decide to kill her right then and there—just reach over and grab a . . . a . . .

Well, one thing—he wasn't living on the street; she had his address. And he wasn't totally feebleminded; he'd sent a fax. Whatever he was, at least what he wasn't was everything except that. And the main thing he wasn't, for absolute certain, was a guy who'd been mashed by a bus.

"Would you like a hankie?" the lady in the seat next to Francie's asked, and Francie realized that she had wiped her eyes and nose on her sleeve. "I have one right here."

"Oh, wow," Francie said gratefully, and blew her nose on the handkerchief the lady produced from a large, shabby cloth sack on her lap.

Despite the shabbiness of the sack, Francie noticed, the lady was tidy. And pretty. Not pretty, really, but exact—with exact little hands and an exact little face. "Do you live in New York?" she asked Francie.

"I've never even been there," Francie said. "My roommate from school invited me to visit once, but my mother wouldn't let me go." Jessica's family had a whole apartment building to themselves, Jessica had told her; she'd called it a "brownstone." It was when Francie had foolishly reported this interesting fact that her mother put her foot down. "Actually," Francie added, "I think my mother was afraid. We had a giant fight about it."

"A mother worries, of course," the lady said. "But it's a lovely city. People tend to have exaggerated fears about New York."

"Yeah," Francie said. "Well, I guess maybe my mother had exaggerated fears about a lot of things. She—" The box! Where was the box? Oh, there—on the rack. Francie's heart was beating rapidly; clashing in her brain were the desire to reveal and the desire to conceal what had become, in the short course of the conversation, a secret. "Do you live in New York?" she asked.

"Technically, no," the lady said. "But I've spent a great deal of happy time there. I know the city very well."

Francie's jumping heart flipped over. "Have you ever been to West Tenth Street?" she asked.

"I have," the lady said.

Francie didn't dare look at the lady. "Is it a nice street?" she asked carefully.

"Very nice," the lady said. "All the streets are very nice. But it seems a strange day to be going there."

"It's strange for me," Francie said loudly. "My mother died."

"I'm terribly sorry," the lady said. "My mother died as well. But evidently no one was hurt in the accident."

"Huh?" Francie said.

"Amazing as it seems," the lady said, "I believe no one was hurt. Although you'd think, wouldn't you, that an accident of that sort—a blimp, simply sailing into a building . . ."

Francie felt slightly sickened—she wasn't going to have another opportunity to tell someone for the first time that her mother had died, to learn what that meant by hearing the words as she said them for the first time. "How could a blimp just go crashing into a building?" she said crossly.

"These are things we can't understand," the lady said with dignity.

Oops, Francie thought—she was really going to have to watch it; she kept being mean to people, and just completely by mistake.

"'How could such-and-such a thing happen?' we say," the lady said. "As if this moment or that moment were fitted together, from . . . bits, and one bit or another bit might be some type of mistake. 'There's the building,' people say. 'It's a building. There's the blimp. It's a blimp.' That's the way people think."

Francie peered at the lady. "Wow . . ." she said, considering.

"You see, people tend to settle for the first explanation. People tend to take things at face value."

"Oh, definitely," Francie said. "I mean, absolutely."

"But a blimp or a building cannot be a mistake," the lady said. "Obviously. A blimp or a building are evidence. Oh, goodness—" she said as the bus slowed down. She stood up and gave her sack a little shake. "Here I am."

"Evidence . . ." Francie frowned; Cynthia's red jacket flashed against the snow. "Evidence, of, like . . . the future?"

"Well, more or less," the lady said, a bit impatiently, as the bus stopped in front of a small building. "Evidence of the present, really, I suppose. You know what I mean." She reached into her sack and drew out some papers. "You seem like a very sensitive person—I wonder if you'd be interested in learning about my situation. This is my stop, but you're welcome to the document. It's extra."

"Thank you," Francie said, although the situation she'd really like to learn about, she thought, was her own. "Wait—" The lady was halfway down the aisle. "I've still got your hand-kerchief—"

"Just hold on to it, dear," the lady called back. "I think it's got your name on it."

The manuscript had a title, *The Triumph of Untruth: A Society That Denies the Workings of the World Puts Us at Ever Greater Risk.* "I'd like to introduce myself," it began. "My name is Iris Ackerman."

Hmm, Francie thought: Two people with situations, sitting

right next to each other. Coincidence? She glanced up. The sickening thing was, there were a lot of people on this bus.

"My name is Iris Ackerman," Francie read again. "And my belief is that one must try to keep an open mind in the face of puzzling experiences, no matter how laughable this approach may subsequently appear. For many years I maintained the attitude that I was merely a victim of circumstance, or chance, and perhaps now my reluctance to accept the ugliness of certain realities will be considered (with hindsight!) willful obtuseness."

Francie's attention sharpened—she read on. "Certainly my persecution (by literally thousands of men, on the street, in public buildings, and even, before I was forced to flee it, in my own apartment) is a known fact. (One, or several, of these ruffians went so far as to hide himself in my closet, and even under my bed, when least expected.)

"Why, you ask, should so large and powerful an organization concentrate its efforts on tormenting a single individual? This I do not know. It is not (please believe me) false humility that causes me to say I do not consider myself to be in any way 'special.'"

Francie sighed. She rested her eyes for a moment on the weedy lot moving by out the window. Not much point, probably, trying to figure out what Iris had been talking about. Yup, she should have known the minute Iris said the word "blimp."

"I know only," the manuscript continued, "that there was a moment when I fell into the channel, so to speak, of what was ultimately to be revealed as 'my life': In the fall of 1965, when I was twenty years old, I encountered a mathematics professor, an older man, whom I respected deeply. I became increasingly fascinated by certain theories he held regarding the nature of numbers, but he, alas, misunderstood my youthful enthusiasm, and although he had a wife and several children, I was soon forced to rebuff him.

"I continued to feel nothing but the purest and most intense admiration for him, and would gladly have continued our acquaintance. Nevertheless, this professor (Doctor N.) terminated all contact with me (or affected to do so), going so far as to change his telephone number to an unlisted one. Yet, at the same time, he began to pursue me in secret.

"For a period of many months I could detect only the suggestion of his presence—a sort of emanation. Do you know the sensation of a whisper? Or there would sometimes be a telltale hardening, a *crunchiness*, near me. Often, however, I could detect nothing other than a slight discoloration of the atmosphere . . . And then, one day, as I was walking to the library, he was there.

"It was a day of violent heat. People were milling on the sidewalks, waiting. One felt one was penetrating again and again a poisonous, yellow-gray screen that clung to the mouth and the nostrils. I had almost reached the library when I understood that he was behind me. So close, in fact, that he could fit his body to mine. I had never imagined how hard a man's arms could feel! His legs, too, which were pressed up against mine, were like iron, or lead, and he dug his chin into my temple as he clamped himself around me like a butcher about to slash the throat of a calf. I cried out; the bloated sky split, and out poured a filthy rain. The faces of all the people around me began to wash away in inky streaks. A terrible thing had happened to me—A terrible thing had happened—*it was like water gushing out of my body.*

"Since then, my life has not belonged to me. Why do I not go to the authorities? Of course, I have done so. And they have added their mockery to the mockery of my tormentors:

Psychological help! Tell me: Will 'psychological help' alter my history? Will 'psychological help' locate Dr. N.? Any information regarding my case will be fervently appreciated. Please contact: Iris Ackerman, P.O. Box 139775, Rochester, N.Y. Yours sincerely, Iris Ackerman."

Enclaves of people wrapped in ragged blankets huddled against the walls of the glaring station. Policemen sauntered past in pairs, fingering their truncheons. Danger at every turn, Francie thought. Poor Iris—it was horrible to contemplate. And obviously love didn't exactly clarify the mind, either.

You had to give her credit, though—she was brave. At least she tried to figure things out, instead of just consulting, for example, the wall. To *really* figure things out. Francie blew her nose again. For all the good that did.

Any information regarding my case will be fervently appreciated. But this was not the moment, Francie thought, to lose her nerve. The huge city was just outside the door, and there was no one else to go to West Tenth Street. There was no one else to hear what she had to hear. There was no one else to remember her mother with accuracy. There was no one else to not get the story wrong. There was no one else to reserve judgment. Francie closed one hand tightly around her new handkerchief, and with the other she gripped the handle on her box. The city rose up around her through a peach-colored sunset; now there was no more time.

The man who stood at the door of the apartment (K. McIntyre, #4B) was nice-looking. Nice-looking, and weirdly unfamiliar, as if the whole thing, maybe, were a complete mistake, Francie thought over and over in the striated extrusion of eternity (that was then and this is then; that was now and this is now) it had taken the door to open.

She was filthy, she thought. She smelled. She'd been wearing the same dress, the same socks, for days.

"Can I help you?" he said.

He had no idea why she was there! "Kevin McIntyre?" she said.

"Not back yet," he said. His gaze was pleasant—serene and searching. "Any minute."

He brought her into a big room and sat her down near a fireplace, in a squashy chair. He reached for the chain of a lamp, but Francie shook her head.

"No?" He looked at her. "I'm having coffee," he said. "Want a cup? Or something else—water? Wine? Soda?"

Francie shook her head again.

"Anyhow," he said. "I'm Alex. I'll be in back if you want me."

Francie nodded.

"Can I put your package somewhere for you, at least?" he asked, but Francie folded her arms around the box and rested her cheek against its plastic wrapping.

"Suit yourself," the man said. He paused at the entrance to the room. "You're not a very demanding guest, you know."

Francie felt his attention hesitate and then withdraw. After a moment, she raised her head—yes, he was gone. But then there he was again in the entranceway. "Strange day, huh?" he paused there to say. "Starting with the blimp."

The night before Francie left school, when she'd known so much more about her mother and her father than she knew now, she and Jessica had lain in their beds, talking feverishly. "Anything can happen at any moment," Jessica kept exclaiming. "Anything can just *happen*."

"It's worse than that," Francie had said (and she could still close her eyes and see Cynthia coming up that hill). "It's much, much worse." And Jessica had burst into noisy sobs, as if she knew exactly what Francie meant, as if it were she who had brushed against the burning cable of her life.

Her body, Francie noticed, felt as if it had been crumpled up in a ball—she should stretch. *Strange day*. Well, true enough. That was something they could all be sure of. This room was really nice, though. Pretty and pleasantly messy, with interesting stuff all over the place. Interesting, nice stuff . . .

Twilight was thickening like a dark garden, and paintings and drawings glimmered behind it on the walls. As scary as it was to be waiting for him, it was nice to be having this quiet time. This quiet time together, in a way.

Peach, rose, pale green—yes, poor guy; it might be a moment he'd look back on—last panels of tinted light were falling through the window. He might be walking up the street this very second. Stopping to buy a newspaper.

She closed her eyes. He fished in his pocket for change, and then glanced up sharply. Holding her breath, Francie drew herself back into the darkness. *It's your imagination*, she promised; he was going to have to deal with her soon enough—no sense making him see her until he actually had to.

ACROSS THE LAKE

At first, what Rob saw from the back seat appeared to be projections of stone on the bluff just above—columns of lava, or basalt. Then the smoky morning split into gold rays, the black forms flickered human/mineral, human/mineral, and a shift of sun flashed against machetes, lighting up for one dazzling instant the kerchiefs tied over faces as masks, and the clothing—the wide, embroidered Indian trousers that Mick and Suky were headed toward the village to buy.

"Hoo hoo!" Mick said. "Worth the trip?" But his hand, extended for Suky's cigarette, was unsteady. How long, Rob wondered; how much longer until they reached the village?

When they arrived, he would eat something with Mick and Suky, maybe even check into the hotel, but he would look around for some way to get back to town immediately. There would be other tourists with cars, and there was supposed to be a boat, a little boat that carried mail across the lake, between town and the village to which they were going on the far side. In any case, he could hardly say it was Mick and Suky's fault that he had come; the fact was, he had knowingly—no, eagerly—given himself over to them, to these people he never would have dreamed of getting into a car with at home. And if something happened—if the guerrillas reappeared, or if there were robbers, or if he got sick, or if, most terrifying of all, they were stopped by the army—he would have only himself to blame.

Suky's small, tanned arm, draped across the seat, sparkled faintly. Her shoulder, the back of her neck . . . The car fishtailed and Rob turned his gaze to the steaming lake. Himself, himself to blame, himself, only himself. Perspiration—forming below the surface, squeezing its way up to collect in basins around each gold stalklet of a hair, in tiny, septic, bejeweling drops.

According to Mick, the crumbly, bunkerlike building they checked into was the village's premier hotel, the dirty pavilion where they sat now under a swarming thatch was the village's premier restaurant. "Only restaurant," Suky amended lazily. "Well, yeah, there's one other, but Mick got a wicked parasite there last year."

What difference did it make? Rob would be back on his way to town soon enough.

"Chicken everyone?" Mick said. "Always tasty, always safe." He put down the sticky menu and turned with a little bow to the child who was swinging idly against a chair, waiting to take their orders. *"Tres pollos."*

The child considered Mick before responding. *"Pollo no hay,"* he said impassively.

"Pués," Mick said, *"pescado. Bien fresco."*

"Pescado no hay," the child said.

"Bueno"—Mick folded his arms and leveled a ferocious grin at the child—*"Carne."*

The child stared back.

Suky yawned. *"Qué hay?"* she said.

"Frijoles," the child said, already wandering off. Pleased,

Rob wondered, because he could offer them beans, or because he could offer them nothing else?

The pavilion sat on a rise overlooking the muddy road, and beyond that, the lake. In front, just next to each of the poles that supported the thatch, a soldier stood, aiming a rifle at the shabby ladinos walking below, and the soundless Indians, in their elaborate, graceful, filthy textiles. From town, the lake had seemed blue, and the air over it tonic, a pure ether in which the volcanoes and the hills presided, serene and picturesque. But on this side the air was green, heavy with a vegetal shedding, sliding, with a dull glint, like scales. The water, the volcano, the dense growth, and the crust of tin-roofed shacks that covered the hills all appeared to be discharging skeins of mist that made everything waver, as though Rob were under the lake, here, looking up.

"A gourmet paradise it may not be," Mick said. "But you've got to admit it's beautiful."

Incredible. Was Mick aware of his callousness? Even if you were to succumb to some claim of the dark and protean landscape, you could hardly ignore those soldiers. Their faces were smeared with anarchic black markings, and their eyes glittered red with exhaustion or hatred, or illness.

Of course, Rob was not unprepared for some kind of unpleasantness. The other day in town, when Mick had pointed across the lake to the village, Rob's insides had registered a violent but incoherent response. He'd heard vague but alluring mention of the area—its unparalleled weaving and embroidery, its ancient indigenous religions. He had the impression of an iridescence. But someone had referred to guerrillas, and someone else had told him about the people, Indian peasants, who had been untouched by centuries of change but who now, during planting and harvest seasons, were taken off to labor on the eastern plantations under military guard. "It sounds really interesting," Rob had said politely to Mick.

"Interesting," Mick said. "It's sensational. Very dark, very magical."

Suky sighed then, Rob remembered. And he had said something about how he'd like to get there one day, and then Suky had said, "So why not come with us? We're going Wednesday."

Wednesday. Rob stared at her while she rooted around the bottom of her drink with her straw. "Why not?" she said. She looked up at him and pushed her drink aside. "This is a great time to go. Some general's up in the States, lobbying Congress for more aid, so the army's making kind of a point these days of not killing gringo tourist college boys." She had smiled then briefly, showing her funny little sharp, uneven teeth.

Shame (as though Rob were on the brink of doing or thinking something unworthy) abruptly presented him with another memory: his parents, with boxes of slides, resulting from various travels, which they showed on a screen in the living room to himself and his sister, and sometimes to others in the community who were considering similar adventures. His parents were vigorous and inquiring—much more energetic, physically and intellectually, than he was. There had never been any place, as far as Rob knew, they hadn't wanted to go. And although they had made a show of disapproval about the casualness of Rob's plans this summer, Rob could feel their pride, their eagerness to see new places through his eyes. If only he had their stamina. Bad weather seemed only to intensify their interest in the way other people lived. And bad food, and bugs. Only two or three times, as Rob remembered, had their trips worked out badly. Their sunny temperaments seemed damaged on those occasions, when they had come home plaintive and baffled. Which trips had those been? Haiti? The Philippines? Rob was no longer sure—the slides had stayed in their boxes.

The infant waiter reappeared, shoving three plates of rice and beans onto the table and dropping a plate of tortillas into the center so that it buzzed. *"Dos más, Pablo,"* said a voice from over Rob's shoulder. Then, *"Welcome, welcome."*

The owner of the voice was probably no more than thirty, just a few years older than Mick and Suky, but his weighty graciousness insisted on a wide margin of seniority. He held one hand out to Mick, and with the other he decorously reached a chair for the sphinxlike Indian girl who accompanied him. *"Y, Pablito,"* he called to the child, *"dos cervezas."*

Drugs, most likely, Rob thought. Rob had seen men like this in towns en route. But usually they kept to themselves, hanging around in clumps, or with various counterparts—burly, scarred Latins, or older good-for-nothings from the U.S., '60s casualties with greasy, faded ponytails, whose clattery frames and potbellies would have devolved from bodies as supple and powerful as this man's.

Rob started with dismay—his plate had been washed! A universe of disease trembled in a droplet of water on the rim. Think sick, get sick, was what Mick said, and that was probably true in some way, although the corollary—think healthy, stay healthy—seemed less of a sure thing.

"Rob, Suky, hey—" Mick was poking Rob on the arm, pointing to the beers Pablo was setting down in front of the newcomers. "Now this is smart. See what Kimball is doing?"

Kimball who? Who Kimball? Bad, Rob thought, not good—he had failed to control his attention. He channeled it now, with effort.

Despite the impression he made of size, this Kimball person was not tall, Rob saw—just rather broad, and well put together. Although his features were somewhat sharp and his dark blue eyes small, there was a suggestion of largesse, or costliness, possibly, about his creamy skin and loose black curls. And Mick had certainly fallen in behind him with disgusting alacrity. Astonishing, really. Lofty Mick, dignified Mick—but sensitivity to rank, evidently, was fundamental to this aristocracy of wanderers.

"People don't realize how easy it is to get dehydrated," Mick was saying showily to Rob. "Listen. The juice here is great. If you don't want to drink beer, you should have some juice, at least." But Kimball could obviously care less, Rob thought, who was a beer drinker and who was not; even though all the other tables were empty, he kept craning around as though he were expecting someone.

"I'm not thirsty," Rob said.

Suky's eyes were closed, though Rob thought he saw a mocking little smile flicker across her mouth. So what? He wasn't thirsty; he could wait—he had three safe bottles of water back at the hotel, in his pack, the weight of which had given Mick occasion to marvel, satirically, as they'd climbed into the car.

"Suky?" Mick said.

"Beer," she said.

"Well, I'mna have beer, and I'mna have juice," Mick said with infuriating cheer. "Pablo—" he called.

Was that really the child's name? Rob wondered. Or some demeaning generic business. And what was this Indian girl's name? Had she even been introduced? Her expression hadn't altered by a blink so far as Rob had observed, since she'd sat down. *"Señorita,"* he said, *"vive usted aquí?"*

Kimball turned to contemplate Rob. "She don't speak Spanish," he said. He put his arm around the girl and said something into her ear in a language full of *sh* and *z* sounds. The girl laughed—a tiny, harsh glitter. "But, yeah—" Kimball turned back to gaze at Rob. "She wants you to know. She does live here."

The girl's eyes passed over Rob with a smoldering chill, like dry ice. She was even more terrifying, Rob thought, than Kimball. What was it about her? If only he'd asked Meredith along. She'd had the summer free; she'd hinted. And if she were here, she'd know what was upsetting him—she always did. Sometimes, as Meredith pointed out, it was nothing more than beauty. "Rob, that's *beautiful*, don't you see?" she would say. Or: "That woman's not weird-looking, she's *beautiful*." Then Meredith would laugh and rub her head against his, and he would see: whatever it was, was only beautiful.

He sighed and put down his fork—he had tried to eat something, but both the rice and the beans had a scorched, compost taste. Suky glanced at his plate, at him. She took a sip of her beer, and stretched her arms high over her head. It was appalling, the way so many girls traveling around here dressed. With grimy bits of underwear showing, or worse, like Suky, with none, Rob observed as she adjusted the strap of her sluttish camisole, to show. What did people think about their country being turned into a private beach? What could the Indian girl, for example, be thinking? When Meredith traveled (Rob knew, though they had never yet traveled together) she took particular care to dress respectfully. Especially if she were going to some Third World country, where, as she'd said to Rob, the inhabitants had little to offer one another aside from courtesy.

Rob brought his mind to the table again, and found Mick entrenched in a boast-fest—the places he and Suky had gone hunting textiles to sell in the States, the foods they'd survived, the dangers they'd faced . . . Still, if he were to be honest with himself, Rob thought, he would have to admit that Mick and Suky had an effect on him even now. From the moment he'd met them, he'd contorted himself into all sorts of ridiculous postures—misrepresenting and stifling reactions, even exaggerating. And even now, when Mick was evidencing worm-like, sycophantic tendencies of his own, Rob couldn't control a desperation for their good opinion. Pathetic, but true.

He'd seen them as soon as he disembarked in town from the bus. There they were, at a food stand, joking with the proprietor in Spanish far too advanced for Rob. They were clearly Americans, and he was pining for the sounds of American English, but really, it was something about their appearance that had stopped him—the way they looked together; their slightly feral, miniaturized quality, fastidious and carnal at once.

Although he'd been able to see from where he was standing the hotel recommended by his student guide book, he lingered near them, waiting to ask for their advice. When they finished their conversation, they directed him, without interest, to a hotel in the opposite direction from the one he was facing.

Their indifference had been disorienting. His sincerity, his good nature (and his looks, he conceded uncomfortably) generally made people attentive. But these two! It was hard to tell if they were even listening. *Most* people made an effort to show by their faces that they understood, were interested in, what one was saying. An unwelcome indignation branched quickly through Rob as he remembered this first encounter, clearing a path through which embarrassment then shot treacherously; he'd just been tricked by his *own brain* into thinking something distasteful—that the facial expressions displayed by most people, by himself, were social signals, like clothing.

The town was small, and over the next several days, Rob had seen Suky and Mick a number of times. They would nod from the sanctum of their unwashed majesty, and Rob was reminded, each time more keenly, that although they were the largest and most vivid figures in his small universe here, he was no more than a mote, for them, in a vast swarm of tourists.

But Sunday, they'd appeared at an overcrowded restaurant where Rob was sitting, and stood for a moment in the doorway. Rob gestured, more out of civility than hope, to the empty chairs next to him, but they made their way over and sat down without surprise or thanks. And when Mick put a leaf of lettuce and a slice of tomato—both virtually leaping with microbes—right onto his hamburger, Rob, giddy with happiness, had thrown caution to the winds and followed suit. How pure the lake had looked from that side, Rob thought again. He had a perfect view of it from their table, and had noted, he remembered, the way its surface reflected with such certainty the volcano and the little hills—the hills where he sat sweating, now.

Bali, blah blah blah—Mick was still going *on*; hill tribes, Panama, opium, blah blah—Rob had heard this all not three days before. Though no question Mick was a better performer for a worthier audience.

Worthier, but possibly less impressionable. Kimball merely rubbed his chin, frowning distantly. Only at one moment did his expression change. One of the soldiers had turned slightly; he seemed to be glancing up at Kimball. Did Kimball nod? It seemed to Rob he'd lowered his eyes a fraction of a second. Had something happened? No, there was only a young Indian walking quietly along the road below. Suky was squirming restlessly, her peculiar yellow eyes fixed on the lake, as she twisted a strand of her springy hair. Jealous, probably, Rob thought, for Mick's attention, and he was taken unawares by a harsh little clout of sympathy.

"We've come across a couple of times now," Mick was saying. "But we haven't had a whole lot of luck. Hard to find quality these days. Old stuff's in shit condition, new stuff's just plain shit . . ."

Kimball rested his fingertips together, indicating the Indian girl with a movement of his head, and Rob became fully aware of the fine, even stripe running through her clothing, the softness of the fabric, the yoke of her blouse, where flowers and jungle animals—jaguars, monkeys, snakes—bloomed and sported in a heavy embroidered wreath.

"I was noticing," Mick said.

"Made it herself," Kimball said.

Mick eyed the blouse sideways, then reached out and rubbed an edge of the fabric between his thumb and forefinger.

"Family does great work," Kimball said.

"Great piece," Mick said. "Yeah." He stared at the girl smokily.

Kimball leaned over to the girl and they spoke in low voices, as if, Rob thought, anyone else could possibly understand the preposterously arcane language they were speaking. "Listen," Kimball said. He pushed his empty plate aside. "She says when are you leaving? Because this is it—we could go check out her family's stuff, and then she and I could catch a ride with you back into town."

"Ideal," Mick said.

"Except we're sort of tight," Suky said.

"We can fit them," Mick objected. "No problem." He glanced at Rob.

"Sure," Rob said. "Of course."

"We've got a lot of luggage," Suky said, looking at Rob evenly. "Why don't you take the mail boat?" she said to Kimball. "It would probably be a lot more comfortable."

Rob felt himself flush. However comical Suky and Mick had found his pack, it would hardly prevent Kimball and the girl from sitting in the back seat with him.

Kimball was emitting a fog of absentmindedness. "Problem is," he said, "we got a business appointment—we got to get all the way to the capital by morning."

"See, so we couldn't help you out in that case," Suky said. "We're not going back to town until tomorrow."

"Huh," Kimball said. He reached over to the Indian girl's plate and wrapped a spoonful of her beans in one of the sour, hay-flavored tortillas. "Well, no sense our taking the boat anyhow," he said. "We'd get to town too late to go straight on. So we might as well spend one more night here, then squeeze in with you tomorrow."

"What about your appointment?" Suky said.

Kimball scooped up the remainder of the girl's meal. "Appointment'll just have to wait one day, because we're sure as shit not going to do the road from town to the capital after dark."

"After dark!" Mick said. "Hey, guess who we saw this morning. On *this* road. In broad daylight."

Kimball put his beer bottle down on the table and looked at Mick. "Who?" he said.

"The muchachos," Mick announced.

"You know this?" Kimball said, and only then did Mick appear to notice his unwavering stare.

"What he means," Mick said, turning to Rob as though it were Rob who'd committed some kind of faux pas, "is that around here you're never sure. Army dresses up like the guerrillas, guerrillas dress up like the army . . ."

Kimball was looking from one of them to another. "They didn't stop you?" he said.

"They were gone," Mick said. "They were there, and then they were gone, *vanished*."

Really, Rob thought, there really couldn't be any question of who it had been, standing mere yards from them this morning. Oh, anyone could put kerchiefs over their faces, but who could learn to become invisible? Only people who had lived in the mountains. Only people who had been hunted in the mountains like animals. "See, look at Rob," Mick said. "He still looks like he saw a ghost."

Rob turned to Kimball, disregarding Mick's witticism. "Are they stopping people? You know, I heard they were, some places. I met a kid in San Cristobal who told me they stopped him, I don't know if it was here, really, and took his last fifty dollars. He said it was the worst experience he ever had. Not the money, obviously, but when he felt the gun, sort of rubbing against his hair, he said it was like a switch on his head, and everything lit up with this strange, glowy light and became completely lucid, like one of those little glass things." Rob remembered the kid's voice, his white, wondering face. "He said his life had always been all dark and confused, but right then he could see how it all fit together, and his whole life made perfect sense. And the sense it made—the sense it *made*—was that it was completely, totally pointless."

The others looked at him. Then Suky smiled and slid a cigarette out of her pack.

"Of course," Rob said, "he was glad it wasn't the army."

"Excuse me, dear," Kimball said to Suky. "You got extra?"

She inhaled luxuriantly, then handed Kimball her cigarette. "By the way," she said to him. "How did you happen to know we came by car?"

Kimball gazed at her in sorrow. "How else could you have

gotten here before the mail boat came in?" he asked reasonably. "Besides," he added. "I saw you drive up."

"Hey, lookit," Mick said. "No soldiers." And in fact they had disappeared from in front of the restaurant.

Kimball squinted down at the lake. "Yup, and the mail boat's coming in," he said. He glanced at his watch—an incongruously expensive one, Rob saw. "On the dot, give or take."

"Fabulous," Suky said. "Hours of Pantsuits before we've got the place to ourselves again."

Kimball twisted around in his chair to look full at her. "You know what?" he mused. "You kids are nice kids. You got a sense of propriety, and that's something that appeals to me. So what I'm saying is, if you've *got* to stay over tonight, I want you to do me this favor. I want you to take care of yourselves, and stay inside."

"Can't," Suky said. "Rob and I have tickets for the opera."

Mick looked annoyed. "Very funny," he said.

Kimball smiled indulgently. "Now, *her* family"—he pointed at the Indian girl—"barricades themselves in."

"No shit," Mick said. He pursed his lips and examined his juice glass. "'Barricades.'"

"Hey, now," Kimball protested, as though Mick had maligned the girl's family. "These are good people."

Mick nodded gallantly at the immobile girl. "I don't doubt that for a second," he said. "But, what you're . . . I mean, if there's actual . . . *conflict*." He turned the glass in his hands. "What do you say, Suke?"

"Besides." Suky smiled sweetly. "Rob wants to stay, obviously. Rob wants to see conflict."

"No conflict," Kimball said. "Oh, sure, the odd incident, naturally, now and again, but the real problem around here"—he lowered his voice—"is *brujos*. There was one recently, changed himself into a wild boar nights. Rampaged, was tearing up everyone's little plots of corn and beans, went after people whenever he got the chance." He studied Mick for a moment. "Now, Micky. We know that anybody who's out at night is up to mischief. I know that as well as you do. A person who's out at night is not a reliable human being. But things happen, and you got to take that into consideration. Someone's old lady gets sick, they have to get water from somewhere. A kid wanders out. You know how it is. And this *brujo* chewed up some folks something awful, they say, before they shot it one night in a cornfield. And in the morning? When the sun came up? The body turned into the sweetest old man you'd ever want to meet. One of our next-door neighbors." He sighed and shook his head. "But you know what?" He looked up as though surprised. "Rob—Suky—Are you listening? Because this is the interesting part, now. *Afterwards*, there were a lot of people who said that sweet old man and his wife were *guerrillas*."

Suky was looking at him thoughtfully. "No shit," she said, after a moment.

"No shit," he said. He stood, studying the empty spots where the soldiers had been, and hitched up his jeans. "Hey—" He whistled. "Pablito—"

"A buck fifty apiece," Mick said, when the bill was analyzed. "Can't beat that." He drained his juice, set the glass purposefully on the table, and stood. "Sure. We'll try to give you guys a hand, go back today if we do good business early—no real need to stay over, then. So, ready?"

"I think I'll just hang around," Rob said. "Explore."

Mick and Suky looked at him blankly.

"Okay, professor," Kimball said. "Explore away."

Now that Rob had succeeded in obtaining solitude, he found he had no idea what to do with it. The prospect of finding a ride back, which in the car had seemed so reasonable, was obviously absurd; he had noticed no other cars in the village. And who could he even ask? Pablo was at his elbow, staring at the little pile of money on the table. "*Sí.*" Rob nodded. "*Gracias.*" Pablo's eyes glinted as he seized it.

He could consult the man who had checked them in at the hotel, Rob thought. Though that didn't seem too promising. For a hotel keeper in a village to which few surely traveled, the man had been remarkably—not actually rude, Rob thought, but, well, ... *preoccupied.*

There was one other party of guests at the hotel, Rob remembered. Three unsmiling button-faced blonds, of which one or two seemed to be boys. He could ask them. A good idea.

But when he imagined himself strolling back and finding them, a feeling of weakness overtook him. Their presence in the hotel's sunless courtyard earlier had been ghostly and forbidding. The hotel keeper had gestured to an enclosure beyond them—the shower, he explained. A shower! But Mick had been jittery and discouraging. "It'll be freezing, man. Let's go get some lunch—it'll warm up later." But Rob stood his ground—he'd earned the right, he felt, in the car. So Mick and Suky waited while he fetched the stiff little towel from his room—his cubicle—and disappeared into the shower stall. Instantly he was back in the courtyard, humiliated; the shower was *literally* unbearable. Mick had doubled up, and the blonds looked at him out of their button faces. But perhaps the blonds simply hadn't understood—they were foreigners. Well, foreigners, of course, but what he meant, he corrected himself, was, not American.

Rob gazed out at the watery sky, the cloudy lake. At the very worst, he'd only have to wait until late afternoon. Either Kimball would have succeeded in convincing Mick and Suky to return to town today, or he could take the mail boat by himself. Which was by far the more appealing alternative, actually—he was certainly in no hurry to be out on that road again. Anyhow, the urgency to leave had passed. There was something—well, something *correct* about being where he was. After all—the thought rose up dripping—it *was* where he was . . .

He had wanted to go, while he had the chance this summer before starting grad school, someplace very far away. Whenever his parents came home from their trips, they sparkled with things it was impossible to say. In fancy books of photographs you could see clues, hints, in the glossy pages, where boats rocked in the harbors of seaside towns, streetlamps spread a soft glamour through the rain of antique cities, where men and women of distant nationalities hunkered in the circle of the lens, enticing and resistant.

Since the beginning of summer he'd wound his way down and down and down, in buses throbbing with peasants and chickens. His heart had pounded at each blue and gold drop to the valley floors, at the crude white crosses marking death along the roads, at the shining, disinterested God-filled air, through which he had expected, at every moment, to plummet, along with his fellow passengers, bouncing in their tinny container from peak to peak. And he had felt, all the time, that he was following a trail of instructions that would lead him as far as it was possible to go.

Now here he was. As far as it was possible to go. The end of the trail, where the world trickled out into mud.

If Meredith were here, she would show him how to find

the beauty of this place as though it were a photograph. Through her eyes, it would acquire coherence, meaning, intelligibility. The lake with its sudsy rolls of fog—Meredith would know facts about it: its size, its depth, its geological origin. She would have researched the social organization, the language, the economy of these silent, unreadable villagers. She would smile, now, and coax him to his feet.

Oh, if only he could just go back to the hotel and have his shower! But he imagined Meredith's bewilderment: *You got all the way there and didn't even see the market? Or the church?* She shook her thick gold-brown hair and laughed. *You just took a shower and went back?* No, she didn't laugh—her white smile dimmed when she saw his face.

All right. So, market, church, *then* shower and return. A few tourists were struggling up the hill—evidently Suky had overestimated the impending plague. They would be headed for the market themselves, Rob reasoned, as he lost sight of them in the thicket of tin roofs and little hills.

But despite the intricacy of paths and turnings, the market turned out to be no more than two minutes' walk from the restaurant. Indian clothing hung from stalls, and careful heaps of dwarfed and fly-specked mangoes were displayed on crates.

Pale, smiling people, determined, apologetic, wearing squashy hats to protect them from the sun, aimed cameras at undersize children and their glowering mothers. Even worse was the dickering at the stalls. The scene had a sickening familiarity. It was like seeing as an adult one of those frenetic, mean-spirited, sentimental TV shows Rob had watched as a child. "They want you to bargain, they expect you to. It's insulting if you don't," one woman was informing her shame-faced husband. "Twenty dollar," she said to the shop owner, believing herself, apparently, to be speaking a foreign language.

The shop owner was a large woman. Some automatic function was releasing rage evenly into her face. She held out for inspection a pair of trousers, embroidered with rich tiers of parrots and ice-cream cones, while the customer deliberated—with shrewdness and forced gaiety—as though she were trying on hats in Paris.

It was a large, rusty stain on the side of the trousers that decided the matter. The shop owner was adamant. The stain would wash out, she insisted without a trace of credibility. The customer was knowing, regretful. As she walked away, strength of character lighting up her face, the shop owner hissed after her. The retreating customer's step did not quicken, though her expression toughened slightly. Rob, rooted to the spot, waited for her skin to blossom with hemorrhages, her flesh to turn to pulp, her hair and teeth to spring out onto the mud.

Why did he feel he must redress the imbalance between buyer and seller? It was a stupid and superstitious impulse, he told himself. Humanity everywhere was at ease with the barbarism of his countryfellows. And how not? It was simple—one had power and money on one's side; inevitably every act one committed was predicated on that fact. If he were to give in and buy something now, his transaction would be predicated on that fact as well.

It was true, he thought. He could buy or not buy; he could exercise his power and money or refrain from doing so, and that was the extent of his choice. But the notion only fanned the agitation threatening to rattle him like a dried gourd should he leave the market with nothing.

At the nearest stall he gathered up, roughly, like a criminal, several sashes and a pair of trousers, the inferior work-manship of which suggested a low price. He paid what was asked and left before the incredulous saleswoman could de-termine whether he ought to be addressed with mockery or with pity. Had his gesture alleviated in the least degree the disarray of his pulse, his breathing, his glands? No.

Mick had been right, he thought; he should have ordered some juice. His lightheadedness might well be dehydration, in part. But at least he'd managed to see the market already, and the church could not be far. He would take his dutiful glimpse, return to the hotel to drink some water and take his shower, and by that time Mick and Suky might be ready to leave. He tucked his purchases under his arm, noting that these new trousers of his were marred, too, by rusty stains. Should he deposit them by the side of the road? No point in that; whatever was on them was on him now, as well.

The church was not around the first turn he took, nor the second, nor the third. Around the fourth, little huts petered out into a foggy scrub. Figures were moving in the mist—women with water jugs on their heads and babies, wrapped in shawls, on their backs. Below, the gray lake and gray sky ex-changed their vapors.

Something bulged from the scrub! No, only an old man, coming toward him. Sometimes these Indians looked a little pathetic, Rob thought, in their wide trousers, in all their loose, swaddling clothing. Clownish, almost, like patients. *"Señor,"* Rob called. *"Iglesia? Dónde está, por favor?"*

The old man approached Rob teeteringly. He held an old straw hat by the brim, and his expression was quizzical and humorous. Again, Rob asked where the church was, but the old man gave no sign of understanding, even of hearing, the question.

Moisture made his large black eyes radiant, his gaze penetrating but unspecific. His face was a patchwork with deep seams. His mouth had simply been left open, like a doorway, and inside, stumpy teeth tilted at random intervals. Yet the effect was pleasant, even soothing. Rob felt as though a thrumming sleep were beginning to enfold him as he watched the man approach. *"Iglesia,"* Rob said again. The word was a wooden ball, rolling on a wooden floor. It rolled toward the old man, who reached out, and Rob remembered, just in time, to retract his hand.

The old man paused in front of him, swaying. Drunk, Rob decided. In several places along the road this morning, they had seen figures sprawled out in the mud. "Drunk," Mick pronounced at the first. And at the third, "Shit, all of these drunks."

The man's face crinkled up, as though he and Rob were the oldest of friends. It wouldn't hurt to let him hang on to my sleeve, Rob chided himself. He couldn't stop looking at the man—it was as though he really had fallen asleep.

But the man had lost interest in the arm Rob now offered. His mouth moved, and the silky sounds of the language of the village were slipping around Rob. Yes, like patients, wandering in the mist. *"No entiendo,"* Rob said, remembering that he was supposed to understand. The man smiled in agreement and nodded. They were both smiling, Rob observed with a mild, puzzled interest.

The old man pointed to a hovering strip of fog. "No," Rob said, smiling still, as the word breathed in and out—no, no—a sail, or wing, in front of him. But the old man beckoned, and retreated a few steps, looking at Rob.

Several yards off the path a cluster of freshly painted wooden crosses rose up from the mud. The man watched Rob, feeding out the silken cord of his language. *"No entiendo,"* Rob said again, smiling just the way the man was smiling. *"No entiendo . . ."*

Each declaration of Rob's ignorance seemed only to amuse the old man more. He nodded, held up a finger, then stood very still and bowed his head, as though he were preparing a recitation, or prayer. He looked up roguishly to check on Rob's attention, then bent over and picked up an imaginary bundle. Watching Rob playfully, he rocked the bundle in his arms, then replaced it on the ground.

He held his finger up again, waited for Rob to nod, then drew himself erect and saluted at someone beyond Rob. As Rob struggled with the thick air for breath, the old man aimed an imaginary gun at the spot where he had laid the bundle, and pulled its imaginary trigger. *"No entiendo,"* Rob said, as the performance began all over. "I don't—" But the old man persevered in his nightmarish repetitions. Behind him the crosses gleamed like bone, new and white, as Rob scrabbled in his pocket for small bills; when he thrust some at the old man, a handful of change fell twinkling in the mud.

One more turn and Rob was at the church. It was enormous, ludicrous. Inside, the streaked blue-green paint and distant ceiling made it seem the size of a stadium. Rob's empty gut kept turning slowly inside out, like a sock. He was covered with a chilling sweat.

Aromatic grasses and flowers were scattered on the vast, cracked concrete floor. Here and there groups of Indians squatted, chanting over smoking vessels. A child skittered by him, cawing and waving his arms in play flight, or mental illness. The chanting spiraled high, modal, nasal—looping back, around the new Spanish god who starved on the altar, looping forward into the dark future . . . Rob wiped the sweat that was leaking into his eyes. Good heavens—the three button-faced blonds from the hotel were parading far down the nave, one of them holding, in both arms, a monstrous pineapple. A *pineapple*! Saints, dressed in embroidered trousers and battered straw hats, looked lustfully down at it from their niches, the hunger in their plaster eyes exaggerated, Rob saw as he felt about for something to lean on, by the kerchiefs— the guerrilla masks—the worshippers had tied across their saintly plaster noses and mouths.

His room faced the lake. The glass in the window was broken and filthy, but that hardly mattered since the window could not be closed, and from where Rob lay he could see clearly. Perhaps the old man had only . . . There were a few shacks scattered along the marshy strip between the hotel and the lake, and children played near the docked mail boat. Rob closed his eyes, and the children's voices floated up to him, intimate and allusive, like dreamed whispers in his ears. He had been lying there for some time. Two hours? Three? It was impossible to guess; the children's voices rose and fell, measuring nothing.

When Rob came in, he had slowly, carefully, drained one of his three bottles of water. Then he'd gone back downstairs to the shower stall, where no trickle, of any temperature, was to be coaxed from the faucet. The hotel keeper was outside, at the door, staring up into the hills. He waited courteously for Rob to struggle through his question in Spanish. "Generator," the hotel keeper answered in English, and made an unmistakable gesture of termination before he returned to squinting up at the hills.

Graffiti were scratched into the dirt and old paint on Rob's wall. *Hi,* one said. *My name is Bob I like this place I am American so all here stinks The toilet doesn't work Too All here is disgusting I like Indians I like I like most one good dead Indian The food here in this place is disgusting All here is dirty dirty dirty Bye bye Your Bob.*

Rob stared at it stunned, then laughed. An American named Bob! Oh, sure. Some German, more likely. And they had nerve to talk. A *lot* of nerve. Besides, Rob thought, the toilet worked perfectly. Or at least, he pointed out to himself, it had while the generator was functioning.

His flat little pillow smelled of mildew. So did the shelf of uncompromising lumps that was his bed. He tried to isolate the strains of the odor, the ornate tangling of growth and decay; he concentrated as his body dripped from the heat into the mattress and plumes of gray light spread, confusing the water, the sky, the volcano. Where were Suky and Mick? If only Suky and Mick would walk in now, and they could all go back to town!

He closed his eyes and the village lay before him. For a moment the market stalls, the tin-roofed huts, the children looked pretty, and exotic—*beautiful.* But smells, rising up from the scanty heaps of rotting food set out for sale and from the tottering, fly-plagued animals, were saturating the glossy surface, causing it to decompose into a deep welter. The smells were making Rob soft, seeping into his body, allowing the chanting from the church to permeate him, too, and alter the codes of his cells with every tiny, insistent modulation.

He was now not merely dirty, he was contaminated. No, he was a crucible, originating poisons, spreading contaminants backward through his life. His parents appeared in their sunny kitchen. Rob drew himself in, but he could feel filth bleeding through his skin where his body pressed against the mattress.

Down below, a few tourists were drifting toward the dock. The children who had been playing were now harnessing themselves into work, begging caressingly for pencils. Rob could hear them: *Lápiz, lápiz,* in their sing-song Spanish, see them advance, surround, pull at sleeves, undeflected by the stony embarrassment of their prey. Obviously Mick had abandoned his prudent thought of attempting to return to town today, and Rob was actually going to have to get himself onto his feet, and go down to the boat.

In the kitchen, Meredith joined his mother and father. The sink was full of water. A pan bobbed up from under a merry mound of suds, and flashed. At home they hadn't yet noticed how the walls were beginning to stain, and buckle.

He turned over and curled himself around his pillow. Soap bubbles winked, breaking. He located one, and with great caution, introduced the tiny figures of his parents and Meredith into it—the soap vessel yielded and resealed around them. Then the bubble lifted and floated through the kitchen window. A little spasm jerked in his chest; he put his fingers to his eyes; his fingers came away wet and hot. "Knock knock," someone said.

"Who's there?" he said, sitting abruptly.

"Banana." Suky hovered in the doorway. "Listen—" She glanced away diplomatically. "—Two things. Number one: the generator's out. Number two: Mick's sick." Rob stared at her, waiting for the bits of speech to organize themselves into information. For a moment it seemed that she was going to come sit next to him on the bed.

A little bug was clambering insecurely over the strap of her camisole, making its way to the cupid's bow peak of her collarbone. She located it and let it board her finger, with which she conveyed it to the window. Her hands were fine and pliant,

Rob noticed, her nails bitten savagely. A protracted shudder rose the length of his spine. "Sick, how?" he asked.

"Sick, plain old," Suky said. "I guess they put water in that juice this morning, huh." That was all she seemed to have to say. She stood aimlessly in the doorway.

Rob leaned over to sling his pack up on the bed. "I brought some clean water," he said.

"Clever," Suky said, unenthusiastically.

So, what more could he possibly do? "Did you have a good day?" he said.

"Yeah," Suky said. "Really great. And who knows— maybe Mick will stop throwing up eventually and we'll be able to go back tomorrow. I really look forward to the drive, don't you? Through guerrilla country with an informer in the car?"

"Army informer?" Rob stared at Suky. "Kimball?"

"Consultant, if you prefer," she said. "What did you think, he's an anthropologist?" She hugged herself despite the heat. "You and Mick, Jesus." Her hair curled like steam around her neck and temples, her camisole was spotted with damp. From the window past her, Rob saw the tourists assembling at the boat below. *Time to get up, time to get up—* He remembered his parents' cheerful morning voices; the way he had floated, waking from his night voyages, back into his own bed.

"But what we have to do now," Suky said, "is get some candles. The sun's going to set any minute."

"Candles," Rob said. "Candles . . . Oh, listen—better give these to Mick." He held out his two remaining bottles of water. "Before he gets dehydrated."

Suky watched him. "What about you?"

One of the dark blotches on her camisole seemed to be spreading slightly. Or possibly not. "The thing is," he said, "I've got to get down to the boat."

She took one of the bottles of water from him. "Great," she said. Her skin gave off its faint sparkle, her face was expressionless, "So. Well. Bon voyage."

"Wait—" Rob said. "Is there—is there some way I could help?" But she was gone, and the stiffness and insincerity of his voice stopped him from calling after her.

Down at the dock the children clung to him, their eyes huge, their tiny hands searching for his pockets. A skinny monkey of a boatman with bare feet and torn, rolled-up pants was collecting the last fares. Rob squinted back at the village: green, fog, glints of tin. But he! Yes, they were all exposed down here at the dock, pinned behind the hidden crosshairs.

Across the lake a cluster of boxy buildings, all no bigger than his fingernail, floated in a disk of harsh blue. Hard to believe town was so close, that he and Suky and Mick had been there only this morning. Hard to believe that he was simply going back there now, to the loud, junky restaurants; to the strained, moribund, fever-pitch cheer of ladinos and gringos vacationing . . . *Time to get up, time to get up* . . .

He found Suky at the pavilion, sitting over another meal of rice and beans. "I brought a flashlight," he said. He took it from his pack, and held it out as an offering. "I thought you might need it."

She glanced up at him, then held out a sheaf of candles in answer.

A little girl, no more than six, arrived with a Coke for Suky. *"Dónde está Pablo?"* Rob asked. The girl stared at him.

"Reinforcements for the night crowd," Suky explained. "Pablo's in the kitchen, cooking."

Rob looked around; the restaurant was empty except for himself and Suky. "Mind if I sit with you?" Rob said, and waited until Suky shrugged.

Dusk was collecting rapidly, settling in heavy folds around the hills and shacks. All along the road, up and down the paths through the village, points of candles began to move at the stately pace of Indians. The volcano and the low vegetation appeared as a furze against the darkness; the sky and lake blended in a colorless sheen.

The little girl brought rice and beans for Rob. He ate a few bites—it was possible to eat, now that he was no longer hungry. Suky lit one of her candles and stuck it onto the table. The little girl drew close and gazed into the flame; she ran her finger sensuously along one of the other candles and looked at Suky, who shook her head no. The little girl leaned against Suky with a loud sigh, which turned into a yawn. *"Tienes hambre?"* Suky said.

"Hambre," the child agreed, and Suky picked her up. Settled in Suky's lap, the child finished Suky's meal, then Rob's, eating delicately with tortillas. When Suky stroked her glorious, filthy black hair, she responded with a snuffly little intake of breath, and they snuggled against each other, sated and filmy-eyed.

Pablo called from the kitchen; the little girl wriggled off Suky's lap. She picked up one of the candles and looked challengingly at Suky. "All right." Suky sighed. *"Sí."*

"Y para Pablo?" the little girl said.

Suky rubbed her forehead. Was she crying? No, just fatigued, apparently. "Okay," she said, and the child scampered off to the kitchen with her trophies.

The sky at the other side of the lake was still faintly blue; it had been clear the whole of the four, vanished days Rob

had spent there; clear, he thought with tunneled reverbera-
tions of grief.

"I didn't take the boat," he said.

"Is that so," Suky said. She rubbed her forehead again.

"I didn't think I should leave you alone when Mick wasn't
well," Rob said.

"Rob," she said, and he floundered in her amber stare.
"Rob, let me clarify something, please: Fuck you."

Rob sighed. He passed his finger idly through the candle
flame. It had fascinated him as a child—that you could do it
and not feel heat; that any household object might disclose
inexplicable gaps within a supposed sequence of events. *Was
everything he said some sort of lie?*

A dog barked, began to bay. "Shit," Suky said. Candles
blinked out one after the other, and night gushed over the
village as two dogs, three dogs, joined in until a claxon sprang
up in a ring around Rob and Suky. "Let me guess," Rob said.
"Brujos."

Suky pinched out their candle, making the sky huge with
moonlight, and Rob saw what she and the dogs had seen already: a line of black dots, small black shapes moving down the
hills closer and closer, winding off a silent cog—a dark chain of
soldiers, holding their rifles, descending into the village.

"It's okay—" Suky's quiet voice hovered within the wheeling frenzy of the dogs. "It happens every night. Someone we
bought from let it slip to me and Mick today. Remember the
guys we saw out front this morning? Every night they all
come down. The whole unit. And they stay in the village all
night and into the day. But while the tourists are here they
have to evaporate, right? So when the mail boat arrives they
go back up to their barracks to sleep and the tourists stumble
happily around."

On the road below, a few late stragglers hurried past with candles, their faces stark with purpose in the circle of illumination.

"The boat," Rob said. "The mail boat . . ."

"Uh-huh," Suky said. "And now the tourists are gone."

The hotel keeper was still at the door. What was he always watching for, Rob wondered. Could he and Kimball discern one another through the blackness, across the hills, as clearly as if they were facing each other, inches apart? *I saw the village, I saw the market, I saw the church,* Rob insisted to himself, but all he could see now was a limitless dark, screened by the reflection of his own face, its expression of untested integrity, of convenient innocence.

Inside the courtyard the three blonds were feasting, fierce and ceremonial, on their pineapple. One of them hacked off a chunk of it with a long, shining knife, and held it out toward Suky. She paused. A troubling warmth floated off her. She shook her head, as though something had been denied, rather than offered to her. "Suky—" Rob said. She glanced at him, then turned away.

Tatters of shine lay on the center of the lake; the boat would have passed through them long before, and in the electric glare that was town, the tourists would just be tucking into steaks, ordering fancy mixed drinks, turning on the televisions in their hotel rooms . . . But from town, this hotel, the whole village, in fact, would be invisible. Even from Rob's window, the shacks scattered just outside showed only as indeterminate patches of depthless black. Were soldiers, their rifles cocked, squatting there against barricaded doors? *Hi, my name is Bob*, Rob saw. He blew out his candle, but night covered the story that was unfolding below for no other witnesses.

He stretched out on his bed. The darkness around him rustled and whispered, and a satiny gleam from the moon and stars began to collect on his body. In country like this there were probably animals, all kinds of animals, jungly things. Not lions or elephants, of course, but snakes, certainly, and even monkeys, perhaps—the kind that screamed at night—and small nocturnal creatures that looked like big cats or rats and frolicked through ruins of huts where people had recently lived. Just born, they would sleep for a few days in shaded hollows, and then one night unlid their jewel-like eyes.

And when they opened their tiny new mouths, when their new little natures ordained that this one or that one stretch the hinges of its sleek new jaws, what pleasures of discovery there would be! The flickering tongue, the high-pitched howl, the needle-pointed teeth, whatever marvelous instrument it was, discovered anew by each new being, that was the special gift of its species. Yes. Rob's heart pounded as though he'd run to keep an appointment.

When the knock came, he waited for one luxurious moment; the gleam slid off him as he stood.

"Mick wants water," Suky said from the doorway.

Rob cleared his throat. "How is Mick?" he asked. "Puking," she said. "As usual."

"Sit down," he said, breathless. "I've got that other bottle around here somewhere." Again, a long shudder ascended his spine.

Suky rested, propped up on one elbow, while Rob pretended to search. When he could stand it no longer, he retrieved the bottle and a stack of styrofoam cups from their corner. "Here," he said.

Suky reached for the bottle, but he held it back. "Careful, careful," he said, experimentally. "It's all I've got left."

She looked at him sharply, before her face became opaque. When she held out her hand again slowly, he relinquished the bottle.

Trembling, he disengaged two cups from the stack. Suky poured some water into each; the sound was deafening. "Cheers," he thought he heard her say, and their cups scraped together.

He struggled to restrain his uncoiling mind as he traced Suky's collarbone with his finger and blinked back the veil of terror that kept gathering across his eyes. Darkness was reaching out like creepers, unfolding into thick, oily petals, and distant sounds were becoming audible; Rob's thoughts were pattering here and there in darkness. "What's going on?" he whispered against Suky's throat, but her eyes narrowed, gleamed, dilated—already she was gliding off. Those distant cries—something waking now to the fragrance of blood? Levering the straps down from Suky's shoulders, Rob strained to hear, and waited.

SOMEONE TO TALK TO

"Are you going to be all right, Aaron?" Caroline said.

Shapiro saw himself, as if in a dream, standing on a dark shore. "Yes," he heard himself say.

"Are you sure?" Caroline said.

Lady Chatterley leaned herself thuggishly against Shapiro's shin and began to purr. "Hello, there," he said. He reached down and patted her gingerly.

Caroline hesitated at the door, then took a few steps back toward Shapiro, and her delicious, clean fragrance spilled over him. "Your big concert's in less than a month now . . ." She tilted her head and managed a little smile.

Was she going to touch him? Shapiro went rigid with alarm, but she just looked vaguely around the room. "You know, it's supposed to be a beautiful country . . ." She scooped up Lady Chatterley and nuzzled the orange fur. "Chat. Dear little Chat. Are you going to take care of Aaron?" She took a paw in her hand. "Are you?"

Lady Chatterley wrenched herself free and bounded back to the floor. Caroline's eyes—like Lady Chatterley's—were large and light and spoked with black. Her small face was pale, always, as though with shock.

"Shall I help you with your things?" Shapiro said.

There was really only one suitcase, a good one—leather,

old, genteel—which had probably accompanied Caroline to
college; the rest had gone on before. "No need," she said. Tears
wavered momentarily in her eyes. "Jim's picking me up."

The suitcase appeared to be heavy. Shapiro watched
Caroline's thin legs as she struggled slightly with it. At the door
she turned back. "Aaron?" she said.

He waited to hear himself answer, but this time no words
came.

"Aaron, I know this is probably not what you want to
hear right now, but I think it's important for me to say it—I'll
always care about you, you know. I hope you know that."

Shapiro awoke suddenly and unpleasantly, as though a crate-
ful of fruits had been emptied out on him. There was an unfamiliar wall next to him, and the window was all wrong. He
heard footsteps, a snicker. A hotel room wobbled into place
around him—yes, Richard Penwad would be coming to pick
him up, and Caroline wasn't even in this country.

The night had been crowded with Caroline and endless
versions of her departure—dreamed, reversed in dreams,
modified, amended, transfigured, made tender and transcen-
dently beautiful as though it had been an act of sacral purifi-
cation. For a week or so he had been free of her, or at least
anesthetized. But this morning he was battered by her absence; in this distant place his body and mind didn't know
how to protect themselves.

As soon as she'd left that day, he'd closed his eyes. An afterimage of the door glowed. When he'd opened his eyes again,
the room seemed strange in an undetectable way, as though
he were seeing it after a hiatus of years. Hesitantly, he brushed
cat fur from the armchair and sat down.

Six years. Six years of life that belonged to them both, out the door in the form of Caroline's fragile person. If only there'd been less . . . tension about money. Caroline, from many generations of a background she referred to as "comfortable," was deeply sympathetic with, and at the same time deeply insensitive to, the distress of others. "Why not, Aaron?" she would say. "Why don't I just take care of the rent from now on?" Or, when she felt like going to some morbidly expensive restaurant, "I could treat. Wouldn't it be fun, for a change? Of course"—she would gaze at him with concern—"if you're not going to enjoy it . . ." Sometimes, when she noticed him grimly going through the mail or eying the telephone, she would say gently, "Something will turn up."

Though not quite a prodigy, Shapiro had been received with great enthusiasm at the youthful start of his career. He'd been shy and luminously pale, with dark curls and almost freakish technical abilities that delighted audiences. But the qualities he greatly admired and envied in other pianists—varieties of a profound musicianship which focussed the attention on the ear, hearing, rather than on the hand, executing—were ones he lacked. He practiced, he struggled, he cultivated patience, and he was rewarded—minimally. By just the faintest flicker of heat in his crystalline touch.

His curls, pallor, and technique lost some of their brilliance; his audience was distracted by newcomers and dispersed, and a sudden increase in the velocity of the earth's spin dumped Shapiro into his thirty-eighth year. *Aaron Shapiro.* Caroline had been starry-eyed when they'd met, although by that time he'd already moved out to the margin of the city and was beginning to take on private students, startlingly untalented children who at best thought of the piano as a defective substitute for something electronic. Gradually he ceased to be the sort of pianist who might expect to make recordings, give important concerts, be interviewed, hold posts at conservatories. His name, once received like a slab of precious metal, was now received like a slip of blank paper.

"Things will work out," Caroline said, although "things," in Shapiro's estimation, were deteriorating. She touched him less often. Her smiles became increasingly lambent and forbearing. Sometimes she called in the afternoon to say she'd be held up at work. Her voice would be hesitant, apprehensive; her words floated in the air like dying petals while he listened, reluctant to hang up but unable to think of anything to say.

Recently, he'd been silent for whole evenings, reading, or simply sitting. Rent, plus utilities, plus insurance, minus lessons, plus food—columns of figures went marching through his head, knocking everything else out of it. Once, after he'd had a day of particularly demoralizing students, Caroline perched on the arm of his chair. "Things will work out," she said, and touched his cheek.

She might just as well have socked him. "Things will work out?" he said. He was ready to weep with desire that this be true, yet it was manifestly not. "You mean—Ah. Perhaps what you mean is that things will work out for some other species. Or on some other planet. In which case, Caroline, you and I are in complete accord. After all, life moves on."

She was staring at him, her hand drawn back as though she'd inadvertently touched a hot stove. Was that his voice? Were those his words? He could hardly believe it himself. Those stiff words, like stiff little soldiers, stiff with shame at the atrocities they were committing.

"Life moves on," he continued, ruthless and miserable, "but not necessarily to the benefit of the individual, does it? Yes, things will work out eventually, I suppose. But do you think they'll work out for the guy who sleeps in front of our building? Do you think—" The danger and excitement of probing his terror narrowed his vision into a throbbing circle, from which Caroline, imprisoned, stared back. "Do you think they'll work out for me?"

She'd retreated to the other room, and he sat with his head in his hands. Evidently, Caroline herself did not understand or accept the very thing she had just forced him to understand and accept—that he, like most humans, was an experiment that had never been expected to succeed, a little padding around some evolutionary thrust, a scattershot nubbin of DNA. It was a matter of huge biological importance, for some reason, that he be desperate to meet the demands of his life, but it was a matter of no biological importance whatever that he be *able* to meet them.

But that week—that very week—an airmail letter arrived from a Richard Penwad inviting Shapiro to play Umberto García-Gutiérrez's Second Piano Concerto at a Pan-American music festival.

An amazing occurrence. Though one that, having occurred, was—like every other occurrence—plausible. The terrible feeling hanging over the apartment began to evaporate. Shapiro was embarrassed by his recent behavior and feelings, which now seemed absurdly theatrical, absurdly childish. Of course things would work out. Why wouldn't things work out? Why shouldn't he and Caroline go to whatever restaurant she pleased? And enjoy it. Order some decent wine, attend concerts, travel . . . Check in hand, he would lead Caroline into the bower of celebrity and international conviviality from which he'd been exiled. However gradually, in due course things would work out.

In the days that followed, Shapiro felt by turns precariously elated and violently dejected, as though he were emerging from the chaos of an accident that had left him impaired in as yet undisclosed ways. He would catch Caroline gazing at him soberly with her great, light-filled eyes. She mentioned the invitation frequently. "Isn't it terrific?" she said. "Aaron. How terrific." Her voice was tender and lingering—remote, the voice in which, when they'd first met, she'd recounted to Shapiro tales of her idyllic childhood. Then, one evening, when he came home with a guidebook, she said, "Listen, Aaron." And her voice had been especially gentle. "We have to talk."

Shapiro checked the clock by his uncomfortable bed; it would be a relief to go downstairs and meet Penwad. His brain felt unbalanced by Caroline's precipitous entrances and exits; anything to block them. He shut the door of his dark, cramped room behind him, and descended to the restaurant; yes, unbalanced! The corridors themselves seemed to buckle underfoot.

The festival would have been an attractive proposition even at the best of times. Shapiro had played once before in Latin America—a concert in Mexico City many years earlier. The air in the hall had been velvety with receptivity, the audience ideal, and although his piece had been first on the program, they had demanded an encore from him right then and there.

The García-Gutiérrez concerto had furnished other happy occasions in his career. He'd performed its United States première some seventeen years earlier. The piano part was splashy and difficult, perhaps not terribly substantial, but an excellent vehicle for Shapiro; it glittered in his hands. García-Gutiérrez had been there to congratulate him with a quiet intensity. What would he look like now, Shapiro wondered. At that time he'd been handsome—silvery hair, tall, hooded eyes.

How young Shapiro must have seemed, with his abashed, eager gratitude!

Penwad was already downstairs at the restaurant drinking a coffee. He extended, with official enthusiasm, a carefully manicured but stubby hand, and grimaced as Shapiro shook it. "We're pleased we could get you down," he said, and glanced at his palm. "This is our first go at the festival, I think I must have written you, but we're hoping to bring people such as yourself annually, from all over the Americas—especially the States. We're starting out with García-Gutiérrez as our star attraction, you see, because he's a local boy."

On the walls were posters of palm-fringed lakes, frosted volcanoes, and Indians smiling regal, slightly haughty smiles. Interspersed with the posters were magnificent examples of Indian textiles.

"Charming, isn't it?" Penwad said. "Not a—an *ostentatious* place, but we felt you'd find it charming."

Charming, Shapiro thought. Well, probably the other hotels were even worse. He glanced at the walls again. Charming! It was well known, what was happening in this country to the descendants of its earliest inhabitants—massacres, internment, debt slavery, torture—and, *naturally*, the waiters who scurried around beneath the smiling posters, looking raddled and grief-stricken, were Indians, ceremonial costumes draping their skinny bodies.

"People don't tend to be aware how vigorous our sponsorship of the arts is," Penwad was saying. "We're hoping the festival will help to . . . rectify the, ah, perception that we're identified with the military here."

Shapiro's attention was wrenched from the waiters. "The perception that . . ."

"Rectify that perception," Penwad said.

Fee, Shapiro reminded himself. Fee plus lessons, minus rent, minus utilities . . . Well, and besides, there would be the credit. In a program note, even the most dubious event acquired grandeur. And why not? Concerts and exhibitions from the beginning of time had been funded by villains in search of endorsement, apologists, a place in history, or simple self-esteem. "Incidentally," Shapiro said, "who is 'we'?"

Penwad raised his eyebrows. "Who is we?" he said.

"That is, when you say 'we'—"

"Ah," Penwad said. "Well, I'm not including myself, actually. I'm just a liaison, really, between the Embassy and various local committees and groups concerned with the arts."

"I see," Shapiro said, with no attempt at tact.

"So," Penwad said. "We'll get you a bit of breakfast, then go on over to the Arts Center, take a little look around— Rehearsal all day, rather strenuous, I'm afraid. After that we've fixed up a little interview for you—I trust that's all right— around dinnertime. Friday's free until the concert. Joan and I will pick you up first thing in the morning to show you around." He smiled. "Joan has her own ideas, but you must say what interests *you*. Then, after the concert, there's to be a party, a reception for you, essentially, at the home of some friends of ours, very fine people here. Then plane, yes? Very next morning." He already, Shapiro noticed, looked relieved. "Quite a whirlwind."

"Wonderful," Shapiro said. "But no need, you know, to take me over to the . . . Arts Center. Why don't I just grab a taxi?"

Penwad waved his hand. "I'm afraid the Center is difficult to find. Most of the drivers are unfamiliar with it. Besides," he added, "enjoy your company." He narrowed his eyes at his coffee cup, and raised it to his mouth.

There was something anatomical about the Center's great concrete sweeps and protuberances. Like all Arts Centers and Performing Arts Complexes and National Centers for the Performing Arts, though futuristic in design, it had a look of ancient decay, being left over from a period when leisure time and economic abundance were considered an imminent menace. How quaint a notion that now seemed! Shapiro almost laughed to think there had been a period, the period in which he'd grown up, no less, when it had been feared that wealth would soon cause humanity to devolve into a grunting mass sprawled in front of blood-drenched TV screens. But, no—*Art* (whatever that was), encouraged to flourish in its Centers, would prevent people from becoming intractable, illiterate, fat! And all the while poverty was accomplishing the devolution by itself.

"I see you're enjoying the, ah, prospect," Penwad said.

Shapiro became aware that he was staring down over toothy crenellations into a city cleaved by deep ravines and encircled by mountains.

"Those tall buildings are the downtown area, of course," Penwad said. "And to the right and left, obviously, are residential sectors. Our place is over there—that's pretty much where the whole English-speaking community has . . . put down its little roots. And up there on the slopes is what we call the Gold Zone."

Shapiro, shading his eyes, noticed that the ravines below were encrusted with fuming slums. "My God," he said.

"Incredible, isn't it," Penwad said, "what an earthquake can do? You can really see the damage from up here. You probably noticed the floor of your hotel. The Center survived intact, though. We're very proud of the Center. The architect was truly successful, we feel, the way he . . . Yes, actually. You might be interested. A fellow named Santiago Méndez. He's done most of the better hotels in town, and our museum. There was a lecture last year. One of our events. It was explained. The way Méndez— Well, this was some time ago, of course—Joan would be better able to . . . But . . . the . . . combined influences." He gestured toward several concrete mounds. "The modernistic, the indigenous . . . well, *motifs*. A cross-fertilization, as Joan says."

Shapiro hesitated. A bunting-like stupefaction had enveloped him. "Of . . . what?" he asked.

"Of . . . ? What of what?" Penwad asked.

"Of . . ." Shapiro had lost the thread of his own question. "Of what . . . does *Joan* . . . say 'cross-fertilization'?"

"Joan *says* it . . ." Penwad glared at him. "She says it of . . . *motifs*."

The orchestra was from a small, nearby dictatorship, and the musicians had a startled appearance, as though a huge claw had snatched them from their beds and plonked them into their chairs. The conductor, a delicate and intelligent-looking man, welcomed Shapiro with reassuring collegiality, but when he brought down his baton Shapiro almost cried out; the sound was so peculiar that he feared he was suffering from some neurological damage.

How had the conductor come to find himself in his profession, Shapiro wondered. The man's waving arms seemed to be signalling for help rather than leading an orchestra. The poor musicians clutched their instruments, staring wildly at their sheet music as they played. But then it was Shapiro's entrance; notes began to leap froggily from his own fingers, and he understood: clearly the hall was demonic.

How to outwit these acoustics? As if this concerto were not difficult enough under the best of circumstances, with all its flash and bombast! But, of course, there was always something. Even in the loftiest, the most competently administered concert, catastrophes invented themselves from the far reaches of possibility. The piano bench would fall into splinters at seven forty-five, or the other musicians turned out to have a new version of the score, three measures shorter than one's own, or there was a bank holiday and it was impossible to retrieve one's tuxedo from the cleaner's—catastrophes far beneath the considerations of music, and yet!

How synthetic the concerto sounded in this inhospitable hall! Shapiro was surprised to find himself disliking it so. He had never tremendously admired it, exactly, but he'd always enjoyed playing it: he'd enjoyed the athletic challenge of its surface complexities; he'd enjoyed the response of the audience. It was *affirming*, people said upon hearing it, and their faces had the shining, decisive expressions of people who feel their worth to be recognized. *Affirming*, Shapiro thought, as sound sloshed and bulged, gummed up in clumps, liquefied, as though the air were full of whirling blades.

The interview that had been arranged for Shapiro was with an English journalist named Beale. An interview: implied interest on the part of someone. There would be clippings, at least, and, perhaps, therefore some shadowy retention of his name in the minds of those people—"we"—who put these festivals together.

Shapiro located Beale in a restaurant of the hotel, much

larger than his own, where they'd been scheduled to meet. "Are you tired of it?" Beale inquired anxiously. "I was hoping not. In my opinion it's the best food in town, and the station will reimburse if it's an interview."

Beale's head was an interesting space-ship shape. Colorless and sensitive-looking filaments sprouted from it, and his ears looked like receiving devices. Sensors, transmitters, Shapiro thought, noting Beale's other large, responsive-looking features and his nervous, hesitant fingers. Beale's suit was faintly mottled by traces of stains; his shirt, from the evidence of his wrists, was short-sleeved, and he wore, incredibly, a tie that appeared to be made of rope.

"I'm not tired of it yet," Shapiro said. "I've never been here."

Beale squinted distrustfully at Shapiro. "They didn't put you here? They put a lot of guests here . . ."

Shapiro glanced around. So this was where they'd put an *important* musician. It was ugly and grandiose, with slippery-looking walls—the very air seemed soaked with a venal, melting luxe. "Santiago Méndez?" he said.

"Oh, you're good," Beale said with delight. "Seriously. If they bring you down again, insist. Nice, isn't it? They all speak English, and the furniture doesn't just"—he lunged toward Shapiro in illustration—"loom up at you. Now, will you drink something?"

Shapiro saw that two glasses already sat in front of Beale, one emptied and the other containing hardly more than a gold film. "Just water, thanks," Shapiro said.

"Oh, you can, here," Beale said. "Rest assured. Ice and all. I, on the other hand," he informed a waiter, "will have a whiskey, why not."

"And perhaps we could order," Shapiro added. Well, at least someone had seen fit to arrange a party for him.

Beale studied the menu worriedly, running his finger along the print. He had quantities of advice for Shapiro about it but seemed unable to make up his own mind. "A nice chop, perhaps," Beale said. "You know, this is the one place where it's perfectly safe to eat pork. That is if you—" His eyes blinked and reset themselves furiously, like lights on an overtaxed instrument panel.

While Beale entrusted his order to the waiter, Shapiro's attention wandered to posters on the wall. Plenty of charm here, too: more lakes, more volcanoes, more smiling Indians . . . Beale dove abruptly beneath the table, resurfacing with a tape recorder as primitive-looking as a trilobite. "I hope you don't mind if I . . . There are several publications that are reasonably, well . . . friendly to me, but mostly I do radio."

"Radio," Shapiro agreed politely. "And this would be for . . . the English-speaking community, I presume."

Beale looked at him blankly. "Not really. There are telephones for that sort of thing. Oh! No." His voice became gluey with attempted modesty. "No, this is a show back home in England, you see. They often ask me for a little story."

England. So, this was a bit more promising. "A show . . . about the arts," Shapiro suggested.

"The arts?" Beale said. "Well, there's not really too much scope for that sort of thing here. This country isn't just churning out the artists, you know. Not a very . . . well, 'favorable climate' I suppose is the expression. Actually, it's a show about just whatever happens to come up. I was glad when your Embassy called and put me on to this one, because there's not really a fantastic amount. You can file only just so often about dead students before people get sick of it. Still, don't think I'm complaining—I'm lucky to be here at all. When I was young, I was simply frantic to get to this part of the world. Astonishing place. Have you had much chance to get around? See the sights, meet the people?"

"I got in last night," Shapiro said.

"Ah," Beale said. "Oh, yes. Well, it is truly staggering. Very beautiful, as I'm sure you know. And the highlands—when I first came it was like the dawn of the earth up there, really. Oh, if I could only . . ." He sighed. "You know, the Indians here had simply everything at one time. A calendar. A written language—centuries, centuries, *centuries* before the Spanish came. And all sorts of other magnificent, um—appurtenances. While *we* were still running around in—" He cast a veiled glance at Shapiro. "Yes. Well, and the Spanish actually destroyed it all. But you know that. Burned their books, herded them into villages with Spanish overseers. Isn't it amazing? The written language was actually *destroyed*, do you see. The calendar, the architecture, the books . . . And so, I mean, we're slaughtering these people and so forth, but we don't really know anything about them. And if they know anything about themselves they're not letting on. Who *are* they? That is, who are *we*? I mean, *they're* here, *we're* here . . . It's just terribly *strange*." He smiled a misty, wondering smile, then frowned. "Oh dear. *Anyhow*, I tried and tried to get people to send me here. They said, 'But *why*? Where *is* it? Nothing *happens* there.' Then, fortunately, there were all these insurrections and repressions and whatnot, and that created demand, and so now I've been here over fifteen years!"

Shapiro opened his mouth; a blob of sound came out.

"I tried to reach García-Gutiérrez yesterday," Beale said. "But I gathered he hadn't arrived yet. He lives in Europe a lot of the time now, you know. They told me he'd be in today, but I thought I'd talk to you instead. I'm sure he's a wonderful composer. They say he is. But, to tell you the truth, the man gives me the shivers. I've seen him around, at parties here, and I just don't like his sort. You know what I mean—well-fed, a bit of a dandy. *Suave.* Eye always on the main chance. A big smile for every colonel. Ladies all love him. Government always showing him off like a big, stuffed . . ." Beale brooded at his drink, then waved over a new one. "Anyhow," he said unhappily, "I've got you."

Shapiro took a sip of water. He would have liked a drink, too, but alcohol affected him unpredictably. Even Beale's alcohol seemed to be making Shapiro mentally peculiar. "Let me ask you," he said. "It isn't actually dangerous here, I suppose."

"Dangerous?" Beale said. "Why? What do you mean? Not for *you*, it isn't. You know"—he sat back and looked at Shapiro with drunken coldness—"I find it *most* comical. How Americans come down here, and they talk about danger. And they talk about *this*, and they talk about *that*. Well, I don't endorse slavery and torture myself, but who are you, may I ask, to talk? Dare I mention who kicked off all this ha-ha 'counterinsurgency' business here in the first place? Dare I mention whose country it was that killed *all* their Indians?"

"Now, look—" Shapiro began.

"A thousand apologies," Beale said. "How true. You're no more responsible for your country than I am for mine. But all this simply jerks my chain, I'm afraid. It simply does. And I mean *dangerous*! I mean this place is hardly in the league of—I mean, one's forever reading, isn't one? How some poor tourist? Who's saved his pennies for years and years and years. Who then *goes* to New York, to see a show on your great Broad*way*, and virtually the instant he arrives gets stabbed in the . . ." He took a violent gulp of his drink. "The—"

"Liver," Shapiro said.

"*Sub*way," Beale said. "Yes." He beamed at Shapiro in surprise. "I don't know why that's so difficult to . . . Oh, look," he exclaimed, as the waiter set down their plates. "Oh, my darling! That *is* nice." He extracted a pair of glasses from his pocket, put them on to peer at his plate, then removed them to clean them on his ropy tie.

Shapiro took a bite of his meal, but Beale's grubbiness had damaged his appetite.

"Of course the highlands are another story," Beale said. "The highlands, the whole countryside, really—still sheer carnage. But here in the city it's just sporadic violence. Of a whatsit sort. Really, about the worst that can happen to you here is Protestants. Random. Of a random sort."

"Protestants?" Shapiro said.

"Evangelicals," Beale said. "So bloody noisy. Haranguing in the streets, massive convocations every which place, speaking in tongues—YAGABAGABAGAGABAGAGA." He sighed. "Now, don't think I'm prejudiced, please. I'm Protestant myself. But that's the point, isn't it? That one can slag off one's own group, though one would never— That is, I, for instance, would never, oh, say, call . . . a Jew, for example, a 'kike'—that's *your* prerogative. But all that shouting is simply not the point of speech. I mean, the point of speech is— Well, that is just very simply not the point. And it can be terribly, just terribly annoying when you're trying to conduct an interview or what have you, as you and I are here today."

"Perhaps . . ." Shapiro began with difficulty. "That is, perhaps, speaking of the interview, perhaps there's something you'd like to ask me."

"Ah," Beale said. "Right you are." He smiled, then frowned. "But the thing is, old man—I'm afraid I'm not all that familiar with . . . If you could help me out a bit. That is, perhaps we'd best stick to rather general concepts."

Shapiro nodded. "If you wish. What . . . for example, were you thinking we might—"

"Yes," Beale said. "Hmm. Well, I suppose we might talk about your . . . oh, impressions, for example, of the country . . ."

Shapiro looked at him. "I only arrived last—"

"Last night," Beale said impatiently. He drummed his fingers on the tape recorder. "Well, but just generally, you know. Just something . . . spontaneous."

Shapiro pressed his fingers to the corners of his eyes.

"Not acceptable. I see, not acceptable," Beale said, bitterly. "Well, in that case . . . we could talk, for example, about what it feels like to come down here as an American."

"As an American?" Shapiro said. "I'm not *down* here as an American. I'm not down here *as* anything. I'm down here as a *pianist.*"

"Yes," Beale said. "Quite."

Heat began to creep over Shapiro's skin as Beale stared at him.

"You know," Beale said, "I've always wondered. And this is something that I think would be very interesting to the radio audience. How do instrumentalists feel about their relationship—that is, via music, of course—to the composer?"

"What are you—" Shapiro began.

"Well, the very *word*—" Beale said. "That is, the word *literally*, well, it literally *means*—well, instru*ment*alist. I mean, you're a—"

"Excuse me," Shapiro said. "I've got to . . . get to a phone."

Shapiro fled into a system of corridors and polyp-like lobbies or reception rooms. Oh, to be alone! The men's room?

Maybe not. Well, actually, there was a phone booth. Shapiro sat down inside it, shutting himself into an oceanic silence. Beyond the glass wall people floated by—huge, serene, assured, like exhibits. Shapiro leaned against the wall. He rested his hand on the phone as though it were the hand of an old lover. Absently, he stroked the receiver, then lifted it, releasing a loud electronic jeer—the sound, as silence is not, of emptiness. He would tell Beale that he was unwell, that he had to go rest.

Shapiro paused at the entrance to the restaurant. Beale was sitting at the table alone, his narrow shoulders hunched and his spaceship head bent over the tape recorder as he spoke into it. There was urgency in Beale's posture, and his face was anguished. What could he be saying? Shapiro took a step closer.

"Ah!" Beale said, clicking off the machine with a bright smile, as though he'd been apprehended in some mild debauchery. "Get through?"

"Excuse me?" Shapiro said.

"Get your call through?"

"Oh," Shapiro said. He sat down and passed his hands across his face. "No."

"No," Beale agreed with unfocussed sympathy. "Oh, it's all so difficult. *So* difficult. Now—" He smiled sentimentally. Amazingly, he appeared to have completely forgotten he'd been in the process of attacking Shapiro. "Not to worry— we're going to get a very nice little segment about you. In fact"—he twinkled slyly—"I've already done something by way of an intro. Your name and so on, you're down here for the festival, you'll be playing the García-Gutiérrez . . . Hmm." He removed his glasses to study a crumpled piece of paper. "And, let's see." He turned on the machine and spoke into it again. "You've played the piece before with great success . . . Mr. Shapiro, I understand." He nodded encouragingly and indicated the machine.

Shapiro looked at it. "Yes," he said, wearily.

Beale gave him a wounded glance. "In fact, you premièred the piece in the U.S., I believe."

Shapiro closed his eyes.

"Yes," Beale said. He took a deep breath through his nose. "Well, *any*how, that was back in, let's see . . . nineteen . . . goodness me! You must be very fond of it."

"Well," Shapiro said, "I mean, it *is* in my repertory . . ."

Beale emitted a giggle, or hiccup. "I have a set of little spoons," he said. "Tiny little silver things. For olives or something of the sort, that someone gave a great-aunt of mine as a wedding present. And somehow *I've* ended up with them."

Shapiro opened his eyes and looked at Beale.

"Well, I don't throw them out, I mean, do I?" Beale said. "I say." He frowned. "Are you not going to . . . ?" He waved at Shapiro's plate.

"No, no," Shapiro said. "Go ahead. Please."

"Thank you." Beale switched off the tape recorder and placed Shapiro's full plate on top of his own empty one. "We'll go on in a minute. And I think we'll get something nice, don't you? Most people like doing radio. It's a lovely medium, lovely. Do you know what I especially like about it?" He interrupted himself to eat, then continued. "One meets people. Oh, I know one does in any profession—it can hardly be avoided. But I mean one *goes out* to meet people, on an equal basis. The voice—it's freeing, wouldn't you agree? Yet intimate. There one is, a great glob of . . . oh . . . pork pie!" His eyes gleamed briefly with lust. "But I mean all one's qualities and circumstances just . . . globbed together, if you see what I mean. The good, the bad, the . . . pointless . . ." He paused again, and rapidly forked food into his mouth. "But with radio, you see, there's a way to separate out the real bit. And all the rest of it—I mean one's body, one's face, one's age . . . even, even"—he glanced around as though bewildered—"even the place where one is sitting! Well, one is free of it, isn't one? One sees how free one really is.

"Great *leaps*. Teleportation. The world is so . . . *roomy*. So full of oddments. But there's that now-you-see-it, now-you-don't quality about life that makes one so very nervous. Danger, as you pointed out just now, yourself. Danger simply everywhere. Everything destroyed, lost, forgotten . . . Well, that's what they want, you know, most of them. *'There's nothing about it in the reports,'* they'll tell you. They'll say it straight to your face. Of course there are ghosts, people say. I suppose that's some help. But a ghost is simply not terribly . . . *communicative*. They haunt, they grieve, that sort of thing. But it's all rather general, you see. Because they don't much really talk.

"Oh, didn't you just love it when you were a boy? It's raining outside, your mum's still working in the shop, you haven't a friend in the world, then you turn on the radio, and someone's talking—to *you*. Oh, my darling! Someone is talking to you, and you don't know, before you turn that radio on, who will be there, or what thing they've found to tell you on that very day, at that very moment. Maybe someone will talk to you about cookery. Maybe someone will talk to you about a Cabinet minister. And then that particular thing is *yours*, do you see what I mean? Who *knows* whether it's something worth hearing? Who *knows* whether there's someone out there to hear it! It's a leap of faith, do you see? That both parties are making. Really the most enormous leap of faith." He paused to devour the food remaining on Shapiro's plate, and then looked helplessly into Shapiro's eyes. "I mean, I find that all enormously, just enormously . . . ." He shook his head and turned away.

Shapiro set his alarm for 6 a.m., and slipped out of the hotel before Penwad could come for him, consequences be damned. *Ha-ha*—the day was his! Screechy traffic flew cheerfully through the streets, and toxins gave the air a silvery, fishlike flicker as the sun bobbed aloft on waves of industrial waste.

Shapiro walked and walked. He passed through grand neighborhoods, where armed guards lounged in front of high, white walls. And he passed through poor neighborhoods, where children, bloated with hunger, played in the gutters, their eyes dreamy and wild with drugs. Beyond the surrounding slopes lay the countryside—the gorgeous, blood-drenched countryside.

In some parts of the city Indians congregated on the sidewalk. Some sold chewing gum or trinkets on the corners, some seemed to be living the busy and inscrutable life of the homeless. Their clothing was filthy and tattered, but glorious nonetheless, Shapiro thought, glorious, noble, celebratory— like the banners of an army in rout.

Shapiro considered them with terror. The destitute. People who were almost invisible, almost inaudible. People to whom almost anything could be done: *other* people. At home, in the last five or ten years they had encamped in Shapiro's neighborhood. At first he thought of them as a small and temporary phenomenon. But now they were everywhere—sleeping in parks or on the pavement, ranging through the city night and day, hungry and diseased, in ragged suits and dresses acquired in some other life.

Everyone had become used to them; no one remembered how shocking it had been only a few years earlier to see someone curled up in a doorway, barefoot in freezing temperatures. Most of the time they were just a group at the periphery of Shapiro's vision. But when a student failed to show up for a lesson, or no concert work materialized, or the price of the newspaper went up, or some unexpected expense arose, Shapiro's precious hands would tingle. Injury? Arthritis? Even as it was, daily life was beginning to eat away at Shapiro's small savings. And at such times Shapiro would see those *other* people with an individualized and frigid clarity, would search their faces for proof that each was in some reliable way different from him, as though he were a dying man approaching the gauzy crowds waiting for judgment.

And they—what were they seeing? Perhaps he and his kind seemed a ghostly population to *them*—distant, fading . . . Perhaps at some terrible border you'd simply leave behind everything that you now considered life, forget about once precious concerns, as though they were worn-out shirts or last year's calendar or old lists of things that long ago it had seemed important to accomplish.

Oh, it was probably true, as Caroline had sometimes said, that his fears were irrational. That he'd always find some way to manage. But when the door closed behind her that day he ought to have understood—yes, he thought, that was the moment he ought to have understood—that success, the sort of success Penwad's letter seemed to promise for him again, was something he could just, finally, forget about.

But he had understood nothing; he'd simply sat there numb—for hours—until Lady Chatterley threw herself forward in a frenzy of carpet shredding. "Stop that," he'd said. "Stop, O.K., please?" He'd flicked a finger at her rear, and she'd leapt, snarling. The truth was he had always been a little afraid of the cat. She was Caroline's, but Jim, evidently, was allergic.

Shapiro supposed that, to whatever extent Caroline was thinking about *him*, she would be imagining him in debonair company here, taking part in animated and witty conversations of a sort no living person had ever experienced. Shapiro felt short of breath, as though Caroline were suffocating him with a pillow. "This is a wonderful opportunity for Aaron," she could be assuring Jim at this very instant. "Really it is." Oh, yes. *He*, Shapiro, must be happy so she could be.

An Indian child playing nearby in the street skinned a knee and howled for his mother. Shapiro felt an almost uncontainable sorrow, as though he were just about to cry himself. But to cry it's necessary to imagine the comforter.

Caroline had never cared what things were really like. He'd once overheard her saying thank you to a recorded message. Everything was nice, pleasant, good. If he spoke truthfully to her, she couldn't hear him. She despised no one. Those who were not nice, pleasant, happy simply ceased to exist.

Shapiro was ravenous. He entered an inviting little restaurant. Inside, it was very dark, but low-hanging, green-shaded lamps made a pool of light over each table.

The waiter spoke no English, but was agreeable when Shapiro pointed at a nearby diner's plate of soup. But there had been a time—truly there had—when Caroline actually loved him, had been fascinated by him, not just by his reputation. For a moment he saw her distinctly. She stood holding Lady Chatterley, gazing into space with a baffled sorrow. "Caroline—" he said.

Had he spoken aloud? Three men at a neighboring table were staring at him with a volatile blend of loathing and amusement. All three were mammoth. One appeared to be a North American; he and one of the others wore pistols, visible even in the restaurant's pleasant gloom, beneath their shirttails.

The waiter, bearing soup, interposed himself; Shapiro gestured fervent thanks. He took a spoonful of the soup. It was clear, and delicious. *Food*, he thought.

Plus rent. Plus utilities . . . Yes, tonight the stage of a concert hall, a tuxedo. A party, champagne, adulation. But tomorrow it was back to cat fur.

The waiter arrived with a second plate for him, huge and unexpected. A pretty selection of things that seemed to have been cooked in the broth. Mmm. Shapiro leaned into the light of his hanging lamp to poke around at it—carrots, onions, white beans, cabbage, celery, a small . . . haunch, something that looked . . . like . . . a snout . . .

One of the men at the next table chuckled softly. Shapiro glanced at them involuntarily again, and they stared back, their faces framing the teardrop of light from their hanging lamp. Then one of them, still staring, reached up and unscrewed the bulb.

The enfeebled musicians threw themselves on García-Gutiérrez's last, idiotic, triumphal chord. What had happened? Shapiro felt as though he'd awakened to find himself squatting naked in a glade, blinking up at a chortling TV crew that had just filmed him gnawing a huge bone. Had he played well or badly? He hardly knew. He'd played in a frenzy—the banal sonorities, the trivial purposes, the trashy approximations of treasures forged in the inferno of other composers' souls. Lacerating ribbons of notes streamed from his hands as he tried to flog something out of the piece, but it had simply sat there over them all—a great, indestructible, affirming block of suet.

The sparse audience stopped fanning themselves with their programs and made some little applause. Seething with confusion and misery, Shapiro stood to take his bow, and caught a glimpse of a man who could only be García-Gutiérrez, opaque and dignified in the face of tribute. At the sight, Shapiro reexperienced the frictional response of his skin, seventeen years earlier, to the man's blandishments, like an acquiescence to unwelcome sensual pleasure.

Outside, Penwad resumed his post at Shapiro's elbow. "We'll just stick around here for a few minutes," he said nervously, "then round everyone up and get going to the reception. Oh. I don't believe you've met. Joan."

"That was lovely," Joan said. "Just lovely. You know, we looked for you at your hotel today. We felt sure you'd want to see our Institute of Indigenous Textiles."

"Oh, Lord—" Shapiro floundered. "Yes! No, absolutely. I—"

"We left messages at the desk," Penwad said.

"Well," Joan said. "Those *people* at the desk . . ."

Night had ennobled the Center. Musicians and members of the audience milled about in the uncertain radiance of stars and klieg lights. A slow, continuous combustion of garbage sent up bulletins of ruin from the hut-blistered gorges, which were quickly snuffed out by the fragrance drifting down from the garlanded slopes of the Gold Zone.

Penwad pointed out various luminaries. There was a Cultural Attaché, a Something Attaché, several Somethings from the Department of Something—it was all a matter for experts.

"And do you see the lady over there?" Joan said, nodding discreetly in the direction of a stunning woman with arched eyebrows and a blood-red mouth. She was bending toward a boy who appeared to be about fifteen. "Our hostess. The reception for you is at her house. And her son. Well, as you see. They're identical. You'll enjoy talking to him. Perfect English—he's going to boarding school up in the States, and he just loves it. He loves to meet our visitors. The father's cattle, you know. Special, special people. Josefina's a marvel. You're not going to believe the house. She's a real force behind culture here. And, you can imagine, *some* of these wives . . ."

"Wonderful people," Penwad said. "And of course *you* two know each other from way back."

García-Gutiérrez had joined them, murmuring thanks to Shapiro. He was as handsome as before, though he'd be over sixty—a great tree of a man, at which age was hacking away fruitlessly. His loaflike body was still powerful; his long arms and legs, the musculature so emphatic one felt aware of its operations beneath the very correct clothing, the straining neck and jaws, the hooded eyes. "I feel that you brought something new to my music tonight," he was saying. "Something of a darkness, perhaps." In the man's lingering examination Shapiro felt the blind focussing, adversarial and comprehending, the arousal of the hunter. "Very interesting . . ."

Oh, that night seventeen years earlier! When it was reasonable for Shapiro to assume that he himself was going to be one of the favored. That he, too, would be respected, dignified, happy . . . The audience that night! How gratifying Shapiro had found their ardor then, how loathsome now, in memory. How thrilled they had been, seeing their own bright reflection in all the weightless glitter.

"We'll talk more, you and I, at the reception," García-Gutiérrez whispered, and glided off with Penwad and Joan to a huddle of musicians, who watched their approach with alarm.

Shapiro's heart jumped and blazed. People were beginning to float toward the parking lot. He played *better* now than he had then, but it made no difference—*no difference at all*. And those nights at the stage door; the faces, golden in the light, diamond earrings winking in the gold light . . . All the beautiful women. Gone now. No matter. What was it they'd adored? Those ardent glances, warm in the glow of his fame, the first shock, at the stage door, of Caroline's great, light eyes. *Affirming, affirming*—oh, what was he to *do?* They couldn't even put him in the decent hotel! Caroline was walking down the street. She wore a dainty little dress. The sun was on her hair, but black shadows swung overhead, and battling armies clanged behind her in the dust. Men and women lay on the sidewalk, their torn clothing exposing sticky lesions. One of them shifted painfully and held out a disintegrating paper cup. Caroline paused, opened her purse, and took out a quarter.

"Are you all right?" someone asked. Shapiro blinked, and saw the boy, the son of the woman who was having the reception. "You must be famished." He regarded Shapiro with the merry, complicitous look of a young person who anticipates approval. "What a workout for you, I think, that piece of G.-G.'s. But we'll have plenty of food back at home—the cooks have been racing around all day. Oh! Well, look at this. *He's* smart. He brought his own." The boy directed an amused glance toward Beale, who was ambling toward them, disemboweling an orange.

"Hello," Shapiro said. The boy's tone—despicable. He hoped Beale hadn't caught it.

"Would you care for any?" Beale said. "I'm afraid it's somewhat . . ." He nodded to the boy, who nodded distantly back. "You know," he said to Shapiro, "I'm sorry if I lost my bottle a bit last night. I tend to go on, from time to time, about one thing and another. Hope I said nothing to offend."

"Not at all," Shapiro said. *It made no difference at all.*

"Good good." A pink and rumpled smile wandered across Beale's face. "Goody goody."

Beale was making a complete mess of his orange. A small piece of peel had lodged in his webby tie. The boy was looking at it. "Oh," Beale said, glancing up. "Sorry. Difficult to handle. You know, it's strange about oranges, isn't it? They're so alluring. Irresistible, really. I mean, that color, for example—*orange.* And the *glossiness.* And that delicious smell they have. But it's all very strange. I mean, what good does it do them? They can't enjoy it. At least, so one supposes. All their deliciousness, do they get any fun out of it? No. It only gets them eaten. Isn't that strange? I mean, what is it for, from their point of view? I suppose you might ask the same of a flower. Flowers have sort of got it all, don't they. Looks, scent . . . But they have absolutely no way to appreciate that!" He giggled. "For all we know, they think of themselves as grotesque."

The boy was considering Beale with a dreamy, meditative look. His stare idled among the stains on Beale's suit. "Excuse me," he said. He smiled briefly at Shapiro. "I should go find some of our"—he glanced at Beale—"guests."

Beale gasped. "Did you hear that?" he said. "Little swine. Vicious little prick. As if I were going to crash the party! As if anyone *could* crash their fucking miserable party—they'll have half the fucking *army* at the gate."

"Mr. Shapiro, Mr. Shapiro," someone was calling.

"It's Joan," Shapiro said, hesitating. He heard his name

again. "Just a moment!" he called out. "Just a moment," he said to Beale. "I've got to—"

"Little putrid viper," Beale was saying, as Shapiro hurried off.

"We're ready to leave now," Joan said cheerily as Shapiro approached. "Everyone's gone down to the parking lot."

"Just a moment," he said. "I'll be right—"

"Don't be long," she sang with warning gaiety, and tweaked the lapel of his tuxedo.

"I'll be right—" he said. A tuxedo! He might just as well be wearing grease-stained overalls with his name embroidered on the pocket. "One more minute." He hurried back to find Beale, but Beale had disappeared.

"Hello?" Shapiro said. "Hello? I just wanted to—" But where could Beale have gone to? How arrogant that young boy was! How— Well, and the fact was, Shapiro thought, a man in livery could hardly afford to turn up his nose at a sloppy suit. "Hello?" he said again.

For a moment there was just a gentle surf of night noises, but then Shapiro made out Beale's voice, faint, very faint. Following the sound, he saw Beale, a dark shape, crouched in the corner of a concrete trough that must have been intended as some sort of reflecting pool.

Beale was speaking into his tape recorder. His voice had a stealthy, incantatory tone. "And now . . ." But the little noises of the night were washing away his words. ". . . take you to the party I promised you. It's . . . prominent family here."

There was an oily stain, or fissure, Shapiro saw, at the bottom of the trough. "And any important artist from . . . And what a beautiful . . . high, white . . . and tasteful objets d'art. But tonight . . . to take you out into the . . ."

Shapiro stood as still as he could and strained to hear.

"How lovely it . . ." Beale crooned into the machine. "Fountains, flowers . . . And . . . of chirpings! Croakings! Can you hear, my darling?"

Beale held the tape recorder up in the lifeless trough. Shapiro shuddered—a slight chill was coming down from the mountains.

"And those other sounds—do you hear?" Beale said. His voice was growing louder or Shapiro's ears were adjusting, seeking out the words. "The little plashings?" Beale said. "The fountain, yes, but what else? Not Spanish. But a language, yes! Just so. A language that's much, much older.

"Yes, because we're right across from the servants' quarters. And right there, on the servants' portico, the children are playing. The Indian children. Their mothers are all inside, serving little goodies to the guests. Can you hear the chatter behind us, of the guests?" Shapiro closed his eyes. Yes, he could hear it, the chatter, the pointless chatter. And smell the orange-scented garden. Yes—and he could see the children, just beyond the fountain, with their black, black hair, and shrewd, ravishing little faces.

"Good," Beale said. "Yes. And one of the children has a piece of stone or crockery. The others whisper together. They're joining hands—they seem to be inventing a game, don't they? Or reinventing. Some sort of game. Maybe they remember . . ."

Shapiro's name floated up from the parking lot. They were beginning to shout for him. *Yes, yes*, he thought fiercely, and held up a hand as though both to forestall and to shush them. *In a moment* . . . He sat down, as quietly as he could manage, on the cool concrete. Another moment and he'd go.

"When I first came to this country," Beale was telling the tape recorder, "the sky was a blue dome over the highlands.

People had more food then, and weren't so afraid. When you went hiking through the villages, suddenly there would be a waterfall, and fifty, a hundred, two hundred women, swaying along the mountain, coming to do their washing."

Ah! Along the mountain, coming closer. Their faces were in shadow still, and indistinct. But any minute, any minute now . . .

"I wanted to speak to them," Beale said. "But how could I? I was only an apparition! But—are you listening, my darling? I know they're still there—they'll always be there, beyond the curtain of blood." Beale stretched himself out in the trough, tucking the tape recorder under his head like a pillow, and a delicious sensation of rest poured into Shapiro's body. "I'm tired now." Beale patted the tape recorder. "I think I'll sleep. But it's going to be all right. Because the first thing. In the morning. When the sun is up again and shining? I'll start back off to them. And finally we'll speak. Please be there with me. They'll be so happy. I know they will. Because everyone has something, some little thing, my darling, they've been waiting so long to tell you . . ."

TLALOC'S PARADISE

The young American at the door was looking for a place to rent; Jean knew that as soon as she saw him. No, almost that soon, but in fact she was first seized, facing him there, by the violent and irrational certainty that he had come to tell her something—that he'd come down from the States to tell her something about Leo.

It was a moment before she began to thaw out and catch up with the boy's disorderly excuses. His name was Mark something, he was telling her; he'd been talking to a man in a café near the square. This man had said she and her husband were likely to know if there were a place available. He was sorry to just show up at her home like this, but he'd gone to the shop earlier and found it closed. He'd tried to phone, of course, but the phones just didn't seem to *work*, and since the man in the café had given him directions to the house . . . How did people manage, by the way, with these phones? Though that was part of the charm of the country, wasn't it?

He looked at her, and immediately began to apologize again: a cliché; it must be no end irritating to hear this sort of thing constantly. And the fact was, he rarely found himself anyplace where phones did work. But sometimes one just opened one's mouth, and out came some—

"Of course," Jean said. "Well, and besides." He was large,

and almost puffy, as though with fatigue, or some mild, chronic inflammation. "Anyhow, I don't think anyone would argue that malfunction and charm are related, at least here."

"Hmm." The boy frowned. "'Related.' Right. *Complicated* . . ."

"I'm afraid I don't know of any places at the moment," she said. "Leo would, probably, but you'll have to come back. I'm sorry. I'm afraid he's up in the States right now."

"Ah," the boy said.

"I'm sorry," Jean said. "You just missed him. He only went up this morning."

"Well." The boy frowned again, nodding. "Thanks. Too bad. Oh— Should I come back sometime? Yes, you said that, didn't you."

"Some other time," Jean said. "Yes."

"So," he said. "I'll try again next week?"

"Fine," she said.

He was so big, just standing there.

He ducked his head. "Well," he said. "Thanks."

She sighed. "Would you like to come in?"

Inside, he seemed even larger, and more formless, as though her fatigue were allowing him to spread into the far reaches of the large room. "Did you take the bus?" she asked, attempting to anchor her attention to one spot.

He had. He was pleased to be asked, she saw; the ride was short—she and Leo were no more than twenty minutes from town—but it was confusing, and, for strangers, difficult to negotiate. Clearly the boy was a good traveler—he'd found her after only one day in town. Though he'd been in the country, he seemed to be saying now, for several weeks.

As he talked, his shadowy bulk moved here and there, beyond the soft canopy of lamp- and candlelight, vaguely inspecting her emissaries, as it amused Leo to call them—the tall figures she'd constructed over the years, of various materials. "The man in the café *mentioned* you were a sculptor," the boy said, as though it were astonishing that this should, in fact, be so. *Mark*, she reminded herself. They looked like they were loitering there, in the dim margins, or massing.

"Welded?" the boy said.

"That one, yes." Fine, something she could talk about almost automatically. "A number of the early ones are, but I haven't worked in metal for years."

He hovered near one of the figures, peering. "Interesting," he said.

His caution made Jean smile. "You don't have to . . . I have no great stake in their quality, as it turns out."

Each had represented—witnessed and represented—pressing matters; attitudes, preoccupations . . . Pressing at the time. But eventually each figure was merely subsumed into the slowly expanding crowd. "It's just something I enjoy."

"Mmm." Mark frowned. "Enjoy . . ."

It wasn't his size, exactly—it was his obstacle-like quality. Still, Jean reminded herself. New places. Things abruptly inflating with a puzzling significance, or, just as suddenly, draining of any significance at all. She remembered: Herself and Leo, sitting gingerly, like this boy, wary lest some chance phrase burst into flames . . . "There shouldn't be much of a problem with a house for you," she said. "You're off-season, and there are a few vacation places Leo's been looking after."

Actually, there were probably some things she should take care of herself—plants, lights to outwit the tireless thieves . . . Neither she nor Leo had given any of that a thought in all the chaos of booking his ticket, getting in touch with friends in

San Antonio, getting him on the plane. "When Leo's back he'll . . ." She sighed.

"I'd hate to have . . . I mean, well—a *house.* I hadn't really been thinking of a whole— And I'd hate to have . . . your husband go to trouble if—"

"Leo likes it," Jean said. "Can you imagine? Well, who knows. Maybe that's the sort of thing you like, too. I can't stand it myself. Dealing with the propane, dealing with keys, dealing with cleaning girls. But I suppose it makes Leo feel . . ." She picked up a cushion near her on the sofa, looked at it, then let it drop. "Well, he likes it, that's all. That's all."

Mark took a deep breath. "Also, the price is something I'd . . . I mean, I don't have all that much—"

"Of course," Jean said. No, obviously this boy wouldn't have any money. "Well, that's something everyone down here . . . Anyhow, owners tend to want someone just to . . . Actually, you know, I've probably got all kinds of keys around here somewhere. Of course, even if I could find them I wouldn't know what key was what. Leo always says he's going to label, but you know how it is. *Years* go by . . ." Her head felt rubbery. She pushed her hair back; she'd forgotten to wash it in the morning.

The boy was watching her. "Oh, listen," she said. "Would you— How stupid I am tonight. Mark. Would you like something to drink?"

"Yes," he said. "Sure, great. Oh, but maybe you— God, it's late. I hadn't—"

"No," she said. "Believe me. I never sleep till two."

"Well, great, then," he said.

He kept his eyes lowered; he seemed almost afraid to look at her. But when he did, the intensity of his scrutiny was outrageous, practically comical. What did he suppose it was that licensed him to display such curiosity? The fact of his youth? His status as newcomer? There was nothing to prevent her from being annoyed, Jean thought, just as he blinked, and turned his gaze to the French doors.

She watched his large, moist eyes. "So," she said. "What's up?"

He shook his head and turned back to her, looking bewildered. "Lots of stars . . ."

"Oh, lots," Jean said. "Always. Very busy at night."

So busy. She'd never gotten over it—that sky, this room, dim and glossy with tiles and Mexican mirrors; all the faces amid the complex refractions—the faces of those figures of hers, of the pre-Columbian pieces and the masks she and Leo had scattered around; the brilliant Mexican night beyond the doors, with its festive, agitated stars and roses. Sometimes she and Leo stood here stricken, with all of that right around them, as though it were something that had eluded them . . . "Oh, heavens," she said. "Sorry. Usually I'm a bit more— Listen, all I can offer you is Canadian Club. Well, there's beer or tequila, but you'll get deeply sick of those if you're sticking around. We always used to have these great, sloshing reservoirs of alcohol, but I'm afraid we seem to be down to bedrock. The dreadful truth is, we're utterly at the mercy of whatever anyone grabs on the way through duty-free."

He'd picked up a small stone carving from the coffee table. "Actually, I don't really drink," he said, turning the figure over in his hand. "Do you have a Coke, or something like that? But really, I don't want to keep you up."

How often was she supposed to ask him to stay? "Pre-Columbian," she said. "Not a very good piece, and in terrible condition, but I like it."

"A big personality," he said.

"Oh, yes," she said. "That's Tlaloc. Very important—A harvest-cycle type. In charge of rain, also militia. He has this special little heaven you got to go to if you were a warrior, or died of drowning. A friend of ours brought it the last time he came through. He has great luck finding interesting ones. We have a little Olmec lady he brought us. And the one over there's Chac-Mool, the messenger. Who carried the sun around—Corrigan brought us that, too. And in fact he's responsible for most of our masks."

She reached over for the figure Mark was holding. It lay in her palm as she looked at it. "Good lord, you're dying of thirst, aren't you. You'll have to— I was up at the most horrible—"

"I'm sorry," Mark said. "You must be—"

"Mark, you know, people don't get *tired* when they get older, they get *impatient*. Oh, look—" Right, hardly his fault that she—"Is Sprite okay? Didn't even know we had it."

"Perfect," he said unhappily. "Sprite."

"Sprite it is." It had been a long time now since Corrigan had last been through. He hadn't even been living in his Mixtec village then, just out in the desert by himself. And he'd seemed to be floating, ever so slightly away from them. She'd thought perhaps she was imagining it, but looking back she was sure. Of course eccentricities often began as choices, or tools, or positions. But they could take you captive . . . "You're not going to have some sort of religious crisis, Mark, are you, if I have a drink?"

"No—" He cleared his throat. "Oh, not at all. I mean, I used to drink, myself."

"You used to?" she said. "My God. How old are you?"

"Twenty-eight." He looked at her. "Is that—"

"Reasonable," she said. "I suppose. And neutral. Insofar as I'm concerned, at least."

"Strange," he said. "Isn't it? Such a narrow range. I mean, I can't tell at all how old you are. And then it just closes up behind you again, doesn't it. I mean, I can't tell if someone's seventeen or twenty-two."

"Seventeen or twenty-two," Jean said. "Ha. I can't tell if someone's seventeen or fifty. Jesus, you know, if the truth be told, I *loathe* CC. And you know what else? I can't even remember who the cheapskate was who . . . You see, at one time we used to have all sorts of . . . Ah, well. The fact is, people simply don't come down here the way they used to."

"No." He frowned. "I suppose not."

Twenty-eight. Yes, she could see it. He was boyish-looking, and easily unbalanced, but a backlog of worry seemed to slow, or blur, his movements. Although his features were unremarkable and blunt, his expression reflected with great purity the finest modulations of his embarrassment and confusion. Her filthy hair! Her undisguised rancor! Well, all something for him to contemplate, wasn't it; Jean noted dispassionately the thorny little tendrils of amusement uncurling within her at the consternation she was causing her guest.

"When is—when is your husband expected back?" he asked.

"It shouldn't be long," she said. "He's just up for tests."

"I'm sorry," he said. "Is that bad?"

She rubbed the bridge of her nose. Amazing, the tiny, tiny things you could do to make yourself feel better. Rubbing the bridge of your nose, your temples . . . There was some spot on her palm where Leo could rest his thumb, and the muscles of her back and neck would relax . . .

"I'm sorry," the boy said again.

"It's just tests," Jean said.

She propped her feet—nice feet, small feet, even in their

funny sneakers—against the coffee table and leaned back, looking at the ceiling. Mark had gotten his hands into the middle
of some futile gesture; from the corner of her eye she watched
him trying to resolve it.

"Anyway, though, it still is interesting," he said. "Isn't it."

"Yes?" She lifted an eyebrow. "What is?"

"This place." He squirmed, but persevered. "This country. Even though people don't come here as much. It's still
interesting."

"Ah," Jean said.

"The man in the café was interesting," he offered after a
moment.

Jean meted out a glance of enquiry.

"The man who told me about you and Mr. Soyer."

"Ah, yes."

"He was German, I think. Well, I mean, he was."

"Plenty of Germans around," Jean said.

"This one was old—"

"Plenty of old Germans."

"A real character. He kept making these sort of . . . dark
allusions. You know, he'd say, 'The *coffee* at this place is better
than the *coffee* next door. Have you *tried theirs*?' It was as though
he was a spy, and I was a spy, too, only no one had bothered to
let me know."

Jean laughed abruptly. Beyond the seismic dislocation of
her body she saw the boy peering at her with hope.

"And then for hours afterwards," he said, "everything
seemed like that. As though everyone was telling me something else."

"Sounds like Schacht," Jean said.

"Actually, though, you know what?" Mark said. "Everything *is* like that, sort of, isn't it? I mean everyone *is* telling

you . . . *is* telling you— Oh, and he had a kind of funny eye, I think, too."

"Yup," Jean said. "Schacht." Schacht sat at the cafés all day, a hairy disk of a spider, hors de combat. His legs dangled from his chair and one eye would drift enigmatically in and out of alignment while he waited for Mexican boys. A sufficient number were on hand, always, desperate for a meal— the price was no greater than an hour or two of boredom and the humorous remarks of one's friends.

"He was sort of nice, though, I think," Mark said. Jean looked at him, but his face had gone deceptively blank. "He seemed lonely."

"Lonely," Jean said. "Well, if you can't really talk about your life—I mean, people manage to believe all sorts of things about themselves, don't they. And it's very isolating to have an official view of your life with something else locked up somewhere."

"Do you—" A slightly gluttonous shine appeared in Mark's stare. "God. I've never actually met anyone from that—"

"Well, who knows, really," Jean said. She and Leo always referred to Schacht as "the Nazi," but his hand, as it clung to hers in greeting, was the hand of any old man—tremulous and age-spotted. "Actually, though, it's interesting—there's a place here, in town. Run by an Austrian family. And all the old Germans and Austrians in the area sit around shoveling down great slabs of swine and what-not, that's cooked and served by Mexicans. And they're all schmoozing away in German. Pretending, believe it or not, that they were born in Mexico, or that they were in this or that resistance. Oh, I mean there are bound to be a few old Jews, and a few old déclassé aristos from one side of the fence or the other, and maybe one or two of them really did hold a match to party headquarters at Berchtesgaden or whatever. But that was simply not the story with most of them, obviously—the place is swarming with fake passports and fake histories. But whoever those people were once, they're all sitting together now, missing the same real pastries, the same real streets . . ."

Mark nodded. "Oh, strangeness," he said. "Opacity."

As he and Jean raised their glasses to one another she saw a little heap—translucent, gelatinous, torn things. Memories, discarded by the barbed wire under a tiny, oil-colored sun. A little heap, growing on the icy soil as a shivering procession filed, naked and desperate as angels, past the guard post, where meaningless new memories were being issued. "Anyhow." Jean closed her eyes. "Pardon me, but another burning question—what's brought you down?"

"Oh, me." Mark shook his head. "Well, me. All right, let's— So who am I, what am I doing here, what—hmm. Okay, I was studying. Engineering, which is not such a ridiculous . . . But then I was finished, and I realized, my God, you know. This is my *life*, which I sort of hadn't grasped until then. And also at the same time, more or less, my father died. And I realized I hadn't known too much about him. And everything that I didn't know actually didn't *exist* any longer. And what did still exist was any little thing I did happen to know . . . And everything was just *flying* off the face of the earth, just flying *off* . . . But I didn't know how to . . . But anything less just seemed pointless. So I began to just sort of rush around, I guess. For a while I was catching salmon. For big companies off the coast of Alaska." He looked at her. "It's amazingly hard."

She nodded.

"And then I was working in the oil fields. Along the Amazon. Which isn't so easy either, in fact." He stared at the little stone carving on the table. "Anyhow, my Spanish isn't that bad. So." He looked out the doors again, voyaging.

"Where did you stay last night?" Jean asked quietly.

He sighed hugely, coming to rest. "Oh, I've put myself at El Parque. It's kind of a splurge. I mean, the room is fairly primitive—except for the bugs. Those bugs—wow, *advanced*. But I've got a view. I look right out onto the square, you know? So this morning I ran out to the market for oranges and bread, and then I came back and had breakfast on my balcony."

Jean leaned back and smiled.

"That square," he said. "It's really . . ."

"Hypnotizing," she said. "I know. And the incredible thing is, it simply never changes. It's absolutely eternal. Every day, decade after decade. The children, the old people, the band in the bandshell, the flowers, the fountains . . . Except that the children are always new children and the old people are always new old people and the flowers are always new flowers . . . The sun comes up, the sun goes down—all these years, and we've never gotten tired of it . . ."

"How many years?" Mark leaned forward. "Incidentally."

Jean regarded her glass—the answer seemed to be sleeping, deliciously, at the bottom of her drink. "Well," she said, slowly, "the fact is. We came down in the fifties."

"Mm," he said, with tact so inept that she laughed out loud.

"Yes, hundreds of—"

"Not at—"

"Anyhow," she said, "a lot of us came down then. Terrible things were going on in the States. Comparatively subtle, but nonetheless . . ."

"Oh, right," he said. "My mom and dad used to tell me. How everyone had to look exactly alike, and everyone had to be completely happy . . ."

"Yes . . ." she said. "Well, listen, Mark. You probably don't know much about it, but there were these sort of mild purges . . . You know, nobody was going around killing anybody, so it was all very vague and insidious. It was sort of a warning, really. Later everyone laughed about how absurd it all was, but I tell you, Mark, people just kept on being very, very careful. In their actions and in their thoughts, without actually remembering, or even knowing, exactly why."

He squinted at her, as though he could extract her meaning by looking. "Yes," he said. "Oh, actually, you know, I had a cousin, or something. No. My mom's uncle, Frank, she told me. She was still absolutely furious. The FBI came to the house, and Frank lost his job. But"—Mark looked at Jean with surprise, as though it were he who was hearing the story for the first time—"he wasn't a *Communist*. He was an ichthyologist."

Jean looked at him. "Oh, yeah. Well. Anyhow, Mexico had a lot of glamour at that time. You know, that luster that moves around from place to place. Jesus, Mexico City—You can't—So jaunty. And pretty and chic. And the whole, strange, gorgeous country. The way those names sounded to us—Chiapas, Cuilapan, Pátzcuaro, Tepotzlan, Ixtlán del Rio . . . Imagine how that felt—going where words like that were still alive! And all these fresh memories of bandit-saints and campesino intellectuals and painter-revolutionaries. And wild people from simply everywhere, those people who always go places to start things new . . . There was this one woman—a sort of Russian Gypsy Jew, truly stunning. She'd arrive on horseback. All this *red* hair. Men were simply shooting each other by the score . . ."

Mark nodded respectfully.

"Boring, boring," Jean said. "I know. Jesus Christ, we don't even get *movies* anymore. The currency's so fucking rotten they can't even import movies." She rested her fingertips against her eyes; if she could only keep herself from *talking*, maybe he'd . . .

"Mexico City—" But there was his voice again. Soft, relentless. "Mexico City's gotten pretty difficult, I guess."

"The thing is—" Jean looked at him. "She *died* a week or so ago. Someone happened to tell us. We only heard by chance. She drank. I mean, she was old—considerably older than, than we are—But, I mean, she fell. She fell down the fucking *stairs*."

Mark reddened. "Wow, that's—"

"Isn't it just," Jean said. "Anyhow, difficult, difficult. Yes, difficult, now, Mexico City. We all started off there, of course. Then most of our friends just went back up, but some stayed, and we came down here. For a long time we lived right in town. Our friend Corrigan—the mask guy?—lived right next door to us. Then he moved out here, long before we did. Now he lives way off in hell-and-gone by himself. Well, not by himself in his opinion—he's got one of those hateful little, those dogs. An esquintle, it's called."

"Oh, yes," Mark said. "One of those—"

"It's Aztec, he says, so he speaks to it in Nahuatl."

"Oh." Mark frowned. "That's funny."

"Funny," Jean agreed. "So, Mark. I'm having another of those delicious— How about you? More yum-yum Sprite?"

"Well. Don't mind if I—" He handed her his glass and wiggled his eyebrows elaborately.

"Such talent," she said. "It's actually been a couple of years, now, since we've seen him. I mean, I'm sure he's fine. Always up to his . . . In fact, we heard he was trying to generate his own electricity. Out of old socks, you may be sure, or something."

For a moment her voice split into harmonics, exposing a chord of other voices, crowding the room. Then a blinding sheet of desert light fell, and against its silence the tiny, distant figure of Corrigan was walking, walking . . . Jean closed her eyes. "The last time we saw him, he was teaching it Mixtec, too."

"Pardon?" Mark said.

Jean shook her head.

"Those stars . . ." He stood and went to the French doors.

There was no haze at all, Jean saw, or softness in the air. The stars snapped brilliantly against flat black, as if this were to be their final appearance.

"Strange," he said. "That people would get it into their heads that those things determined what went on down here."

"That anything determined what went on down here," Jean said.

He stood, looking out at the night. "Who are the women in red?" he asked.

Jean stood in alarm. "The women—"

"No, sorry," he said. "Not—"

"Oh—" She flopped back down.

"Not here. I meant the women in the square who wear those long red—"

"Yes, yes—" She'd known just who he meant. But for an instant she'd thought he was *seeing* them; that they'd come up here for some reason. For her.

"No, sorry, just—I watched them all day. The way they glide. Up and down in the square. I couldn't imagine who—"

"Yes," she said. "Indians. I mean, obviously."

"They look— They don't look—"

"No, not exactly real. A Tzotzil group, but I don't . . . They're not really from this area; they seem to be . . . well, 'displaced' is how people . . . God, Leo did the most marvelous paintings of them in the square at one time. I wonder—"

"I'd love to see them." Mark squinted eagerly past the fuzzy goldish mass of light in the center of the room.

"Ah, well," Jean said. "There aren't any here, in any case."

All this talk of hers, this evening; all this noise. And now she seemed to have implied this boy should come back. For more talk, more noise. "Actually, I think Leo probably threw all that stuff out when he gave up painting."

Mark started to speak, then stopped.

Jean shrugged. "He didn't think he would ever be good enough," she said clearly.

After a minute Mark spoke. "That's very courageous."

"Is it?" Jean said. "Oh, listen. Courageous, cowardly, who knows. It actually wasn't very painful for Leo to give it up. He just stopped, the same way I just continued. People have different ways of holding on to things. Our friend Corrigan, for example. In a sense he's the most acquisitive person I've ever met. If he sees something that interests him, an unusual mask, for example, or one of those pieces like that little thing on the table, he'll go to any lengths to get ahold of it. But then he just gives it away again as soon as he possibly can. The fact is, it makes Leo happy to give things up. It's a kind of exercise, I suppose. He's never so happy as when he's giving something up, or leaving something behind." The phrase sounded flat to Jean, as she heard herself saying it now, or sententious. Was it true, she wondered— Had it been true at some point? Or was it just something rather like the truth that she and Leo had settled on?

Mark was watching her intently. "Tell me something," he said. "Do you ever think of going back?"

"Back," she said. "And what would that mean, 'back'?"

Every day, how many species was it that disappeared, now, forever? There was some horrifying statistic—it used to be four hundred a year, she had read somewhere; now it was hundreds every day. And cadres of botanists, zoologists, anthropologists, God only knew what, swarming over the globe with instruments of every sort, praying to catch sight of one rare, precious organism or another as it died. "Oh, of course it's very nice to think—very seductive—that you have some sort of 'home' somewhere, that you could return to, that would make some kind of sense of your life. And Leo and I have always prided ourselves, I suppose, on resisting that. Because, a *place*—I mean, what is that? A place. What you leave, what you go to; here or there, 'home' or 'foreign'— Well, it's all based on, on the most fantastic misunderstanding, isn't it."

But was that true, either? Chiapas, Cuilapan, Pátzcuaro, Tepotzlan, Ixtlán del Rio—ancient fragments irradiated by an ancient light. Yes, what she and Leo had left behind vanished with their departure, and what they'd wanted here had vanished, too. Vanished, not into the past, nor into some relinquished area of fantasy, but into the future. Into the future. Evidence of a continuity, of a fugitive precision would appear without notice—a swift concentration of the afternoon into heavy, golden shapes; a face like a key, glimpsed in the market; a perfect, trembling balance in the square as seen for an instant from a balcony . . . . promises.

The nights here still smelled like honey. Jean could still be made happy by the braying of a neighbor's burro. Back when Mexico City had faded and they'd come out here, the nights always smelled of honey and woodsmoke, the days of chocolate and earth and peppers—rich anchos and poblanos in sacks at the market. How clean everything had been! The revolution had left the campesinos as penniless as ever, as clean as bones. They'd worn white; the coarse-loomed cloth showed up in the fields miles away. Roosters woke you, cacti bloomed in the churchyards. Toxins from new industry and traffic seeped into the earth, corroded the organs of the children. One murderous poverty replaced another. Refugees appeared, Indians, fleeing internment and slaughter in Guatemala and the secret wars up here, out in the muffled desert. Corrigan used to bring word of skirmishes. From time to time rumors would flicker through town. Alicia, who cooked for them, might let something slip, or Ramón, who brought the great jars of water. Once in a while, someone was said to disappear—someone's cousin, someone's son . . . The Tzotzil women moved back and forth across the square, in constantly changing configurations of blood red against the white walkways. They approached as you sat by the fountains, under the elegant palms. They stretched out their arms. You could hardly hear their voices. They looked past you, at something that happened in the distance. The tourists, dazzled by the beauty of their clothing and unearthly, famished faces, dropped small sums into their hands. Who were the women in red, they asked.

One shrugged: They were widows.

Often now—whispers of special forces deployed in the desert. Sometimes one would hear faint, high tones in the night, like bullets striking rock— "Was that the phone?" Jean said.

"No," Mark said.

"Ah," Jean said.

"Yes." He stood. "It's late. I'll leave you." His soft voice floated next to her ear. "Thank you, Mrs. Soyer, you've been—"

"Jean," she said. "Hardly." She closed her eyes, and the room blazed again with desert light. Why hadn't she gone up this morning? So long ago, that bright sun. The Tzotzil women would be dozing now, wrapped in lengths of red. Schacht, having a final tequila while he gazed out at the dark square. And up there— The suffocating imminence of drugged sleep? Rapid footsteps down the corridor? Whatever was happening in that white bed, she would wake up here in the mornings, she would go to the shop. She would come home and eat the food Alicia had prepared, have a drink, look at the stars . . . It had seemed ridiculous, in all that sunlight, to think of going along. Ridiculous, and imprudent, as though panic itself were malignant. All yesterday he had done his little tasks around the house, around the yard. Even this morning— He'd looked up at her from his gardening, shading his eyes against the sun, with the trowel still wedged in the earth—

"So then." That soft voice. "Next week."

"Next week . . ." Jean repeated, but for moments she couldn't think what the boy was talking about.

ROSIE GETS A SOUL

Rosie dips her brush into the dark-green paint and makes a careful little curve with it on the wall. She does it again, and then she does it again. Jamie was right—a monkey could do this.

When the green dries, Jamie will show her how to add another color, and, when that dries, another. And pretty soon, at the rate Jamie is painting, there will be three lush tiers, high around the room, of curling vines and flowers. Fruit, or some such shit, is going to go up there, too.

Morgan, the ridiculously handsome decorator, is out in the living room, discussing this, *the concept*, with Jamie, no doubt driving him nuts. Not for one second could even the dimmest person alive mistake Jamie's attitude about the whole thing for enthusiasm. Poor Morgan.

The blue sky and water lie seamlessly just outside the window, across from Rosie's little scaffold. Sometimes Rosie takes a moment to rest her mind and her aching arm, and lets herself float out there until the whir of time going by in the room recalls her to her task. It's warm enough now so that a few little sails and wisps of cloud glide over the blue. When Rosie arrived in this city, it was winter, and the water and the sky looked like liquid metal.

This whole apartment is gleaming and slidey. You could

be inside a bubble, here—a dark pearl, hanging in the middle of the sky. Monday, Tuesday, Thursday, Friday: four mornings a week Lupe comes to clean and launder and put things in order. The floors have been bleached almost translucent, and stained, and a crew of other painters has done something to the walls to make them dark and glassy, so that Jamie's leaves look like they're twining right in the air. Every afternoon when Rosie and Jamie open the door on their way out, Rosie is shocked to see that they're in an ordinary apartment building, where other people live—just ordinary people.

Almost thirty years old, Rosie thinks, and this is where she finds herself—on someone's bedroom ceiling. Can it be true? But here's the corroborating smell of the paints and mineral spirits, the feel of the brush against the hard surface, and, even more surprisingly, that little mark on the wall afterward: Rosie did this . . .

The people have moved in, although Jamie and Rosie still have the bedroom to do. The important thing was to have finished the smallish room—office, study, whatever—where the man frequently works, on a sleek assemblage of technology which Rosie watched arrive. The woman works in an office nearby, evidently, when she's not traveling.

"Not to worry," Morgan said to Rosie and Jamie. "They won't get in your way." He meant, obviously, that Rosie and Jamie had to figure out how not to get in *their* way. If he'd been talking to her, Rosie thinks, that's pretty much how he would have put it. But, hey—he wasn't talking to her.

Of course they'll be pleased to see the last of Rosie and Jamie, these people. These people, obviously, like to keep things moving along. Already, pretty little objects have been placed out on tables and shelves, and a shining silk slip has been slung over a French screen in the bathroom—things like that. But framed pictures still lean against walls, and so do mirrors, which ambush Rosie with her own pale, fugitive presence.

Really, it would be just about impossible for anyone to get seriously in anyone else's way here. The place is too large; the thick padding of money soaks up disturbance. The other day Rosie felt something behind her, and when she twirled around, Lupe was right there, working.

So Rosie has seen the maid, but she's never seen the man or the woman who actually live in this place. Maybe they can't be seen by ordinary eyes, is what Jamie says; maybe they're just too special.

In the broad marshes between waking and sleep, where Rosie used to watch pictures fold and unfold like flowers, she is now plagued by visitors. Here's a woman carrying a parcel from the German butcher shop around the corner. Blood has soaked through the waxed wrapping, staining the string that ties it. She models herself for Rosie: print dress; lumpy, shifting contours; resentful smile fading after some encounter. Several pretty hookers, one black, the others maybe Polish, totter about in platform shoes, on beautiful, spindly legs, laughing together, ruined, it looks like, every which way. A man in a hurry—good-looking, preoccupied, pleased with himself, *spoiled*, Rosie thinks—pulls up the collar of his expensive raincoat against the stinging drizzle.

The visitors assemble around Rosie and draw closer. When she sits up irritably, they scatter to the corners of the room, then draw back, flaunting themselves and their lives—their lives which are so particular and binding, as heavy as crowns and gold chains and royal robes. The weight falls across Rosie's mouth and nose as she lies back down to sleep. She can hardly breathe.

People always say, you can't run away. It's one of those things Rosie's heard a million times: Whatever it is you're running from, people say, you're sure to bring it with you. But that's not her problem, Rosie thinks—not at all. Unless what she always had was nothing.

When she came to this city and left what—at least, in her opinion—was quite a lot, back at Ian's, there must have been something in her mind which made it possible for her to leave: she must have thought that while she (as it had suddenly come to appear) was taking time out the shuttle kept on moving back and forth; she must have thought that she could weave herself back into the web whenever she was ready; she must have thought it would be obvious what she was supposed to do next; she must have thought she'd just find herself doing whatever it was people did. Who knows what she was thinking? Whatever it was, she was wrong.

Once in a while she resorts to the notion that Ian is back there wishing her well, in whatever manner he can. She *draws strength* from that, she thinks. Oh, well; shit.

No doubt he'd been incensed to find her gone. Still, she left all her effects—the pretty suède pouch containing her syringe, her silver spoon, her rubber tubing, everything—right there on the pillow, so he'd see right away, and he'd know, more or less, just what she'd be going through. Better than leaving a note, Rosie thought—she just didn't know what more to say.

From time to time she regrets not having told Ian she was leaving. But what was the point? She was leaving. And Ian would have said no, stay, he'd help her to stop; hadn't he always told her to stop? Just what she needed, Rosie thinks—Ian in charge of her free will.

It's not Ian's way to lie, but Rosie has to wonder what he really wanted from her. All that talk about his clients—their weakness, their needs, the things they pretended to themselves. But the whole point, Rosie thinks, is that, high, she was as strong as wire, she needed nothing, and she never had to pretend a thing. All that talk about Rosie abusing her body (with not a word, of course, about what her body was doing to her!), but how did Ian think he'd met her, if not selling her and Cathy what they'd started snorting during lunch hour, years ago? The truth is, Ian could afford to say anything at all that made him feel righteous: it seemed he could count on her not to stop.

Another one of those things that Rosie's heard for years and years is people asking other people, *Why did you start taking drugs?* You turn on the *tele*vision and you hear that. But this is not a real question; it's just a sticky, juicy treat. Pornography. The shining faces, the eager and self-congratulatory answers—everyone feels great, everyone's rubbing it in their hair. My mother, my father, whatever—not real answers, but the question's not a real question. *Why did you start taking drugs?* Not a real question. Here, the real question: *Why didn't you, dear?* No. The real question: *Why did you stop?*

Not long before Rosie left, Ian took her on a call to some clients. There was an architect, and a man who owned a restaurant that the architect had designed, and their wives. It was an occasion, a birthday party, of sorts. Ian, as usual, wore his English hat with his initials stamped in gold on the inside band, and he carried his good briefcase. Very impressive, no doubt, to the hopheads stumbling around River Street, but the architect and the restaurateur were wearing suits obviously woven of fibers plucked for them personally from some rare beast. One of the wives wore a suit as well, a tiny little black thing, and the other wife wore a tiny little black dress. The house, which the architect had designed, was glaringly white. Almost the only color in it, aside from the soft green of Rosie's longish, graceful dress, was a huge crystal vase of roses, dark, dark red, like a blackening heart.

Ian had been called in to supply the birthday present—for the architect, as Rosie remembers, though all four of those people were pretty jacked up, controlled and furtively absent, like kids who have planned to sneak out and have sex.

The whole thing is even worse to remember than it was when it was happening. Ian and his *database*; earlier that evening he'd called the architect and the restaurateur up on the screen to make Rosie look. Lists of accomplishments vibrated in the synthetic blue depths. "Prominent people," Ian had said.

The lowered eyes, the swinishly clean whiteness, the hair like sculpture—Rosie practically gags, thinking of it. Never has she heard the words "my wife" used so often in so short a time. At moments the two couples had behaved as though Ian and Rosie weren't there; at other moments they were terribly, terribly polite—as if Ian and Rosie were the stableboys, called away from rolling in manure to come into the house for, say, a Christmas eggnog. What a waste of good drugs.

Ian had hustled Rosie along. They were just going to drop by on this thing, he'd said; they'd be home in good time, he meant, before she got uncomfortable. But then he was talking and talking. He knew about everything, of course. He knew about the new restaurant and other buildings the architect had designed, the wine they were all drinking, the variety of rose in the big crystal vase. Naturally he knew about the house—building techniques, materials . . . pretty much whatever could be known.

Rosie could perfectly well have excused herself and emerged decorously from the bathroom in mere minutes, in a much more accommodating frame of mind—she'd tucked her pouch prudently in her purse—but Ian would have gone absolutely nuts.

The little thorns of his voice caught and caught at her. She made herself get up, cross the room, and examine the bookshelves. In all those shelves there were about ten books—the tall kind, with pictures. She opened one: photograph after photograph showed a nude girl strapped down, with medical equipment inserted into her. Rosie closed her eyes, as if to bring the ocean, and a whooshing sound came up around her. Cars, obviously, going and going outside on the highway. When she turned around again, Ian was nowhere to be seen.

She found him standing in the long sweep of the kitchen. His briefcase was open and his scales were out on the table. The wife in the suit was there, too, counting out money, slowly and carefully, her head tilted down as she watched the bills leave her hands. Her thick lashes were very dark against her skin, and her smooth hair was pouring slowly forward. Ian leaned against the refrigerator, not touching the money, of course, or even looking at it. "I have to get back," Rosie said. Ian glanced at her, and his glance held. "Right," he said. "With you in a sec."

The others seemed not to have moved while Rosie was out of the room. The air was fantastically still. "It's going to storm," she said, but none of the others responded. Perhaps she hadn't actually spoken.

"Where's Ashley?" one of the men said.

"Out in the kitchen," the other man said. "With the

Connoisseur. Your competition." And they made that little pause that stands for a laugh.

On the way home, Ian was calm, and happy, telling Rosie about a building in Seattle that the architect had designed. Yes, Rosie kept saying; that's great, yes. It was like listening to the happy stories of a child who doesn't yet know his home has been destroyed in a fire.

How could he have been such an idiot? And those people! How pleased they were with themselves—with all their things, with all their accomplishments. *My wife, my wife . . .* So pleased to have used their time so well. Those people had treated their lives so well, tending them and worshipping them and *using* them (however moronically), and she had just tossed hers into the freezer, like some old chunk of something you didn't exactly know what to do with. But why should her life be more despised than theirs?

Yeah, you've got to *play your cards right* with time, Rosie thinks. It's not merely the thing that kills you; evidently it's also the thing that keeps you alive. You can inoculate yourself against it, you can rid yourself of it, but then where are you? Not dead, true, but not alive, either; you've got rid of the thing inside you that pulls you along toward the end of the line, but don't you want to go anywhere? Because if you want to go somewhere, the end of the line is the only available destination.

The trees by the side of the road had begun to rustle anxiously, and a peal of thunder tore open the sky, exposing a jagged edge of lightning. When the sky went black again, it was as if a fissure in the earth had been revealed.

On one side of the chasm was the house with the architect and the restaurateur and their wives, and Rosie's school friends, and the others in her office, and stadiums full of

people, and the students traveling in packs through Europe—
all the people in the world, in fact, studying and working and
playing sports and having colds and running errands and doing whatever it is humans do. And on the other was Rosie,
sitting in her little bathroom, cleaning her syringe. All those
people rushing around, but they can't touch Rosie. Their
awful thoughts and desires, their disdain, their demands—
nothing coming from them can stain or damage Rosie; she
never changes, never gets older, just dries out into nothing as
she cleans her syringe in a glass of pure spring water.

Poor Ian—how could he ever have expected to protect
her when he couldn't begin to protect even himself? In just
one instant that evening Rosie had been shown both of them
with perfect clarity.

"Look at that," he said, as water poured from the sky.
"Just what we need."

If he'd actually cared about her he wouldn't have taken
her along to meet those people. At least, not in the condition
she happened to be in. Because by the time you see there's a
decision to be made, you can be pretty sure it's a decision you
already have made.

Rosie thinks so often these days of people, children, who
have had to leave the country where they live. What it must
be, that last morning, pressing every detail into your brain to
preserve it on your long journey—the journey that's going to
last for the rest of your life. The color of the light that day, or
the feel of the air, a certain little shrub in the park you always
pass on your way home from school, the tender little waves
that reach out for the boat as you embark—all those precious
things which once breathed and lived in your casual attention,

no better than powdery old petals pressed in a book: you've left your country for good.

That last night, proceeding through her bedtime ritual as always, she thought at every step: *This.* And *this.* Her cup of good cappuccino sat in front of her, and the rubbing alcohol, and the glass of Evian water. Her hairbrush was waiting, and the clean, clean sheets.

Opening the white-paper bindle; pouring, more carefully than ever, the contents into her silver spoon; drawing the water all the way up into the syringe and discharging it gently over the pure white powder. The match bursting into flame, the softly boiling solution, the needle pointing heavenward to coax the air bubble up and out, the bubble moving higher, higher . . . the precious liquid glittering for a moment at the tip. The rubber around her arm, good and tight, the pumped vein rising, the seeking needle, the stunning penetration, the drop of hungry blood, released to commune in a faint whorl with the contents of the barrel and plunge back into her body, step by teasing step: the first floating radiance with its delicious burn, the second, and, finally, the third, lighting up the splendid corridors.

After swabbing the site of the injection and sluicing the pure water through the syringe, she put the cap on the bright point for good. She brushed her hair over and over, watching her reflection, went into the bedroom, and lay down to sleep, as if on a bier.

In the morning, Ian gave her a little kiss, checked his E-mail, and went out on rounds.

Rosie had planned well; she'd contacted Jamie, checked schedules, looked at maps, and so on, but it came on quickly, the outrage of her body. It was as if she'd swallowed in her sleep a sleeping bird that awoke, then panicked, and by the middle of the day all those plans of hers were rearing up in shivering columns, swaying and crashing back down. Could her hands actually have been shaking the way she saw them shake? And what on earth was happening with her legs!

How did she get out that afternoon? Practically crawling, through the air's hammer blows and sirens, her vision all fretted and dazzled, falling away in glaring planes, past the razor-sharp, poison-colored blades of grass growing by the house . . .

How far was her foot from the step, the step from the ground? How big was the doorknob? She'd had to jam her things into the duffel with her fist. In the cab to the station, for all she knows she was screaming.

She was a reverse pioneer. The train brought her in from the western edge, steaming east toward the plains. The settled territories flickered by the window like film, into oblivion, as the vacuum of Rosie's brain stripped off the names of the towns, and then the towns themselves.

She stopped for some days, as she'd planned, to let the worst of it come up and drain away before she presented herself to Jamie. Not much she remembers about *that*: a room up some stairs, stumbling down to get Cokes, or once in a while, when the nausea gave over a bit, a sandwich; cold sweats in sheets that absorbed nothing and slid around on the mattress.

The configuration of wrinkles on the sheet, the untied shoelace of the waiter downstairs in the coffee shop, the little stain on the plastic lid of her Coke, the sickle of dust on the bureau, echoing the curve of the ice bucket—details hung at the forefront of her attention, like inadequately assimilated commands. In the halls, the Asian maids congregated by their filthy canvas bins full of used linens, talking for hour after hour in a cool, rippling language that blended with the noise of machines working on the pavement outside and of the televisions in the nearby rooms. Sometimes it seemed to Rosie that she could almost understand, that if she could only assemble the elements of her brain properly . . . and then sometimes a slippery phosphorescence would irradiate the sounds, and she did understand: they were whispering stories, complicated, tiresome, and interminable, about talking animals, underground kingdoms . . .

One morning, she woke up to silence. The thrashing wings inside her had drawn back, folding into a painful little lump in the region of her lungs. She stood looking at the long mirror in the thin sunshine that came through the window. Well, well; so this is what the person who had risen from the bed looked like—skim-milk pale, much younger than she really is. The drug-becalmed marble glow of her skin has moderated into a petal-like softness, as if she'd just been born. Her body is thin, unmuscular, childish—unmarked except for the raised, red dots on her arm.

How had she ever had the nerve to call Jamie, she wonders. She wouldn't have it now. Fortunately, though, at the time she'd been desperate; fortunately, she hadn't been thinking clearly. And who else could she have called, anyway—Mona McCauley? With her house and her husband and her dog and her child? Lexi Feld?

Jamie was two years older, and he had been kind, all through school. It had been obvious that he'd be going on to college and obvious that Rosie wouldn't; God knows, her mother had never had that kind of money, and, assuming her father did, it would go, presumably, to his younger children, wherever. So there'd always been plenty of differences between her and Jamie, but there are differences which when you're young, she thinks, run all up and down your life that you still assume are just incidental.

After school, Jamie had gone on to college, and then to art school, and by then Rosie had pretty much lost track of him. Bits of news came back, through one person or another. Jamie was still painting. But not (people were quick to point out) making any money at it. And there was Vincent. Who moved in, and, fairly recently, had moved out.

With every phone call Rosie had made to trace Jamie, it became more of a certainty that she really was going to leave. But leaving was one thing, she realized when the taxi let her out at a real house, and she rang the real bell of Jamie's apartment, and she walked up the two flights of real steps, and arriving was another.

Of course you could forget about your past, but then—how funny—there's someone on your doorstep ten years later: *Hey, didn't you drop something?* She and Jamie looked at each other as if they were studying a map, an aerial map of all the years that the mirror Rosie had studied earlier was not able to see.

In the morning, Rosie awoke in a dark-blue room. She was in Jamie's apartment. Yes, and the room, obviously, must have been Vincent's. There was nothing in it except a bed, a light, and a painting. A door opened into a small closet with a few shelves and a place to hang some clothes. Rosie has since noted that the painting is the only one in the apartment. It's by Jamie; this she knows from the signature. Most likely, it was a gift to Vincent.

Rosie paused in the kitchen doorway. Jamie was sitting at the table, beyond a pillar of dusty light, drinking coffee, and just staring out. He was wearing a heavy kimono—faded red silk, covered with designs of clouds and birds.

Impossible: Her ten-years-later self, in underpants and a tank top, standing at the door of a place that's Jamie's kitchen. But maybe that's what life is always like. All the time, for everyone. Maybe any moment you could say, this is normal; it's just what's happening. And you could equally well say, this is the strangest thing that ever could be. Probably so— it'll just depend on where you start the story.

She stood for a moment, shivering, feeling her body taking up space, pushing the air around in ways that were unfamiliar to the room, sending off its tiny, continuous demands. Jamie's face had changed so much, really; by more than just time. Well, but what would that be—*just time*? "Morning," she said.

Jamie glanced up. "Morning," he said. He indicated her arm. "Very chic." Then he wandered out and returned with another kimono—also heavy old silk, but blue, with designs of waves and flowering trees. "Here. Say yes to shame."

He sat again, folded his arms, and rested his head on the table. It looked as though he were exhausted, too, although, throughout the long night, Rosie had pictured him luxuriously asleep in the next room—his silky hair, his comfortable, appealing body, which her body had had sex with a few times back in high school, before Mr. Tomlinson showed up and settled the matter for Jamie once and for all.

Jamie opened his eyes and considered Rosie in the kimono. "O.K.," he said, and sighed. "Well, that's all right."

He took her through the frozen city. The neighborhood, with its Polish, Greek, and Hungarian bakeries, the hardware store, the German butcher shop, the fish market, the bank, the stationery store. Then farther afield to bars with sad pianos, and coffee shops that stayed open all night, to a bookstore with its webs of old light, to several little neon-festooned night clubs in a jaunty row, and to the downtown, where he and Rosie are working now, with its gentlemanly old office buildings and shining towers. What has all this to do with her? Once, glimpsing a cluster of blue needle caps discarded in a gutter, she is blinded for a moment; she might as well have glimpsed a company of angels departing the earth forever. Yes, this was where she lived; this barren, icy planet was where she lived now.

She was still feeling far from recovered—though who was to say what "recovered" felt like? Her legs were still subject to involuntary actions; her body rebelled against its new unprivileged condition with small colds, infections, and rashes. Going to the corner for ice cream, washing a dish or two— for the first weeks anything might take her most of the day. She'd get lost no farther than a block from the apartment. Things slipped from her grasp, as if her hands had been confiscated and exchanged for paws. No amount of clothing was adequate to keep her warm or to locate her in space. She spent most of her time in Vincent's room, in bed, wearing Vincent's kimono. It was fantastically difficult to bathe; the prospect of water next to her skin brought her nerves right up to the surface, and Jamie's best towel could have been sandpaper. Her hair became stiff with grime. By way of encouragement, Jamie bought her a little rubber duck. She saw its sunny shadings and its calm, blue eyes, and she rocked unsteadily on her feet. "Jamie—?" she said.

"Drug-crazed twisto," he said, and put an arm around her.

They went on the little train, winding quietly among lines of laundry and fire stairs. They stared into back windows at people staring out at them just as they stare out from

Jamie's kitchen window at the people going by on the train.
Rosie leaned back and closed her eyes. A voice near her said
to someone, "This is my stop."

"How does he know?" Rosie said.

"Well, I guess it's on his card," Jamie said.

Rosie opened her eyes.

"His card, the little card they give you that tells you what
your stop is." Jamie looked at her. "Oh, didn't you get one?"

The train is audible from Vincent's room, but the tracks
run by the back of the apartment, just outside the window of
the kitchen. The people on the train stare into the window as
they go by, and Rosie and Jamie stare back. *Who are they? Who
are they?*

Beyond the tracks are the backs of other houses, hung
with a dirty lace of fire stairs. From Vincent's window and
from Jamie's what you see are the fronts of the houses—turrets
and complicated shingles—all dilapidated, with the oily gold
light spreading out at night in the windows, and the grape-
colored shadows.

Nights, Rosie fades in and out, echoing with footsteps
and whispers, traces of invisible inhabitants. She lies awake in
Vincent's room with its peeling, dark-blue paint, and the city
breaks up into pieces, like a puzzle. All the various neighborhoods that Jamie showed her, the little train, the narrow
tracks with street lights drooping over them tenderly, like dying flowers, this tiny, dark-blue room, the downtown—that
shining wedge that pushes up from flatness and drops off in a
sheer glass-and-steel cliff by the water. It floats through the
darkness now in a bright sphere. The windows are cold and
starry; green tendrils wind around the bed.

The pieces of the city stream off into the darkness, and
even in her sleep, the watery, transparent kind of sleep she has

these days, Rosie listens for the little train to start up in the morning, swinging through the city, fitting the pieces back together.

There are some things, Rosie thinks, that she ought to have dealt with long before she did. To be fair, of course, she's had her hands full just standing upright. Just trying to work up some traction. Just dealing with the fact of herself, which pops up in front of her every day when she awakes, like some doltish puppet. So certain other worrisome items have just slid right off the agenda.

Jamie didn't make a living from his paintings, it true. He did other kinds of painting, Rosie learned, to make money. From time to time he'd spend a few days or a week on the job, getting up early in the morning and going off to work in some rich person's home. But when he wasn't making paintings in his studio, Rosie noticed, Jamie became very . . . distant. *Estranged* . . . How long would it be before he got sick of her and tossed her out? It was a miracle he'd taken her in in the first place.

What on earth was she going to do when he didn't feel like taking care of her any longer? She hadn't meant to just throw herself in a heap on his floor. On the other hand, she hadn't meant not to; she hadn't meant anything at all—she was just scrambling. And now she was going to have to get some money together, herself. And fast, too—she'd almost gone through her savings.

Maybe the best thing about drugs, Rosie thinks now (or, on the other hand, maybe it's the worst), is the way they unhook you from that stupid step-by-step business—first one moment, then the next, then the one after that. No skipping, no detours, no time off. Which is what she's had to live through for all these long, recent months, and what she'll have to live through, now, every day until she dies. No wonder she hadn't particularly minded working in an office before. Beginning of day, end of day; pure-white time in between. The hands of the clock might sleep or twirl—that was discretionary.

But the laws of human time must have registered on some template lying around in Rosie's brain, because, facing the prospect of going back, Rosie remembers herself as a miner, hacking her way through the stony mass, instant after intolerably boring instant.

And if only boringness were the whole problem! Again, Rosie's memory offers up things Rosie didn't even notice at the time: the sadness of herself, the sadness of all the others—the secretaries and clerks, working away like mice in their little cubicles, at their endless, miniature tasks, their careful clothes and clean hands, *Good morning, good morning, how was your weekend?* And Mr. Gage and Mr. Peralta in their horrible suits and ties, appearing at the doorways of their offices with sheaves of paper, the light from their windows flashing into the fluorescent light over Rosie's desk.

How polite everyone was, and how cheery! Their cheerfulness lay like boulders over geysers of misery. *Have a nice night. See you tomorrow.* By five in the evening you were abrim with filth.

Rosie asked Jamie: Did he know of any jobs? Any people who worked in an office?

"Are you out of your mind?" he said.

Fine, she thought; that was her opinion of the whole thing, too, obviously.

"You don't want to do that," he said. "You'd hate it."

"Really," Rosie said.

"Why are you pissed off at me?" he said.

"I'm not," she said. "Pissed off at anyone."

"Well, good, then. Hey, where are you going? Aren't you going to say good night, at least?"

"Good night," Rosie said. "So you think I should be a doctor, right? You think I should be a famous artist."

Jamie looked at her. "Wow, Rosie . . ."

Rosie put her hands over her ears. "Look, Jamie. Could we just not talk about this, please?"

The next day she apologized, of course.

"Hey, I was thinking last night," Jamie said. "Now please don't get pissed off again. But maybe you could be my assistant."

The room dimmed. "I know you're trying to help me," Rosie said laboriously, as if she were picking her way through the words in the dark. She was silting up, her blood was draining out. She should have stayed back there, she thought, where the spears just bounced right off. "I appreciate everything you've done to help me. But listen, Jamie . . ." She put her head in her hands.

". . . 'Listen, Jamie'?"

"Well, I *can't*. Obviously."

"Can't what? Let's see. Can you . . ." He plucked a paintbrush from a jar sitting beneath the kitchen table, and prodded her with the handle. "Perfect," he said, as her hand closed around it to push it away. "Great reflexes."

"Oh, Jesus," she said. "Should I show you how I draw a house? I never even learned to finger paint."

"Rosie, we are not talking Sistine Chapel, here. Do you know what these jobs are about? The whole thing is ridiculous.

A lot of these people like to think that there are only a few special people—really *gifted* people—who can do this shit. They get So-and-So, you know? Or So-and-So. *Artists.* But anyone could do it, a monkey could do it. Plus, do you know what kind of stuff they want? Once, I was flown to the Cayman Islands to paint an extra inch of rug on some guy's floor. Once, I had to marbleize all of some lady's toilet-paper holders."

"You think anyone can do it because you can do it," Rosie said.

"Wrong," Jamie said. "I think anyone can do it because anyone can do it. Especially the easy parts, which I'm going to show you, foolproofily, how to do. Look, how do you think people get to be able to do a thing? First they pretend they can do it, and then they do it, and then they can do it."

Rosie stared; he wiggled the brush. "The main thing you've got to learn is to stay out of the medicine cabinet. Hey, lighten up—that was a joke."

The first job was an hour's drive distant, and there were four of them—Jamie and Rosie and Marina and Jean-Michel, squashed into Marina's red pickup truck. Marina and Jean-Michel looked at Rosie. What had Jamie said to them? "Great," Marina said. "A new face. Someone to bore with our war stories."

The sun was round and yellow. The city melted away. Lawns and trees and driveways flowed by. Massive houses sat behind hedges. The houses looked like pictures from travel posters: Spanish, Rosie thought; Japanese; English, maybe from some other century. "Where are we?" she said.

"We're dead now," Marina said dreamily. "This is the

land of the dead. Unfortunately, this civilization wasn't worth preserving, so all these people fell into their pools and died. Isn't that sad?"

"Darling—" Jean-Michel sighed. "It's not for us to judge these people. Scum though they be, it's just not our job to judge them."

"No?" Marina looked at him with enormous gray eyes. "So, what is our job?"

"Our job," Jean-Michel said. "Our job . . . Right. Well, our job is to make a mockery of our God-given talents."

"Oh, yeah . . ." Marina said. "Right . . ."

Rosie sighed; she was never going to be able to do this stuff . . .

The red truck rattled and screeched into a driveway; the house at the end of it looked shocked into its whiteness. With noisy rapidity, Jamie and Marina and Jean-Michel unloaded pails and jars and stained rags and cloths, wooden sticks and cans and huge, old sponges, heaping it all up in the driveway like booty. Rosie blinked. "Trash," Jamie said into her ear. She looked at him. "Trash," he said again, as if he were patiently teaching a parrot.

The lady of the house came out and greeted them nervously; her glance snagged on Jean-Michel, as if she'd been briefly hypnotized by his elaborate mass of little braids. She probably didn't see too many black people out here, Rosie thought, who weren't in uniforms. "I'm so glad you could come," the lady said confusedly. Jean-Michel inclined his head, disengaging her stare with kingly ease.

Upstairs, the four inspected a room where they were to paint a border of stenciled sheep, and a blue ceiling with white clouds, and then another room, where they were to make a border of stenciled flowers.

"For this she needed *us*?" Marina said.

Jamie shrugged. "It's only our prices that can justify the misery of her husband's existence."

A carton stood in the corner of the room, containing a whole little life—a jumble of soft toys and dolls, and a small, fuzzy blanket. "Hey, wow—" Rosie said, and the three others wheeled around.

"I was just *looking*," she said.

"No, I know," Jamie said, as Marina and Jean-Michel returned to setting out their tools. "Just, it's . . ."

"Fine," Rosie said. "So I won't look."

Jamie gave her a stencil and a round brush, and showed her how to hold them both and to pat the paint onto the wall instead of stroking it on.

It was hard. You had to hold the brush just right and the stencil just right or you'd smear or drip. Rosie's heart pounded in her ears as she lifted the stencil from the wall. "Right," Jamie said. "Perfect."

Did children really like these little sheep? Or was it just the sort of thing adults insisted they like. Would Rosie have liked sheep on her wall when she was little? Sheep: She doubted they would have applied. She doubted these petrified-looking creatures would have improved her dreams any. She liked them now, though, poor things. Now it was easy enough to imagine them jumping over their fences, on their way off to slaughter . . .

Painted sheep, stuffed animals, ribbons, sweet little-girly things—it reminded Rosie of sitting in the pretty bathroom back at Ian's with her cappuccino and her bottle of rubbing alcohol and her needle and her hairbrush. "You're doing good," Jean-Michel said, and she jumped.

"Thanks," she said, flushing with rage and shame. Yeah, thanks. She knew perfectly well she was a charity case.

The others laughed and joked—they didn't even have to concentrate, though it was all Rosie could do to remember what, out of all the rags and brushes and stencils and containers she had to juggle, she was holding in what hand. "Oh, no!" she said; she'd blurred an edge. "No problem," Marina said, quickly dipping a rag into some thinner and dabbing it expertly against the wall. "See? All better now." Without looking at Rosie she returned to her own section of wall.

But, after the third time Rosie smeared, Marina sighed loudly. "Sorry, but stencils are not the easiest way to start," Marina said. She looked at Jamie. "You've got to be really, really careful with them."

"We've got too many people doing this anyhow," Jamie said. "What we really need are some clean brushes."

He showed Rosie how to clean the brushes and lay them neatly out on a rag to dry. Fuck you, she thought; fuck you, fuck you. But the fact was it wasn't all that easy to clean the brushes, either. You had to swish them around in a little jar of thinner, Jamie explained, and just keep changing to new thinner until it stayed clear. Changing it over and over, and over and over and over. And obviously, Rosie thought, the thinner was never going to stay clear.

Marina was applying two bands of blue tape to the wall, in order to paint a thin pink stripe between them; the space between the bands didn't vary by an iota, as far as Rosie could see. Marina and Jamie and Jean-Michel were working away, bending and reaching, with unhurried, engaged precision as the toxic incense of the paint rose up and swirled around them. Their hair was bound up in brilliant scarves, and their clothing and the exposed parts of their bodies were smeared with glistening colors.

There were times Rosie missed her needle so much she could have burst into tears. She'd done just that, in fact—over coffee at some counter, in line at the bank where she went to open a tiny checking account, and once simply walking down the street she'd sobbed loudly, as if she'd been flung at the wall of a prison.

For a few moments the tears would dissolve the distance between herself and her bartered immortality. When the tears were gone, the distance was back, as solid as before. But each time it happened, she felt a bit better—she'd had a little visit.

"How's it going?" Marina said brightly, not waiting for an answer. All friendly solicitude now that the walls were out of harm's way.

Rosie wandered into the bathroom they'd been instructed to use. Oily stains were ingrained all up her arms—phantom badges she had no right to wear. Her skin was already sore and stinging from the turpentine she'd rubbed on it, but she worked at the stains with soap, and then shook her hands to dry them. Were they allowed to use the towels? The lady hadn't said; best not to. Rosie checked the mirror again, and smiled at it falsely. There. All better now.

Stay out of the medicine cabinet. Some joke. Well, what did people like this keep in those things? Jamie had aspirin, and that was about it. These people were more serious, of course. Serious people: Rogaine, Aldomet, Propanolol, Zovorax, Imodium, and oh—there. Fiorinal. Marina with that blue tape! The patience of a robot.

The bottle of Fiorinal was in Rosie's hand, she noticed. She looked at it, and replaced it in the cabinet. She stared into the mirror, then smiled falsely at it once again. Ha—a person. But what a disappointment that *she* was the person she'd turned out to be. She reached for the bottle, opened it, and shook about half its contents out into a Kleenex.

She found Jamie and the other two in the second room they were to paint. The lady of the house was with them. "Well," the lady said. "Now I want *her* opinion." She turned to Rosie. "He's almost got me convinced. And these people"—she indicated Jean-Michel and Marina—"agree with him." Jean-Michel, Marina, and Jamie stood by, splendid, like rabble in their raggy work clothes, their eyes gleaming and their faces streaked. "You've seen the samples, I'm sure. Let's hear what you think."

What samples? Rosie glanced at Jamie.

"You can be perfectly honest with Mrs. Howell, Rosie," Jamie said.

"I can't do any worse than I'm doing now," the lady said.

Rosie gasped, as though she'd been slapped. *Oh, no?*

"Well, Mrs. Howell," Rosie said slowly, "It's your house, after all, and no matter what *we* think it's you who—"

"I see," Mrs. Howell said. "So. Four against one."

Over Mrs. Howell's shoulder, the others smiled.

Rosie learned a lot there, she thinks. Well, at least she learned something. And though this place downtown is only her second job, she can clean the brushes without wrecking them or going insane, she can stir the paints and put them out and straighten up at the end of the day without making a mess, she can maneuver her scaffold around with a modicum of authority, she always remembers to lock the wheels on Jamie's so he won't go flying through the window, she can navigate the treacherous shoals of someone else's rooms without dripping, spilling, or breaking a thing, she can manage (once in a while) the huge, necessary array of implements and liquids simultaneously, she's learned to become invisible at will, and, best of all, she can actually do a bit of the painting, even though this job's so much fancier and more complicated than the one in Mrs. Howell's house.

It's beautiful, what Jamie's done, in Rosie's opinion—no matter what Jamie has to say about it himself. And it's all but finished. Even the garlands near the bedroom ceiling are all but finished now.

It was Jamie who painted the forms of the leaves and flowers and fruit, of course, and it was Jamie, of course, who drew them all on the wall in the first place. And Jamie did the complicated shadings and details. But Rosie actually painted a lot of the veining on the leaves and most of the stems, and today Jamie's going to show her how to make highlights. Without Marina and Jean-Michel around to make her feel terrible, Rosie can manage reasonably well.

A couple of days later Jamie asks Rosie to work the whole following week all alone. "There's really nothing left for me to do, now that you're so expert with the highlighting."

"But I can't," Rosie says. "I can't do it if you're not there. How am I supposed to know what to do?"

"I'll draw you a map," Jamie says. "Look. You know how to do the grapes, right? You know how to do the plums, you know how to do the pears . . . It's just a question of where."

"But that won't take much more than a day or two anyhow," Rosie says.

"And there are a few other things that have to be done," Jamie says. "Look, Rosie, there's some stuff of my own I really want to work on, and I'm going to go truly nuts if I don't get to it right away. And you know what'll happen if we both disappear. I mean, they'll absolutely send in the Marines."

"But—" Rosie says.

"You can," Jamie says. "I've seen you work. Rosie, you can do everything that's going to be required this week. You can do the highlights, you can stand around on the scaffold looking fabulous, and I know you'll treat all their tastefully priceless shit with the . . . the reverence it . . . Have I ever asked you for anything else? *Anything?* Please. I'm under a lot of time pressure. And besides. Well, look. Actually, also, I've met someone."

Rosie stares, trying to let all the meanings of the words come to her, through a closing gate of panic. "Oh," she says. "Well. So, I mean, do you need Vincent's room back?"

Jamie stretches, and yawns. "Hey," he says in rebuke. "Besides. I doubt this thing with Trevor is going to work out."

By Monday afternoon she's already finished the highlights, and, as instructed by Jamie, she's working with the blue tape, making a thin gold line around the cornice.

According to Jamie, this bit is the easiest of all. Just a thin gold line! It hardly even requires a monkey—a one-celled organism with an opposable thumb would do. Right. Of course, it's all but impossible to get the tape on straight, to keep the interval between the strips even, to restrain yourself from diving down onto the bed to relieve your aching back and arm, to work the tape off at the necessary glacial speed rather than yanking down the whole damn wall . . . A thin gold line. The horizonless depth. Tiny little boats, bobbing . . . Rosie is gazing out the window when the door opens and a woman strides in. "Sorry," the woman says. "Have to get some things. Hope I won't be in your way."

How very tactful, Rosie thinks. But she stays put: do they want her to work or not?

What you can do if something belongs to you! The way

you can behave! Rosie always slips into this room, taking care not to disrupt the serenity so carefully tended by Lupe, but this woman just plunges right through it, as though she'd arrived by diving board. Now she's tossed a suitcase right down on the bedcover—that fragile bedcover. But why not? The suitcase itself is clearly leather, probably as fine-grained as silk.

The woman goes back and forth between the suitcase and the closet. This is the first time Rosie has seen the closets open. The hangers are the puffy, satiny kind, and the suits and blouses on them are delicious colors: colors that could be worn only by someone who expects people to be glad to see her—coral, pale yellow, the most shamelessly pretty blues. There are plenty of built-in drawers in the closet, too, which must have taken someone a lot of time to make, and racks and racks for shoes.

The woman pauses to consider. Her eyes come to rest on a tiny lacquer box sitting on the table. She scrutinizes it for a moment, then reaches out and repositions it, almost imperceptibly.

As if Rosie would have gone near the thing! The woman's cream silk blouse is escaping from her skirt. She tucks it back in, and Rosie can't help noticing the little bulge of flesh over the waistband. She did not ask to be up here watching this!

Flop! Into the suitcase with a dark-blue suit. Now a yellow one. Rosie is surprised by something, she notices; what is it? Ah—it's the woman's appearance. Well, she does have good legs, this woman, that's for sure; anybody might be jealous. Anybody at all. And her hair—thick, glossy, dark gold, like something with a lot of calories. People must just plunge their hands in and grab fistfuls.

But she isn't actually beautiful. And, Rosie judges, she probably never really was. She must be around forty, and she looks like she's been used to getting her way every minute of those years. Well, of course. And maybe people say she's beautiful without actually looking. But if she were just a few pounds heavier, Rosie thinks, everyone would see how it worked: sheer brute force. No one would mistake it for charm or ability or intelligence, let alone beauty.

The woman rolls the two suits up into plastic bags—no question she knows what she's doing. She jostles everything about in the suitcase, roughly and expertly, snaps the bright clasps closed, and clicks on a little lock. She pulls her suit jacket from the closet and puts it on. Goodbye, little bulge! "Harris—" she calls. She stops to listen and then sighs with exasperation, as though she were an actress in a play. "Harris?" And Rosie's the audience. The woman picks up the suitcase and hurries out of the room.

Well, she's gone.

But the sliding door of the closet is still open. It looks as if someone had slashed the wall, and its insides are all exposed, spilling out of the cavity. A scent, too sweet for Rosie, swells out from it, as if it were warm.

The room vibrates with silence, as though the woman had slammed the door on her way out. There are a few slight dents in the bedcover, and on it is something green—a cool green. Rosie wipes her hands with a thinner-drenched rag and climbs down from the scaffold, her legs shaking a little, to look.

It's a pair of gloves—palms up, wrists tilted away from one another, fingers of one adjacent to the fingers of the other, all slightly curled, as though the body they belonged to were responding to someone's touch.

Rosie stands, looking; she glances at her own hand: clean, to all appearances. She extends it and picks up one of the gloves, holding it gingerly between her thumb and index finger. It's amazingly pliant and soft—slightly adhesive.

And so small! Is it possible that this woman's hand is smaller than Rosie's? *Ladies . . .* used to use talc to get those things on: Rosie observes this fact her memory offers up as if it were a strange object for which she's just discovered a fascinating use. How tight those gloves must have been—slick smooth, no bones, no veins . . .

The door opens; a man is standing in front of Rosie. Saying something; saying, *Sorry*. Loops of silvery black curls; expensive raincoat folded over one arm. "Sorry, my wife says she forgot her gloves." The glove is dangling from Rosie's hand. He sees it. He's looking at it. What if he tells Jamie? What if he tells *Morgan*? "I was just—" Rosie begins, and her throat shuts down.

"Ah," the man says. "Kind of you, but you wouldn't have found us in any case. That parking lot's the size of France."

Without moving from the spot, he extends his hand. His eyes are almost black. Watching him, Rosie reaches the second glove from the bed and then steps forward to drop both into his outstretched palm.

"Thanks." His hand closes around the gloves, and he smiles. "Thanks very much."

On Tuesday the room seems different. To the eye, it's as usual: Lupe has been here, the closet door is closed, the bed is traceless. But something is altered.

Rosie reruns the scene that took place right here the day before, trying to slow it down so she can search into its folds

and crevices. But with each repeated exposure the scene slips
more out of control. Rosie knows very well, for instance, that
she was not watching from far above as the man extended his
hand. She could not have seen her hair escaping from the
scarf it was bound up in. She could not have seen the glistening smear of fresh paint just under her own ear at her jawbone
any more than she could have seen herself standing there,
staring, dropping the green gloves into the outstretched palm.
She could not have observed her T-shirt flutter slightly with
her breathing.

There's only tinkering left—cleaning up her mistakes and
blotches, and she might as well refine some of the highlights
and some stems that now look amateurish to her. In the late
afternoon, she organizes things for the following day, putting
lids on cans and cleaning brushes, and goes to wash up and
change out of her painting clothes. The splendid silk slip is
still hanging over the screen in the bathroom. Rosie looks at
it. She turns away, concentrating on cleaning off the paint she
always ends up streaked with, even under her clothing, in
the most improbable places, but the slip behind her seems to
have some claim on her today; she'd just as soon she'd never
seen inside that woman's closet.

When Rosie gives the slip just the gentlest tug, it tumbles
down, twinkling, into her hands. The slip pours tremblingly
around her body, transforming it into a thrilling landscape, all
gleams and shadows. Her skin looks an edible white. And the
way the thing feels! Rosie lifts her arms; it slides against her.
Her painting clothing—shoes, T-shirt, jeans, underwear—lies
in a heap at her feet.

How does that woman look in this? Easy to imagine.
Rosie pictures that hair of hers, swooshing around, Harris's
hands in it.

She closes her eyes to erase the scene. She takes the slip off, sniffs it to see whether her body has left any trace of paint or mineral spirits on it, replaces it carefully over the screen, and breathes in and out to calm her pounding heart. Then she puts on her clean clothes, and returns to the bedroom to collect her things. Out the window, the sails float, so far away. One detaches itself from the blue and flutters off—not a sail, a gull.

"Didn't mean to startle you—" a voice says behind her. "I thought you'd gone."

Rosie spins around. "Actually," she says, "I thought *you'd* gone."

Harris blinks, evidently searching his mind. "Oh, I see," he says. "Other day, yesterday, whatever it was? Just giving Elizabeth a lift to the airport."

Rosie stares. The way she just spoke to him!

He seems not to have noticed, though. "I usually do," he's saying, as if this would clear up some confusion. "She says it's the only time we see each other anymore. Not completely a joke . . ." He frowns. "Will it bother you if I grab a tie?"

Will it *bother* her? Rosie closes her eyes again for a moment.

Harris pulls a lustrous sheaf of ties from his closet and leafs through it, extracting several. He holds one up to himself, peering at the small mirror over the dressing table.

Sight, sound, smell, taste, touch, Rosie thinks. All of that, and you don't have the faintest idea what's going on with another person. "This one, I think," he says. "Yes?"

She watches as he makes the knot, his collar up, concentrating—his eyes on her face, as if she were the mirror. It's impossible for her to turn away from the rapid, complicated performance.

"Really hate this," he says, turning down his collar and smiling quickly at her.

She feels slightly dizzy. "You hate . . ."

He gestures, as if the whole thing were simply too difficult to explain. "Oh, putting on a tie at this hour." He looks at her, apparently for sympathy. "A meeting. In a bar, if you please. Downsizing—this is what it comes to. Now that we're all laptops and cellulars, there's no place that isn't the office. Bar, apartment, plane, car, street . . . I liked it better when you went somewhere, didn't you? Well, you're too young to remember. But you used to *go* somewhere. There was your desk, there was your secretary. And then, the point is, you left."

Rosie looks at him uncertainly.

He smiles. Oh—this is his home! She picks up her backpack. "Well, goodbye," she says.

"Goodbye," he says. "By the way, why don't I know your name?"

"It's Rosie," Rosie says.

"Rosie," he says, and turns briefly back to the mirror. "Rosie. Well, good. Now we have a basis."

It's Lupe's day off. And Harris, evidently, is not by nature a housekeeper. The cover has been thrown sloppily over the bed, and a thick book is propped open, pages down, near a pillow. A tumbler containing what seems to be the watery remains of a whiskey sits on the floor by the bed next to a cup holding some boiled-smelling coffee. A robe lies open over the little chair.

Rosie squints at the book's cover. Some sort of fancy thriller, it looks like. About high finance. No sign of Harris himself. Maybe he's in his study. Maybe he's out . . .

Does Rosie hear someone? Yes, someone's come in. But—oh, no!—it's *Morgan*. And of course Jamie's not around to deal with him. "Hello, there," Morgan says, inattentively, as he wanders into the bedroom. Does he happen to remember who she is? "How's it going? Everything fine?"

He glances around, and Rosie does, too. The glass, the bed, the robe . . .

"Looking good," Morgan comments, vaguely. He stands back from a wall, scrutinizing it, then approaches. He takes a fabric swatch from his briefcase, tacks it up by the window, stands back, and approaches again. "Very, very good. So. She'll be back Tuesday night, I understand—after the holiday. I'd assume she'll be pleased, but of course she'll have to look at it. And if there are no adjustments, perhaps James will want to go ahead and seal it on Wednesday? Do you think?"

"I guess . . ." Rosie says. "So, where did she go anyhow?"

"Sorry?" Morgan raises his eyebrows slightly.

Rosie looks at him.

"Oh," he says. "Business, I suppose."

"She travels a lot . . ." Rosie suggests.

Morgan is loftily forbearing, as though he were waiting for a child to conclude a tantrum, but after a moment he concedes. "Some high-end international-hotel concern, I believe. Well—" he looks at Rosie, then away. "And where might James be?"

Where indeed? Jamie didn't get around to mentioning what she was to do in this contingency. "Actually," Rosie says, "he's sick."

Terror ripples in the depths of Morgan's beautiful face, and tears spring, astonishingly, into Rosie's eyes; it's as if Jamie really were sick. "It's nothing much, I'm sure," she says. "We ate at the Golden Calf last night. Big mistake."

"I see," Morgan says.

Obviously he's realized she's lying. "That's too bad. Well, do ask him to give me a call if he has a moment. No, never mind, don't bother."

"Morgan asked if you want to seal it Wednesday," Rosie says that night.

"I know," Jamie says. "He called."

"Will that take long?" Rosie asks, though she pretty much knows how long it will take, since she and Jamie sealed the other rooms.

Jamie shakes his head. "A couple of hours, maybe. How's it been going, by the way? Any problems?"

"Problems?" Rosie says. "Painting a line?"

"Well . . ." Jamie says. "Listen, if you've finished, there really isn't any reason for you to go back tomorrow."

"I've got a bit more to do, anyhow," Rosie says.

"It's great you were there when Morgan came by. He won't show up again, probably."

A basis! Rosie is thinking—she'll probably never catch another glimpse of that person. And did he simply assume she'd know *his* name? Of course, the fact, ha-ha, is that she did happen to.

"And in case I haven't thanked you . . . This has really been great for me. I've gotten a lot done."

A lot of what? "I'm going to make some tea," Rosie says. "Want some?"

"No, thanks," he says. "I want to wash my hair. You got any immediate plans for the tub?"

Rosie wanders into the kitchen. She's got into the habit of thinking of this as her life, but what is it, really? An accident, a coincidence—nothing. And now Jamie's letting go.

Already, in fact, she's being completely colonized by the

first person to happen by. Concentrate, she tells herself. Put the water in the kettle, put the kettle on the stove, turn the burner on, reach yourself a tea bag, and drop it in the cup.

This is one good reason why people take care to have a past, Rosie thinks. So their minds are full of stuff—big, heavy things. Anchors, buoys, urns, old statuary, armoires, lots of clutter, lots of buffers, so that some perfect stranger can't just wander in and use up all the space.

Take a seat, she'd like to say. There, over in the corner, in the shadows with all that old junk. I'm making tea just now; don't loaf around there in the middle of the room, please. Take a seat in the back, and I'll be with you when it's convenient.

Unfortunately, though, he's a spreading blob. She doesn't have any shapes to think of him in; she doesn't know anything about him. She can't make any observations about him, she can't have any opinions about him, and she certainly can't push him out of her mind—he just oozes back around the slammed door.

In fact, it seems to Rosie that all her resistance is just getting him more entrenched. Why not relax a bit? Why think every second about how much she's thinking about him? Maybe she should just give him full run. Let him lounge around and put his feet up—she's bound to get sick of it after a while, and throw him out.

"Hey, Rosie—" Jamie calls from the bathroom. "Can I borrow your duck?"

"Help yourself," Rosie calls back.

Or, one thing that Ian used to do when he got stuck on something was just sit himself down in front of his computer and sort things out. *It's right there,* he'd say, *in your mind. What's keeping you hung up? What do you know that you don't know you know?*

"Instrumental meditation," he'd called it. "A technique."
Taught to him by some simpleton of a therapist he'd boasted
about knowing. *Taught*, Rosie thinks. *Technique.* How's that
for something to get taught—making a *list*?

Ludicrous. Still, what's there to lose? Rosie locates some
lined yellow paper in the kitchen, and brings it into Vincent's
room along with a cup of tea. She takes a sip of tea and stares
at the piece of paper. Well, you can see why Ian likes that
computer of his so much—it's a crystal ball. All that information swimming around in that blue cyberspace, ready to jump
to the right bait and get reeled up to the surface of the screen.
Whereas you can be sure nothing's going to just appear on
this piece of paper.

Rosie sees Ian tapping the silent keys to make a list. He's
replaced by Harris, at his screen, sending out the orders that
raise up and demolish the invisible empire.

"Hey," Jamie says, pausing at Vincent's door, a towel around
his neck and his hair dripping wet.

"Which of them makes more money, do you think?"
Rosie says.

"Er . . ." Jamie says.

Oh, great, Rosie thinks. Why not just make a general an-
nouncement? That she's actively thinking about some people
who are hardly aware of her existence. That before she'd even
laid eyes on them, her mind had gone so far as to form expectations of them, without her permission, and even without
her knowledge. "Those people we're working for. I was just
wondering today—which one do you think makes more?"

Jamie shrugs. "You can't count that kind of money. It's
indivisible. No metal coins, no flappy little bills. It's abstract.
It's a construct. It's outer-space gunk. Their bank accounts are
just big, mad-scientist thingies, with gunk gurgling around in

the tubes. People like that can't even buy a hot dog on the street."

"She's not beautiful," Rosie says.

"Huh," Jamie says. "And so?" He sits down on the bed, next to Rosie, and she takes the towel from him to dry his silky hair. "Mmm," he says. "That feels good."

True: *And so?* She's going to miss Jamie one of these days. She misses him now.

"So, why do you think they got married?" Rosie says, stanching a little rivulet of water behind his ear.

"Rosie, I'm surprised at you. 'Why'—now, *that's* a question that won't take you there. Why did they get married? Why does anybody marry anybody instead of anybody else? Why does anybody anything?"

Rosie lowers the towel, thinking.

"Besides, judging by the archaeological evidence, they're perfect for each other. Don't stop, don't stop! The two least interesting people on the planet."

Also true: *Why*—a completely primitive concept. Still, why *does* anybody anything, Rosie thinks, looking around the next day at the pure, breathing silence of the bedroom. Why does this person want to be with that person rather than with any other? Why did Lexi Feld get together with Arnold Schaefer? Because he was blocking her path? To Rosie neither Lexi nor Arnold ever seemed to have much in the way of attributes, let alone allure. What is it about the mere sight of Jamie that does to Morgan the strange things it does? What could have been so special about Vincent that to this day Jamie never says a word about him? What on earth could it be about some stranger, who does not, in fact, seem particularly interesting, that keeps Rosie's attention nailed to him? And why *did* he marry that woman?

Lots of people want to have a dog around; others prefer cats. Once in a while, someone goes into the pet store and comes out with a mynah bird or a snake or a miniature African hedgehog. And even about this matter, which should be pretty simple to figure out, what do people say? They say, "It doesn't shed"; or, "You can walk it"; or, "You don't have to walk it"—whatever. In other words, no one has a clue why it's some particular creature rather than another that causes them to exclaim, "Oh, hey, now—that's for me!"

Rosie's hungry, she notices. This whole Thursday has gone by as if it had been poured slowly into sand. It would be nice to have a bite with Jamie tonight, but he's sure to be at his studio, or with Trevor. No matter. She looks around— still a few smears left to clean up.

She'll do it tomorrow, though. It's taken her all day to do about fifteen minutes worth of work. Because when you're waiting, she thinks, waiting is all you can do.

So much for all the wasted head space. By afternoon of the following day, Rosie has pretty much resigned herself—*really*, she thinks—to the idea that she's not going to be running into Harris again. Obviously she's not going to run into him. She hadn't actually thought she was going to run into him anyway. And she just isn't.

How stupid this has all been. What had she actually hoped to gain by sacrificing the magic hum of her blood, anyway? Ordinary human experience? Ordinary human experience— something, obviously, only an elephant could survive.

Not a sound in the place other than the creakings of the

scaffold as Rosie clambers up and down, the comforting little clicks of the paint-can lids as she removes and replaces them, and the handles of the brushes against the jars of paint and mineral spirits. Tarnished gold veils are beginning to drop through the blue at the window; soon, the planet will turn its back on the day.

In half an hour she'll be gone. Rosie finishes cleaning up slowly. She could just take the little train back to the apartment. Or she could walk around for a while, stalling in the grimy air, or hang out at a bar, watching the early-evening drunks ricochet between desperation and pointless hope . . .

The room glitters with cool shadows, like a garden on the last day of summer. She should have used her time here better—her time on this job. On Wednesday, she'll return with Jamie, and within a few hours everything she's been doing with her day will be sealed off from her. And then what? In these weeks Jamie's done some brand-new paintings; in these weeks Jamie's acquired a brand-new lover.

Rosie goes to wash up and change out of her painting clothes. The silk slip is hanging over the screen, of course, glimmering, winking at her. She turns away, as if she'd encountered in genteel company someone with whom she'd once had a sordid affair.

Just one last look at the view that will cease to be hers, today, the moment she shuts the door of the apartment behind her. Bright days out on the water, indigo nights . . . Oh, yeah—memory! *Now* Rosie gets it; *memory*—the thing humans get to keep, a little travel kit to bring along with you. A little substitute for eternity. Pathetic. Rosie looks at her hands, her arms, every part of her body she can see that isn't covered by her dress. No fresh paint, she's certain. She sits down as gently as possible on the bed, and after a minute or two leans back against the cloud of pillows.

She can see only one sail now, in the darkening blue. Someone out there, gliding farther into the darkness, a hand trailing in the water, edged with light . . .

Later, Rosie once again finds it impossible to recapitulate in any way that seems trustworthy the thing that happened next—the last, unexpected entrance of Harris.

Unexpected? Of course not. Shocking, yes, but not unexpected. And there it all is, over and over—a wedge of dark where the door is opening, herself against the pillows, his hand resting on the doorframe, his watch flashing against his wrist—as though it were all being reflected in the falling pieces of a shattered mirror. Rosie sits herself up fast, speechless.

They stare at one another. "Not feeling well?" he says.

"No, no—" she says, her heart pounding. "I'll be fine in a moment—"

"Mmm," he says. He shakes his head, as if he'd fallen asleep for an instant. "Probably best to be still." He runs a hand through his black-and-silver hair. "Very pale. Migraine? Do you get migraines?"

"Not often," Rosie says, truthfully.

"Sometimes tea works," he says. "They say not, but what do they know? I say it does."

The kitchen is a million miles away. Of course Rosie can't even hear Harris there, clattering around, let alone see him. And yet this, too, is something that happens later: watching him search for the teakettle, the cup, the saucer, observing his intent expression as he fills the kettle at the tap, waits for it to boil . . .

And then he returns, with a pretty little tray. "There," he says, pleased.

The tray holds a tiny china teapot, the most beautiful cup and saucer Rosie's ever seen, a paper napkin, a silver spoon, a small silver bowl of sugar, and a little dish containing various sorts of tea bags. "This is not the way it's done," Harris says. "I do know that. And, to tell you the truth, there are boxes and boxes of the real thing out there—the stuff in shreds. But all that paraphernalia! The little mesh things . . ." He presents her with an expression of cheery bewilderment. "I don't know why we've got that stuff, anyhow. Neither of us drinks it. Just to persuade Lupe we're legit, I suppose. Oh, Christ—lemon."

"This is perfect," Rosie says.

"Just as well," Harris says, sitting down in the little chair. "Probably is no lemon."

Rosie selects a tea bag and puts it in the cup. She looks up at Harris; he's watching her. She pours the water out from the teapot, and nearly chokes from the stench of synthetic fruit. Harris frowns worriedly. "O.K.?" he says.

Rosie nods. "Perfect."

"Things really do fall apart back there when Elizabeth's away," he says. "Not that Elizabeth's all that domestic. But she is very . . ."

Rosie looks demurely at her teacup.

". . . well organized," he says. "Funny to remember, but there was a time, back in our very first place, when we used to cook a lot. Penthouse, *miles* of terrace. That was all back then, when people did that. You wouldn't remember, probably. Maybe your parents were into it."

Jesus fucking Christ, Rosie thinks. Who on earth might he imagine her parents to be?

"Little dinner parties," he says. "Sort of a blood sport. Everything just right. Very competitive. Stakes escalating . . ." He laughs. "Seriously, though, it was grim . . ."

And how on earth old does he imagine her to be?

He's got the facts all wrong. But, Rosie thinks, only the facts. This man has some quality that works like intuition. It's confidence. Or generosity of a sort. He seems to believe he has only to say something in order for her to understand it; that he'll understand whatever it is she might say . . . .

He's tapped into some great, generous reserve—the ocean that flows around everyone, between everyone, rolling like a heartbeat, making big, comforting, heartbeat sounds, oceanic sounds . . . approbation, pleasure . . .

Mr. Gage and Mr. Peralta, the men she used to work for, were so nervous—as if they were afraid that she or one of the other secretaries would suddenly speak up. *Calm down, guys,* Rosie could have told them; *no fear of that. What do you think those suits of yours are for?* Those sad, furry suits . . . . The shirt Harris is wearing right now probably cost what any of those suits did.

"I wonder where these things disappear to," Harris is saying. "These trends, or whatever you want to call them. You do something all the time, and then one day you're telling somebody about the things you used to do. It's peculiar, getting older." He smiles at Rosie. "I'd advise against it. Oh, well, who has time for those little dinners? Who can afford that sort of thing these days? More expensive than eating out every night. Which is pretty much what we do now. Well, or order in, actually. Elizabeth gets sick of it, but to tell you the truth I'd much rather have Chinese in those cardboard things than one of those grand—just something from the deli. A sandwich . . ."

"Pastrami sandwich," Rosie says.

"Pastrami sandwich," he agrees. "In bed. Hmm!" He stands up impatiently, and walks over to the window. "Light so late."

Rosie looks at him. "I should probably leave," she says.

"No, no," he says. "Not at all. Finish your tea."

For a moment there's disastrously nothing to say. It would be rude to just run now, Rosie thinks; it would make him feel that he'd been rude. "Aren't you going to have some, too?" Rosie manages. "Tea?"

"Hmm," Harris says. "Or something. Now, that's a thought."

Rosie swings her feet over the side of the bed.

"Easy does it," he says.

What he seems to want, it turns out, is not really to hustle her away but to resettle her in the living room. "More comfortable here, yes?" he says. "Less like death's door."

She's curled up on some divan-type thing, and he's given her an astonishingly soft little blanket—*cashmere*, she thinks—to tuck around her feet.

"So, tell me," he says, as he makes himself a drink. "Tell me something. Who are you? What are you?"

Rosie looks at him.

"Quite a sight, you realize. Strolling into your own room and there's a dying artist on the bed."

"I'm feeling better," Rosie says.

"Good," Harris says.

"Really much better."

"I notice," Harris says, "that you're evading my subtle but probing questions. No matter—I'll try another. Are you . . . let's see . . . in art school?"

Rosie hesitates. "Actually, I'm not in school at all anymore."

"Um-hmm," he says. He waits for a moment, taking a sip of his drink. "So, you are no longer in school, and now you are . . ."

Rosie shakes her head, and gestures helplessly.

"Biding your time," Harris says. "Just biding your time . . ."

"Yes . . ." Rosie says.

"And painting while you're doing it . . . That's a nice thing to be able to do—paint . . ."

Rosie looks down at the undrinkable reddish liquid in her teacup.

"But it must be very interesting, what you do," she says.

"Not really," he says. "It's really rather boring, most of the time over here on our side. Tense, but boring. Elizabeth gets some of the fun—travel, dinners, armies at her command . . . I just sit here." He smiles at Rosie. "Oh, not to complain. The *situations*, I suppose you'd call them, in my line can be quite . . . There are some real pirates out there, I'll tell you. Rascals. Real buccaneers. Of course, you don't know how some of those characters can live with themselves."

He doesn't *look* bored, Rosie notes; a little smile has crept over his face as he thinks about it all.

"Much better to be a painter," he says. "You've got to be able to look at yourself in the mirror. Well. And is that your beau?"

"My . . . ?" she begins.

"The other painter. Your beau?"

"Oh," she says. "Jamie?" Harris is holding his drink up so that the ice casts strange reflections on the wall. "No, Jamie's just a friend."

"Ah ha," Harris says.

The potent, otherworldly aroma of paint pervades even this room faintly. Rosie leans back, shutting her eyes, and breathes it in. Maybe it's coming from her.

"I understand, from the decorator, that he's very serious about his art."

"Very," Rosie says, happily; Harris doesn't even know

Morgan's name! "But people don't buy his paintings much. It's discouraging . . ."

"Of course," Harris says. "It must be hard not to lose heart . . . but I suppose you all must really love what you do."

Rosie bows her head. Poor Jamie; lucky Jamie.

It's twilight, she notices—twilight has drifted into the room like a fragrance, entwining with the smell of the oils. "So. You're feeling better?" Harris says.

"Oh," Rosie says. "I should—"

"Because if you are, maybe you'd like a drink."

She looks at him. "Well, yes, actually. Actually, I would."

He pours another for himself and one of whatever it is for her. "I drink so rarely these days," he says. "Mostly when Elizabeth's away. The thing is, drinking makes me crazy for a cigarette."

Rosie smiles.

"Would you be horrified?" he says.

She shakes her head.

"Because I happen to know where Elizabeth hides them."

He leaves the room and comes back in a moment, flourishing one. "We quit together years ago, but I happen to know she still sneaks one from time to time." He wiggles an eyebrow at Rosie. "The sneak. Oh, damn—" he says, looking around.

"Matches?" Rosie says. "I've got matches—" She dives into her backpack. She's sure there are some in there, from the old days. She comes up with a matchbook, opens it, bends a match over, and strikes it, holding it out for Harris.

For an instant, his eyes flicker over the matches, half of them creased and blackened, then he inclines toward them and inhales, bringing the cigarette to life.

He leans back, eyes closed, and exhales a rich plume.

"Fantastic," he says. He opens his eyes and smiles at her. "Back to the subject. So. Where were we? Artists: not losing heart. Other painter: not your boyfriend . . ."

"Well," Rosie says. "I was going out with someone, but we broke up this winter."

"Pity," Harris says.

Rosie shrugs. Another life. Had she even really cared about Ian? No—her magic blood saw to its own cravings.

Harris is looking at her. "Artist, too?"

"Oh, no," Rosie says. "Ian, never."

"And what was his field?"

Rosie frowns. "Well," she says. "Commodities, basically."

Harris inhales, and exhales luxuriously again. "Not for you, was it?" he says. "You found the life restricting?"

"Yes, I guess . . ." Rosie says. "I was . . . Actually, I felt as if I weren't even alive . . ."

"Ah," Harris says. "That's the choice, isn't it. That's the question. I'm sure it seems very hard to you, an artist's life. Restlessness, fear, discouragement . . . despair, yes? Even despair. While for people like me or your ex, it all seems to be under control. And in many ways, it all is under control. I'm sure you artistic types think we have it easy, and we do—aside from the normal quota of human misery, of course. But it's all *settled*—it's settled. We've answered the questions a certain way, we've made our choices. But then what? Not to say we aren't . . . Not to say . . . which is all very well, but come my age a lot of men look around and say, '*Wait*, this is my life, it's my only life, the only one I'm ever going to have.' I know men whose lives were just perfect. Men who had a perfect life and just threw it all over. Left perfect wives, perfect jobs, perfect families . . . Because they just couldn't resist some impulse. To spoil the perfect thing, is what some people say. But I think it's more the thought of . . . we're all going to *die*, do you see? Think of it, Rosie—the cold, the stillness, the *finality* . . ." He stubs out his cigarette. "Well. But you must know men like that."

For a moment they sit in silence. "It's dark," Harris says, in surprise, and switches on a lamp. "There. *Let there be* . . . You know, I've got so much stuff here I bet you'd really appreciate. Elizabeth and I aren't collectors in any serious sense of the word, but we have picked up some awfully good things over the years, in my opinion. Should we see if you agree?"

He takes her through the apartment, turning on little lights over paintings and drawings, which are now hung on all but the bedroom walls, and speaks of each one knowledgeably and lovingly. His hand rests on her shoulder, her wrist, the small of her back, as he shows her around, causing tears to come to her eyes and cruel little flames to flick at her bones, snapping around them like a lash. "What do you think of this?" he says, pausing in front of a painting.

Rosie's eyes clear, and the painting appears in front of her. "It's wonderful . . ." she says, surprised. The painting's alight; the whole room is alight. "Really wonderful . . ."

"Yes, it's wonderful," he says. "That's right. This is the one." He gives her a pleased, brief little hug. "You're very easy to talk to," he says. "It's absolutely frightening. I wish you didn't have to go."

She stares at the painting in front of her. Its shapes leap and dance as Harris rests his hand on the back of her neck.

"I just can't tell what's in your mind," Harris says. "It's an attractive quality, you know; I'll bet you're very attractive to men."

She shakes her head, slowly. Hot shame creeps up her skin as she thinks back to the sort of men she used to be attractive to, in the days when it was easier just to fuck the guy instead of having the tedious discussion about why you weren't going to and then doing it anyhow, to get him to leave. "A long time ago," she says, "there were a lot of men. But then, thank God, Ian came along."

"Hmm," Harris says. His hand drops away. "Well," he says again. But this time clearly, it's an instruction: "I wish you didn't have to go . . ."

Rosie's heart plunges. "I wish I didn't, too," she says, and steps obediently to the door.

He holds it open and smiles, but when she looks up at him to see what she's done wrong, his smile fades, and he folds his arms around her. "Going to be here this weekend?" he says into her ear.

She rubs her cheek against his marvelous shirt; her heart is beating so furiously that for a moment she can't speak. "Do you want my number at Jamie's?" she says.

"I do," he says, and releases her. "I certainly do. Maybe we can . . . grab a pastrami sandwich—I'll be at loose ends here till Tuesday evening."

Paper is waiting at a little maple desk. Rosie writes out her number, and when she hands it to him he puts his arms around her again, adjusts her slightly, and gives her a kiss more debilitating than whole encounters she's had in bed; so graphic that, hours later, she's still trembling.

But he doesn't call. It's Sunday evening, and he still hasn't called. Of course, it's really only been two days. No, one day, really—Saturday.

And yet there's only Monday to go. Well, Monday, and Monday night. And Tuesday, of course—Tuesday during the day . . . before Elizabeth returns. At least during the day after Lupe leaves.

"Think you might eat something ever again?" Jamie says, on a visit to the apartment. "Just as a favor to your fans? Or are you intending to spend the rest of your life in this room?"

Rosie rolls over in bed to face the wall.

He sighs. "Want to tell me what's the matter?"

"Nothing's the matter," she says. "Nothing. Just nothing."

After Jamie leaves, she gets herself into the tub, and stays, for hours, with her friend the duck bobbing blankly between patches of suds on the water's dirty surface. Her skin is tormented from thinner, but she scrubs away at it, crying.

Her friend the duck! She grabs it and hurls it into the corner, near the toilet. Could he have lost her number, possibly? Did he expect *her* to make the call? Well, but maybe he did, actually . . . What he'd said was he'd be at loose ends "until Tuesday evening." And, actually, he might not have put it that way, in fact, exactly, if he *wasn't* expecting her to make the call.

When after the fourth ring he picks up the phone, she can hear a little scrap of voices even before he says hello; obviously he's in the middle of dinner, or something. A conversation. Rosie uses her thumb to cut the connection, soundlessly. A jolly enough dinner, that's for sure—they were laughing, all of them, whoever they were. Well, not *all* of them, exactly—the *others* were laughing; Harris, the fact is . . . was *chewing*.

Three cheers for Mrs. Howell's Fiorinal. It's eradicated the time perfectly. And Rosie has finally, after all these months, got a truly decent sleep. Two dear little pills took care of Sunday night, then three eliminated Monday, and only five more, actually, were needed to roll Wednesday morning right up to Rosie's bedside.

For several hours now, Rosie has had to stand up and walk and talk—and she's been able to, though her hangover still makes an odd, gauzy curtain over everything in view. Just as well: the view has included Elizabeth; the great, rumpled bed, all its noisy turmoil exposed in the glare of Lupe's day off; and, of course, Harris. Who could not have been friendlier or more pleasant, to Rosie and Jamie as well as to Morgan.

The five of them have stood together, looking at the bedroom walls. There's no doubt that Morgan is satisfied, although, Rosie notes through her hangover, he's more muted—softer—than usual; it'll probably be some time till he runs into Jamie again. And Elizabeth is clearly pleased, in her surgical way. And, naturally, it's all just fine with Harris.

They're quiet for a minute or so, turned toward the glinting blue out the window as if a trance had fallen over them. Elizabeth speaks dreamily into the silence. "Let's get a boat next summer, darling. Let's get a boat and go sailing off, right into the sky . . ."

"We'll discuss this," Harris says.

Elizabeth laughs. "Sloth," she says affectionately. "You know you'll love it . . ."

They make their goodbyes. Morgan delivers his gracious little speech of thanks to Jamie, and, as Elizabeth begins her gracious little speech of thanks to Morgan, Harris takes Rosie's hands in both of his and looks at her. "The important thing," he says in a low, vibrant voice, "is to keep painting, Rosie . . . Trust your talent. Trust your future." And he gives her a special little smile—formal, final, but just for her. She'll see that smile more vividly, she knows, in the starkness of memory, when the curtain rises.

"It's been real," Jamie says to a wall, and turns to Rosie. "Ready?"

"Just a moment," Rosie says. "Let me wash my hands."

The slip glimmers as though it's been waiting for her; it tumbles into her arms as she touches it. A rescue? Oh, no, not at all. Rosie stuffs it violently into her backpack as she will later stuff it violently to the rear of Vincent's dusty shelves, and then, she assures herself, she'll never give these people another thought.

But what will *they* think, Elizabeth and Harris? Or, to put it more precisely, what will Elizabeth think, and what will Harris think? Because—Rosie removes a fleck of paint from the faucet—they'll be thinking about her, all right. They will. Yes, *let* them think about her . . .

MERMAIDS

"Good? Not good?" Mr. Laskey said. "What do you say, girls?"

"Kiss kiss," Alice said, making two spoons kiss, and Janey was just staring rudely into space, so it fell to Kyla (as it had all day) to make things all right. "It's perfect," she assured Mr. Laskey, and, true, the old-fashioned gleam and clatter, the waitresses in their pastel uniforms, the glass dishes with their ice-cream spheres, the other little groups of wealthy tourists and even New Yorkers, all of this would be exactly what her mother was back home picturing.

Spring vacation had been hurtling down toward Kyla for weeks and weeks, at first just a fleck troubling the margin of her vision, then closer and larger and faster until it smashed into place, obliterating everything that wasn't itself, and Kyla's mother was dropping her off at the Laskeys', where they were waiting for her, and Mrs. Laskey was smoothing Janey's dress and giving little Alice a hug, and for one fractured and re-peating moment Kyla was saying goodbye to Richie Laskey, and then the car door shut Kyla in with Alice and Janey and Mr. Laskey, and Mrs. Laskey and Richie were waving goodbye, and Alice began to cry at the top of her lungs, as though she were being snatched away by killers. "Oh, grow up, Alice," Janey said.

The airport was gray and shiny, like a hospital where Kyla was to be anesthetized and detached hygienically from home. A corridor of shiny gray time sucked her in along with Janey and Alice and Mr. Laskey, and then the crowd in which they were to be conveyed away compressed itself into the tube of the airplane.

"You get the window seat," Janey said to Kyla. "You're the guest."

Seven days, Kyla had thought; seven days before she could go home, seven days of being the guest, seven days of having to have a good time—even though she was with Janey Laskey. "That's okay," she said. "Take it if you want it."

"You take it," Janey said. "I've been on lots of planes before. I get to go on planes all the time."

Kyla looked around for Mr. Laskey, but he was already settled into the seat across the aisle from Alice, and one of the stewardesses was leaning over him, laughing and laughing, as he told a joke about a fox and a bunny rabbit. And Kyla would have taken the window seat then (because someone should show Janey she couldn't always get away with that sort of thing) but the thought of her mother's pleading look intervened, so she just shook her head and sat down, thunk, where she was.

Janey shrugged. "Okay," she'd said, squishing her porky rear end past, to the good seat, "I guess some people don't like it. Some people are scared to look out the window." She opened the big book she was carrying and squinted down at it, following the print with her finger; her thin hair, the color of cardboard, drooped forward; obviously she should be wearing glasses.

Poor Janey. "What's your book about?" Kyla asked.

Janey jumped slightly. "Oliver *Twist*?" she said, and looked at Kyla. "Is about orphans."

"*Sor*-ry," Kyla said.

Air whooshed through some little spouts above them, the lights flickered, and a heartless angel's voice instructed them to strap themselves in.

No, Kyla thought. No no no no no. She closed her eyes; the gravity of her will flowed around the seats and into the little compartments: *The plane was growing heavier and heavier*—it would sit, the plane, heavy with her will; darkness would come; someone would open the door, and they could all go home. But for one instant there was a flaw in her concentration—or was it in her sincerity? Her will was flicked aside like an insect and the plane rose, through a great roaring.

The stewardess returned to make a big fuss over Alice. "Kindergarten, *already*?" she sang out, amazed, to Alice, who confirmed this with a gracious nod. The stewardess straightened up, twirled a bit of stray hair around her finger and tucked it back into place, smiling brilliantly at Mr. Laskey. Janey stared at her with loathing and then turned to the window.

"Guess what you can see from up here," Janey turned back to say to Kyla. "You can see the bodies in the lagoons."

"There are no bodies in the lagoons," Kyla had said firmly, for Alice's benefit, but Alice was playing happily with the safety instruction card, like someone who has no troubles in the world.

"They look just like mermaids, except they're face up," Janey said. "Their hair floats, and their legs are green and slimy."

"*Don't*," Kyla said.

"*Eleven-year-old Courtney Collier disappeared from the mall at ten o'clock this morning while her mother was buying a new tie for Mr. Collier,*" Janey said. " '*Courtney was a beautiful little girl,*' authorities said. '*We're totally positive it was a sex crime.*' "

Seven days; seven more days. Minus the three hours and

fifteen minutes between getting from the Laskeys' house to wherever it was they were now. Minus this second. Minus this second. Kyla leaned across Janey to see: Naturally there were no dead girls. You couldn't even see the lagoons—all you could see were clouds.

Now most of that seven days was over with. Sunday night Kyla had settled into the room she was to share with Janey and Alice, with the blue carpet and the alien blue-flowered wallpaper, and she'd carefully put her clothing into a bureau drawer or hung it on the hotel's heavy wooden hangers—how strange it looked on those hangers in that big, dark closet that smelled like wood and furniture polish and very faintly of other people, though nobody in particular. Then she and Janey had to play Brides with Alice to calm her down and they had all gone to sleep.

"I want you girls in bed early," Mr. Laskey had said, "except on the nights we've got tickets. And there are going to be some serious naps around here. Agreed? The days will be pretty strenuous, and I don't want to arrive back home with three little zombies. Now. I'll be right next door, but I'm looking forward to a little stress-reduction myself, and you have an entire hotel staff downstairs at your disposal. Kindly take advantage of that unusual fact. If you need anything, Donald will be at the concierge's desk every afternoon and night."

And it *had* been . . . strenuous. On Monday evening they'd gone to a restaurant with waiters in tuxedos, where Kyla had worn the new party dress her mother had gotten her for the trip, and Tuesday night she'd worn the dress again, when Mr. Laskey let them stay up late and they'd gone to a show with poor people who were singing and dancing. And yesterday evening they had gone to another amazing restaurant, in Greenwich Village, where everyone—all the waitresses and all the customers—looked like models. And during the days they'd gone to the Empire State Building and the Planetarium and the Statue of Liberty and the Museum of Natural History and various other museums (which Janey claimed to enjoy) and they'd walked in the big, dirty, interesting park with the little fringe of silver buildings at the edges, and they'd gone in a horse-drawn carriage, and had taken a boat around the whole island, and along with all that there had been a revolving display of fascinating delis and coffee shops and people you couldn't believe had even been *born*, and long, sludgy naps in the sad blue room where it seemed Kyla had been living with Janey and Alice forever.

So now there was only tonight and then Friday and then Saturday, and on Sunday they'd get back in the plane, and on Monday morning Kyla would wake up in her own bed and all the big blank obstacles that at one time had been between her and home would have dissolved into a picture she could remember for her mother at breakfast.

Because at the time something was happening, of course, you didn't know what it was like. At the time a thing was happening, that thing was not, for instance, *New York. New York* was what her mother was at home picturing. The place where you actually *were* was a street corner with wads of paper in the gutter, or it was standing there, facing the worn muzzle of the horse that had pulled your carriage, or it was sitting in front of a little stain on the tablecloth. *It* really wasn't *like* anything—it was just whatever it was, and there was never a place in your mind of the right size and shape to put it. But afterwards, the thing fit exactly into your memory as if there had always been a place—just right, just waiting for it.

On Monday morning, she would be home. She would be telling her mother over breakfast all about *New York*. And Kyla would know—because she'd be remembering it—just what *New York* was *like*. But today was the biggest obstacle so far. She was so tired that her body kept forgetting to do things in its usual way—even to sit in its chair properly, and Alice was easily upset, as though the nightmares that had plagued her all night long were rustling and hissing at her feet. And Janey was behaving . . . *abominably*, so Kyla had to be extra careful about everything. "It's just perfect," she said.

"Yes, this, girls, is New York as it used to be," Mr. Laskey said. "Genteel, clean, gracious . . ." He sighed. *"Oh, where are the snows . . ."*

Janey rolled her eyes.

It was preferable, Kyla thought, when Janey just *said* whatever horrible thoughts were in her mind. Otherwise, they just leaked out and dripped all over *your* mind . . .

"Try to have a wonderful time, darling," Kyla's mother had said. "And make sure to remember everything for me." And she looked at Kyla so sadly and sweetly.

Her mother was far away now. And tiny, standing there and peering through a dark distance for Kyla. Oh, why did her mother look so sad? Why? *Kyla* knew: because of her, because she had made her mother feel bad. She had made her mother feel—and this was a fact—as though she had forced Kyla to go on this trip against her will. And now, there was her mother, tiny and fragile across the miles, straining anxiously, as if Kyla had become lost right in the field of brilliant stars that at home shone so sparsely and coldly and far away.

Mr. Laskey raised his hand in the air to summon a waitress. "We'll see if the ice cream is as good as it used to be," he said.

"When Grandfather Laskey used to bring you here," Janey intoned.

Mr. Laskey hesitated. "Yes, Jane . . ." he said seriously, as though Janey had brought up some interesting point (but soon, Kyla thought, and her insides felt odd and sparkly, Mr. Laskey was going to decide to get angry) ". . . when Grandfather Laskey used to bring me to New York—"

"—on business!" One of Alice's spoons said enthusiastically to the other.

Janey snickered.

"Put those spoons down, Alice," Mr. Laskey said. He signaled again for a waitress. "It's not nice."

Alice dropped her spoons on the table and put her hands over her face. "Aha," Mr. Laskey said as a waitress appeared. "There you are."

The waitress smiled unhappily around the table. "What pretty blue eyes," she said to Alice, who was peeking skeptically through her fingers.

The waitress turned to Kyla first. She would be supposing, Kyla thought, that Kyla was one of them—that she belonged to the handsome man who only had to raise his hand in the air to bring over a waitress. Kyla, and not Janey. Because no matter how much Mrs. Laskey paid for Janey's clothes (plenty, Kyla's mother said), Janey always looked as if she'd been dressed out of some old lady's trunk. Yes, the waitress was smiling in such a kind and unhappy way—she must be admiring Kyla's soft brown hair, the dainty little skirt and sweater her mother had chosen for her at Baskin's. The waitress herself was not pretty at all. Although that, of course, made no difference. Just, it was what Kyla could feel *Janey* was thinking. "I'm sorry," Kyla said. "I haven't decided."

"So what can I get you, doll face?" the waitress asked Alice.

"What will it be for Alice?" Mr. Laskey said.

"Ice cream for Alice," Alice confided huskily to the waitress.

"Yes?" Mr. Laskey said. He smiled at the waitress. "Are you sure? Or do you want cinnamon toast?"

Alice looked at Mr. Laskey uncertainly. "Cimona . . ." she began, and halted warily.

"Do you know, Alice," Mr. Laskey said, "that this is one of the few places on the planet, along with our hotel, that still has cinnamon toast on the menu?"

He looked at the waitress, who made a little giggle and then looked surprised at herself. "That's right," she said.

Mr. Laskey tugged a lock of Alice's soft hair. "She's been eating nothing but cinnamon toast since we got to New York," he said. "Haven't you, Alice?"

Alice appeared briefly puzzled, then nodded vigorously.

"Good old Alice—sucking up to everyone as usual," Janey remarked, in some neutral area between audible and not audible.

Mr. Laskey's expression wavered, then settled down. "And what's your pleasure, Kyla?" he said. "Decided yet?"

This was always a terrible moment, and it was one that occurred about three times every day. Her mother had told her to be especially careful not to order the most expensive thing on the menu, but it didn't seem that the price of something was what Mr. Laskey was particularly thinking about.

She shook her head, watching him.

"Well, I'm having a hot fudge sundae," he said. "Why not join me?"

She felt herself beginning to blush. "Okay," she said.

"Good girl," he said, and Kyla tossed her hair back.

"Alice . . . Alice . . ." Alice began.

"Chill out, Alice," Janey said.

"You want cinnamon toast, sweetheart," Mr. Laskey said.

"Oh," Alice agreed cheerfully.

"Janey?" Mr. Laskey said.

Janey turned to him with the look she could make that was as if she were gazing at something on the other side of a person.

"A promise is a promise," Mr. Laskey said. "Would you like a hot fudge sundae, too?"

Janey continued to stare at him as red waves came up into her face. "Fruit salad," she said.

Mr. Laskey looked down at the table as if it were an old, old enemy. "I'd like the fruit salad, *please*," he said.

A promise is a promise. And what it was that had been promised—Kyla had been there; she had heard it—was *anything we like.*

It was a night she'd had to sleep over at the Laskeys'.

"I hate going to the Laskeys'," she'd said.

"Well, where will we put you, sweetie?" her mother said. "Because you've had too many sleepovers at Ellen's lately."

Kyla hesitated. "Could we call Courtney?" she said.

"Oh, no, sweetie," her mother said. "I don't think so, do you?"

"Why not?" Kyla said.

"Well, we don't really know the Colliers very well, do we? We can't ask them for favors."

Favors, Kyla thought; was she a "favor"?

"Besides, we don't really know what kind of people they are."

Kyla looked at her mother. "They're nice," she said.

"I'm sure they are, sweetie," her mother said. "But, no."

"Why do I have to sleep over at anyone's?" Kyla said.

"Oh, because," her mother said. "I'm going out to dinner with a friend."

"But—" Kyla said. "So why can't I just stay home by myself? Until you've eaten dinner?"

"And what would you do for dinner?" her mother said.

"I could have something," Kyla said. "From the microwave. Just like I do when you work late."

Her mother stroked her hair. "Just *as* I do."

"Why not?" Kyla said.

"Well, darling—" Her mother smiled gently. "Because I need time to see my friends just as you need time to see your friends."

But the point was, Kyla thought, she didn't need time to see her friends. All she and her friends had was time—time and time and time. Waiting through the long, dull afternoons, the whole funnel of Kyla's memory, playing upstairs with the dolls or games or trading cards they'd been given to play with, doing each other's hair, pretending Brides or Baby or Shopping just like Alice did now, pretending—there was nothing else to do—that they were pretending, until it was time to come back down for milk and cookies or for one of them to be taken home. Waiting to understand the point of the dolls or games they'd been presented with, waiting for the afternoon to turn into night or for Sunday to turn into Monday, or for August to turn into September, or for nine years old to turn into ten and ten to turn, heavily, into eleven. Waiting alone in front of the television for the long evenings to fall away. Staring at the screen as if they were staring through periscopes for land, and in the dim evening rooms, the world, the distant world—which was what they must be waiting for—approached, welled into the screens, and the evening fell away in half-hour pieces. And then, finally, there was bed, and another long day had been completed. "What friend do you need time to see?" Kyla said.

"Stand up straight, darling," her mother said. "You don't want to look like Margie Strayhorn, do you? Doctor Loeffler."

Dr. Loeffler—Kyla stared. Dr. Loeffler had come over the week before and filled up their pretty living room, which he was much too big for, and her mother had made Kyla sit there for no reason at all. And the whole time—while Kyla looked at the shiny black hairs on the backs of his hands—this Dr. Loeffler had had a little smile, as if something were funny, or ridiculous. "You were planning this!" Kyla said. "Why didn't you tell me before? You knew you were going to do this!"

"Darling," her mother said with a breathless little laugh. "What do you mean?"

A tear had squirted into each eye, and yet the thing that Kyla meant, which had been so clear the instant before, was gone—simply gone—as if a hand had materialized and closed around it. "I don't like Dr. Loeffler," she said.

"Sweetie," her mother said, and no trace of the laugh was left, "you mustn't be so severe—you only met him once. Dr. Loeffler's a very fine man— He's only forty-two years old, and he's the head of the entire division of internal medicine at Hillsdale."

"*Only* forty-two years old," Kyla said.

"Don't be such a *cross* old thing," her mother said happily. "Besides, maybe the Laskeys will give you spaghetti again."

The Laskeys had not, however. Instead, there had been some sort of meat with a strange dark sauce and a fancy name.

"How was everyone's day?" Mr. Laskey said—which was what he said first thing every time Kyla had ever had dinner at the Laskeys'. He looked around the table. "Richard?"

Richie raised his serious dark eyes and then lowered them again. "Fine," he said.

"Yes?" Mr. Laskey said. He waited, his fork in his hand.

Dinner had only begun. Soon Mrs. Laskey and Janey and Alice would be crying and shouting, and then there would be after dinner, when Kyla would have to play with Janey, and then there would be morning, when she'd have to play with Janey yet again, before her mother came for her.

"Biology was interesting," Richie said. "We're studying the wheat rust cycle."

"Very good," Mr. Laskey said. "And what about calculus? Didn't you have a test the other day? I never heard how that went."

"That's a third-year class," Mrs. Laskey said. "Isn't it enough that—"

"It went fine," Richie said. "I got an A."

Mr. Laskey nodded. "There you go," he said. "You see?"

Chew slowly, one of Kyla's teachers had said once. *Your stomach has no teeth.* But what she was chewing, she thought, was the body of an animal, with blood cooked into it.

"And track?" Mr. Laskey said.

"Okay," Richie said.

A silence rose separately from Richie and Mr. Laskey and consolidated.

Richie was so . . . dignified, really, was the word, Kyla thought. Everything about him was clean and dignified. Even the way he ate—as if food were clean, as if all the frantic things your own animal's body did with it, with even the body of other animals, was just clean and ordinary.

"*Alice*—" Mrs. Laskey said, and the block of silence over the table became porous and dissolved.

"I came in ahead of Nelson Howell today," Richie said.

"What did I tell you," Mr. Laskey said.

"—You don't have to kill it, Alice," Mrs. Laskey said. "It's already dead."

"I did my report on Native Americans today," Janey said loudly. "Miss Feldman said it was the best report."

Kyla glanced inadvertently at Richie.

"Mother," Richie said, "Jane's prevaricating again."

"I am not!" Janey said. "It was really interesting. In lots of tribes the girls—"

"Pre . . ." Alice began, scowling quizzically at Mr. Laskey. "What does—"

"Absolutely nothing, Alice," Mr. Laskey said. "In this case."

"In *lots* of *tribes* the girls bleed and they go out to little—"

"*Not* at the table, Jane," Mrs. Laskey said.

"Janey made it up?" Alice said.

"No," Mr. Laskey said. "Yes."

"They *do*," Janey said. "They—"

"You heard your mother," Mr. Laskey said. "Not at the *table*." He turned to Kyla. "And what about you? Did you do a report today, too?"

"I did mine last week," Kyla said. And then, because it looked like Janey was about to erupt again, "It was about ballet dancers."

"Bal*let* dancers," Mr. Laskey said. He dipped his head as if he were tipping a hat.

"Bal*let* dancers," Janey said. "Yeah, wow, bal*let* dancers. Well, throw *you* a bone."

Mrs. Laskey snorted.

"Now," Mr. Laskey said. "Who wants more of this excellent . . . This . . . Kyla?"

"No, thank you," Kyla said.

"The child eats nothing," Mr. Laskey said admiringly. "She will vanish into thin air."

"More for Alice!" Alice shouted, flinging herself at the serving plate.

"Alice," Mrs. Laskey said, "kindly restrain yourself—look what you've done to your father's tie."

"Plus guess what, Alice," Janey said. "Your table manners make us all puke."

"Jane," Mrs. Laskey said warningly, "Alice—"

"Incidentally," Richie said. *Incidentally*, Kyla thought. "Scott Ryerson invited me to go skiing with him and his family over spring vacation."

"I want to go, too—" Janey said.

"Oh, were you invited as well, Jane?" Mr. Laskey said.

"Mother," Janey said. "Why does Richie always get to do everything?"

"Nobody said anything about—" Mr. Laskey said.

"But Alice and I never—" Jane said.

"Stop that this instant," Mrs. Laskey said. She turned to Alice, who was plucking at her. *"No,"* she said. "And I am not going to ask you one more time to behave."

Mrs. Laskey's fury was always like a gun pointing at the table; it made you tired, Kyla thought, waiting for it to go off. Her own mother never raised her voice, and she was always kind and patient. Everyone knew how patient she was. Lots of people said it was why (and the other people said it was because) she was such a good nurse. But that was frightening, too. No matter how angry Mrs. Laskey got, it was better than the look of disappointment her own mother got when Kyla did something wrong. Because when people got angry, they were angry and then they stopped being angry, and it was something that went from them to you. But when people were disappointed in you, it was something that went from you to them. You did something to them. It was as if you had made a hole in them, or had gotten a spot on them that could never be taken away.

"Where do Scott's people ski?" Mr. Laskey said.

"See, Mother?" Janey said. "Mother, don't you—"

"Jane," Mrs. Laskey said. "If I don't get—"

"All right," Mr. Laskey said, and everyone stopped talking. "Yes," he said, quietly. "Fair enough. Janey, your point is well taken. And has given me an excellent idea: Rich will go skiing over spring vacation, I will take you and Alice to New York, and your mother—your *mother* will have one entire week of peace, all to herself."

Mrs. Laskey put down her fork. "Excuse me?" she said.

Richie continued his pristine eating. "Correct me if I'm wrong," Mrs. Laskey said, slowly, "but weren't you just in New York?"

"On business," Mr. Laskey agreed pleasantly.

"And now you propose to go right back," Mrs. Laskey said.

"Not *right* back," Mr. Laskey said. "No."

"May I please be excused?" Richie said.

"You may," Mr. Laskey said. "In the future, please do not interrupt."

"I'm sorry," Richie said.

"Apologies accepted," Mr. Laskey said.

"And when did you become so enamored of New York?" Mrs. Laskey said. "The last time you and I were there together, *hellish sewer*, I believe, was what you . . . It's a filthy place, and you loathe it, and you are now proposing to go right back and expose the girls to it, for what reason I cannot—"

"*As* you know"—Mr. Laskey overrode her—"As you *know*, Carol, the events of my childhood upon which I look back with the greatest affection are those trips I took to New York with my father. As you know, I consider those excursions to be the single most meaningful experience of my childhood. It was during those trips that I felt closest to my father and learned to honor his values . . ."

Mrs. Laskey was staring at him incredulously. "His *values*," she said. She picked up her glass of water and drank until, to Kyla's amazement, the glass was empty. "I should go with you," she said. "That's what I should do."

A long, long look, arcing between Mr. and Mrs. Laskey, was pierced by a rising wail from Alice.

"Alice—" Mr. Laskey said. "What's the matter, sweetheart?"

Alice put her head on the table as though it was about to be chopped off. "It's all right, darling," Mrs. Laskey said. "You're just tired."

"Soon to bed," Mr. Laskey said. "But first, what's for dessert? What kind of ice cream do we have back there? Ice cream, Kyla?"

"No, thank you," Kyla said, because before you knew it you could turn into a clump, like Janey.

"Yes, please, chocolate," Janey said.

"There's some fruit for you," Mrs. Laskey said. "Remember those five pounds."

"Daddy—" Janey said.

Mr. Laskey glanced at Janey; his glance held and sharpened. "Your mother has spoken," he said.

"And *you* can take it easy, too," Mrs. Laskey said. "I don't want to get a phone call from New York telling me you've dropped dead in your hotel room."

"I don't want to go to New York," Janey said suddenly.

Mr. Laskey took Janey's wrist and Kyla heard her quick intake of breath. "You cannot have it both ways, Jane," he said. "You cannot complain that Rich has privileges and then behave like a prima donna yourself. Of course you want to go to New York. We'll have a wonderful time, if you'll just stop this nonsense." He released her wrist and patted her hand. "We'll treat ourselves like royalty. We'll do anything we want and have ice cream whenever we want. A trip to New York City! Isn't that ideal? Ideal, girls? Ideal, Alice?"

Upstairs in her fancy bedroom Janey had more toys than anyone, a whole closet stacked with games and toys, and dolls, too. She was *spoiled*, Kyla thought, and that was a fact. But the only thing she ever wanted to do was play Scrabble or read one of her great, thick books. Or worse, talk.

"My Great-aunt Jane who I was named for," she said, "used to have a mansion in New York. She had a lot of famous paintings, that you see in books, and jewels. Unfortunately, she passed away, or I'd get to stay there when I go to New York."

"What happened to all her stuff?" Kyla said. Oh, why was she doing this? Encouraging a person who couldn't help lying was worse than *being* the person. "How come you don't have it?"

"Because unfortunately," Janey said, "her husband gambled it all away. At the . . . gaming table. So we'll have to stay at a hotel, like the Plaza, or the Carlyle. But places like that are all right."

"Do you stay at those places a lot?" Kyla said.

"Well, not just actually," Janey said. "But whenever my parents go anywhere, they always write me letters about it and bring me back . . . mementos. When they went to San Francisco this fall they brought me back a whole huge suit-case full of presents."

"That's nice," Kyla said. She stood up and stretched. "I don't feel like talking anymore."

"So what?" Janey said. "Neither do I. I want to read my book."

And then, in the morning, of course there was Scrabble. Kyla could see Richie out in the front yard with John Hammond and then, finally, her mother's car.

"My mother's here," she said. "I'm going down."

"Relax," Janey said. "She'll call up for you when she's ready. We've got time for one more game at least."

"You're cheating," Kyla said.

"*Cheating!*" Janey yelped.

" 'Sosing' is not a word," Kyla said.

"It is, too," Janey said. "It means to send an S.O.S. Be-sides, you have to say something when the person does it."

"I'm not playing anymore," Kyla said.

She wandered down to the living room, where her mother was talking to Mrs. Laskey.

"Good morning, sleepyhead," Mrs. Laskey said.

"Hello there," her mother said, as Kyla leaned on her arm. "Have a good time?"

Kyla nodded.

"We'll go in just a minute, sweetie," her mother said, "but first I want to talk to Carol a bit. Now, run on back upstairs, quick like a bunny."

Kyla freed herself from her mother's careless arm and wandered out to the hall, where she inspected Mrs. Laskey's collection of little crystal animals.

"I *saw* him get the idea," Mrs. Laskey was saying. "I saw it happen. And then he hauled in this load of horse shit about his father—his father's *values*—as vile an old swine as ever lived. What a genius Dick has for exploitation! He exploits his children, he exploits his poor old dead disgusting father . . ."

"Well, Carol," Kyla's mother said carefully, "you have been dying for a break. And this is the . . . And besides, he probably does want to spend some time with—"

"Dick?" Mrs. Laskey snorted. "That's very funny, Lorraine."

"Well, that's what I mean," Kyla's mother said, encouragingly. "After all, it's not something he does very often."

"And poor Janey," Mrs. Laskey said. "That poor kid is a born stooge. She was so *cute* when she was little. Of course, he simply adored her then. Now, there's nothing the poor child can do to—"

"She just needs friends," Kyla's mother said. "If she just spent more—"

Oh, no! Kyla thought.

But fortunately Mrs. Laskey had interrupted. "The worst thing," she was saying, "is you can see the man operating from a mile away."

"Well," Kyla's mother said, "of course this is a side of Dick I never—"

"*And* it's compulsive," Mrs. Laskey said. "He doesn't even know he's doing it. Do you know, I actually used to feel flattered by it?"

"Still," Kyla's mother said, "it is a wonderful opportunity for the girls. I only wish Kyla could—"

The little glass owl Kyla was examining almost slipped from her hand, but Mrs. Laskey had interrupted again.

"I used to feel flattered that he would expend so much energy just to manipulate me," she said. "That's how pathetic I was. That's where my self-esteem level was. But then I realized he was expending the same amount of effort manipulating everybody. He can't just *buy* a quart of milk, he has to get the store to *sell* it to him. But he's really got me over a—I'd just love to call him on this, but I don't dare give him a reason to—"

"No, no," Kyla's mother said. "At this point, I don't think you want to do anything to—"

"*New York,*" Mrs. Laskey said. "All those filthy people from God only knows where . . . I just wonder how long this has been going on."

"Carol," Kyla's mother said. "I'm really serious. I really don't think it's prudent to jump to any . . . And besides, it's bound to be a wonderful learning opportunity for the girls. I only wish I could give Kyla an opportunity like this. And if anyone deserves a little time to herself, you know it's you."

Mrs. Laskey sighed loudly, and for a moment—since nothing else was happening—Kyla wondered if she could go back into the living room to get her mother. But then Mrs. Laskey laughed. "So, speaking of duplicitous sons-of-bitches," she said, "how was last night?"

"Why do you have to do it?" Ellen had said.

"I don't *have* to . . . ," Kyla said.

"You *want* to go on spring vacation with Janey Laskey?" Ellen said.

It was already the end of February. Snow from a recent storm still covered the ground and lay along the branches, and the sky was a glassy blue. But Kyla could feel spring marshaling strength right behind winter's fortifications.

"I feel sorry for her," Kyla said.

"I feel sorry for her, too," Courtney said.

"Well, I feel sorry for her, too," Ellen said. "When she's not around. But it's really hard to feel sorry for her when she is around."

"She's troubled," Kyla said.

"*Kyla—*" Ellen looked at her. "'She's troubled.'"

"Besides," Kyla said. "I get to see New York."

"New York's great," Courtney said. "I used to get to go all the time. It's the worst thing about moving here."

"We'll probably stay at the Plaza or the Carlyle or someplace like that," Kyla said.

"I still don't see why your mother's making you do it," Ellen said.

"She *isn't*," Kyla said. She looked at Ellen in bewilderment. Oh. Of course. *Ellen was jealous.* "She just wants me to be able to go to all the museums and the ballet and that stuff. And Mrs. Laskey's her friend . . ."

"Kyla's mom is so sweet," Courtney said dreamily, and Kyla looked at her with gratitude; she was so pretty, sprawled out on Ellen's bed. The prettiest girl in school, and she was *their* friend—Kyla's and Ellen's. Her short blond hair fluffed out evenly, like a dandelion. Her blue eyes—lighter than the sky—reflected nothing.

"But why does your mom like Mrs. Laskey so much?" Ellen said.

"*Ellen,*" Kyla said.

"They have bags of money," Courtney said. "They have a big, huge money bin in their basement, my dad says."

"I think Mrs. Laskey's crazy," Ellen said. "My mother doesn't like her at all."

"My mother feels sorry for her," Kyla said. And then she said the thing she was never supposed to say, not about anyone, or was even supposed to know. "She used to be in the clinic where my mother works."

"I bet she takes pills," Courtney said. "You know the way she's all puffed up?" She studied her fingernails and frowned. "Mr. Laskey's handsome, but I'd hate to be married to him. They came to my parents' cocktail party last week, and Mr. Laskey and Peter Nussbaum's mother were flirting away like crazy."

"Really?" Ellen said.

"Mr. Laskey was flirting with everybody," Courtney said.

Kyla looked at her. Flirting. Flirting, actually, was when you . . . "What was he doing?" she asked.

"Just . . ." Courtney said. "Just nothing. He was flirting. He was flirting with my mother, too. I bet he flirts with your mother."

"No he doesn't," Kyla said, and her heart veered.

"Rich Laskey is nice, though," Ellen said.

"Rich Laskey?" Courtney said. "Rich Laskey is *gorgeous*. But you know what? He looks exactly like Mr. Laskey, actually."

Ellen and Kyla looked at her. "Yikes," Ellen said. "That is so *strange* . . ."

Outside, the air was as clean as an apple, and the crystal branches were glittering. Kyla shut her eyes, to keep Mr. Laskey's face from Richie's, but the two merged unpleasantly. "I'm sick of sitting around," she said. "Let's go outside."

"It's cold," Courtney said. She shifted on the bed and sighed.

"What should we do?" Ellen said.

All around them were Ellen's toys and games. The television sat, opaque, in the next room. Dark, Kyla thought, but still seeing—still receiving everything that was happening. You could turn it off, but that only meant that *you* couldn't see, behind its darkness, what it was seeing. Sometimes at night, when you had to turn it off to go to sleep, you could feel the world seeping out from the blocked screen—the hot confusion of laughter, the footsteps pounding like a giant, besieged heart, the squealing tires, the eruptions of gunfire, and fearful pictures you couldn't help staring at before they vanished, and people at desks, smiling as though you'd imagined all the rest of it—rising up on all sides of you, staining the evening with the smells of blood and perfume and metal, staining the helpless moments before sleep, and your dreams, and the tattered edges where you broke through into morning.

"I know what we can do," Courtney said. She propped herself up lazily on an elbow. "One of us can pretend to be Richie Laskey."

How nice it would be to be at home, Kyla thought, in her own room. With soft darkness outside and her mother right downstairs . . .

Ellen was looking at Courtney strangely. "How do you mean?" she asked.

Then Kyla turned to Courtney, too, and her heart veered again.

"It's easy," Courtney said. "I'll show you."

"Okay," Ellen said.

The sounds of Ellen's mother moving around downstairs were fantastically loud in Kyla's ears.

"We'll take turns," Courtney said.

"Okay," Ellen said again.

Kyla heard Ellen speak, but she couldn't take her eyes off Courtney.

Courtney was watching her. "I'll be Richie," Courtney said. The clear blue silence of her eyes was like the silence of a clock. "Kyla first." She held out her hand. "Okay?"

"Why do I have to go to New York with the Laskeys?" Kyla said.

"You don't have to, darling. Of course." Kyla's mother looked surprised. "I didn't realize you were so upset about it. I was just so astonished when the Laskeys offered—it's extremely generous of them. Of course, I knew Carol would be so happy if Janey had a friend along, but I only accepted because it seemed like such a wonderful opportunity for you."

If her mother knew that Janey lied all the time and used words like *buns*, and *piss*, and even worse things, she might not think the Laskeys were so wonderful. And if she only understood how Janey really treated her when she came over to their house for dinner—that blank *yes, thank you, no, thank you*—You could feel exactly what Janey was thinking, that Janey was thinking about Kyla's mother as if she were the maid.

"I know Janey isn't your favorite person," her mother said.

"I hate Janey," Kyla said.

Her mother waited for a moment. "I know Janey isn't your favorite person," she said again. "But your kindness to her means so much. I'm very grateful, and I know her mother and father are, too."

"I feel sorry for Mrs. Laskey," Kyla said.

"For Carol?" Kyla's mother looked at her with amusement. "Carol's one of the most fortunate women I know. She's just as capable as anything—you don't remember that house when the Fosses owned it. *And* she has the means to enjoy her life, which is very important, darling, as I think you'll find one of these days, though, of course, there are other things that are more important, aren't there. And she's so *attractive*. I happen to know she hasn't done a thing to her face. You're very unusual, darling—most little girls would want to be just like her."

"I'd hate to be married to Mr. Laskey," Kyla said.

"Would you, darling?" Her mother laughed a little. "Well, fortunately, that's nothing you have to worry about. But it could be worse, you know. Dick is demanding, I suppose, and you could say he's a selfish man—or self-involved—but he's cultured and he's broad-minded and he's attractive and he's energetic and he can be loads of fun. And he's certainly a good provider. All in all, he's what I'd call a good catch."

Kyla looked around at the pretty living room. Didn't her mother even like it? It was so much sweeter than the Laskeys' big white glassy house, with all its ugly paintings and statues— *sculptures*. "Wasn't my father a good catch?" Kyla said.

Kyla's mother stroked Kyla's hair. "Your father's a very fine man," she said. "He has a kind and generous heart, like you. He just . . . lacks ambition. I suppose it's a good quality to be content with things as they are, but not when you're the father of a young child. It used to—" She stopped, and laughed a regretful little laugh. "The fact is, your father and I just never really belonged together. Although"—she smiled at Kyla—"if we hadn't been together, I wouldn't have you, would I, darling? And speaking of you, what do you want to do this afternoon?"

"Stay here," Kyla said.

"Oh, darling. It's Saturday. You can't just stay in and mope around all day. Isn't there any special thing you want to do? Don't you want to call Ellen?"

"No," Kyla said.

"Or Courtney?"

Kyla shook her head.

"Don't you like your friends anymore?" her mother said. "You haven't seen Ellen or Courtney in so long."

Kyla leaned against her mother's coolness.

"Don't *cling*, darling," her mother said. "You're getting much too big."

Kyla jumped away. What if her mother were to see what she herself had seen only this morning, in the mirror, for the first time? She was getting big. It was possible, after all, that she would get those legs that bulged out. Or the horrible little stomach that Judy Winner's sister got when she went into high school. Little things seemed to be happening to her face, too. In the mirror that morning, it had looked as if someone else climbed into her face during the night and was stretching it out into their own. And where was *her* face going? The face that her mother loved? She turned away.

"All right, darling. Please don't sulk." Her mother sighed. "You don't have to go to New York. I just want more in the way of advantages for you than I ever had—I want you to have an exciting life."

"But your life *is* exciting," Kyla said. She stared at her mother. "Isn't it, Mother? Isn't it? Your life isn't boring. Isn't your life exciting?"

"My darling," her mother said, and Kyla saw that there were things happening to her face, too. "My good, kind little girl."

"Janey," Mr. Laskey said, "just eat that nicely, please, like an adult. If you didn't want fruit salad you shouldn't have ordered it."

"Want fruit *salad*," Janey said. "I didn't want to come on this *trip*."

"That's not how I happen to remember it," Mr. Laskey said.

"I *wanted* to go skiing with Richie," Janey said.

"When, like Rich, you are fourteen," Mr. Laskey said, "and when, like Rich, you have a friend whose parents own a condo in Vail, then, like Rich, you may go skiing."

"When, like Rich, I am a boy," Janey said.

The waitress loomed hopefully. "How is everything?" she said, looking at Mr. Laskey.

"Just fine," Mr. Laskey said irritably. Then he seemed to remember who she was, and smiled. "Everything just as good as it used to be." He nodded commendingly.

"Well, that's nice," the waitress said. She appeared to be waiting for him to say something more.

Janey cast a small, contemptuous smile at her fruit salad, but Alice burst into tears.

"What's the matter now, Alice?" Mr. Laskey said.

"*Anything we want,*" Alice announced belligerently.

"You have what you want," Mr. Laskey said, looking bewildered.

"What do you want, Alice?" Janey said. "Just calm down and tell me."

"You said you wanted cinnamon toast," Mr. Laskey said.

"No!" Alice roared. She pointed at Kyla's sundae. *"That."*

Mr. Laskey sucked in his cheeks and stared at his own

sundae. "Miss? Miss?" he called. "One more hot fudge sundae, please. For the young lady."

Alice's noisy tears were absorbed into the general cheerful clatter of the restaurant. But it was amazing, Kyla thought, how loud the voices of little children were. Whether it was joy or sorrow or terror, you could hear them screeching blocks away. Not just Alice, though she did seem prodigious, but all little children. It was nature, probably; it was nature that made Alice loud and it was nature that made Alice cute. Nature made little children helpless, but nature protected them, too, with loudness and cuteness. Kyla herself had probably once been able to produce sounds just like Alice's, and she'd never even noticed! And now, no matter how much she might want to let out a howl that would bring the whole neighborhood running, there wasn't a chance of it. Because the minute people struggled to get a bit free of nature, and could begin to take care of themselves, the point was, they stopped being loud, and they stopped being cute.

"All right, now," Mr. Laskey said as the waitress put an enormous hot fudge sundae in front of Alice. "Does everybody have what he or she wishes? Is everybody happy?"

"You bet, pal," Janey said.

"Jane," Mr. Laskey said. "Are we having some kind of problem today?"

Janey held his gaze for a moment and then looked away. "No," she said.

"You're sure," Mr. Laskey said.

"Yes," Janey said.

"Because," Mr. Laskey said, "if there is a problem, maybe you'd like to tell me what it is so we can clear it up right now."

"There isn't," Janey said.

"Isn't what?" Mr. Laskey said.

"Isn't a problem," Janey said.

"What was that?" Mr. Laskey said. "I didn't hear you."

For a moment Janey didn't speak. "There isn't a problem," she said finally, in a low, dead voice.

"That's my girl," Mr. Laskey said. "All problems forgotten. Now—" He looked at his watch. "We'll go back to the hotel for a three o'clock nap, then we'll get up at five-thirty, and at six forty-five we'll have had our baths and be ready to go. Everybody with me?"

"I'm with you," Janey said. "You mean we have to have a two-and-a-half-hour nap."

"Aha," Mr. Laskey said. "Another mathematician in the family."

"A two-and-a-half-hour *nap*?" Janey said.

"No!" Alice said in alarm. "It's ideal!"

"You're confused, Alice," Janey said.

"On the contrary," Mr. Laskey said. "Do you know what an adult is? Jane? An adult is someone who's learned to delay gratification. We're going to the ballet tonight, and we're going to have a very late night. In short, this is non-negotiable. But the question is, we have time for one quick activity before our nap, so what do we all want to do?"

"We all want to go to the children's zoo," Alice said.

"We all want to go to the Museum of the American Indian," Janey said.

"Kyla?" Mr. Laskey said.

"Either's fine with me," Kyla said. *She* just wanted to go home.

"Well," Mr. Laskey said, "we were just at the Museum of the American Indian yesterday. Besides, it's very, very far away—I'm afraid it's impracticable."

"It's only one-thirty," Janey said. "We have time."

"Let me be the judge of that," Mr. Laskey said.

"But it's only one-*thirty*," Janey said.

"I think we all heard you," Mr. Laskey said. "And *I* said, let me be the judge of that."

"Children's *zoo*, children's *zoo*," Alice chanted.

Mr. Laskey peered at Alice. "Are those dark circles I see?" he said. "Didn't you sleep well last night?"

"No," Alice said nonchalantly.

Mr. Laskey looked at Janey. "What does she mean?" he said.

Janey and Kyla looked at each other. "She had night-mares," Janey said. "She kept me and Kyla awake all night."

"Is this true?" Mr. Laskey said.

"Janey wouldn't let me call mommy," Alice said.

"Did you want to wake mommy up?" Janey said fiercely. "Is that what you wanted, Alice?"

Alice hung her head, and large tears began to form in her eyes. "No," she said in a little voice. Though actually, Kyla thought, Janey was no mathematician at all—it wouldn't have been much past ten at home when Alice first woke them.

"What upset you, Alice?" Mr. Laskey said. "Was it the museum yesterday? Was it the Indians?"

"You weren't there," Alice said. Her shoulders were bowed and she stared at her melting sundae, tears sliding from her wide eyes. "The pond was there, and ice was on it, and it opened up, and you were thin air."

"I'm here, sweetheart. It was just a nightmare. I'm right here."

"That's what I told her," Janey said. "I told her it wasn't real."

"I was—" Mr. Laskey began. Then he looked at the wall, as if something had suddenly appeared there. "Jane," he said,

"I'm proud of you. I'm gratified that you took responsibility and stayed calm."

Janey stared straight ahead; amazingly, it looked as if she was about to cry.

"And you know what?" Mr. Laskey said. "I have a thought. I think what we should do before our nap is to get Mommy a present. Isn't that a good idea?"

Janey and Alice nodded soberly.

"We'll get Mommy a present to show that we're thinking about her and to congratulate her for having two such good girls. Now, I'm just going to make a phone call, and when I come back Alice will have finished her sundae and we'll march along."

"We'll call Mommy?" Alice said, still furrowed and dubious.

"We'll call Mommy when we're all together," Mr. Laskey said.

"When . . ." Alice said, and shook her head slowly.

"When we can be all together at the phone in the hotel," Mr. Laskey said.

Well, it was true; Janey, of all people, had taken responsibility last night. There had been no alternative. When Alice awakened for the second time, rattling as if in the grip of a high fever, and could not be consoled, Kyla had said to Janey, "Should we get your father?"

"I don't know," Janey said. "Daddy said if we needed anything we should ask Donald."

Alice, in a damp heap, continued to sob. "But what do we need?" Kyla said.

"Hmm," Janey said. She and Kyla looked at each other. "True . . ."

"*Daddy Daddy Daddy Daddy,*" Alice screamed.

"Be quiet, Alice, *please,*" Janey said. "You're going to wake up everyone in the hotel."

"*Daddy——*" Alice screamed again, at an increased volume.

"All *right,*" Janey said. "I'll get him."

But she was not able to rouse him either by knocking on his door or—when Kyla located a plastic card that told you how to call the other rooms—by telephone.

Kyla could hear her own heart pounding, or maybe it was Janey's, as they both snuggled against Alice on the little cot. What if Mr. Laskey had actually had a heart attack? What if he was lying there dead in the next room?

"Hey, Alice, let go," Janey said. "I'm going downstairs to get you a cup of hot milk, and then you're going to sleep."

Janey put her coat over her nightie and went out the big wooden door of their room, and Kyla remembered that there were many other people, in many other rooms, all around them. Beyond the sad blue flowers on the wallpaper, in fact, millions of people, who couldn't help them at all, slumbered on in the twinkling city. At least Alice was still cute, lucky for her; Kyla thought of the new plainness spreading like an illness through her own face. *Don't cling,* her mother had said. "Do you want to play something, Alice?" Kyla said, when Alice grew quieter. "Do you want to play Baby?"

Alice hiccuped. "No!" she shrieked.

And then Janey had returned, with, in fact, a big mug of hot milk. "Here, Alice," she said.

Alice accepted the mug and held it out to Kyla. "Baby drink," she said, and hiccuped again.

"Stop that, Alice," Janey said. "You drink that yourself. Pronto. Donald made them put honey in it for you, wasn't that nice? So I want you to say thank you to him the very next time you see him."

Janey sat down stiffly and looked out the window while Alice drained her milk with gulps and sighs and, finally, a little belch.

"Donald said nothing can wake him up when he's asleep," Janey said. "He said once there was a burglar in his apartment and his roommate screamed and called the police and the police came and he slept through it all."

Kyla nodded, though Janey was still looking out the window.

"Lucky Richie," Janey said.

"For sure," Kyla said. And then it was as if Janey had lifted a curtain, and what was there—and had been there all along—was Richie. But Richie blending back and forth with Mr. Laskey—blending with Mr. Laskey helplessly because she had done something to him. She had done something to him, with Ellen and Courtney; she had let something happen to Richie.

The next morning when they got up and got dressed, Janey was still frozen slow and pale. But then there was Mr. Laskey, reading his newspaper at the breakfast table, just as always. "Daddy's here!" Alice observed superfluously. Janey paused; Alice scampered ahead to the table, and Janey went right into the cross mood that had lasted her all day.

"There," Mr. Laskey said when the bracelet they had all—including Kyla—chosen for Mrs. Laskey was put into its beautiful little velvet box. "I think Mommy's going to be very happy with that."

And no wonder, Kyla thought—delicate strips of gold, flashing with stars. It wasn't fair—it would look so much prettier on her own mother. And her mother deserved it, which Mrs. Laskey did not, and her mother would have been so much more grateful to have it. Kyla could just see her mother's face, radiant with surprise and love, if Kyla could present her with just such a little velvet box.

Mr. Laskey raised his hand in the air again, and this time what appeared was a taxi. They all climbed into the back seat quickly enough—Kyla landed a bit sideways between Janey and the door—but when Mr. Laskey gave the address of their hotel, the driver shook his head in disgust. "You'd be better off walking," he shouted over the loud fuzz of his radio. "The whole East Side is a nightmare."

"Thank you for your concern, sir," Mr. Laskey said. "But we'll keep the taxi. It's a good fifteen blocks, and the little girls are tired."

"You're absolutely positive," the driver said. He turned down his radio. "In three more blocks we're not going to budge."

Mr. Laskey smiled. "I understand, sir," he said. "But what do you suggest? We're too tired to walk, and our hotel's on the East Side."

"What I suggest, sir," the driver said, "in that case is, you move to the West Side."

"Ha, ha, ha," Janey said.

"Because furthermore," the driver said, "once I get into this shit I'm not going to be able to get out."

"I'll bear your difficulties in mind, sir," Mr. Laskey said.

"It does me good to hear you say this," the driver said, "because in a situation like today I starve."

The cab, which had been hurtling from side to side, causing Alice to turn a delicate green, was indeed slowing down almost to a standstill. "It costs me more to hire the fucking car on a day like this than I can make."

"I will, as I've said, sir, bear that in mind," Mr. Laskey said.

"Jane, human beings do not lead difficult lives for your personal amusement. Our driver is understandably anxious, but once we get past the bridge traffic everything will be fine."

But within one more block they had entered a solid mass of honking horns in which Kyla's fatigue seemed to entrap her like amber. And after a time Mr. Laskey leaned forward. "What's the problem, driver?" he said. "We haven't moved for twenty minutes."

"What's the problem?" the driver said. "The problem is we aren't moving. Or, wait—you mean to ask what's *causing* the problem."

"That was my intention," Mr. Laskey said. A pulse had begun to throb in his forehead. "Yes."

The driver turned around and stared at Mr. Laskey. "Oh, hey—" he said, and struck the side of his head with his palm "—I get it! From which, ah . . . *planet* do you folks hail?"

"Perhaps you'll be so kind . . ." Mr. Laskey said.

"With pleasure," the driver said. He turned the radio up savagely, but it was almost impossible for Kyla to hear through the static and the honking what it was saying. There was an apartment building, somewhere near their hotel, and there were policemen—

"Who?" Janey was yelling over all the noise. *"What did he do?"*

" 'Who?' " the driver yelled back. " 'What?' Incredible. Every radio station in the city. Every television network in the universe. More blood per cubic foot than the siege of Stalingrad. Where are you from, folks, seriously now—New Jersey?"

"Tell me, tell me, tell me!" Janey was shouting.

"This is not important, Jane," Mr. Laskey said.

"Not important," the driver said. "Right. Not important.

Well, of course it's not important. You types really stick together, don't you? Sure, if the guy's rich enough, if the guy's
handsome enough, if the guy remembers what kind of mineral water each of his patients drinks, it's just not *important* if
he bludgeons his wife to death with a floor lamp, is it. It's not
important that he pulverized her."

"I don't think this is strictly—" Mr. Laskey began.

"Oh, pardon," the driver said. "I have the honor of ad-
dressing a gentleman of the law, I'll wager. It's been *alleged* that
this guy liquefied his wife; it's been *alleged* that the neighbors
waded in through body parts; it's been *alleged* that he fled, dragging his poor little child with him, to his girlfriend's apartment
where the cops later found a sweater, all gunked up with hair
and blood that allegedly matches his wife's; and now it's being
alleged that he's up on the roof with this kid and he's—"

"Sir, I do not think—" Mr. Laskey said, and Alice began
to cry.

"Nothing's going to happen to you, Alice," Janey said.
"No one cares about *you*."

"That's right, Alice," Mr. Laskey said. "Nothing's going
to happen to any of us."

"Oh, hey—" The driver turned around. He looked into
Alice's eyes and took her hand. "Hey, I'm sorry, darlin'. It's
going off, right now." He turned the radio off. "Click, right?
No more depressing stories."

"Sir," Alice said, and rubbed her cheek against his hand.

Mr. Laskey sighed. "Alice, sweetheart," he said, "let the
man drive."

"Why did he do it?" Janey said. "Daddy?"

"We'll never know, Jane," Mr. Laskey said. "Normal
people can never penetrate the mind of a sick individual." He
rolled down his window and thrust his head out.

"The wife was trash," the driver said. "What do you want to bet? A slut. A nag. A gold-digger. All the same, he should've just divorced her."

"Girls—" Mr. Laskey looked at his watch. "I'm afraid it would be a great deal faster to walk at this point."

"Hey, listen to this guy, kids!" the driver said. "The original rocket scientist. *It would be faster to walk!* When do you think Mr. Wizard got a chance to perform the calculations? Say"—he turned around with raised eyebrows—"how's *right here* for you folks?"

"Do we get to pat the goaties?" Alice said as Mr. Laskey opened the door.

"Alice," Janey said, "you're confused again."

Mr. Laskey handed the driver a bill. "Here you are, sir. I sincerely hope this will recompense you for your time."

"And I, sir"—the driver dropped the bill into the gutter—"sincerely hope *this* will encourage *you* to reinsert your patronizing shit back up your butt, where it came from."

"The second we get inside," Mr. Laskey said as they straggled up the steps to the hotel, "I want you to get yourselves upstairs—It's way past three. Way, *way* past three," he added, shaking his head ominously. "And I want you to wash those hands. Alice's especially."

"Her hands are clean," Alice said loftily. "She washed them after lunch."

"That was after lunch," Mr. Laskey said. "You've touched God knows what since."

As they stepped inside the hotel, five or six young men in uniforms—bellboys and desk clerks—swiveled away from a small television on the front desk. Their eyes, brilliant with excitement, dimmed immediately into courteous greeting. "Hello, Mr. Laskey," one of them said. "Horrifying, this business, isn't it?"

"Horrifying," Mr. Laskey said, glancing at his watch irritably. "Come *along*, girls."

"Oh, Mr. Laskey——" Donald disengaged himself from the group and hurried over.

"What's that?" Mr. Laskey frowned back at Donald.

Donald hesitated.

"Yes?" Mr. Laskey said. He paused, looking at his watch again, and Alice bumped into his leg.

"That is," Donald said, "Miss Shawcross was here for you. I'm afraid she just left."

"Didn't she get my message?" Mr. Laskey said.

"I don't know, sir," Donald said.

"My mother's on the phone?" Alice said.

"Shut up, Alice," Janey said.

Alice tugged Mr. Laskey's sleeve. "Janey said, 'Shut up, Alice,'" she reported.

"Be quiet, Alice," Mr. Laskey said. "But I left her a message at her office. Didn't she get it?"

"I don't know, sir. She didn't say."

Alice sat down suddenly on the carpet.

"Your dress, Alice!" Janey exclaimed. "Get off your butt. Mother would kill you!"

"My mother would kill *you*," Alice said, but she scrambled to her feet, swatting at her rear end.

"How are my girls?" Donald said. "Imaginations cooler in the light of day?" He winked at Janey, who gazed serenely at a point on the other side of his head.

Mr. Laskey appeared to wake from a trance. "Don't we say hello to people who say hello to us?" he said.

"Ah, Stan—" Donald said, and one of the uniformed men wrenched himself away from the TV screen to open the door for a man with a briefcase, and the blaring of horns entered the lobby.

"This is the damnedest business," Mr. Laskey said. "God damn it."

"Horrible, sir," Donald said. His eyes flicked eagerly toward the TV. "Incredible what a human being can do, isn't it?"

"You can play with your toys, Alice," Janey said. "You don't have to just lie there."

"Yes, I do," Alice said. "It's nap time." A large tear trickled from each eye.

"What's the matter?" Janey said. "Are you afraid to fall asleep? Are you afraid of having another nightmare?"

"I want to go home," Alice said. "I want to see Mommy. I want Billy and the big rope."

"Is she all right?" Kyla said. "What does she mean?"

"Oh, nothing," Janey said. "She gets Billy Jacobs to tie her up."

"I don't feel well," Alice said. She rolled over into her pillow.

Kyla looked at Janey. "Should we get your father?" she said.

"No," Janey said. "She's playing. Are you playing, Alice?"

"Yes," Alice said mournfully. "I'm playing Disease."

"Nurse—" Janey said. "The patient in bed number one has a horrible disease. She needs a sleeping potion."

"Right away, Doctor," Kyla said, and poured a glass of water in the bathroom.

Alice fell asleep before she even finished her water, and

Janey picked up the big book she'd brought along, but Kyla looked at the dark TV screen. "Don't you want to see what's happening?" she said.

"No," Janey said. "I'm reading."

Kyla stood up and looked out the window. But of course there was nothing to see except tall apartment buildings, where everyone would be watching television to see what was happening. And below, nothing but stalled traffic stretching on and on, lines of cars like strands of colored beads. Lots of blue and green and black, more yellow, not so many red . . . If there were fewer than fifteen red, it wouldn't happen. If there were more than fifteen . . . The steely hand on the child's shoulder, the caress of metal against soft hair, the entire universe exploding in her skull, vanishing into thin air. The entire universe exploding—the universe—how many times was Kyla going to have to see it? To hear it? "*Please* let's turn it on," Kyla said. "Just for a second."

"*No,*" Janey said. "I don't want Alice to wake up. I don't want Alice to freak out again. My father said we should rest, because we're going to the ballet tonight. My father's the one who's paying for this hotel. My father's the one who paid to bring you along."

"*I* know," Kyla said.

"Stuff like this happens all the time," Janey said. "Even at home. There was this person at home, in fact, who was a famous judge, but his wife was a secret drug addict, and he was afraid someone would find out. So one day he said, 'Goodbye, dear, kiss kiss, I'm going away on a trip to get lots of presents to bring home to you, and I'll be back in a few days.' So he drove his car down the street and waved to all the neighbors and he put a plastic bag over his clothes so he wouldn't get blood on his tie, and he snuck back. Lucky for him, it was the coldest winter in a hundred years, and there were icicles hanging from all the trees and houses. So he opened the door and dragged his wife outside and snapped off the biggest icicle he could reach and he stabbed it into her stomach stab stab, and there was splash splash blood all over the place and his wife tried to scream but she was dead. And then the judge snuck back to his car and drove to the airport and flew away. And the next day the sun came out and all the blood and the murder weapon melted into the ground."

"So how did they catch him?" Kyla said.

"How should I know?" Janey said, and turned back to her book. "Nobody, ick, talks about it, obviously."

From down below the soft tumult rose gently, like the sounds of a beach, Kyla thought, when your eyes are closed. What was going on out there? What was happening? Everybody else could see. Donald was watching, and the taxi driver and the waitress would be somewhere by now watching, and all the people in all the other rooms of the hotel and in the little buildings out the window, and Miss Shawcross, and far away, in the mountains, Richie was watching—Richie was watching helplessly—and across the body-choked lagoons, Mrs. Laskey and Ellen and Courtney were watching, and her mother and Dr. Loeffler, twisting together on the sofa, were watching, their blood pounding and their eyes shining—

No—her mother was alone, pale, sitting bolt upright and trembling for the poor little child, *not* with Dr. Loeffler, that was what *Janey* thought; Kyla sprang up and turned on the television. ". . . to de-lethalize the situation—" a voice was saying. Janey reached the dial before the picture even came on, but Alice was awake already, and crying. "Thanks, Kyla," Janey said. "Thanks a lot, old buddy."

"I'm sorry—" Kyla said.

"Where's Daddy?" Alice roared. "Where's my daddy?"

"Hush, Alice," Janey said, curling up beside her on the cot. "Daddy's asleep in the next room."

But Alice had begun to scream. "Should we get your father?" Kyla whispered. "Do you think we should go get your father?"

"Our father's asleep," Janey said. "Our father's resting. Our father's asleep in the next room, and he doesn't want to be bothered, and plus, she's going to get over it."

ALL AROUND ATLANTIS

When do I think about you? Never, these days—almost never. When I was what, about twenty, I suppose, I finally got around to reading the little book you'd written about Sándor. It only took an afternoon, and when I finished, I put the book away, along with various old, disorderly feelings, and just left the whole clutter for about thirty years' worth of dust to settle over.

Well, except for once, when Neil (a person who used to be my husband) returned from a business trip to somewhere and mentioned that he'd happened to catch a glimpse, on some highbrow TV talk show, of a man—perhaps the man I'd mentioned at some time—who seemed possibly to have been something of an authority on my uncle, or my mother's uncle, or whatever it was Sándor had been to me. Naturally, that sort of called you up for a bit, and then you sank back out of my thoughts again.

But you know what, Peter? Yesterday at the service, I turned around at exactly the moment you showed up and slipped into the back row. So what do you think of that?

After the service, I walked through the park. It was raining and the sky was a kindly color, soft and gray. The fountains were steaming in the cold. I was glad for the mournful, commiserating weather—the gentle, chilly rain and the vaporous air. I'll bet you were annoyed, though. You were probably scrambling for a taxi, running home for a hot shower and a nice, relaxing something or other before cocktails or a dinner. Or maybe you ducked in someplace to brood over a cup of coffee. Or not to brood.

In the park we were all bundled up. Everyone was wearing big, dark coats and silly, serviceable winter hats. I'd grabbed that beautiful old challis scarf of Lili's—remember it?—from her closet to wrap around my head because I left my own particular silly, serviceable winter hat on the plane, in some fit of pure hysterical disorganization.

The children were covertly testing their galoshes in the puddles, and the adults were all soldiering on with big, black umbrellas. And then something happened. The rain got gentler and gentler, and then even gentler. And then it simply stayed where it was, hanging in the air like a beaded curtain. Everything halted; the world was between breaths—no motion, no sound . . .

And when the world started up again, what was falling was snow—large, airy clumps of it, like blossoms tumbling silently from a bucket.

In a moment everything was covered with big, white blossoms—us, the trees, the ground . . . The umbrellas looked like parasols. Everything was silent. Everything was muffled and remote, as though it were a picture. A distant brightness and the scent of flowers swelled into the air, and my heart fluttered as though I'd awakened in a picture of something that had existed briefly a long time ago—a memory.

But whose memory was it? Not mine, exactly; it wasn't a memory of mine.

Did you look for me yesterday? Well, of course, you might not have recognized me. I wish I hadn't been so timid! But *did* you look for me—did you have some thought like, *Yes, Anna must be here . . .* ?

Imagine, talking about Lili all these years later! What would you have said, I wonder. For that matter, what would I have said, myself?

Because now, of course, we're the same age, you and I, but the gap between us used to be so large! Especially when you first appeared—my eleven or twelve to your eighteen or nineteen. And naturally I developed a habit of thinking of you as the given—immutable, an adult; and I, a child, as open to scrutiny, correction, evaluation . . . So it didn't even strike me until last night, hours after catching that glimpse of you (and then it struck me forcibly), that you probably didn't even notice, back then, the things that felt, from the inside, like *me*—what constituted *me*.

Did you ever hear that once when Lili cut her finger I fainted? The fact is, I've been waiting my whole life for her death. When I was little, years before you arrived, I used to watch her so intently . . . making breakfast, getting dressed for work . . . as though it was only my vigilance that would prevent her from vanishing off the face of the earth.

Even years after I left home, I knew when she was sick, I knew when she was frightened, I knew when something had happened to cause her pain. When the phone rang, I knew if it was Lili who was calling. And I thought surely that when she died a jagged line would streak through my heart, cracking it in two.

Well, as it happened, not at all. When the time came, as it happened, I was out in the desert, working quite serenely on some old bits of a pot, trying to grasp what they had to say about a group of people who seem to have once lived in that area, in vast pueblos. The sky was just *shining*, Peter—shining and blue—but all day long, messages were flying around right over my head.

And when I got back to Albuquerque, my answering machine was choked with frantic calls—Lionel's, from Brooklyn, my son, Eric's, from L.A. . . .

But how did *you* hear, I wonder. I doubt your heart cracked in two. Did you learn from a colleague at whatever university you're adorning these days? Or maybe one of those old men who sit all curled over on the park benches like fallen leaves spotted you and beckoned you over. Or maybe you saw the tiny notice in the *Times*; I imagine you've begun to check the obits these days, yourself.

A jolt, yes? Sándor, Lili, the apartment, even the sullen, dark-haired child who was me, shoved out onto the stage in front of you. I can just imagine your face: Human feelings! Right there for anyone to see—irritation, smugness, mortal panic, regret . . . I'm sure you cleaned it all up immediately, but it must have hurt, really, didn't it? I'd love to know that it hurt.

Oh—the synagogue, I hasten to add, was Lionel's doing, not mine, obviously. It was all arranged by the time Lionel got ahold of me. It was what your mother wanted, he said, pre-emptively. I'd absolutely sworn myself to niceness, Peter, but I'm afraid I let a long silence speak for me.

She'd have been appalled, yes? Or—what do you think?—maybe she'd just have gotten a big laugh out of the whole thing. Or is it possible that *was* what Lili wanted? Vaguely, I suppose. Who knows what sort of thing people simply suppress for decades. Or maybe she was hedging her bets there at the end. But, still—a synagogue? I doubt she'd set foot in one more than half a dozen times in her life—and as a tourist, at that. Certainly we were no more religious—she and Sándor and I—than potatoes! Not to doubt Lionel's word, of course. He's as honest as someone can be who can't distinguish what he'd like to be true from the evidence in front of his face.

It's pretty startling to see Lionel (of all people!) coming out of Lili's old room in his bathrobe, that's for sure. But I have to say he was good to her, after his fashion. He outwaited all the others, and eventually she was ready to be taken a little care of. She was pretty tired by then. You would have been surprised. Really, Peter—surprised.

A saint, is what Lionel says, missing the point, as usual. And what I say is, all right, make people into saints if that's what you want; there are worse things to do, I suppose. But I can't help thinking that what Lili really died of was boredom.

Actually . . . I wonder now; I'll bet you don't even re-member Lionel. That is, I think there wasn't ever a time in my conscious life before Lionel was around, but he wasn't around all that *much* till fairly recently. (Well, "recently." You know what I mean—the last couple of decades.) But even when Lionel was around, I doubt you noticed.

Sorry. I exaggerate. I do you an injustice—you and Lionel both. I'm sure you noticed. I'm sure you noticed something taking up the best chair. Let me remind you—Lionel: Lionel drank his tea; he praised the pastry (even when he brought it himself); he'd suddenly speak up and drop onto the conversa-tion some weighty, worthy, immovable subject that left every-one speechless; he actually seemed *delighted* when Mrs. Spiegel dropped in from across the hall ("for just a little moment," as she always put it) . . .

But the fact is, Lionel sort of actually came into his own

on those occasions when Lili disappeared into her room; at some point during those episodes, Lionel used, without fail, to show up, hesitating in the hallway, whispering, clearing his throat, clutching a basically useless offering of soup or coffee cake to be left at the door of Lili's room.

During the period you were around, I know it didn't happen so often—that Lili would just *vanish*, into the darkness behind her door. Oh, there were a couple of episodes, yes—and you, like everyone else, faded away, to leave us in "peace"—but when I was little, before you sat yourself down in our life, it was a pretty frequent occurrence.

Could you have known what that was like for me? I always, I think, simply assumed you did. But, really—how would you have?

That silence! I could cry, of course, but Lili was falling through darkness, down to a world where I couldn't be heard or seen.

The whole apartment was silent when Lili was in her room. No visitors, obviously. There would only be Sándor, working in his room, or taking me back and forth to kindergarten or grade school, trying to entertain me with cards or alphabet games, and to make our small meals cheerful. Did I want to go out and play? No.

Go out? Go out and play, when Lili might just dematerialize forever in my absence? So you can imagine the state I'd be in, back in the days I was small, when Lili would reemerge from her room, as affectionate as ever, utterly tranquil, as though there'd been no break in continuity whatsoever.

I was in sole possession of that terrible silence then, and our apartment was full of conversation again, and laughter.

Constant visitors! All those men! Where could Lili have found them? There sure aren't any around *these* days. Not that I much mind, Peter. But every country in Europe must have been represented, serially, on our sofa, wouldn't you say? And then there were those big, rectangular Americans, too! But maybe you never noticed *any* of Lili's admirers, come to think of it—even the handsome, boastful ones. To you, I'm sure, all of them would have been . . . just . . . *old*. And really, it was Sándor you were there for, wasn't it.

Actually, of all those far-ranging types of men, there was only one that Lili had no use for: Lionel's—that worried, de-liberate, "cultured" type. She liked men who were fun—who drank whiskey, who would take her out dancing or to hear jazz, out into the world.

It never occurred to me until much, much later, of course, to marvel at the way she kept moving. She *worked* so hard, too. I think she'd cut back a lot by the time you showed up, but when I was very small she put in outrageous days at Dr. Weissbard's office. Doing, I believe, the most tedious possible chores—the files, the phones, the bills, the checks, the ap-pointments . . . Sándor would take me to school and pick me up, and sometimes one of Lili's admirers would be drafted to take me to the park or the skating rink, but Lili managed to make me breakfast and dinner, she read to me before bed . . . It wasn't until I had Eric and was working myself that I had any idea how much energy it all must have taken.

I never heard her complain. And I'd be very surprised if you did, Peter. I remember once trotting along behind her when she went into the kitchen for something to put a bunch of flowers in. She looked at the flowers as if to solicit their views on the matter, shrugged, and dropped them into a vase; I think no matter where she'd found herself, she would have experienced her life as a faintly comic, wholly inexplicable spectacle that was being rolled out in front of her.

Did it charm you? Did it irritate you? Did you find it childish? *You*, of course, were an adult. Oh, and here's something else I remember, as if it were holy—Lili stretched out, frowning studiously at her fashion magazine, absently reaching out an arm for me to tuck myself under while I waited for the verdict: *No, this is not elegant* . . .

Well, she was so young; she was scarcely nineteen, I think, when I was born. But one could hardly consider that frivolity of hers an adjunct of youth, could one? I, personally, at least, consider it to have been an act of courage and gallantry—a radical choice.

Fairly early on in my marriage (when it seemed worth it to me, I suppose, to bid for Neil's sympathy regardless of the cost) I confided in him what I'd never tried to confide in anyone else: the sheer terror of those days when Lili would retreat into her room. The moment the door closed, I told Neil, I knew perfectly well Lili was somewhere I simply did not yet exist; anything might happen to her, and there I was, on the other side of the wall, being absorbed into that obliterating silence.

So, what was Neil's response? Naturally enough, he seized the opportunity to point out that I had "personal problems." "And no wonder," he said. Yes, yes, any question would kill her, she was going to disappear into her bedroom one day and just die there, of suffering. No wonder I had nightmares! No wonder I had migraines! "Because she never once just sat you down," he said, "to have a normal conversation about her past situation. She just simply allowed that whole thing to develop instead—that atmosphere of violence and danger."

Oh, Neil had a point or two, I suppose; I've had my share of "personal problems." But what other kind of problem can a person have? And a lot of those problems simply faded away, along with the vestigial nightmares and migraines, after he and I got ourselves together to file for divorce.

It's strange to think my dreams wouldn't have been visible to you at a glance. I was still having them at the time you showed up, after all—almost every night. As soon as I closed my eyes, the dark pools behind them deepened; I floated, was caught, and down I went—toward the scream of the train. The bolt rang shut across the door like the report of a pistol; my shattered vision recomposed into silence and the small white disk of the sun. Through the slats, the silent figures in the fields; the small white disk of the moon, light beating down like nails on the silent insects that scurried, slowed, stopped . . .

How many mornings did I stand at the kitchen door when I was little, trailing a blanket, throbbing with nausea and cold, as the silence of my dreams—a silence like a chloroformed rag—thawed slowly, until I could hear the spoon against the table, the juice pouring into the glass . . . . Sándor poured a bright arc of juice from the beaker; Lili's long, restless hands spread the toast with delicious unsalted butter. Was that really Sándor? Was that really Lili?

The night's dense net was lying slack and invisible around us in the sunlight.

Lili could always feel me looking, and she'd turn anxiously.

I approached, hesitated, and leaned myself abjectly against her. *Bad dreams?* she said.

She was made out of glass, my mother, wasn't she? Out of pale silk. I straightened myself up and shook my head: no.

But Lili turned to the window that looked out onto nothing—onto the brick of the airshaft. Her fingers were pressed at the corners of her closed eyes.

Yes, I had nightmares—children do. After all, it takes some time to get used to being alive. And how else, except in the clarity of dreams, are you supposed to see the world all around you that's hidden by the light of day?

But I also had dreams that were just like heaven: A little lake with leaf-shaped boats . . . a tiny theatre with amazing, living puppets—yes, the most marvelous park, elegant in the snow, against the gray sky, like a deserted palace, or twin-klingly awake again in spring, the trees all in flower . . . blossoms scattering on the surface as I broke back up through the reflections.

And there were other dreams, too, those dreams that just *twist*, you know—a sunny meadow, the black shadow . . .

I sometimes watched you. Did you ever know that? When you began sacking out on our sofa now and then. Tossing about, emitting your little sleep-smothered bleats of terror. I stood watching you, breathing stealthily, afraid to break into those dreams of yours; who knew what would come pouring out?

Sleep was a serious business in that household! You prob-ably heard Lili or Sándor, every once in a while, murmuring breathlessly, pleading . . . Even Walden Tócska, poor thing—flopping and twitching, whimpering in his little bed and sending up smelly eddies of hair . . .

Sweet dreams! Get some rest! Sándor and Lili and I going

our separate ways, the dark pools opening, the whisper of the
trawling nets. And then mornings, watching, walking forward to join Sándor and Lili behind the thin screen of daylight, sitting all together in the kitchen, buttering the toast . . .
More juice? Yes, thanks. And the jam, please.

Those mornings were like a seam, joining two worlds,
one invisible by night, one invisible by day.

Now, how's this for a thought: Suppose you and I had spoken
yesterday, after all. And suppose we'd wandered out together,
talking. Suppose we'd strolled over, you and I, to this coffee
shop where I've imagined you ducking in out of the rain.

I can see you—some version of you—looking at me with
incredulity: But what could have been in my brain at that
time, you might have asked me; how did I account for my
existence? Did I think I was descended from . . . pilgrims?
From a distinguished line of, what—cowboys?

Well, now, it's true that none of those people who hung
around our little apartment talking, talked much about their
"past situations," as Neil put it. That prohibition relaxed, of
course, as time went by, but when I was little, no adult I encountered ever spoke in any personal way about the years of the
war or the decade or so preceding it. And you can be sure that
none of the others inquired!

It seemed perfectly natural to me, when I was a little girl,
that English was the language of choice for our visitors—most
of whom were not madly comfortable in it, to say the least; of
course they spoke English—that was what people *spoke*. And
perhaps you simply took it for granted in your own way, when
you eventually showed up; for you, I suppose, English was just
one more language to explore and then inhabit.

But for those others, obviously, it was altogether a different matter, wouldn't you say? A language so new, so clean, so devoid of association and overtone as to be mercifully almost unlike, I'd suppose, human speech.

But new and clean as it was, and new and clean as I was myself, I could detect—trembling there in the depths of those accents—clues and evidence; it was as if iron vaults, sunk to the bottom of the sea, couldn't prevent the radioactive waste buried in them from transmitting its toxic, shining signals.

The child should be out in the fresh air, Mrs. Spiegel would lament from time to time. *It's not healthy to be all the time indoors!* But Lili would only smile, as if she hadn't quite heard, and put an arm around me. And I curled up closer, to listen.

But, you know, Peter, despite what people say about children (their unerring ear for truth, their piercing vision—all those platitudes), children can't pluck actual specifics out of thin air.

Where did I come from? Frankly, children are philosophers and theoreticians and seers only by default; they're so ignorant they *have* to be philosophers and theoreticians and seers. It's not that children disdain hard data, it's not that they're too lofty for it—on the contrary, they're dealing with as much hard data as they can! Think how much hard data is entailed in just getting the applesauce to stay on the spoon!

Where did I come from? "Europe," all right? That's what I was told, and that was plenty. Mrs. Spiegel might have been happy to share with me her exhaustive knowledge about who in the neighborhood purported to be from Vienna or Budapest or Berlin though they were actually from some miserable shtetl near Lwow, but frankly, Peter, when I was four or five or six, I had other things to worry about! "Europe." That was plenty. "Hungary." *Plenty.*

My first words were Hungarian. Naturally; I was almost one and a half when we left. By the time I was seven, I didn't speak *any* Hungarian. By the time I was twelve, I couldn't—as you may or may not have noticed—understand it!

Isn't it strange? If we can remember, why can't we remember everything? Why can't we remember where we once were? The words we once understood? Little snippets of conversation we heard? If I, for example, can remember back forty-seven or so long years, why can't I remember back forty-nine? Just a few little years more? Why can I not remember my father? I spent almost a year of my life in his presence "over there" until he "developed problems" and evidently blasted himself into literal fragments of despair. So why is it that what I have with me now, instead of a memory, is a solid space that nothing—no memory—can occupy?

I'll tell you what I think. I think we can't remember all the way back because God (to speak metaphorically) arranged it that way. And God arranged it that way, in my opinion, so we can be deceived.

> These highly compressed, enigmatic, and largely private lyrics, anticipatory, even premonitory, in their elegiac tone and obsessive cataloguing of a world which was not yet lost, reflect, inevitably, their broad cultural contexts. Certain theoretical orientations, therefore, may be comfortably invoked with a view to illuminate . . . (etc., etc.).
>
> —From *Atlantis: The Poetry of Sándor Szabados*, by Péter (orthographical-marks-fetched-up-from-the-murk-and-pasted-back-on-for-credibility) Kövi

The cover's faded now, you know; the paper has discolored. No matter—I'm sure the book stays modestly in print.

And how did I feel about it, how did it seem, your little book, when I took a look at it again last night after all these years? That is, aside from the embarrassingness of the prose? Well, you can count on me, Peter, of course, not to be able to identify a lot of the distortions and inaccuracies a book like that is sure to be rotten with. And it's hardly original, I know, to observe that biography is bound to be at least as much about the author as it is about the subject. Yes, that's *not* an original observation, I know. And, all right, your book isn't biography, anyway—it's a translation, plus a "critical appreciation" (or some such slithery disclaimer), which "inevitably" entails "illumination" of the subject himself. Well, I know, Peter.

Oh! But how did I *feel* about it! Hm. All right, yes—how did I feel . . .

Well, I'd have to say . . . . I felt . . . *ambivalent.*

Were you aware, Peter, how Sándor responded to Mrs. Spiegel's admiration? Were you aware how completely insane it drove him? "The genius," as she sometimes referred to him. He could detect her footfall with absolute accuracy, as if the two of them were in the forest, and he'd fade instantly into his room for hours, to write, or to read his Thoreau or Dickens or Auden or Stevens, while Mrs. Spiegel chattered on emptily with Lili in the kitchen, stalling. "Did I hear something?" she'd say, glancing over her shoulder. "No."

Oh, Peter. How he hated to hear her go on about his "brilliance," his "originality," his "place in European letters"! Even when his work was available in German, I once heard him say to Lili, could Mrs. Spiegel have—in any meaningful sense of the word—"read" any? The woman's brain, unfortunately, was a Möbius strip of clichés; things went in, he assumed, in working order, but emulsified there, through a continuous, twisting process of Mrs. Spiegelization. Besides, *what* place in European letters? No Europe, no letters, no place. He had no place anywhere but in our apartment, thank you, he added to me. And that was the only place he wanted.

I remember the way Lili patted his arm, and smiled the lazy, inscrutable smile that kept all those men prisoner on our sofa or tamed them to the yoke of irksome tasks and errands, like picking up groceries or fixing the lamp or taking me to the playground.

When you first met us, were you flabbergasted that Lili never became irritable with Mrs. Spiegel? That Lili always had time for Mrs. Spiegel? Did you realize that Lili actually chided me for mimicking the irresistibly mimicable Mrs. Spiegel? Did you marvel how the two of them used to sit at the kitchen table over interminable tea and cookies?

When I was little I used to sit there at Lili's side, supplied with cookies, myself, and a teacup filled with milk. It made me truly sick, Peter, it made me furious, to look at Mrs. Spiegel's arm, just lying there casually on the table—her sleeve riding up over the blue brand that looked so similar to the numbers stamped on the meat at the grocery store: Did Mrs. Spiegel want to be a human being, or did she prefer to be a slab of meat? The truth is, it was as though that dark number of hers could activate Lili's, even under the "decent" (as I felt) cover of her clothing or bracelets.

They never spoke about the past, really, either, those two. At least when I was around, they never, to use Neil's formula, had "a normal conversation" about their "past situation."

And what do you suppose he *meant* by that, Peter? *A normal conversation about her past situation*—It seems to be one of those things words can construct independently of meaning, doesn't it? Because how could there have been such a thing?

In fact, I don't remember anything that sounded particularly like "a normal conversation" about *anything*! Mr. Korda's arthritis, what the hairdresser said about her son's girlfriend— no subject was sufficiently mundane as to resist a septic influence.

I submit to you, Peter, this example: The day Lili found Walden Tócska in the street and brought him home. Well, as you would imagine, Mrs. Spiegel was simply horrified. "But, darling!" she said. "The beast is filthy!"

Not so, Lili said. That very morning, we'd gone to the vet, where Tócska had received numerous shots and his leg was bound up; we'd bathed and deflead him all afternoon.

But there was no telling where an animal like that had been! What habits it had acquired, or what secret diseases, clever enough to evade the vet's medications, it might be harboring, to spread among us at any instant!

Absurd, Lili said; not scientific. Besides, every child should have a pet, and clearly—she shot a guilty look at me— Anna already adored this dog.

Adored, Mrs. Spiegel protested—though I'd steeled myself to pat, illustratively, the great, snoring, quivering heap of hair—it was completely obvious that, on the contrary, the child was terrified!

Lili inhaled deeply, and put her palms down on the table in front of her. "Lise, are you saying that poor dog should be . . ."

No, but of course not! Mein Gott! (And both women, Peter, had gone absolutely white.) Mrs. Spiegel hadn't *meant* . . . She had only meant . . . She had meant only . . .

And then, Peter, there was just a long, long silence, which Lili brought to a close with a sigh, and that was that.

I mean, *Lili* allowed something terrible to develop? It was *Lili* who created an atmosphere of violence and danger? *Lili* was responsible for an atmosphere of violence and danger?

If the silences around our household were vivid and eloquent, was that Lili's fault? Look, I said to Neil, we were all careful back then. And wouldn't you have been, in my place? It was as if Lili were sleepwalking over the abyss of her own life. What if she were to wake? What if I were to wake her?

What about us, I asked him—Did he think he and I were starting Eric out on some perfect, pure, unpopulated, white-sand beach? Did he actually believe Eric was not going to bear some indelible, if illegible inscription?

Neil looked at me steadily, wagged a finger, and lowered one eyelid. I'll get back to you on that, he said.

I wonder what impression I made on you at first. Oh, I know, Peter, none. But I mean, by the time you showed up, I sup-pose I wouldn't have been all that worrisome; I'm sure I re-sembled a child: I was taking piano lessons, I had my friend Paige . . .

Of course, I had no friends *but* Paige. I sometimes imag-ined my schoolmates rising up unblinkingly to tear my arms and legs from the sockets with a juicy pop and stuff my slippery remains under the bulgy asphalt of the playground. I was even afraid of our poor, raddled dog. You were forced to notice even-tually, of course, that, for someone so scowling and skinny and unwholesome, I was an amazingly poor student; that I couldn't fix my attention on anything, that I seemed actually impervious to information; that all facts, the whole world, disassembled into identical meaningless units and slid off my brain into a heap of smoking rubble. That my sole talent—and it wasn't pronounced!—was for satirizing my mother's suitors.

So, did you ever happen to observe how surprising it was that such a child had become interested in playing the piano? Especially in view of how little ability, I'm sure, I demonstrated.

Well, in fact, I had not been interested in playing the piano. There was a sound, however—partially embedded in a piece of chamber music that I overheard one day on a neighbor's radio—by which I was utterly bewitched. The other voice, speaking to me from just beyond articulation . . . my unknown twin . . .

I hung around our school orchestra a bit, traced the sound, and announced at home that I wanted lessons. Music lessons? All right, good, Lili said. But why the viola? Why not the piano? On the piano one could accompany oneself. Pianists were always in demand. The repertoire was splendid and inexhaustible. We might even manage to find a small piano, second-hand, for ourselves . . .

Ourselves . . . "Did you ever play the piano?" I asked, beadily.

Lili, of course, went instantly vague. Oh, she said, not well. But how did you learn? Mmm, we all played a bit. We? Oh, you know, just . . . girls . . . of our class . . .

I stared around at the boxy furniture, the threadbare rug, the pad of scratch paper lying on the table that said, Dr. Martin Weissbard, Optometrist, and Lili drifted off toward her room.

She wants to play the viola? was what Mrs. Spiegel had to say. No, darling! She wants to play the violin!

Lili shrugged. She says she wants to play the viola.

Impossible! Mrs. Spiegel turned to me: The viola was for girls who wanted to play the violin but weren't gifted. Surely I was gifted! Therefore—she turned back triumphantly to Lili and Sándor—I wanted to play the violin!

Such a word, Sándor said. Gifted. Not to be used in front of a child.

And besides, Lili said. She wants to play the viola.

I was just sitting there, Peter, watching the three of them as they debated, and I had an extremely strange sensation. It was as if it had been given to me to see them in the vast, unruly time before I was alive, weighing and meting out, like beings in an old story, a fairy tale, the destiny of a child, soon to be born—the destiny with which that child was to be equipped against the time when they themselves have become weak, have become mere human beings.

No, I said, and the three of them stared as if I'd dropped in by parachute. I want, I announced into the silence, to play the piano.

Lili and I looked at one another for a long moment. Well, she said comfortably to Mrs. Spiegel, so there we are.

And that's how I met Paige. You didn't imagine I'd met Paige at my school, did you? There *were* no girls like Paige at my school. I met her at music school. And if she and I hadn't become friends, Peter, you would have come into a very different situation, I can tell you—at least in regard to me.

What Paige was doing taking up the violin, I couldn't say. No—what I couldn't say is how she would have *heard* of a violin, in that family of hers. But I don't think she had any more interest in music, per se, than I did. I suppose she was just determined, however briefly (and in whatever manner was available to a ten-year-old who would have been slaughtered if she hadn't behaved "nicely"), to be a mutant.

I don't think you ever met her mother; you weren't around yet the time Mrs. Chandler came for tea. A ritual inspection, I have to presume, which, I have to presume, we failed. Mrs. Chandler was wearing a suit of a kind I'd never seen outside Lili's magazines; the driver was parked downstairs, waiting between a row of garbage cans and a game of stickball. That incredibly courtly old man had just dropped by—Mr. Kecskeméti—and Mrs. Chandler couldn't understand one word out of his mouth. At first she kept saying, Pardon me? Pardon me? And then she gave up and simply carried on her side of the conversation as an improvisational solo. Mr. Kecskeméti was totally bewildered, Lili proceeded to forget her English, Sándor basically left the planet, and Paige and I were clutching each other with merriment.

In Paige's family, there wasn't a loose end in sight. Everything was hermetically sealed; her parents had encased themselves in a veneer of propriety so effective you could have lain right down on their floor, screaming in agony, and never have been heard by a living soul.

I, of course, was a walking loose end. And Paige spotted me immediately: something at last to unravel! And not to be vain, but I must have looked worth unraveling—I suppose it was the very weaseliness of my demeanor that was so promising. And once Paige had set her sights on me, she went about me the way she went about everything—calmly, inexorably, sure of success: Why can't you come over and practice with me? Won't your mother and father let you? Well, next week, then. Or the week after that. So, if it's too far, I'll come to your house. My mother won't mind—she'll have the driver bring me.

So, there was Paige—sitting right in our living room. And needless to say, I was numb with embarrassment. But on whose behalf? On behalf of everyone who'd ever been born, I suppose. Though to my astonishment, all parties other than myself appeared to find everything perfectly natural.

Lili was delighted, of course, that I'd found a friend—so well-mannered and self-possessed a friend at that. Sándor was fascinated by the black velvet headband in Paige's glossy, American hair, her perfect impenetrability, her sudden (calculated, I was quick to inform him) dimplings. Mrs. Spiegel adjudged her gifted—not unbecomingly gifted, but gifted. And Tócska! Poor Walden Tócska, who flattened himself against the wall whenever I appeared, heaped his great bulk across Paige the moment she sat down on the sofa, and wheezed with love as she crooned to him and ran her fingers through his nasty fur.

Paige herself was aglow. I guess she'd had something rather concrete in mind for us ("exotic" or even "colorful," I'm afraid, is how she might have characterized us in later years) and we must have accorded satisfactorily to her specifications—the accents, Sándor's marvelous white hair and elegant posture, my blond, stunning, soigné mother, the mere functionality of the furniture, the noisiness of the street outside, the casually shifting landscape of visitors, the—the-what-was-that-thing-called, Paige asked Lili, the delicious thing with the apples? And how ever could Lili have *made* it!

Oh, one learned, Lili said absently; she'd often watched the cook . . .

Paige and I practiced our duets, and then Lili would give us a snack. Paige would be all smiles and dimples, while I watched

Lili tremulously, hoarding the sight of her as she took the glasses for our milk down from the cupboard . . . the plates . . . It was as if Lili were about to undergo, unknowingly and at my hands, an operation which would either save her life or kill her.

Because as soon as Paige and I were alone in my room, Paige would get right down to business: *What* cook? Well, then, what was my mother talking about? Where were she and Sándor from? Who had taught her to play the piano? So why *didn't* I ask? Why had she stopped playing? Well, so why did her whole education stop? Then why did she have to go away? But didn't she have to go to school there? So why did her mother and father let her go? But anyone could get off a train—they must have come with a car! What had she done wrong? But that was impossible—she couldn't be! Didn't I know what they looked like? Like Kathy Frankel, or like that girl with the bassoon, Risa Loeb. Well, we didn't eat funny food, did we? Anyhow, what did that have to do with it? So what did their friends do then? Their neighbors? The cook?

And where was Sándor when she was away? Did he go with her? But no one could really live in someone's closet— how would you go to the bathroom? And where were all the others? The *others*—like Lili's mother and father; I had grand-parents, didn't I? Or aunts and uncles—didn't Lili at least have a brother or a sister?

Paige and I stared at each other, and then I exclaimed: *No*, breathless, as though running at top speed I'd smacked right into an invisible wall.

Of course not, I said. Obviously Lili had no brother or sister.

Paige frowned. But anyhow, she said, what happened to the piano?

It was very much a common enterprise that Paige and I pursued on those afternoons. It was Paige who could lower me down into the world I couldn't reach by myself, and Paige who could haul me back up, to tell what I had seen. But she couldn't go down there herself. And she couldn't see it—not even at second hand, as a nightmare, the way I could, or even as a migraine. It was up to me to tell her what was there; Paige couldn't see that world at all.

We'd stare at one another, concentrating, going over and over it, straining to fit fragments together—straining to look all around, to see its landscapes, its weathers, its populations . . . Sometimes both of us fell asleep, quite suddenly, like travelers. Often we found ourselves at a cul de sac and had to discard a question or an answer in order to proceed.

But slowly, slowly, from the shadows of overheard conversations, as I felt my way around the shapes of skirted subjects, pictures began to distinguish themselves from the welter of my dreams, refining and embellishing themselves; Paige and I watched, as though we were watching a photograph immersed in a solution developing details from a blur.

What did it look like, Paige asked, staring at me.

I lay across the bed and closed my eyes.

Suppose I'd been able, Peter—by bending my entire self to it—to imagine adequately some tiny element. Just, let's say . . . oh, one barb of the wire fence. Its taper, its point, its torque, its dull gleam altering with the play of the searchlights, the small rag of flesh, the faint, high, venomous raging of the current . . .

Fix it in your mind, I'd instruct myself; focus in on it . . . Can you see it—really see it? Yes? And now—*Step back!*

I don't know, I said, though by then I could hear the boots in the courtyard, smell the dank, urgent anxiety of the dogs, see the beautiful boy . . . Did he sense me through the layers of time, struggling back for him? No, it was something quite different he was waiting for, his eyes huge and blank, growing dull, but still stormy blue, like the ocean. Like Lili's.

Oh, I just fry with shame, Peter, when I think of it. Of course, I felt plenty of shame at the time—Lili's shame, probably, the shame of the body; the shame of the disgusting things that can be done to your body—the disgusting ways your body can be made to fail—by someone whose body is itself intact.

But eventually (unclearly, of course, at first—as an uneasiness or unhappiness) a different shame began to emerge from behind that one: the shame of what Paige and I had been doing. Was I exposing Lili needlessly? Was Paige's interest trivial or merely morbid? Was mine? Had I been using Paige, and to do something that I was too weak or too cowardly to do myself or that I had no business doing in the first place?

I discussed it with you, actually. Constantly, in fact, for some years—in imaginary conversation. And what it seemed to me you had to say on the subject, was, basically, that we all live in one world; that everyone is exactly the same distance from the core of the earth. That it was, therefore, if for no other reason, very much my business. And that Paige—even after her nerve gave out and she buckled down to being a socialite—was no less involved than I was in everything that had ever happened.

Well, I still fry with shame, Peter, as I say. But this notion of yours (that I feel almost certain would be yours) does provide some consolation; and actually I think you've got a point.

One time, just one time, I went to dinner at Paige's house. House, yes! Right in the middle of the city! With great, tomb-like beige-and-gold rooms, old, gold-framed—*ancestors*, Paige said, spying down from every wall, massive, closed, oak doors . . .

There was the desolate sound of the dinner bell, and then the maid brought the serving platters around to the five of us—Paige, her older sister Pamela, their parents, and me—docking, departing, docking . . . we might have been towns on the shore of a huge lake. And just as the platter of steak completed its stately voyage, Mr. Chandler's head lifted slightly, as though he had caught a scent. Very unusual, my name—what sort of name was it?

I looked frantically at Paige. "He wants to know where you're from," she said, coolly. "Anna's parents come from Hungary, Daddy."

Mr. Chandler's fork hesitated in the air; his head rotated toward me like a planet. Were my people in Budapest? There was a family friend in Budapest—a prominent person, an elderly, highly respected woman— If my people were there, perhaps they knew her . . .

His stare was cold and flat, a dull blade . . . What *had* happened to my mother's piano? Because Lili had nothing, not even a locket . . .

"Mummy," Pamela said, "I don't think Anna eats meat. Do you eat meat, Anna?"

A ring was collecting around the bloody lump on my plate, soaking the potatoes red. "Oh, dear," Mrs. Chandler said.

"No, I do," I said. Paige was watching carefully, consideringly, as I sank my ornate silver fork into the steak. "Really . . ."

You might not have taken much notice of Paige, Peter, but Paige took plenty of notice of you. It was as if she'd been waiting to see what we really added up to—and *voilà*, yes? It was you.

She insisted to me you were beautiful. No, I said, you were—and this was the very word—creepy. The most beautiful person in the world, Paige said. Next to Sándor, of course, but Sándor was too old for her.

I didn't see why, I said. In only one more year we'd be in high school and her parents would let her go on a date, and Sándor would only be sixty-two. Though naturally by then Mrs. Spiegel might have nabbed him.

Paige's sigh fluttered like a long silk scarf. She said: I have nothing but pity for mean-spirited people.

Well, how would you have felt if I showed up from nowhere at *your* home the way you did at mine? The fact is, you just slid right in there, and then *I* was the stranger.

I was asleep; I woke up suddenly, the way children do when something is wrong. My room was unfamiliar in the dark. I listened, but there was only the usual slightly eerie lullaby of voices and laughter from the living room.

I reached for my clothes, which I'd slung over the chair, and I crept down the hall, blinking in the light.

Oh, my, Peter—how unfed and pretty you were! So different from the sleek, the . . . oh, let's say "personage" I got a glimpse of yesterday. You were like a weedy little flower poking its way through a crack in the pavement. Even your clothing, your dark little jacket, your trousers, your shirt, were as thin as ragged petals.

But what on earth was happening in that room? It was as if

my ears were scrambling what they picked up—just ever so slightly—before passing it on to me! Was I, in fact, still asleep? Ah—no, you and Sándor and Lili were speaking Hungarian . . .

I remember your small, pointed chin and huge, sleepy, skeptical eyes. You looked as though you might bite if someone tried to pet you. I remember your hair falling around your face in black squiggles, and your white, white skin. As white as mine, but bad—a catalogue of privations. The faintest ray of daylight would have scorched you lifeless.

You lifted your eyes to me; you seemed entirely unsurprised to see me there, peeking out from the entranceway. Sándor was speaking—I heard a cataract of water as you and I gazed at one another.

I wonder what it was you were seeing. In my jeans and plaid shirt perhaps I looked like a boy, myself—a delicate little boy; perhaps you were gazing at yourself, younger, in some vision of alternate possibilities. It certainly seemed to me, as I stood there—the happiness of your conversation deafeningly amplified by the unrecalled language—that the three of you were together in a vivid, hardy, enclosed past, and that I was looking on longingly, dissolving into the shadow of an unsatisfactory and insubstantial future.

What did you want from us? You'd arrived in the country, I gathered, some two years earlier, equipped with that most powerful item—a slip of paper, on which were a few names and addresses. Your formidable gift for languages provided you with sparkling English in no time. You'd distinguished yourself at college and had already catapulted, at your tender age, well into graduate school. In short, you had plenty. So couldn't you leave us alone?

No, Lili said. What was the matter with me? It was a marvel, a blessing that you'd come to find Sándor, that you'd tracked him down. That you intended to bring his work into English; it was the most precious gift possible that Sándor (according to you) once again represented something to young people back home.

"Home," Sándor said mildly. And just what was it he was said to represent, he mused, wandering back into his room.

But why did I think, Paige asked me, when we first discussed you, that every single person who was in this country had "escaped" from some place? "Maybe he just *left*, you know, Anna."

In school I learned simple facts: *such and such a country is rich in natural resources; a railroad was built between this place and that; the area was contested*—"simple facts," staggering volumes of blood.

Paige was too polite to say it in so many words, but I'm sure it had occurred to her, nearly as often as it had occurred to me, that everything I said in my room was a lie. Actually, I don't think it was until I was in high school that the particular tragedy which Paige and I had struggled to fathom on those afternoons cooled down into Facts, which people spoke of publicly, as if what my mother experienced in her room were a matter of dates and numbers, a distant aberration.

Your own, much more modest, catastrophe was quite a different thing. Now, there was a disaster one could *speak* of; the sort of disaster that might be experienced by human beings like ourselves; victims we could all—including Mr. and Mrs. Chandler—endorse! I must have been right, Paige told me excitedly, only a few days after her Doubts, you probably escaped—there'd been *Communists* swarming all over Budapest!

How gratified you would have been to hear Paige's conjectural account of your escape, lined as it was with monuments to you—You Scrambling Over Tanks in the Streets, You Dodging Bullets, You in Hand-to-Hand Combat with Soldiers . . .

"Peter?" was what I said. "I'll bet Peter was hiding under the bed."

You, of course, having brought it with you, were unable to appreciate the new atmosphere of industry and purpose that permeated our apartment. Which seemed to be twice as full of people as it had been, though in fact the only newcomers were you and some intermittent girlfriends of yours.

And, oh, what a dilemma you posed for Mrs. Spiegel— Too bad you never got to hear her fretting to Lili in the kitchen! On the one hand, she was elated: Finally they'd come to rescue Sándor from anonymity! On the other hand, *they*, she'd remember, was *you*. Disorder saddened her and made her fearful, and the truth is, Peter, even if you hadn't been a mere student, you were a little raffish for her taste, really. A little oblique.

But Lili! Seriously, Peter, no sooner had you arrived, it seemed to me, than there was a rapid diminution in her sensitivity to the idiotic. *Time to stop practicing, girls*—Do you remember the way she'd say that? *Peter and Sándor have work to do.* Do you remember the way she enumerated our accomplishments to her bored and irritated beaux—Sándor's accomplishments, your accomplishments, even my accomplishments. And I can promise you, Peter, those guys were

every bit as impressed that you'd read Herzen, Gombrow-
icz, and Freud in the original as they were that I could play
To a Wild Rose on the piano!

Sándor himself never would have demanded silence. Sándor wasn't a show-off. Don't you agree? Peter? But Lili was
suddenly never without an ornamental book. Oh, all right,
without a book, I mean. And do you remember those funny,
unconvincing horn-rims she brought home one day from the
office?

Once I came upon you reading to her. In Hungarian,
naturally. That day it was she who was stretched out across
the sofa, and you were sitting in an awkward, straight-backed
chair next to her. Neither of you even noticed me come in!
And I was simply stunned, I have to say, by Lili's dreamy,
unformed expression, as though she were still only a girl, to
whom anything might yet happen.

Oh, look. Do you think I grudged my poor mother pleasure? Well, I didn't! And obviously it was a tremendous relief to
me that there were so few of those episodes, during that time,
in her room. But how deeply, deeply unfair it all was. There
you were, conducting Sándor and Lili back and forth between
me and the world that had more than *wished* them dead so long
before. And how eager they were to see that world; how much
you had to show them! What everyone had been doing, what
everyone had been saying, in the years since they'd left. So
many questions, so much talk! *Europe.* Who cared? I didn't
even *exist* there. We'd been going along so happily where we
all actually did live—America; I had welcomed Lili into
America—that was what I'd been born to *do*.

I was the *American* on the premises! That was my position
and it was an exalted one. But the moment *you* come sauntering along, my position and I get a demotion! What's that all
about, please?

Sándor, at least, didn't think you were so very wonderful. Sándor didn't just jump up from his desk and throw open his door every time you came over. Sándor wasn't looking to you for some muzzy little miracle. Sándor hadn't lost his sense of humor.

Oh, yes, I know he sat with you in his room . . . "working" (as I thought of it) hour after hour. But it was clear to *me*, at least, that he was indulging you. That he lent himself to your purposes out of sheer respect for the surrealism of . . . reality. It's true, Peter— He shook his head: *No good will come of this*, he said—as though he had no power over the matter at all, as though it were all a fait accompli. He seemed to be standing on a bridge, watching himself be carried along on the currents below.

I shook my own head in sympathy; things had been thus far ideal for him, I felt—sitting outside on the benches with the other déclassé Europeans, gossiping, reminiscing, playing chess . . . coming back in to write, for a few hours, in a language that few around him could even read, or to read in a language that he would never speak with complete ease . . . What more could anyone ask, Sándor and I agreed on one of our walks—he had a very good life.

I happen to remember, Peter—do you?—the occasion on which it seemed to occur to Lili that you, like her suitors, could be put to practical purpose. It was an afternoon when you were still draped over the sofa, following several hours of "work." Yes, Lili proposed, she and Sándor, if you would consent to stay and look after me, could go out simultaneously.

I can still see your momentary look of astonishment! And recall my own little frenzy. But of course they could both go

out, I objected; I was virtually fourteen! I was actually starting *high* school and I certainly didn't need looking after!

Imagine how I felt when Lili's gaze rested absently on me
for only an instant, and she said, "No, you don't mind, Peter?
A few hours only?"

You closed your eyes, haughtily. I longed to clamp my
teeth around your ankle. Lili riffled your hair; you opened
your eyes, sniffed, and closed them again.

I remember you and Tócska on that evening, and subse-
quent ones, padding around after Lili and Sándor had left,
humiliated and sorrowful. I generously offered to entertain
you by turning on the TV, and was rewarded by a blank look
that sent me flouncing off. You, I'm sure, remember none of
it (your nubby little sweater, the way you lay on the sofa,
reading, with your feet up rudely on the arm, some coffee
with hot milk you made once and shared with me—its profound, mysterious taste) . . . but I, Peter, remember it all, with
a special, ringing clarity. I was—I admit it—that happy.

Perhaps your own demotion—from severe scholar, or
from spoiled princeling—to domesticated animal, gave you
some feeling of solidarity with me. I couldn't say, of course,
but I certainly remember the moment you abruptly put down
some journal you'd been reading and looked at me narrowly,
as though I were a specimen that had just been brought to
your attention.

"Why are you such a barbarian?" you said. "Why are you
having trouble with your math? It's impossible that you're
an actual imbecile, but look at you—you're always staring as
though you've been lobotomized!"

" 'Lobotomized'?" I scoffed.

"And your vocabulary"—you invited me to marvel with
you—"your vocabulary is a disaster."

You demanded to see my math text. I can see you this instant, plucking it disdainfully from the pile of schoolbooks on my bedroom floor and thumbing through it, frowning. What page was I on, you wanted to know.

Why? Were you so great at math?

You were great at everything, you said, squinting at the book as you settled yourself on my bed. Or hadn't I noticed? No! Off! Who was I to sit next to the great You? I was to grovel respectfully in the little chair over there.

So how was I supposed to see the book, please?

Hmm, you conceded. A plausible argument; evidently the situation wasn't hopeless.

"Anna's doing so well at school," Lili boasted to Mrs. Spiegel. "Thanks to Peter."

You and I looked up at one another from whatever we were reading, and glowered. Mrs. Spiegel drew back. "So sweet," I can remember Lili saying, imperturbably. "Aren't these two? So dear."

When I cried with frustration, alone with you in my room, and hurled my book onto the floor, you waited, you retrieved the book, and you explained again. Don't be so frightened, you told me. Don't be so impatient. Don't fight so hard against it; if you want to know something you don't already know, you have to let yourself change.

It was quite natural, don't you think? That we began to speak of Lili and Sándor. How, in fact, could we have avoided it?

Were you surprised to find how little I knew? That I knew virtually nothing at all about either Lili or Sándor? I wonder at what point it dawned on you that I was only then learning—and from *you*—how Sándor had been smuggled out of Berlin after his brief stint in hiding, with the best fake papers money could buy; how, at the end of the war, Sándor haunted the agencies, going daily to study documents, sign papers, scour the records for anyone who might be left. How, when Sándor went to meet the stranger who was to arrive on the boat, it was Lili who appeared, wearing a little navy-blue coat presented to her by some organization or another, carrying a small suitcase and a one-and-a-half-year-old child.

Her cousin's uncle? I said.

Anna, you said. I could see my own shock in your face as I stared at you, measuring the great, blank space that lay between Sándor and Lili.

And what could have gone through your mind when I asked if you knew whether I might have cousins somewhere, myself: when you realized that the only person there to answer was you; to inform me that (as you'd gathered from Sándor) my father's large family had been eradicated, and that in Lili's there had been only the one other child.

Another child? "Oh—" I remember saying. "Her brother . . ."

It collected in the room as we lay there, stretched out—the pink and silver city; the river, reflecting the pink and silver sky, the sleepy stone lions guarding the tunnel through the mountain, the lights twinkling on in the dusk below the castle, the twinkling bridges, the stone, the tile, the arches, the marble, Europe and Asia washing over each other, converging and diverging, the park, glorious with its drapery of snow or blossoms, the cafés, the Gypsies, despised and magical, playing music in the streets, the crowds strolling, laughing, drinking, dancing . . . or at least that's how it must have been, you said, while Lili was growing up.

It was over, of course—all changed by the time you yourself were growing up—gutted, buried. A gray city now, the ghost of itself.

Lying there, side by side, you and I explored the rainy park, the broad, silent avenues, searching for the big house with the piano and the cook, searching through the ghost city for the missing—you searching for the living city, I for traces of Lili. We were ghosts in the ghost of Lili's city, just as she and Sándor were ghosts in mine.

And you were the stranger, then, everywhere . . . Where was your home, Peter? Were you frightened? I envisioned my own fear rising from my body, encased in a luminous globe— you accepting it into yourself as though it were precious; it left a rift in me like a wound. I remember the springy feel of your hair against my cheek; once in a while I dared to reach out one hand and touch my fingertips to yours. Were you aware of my hand? Whose did you think it was—a girl- friend's? My ghostly mother's? The missing boy's? Mine?

How often did we talk like that? Every afternoon for a while? Every few weeks? Maybe, in fact, it was only once.

Because at a certain point you were just *there*; at a certain point, as long as I could imagine you alive in the world, going about your business, I no longer required for our conversation— which was so necessary to me—your physical presence.

You know, Peter, Paige was much more grown up around that time than I was. I'd go so far as to say she was actually infatuated. She was getting rather dignified, in her way, and she'd all but stopped talking to me about you.

I could at least point out to her, I felt, that you were vain, *not* pleasant, and that you had a different girl tagging along behind you all the time.

Yes? she said, in an idle manner. And what kind of girls did you especially like?

Oh, who could tell, I said. You probably didn't notice what any of them were like. And you dropped them all, anyhow. Or maybe they just got sick of you bragging.

In fact, though, you liked a very distinct type of girl at the time, didn't you. I wonder if you still do. Of course, we don't really produce that type any longer; probably even Europe doesn't—at least, not in quantity. Fragile, restless, sloe-eyed, ill-tempered, *very* squeamish, in their little striped T-shirts, as if someone had just handed them a sickeningly poor translation of Sartre . . .

Those girls! Did you get around to marrying one of them? Maybe you married a whole bunch of them. Or maybe you never bothered yourself about getting married at all. Maybe you married that girl you brought to the party someone gave when your book about Sándor finally came out. Did you, I wonder. That girl had her hand on your sleeve every second.

That afternoon with Voitek, which changed a lot of things for you—it changed some things for me, too, you know.

Didn't you always think, when you were young, that real time starts the year you're born? You're born, and then time begins to move—forward. Didn't you think that there's sort of an ocean of space that separates you—but *completely*—from the big lump of everything that went on before?

Were you particularly aware of Voitek? I wasn't, as far as I remember. I don't think Lili had been seeing him long. And she didn't seem all that interested in him, really—maybe she just felt a little sorry for him. Or, anyway, he was just . . . there. Thinking about it now, I can see that he was very good-looking, but at the time he just seemed to me like a large—like a large apparatus of some sort, humming with silence . . . Like, in retrospect, an atomic reactor.

It started with Tarot cards, that day—isn't that right? I think Paige had seen a deck of them somewhere, and was sort of going on . . . to impress you, it seems fair to say: *Didn't we believe there were cultures that were special? Didn't we believe that there were people who had learned how to*—oh, I don't know—*to harness invisible currents, to see something, the future, in cards, in your hand . . . ?*

I don't really remember what all she was saying, but I remember it seemed so persuasive to me, *fascinating . . .*

And the first thing I do remember clearly is the way Lili simply cut Paige off—how shocking that was: *This is not interesting, a movie would be interesting. Voitek? A movie?*

Paige was simply stunned, and I remember looking at Sándor, for help, because he really did like Paige, you know, and always listened so seriously to all those ideas and opinions of hers—but instead he just made that little bow and said something to the effect that he himself could see clearly into his future, by looking at his hand or by not looking at his hand, that it was the past that was opaque, it was the past that only special insight could reveal, and as for what was going to happen tomorrow, I think he said, *that* was something anyone at all could see if he would only consult his memory of what had happened yesterday, and now, if we would excuse him . . .

Of course by then I could feel it on my skin, in my body. But Paige was simply *lost*. Everything was happening so fast, and she was talking and talking, something, something about the Gypsies, *didn't you adore them? didn't you love to see them, at least, and talk to them?*

And obviously it was to pacify her that you grabbed her hand and looked at her palm and said—goodness knows what you said, yourself—that yes, you'd known some, you'd learned all sorts of this or that: *I see a concert hall . . .* I remember you saying, and then Voitek saying, *This guy sees a concert hall; I see a two-car garage in Bronxville . . .*

Of course he'd intended no more than a flippant little end to the business, I'm sure, but instead of sealing something shut, it tore something open, and where was Voitek then?

Where were we all? And how many people were in that room? Millions, yes? Literally millions of people had been there all that time, just waiting to be recognized.

And who, in particular, was Voitek seeing, I wonder, in the white stillness of your face, when he started to scream, *yes you adored them, "adored" them, shit, shit, opportunist, coward,* or whatever it was, exactly, until it became really impossible to make it out because it was all in Polish, I guess, except for a word here and there of German.

Thank heavens for Lili, yes, Peter? Because you didn't even have the presence of mind to duck. And thank heavens, too, that evidently Voitek had some dim awareness it was Lili, out of all that vast crowd, who'd touched his arm. Otherwise, he would have killed her, I'm sure, within moments.

Was it I who went to the door? Usually that's how I remember it, but sometimes in my memory it was you. Actually, I suppose, it could have been any of us, but usually I remember myself, threading my way toward the pounding on the door through the whirlwind of debris that had just been

our possessions, and the curiously weightless way it was flying around, as though our apartment had only been waiting for one touch to send it wheeling, in splinters, through
the air.

But the thing I always remember in exactly the same way
is how Mrs. Spiegel just stood there in the doorway as those
guys tore in and tackled Voitek. I'm sure neither Lili nor Sándor ever forgot it, either—the uniforms, the truncheons, the
sound of Voitek's head as it hit the wall; the utter absence of
expression on Mrs. Spiegel's face . . .

And what was I thinking as I watched Paige cry? I was thinking
about the way she looked, crying. I wouldn't have imagined
that something so extreme, so complete, could happen to someone's face from the inside. Paige's pretty face—where was it?

I wonder if she ever noted that she got her date with Sándor. Because I gathered, eventually, that after he called her
mother, Sándor took Paige to the coffee shop to wait for the
driver, and the two of them had a soda.

He certainly did his best to get me out of the wreckage,
too. And if you hadn't offered to stay with me, I would have
had to leave. But how could I have left? I knew Lili would go
to her room. I knew she would, and she did, and then there I
was, evaporating, and she was on the other side of the wall,
unreachable, spiraling back down . . .

I guess I never really had a chance to thank you. But obviously you understood how serious I was when I asked you
to leave me alone and go check on Lili. I know it took courage, Peter, to open that door and go in.

And once you had—do you know?—I calmed right
down. I stopped shaking, and that blinding silence dimmed. I

raised my head and opened my eyes. There was the world, all around me—the sky, the earth, a bird, a voice . . .

Did it ever occur to you to wonder what happened when Sándor came back? Well, he looked around mildly for a moment, and he asked how I was. I realized I was holding a book you'd stuck in my hands when you'd gone in to see Lili. I was fine, I said. And Lili? What about Lili? And Lili was fine, too.

Sándor glanced at Lili's door. "She's all right," I said. "Really. She's fine."

"Yes?" he said, and hesitated. "Well. So, what would you say to a movie?"

Lili was perfectly serene when I came in for breakfast the next morning—as serene as you found her when you eventually joined us yourself, looking disheveled and mightily confused. I hope I didn't snicker, Peter, when she said she was glad you'd stuck around, that there was a lot of cleaning up to do.

You, though! You were really insufferable, there, for a while, were you aware of that? I don't know who you thought you were—my brother? my father?

I suppose you were just panicked, really. These days no one bothers even to remark on a very young man and an older woman, but it certainly was a novelty back then.

With all due respect, Peter, I have to say that I don't really attribute Lili's happiness in those days to any individual qualities of yours; no doubt any pretentious twenty-one-year-old Hungarian would have done as well.

But I very much doubt that anyone else at all could have parlayed, as you eventually did, some translations and what amounted to a small essay into so much celebrity for Sándor (and celebrity, consequently, my point is, for . . . well, you get my point, I'm sure).

Of course it was just one of those moments, wasn't it, when attention was on such things, when even writing as rarified as Sándor's was likely to be hijacked—and by just about anyone. Absolutely every poor shnook seemed to be out there scrounging up some piece of art with which to beat up some ideological adversary or intellectual competitor, something that could be said to validate some thesis, or buttress some argument, or represent some something or other—an indictment of totalitarianism, or an indictment of repressive capitalism, or these particular currents of psychoanalytic thought, or those particular currents of Marxist thought, or an esthetic of the elite, or an esthetic of the people, or currents of Jewish mysticism, or an expression of Christian acceptance, or an expression of Buddhist acceptance . . . .

Now, of course, no one wants art for any purpose whatsoever—let alone for its own. But that was the moment, wasn't it? And you seemed to have a perfect understanding of just how to exploit it, how to take it all as far as possible. Something so very exactly what Sándor never wanted.

Hypocrite, you say; ingrate—*Goneril* couldn't have put it better. What do I think you should have done? Surely I can't mean to vilify you for having had a few *thoughts* about work to which you were so devoted! And don't I think a readership deserves something useful in return for its admiration? Besides, anyone whose stance (like Sándor's) is fastidious high-mindedness is simply demanding that others be exploitative on his behalf. Also, who am I to say that you *were* in any way exploitative? Were you not, in fact, entirely sincere in your efforts to bring Sándor's work to a wider and more receptive audience?

Did it mean nothing to Sándor to make contact with the living? Or that his lyric, glimmering salvagings from a lost world were received with deep gratitude? Did it mean nothing to Lili that her life, too, was in some measure reclaimed? What did I wish for them—that they be eternally voiceless, adrift? Plus, where did I think my tuition came from, and how did I think I would have gotten into college in the first place, the way I'd been going on without you?

All right, I give up, you win, thanks. But *Sándor*? A *bastion* against *Communism*? Oh, please, Peter. For shame.

A paradox, as Sándor once said; a conundrum. If no one was listening, at least no one misheard you. If what you made was of no value to anyone, no one stole it and went running off; no one bothered to colonize it and set up little flags. It was his home, he said, his work, and all *I'm* saying is that it seems very hard, that a man who was exiled so many times over was harried again, and in his most intimate refuge.

I'm not going so far as to say it killed him, Peter. Of course not! It merely exasperated him; obviously it was his *life* that killed him.

Some months, I suppose, after you'd more or less dropped out of sight, I was just sitting idly, in our apartment, gazing out the window at the dark sky and dreary rain, and I saw the reflection of Lili's face overlap mine as Lili came and sat down next to me. "Poor Anna," she said. "Do you miss Peter?"

I shook my head.

"No," she said, and in the window I watched drops of rain trickle unevenly over our reflections as Lili stroked my hair. "Good. Well, I don't miss him, either."

Naturally, no liaison between you and Lili could have lasted forever. That was understood. You were very young—

Sándor and Lili were careful to impress this notion on me;
your life was moving very fast.

But still, you might have come around a little more often,
Peter. Lili would have liked to see you, you know. After all,
you were family.

Enjoyable, and even appropriate as it is, to mock Lionel, I do
have to say that in a way I'm not horrified through and *through*
that he arranged yesterday's service the way he did. I certainly
wouldn't have done it, myself, but I wasn't entirely sorry, I
must admit, to see that dark, strange, creaky, stained-glass
spaceship swoop down through the millennia to reclaim Lili.
Though it was impossible, of course, to say anything of the
sort to Lionel when I got up this morning, and there he was,
first thing, in the kitchen.

Fortunately, he didn't want to see me any more than I
wanted to see him. To Lionel, obviously, every presence is a
presence that isn't Lili. He fussed around making a breakfast,
and both of us pretended to eat it, and then Eric called, to see
how we were doing, and to say again how sorry he was he
couldn't be here with us.

"I hope he knows," Lionel said, after we hung up, "how
many people loved his grandmother."

It *is* a beautiful day, isn't it? Lionel was right. Not warm, certainly, but just so bright! The benches along the avenue are
filling up with old men and old women, sitting out in the
sun—do you remember?—just the way they used to all those
years ago.

When I visit Eric in Los Angeles, he takes me driving
way out, to those elastic, self-generating peripheries, where

the most recent immigrants are hoping to establish a life for themselves, and I marvel at everything, as though we were coasting down into the future.

Ma, Eric says, not every manicurist or waiter here used to be the most promising poet or physicist in Nigeria or Guatemala or Korea, you know.

Well, yes. I do know. But a few of them must have been something of the sort. And then, the point is, what about the others?

These old men and women have probably been coming out in the spring for half a century to sit on the very same benches. They're probably the very same people I used to see around here in my childhood. And let me tell you, Peter, they looked every bit as old to me then as they do now!

They're like little birds, perched on a phone wire, cheeping away from time to time in a sheer exercise of being alive, blinking in the indifferent American sun. They sit in the sun, they buy their few groceries, they play chess, they gossip. A few of them must get themselves to an occasional chamber-music concert. I suppose they still read their newspapers in Yiddish, in Polish, in Hungarian, in Czech . . . This spring, the next spring, maybe one more . . .

The elevated train still clatters by in the distance, and the old people gaze out through the traffic and fumes as if they were gazing across the Atlantic. If the great empires of Europe exist anywhere now, I guess it's right here, on these benches.

He seems to be a nice man, Eric, and I think things are working out pretty well for him. Neil was a very good father, I have to say, for what it's worth. Neil, in fact, is not such a bad human being—he and I just have various complementary horrible qualities. I, obviously, am possessive, jealous, resentful, dependent, quick to censure, slow to forgive . . . and there's not all that much I've been able to do about it, I'm afraid, other than keep my distance. On my own, in fact, I'm perfectly all right.

I *am* grateful, Peter (and if we'd had that cup of coffee yesterday, I hope I would have told you so) for the few sentences in your book that pertain to Lili. Because her mother's jewelry, the silver, the piano, the house—all that stuff must have belonged to the neighbors for a long time now. Or, actually, I suppose, to their children. Except what's just floating through Europe these days, from one antique dealer to another.

So, aside from those few sentences of yours, what's left? The challis scarf, a few strings of beads, some inexpensive furniture, bought on Lili's small salary or given to her by those admirers of hers, or organized by some relocation agency or charity . . . That's pretty much it.

Yes, so obviously I'm grateful. Well, I'm sure you know that.

I hope you'd be glad to know that I'm well—that I'm fortunate in my work, that I'm happy enough . . .

The time Neil told me he'd seen the talk show where there was someone who might have been the person he thought I'd mentioned, I asked him so many questions! *What did he look like? What was he saying? Did he say where he was living?* And I must have sounded frantic, because Neil stopped answering and just looked at me. He didn't know, he said slowly; he hadn't been paying attention. He'd simply *happened* to turn the show on while he was rummaging around in his suitcase for a presentable shirt, and he couldn't remember one single thing about whoever it was he'd happened to see.

Oh, I said, after a moment. Well. And I turned away to escape Neil's stare. There was really no need to have seen you myself; I knew it was you, and at least I knew you were safe.

ACKNOWLEDGMENTS

Profound thanks and a big hug from me, too, to the D.A.D.D., Berline, and Joachim Sartorius; profound thanks and respectful salutes to both the Ingram Merrill Foundation and the American Academy of Arts and Letters; and thanks, hugs, and salutes to Amy Hotch, Andras Nagy, and Libby Titus.

TWILIGHT OF

THE SUPERHEROES

For my darling Wall

TWILIGHT OF THE SUPERHEROES

NATHANIEL RECALLS THE MIRACLE

The grandchildren approach.

Nathaniel can make them out dimly in the shadows. When it's time, he'll tell them about the miracle.

It was the dawn of the new millennium, he'll say. *I was living in the Midwest back then, but my friends from college persuaded me to come to New York.*

I arrived a few days ahead of the amazing occasion, and all over the city there was an atmosphere of feverish anticipation. The year two thousand! The new millennium! Some people thought it was sure to be the end of the world. Others thought we were at the threshold of something completely new and better. The tabloids carried wild predictions from celebrity clairvoyants, and even people who scoffed and said that the date was an arbitrary and meaningless one were secretly agitated. In short, we were suddenly aware of ourselves standing there, staring at the future blindfolded.

I suppose, looking back on it, that all the commotion seems comical and ridiculous. And perhaps you're thinking that we churned it up to entertain ourselves because we were bored or because our lives felt too easy—trivial and mundane. But consider: ceremonial occasions, even purely personal ones like birthdays or anniversaries, remind us that the world is full of terrifying surprises and no one knows what even the very next second will bring!

Well, shortly before the momentous day, a strange news item appeared: experts were saying that a little mistake had been made—just one tiny mistake, a little detail in the way computers everywhere had been programmed. But the consequences of this detail, the experts said, were potentially disastrous; tiny as it was, the detail might affect everybody, and in a very big way!

You see, if history has anything to teach us, it's that—despite all our efforts, despite our best (or worst) intentions, despite our touchingly indestructible faith in our own foresight—we poor humans cannot actually think ahead; there are just too many variables. And so, when it comes down to it, it always turns out that no one is in charge of the things that really matter.

It must be hard for you to imagine—it's even hard for me to remember—but people hadn't been using computers for very long. As far as I know, my mother (your great-grandmother) never even touched one! And no one had thought to inform the computers that one day the universe would pass from the years of the one thousands into the years of the two thousands. So the machines, as these experts suddenly realized, were not equipped to understand that at the conclusion of 1999 time would not start over from 1900, time would keep going.

People all over America—all over the world!—began to speak of "a crisis of major proportions" (which was a phrase we used to use back then). Because, all the routine operations that we'd so blithely delegated to computers, the operations we all took for granted and depended on—how would they proceed?

Might one be fatally trapped in an elevator? Would we have to huddle together for warmth and scrabble frantically through our pockets for a pack of fancy restaurant matches so we could set our stacks of old New York Reviews ablaze? Would all the food rot in heaps out there on the highways, leaving us to pounce on fat old street rats and grill them over the flames? What was going to happen to our bank accounts—would they vaporize? And what about air traffic control? On December 31 when the second hand moved *from 11:59:59 to midnight, would all the airplanes in the sky collide?*

Everyone was thinking of more and more alarming possibilities. Some people committed their last night on this earth to partying, and others rushed around buying freeze-dried provisions and cases of water and flashlights and radios and heavy blankets in the event that the disastrous problem might somehow eventually be solved.

And then, as the clock ticked its way through the enormous gatherings in celebration of the era that was due to begin in a matter of hours, then minutes, then seconds, we waited to learn the terrible consequences of the tiny oversight. Khartoum, Budapest, Paris—we watched on television, our hearts fluttering, as midnight, first just a tiny speck in the east, unfurled gently, darkening the sky and moving toward us over the globe.

But the amazing thing, Nathaniel will tell his grandchildren, *was that nothing happened! We held our breath . . . And there was nothing! It was a miracle. Over the face of the earth, from east to west and back again, nothing catastrophic happened at all.*

Oh, well. Frankly, by the time he or any of his friends get around to producing a grandchild (or even a child, come to think of it) they might well have to explain what computers had been. And freeze-dried food. And celebrity clairvoyants and airplanes and New York and America and even cities, and heaven only knows what.

FROGBOIL

Lucien watches absently as his assistant, Sharmila, prepares to close up the gallery for the evening; something keeps tugging at his attention . . .

Oh, yes. It's the phrase Yoshi Matsumoto used this morning when he called from Tokyo. *Back to normal . . . Back to normal . . .*

What's that famous, revolting, sadistic experiment? Something like, you drop the frog into a pot of boiling water and it jumps out. But if you drop it into a pot of cold water and slowly bring the water to a boil, the frog stays put and gets boiled.

Itami Systems is reopening its New York branch, was what Matsumoto called to tell Lucien; he'll be returning to the city soon. Lucien pictured his old friend's mournful, ironic expression as he added, "They tell me they're 'exploring additional avenues of development now that New York is back to normal.'"

Lucien had made an inadvertent squawklike sound. He shook his head, then he shook his head again.

"Hello?" Matsumoto said.

"I'm here," Lucien said. "Well, it'll be good to see you again. But steel yourself for a wait at customs; they're fingerprinting."

VIEW

Mr. Matsumoto's loft is a jungle of big rubbery trees, under which crouch sleek items of chrome and leather. Spindly electronic devices blink or warble amid the foliage, and here and there one comes upon an immense flat-screen TV—the first of their kind that Nathaniel ever handled.

Nathaniel and his friends have been subletting—thanks,

obviously, to Uncle Lucien—for a ridiculously minimal rent
and on Mr. Matsumoto's highly tolerable conditions of cat-
sitting and general upkeep. Nathaniel and Lyle and Amity
and Madison each have something like an actual bedroom,
and there are three whole bathrooms, one equipped with a
Jacuzzi. The kitchen, stone and steel, has cupboards bigger
than most of their friends' apartments. Art—important, soon
to be important, or very recently important, most of which
was acquired from Uncle Lucien—hangs on the walls.

And the terrace! One has only to open the magic sliding
panel to find oneself halfway to heaven. On the evening, over
three years ago, when Uncle Lucien completed the arrangements for Nathaniel to sublet and showed him the place, Nathaniel stepped out onto the terrace and tears shot right up
into his eyes.

There was that unearthly palace, the Chrysler Building!
There was the Empire State Building, like a brilliant violet
hologram! There were the vast, twinkling prairies of Brooklyn
and New Jersey! And best of all, Nathaniel could make out the
Statue of Liberty holding her torch aloft, as she had held it for
each of his parents when they arrived as children from across
the ocean—terrified, filthy, and hungry—to safety.

Stars glimmered nearby; towers and spires, glowing em-
erald, topaz, ruby, sapphire, soared below. The avenues and
bridges slung a trembling net of light across the rivers, over
the buildings. Everything was spangled and dancing; the
little boats glittered. The lights floated up and up like bubbles.

Back when Nathaniel moved into Mr. Matsumoto's loft,
shortly after his millennial arrival in New York, sitting out
on the terrace had been like looking down over the rim into
a gigantic glass of champagne.

UNCLE LUCIEN'S WORDS OF REASSURANCE

So, Matsumoto is returning. And Lucien has called Nathaniel, the nephew of his adored late wife, Charlie, to break the news.

Well, of course it's hardly a catastrophe for the boy. Matsumoto's place was only a sublet in any case, and Nathaniel and his friends will all find other apartments.

But it's such an ordeal in this city. And all four of the young people, however different they might be, strike Lucien as being in some kind of holding pattern—as if they're temporizing, or muffled by unspoken reservations. Of course, he doesn't really know them. Maybe it's just the eternal, poignant weariness of youth.

The strangest thing about getting old (or one of the many strangest things) is that young people sometimes appear to Lucien—as, in fact, Sharmila does at this very moment—in a nimbus of tender light. It's as if her unrealized future were projecting outward like ectoplasm.

"Doing anything entertaining this evening?" he asks her.

She sighs. "Time will tell," she says.

She's a nice young woman; he'd like to give her a few words of advice, or reassurance.

But what could they possibly be? "Don't—" he begins.

Don't worry? HAHAHAHAHA! Don't feel *sad*? "Don't bother about the phones," is what he settles down on. A new show goes up tomorrow, and it's become Lucien's custom on such evenings to linger in the stripped gallery and have a glass of wine. "I'll take care of them."

But how has he *gotten* so old?

SUSPENSION

So, there was the famous, strangely blank New Year's Eve, the nothing at all that happened, neither the apocalypse nor the failure of the planet's computers, nor, evidently, the dawning of a better age. Nathaniel had gone to parties with his old friends from school and was asleep before dawn; the next afternoon he awoke with only a mild hangover and an uneasy impression of something left undone.

Next thing you knew, along came that slump, as it was called—the general economic blight that withered the New York branch of Mr. Matsumoto's firm and clusters of jobs all over the city. There appeared to be no jobs at all, in fact, but then—somehow—Uncle Lucien unearthed one for Nathaniel in the architectural division of the subway system. It was virtually impossible to afford an apartment, but Uncle Lucien arranged for Nathaniel to sublet Mr. Matsumoto's loft.

Then Madison and his girlfriend broke up, so Madison moved into Mr. Matsumoto's, too. Not long afterward, the brokerage house where Amity was working collapsed resoundingly, and she'd joined them. Then Lyle's landlord jacked up his rent, so Lyle started living at Mr. Matsumoto's as well.

As the return of Mr. Matsumoto to New York was contingent upon the return of a reasonable business climate, one way or another it had sort of slipped their minds that Mr. Matsumoto was real. And for over three years there they've been, hanging in temporary splendor thirty-one floors above the pavement.

They're all out on the terrace this evening. Madison has brought in champagne so that they can salute with an adequate flourish the end of their tenure in Mr. Matsumoto's place. And except for Amity, who takes a principled stand against thoughtful moods, and Amity's new friend or possibly suitor, Russell, who has no history here, they're kind of quiet.

REUNION

Now that Sharmila has gone, Lucien's stunning, cutting-edge gallery space blurs a bit and recedes. The room, in fact, seems almost like an old snapshot from that bizarre, quaintly futuristic century, the twentieth. Lucien takes a bottle of white wine from the little fridge in the office, pours himself a glass, and from behind a door in that century, emerges Charlie.

Charlie—Oh, how long it's been, how unbearably long! Lucien luxuriates in the little pulse of warmth just under his skin that indicates her presence. He strains for traces of her voice, but her words degrade like the words in a dream, as if they're being rubbed through a sieve.

Yes, yes, Lucien assures her. He'll put his mind to finding another apartment for her nephew. And when her poor, exasperating sister and brother-in-law call frantically about Nathaniel, as they're bound to do, he'll do his best to calm them down.

But what a nuisance it all is! The boy is as opaque to his parents as a turnip. He was the child of their old age and he's also, obviously, the repository of all of their baroque hopes and fears. By their own account, they throw up their hands and wring them, lecture Nathaniel about frugality, then press spending money upon him and fret when he doesn't use it.

Between Charlie's death and Nathaniel's arrival in New

York, Lucien heard from Rose and Isaac only at what they considered moments of emergency: Nathaniel's grades were erratic! His friends were bizarre! Nathaniel had expressed an interest in architecture, an unreliable future! He drew, and Lucien had better sit down, *comics*!

The lamentations would pour through the phone, and then, the instant Lucien hung up, evaporate. But if he had given the matter one moment's thought, he realizes, he would have understood from very early on that it was only a matter of time until the boy found his way to the city.

It was about four years ago now that Rose and Isaac put in an especially urgent call. Lucien held the receiver at arm's length and gritted his teeth. "You're an important man," Rose was shouting. "We understand that, we understand how busy you are, you know we'd never do this, but it's an emergency. The boy's in New York, and he sounds terrible. He doesn't have a job, lord only knows what he eats—I don't know what to think, Lucien, he *drifts*, he's just *drifting*. Call him, promise me, that's all I'm asking."

"Fine, certainly, good," Lucien said, already gabbling; he would have agreed to anything if Rose would only hang up.

"But whatever you do," she added, "please, please, under no circumstances should you let him know that we asked you to call."

Lucien looked at the receiver incredulously. "But how else would I have known he was in New York?" he said. "How else would I have gotten his number?"

There was a silence, and then a brief, amazed laugh from Isaac on another extension. "Well, I don't know what you'll tell him," Isaac said admiringly. "But you're the brains of the family, you'll think of something."

INNOCENCE

And actually, Russell (who seems to be not only Amity's friend and possible suitor but also her agent) has obtained for Amity a whopping big advance from some outfit that Madison refers to as Cheeseball Editions, so whatever else they might all be drinking to (or drinking about) naturally Amity's celebrating a bit. And Russell, recently arrived from L.A., cannot suppress his ecstasy about how *ur* New York, as he puts it, Mr. Matsumoto's loft is, tactless as he apparently recognizes this untimely ecstasy to be.

"It's *fantastic*," he says. "Who did it, do you know?"

Nathaniel nods. "Matthias Lehmann."

"That's what I thought, I thought so," Russell says. "It *looks* like Lehmann. Oh, wow, I can't believe you guys have to move out—I mean, it's just so totally amazing!"

Nathaniel and Madison nod and Lyle sniffs peevishly. Lyle is stretched out on a yoga mat that Nathaniel once bought in preparation for a romance (as yet manqué) with a prettily tattoed yoga teacher he runs into in the bodega on the corner. Lyle's skin has a waxy, bluish cast; there are dark patches beneath his eyes. He looks like a child too precociously worried to sleep. His boyfriend, Jahan, has more or less relocated to London, and Lyle has been missing him frantically. Lying there so still on the yoga mat with his eyes closed, he appears to be a tomb sculpture from an as yet nonexistent civilization.

"And the view!" Russell says. "This is probably the most incredible view on the *planet*."

The others consider the sight of Russell's eager face. And then Amity says, "More champagne, anyone?"

Well, sure, who knows where Russell had been? Who knows where he would have been on that shining, calm, perfectly blue September morning when the rest of them were here having coffee on the terrace and looked up at the annoying racket of a low-flying plane? Why should they expect Russell—now, nearly three years later—to imagine that moment out on the terrace when Lyle spilled his coffee and said, "Oh, shit," and something flashed and something tore, and the cloudless sky ignited.

HOME

Rose and Isaac have elbowed their way in behind Charlie, and no matter how forcefully Lucien tries to boot them out, they're making themselves at home, airing their dreary history.

Both sailed as tiny, traumatized children with their separate families and on separate voyages right into the Statue of Liberty's open arms. Rose was almost eleven when her little sister, Charlie, came into being, along with a stainless American birth certificate.

Neither Rose and Charlie's parents nor Isaac's ever recovered from their journey to the New World, to say nothing of what had preceded it. The two sets of old folks spoke, between them, Yiddish, Polish, Russian, German, Croatian, Slovenian, Ukrainian, Ruthenian, Rumanian, Latvian, Czech, and Hungarian, Charlie had once told Lucien, but not one of the four ever managed to learn more English than was needed to procure a quarter pound of smoked sturgeon from the deli. They worked impossible hours, they drank a little schnapps, and then, in due course, they died.

Isaac did fairly well manufacturing vacuum cleaners. He and Rose were solid members of their temple and the community, but, according to Charlie, no matter how uneventful their lives in the United States continued to be, filling out an unfamiliar form would cause Isaac's hands to sweat and send jets of acid through his innards. When he or Rose encountered someone in uniform—a train conductor, a meter maid, a crossing guard—their hearts would leap into their throats and they would think: *passport!*

Their three elder sons, Nathaniel's brothers, fulfilled Rose and Isaac's deepest hopes by turning out to be blindingly inconspicuous. The boys were so reliable and had so few characteristics it was hard to imagine what anyone could think up to kill them for. They were Jewish, of course, but even Rose and Isaac understood that this particular criterion was inoperative in the United States—at least for the time being.

The Old World, danger, and poverty were far in the past. Nevertheless, the family lived in their tidy, midwestern house with its two-car garage as if secret police were permanently hiding under the matching plastic-covered sofas, as if Brownshirts and Cossacks were permanently rampaging through the suburban streets.

Lucien knew precious little about vacuum cleaners and nothing at all about childhood infections or lawn fertilizers. And yet, as soon as Charlie introduced him, Isaac and Rose set about soliciting his views as if he were an authority on everything that existed on their shared continent.

His demurrals, disclaimers, and protestations of ignorance were completely ineffective. Whatever guess he was finally strong-armed into hazarding was received as oracular. Oracular!

Fervent gratitude was expressed: Thank God Charlie had brought Lucien into the family! How brilliant he was, how knowledgeable and subtle! And then Rose and Isaac would proceed to pick over his poor little opinion as if they were the most ruthless and highly trained lawyers, and on the opposing side.

After Charlie was diagnosed, Lucien had just enough time to understand perfectly what that was to mean. When he was exhausted enough to sleep, he slept as though under heavy anesthetic during an amputation. The pain was not alleviated, but it had been made inscrutable. A frightful thing seemed to lie on top of him, heavy and cold. All night long he would struggle to throw it off, but when dawn delivered him to consciousness, he understood what it was, and that it would never go away.

During his waking hours, the food on his plate would abruptly lose its taste, the painting he was studying would bleach off the canvas, the friend he was talking to would turn into a stranger. And then, one day, he was living in a world all made out of paper, where the sun was a wad of old newspapers and the only sounds were the sounds of tearing paper.

He spoke with Rose and Isaac frequently during Charlie's illness, and they came to New York for her memorial service, where they sat self-consciously and miserably among Lucien and Charlie's attractive friends. He took them to the airport for their return to the Midwest, embraced them warmly, and as they shuffled toward the departure door with the other passengers, turning once to wave, he breathed a sigh of relief: all that, at least, was over, too.

As his senses began to revive, he felt a brief pang—he would miss, in a minor way, the heartrending buffoonery of Charlie's sister and brother-in-law. After all, it had been part of his life with Charlie, even if it had been the only annoying part.

But Charlie's death, instead of setting him utterly, blessedly adrift in his grief, had left him anchored permanently offshore of her family like an island. After a long silence, the infuriating calls started up again. The feudal relationship was apparently inalterable.

CONTEXT

When they'd moved in, it probably *was* the best view on the planet. Then, one morning, out of a clear blue sky, it became, for a while, probably the worst.

For a long time now they've been able to hang out here on the terrace without anyone running inside to be sick or bursting into tears or diving under something at a loud noise or even just making macabre jokes or wondering what sort of debris is settling into their drinks. These days they rarely see—as for a time they invariably did—the sky igniting, the stinking smoke bursting out of it like lava, the tiny figures raining down from the shattered tower as Lyle faints.

But now it's unclear what they are, in fact, looking at.

INFORMATION

What would Charlie say about the show that's about to go up? It's work by a youngish Belgian painter who arrived, splashily, on the scene sometime after Charlie's departure.

It's good work, but these days Lucien can't get terribly excited about any of the shows. The vibrancy of his brain arranging itself in response to something of someone else's making, the heart's little leap—his gift, reliable for so many years, is gone. Or mostly gone; it's flattened out into something banal and tepid. It's as if he's got some part that's simply worn out and needs replacing. Let's hope it's still available, he thinks.

How *did* he get so old? The usual stupid question. One had snickered all one's life as the plaintive old geezers doddered about baffled, as if looking for a misplaced sock, tugging one's sleeve, asking sheepishly: *How did I get so old?*

The mere sight of one's patiently blank expression turned them vicious. *It will happen to you,* they'd raged.

Well, all right, it would. But not in the ridiculous way it had happened to *them.* And yet, here he is, he and his friends, falling like so much landfill into the dump of old age. Or at least struggling desperately to balance on the brink. Yet one second ago, running so swiftly toward it, they hadn't even seen it.

And what had happened to his youth? Unlike a misplaced sock, it isn't anywhere; it had dissolved in the making of him.

Surprising that after Charlie's death he did not take the irreversible step. He'd had no appetite to live. But the body has its own appetite, apparently—that pitiless need to continue with its living, which has so many disguises and so many rationales.

A deep embarrassment has been stalking him. Every time he lets his guard down these days, there it is. Because it's become clear: he and even the most dissolute among his friends have glided through their lives on the assumption that the sheer fact of their existence has in some way made the world a better place. As deranged as it sounds now, a better place. Not a leafy bower, maybe, but still, a somewhat better place—more tolerant, more amenable to the wonderful adventures of the human mind and the human body, more capable of outrage against injustice . . . .

For shame! One has been shocked, all one's life, to learn of the blind eye turned to children covered with bruises and welts, the blind eye turned to the men who came at night for the neighbors. And yet . . . . And yet one has clung to the belief that the sun shining inside one's head is evidence of sunshine elsewhere.

Not everywhere, of course. Obviously, at every moment something terrible is being done to someone somewhere—one can't really know about each instance of it!

Then again, how far away does something have to be before you have the right to not really know about it?

Sometime after Charlie's death, Lucien resumed throwing his parties. He and his friends continued to buy art and make art, to drink and reflect. They voted responsibly, they gave to charity, they read the paper assiduously. And while they were basking in their exclusive sunshine, what had happened to the planet? Lucien gazes at his glass of wine, his eyes stinging.

HOMESICK

Nathaniel was eight or nine when his aunt and uncle had come out to the Midwest to visit the family, lustrous and clever and comfortable and humorous and affectionate with one another, in their soft, stylish clothing. They'd brought books with them to read. When they talked to each other—and they habitually did—not only did they take turns, but also, what *one* said followed on what the *other* said. What world could they have come from? What was the world in which beings like his aunt and uncle could exist?

A world utterly unlike his parents', that was for sure—a world of freedom and lightness and beauty and the ardent exchange of ideas and . . . and . . . *fun.*

A great longing rose up in Nathaniel like a flower with a lovely, haunting fragrance. When he was ready, he'd thought—when he was able, when he was worthy, he'd get to the world from which his magic aunt and uncle had once briefly appeared.

The evidence, though, kept piling up that he was not worthy. Because even when he finished school, he simply didn't budge. How unfair it was—his friends had flown off so easily, as if going to New York were nothing at all.

Immediately after graduation, Madison found himself a job at a fancy New York PR firm. And it seemed that there was a place out there on the trading floor of the Stock Exchange for Amity. And Lyle had suddenly exhibited an astonishing talent for sound design and engineering, so where else would he sensibly live, either?

Yes, the fact was that only Nathaniel seemed slated to remain behind in their college town. Well, he told himself, his parents were getting on; he would worry, so far away. And he was actually employed as a part-time assistant with an actual architectural firm, whereas in New York the competition, for even the lowliest of such jobs, would be ferocious. And also, he had plenty of time, living where he did, to work on *Passivityman*.

And that's what he told Amity, too, when she'd called one night, four years ago, urging him to take the plunge.

"It's time for you to try, Nathaniel," she said. "It's time to commit. This oddball, slacker stance is getting kind of old, don't you think, kind of stale. You cannot let your life be ruled by fear any longer."

"Fear?" He flinched. "By what fear, exactly, do you happen to believe my life is ruled?"

"Well, I mean, fear of failure, obviously. Fear of mediocrity."

For an instant he thought he might be sick.

"Right," he said. "And why should I fear failure and mediocrity? Failure and mediocrity have such august traditions! Anyhow, what's up with you, Amity?"

She'd been easily distracted, and they chatted on for a while, but when they hung up, he felt very, very strange, as if his apartment had slightly changed shape. Amity was right, he'd thought; it was fear that stood between him and the life he'd meant to be leading.

That was probably the coldest night of the whole, difficult millennium. The timid midwestern sun had basically gone down at the beginning of September; it wouldn't be around much again till May. Black ice glared on the street outside like the cloak of an extra-cruel witch. The sink faucet was dripping into a cracked and stained teacup: *Tick tock tick tock . . .*

What was he *doing*? Once he'd dreamed of designing tranquil and ennobling dwellings, buildings that urged benign relationships, rich inner harmonies; he'd dreamed of meeting fascinating strangers. True, he'd managed to avoid certain pitfalls of middle-class adulthood—he wasn't a white-collar criminal, for example; he wasn't (at least as far as he knew) a total blowhard. But what was he *actually doing*? His most exciting social contact was the radio. He spent his salaried hours in a cinder-block office building, poring over catalogues of plumbing fixtures. The rest of the day—and the whole evening, too—he sat at the little desk his parents had bought for him when he was in junior high, slaving over *Passivityman*, a comic strip that ran in free papers all over parts of the Midwest, a comic strip that was doted on by whole dozens, the fact was, of stoned undergrads.

He was twenty-four years old! Soon he'd be twenty-eight. In a few more minutes he'd be thirty-five, then fifty. Five zero. How had that happened? He was eighty! He could feel his vascular system and brain clogging with paste, he was drooling . . .

And if history had anything to teach, it was that he'd be broke when he was eighty, too, and that his personal life would still be a disaster.

———

But wait. Long ago, panic had sent his grandparents and parents scurrying from murderous Europe, with its death camps and pogroms, to the safe harbor of New York. Panic had kept them going as far as the Midwest, where grueling labor enabled them and eventually their children to lead blessedly ordinary lives. And sooner or later, Nathaniel's pounding heart was telling him, that same sure-footed guide, panic, would help him retrace his family's steps all the way back to Manhattan.

OPPORTUNISM

Blip! Charlie scatters again as Lucien's attention wavers from her and the empty space belonging to her is seized by Miss Mueller.

Huh, but what do you know—death *suits* Miss Mueller! In life she was drab, but now she absolutely throbs with ghoulishness. *You there, Lucien*—the shriek echoes around the gallery—*What are the world's three great religions?*

Zen Buddhism, Jainism, and Sufism, he responds sulkily.

Naughty boy! She cackles flirtatiously. *Bang bang, you're dead!*

THE HALF-LIFE OF PASSIVITY

Passivityman is taking a snooze, his standard response to stress, when the alarm rings. "I'll check it out later, boss," he murmurs.

"You'll check it out *now*, please," his girlfriend and superior, the beautiful Princess Prudence, tells him. "Just put on those grubby corduroys and get out there."

"Aw, is it really *urgent*?" he asks.

"Don't you get it?" she says. "I've been warning you,

episode after episode! And now, from his appliance-rich house on the Moon, Captain Corporation has tightened his Net of Evil around the planet Earth, and he's dragging it out of orbit! The U.S. Congress is selected by pharmaceutical companies, the state of Israel is run by Christian fundamentalists, the folks that haul toxic sludge manufacture cattle feed and process burgers, your sources of news and information are edited by a giant mouse, New York City and Christian fundamentalism are holdings of a family in Kuwait—*and all of it's owned by Captain Corporation!*"

Passivityman rubs his eyes and yawns. "Well gosh, Pru, sure—but, like, what am I supposed to do about it?"

"*I* don't know," Princess Prudence says. "It's hardly my job to figure that out, is it? I mean, *you're* the superhero. Just—Just—just go out and do something conspicuously lacking in monetary value! Invent some stinky, profit-proof gloop to pour on stuff. Or, I don't know, whatever. But you'd better do *something*, before it's too late."

"Sounds like it's totally too late already," says Passivityman, reaching for a cigarette.

It was quite a while ago now that Passivityman seemed to throw in the towel. Nathaniel's friends looked at the strip with him and scratched their heads.

"Hm, I don't know, Nathaniel," Amity said. "This episode is awfully complicated. I mean, Passivityman's seeming kind of passive-*aggressive*, actually."

"Can Passivityman not be bothered any longer to protect the abject with his greed-repelling Shield of Sloth?" Lyle asked.

"It's not going to be revealed that Passivityman is a double agent, is it?" Madison said. "I mean, what about his undying struggle against corporate-model efficiency?"

"The truth is, I don't really know what's going on with him," Nathaniel said. "I was thinking that maybe, unbeknownst to himself, he's come under the thrall of his morally neutral, transgendering twin, Ambiguityperson."

"Yeah," Madison said. "But I mean, the problem here is that he's just not dealing with the paradox of his own being—he seems kind of *intellectually* passive . . ."

Oh, dear. Poor Passivityman. He was a *tired* old crime fighter. Nathaniel sighed; it was hard to live the way his superhero lived—constantly vigilant against the premature conclusion, scrupulously rejecting the vulgar ambition, rigorously deferring judgment and action . . . and all for the greater good.

"Huh, well, I guess he's sort of losing his superpowers," Nathaniel said.

The others looked away uncomfortably.

"Oh, it's probably just one of those slumps," Amity said. "I'm sure he'll be back to normal, soon."

But by now, Nathaniel realizes, he's all but stopped trying to work on *Passivityman*.

ALL THIS

Thanks for pointing that out, Miss Mueller. Yes, humanity seems to have reverted by a millennium or so. Goon squads, purporting to represent each of the *world's three great religions*—as they used to be called to fifth-graders, and perhaps still so misleadingly are—have deployed themselves all over the map, apparently in hopes of annihilating not only each other, but absolutely everyone, themselves excepted.

Just a few weeks earlier, Lucien was on a plane heading home from Los Angeles, and over the loudspeaker, the pilot requested that all Christians on board raise their hands. The next sickening instants provided more than enough time for conjecture as to who, exactly, was about to be killed—Christians or non-Christians. And then the pilot went on to ask those who had raised their hands to talk about their "faith" with the others.

Well, better him than Rose and Isaac; that would have been two sure heart attacks, right there. And anyhow, why should he be so snooty about religious fanaticism? Stalin managed to kill off over thirty million people in the name of no god at all, and not so very long ago.

At the moment when *all this*—as Lucien thinks of it—began, the moment when a few ordinary-looking men carrying box cutters sped past the limits of international negotiation and the frontiers of technology, turning his miraculous city into a nightmare and hurling the future into a void, Lucien was having his croissant and coffee.

The television was saying something. Lucien wheeled around and stared at it, then turned to look out the window; downtown, black smoke was already beginning to pollute the perfect, silken September morning. On the screen, the ruptured, flaming colossus was shedding veils of tiny black specks.

All circuits were busy, of course; the phone might as well have been a toy. Lucien was trembling as he shut the door of the apartment behind him. His face was wet. Outside, he saw that the sky in the north was still insanely blue.

THE AGE OF DROSS

Well, superpowers are probably a feature of youth, like Wendy's ability to fly around with that creepy Peter Pan. Or maybe they belonged to a loftier period of history. It seems that Captain Corporation, his swaggering lieutenants and massed armies have actually neutralized Passivityman's superpower. Passivityman's astonishing reserves of resistance have vanished in the quicksand of Captain Corporation's invisible account books. His rallying cry, No way, which once rang out over the land, demobilizing millions, has been altered by Captain Corporation's co-optophone into, Whatever. And the superpowers of Nathaniel's friends have been seriously challenged, too. Challenged, or . . . outgrown.

Amity's superpower, her gift for exploiting systemic weaknesses, had taken a terrible beating several years ago when the gold she spun out on the trading floor turned—just like everyone else's—into straw. And subsequently, she plummeted from job to job, through layers of prestige, ending up behind a counter in a fancy department store where she sold overpriced skin-care products.

Now, of course, the sale of *Inner Beauty Secrets*—her humorous, lightly fictionalized account of her experiences there with her clients—indicates that perhaps her powers are regenerating. But time will tell.

Madison's superpower, an obtuse, patrician equanimity in the face of damning fact, was violently and irremediably terminated one day when a girl arrived at the door asking for him.

"I'm your sister," she told him. "Sorry," Madison said, "I've never seen you before in my life." "Hang on," the girl said. "I'm just getting to that."

For months afterward, Madison kept everyone awake late into the night repudiating all his former beliefs, his beautiful blue eyes whirling around and his hair standing on end as if he'd stuck his hand into a socket. He quit his lucrative PR job and denounced the firm's practices in open letters to media watchdog groups (copies to his former boss). The many women who'd been running after him did a fast about-face.

Amity called him a "bitter skeptic"; he called Amity a "dupe." The heated quarrel that followed has tapered off into an uneasy truce, at best.

Lyle's superpower back in school was his spectacular level of aggrievedness and his ability to get anyone at all to feel sorry for him. But later, doing sound with a Paris-based dance group, Lyle met Jahan, who was doing the troupe's lighting.

Jahan is (a) as handsome as a prince, (b) as charming, as intelligent, as noble in his thoughts, feelings, and actions as a prince, and (c) a prince, at least of some attenuated sort. So no one feels sorry for Lyle at all any longer, and Lyle has apparently left the pleasures of even *self*-pity behind him without a second thought.

Awhile ago, though, Jahan was mistakenly arrested in some sort of sweep near Times Square, and when he was finally released from custody, he moved to London, and Lyle does nothing but pine, when he can't be in London himself.

"Well, look on the bright side," Nathaniel said. "At least you might get your superpower back."

"You know, Nathaniel . . ." Lyle said. He looked at Nathaniel for a moment, and then an unfamiliar kindness modified his expression. He patted Nathaniel on the shoulder and went on his way.

Yikes. So much for Lyle's superpower, obviously.

"It's great that you got to live here for so long, though," Russell is saying.

Nathaniel has the sudden sensation of his whole four years in New York twisting themselves into an arrow, speeding through the air and twanging into the dead center of this evening. All so hard to believe. "This is not happening," he says.

"I think it might really *be* happening, though," Lyle says.

"Fifty percent of respondents say that the event taking place is not occurring," Madison says. "The other fifty percent remain undecided. Clearly, the truth lies somewhere in between."

Soon it might be as if he and Lyle and Madison and Amity had never even lived here. Because this moment is joined to all the other moments they've spent together here, and all of those moments are Right Now. But soon this moment and all the others will be cut off—in the past, not part of Right Now at all. Yeah, he and his three friends might all be going their separate ways, come to think of it, once they move out.

CONTINUITY

While the sirens screamed, Lucien had walked against the tide of dazed, smoke-smeared people, down into the fuming cauldron, and when he finally reached the police cordon, his feet aching, he wandered along it for hours, searching for Charlie's nephew, among all the other people who were searching for family, friends, lovers.

Oh, that day! One kept waiting—as if a morning would arrive from before that day to take them all along a different track. One kept waiting for that shattering day to unhappen, so that the real—the intended—future, the one that had been implied by the past, could unfold. Hour after hour, month after month, waiting for that day to not have happened. But it had happened. And now it was always going to have happened.

Most likely on the very mornings that first Rose and then Isaac had disembarked at Ellis Island, each clutching some remnant of the world they were never to see again, Lucien was being wheeled in his pram through the genteel world, a few miles uptown, of brownstones.

The city, more than his body, contained his life. His life! The schools he had gone to as a child, the market where his mother had bought the groceries, the park where he had played with his classmates, the restaurants where he had courted Charlie, the various apartments they'd lived in, the apartments of their friends, the gallery, the newsstand on the corner, the dry cleaner's . . . The things he did in the course of the day, year after year, the people he encountered.

A sticky layer of crematorium ash settled over the whole of Matsumoto's neighborhood, even inside, behind closed windows, as thick in places as turf, and water was unavailable for a time. Nathaniel and his friends all stayed elsewhere, of course, for a few weeks. When it became possible, Lucien sent crews down to Matsumoto's loft to scour the place and restore the art.

FAREWELL

A memorandum hangs in Mr. Matsumoto's lobby, that appeared several months ago when freakish blackouts were rolling over the city.

Emergency Tips from the Management urges residents to assemble a Go Bag, in the event of an evacuation, as well as an In-Home Survival Kit. Among items to include: a large amount of cash in small denominations, water and nonperishable foods such as granola bars, a wind-up radio, warm clothing and sturdy walking shoes, unscented bleach and an eyedropper for purifying water, plastic sheeting and duct tape, a whistle, a box cutter.

Also recommended is a Household Disaster Plan and the practicing of emergency drills.

A hand-lettered sign next to the elevator says THINK TWICE.

Twenty-eight years old, no superhero, a job that just *might* lead down to a career in underground architecture, a vanishing apartment, a menacing elevator . . . Maybe he should view Mr. Matsumoto's return as an opportunity, and regroup. Maybe he should *do* something—take matters in hand. Maybe he should go try to find Delphine, for example.

But how? He hasn't heard from her, and she could be anywhere now; she'd mentioned Bucharest, she'd mentioned Havana, she'd mentioned Shanghai, she'd mentioned Istanbul . . .

He'd met her at one of his uncle's parties. There was the usual huge roomful of people wearing strangely pleated black clothes, like the garments of a somber devotional sect, and there she was in electric-blue taffeta, amazingly tall and narrow, lazy and nervous, like an electric bluebell.

She favored men nearly twice Nathaniel's age and millions of times richer, but for a while she let Nathaniel come over to her apartment and play her his favorite CDs. They drank perfumey infusions from chipped porcelain cups, or vodka. Delphine could become thrillingly drunk, and she smoked, letting long columns of ash form on her tarry, unfiltered cigarettes. One night, when he lost his keys, she let him come over and sleep in her bed while she went out, and when the sky fell, she actually let him sleep on her floor for a week.

Her apartment was filled with puffy, silky little sofas, and old, damaged mirrors and tarnished candlesticks, and tall vases filled with slightly wilting flowers. It smelled like powder and tea and cigarettes and her Abyssinian cats, which prowled the savannas of the white, long-haired rugs or posed on the marble mantelpiece.

Delphine's father was Armenian and he lived in Paris, which according to Delphine was a bore. Her mother was Chilean. Delphine's English had been acquired at a boarding school in Kent for dull-witted rich girls and castaways, like herself, from everywhere.

She spoke many languages, she was self-possessed and beautiful and fascinating. She could have gone to live anywhere. And she had come, like Nathaniel, to New York.

"But look at it now," she'd raged. Washington was dropping bombs on Afghanistan and then Iraq, and every few weeks there was a flurry of alerts in kindergarten colors indicating the likelihood of terrorist attacks: yellow, orange, red, *duck!*

"Do you know how I get the news here?" Delphine said. "From your newspapers? Please! From your newspapers I learn what restaurant has opened. News I learn in taxis, from the drivers. And how do they get it? From their friends and relatives back home, in Pakistan or Uzbekistan or Somalia. The drivers sit around at the airport, swapping information, and they can tell you *anything*. But do you ask? Or sometimes I talk to my friends in Europe. Do you know what they're saying about you over there?"

"Please don't say 'you,' Delphine," he had said faintly.

"Oh, yes, here it's not like stuffy old Europe, where everything is stifled by tradition and trauma. Here you're able to speak freely, within reason, of course, and isn't it wonderful that you all happen to want to say exactly what they want you to say? Do you know how many people you're killing over there? No, how would you? Good, just keep your eyes closed, panic, don't ask any questions, and you can speak freely about whatever you like. And if you have any suspicious-looking neighbors, be sure to tell the police. You had everything here, everything, and you threw it all away in one second."

She was so beautiful; he'd gazed at her as if he were already remembering her. "Please don't say 'you,'" he murmured again.

"Poor Nathaniel," she said. "This place is nothing now but a small-minded, mean-spirited provincial town."

THE AGE OF DIGITAL REASONING

One/two. On/off. The plane crashes/doesn't crash.

The plane he took from L.A. didn't crash. It wasn't used as a missile to blow anything up, and not even one passenger was shot or stabbed. Nothing happened. So, what's the problem? What's the difference between having been on that flight and having been on any other flight in his life?

Oh, what's the point of thinking about death all the time!

Think about it or not, you die. Besides—and here's something that sure hasn't changed—you don't have to do it more than once. And as you don't have to do it *less* than once, either, you might as well do it on the plane. Maybe there's no special problem these days. Maybe the problem is just that he's old.

Or maybe his nephew's is the last generation that will remember what it had once felt like to blithely assume there would be a future—at least a future like the one that had been implied by the past they'd all been familiar with.

But the future actually ahead of them, it's now obvious, had itself been implied by a past; and the terrible day that pointed them toward that future had been prepared for a long, long time, though it had been prepared behind a curtain.

It was as if there had been a curtain, a curtain painted with the map of the earth, its oceans and continents, with Lucien's delightful city. The planes struck, tearing through the curtain of that blue September morning, exposing the dark world that lay right behind it, of populations ruthlessly exploited, inflamed with hatred, and tired of waiting for change to happen by.

The stump of the ruined tower continued to smolder far into the fall, and an unseasonable heat persisted. When the smoke lifted, all kinds of other events, which had been prepared behind a curtain, too, were revealed. Flags waved in the brisk air of fear, files were demanded from libraries and hospitals, droning helicopters hung over the city, and heavily armed policemen patrolled the parks. Meanwhile, one read that executives had pocketed the savings of their investors and the pensions of their employees.

The wars in the East were hidden behind a thicket of language: *patriotism, democracy, loyalty, freedom*—the words bounced around, changing purpose, as if they were made out of some funny plastic. What did they actually refer to? It seemed that they all might refer to money.

Were the sudden power outages and spiking level of unemployment related? And what was causing them? The newspapers seemed for the most part to agree that the cause of both was terrorism. But lots of people said they were both the consequence of corporate theft. It was certainly all beyond Lucien! Things that had formerly appeared to be distinct, or even at odds, now seemed to have been smoothly blended, to mutual advantage. Provocation and retribution, arms manufacture and statehood, oil and war, commerce and dogma, and the spinning planet seemed to be boiling them all together at the center of the earth into a poison syrup. Enemies had soared toward each other from out of the past to unite in a joyous fireball; planes had sheared through the heavy, painted curtain and from the severed towers an inexhaustible geyser had erupted.

Styles of pets revolved rapidly, as if the city's residents were searching for a type of animal that would express a stance appropriate to the horrifying assault, which for all anyone knew was only the first of many.

For a couple of months everyone was walking cute, perky things. Then Lucien saw snarling hounds everywhere and the occasional boa constrictor draped around its owner's shoulders. After that, it was tiny, trembling dogs that traveled in purses and pockets.

New York had once been the threshold of an impregnable haven, then the city had become in an instant the country's open wound, and now it was the occasion—the pretext!—for killing and theft and legislative horrors all over the world. The air stank from particulate matter—chemicals and asbestos and blood and scorched bone. People developed coughs and strange rashes.

What should be done, and to whom? Almost any word, even between friends, could ignite a sheet of flame. What were the bombings for? First one imperative was cited and then another; the rationales shifted hastily to cover successive gaps in credibility. Bills were passed containing buried provisions, and loopholes were triumphantly discovered—alarming elasticities or rigidities in this law or that. One was sick of trying to get a solid handle on the stream of pronouncements—it was like endlessly trying to sort little bits of paper into stacks when a powerful fan was on.

Friends in Europe and Asia sent him clippings about his own country. *What's all this,* they asked—secret arrests and detentions, his president capering about in military uniform, crazy talk of preemptive nuclear strikes? Why were they releasing a big science fiction horror movie over there, about the emperor of everything everywhere, for which the whole world was required to buy tickets? What on earth was going on with them all, why were they all so silent? Why did they all seem so confused?

How was he to know, Lucien thought. If his foreign friends had such great newspapers, why didn't *they* tell *him*!

No more smiles from strangers on the street! Well, it was reasonable to be frightened; everyone had seen what those few men were able do with the odds and ends in their pockets. The heat lifted, and then there was unremitting cold. No one lingered to joke and converse in the course of their errands, but instead hurried irritably along, like people with bad consciences.

And always in front of you now was the sight that had been hidden by the curtain, of all those irrepressibly, murderously angry people.

Private life shrank to nothing. All one's feelings had been absorbed by an arid wasteland—policy, strategy, goals. One's past, one's future, one's ordinary daily pleasures were like dusty little curios on a shelf.

Lucien continued defiantly throwing his parties, but as the murky wars dragged on, he stopped. It was impossible to have fun or to want to have fun. It was one thing to have fun if the sun was shining generally, quite another thing to have fun if it was raining blood everywhere but on your party. What did he and his friends really have in common, anyway? Maybe nothing more than their level of privilege.

In restaurants and cafes all over the city, people seemed to have changed. The good-hearted, casually wasteful festival was over. In some places the diners were sullen and dogged, as if they felt accused of getting away with something.

In other places, the gaiety was cranked up to the level of completely unconvincing hysteria. For a long miserable while, in fact, the city looked like a school play about war profiteering. The bars were overflowing with very young people from heaven only knew where, in hideous, ludicrously showy clothing, spending massive amounts of money on green, pink, and orange cocktails, and laughing at the top of their lungs, as if at filthy jokes.

No, not like a school play—like a movie, though the performances and the direction were crude. The loud, ostensibly carefree young people appeared to be extras recruited from the suburbs, and yet sometime in the distant future, people seeing such a movie might think oh, yes, that was a New York that existed once, say, at the end of the millennium.

It was Lucien's city, Lucien's times, and yet what he appeared to be living in wasn't the actual present—it was an inaccurate representation of the *past*. True, it looked something like the New York that existed before *all this* began, but Lucien remembered, and he could see: the costumes were not quite right, the hairstyles were not quite right, the gestures and the dialogue were not quite right.

Oh. Yes. Of course none of it was quite right—the movie was a *propaganda* movie. And now it seems that the propaganda movie has done its job; things, in a grotesque sense, are back to normal.

Money is flowing a bit again, most of the flags have folded up, those nerve-wracking terror alerts have all but stopped, the kids in the restaurants have calmed down, no more rolling blackouts, and the dogs on the street encode no particular messages. Once again, people are concerned with getting on with their lives. Once again, the curtain has dropped.

Except that people seem a little bit nervous, a little uncomfortable, a little wary. Because you can't help sort of knowing that what you're seeing is only the curtain. And you can't help guessing what might be going on behind it.

THE FURTHER IN THE PAST THINGS ARE, THE BIGGER THEY BECOME

Nathaniel remembers more and more rather than less and less vividly the visit of his uncle and aunt to the Midwest during his childhood.

He'd thought his aunt Charlie was the most beautiful woman he'd ever seen. And for all he knows, she really was. He never saw her after that one visit; by the time he came to New York and reconnected with Uncle Lucien she had been dead for a long time. She would still have been under fifty when she died—crushed, his mother had once, in a mood, implied, by the weight of her own pretensions.

His poor mother! She had cooked, cleaned, and fretted for . . . months, it had seemed, in preparation for that visit of Uncle Lucien and Aunt Charlie. And observing in his memory the four grown-ups, Nathaniel can see an awful lot of white knuckles.

He remembers his mother picking up a book Aunt Charlie had left lying on the kitchen table, glancing at it and putting it back down with a tiny shrug and a lifted eyebrow. "You don't approve?" Aunt Charlie said, and Nathaniel is shocked to see, in his memory, that she is tense.

His mother, having gained the advantage, makes another bitter little shrug. "I'm sure it's over my head," she says.

When the term of the visit came to an end, they dropped Uncle Lucien and Aunt Charlie at the airport. His brother was driving, too fast. Nathaniel can hear himself announcing in his child's piercing voice, "*I want to live in New York like Uncle Lucien and Aunt Charlie!*" His exile's heart was brimming, but it was clear from his mother's profile that she was braced for an execution.

"Slow *down*, Bernie!" his mother said, but Bernie hadn't. "Big shot," she muttered, though it was unclear at whom this was directed—whether at his brother or himself or his father, or his Uncle Lucien, or at Aunt Charlie herself.

BACK TO NORMAL

Do dogs have to fight sadness as tirelessly as humans do? They seem less involved with retrospect, less involved in dread and anticipation. Animals other than humans appear to be having a more profound experience of the present. But who's to say? Clearly their feelings are intense, and maybe grief and anxiety darken all their days. Maybe that's why they've acquired their stripes and polka dots and fluffiness—to cheer themselves up.

Poor old Earth, an old sponge, a honeycomb of empty mine shafts and dried wells. While he and his friends were wittering on, the planet underfoot had been looted. The waterways glint with weapons-grade plutonium, sneaked on barges between one wrathful nation and another, the polar ice caps melt, Venice sinks.

In the horrible old days in Europe when Rose and Isaac were hunted children, it must have been pretty clear to them how to behave, minute by minute. Men in jackboots? Up to the attic!

But even during that time when it was so dangerous to speak out, to act courageously, heroes emerged. Most of them died fruitlessly, of course, and unheralded. But now there are even monuments to some of them, and information about such people is always coming to light.

Maybe there really is no problem, maybe everything really is back to normal and maybe the whole period will sink peacefully away, to be remembered only by scholars. But if it should end, instead, in dire catastrophe, whom will the monuments of the future commemorate?

Today, all day long, Lucien has seen the president's vacant, stricken expression staring from the ubiquitous television screens. He seemed to be talking about positioning weapons in space, colonizing the moon.

Open your books to page 167, class, Miss Mueller shrieks. *What do you see?*

Lucien sighs.

The pages are thin and sort of shiny. The illustrations are mostly black and white.

This one's a photograph of a statue, an emperor, apparently, wearing his stone toga and his stone wreath. The real people, the living people, mill about just beyond the picture's confines, but Lucien knows more or less what they look like—he's seen illustrations of them, too. He knows what a viaduct is and that the ancient Romans went to plays and banquets and that they had a code of law from which his country's own is derived. Are the people hidden by the picture frightened? Do they hear the stones working themselves loose, the temples and houses and courts beginning to crumble?

Out the window, the sun is just a tiny, tiny bit higher today than it was at this exact instant yesterday. After school, he and Robbie Stern will go play soccer in the park. In another month it will be bright and warm.

PARADISE

So, Mr. Matsumoto will be coming back, and things seem pretty much as they did when he left. The apartment is clean, the cats are healthy, the art is undamaged, and the view from the terrace is exactly the same, except there's that weird, blank spot where the towers used to stand.

"Open the next?" Madison says, holding up a bottle of champagne. "Strongly agree, agree, undecided, disagree, strongly disagree."

"Strongly agree," Lyle says.

"Thanks," Amity says.

"Okay," Russell says. "I'm in."

Nathaniel shrugs and holds out his glass.

Madison pours. "Polls indicate that 100 percent of the American public approves heavy drinking," he says.

"Oh, god, Madison," Amity says. "Can't we ever just *drop* it? Can't we ever just have a nice time?"

Madison looks at her for a long moment. "Drop what?" he says, evenly.

But no one wants to get into *that*.

When Nathaniel was in his last year at college, his father began to suffer from heart trouble. It was easy enough for Nathaniel to come home on the weekends, and he'd sit with his father, gazing out the window as the autumnal light gilded the dry grass and the fallen leaves glowed.

His father talked about his own time at school, working night and day, the pride his parents had taken in him, the first college student in their family.

Over the years Nathaniel's mother and father had grown gentler with one another and with him. Sometimes after dinner and the dishes, they'd all go out for a treat. Nathaniel would wait, an acid pity weakening his bones, while his parents debated worriedly over their choices, as if nobody ever had before or would ever have again the opportunity to eat ice cream.

Just last night, he dreamed about Delphine, a delicious champagne-style dream, full of love and beauty—a weird, high-quality love, a feeling he doesn't remember ever having had in his waking life—a pure, wholehearted, shining love.

It hangs around him still, floating through the air out on the terrace—fragrant, shimmering, fading.

WAITING

The bell is about to ring. Closing his book Lucien hears the thrilling crash as the bloated empire tumbles down.

Gold star, Lucien! Miss Mueller cackles deafeningly, and then she's gone.

Charlie's leaving, too. Lucien lifts his glass; she glances back across the thin, inflexible divide.

From farther than the moon she sees the children of some distant planet study pictures in their text: there's Rose and Isaac at their kitchen table, Nathaniel out on Mr. Matsumoto's terrace, Lucien alone in the dim gallery—and then the children turn the page.

SOME OTHER, BETTER OTTO

"I don't know why I committed us to any of those things," Otto said. "I'd much prefer to be working or reading, and you'll want all the time you can get this week to practice."

"It's fine with me," William said. "I always like to see Sharon. And we'll survive the evening with your—"

Otto winced.

"Well, we will," William said. "And don't you want to see Naomi and Margaret and the baby as soon as they get back?"

"Everyone always says, 'Don't you want to see the baby, don't you want to see the baby,' but if I did want to see a fat, bald, confused person, obviously I'd have only to look in the mirror."

"I was reading a remarkable article in the paper this morning about holiday depression," William said. "Should I clip it for you? The statistics were amazing."

"The statistics cannot have been amazing, the article cannot have been remarkable, and I am not 'depressed.' I just happen to be bored sick by these inane— Waving our little antennae, joining our little paws in indication of— Oh, what is the point? Why did I agree to any of this?"

"Well," William said. "I mean, this is what we do."

———

Hmm. Well, true. And the further truth was, Otto saw, that he himself wanted, in some way, to see Sharon; he himself wanted, in some way, to see Naomi and Margaret and the baby as soon as possible. And it was even he himself who had agreed to join his family for Thanksgiving. It would be straining some concept—possibly the concept of "wanted," possibly the concept of "self"—to say that he himself had wanted to join them, and yet there clearly must have been an implicit alternative to joining them that was even less desirable, or he would not, after all, have agreed to it.

It had taken him—how long?—years and years to establish a viable, if not pristine, degree of estrangement from his family. Which was no doubt why, he once explained to William, he had tended, over the decades, to be so irascible and easily exhausted. The sustained effort, the subliminal concentration that was required to detach the stubborn prehensile hold was enough to wear a person right out and keep him from ever getting down to anything of real substance.

Weddings had lapsed entirely, birthdays were a phone call at the most, and at Christmas, Otto and William sent lavish gifts of out-of-season fruits, in the wake of which would arrive recriminatory little thank-you notes. From mid-December to mid-January they would absent themselves, not merely from the perilous vicinity of Otto's family, but from the entire country, to frolic in blue water under sunny skies.

When his mother died, Otto experienced an exhilarating melancholy; most of the painful encounters and obligations would now be a thing of the past. Life, with its humorous theatricality, had bestowed and revoked with one gesture, and there he abruptly was, in the position he felt he'd been born for: he was alone in the world.

Or alone in the world, anyway, with William. Marching

ahead of his sisters and brother—Corinne, Martin, and
Sharon—Otto was in the front ranks now, death's cannon
fodder and so on; he had become old overnight, and free.

Old and free! Old and free . . .

Still, he made himself available to provide legal advice or
to arrange a summer internship for some child or nephew.
He saw Sharon from time to time. From time to time there
were calls: "Of course you're too busy, but . . ." "Of course
you're not interested, but . . ." was how they began. This was
the one thing Corinne and her husband and Martin and
whichever wife were always all in accord about—that Otto
seemed to feel he was too good for the rest of them, despite
the obvious indications to the contrary.

Who was too good for whom? It often came down to a
show of force. When Corinne had called a week or so earlier
about Thanksgiving, Otto, addled by alarm, said, "We're
having people ourselves, I'm afraid."

Corinne's silence was like a mirror, flashing his tiny,
harmless lie back to him in huge magnification, all covered
with sticky hairs and microbes.

"Well, I'll see what I can do," he said.

"Please try," Corinne said. The phrase had the unassail-
able authority of a road sign appearing suddenly around the
bend: FALLING ROCK. "Otto, the children are growing up."

"Children! What children? Your children grew up years
ago, Corinne. Your children are old now, like us."

"I meant, of course, Martin's. The new ones. Martin and
Laurie's. And there's Portia."

Portia? Oh, yes. The little girl. The sole, thank heavens,
issue, of Martin's marriage to that crazy Viola.

"I'll see what I can do," Otto said again, this time less cra-
venly. It was Corinne's own fault. A person of finer sensibilities

would have written a note, or used e-mail—or would face-savingly have left a message at his office, giving him time to prepare some well-crafted deterrent rather than whatever makeshift explosive he would obviously be forced to lob back at her under direct attack.

"Wesley and I are having it in the city this year," Corinne was saying. "No need to come all the way out to the nasty country. A few hours and it will all be over with. Seriously, Otto, you're an integral element. We're keeping it simple this year."

" 'This year?' Corinne, there have been no other years. You do not observe Thanksgiving."

"In fact, Otto, we do. And we all used to."

"Who?"

"All of us."

"Never. When? Can you imagine Mother being thankful for anything?"

"We always celebrated Thanksgiving when Father was alive."

"I remember no such thing."

"I do. I remember, and so does Martin."

"Martin was four when Father died!"

"Well, you were little, too."

"I was twice Martin's age."

"Oh, Otto—I just feel sad, sometimes, to tell you the truth, don't you? It's all going so fast! I'd like to see everyone in the same room once a century or so. I want to see every-body well and happy. I mean, you and Martin and Sharon were my brothers and sister. What was *that* all about? Don't you remember? Playing together all the time?"

"I just remember Martin throwing up all the time."

"You'll be nice to him, won't you, Otto? He's still very sensitive. He won't want to talk about the lawsuit."

"Have you spoken to Sharon?"

"Well, that's something I wanted to talk to you about, actually. I'm afraid I might have offended her. I stressed the fact that it was only to be us this year. No aunts or uncles, no cousins, no friends. Just us. And husbands or wives. Husband. And wife. Or whatever. And children, naturally, but she became very hostile."

"Assuming William to be 'whatever,'" Otto said, "why shouldn't Sharon bring a friend if she wants to?"

"William is *family*. And surely you remember when she brought that person to Christmas! The person with the feet? I wish you'd go by and talk to her in the next few days. She seems to listen to you."

Otto fished up a magazine from the floor—one of the popular science magazines William always left lying around—and idly opened it.

"Wesley and I reach out to her," Corinne was saying. "And so does Martin, but she doesn't respond. I know it can be hard for her to be with people, but we're not people—we're family."

"I'm sure she understands that, Corinne."

"I hope you do, too, Otto."

How clearly he could see, through the phone line, this little sister of his—in her fifties now—the six-year-old's expression of aggrieved anxiety long etched decisively on her face.

"In any case," she said, "I've called."

And yet there was something to what Corinne had said; they had been one another's environs as children. The distance between them had been as great, in any important way, as it was now, but there had been no other beings close by, no other beings through whom they could probe or illumine the mystifying chasms and absences and yearnings within themselves. They had been born into the arid clutter of one another's behavior, good and bad, their measles, skinned knees, report cards . . .

A barren landscape dotted with clutter. Perhaps the life of the last dinosaurs, as they ranged, puzzled and sorrowful, across the comet-singed planet, was similar to childhood. It hadn't been a pleasant time, surely, and yet one did have an impulse to acknowledge one's antecedents, now and again. Hello, that was us, it still is, goodbye.

"I don't know," William said. "It doesn't seem fair to put any pressure on Sharon."

"Heaven forfend. But I did promise Corinne I'd speak with Sharon. And, after all, I haven't actually seen her for some time."

"We could just go have a plain old visit, though. I don't know. Urging her to go to Corinne's—I'm not really comfortable with that."

"Oof, William, phrase, please, jargon."

"Why is that jargon?"

"Why? How should I know why? Because it is. You can say, 'I'm uncomfortable *about* that,' or 'That makes me uncomfortable.' But 'I'm uncomfortable *with* that' is simply jargon." He picked up a book sitting next to him on the table and opened it. *Relativity for Dummies.* "Good heavens," he said, snapping the book shut. "*Obviously* Martin doesn't want to talk about the lawsuit. Why bother to mention that to me? Does she think I'm going to ask Martin whether it's true that he's been misrepresenting the value of his client's stock? Am I likely to talk about it? I'm perfectly happy to read about it in the *Times* every day, like everyone else."

"You know," William said, "we could go away early this

year. We could just pick up and leave on Wednesday, if you'd like."

"I would not like. I would like you to play in your concert, as always."

William took the book from Otto and held Otto's hand between his own. "They're not really so bad, you know, your family," he said.

Sometimes William's consolations were oddly like provocations. "Easy for you to say," Otto said.

"Not that easy."

"I'm sorry," Otto said. "I know."

Just like William to suggest going away early for Otto's sake, when he looked forward so much to his concert! The little orchestra played publicly only once a year, the Sunday after Thanksgiving. Otto endured the grating preparatory practicing, not exactly with equanimity, it had to be admitted, but with relative forbearance, just for the pleasure of seeing William's radiant face on the occasion. William in his suit, William fussing over the programs, William busily arranging tickets for friends. Otto's sunny, his patient, his deeply good William. Toward the end of every year, when the city lights glimmered through the fuzzy winter dark, on the Sunday after Thanksgiving, William with his glowing violin, urging the good-natured, timid audience into passionate explorations of the unseen world. And every year now, from the audience, Otto felt William's impress stamped on the planet, more legible and valuable by one year; all the more legible and valuable for the one year's diminution in William's beauty.

How spectacular he had been the first time Otto brought him to a family event, that gladiatorial Christmas thirty-odd years earlier. How had Otto ever marshaled the nerve to do it?

Oh, one could say till one was blue in the face that Christmas was a day like any other, what difference would it make if he and William were to spend that particular day apart, and so on. And yet.

Yes, the occasion forced the issue, didn't it. Either he and William would both attend, or Otto would attend alone, or they would not attend together. But whatever it was that one decided to do, it would be a declaration—to the family, and to the other. And, the fact was, to oneself.

Steeled by new love, in giddy defiance, Otto had arrived at the house with William, to all intents and purposes, on his arm.

A tidal wave of nervous prurience had practically blown the door out from inside the instant he and William ascended the front step. And all evening aunts, uncles, cousins, mother, and siblings had stared at William beadily, as if a little bunny had loped out into a clearing in front of them.

William's beauty, and the fact that he was scarcely twenty, had embarrassed Otto on other occasions, but never so searingly. "How *intelligent* he is!" Otto's relatives kept whispering to one another loudly, meaning, apparently, that it was a marvel he could speak. Unlike, the further implication was, the men they'd evidently been imagining all these years.

Otto had brought someone to a family event only once before—also on a Christmas, with everyone in attendance: Diandra Fetlin, a feverishly brilliant colleague, far less beautiful than William. During the turkey, she thumped Otto on the arm whenever he made a good point in the argument he was having with Wesley, and continued to eat with solemn assiduity. Then, while the others applied themselves to dessert, a stuccolike fantasy requiring vigilance, Diandra had delivered an explication of one of the firm's recent cases that was worth three semesters of law school. No one commented on *her* intelligence. And no one had been in the least deceived by Otto's tepid display of interest in her.

"So," Corinne had said in a loud and artificially genial tone as if she were speaking to an armed high-school student, "where did you and William meet, Otto?"

The table fell silent; Otto looked out at the wolfish ring of faces. "On Third Avenue," he said distinctly, and returned to his meal.

"Sorry," he said, as he and William climbed into the car afterward. "Sorry to have embarrassed you. Sorry to have shocked them. Sorry, sorry, sorry. But what was I supposed to say? All that completely fraudulent *interest*. The *solicitude*. The truth is, they've *never* sanctioned my way of life. Or, alternately, they've always *sanctioned* it. Oh, what on earth good is it to have a word that means only itself and its opposite!"

Driving back to the city, through the assaultively scenic and demographically uniform little towns, they were silent. William had witnessed; his power over Otto had been substantially increased by the preceding several hours, and yet he was exhibiting no signs of triumph. On the contrary, his habitual chipper mood was—where? Simply eclipsed. Otto glanced at him; no glance was returned.

Back in the apartment, they sat for a while in the dark. Tears stung Otto's eyes and nose. He would miss William terribly. "It was a mistake," he said.

William gestured absently. "Well, we had to do it sooner or later."

We? We did? It was as if snow had begun to fall in the apartment—a gentle, chiming, twinkling snow. And sitting there, looking at one another silently, it became apparent that what each was facing was his future.

Marvelous to watch William out in the garden, now with the late chrysanthemums. It was a flower Otto had never liked until William instructed him to look again. Well, all right, so it wasn't a merry flower. But flowers could comfortably embrace a range of qualities, it seemed. And now, how Otto loved the imperial colors, the tensely arched blossoms, the cleansing scent that seemed dipped up from the pure well of winter, nature's ceremony of end and beginning.

The flat little disk of autumn sun was retreating, high up over the neighbors' buildings. As Otto gazed out the window, William straightened, shaded his eyes, waved, and bent back to work. Late in the year, William in the garden . . .

Otto bought the brownstone when he and William had decided to truly move in together. Over twenty-five years ago, that was. The place was in disrepair and cost comparatively little at the time. While Otto hacked his way through the barbed thickets of intellectual property rights issues that had begun to spring up everywhere, struggling to disentangle tiny shoots of weak, drab good from vibrant, hardy evil, William worked in the garden and on the house. And to earn, as he insisted on doing, a modest living of his own, he proofread for a small company that published books about music. Eventually they rented out the top story of the brownstone, for a purely nominal sum, to Naomi, whom they'd met around the neighborhood and liked. It was nice to come home late and see her light on, to run into her on the stairs.

She'd been just a girl when she'd moved in, really, nodding and smiling and ducking her head when she encountered them at the door or on the way up with intractable brown paper bags, bulging as if they were full of cats but tufted with peculiar groceries—vegetables sprouting globular appendages and sloshing cartons of mysterious liquids. Then, farther along in the distant past, Margaret had appeared.

Where there had been one in the market, at the corner bar, on the stairs, now there were two. Naomi, short and lively, given to boots and charming cowgirl skirts; tall, arrestingly bony Margaret with arched eyebrows and bright red hair. Now there were lines around Naomi's eyes; she had widened and settled downward. One rarely recalled Margaret's early, sylvan loveliness.

So long ago! Though it felt that way only at moments—when Otto passed by a mirror unprepared, or when he bothered to register the probable ages (in comparison with his own) of people whom—so recently!—he would have taken for contemporaries, or when he caught a glimpse of a middle-aged person coming toward him on the street who turned into William. Or sometimes when he thought of Sharon.

And right this moment, Naomi and Margaret were on their way back from China with their baby. The adoption went through! Naomi's recent, ecstatic e-mail had announced. Adoption. Had the girls upstairs failed to notice that they had slid into their late forties?

Sharon's apartment looked, as always, as if it had been sealed up in some innocent period against approaching catastrophes.

There were several blond wood chairs, and a sofa, all slipcovered in a nubby, unexceptionable fabric that suggested nuns' sleepwear, and a plastic hassock. The simple, undemanding shapes of the furnishings portrayed the humility of daily life—or at least, Otto thought, of Sharon's daily life. The Formica counter was blankly unstained, and in the cupboards there was a set of heavy, functional, white dishes.

It was just possible, if you craned, and scrunched yourself properly, to glimpse through the window a corner of Sharon's beloved planetarium, where she spent many of her waking hours; the light that made its way to the window around the encircling buildings was pale and tender, an elegy from a distant sun. Sharon herself sometimes seemed to Otto like an apparition from the past. As the rest of them aged, her small frame continued to look like a young girl's; her hair remained an infantine flaxen. To hold it back she wore bright, plastic barrettes.

A large computer, a gift from Otto, sat in the living room, its screen permanently alive. Charts of the constellations were pinned to one of the bedroom walls, and on the facing wall were topographical maps. Peeking into the room, one felt as if one were traveling with Sharon in some zone between earth and sky; yes, down there, so far away—that was our planet.

Why did he need so many things in his life, Otto wondered; why did all these things have to be so special? Special, beautiful plates; special, beautiful furniture; special, beautiful everything. And all that specialness, it occurred to him, intended only to ensure that no one—especially himself—could possibly underestimate his value. Yet it actually served to illustrate how corroded he was, how threadbare his native resources, how impoverished his discourse with everything that lived and was human.

Sharon filled a teakettle with water and lit one of the

stove burners. The kettle was dented, but oddly bright, as if she'd just scrubbed it. "I'm thinking of buying a sculpture," she said. "Nothing big. Sit down, Otto, if you'd like. With some pleasant vertical bits."

"Good plan," Otto said. "Where did you find it?"

"Find it?" she said. "Oh. It's a theoretical sculpture. Abstract in that sense, at least. Because I realized you were right."

About what? Well, it was certainly plausible that he had once idly said something about a sculpture, possibly when he'd helped her find the place and move in, decades earlier. She remembered encyclopedically her years of education, pages of print, apparently arbitrary details of their histories. And some trivial incident or phrase from their childhood might at any time fetch up from her mind and flop down in front of her, alive and thrashing.

No, but it couldn't be called "remembering" at all, really, could it? That simply wasn't what people meant by "remembering." No act of mind or the psyche was needed for Sharon to reclaim anything, because nothing in her brain ever sifted down out of precedence. The passage of time failed to distance, blur, or diminish her experiences. The nacreous layers that formed around the events in one's history to smooth, distinguish, and beautify them never materialized around Sharon's; her history skittered here and there in its original sharp grains on a depthless plane that resembled neither calendar nor clock.

"I just had the most intense episode of déjà vu," William said, as if Otto's thoughts had sideswiped him. "We were all sitting here—"

"We *are* all sitting here," Otto said.

"But that's what I mean," William said. "It's supposed to be some kind of synaptic glitch, isn't it? So you feel as if you've already had the experience just as you're having it?"

"In the view of many neurologists," Sharon said. "But our understanding of time is dim. It's patchy. We really don't know to what degree time is linear, and under what circumstances. Is it actually, in fact, manifold? Or pleated? Is it frilly? And what is our relationship to it? Our relationship to it is extremely problematical."

"I think it's a fine idea for you to have a sculpture," Otto said. "But I don't consider it a necessity."

Her face was as transparent as a child's. Or at least as hers had been as a child, reflecting every passing cloud, rippling at the tiniest disturbance. And her smile! The sheer wattage—no one over eleven smiled like that. "We're using the teabag-in-the-cup method," she said. "Greater scope for the exercise of free will, streamlined technology . . ."

"Oh, goody," William said. "Darjeeling."

Otto stared morosely at his immersed bag and the dark halo spreading from it. How long would Sharon need them to stay? When would she want them to go? It was tricky, weaving a course between what might cause her to feel rejected and what might cause her to feel embattled . . . Actually, though, how did these things work? Did bits of water escort bits of tea from the bag, or what? "How is flavor disseminated?" he said.

"It has to do with oils," Sharon said.

Strange, you really couldn't tell, half the time, whether someone was knowledgeable or insane. At school Sharon had shown an astounding talent for the sciences—for everything. For mathematics, especially. Her mind was so rarefied, so crystalline, so adventurous, that none of the rest of them could begin to follow. She soared into graduate school, practically still a child; she was one of the few blessed people, it seemed, whose destiny was clear.

Her professors were astonished by her leaps of thought, by

the finesse and elegance of her insights. She arrived at hypotheses by sheer intuition and with what eventually one of her mentors described as an almost alarming speed; she was like a dancer, he said, out in the cosmos springing weightlessly from star to star. Drones, merely brilliant, crawled along behind with laborious proofs that supported her assertions.

A tremendous capacity for metaphor, Otto assumed it was; a tremendous sensitivity to the deep structures of the universe. Uncanny. It seemed no more likely that there would be human beings thus equipped than human beings born with satellite dishes growing out of their heads.

He himself was so literal minded he couldn't understand the simplest scientific or mathematical formulation. Plain old electricity, for example, with its amps and volts and charges and conductivity! Metaphors, presumably—metaphors to describe some ectoplasmic tiger in the walls just spoiling to shoot through the wires the instant the cage door was opened and out into the bulb. And molecules! What on earth were people talking about? If the table was actually just a bunch of swarming motes, bound to one another by nothing more than some amicable commonality of form, then why didn't your teacup go crashing through it?

But from the time she was tiny, Sharon seemed to be in kindly, lighthearted communion with the occult substances that lay far within and far beyond the human body. It was all as easy for her as reading was for him. She was a creature of the universe. As were they all, come to think of it, though so few were privileged to feel it. And how hospitable and correct she'd made the universe seem when she spoke of even its most rococo and farfetched attributes!

The only truly pleasurable moments at the family dinner table were those rare occasions when Sharon would talk. He remembered one evening—she would have been in grade school. She was wearing a red sweater; pink barrettes held back her hair. She was speaking of holes in space—holes in nothing! No, not in nothing, Sharon explained patiently—in space. And the others, older and larger, laid down their speared meat and listened, uncomprehending and entranced, as though to distant, wordless singing.

Perhaps, Otto sometimes consoled himself, they could be forgiven for failing to identify the beginnings. How could the rest of them, with their ordinary intellects, have followed Sharon's rapid and arcane speculations, her penetrating apperceptions, closely enough to identify with any certainty the odd associations and disjunctures that seemed to be showing up in her conversation? In any case, at a certain point as she wandered out among the galaxies, among the whirling particles and ineffable numbers, something leaked in her mind, smudging the text of the cosmos, and she was lost.

Or perhaps, like a lightbulb, she was helplessly receptive to an overwhelming influx. She was so physically delicate, and yet the person to whom she was talking might take a step back. And she, in turn, could be crushed by the slightest shift in someone's expression or tone. It was as if the chemistry of her personality burned off the cushion of air between herself and others. Then one night she called, very late, to alert Otto to a newspaper article about the sorting of lettuces; if he were to give each letter its numerological value . . . The phone cord thrummed with her panic.

When their taxi approached the hospital on that first occasion, Sharon was dank and electric with terror; her skin looked like wet plaster. Otto felt like an assassin as he led her in, and then she was ushered away somewhere. The others joined him in the waiting room, and after several hours had the opportunity to browbeat various doctors into hangdog temporizing. Many people got better, didn't they, had only one episode, didn't they, led fully functioning lives? Why wouldn't Sharon be part of that statistic—she, who was so able, so lively, so sweet—so, in a word, healthy? When would she be all right?

That depended on what they meant by "all right," one of the doctors replied. "We mean by 'all right' what you mean by 'all right,' you squirrelly bastard," Wesley had shouted, empurpling. Martin paced, sizzling and clicking through his teeth, while Otto sat with his head in his hands, but the fateful, brutal, meaningless diagnosis had already been handed down.

"I got a cake," Sharon said. She glanced at Otto. "Oh. Was that appropriate?"

"Utterly," William said.

Appropriate? What if the cake turned out to be decorated with invisible portents and symbols? What if it revealed itself to be invested with power? To be part of the arsenal of small objects—nail scissors, postage stamps, wrapped candies—that lay about in camouflage to fool the credulous doofus like himself just as they were winking their malevolent signals to Sharon?

Or what if the cake was, after all, only an inert teatime treat? A cake required thought, effort, expenditure—all that on a negligible scale for most people, but in Sharon's stripped and cautious life, nothing was negligible. A cake. Wasn't that enough to bring one to one's knees? "Very appropriate," Otto concurred.

"Do you miss the fish?" Sharon said, lifting the cake from its box.

Fish? Otto's heart flipped up, pounding. Oh, the box, fish, nothing.

"We brought them home from the dime store in little

cardboard boxes," she explained to William, passing the cake on its plate and a large knife over to him.

"I had a hamster," William said. The cake bulged resiliently around the knife.

"Did it have to rush around on one of those things?" Sharon asked.

"I think it liked to," William said, surprised.

"Let us hope so," Otto said. "Of course it did."

"I loved the castles and the colored sand," Sharon said. "But it was no life for a fish. We had to flush them down the toilet."

William, normally so fastidious about food, appeared to be happily eating his cake, which tasted, to Otto, like landfill. And William had brought Sharon flowers, which it never would have occurred to Otto to do.

Why had lovely William stayed with disagreeable old him for all this time? What could possibly explain his appeal for William, Otto wondered? Certainly not his appearance, nor his musical sensitivity—middling at best—nor, clearly, his temperament. Others might have been swayed by the money that he made so easily, but not William. William cared as little about that as did Otto himself. And yet, through all these years, William had cleaved to him. Or at least, usually. Most of the uncleavings, in fact, had been Otto's—brief, preposterous seizures having to do with God knows what. Well, actually he himself would be the one to know what, wouldn't he, Otto thought. Having to do with—who *did* know what? Oh, with fear, with flight, the usual. A bit of glitter, a mirage, a chimera . . . A lot of commotion just for a glimpse into his own life, the real one—a life more vivid, more truly his, than the one that was daily at hand.

"Was there something you wanted to see me about?" Sharon asked.

"Well, I just . . ." Powerful beams of misery intersected in Otto's heart; was it true? Did he always have a reason when he called Sharon? Did he never drop in just to say hello? Not that anyone ought to "drop in" on Sharon. Or on anyone, actually. How barbarous.

"Your brother's here in an ambassadorial capacity," William said. "I'm just here for the cake."

"Ambassadorial?" Sharon looked alarmed.

"Oh, it's only Thanksgiving," Otto said. "Corinne was hoping— I was hoping—"

"Otto, I can't. I just can't. I don't want to sit there being an exhibit of robust good health, or noncontaminatingness, or the triumph of the human spirit, or whatever it is that Corinne needs me to illustrate. Just tell them everything's okay."

He looked at his cake. William was right. This was terribly unfair. "Well, I don't blame you," he said. "I wouldn't go myself, if I could get out of it."

"If you had a good enough excuse."

"I only—" But of course it was exactly what he had meant; he had meant that Sharon had a good enough excuse. "I'm—"

"Tell Corinne I'm all right."

Otto started to speak again, but stopped.

"Otto, please." Sharon looked at her hands, folded in her lap. "It's all right."

"I've sometimes wondered if it might not be possible, in theory, to remember something that you—I mean the aspect of yourself that you're aware of—haven't experienced yet," William said later. "I mean, we really *don't* know whether time is linear, so—"

"Would you stop that?" Otto said. "*You're* not insane."

"I'm merely speaking theoretically."

"Well, don't! And your memory has nothing to do with whether time is 'really,' whatever you mean by that, linear. It's plenty linear for us! Cradle to grave? Over the hill? It's a one-way street, my dear. My hair is not sometimes there and sometimes not there; we're *not* getting any younger."

At moments it occurred to Otto that what explained his appeal for William was the fact that they lived in the same apartment. That William was idiotically accepting, idiotically pliant. Perhaps William was so deficient in subtlety, so insensitive to nuance, that he simply couldn't tell the difference between Otto and anyone else. "And, William——I wish you'd get back to your tennis."

"It's a bore. Besides, you didn't want me playing with Jason, as I remember."

"Well, I was out of my mind. And at this point it's your arteries I worry about."

"You know," William said and put his graceful hand on Otto's arm. "I don't think she's any more unhappy than the rest of us, really, most of the time. That smile! I mean, that smile can't come out of nowhere."

There actually were no children to speak of. Corinne and Wesley's "boys" put in a brief, unnerving appearance. When last seen, they had been surly, furtive, persecuted-looking, snickering, hulking, hairy adolescents, and now here they were, having undergone the miraculous transformation. How gratified Wesley must be! They had shed their egalitarian denim chrysalis and had risen up in the crisp, mean mantle of their class.

The older one even had a wife, whom Corinne treated

with a stricken, fluttery deference as if she were a suitcase full
of weapons-grade plutonium. The younger one was restlessly
on his own. When, early in the evening the three stood and
announced to Corinne with thuggish placidity that they were
about to leave ("I'm afraid we've got to shove off now, Ma"),
Otto jumped to his feet. As he allowed his hand to be crushed,
he felt the relief of a mayor watching an occupying power
depart his city.

Martin's first squadron of children (Maureen's) weren't
even mentioned. Who knew what army of relatives, step-
relatives, half-relatives they were reinforcing by now. But there
were—Otto shuddered faintly—Martin's two newest (Laurie's).
Yes, just as Corinne had said, they, too, were growing up.
Previously indistinguishable wads of self-interest, they had
developed perceptible features—maybe even characteristics; it
appeared reasonable, after all, that they had been given names.

What on earth was it that William did to get children to
converse? Whenever Otto tried to have a civilized encounter
with a child, the child just stood there with its finger in its
nose. But Martin's two boys were chattering away, showing
off to William their whole heap of tiresome electronics.

William was frowning with interest. He poked at a key-
board, which sent up a shower of festive little beeps, and the
boys flung themselves at him, cheering, while Laurie smiled
meltingly. How times had changed. Not so many years earlier, such a tableau would have had handcuffs rattling in the
wings.

The only other representative of "the children" to whom
Corinne had referred with such pathos, was Martin's daughter, Portia (Viola's). She'd been hardly more than a toddler at
last sight, though she now appeared to be about—what? Well,
anyhow, a little girl. "What are the domestic arrangements?"

Otto asked. "Is she living with Martin and Laurie these days, or is she with her mother?"

"That crazy Viola has gone back to England, thank God; Martin has de facto custody."

"Speaking of Martin, where is he?"

"I don't ask," Corinne said.

Otto waited.

"I don't ask," Corinne said again. "And if Laurie wants to share, she'll tell you herself."

"Is Martin in the pokey already?" Otto asked.

"This is not a joke, Otto. I'm sorry to tell you that Martin has been having an affair with some girl."

"Again?"

Corinne stalled, elaborately adjusting her bracelet. "I'm sorry to tell you she's his trainer."

"His *trainer*? How can Martin have a trainer? If Martin has a trainer, what can explain Martin's body?"

"Otto, it's not funny," Corinne said with ominous primness. "The fact is, Martin has been looking very good, lately. But of course you wouldn't have seen him."

All those wives—and a trainer! How? Why would any woman put up with Martin? Martin, who always used to eat his dessert so slowly that the rest of them had been made to wait, squirming at the table, watching as he took his voluptuous, showy bites of chocolate cake or floating island long after they'd finished their own.

"I'm afraid it's having consequences for Portia. Do you see what she's doing?"

"She's—" Otto squinted over at Portia. "What is she doing?"

"Portia, come here, darling," Corinne called.

Portia looked at them for a moment, then wandered sedately over. "And now we'll have a word with Aunt Corinne," she said to her fist as she approached. "Hello, Aunt Corinne."

"Portia," Corinne said, "do you remember Uncle Otto?"

"And Uncle Otto," Portia added to her fist. She regarded him with a clear, even gaze. In its glade of light and silence they encountered one another serenely. She held out her fist to him. "Would you tell our listeners what you do when you go to work, Uncle Otto?"

"Well," Otto said, to Portia's fist, "first I take the elevator up to the twentieth floor, and then I sit down at my desk, and then I send Bryan out for coffee and a bagel——"

"Otto," Corinne said, "Portia is trying to learn what it is you *do*. Something I'm sure we'd all like to know."

"Oh," Otto said. "Well, I'm a lawyer, dear. Do you know what that is?"

"Otto," Corinne said wearily, "Portia's father is a lawyer."

"Portia's father is a global-money mouthpiece!" Otto said.

"Aunt Corinne is annoyed," Portia commented to her fist. "Now Uncle Otto and Aunt Corinne are looking at your correspondent. Now they're not."

"Tell me, Portia," Otto said; the question had sprung insistently into his mind, "what are you going to be when you grow up?"

Her gaze was strangely relaxing. "You know, Uncle Otto," she said pensively to her fist, "people used to ask me that a lot."

Huh! Yes, that was probably something people asked only very small children, when speculation would be exclusively a matter of amusing fantasy. "Well, I was only just mulling it over," Otto said.

"Portia, darling," Corinne said, "why don't you run into the kitchen and do a cooking segment with Bea and Cleveland?"

"It's incredible," Otto said when Portia disappeared, "she looks exactly like Sharon did at that age."

"Ridiculous," Corinne said. "She takes after her father."

Martin? Stuffy, venal Martin, with his nervous eyes and scoopy nose, and squashy head balanced on his shirt collar? Portia's large, gray eyes, the flaxen hair, the slightly oversized ears and fragile neck recapitulated absolutely Sharon's appearance in this child who probably wouldn't remember ever having seen Sharon. "Her *father*?"

"Her father," Corinne said. "Martin. Portia's father."

"I know Martin is her father. I just can't divine the resemblance."

"Well, there's certainly no resemblance to— Wesley—" Corinne called over to him. "Must you read the newspaper? This is a social occasion. Otto, will you listen, please? I'm trying to tell you something. The truth is, we're all quite worried about Portia."

Amazing how fast one's body reacted. Fear had vacuumed the blood right through his extremities. One's body, the primeval parts of one's brain—how fast they were! Much faster than that recent part with the words and thoughts and so on, what was it? The cortex, was that it? He'd have to ask William, he thought, his blood settling back down. That sort of wrinkly stuff on top that looked like crumpled wrapping paper.

"Laurie is worried sick. The truth is, that's one reason I was so anxious for you to join us today. I wanted your opinion on the matter."

"On what matter?" Otto said. "I have no idea what this is about. She's fine. She seems fine. She's just playing."

"I know she's just playing, Otto. It's *what* she's playing that concerns me."

"What she's playing? What is she playing? She's playing

radio, or something! Is that so sinister? The little boys seem to be playing something called Hammer Her Flat."

"I'm sure not. Oh, gracious. You and Sharon were both so right not to have children."

"Excuse me?" Otto said incredulously.

"It's not the radio aspect per se that I'm talking about, it's what that represents. The child is an observer. She sees herself as an outsider. As alienated."

"There's nothing wrong with being observant. Other members of this family could benefit from a little of that quality."

"She can't relate directly to people."

"Who can?" Otto said.

"Half the time Viola doesn't even remember the child is alive! You watch. She won't send Portia a Christmas present. She probably won't even call. Otto, listen. We've always said that Viola is 'unstable,' but, frankly, Viola is *psychotic*. Do you understand what I'm saying to you? Portia's *mother*, Otto. It's just as you were saying, *there's a geneti*—"

"I was saying *what*? I was saying nothing! I was only saying—"

"Oh, dear!" Laurie exclaimed. She had an arm around Portia, who was crying.

"What in hell is going on now?" Wesley demanded, slamming down his newspaper.

"I'm afraid Bea and Cleveland may have said something to her," Laurie said, apologetically.

"Oh, terrific," Wesley said. "Now I know what I'm paying them for."

"It's all right, sweetie," Laurie said. "It all happened a long time ago."

"But why are we celebrating that we killed them?" Portia asked, and started crying afresh.

"We're not celebrating because we killed the Indians, darling," Laurie said. "We're celebrating because we ate dinner with them."

"Portia still believes in Indians!" one of the little boys exclaimed.

"So do we all, Josh," Wesley said. "They live at the North Pole and make toys for good little—"

"Wesley, please!" Corinne said.

"Listener poll," Portia said to her fist. "Did we eat dinner with the Indians, or did we kill them?" She strode over to Otto and held out her fist.

"We ate dinner with them and *then* we killed them," Otto realized, out loud to his surprise.

"Who are you to slag off Thanksgiving, old boy?" Wesley said. "You're wearing a fucking bow tie."

"So are you, for that matter," Otto said, awkwardly embracing Portia, who was crying again.

"And *I* stand behind my tie," Wesley said, rippling upward from his chair.

"It was Portia's birthday last week!" Laurie interrupted loudly, and Wesley sank back down. "Wasn't it!"

Portia nodded, gulping, and wiped at her tears.

"How old are you now, Portia?" William asked.

"Nine," Portia said.

"That's great," William said. "Get any good stuff?"

Portia nodded again.

"And Portia's mommy sent a terrific present, didn't she," Laurie said.

"Oh, what was it, sweetie?" Corinne said.

Laurie turned pink and her head seemed to flare out slightly in various directions. "You don't have to say, darling, if you don't like."

Portia held on to the arm of Otto's chair and swung her leg aimlessly back and forth. "My mother gave me two tickets to go to Glyndebourne on my eighteenth birthday," she said in a tiny voice.

Wesley snorted. "Got your frock all picked out, Portia?"

"I won't be going to Glyndebourne, Uncle Wesley," Portia said with dignity.

There was a sudden silence in the room.

"Why not, dear?" Otto asked. He was trembling, he noticed.

Portia looked out at all of them. Tears still clung to her face. "Because." She raised her fist to her mouth again. "Factoid: According to the Mayan calendar, the world is going to end in the year 2012, the year before this reporter's eighteenth birthday."

"All right," Corinne whispered to Otto. "Now do you see?"

"You're right, as always," Otto said, in the taxi later, "they're no worse than anyone else's. They're all awful. I really don't see the point in it. Just think! Garden garden garden garden garden, two happy people, and it could have gone on forever! They knew, they'd been told, but they ate it anyway, and from there on out, *family*! Shame, fear, jobs, mortality, envy, murder . . ."

"Well," William said brightly, "and sex."

"There's that," Otto conceded.

"In fact, you could look at both family and mortality simply as by-products of sexual reproduction."

"I don't really see the point of sexual reproduction, either," Otto said. "*I* wouldn't stoop to it."

"Actually, that's very interesting, you know; they think

that the purpose of sexual reproduction is to purge the genome of harmful mutations. Of course, they also seem to think it isn't working."

"Then why not scrap it?" Otto said. "Why not let us divide again, like our dignified and immortal forebear, the amoeba."

William frowned. "I'm not really sure that—"

"Joke," Otto said.

"Oh, yes. Well, but I suppose sexual reproduction is fairly entrenched by now—people aren't going to give it up without a struggle. And besides, family confers certain advantages as a social unit, doesn't it."

"No. What advantages?"

"Oh, rudimentary education. Protection."

"'Education'! Ha! 'Protection'! Ha!"

"Besides," William said. "It's broadening. You meet people in your family you'd never happen to run into otherwise. And anyhow, obviously the desire for children is hardwired."

"'Hardwired.' You know, that's a term I've really come to loathe! It explains nothing, it justifies anything; you might as well say, 'Humans have children because the Great Moth in the Sky wants them to.' Or, 'Humans have children because humans have children.' 'Hardwired,' please! It's lazy, it's specious, it's perfunctory, and it's utterly without depth."

"Why does it have to have depth?" William said. "It *refers* to depth. It's good, clean science."

"It's not science at all, it's a cliché. It's a redundancy."

"Otto, why do you always scoff at me when I raise a scientific point?"

"I don't! I don't scoff at you. I certainly don't mean to. It's just that this particular phrase, used in this particular way, isn't very interesting. I mean, you're telling me that something is biologically *inherent* in human experience, but you're not telling me anything *about* human experience."

"I wasn't intending to," William said. "I wasn't trying to. If you want to talk about human experience, then let's talk about it."

"All right," Otto said. It was painful, of course, to see William irritated, but almost a relief to know that it could actually happen. "Let's, then. By all means."

"So?"

"Well?"

"Any particular issues?" William said. "Any questions?"

Any! *Billions.* But that was always just the problem: how to disentangle one; how to pluck it up and clothe it in presentable words? Otto stared, concentrating. Questions were roiling in the pit of his mind like serpents, now a head rising up from the seething mass, now a rattling tail . . . He closed his eyes. If only he could get his brain to relax . . . Relax, relax . . . Relax, relax, relax . . . "Oh, you know, William—is there anything at home to eat? Believe it or not, I'm starving again."

There was absolutely no reason to fear that Portia would have anything other than an adequately happy, adequately fruitful life. No reason at all. Oh, how prudent of Sharon not to have come yesterday. Though in any case, she had been as present to the rest of them as if she had been sitting on the sofa. And the rest of them had probably been as present to her as she had been to them.

When one contemplated Portia, when one contemplated Sharon, when one contemplated one's own apparently point-less, utterly trivial being, the questions hung all around one, as urgent as knives at the throat. But the instant one tried to grasp one of them and turn it to one's own purpose and pierce through the murk, it became as blunt and useless as a piece of cardboard.

All one could dredge up were platitudes: one comes into the world alone, snore snore; one, snore snore, departs the world alone . . .

What would William have to say? Well, it was a wonderful thing to live with an inquiring and mentally active person; no one could quarrel with that. William was immaculate in his intentions, unflagging in his efforts. But what drove one simply insane was the vagueness. Or, really, the banality. Not that it was William's job to explicate the foggy assumptions of one's culture, but one's own ineptitude was galling enough; one hardly needed to consult a vacuity expert!

And how could one think at all, or even just casually ruminate, with William practicing, as he had been doing since they'd awakened. Otto had forgotten what a strain it all was—even without any exasperating social nonsense—those few days preceding the concert; you couldn't think, you couldn't concentrate on the newspaper. You couldn't even really hear the phone, which seemed to be ringing now—

Nor could you make any sense of what the person on the other end of it might be saying. "What?" Otto shouted into it. "You what?"

Could he—the phone cackled into the lush sheaves of William's arpeggios—*bribery, sordid out*—

"William!" Otto yelled. "Excuse me? Could I what?"

The phone cackled some more. "Excuse me," Otto said. *"William!"*

The violin went quiet. "Excuse me?" Otto said again into the phone, which was continuing to emit jibberish. "Sort *what* out? Took her *where* from the library?"

"I'm trying to explain, sir," the phone said. "I'm calling from the hospital."

"She was *taken* from the library *by force*?"

"Unfortunately, sir, as I've tried to explain, she was understood to be homeless."

"And so she was taken away? By force? That could be construed as kidnapping, you know."

"I'm only reporting what the records indicate, sir. The records do not indicate that your sister was kidnapped."

"I don't understand. Is it a crime to be homeless?"

"Apparently your sister did not claim to be homeless. Apparently your sister claimed to rent an apartment. Is this not the case? Is your sister in fact homeless?"

"My sister is not homeless! My sister rents an apartment! Is that a crime? What does this have to do with why my sister was taken away, by force, from the library?"

"Sir, I'm calling from the hospital."

"I'm a taxpayer!" Otto shouted. William was standing in the doorway, violin in one hand, bow in the other, watching gravely. "I'm a lawyer! Why is information being withheld from me?"

"Information is not being withheld from you, sir, please! I understand that you are experiencing concern, and I'm trying to explain this situation in a way that you will understand what has occurred. It is a policy that homeless people tend to congregate in the library, using the restrooms, and some of these people may be removed, if, for example, these people exhibit behaviors that are perceived to present a potential danger."

"Are you *reading* this from something? Is it a crime to use a *public bathroom*?"

"When people who do not appear to have homes to go to, appear to be confused and disoriented—"

"Is it a *crime* to be *confused*?"

"Please calm *down*, sir. The evaluation was not ours. What I'm trying to tell you is that according to the report, your sister became obstreperous when she was brought to the homeless shelter. She appeared to be disoriented. She did not appear to understand why she was being taken to the homeless shelter."

"Shall I go with you?" William said, when Otto put down the phone.

"No," Otto said. "Stay, please. Practice."

So, once again. Waiting in the dingy whiteness, the fearsome whiteness no doubt of heaven, heaven's sensible shoes, overtaxed heaven's obtuse smiles and ruthless tranquillity, heaven's asphyxiating clouds dropped over the screams bleeding faintly from behind closed doors. He waited in a room with others too dazed even to note the television that hissed and bristled in front of them or to turn the pages of the sticky, dog-eared magazines they held, from which they could have learned how to be happy, wealthy, and sexually appealing; they waited, like Otto, to learn instead what it was that destiny had already handed down: bad, not that bad, very, very bad.

The doctor, to whom Otto was eventually conducted through the elderly bowels of the hospital, looked like an epic hero—shining, arrogant, supple. "She'll be fine, now," he said. "You'll be fine now, won't you?"

Sharon's smile, the sudden birth of a little sun, and the doctor's own brilliant smile met, and ignited for an instant. Otto felt as though a missile had exploded in his chest.

"Don't try biting any of those guys from the city again," the doctor said, giving Sharon's childishly rounded, childishly humble, shoulder a companionable pat. "They're poisonous."

"Bite them!" Otto exclaimed, admiration leaping up in him like a dog at a chain link fence, on the other side of which a team of uniformed men rushed at his defenseless sister with clubs.

"I did?" Sharon cast a repentant, sidelong glance at the doctor.

The doctor shrugged and flipped back his blue-black hair, dislodging sparkles of handsomeness. "The file certainly painted an unflattering portrait of your behavior. 'Menaced dentally,' it says, or something of the sort. Now, listen. Take care of yourself. Follow Dr. Shiga's instructions. Because I don't want to be seeing you around here, okay?"

He and Sharon looked at each other for a moment, then traded a little, level, intimate smile. "It's okay with me," she said.

Otto took Sharon to a coffee shop near her apartment and bought her two portions of macaroni and cheese.

"How was it?" she said. "How was everyone?"

"Thanksgiving? Oh. You didn't miss much."

She put down her fork. "Aren't you going to have anything, Otto?"

"I'll have something later with William," he said.

"Oh," she said. She sat very still. "Of course."

He was a monster. Well, no one was perfect. But in any case, her attention returned to her macaroni. Not surprising that she was ravenous. How long had her adventures lasted? Her clothing was rumpled and filthy.

"I didn't know you liked the library," he said.

"Don't think I'm not grateful for the computer," she said. "It was down."

He nodded, and didn't press her.

———

There was a bottle of wine breathing on the table, and William had managed to maneuver dinner out of the mysterious little containers and the limp bits of organic matter from the fridge, which Otto had inspected earlier in a doleful search for lunch. "Bad?" William asked.

"Fairly," Otto said.

"Want to tell me?" William said.

Otto gestured impatiently. "Oh, what's the point."

"Okay," William said. "Mustard with that? It's good."

"I can't stand it that she has to live like this!" Otto said.

William shook his head. "Everyone is so alone," he said.

Otto yelped.

"What?" William said. "What did I do?"

"Nothing," Otto said. He stood, trying to control his trembling. "I'm going to my study. You go on upstairs when you get tired."

"Otto?"

"Just—please."

He sat downstairs in his study with a book in his hand, listening while William rinsed the dishes and put them in the dishwasher, and went, finally, upstairs. For some time, footsteps persisted oppressively in the bedroom overhead. When they ceased, Otto exhaled with relief.

A pale tincture spread into the study window; the pinched little winter sun was rising over the earth, above the neighbors' buildings. Otto listened while William came down and made himself breakfast, then returned upstairs to practice once again.

The day loomed heavily in front of Otto, like an opponent judging the moment to strike. How awful everything was. How awful he was. How bestial he had been to William; William, who deserved only kindness, only gratitude.

And yet the very thought of glimpsing that innocent face was intolerable. It had been a vastly unpleasant night in the chair, and it would be hours, he knew, before he'd be able to manage an apology without more denunciations leaping from his treacherous mouth.

Hours seemed to be passing, in fact. Or maybe it was minutes. The clock said seven, said ten, said twelve, said twelve, said twelve, seemed to be delirious. Fortunately there were leftovers in the fridge.

Well, if time was the multiplicity Sharon and William seemed to believe it was, maybe it contained multiple Sharons, perhaps some existing in happier conditions, before the tracks diverged, one set leading up into the stars, the other down to the hospital. Otto's mind wandered here and there amid the dimensions, catching glimpses of her skirt, her hair, her hand, as she slipped through the mirrors. Did things have to proceed for each of the Sharons in just exactly the same way?

Did each one grieve for the Olympian destiny that ought to have been hers? Did each grieve for an ordinary life—a life full of ordinary pleasures and troubles—children, jobs, lovers?

Everyone is so alone. For this, all the precious Sharons had to flounder through their loops and tucks of eternity; for this, the shutters were drawn on their aerial and light-filled minds. Each and every Sharon, thrashing through the razor-edged days only in order to be absorbed by this spongy platitude: *everyone is so alone!* Great God, how could it be endured? All the Sharons, for ever and ever, discarded in a phrase.

And those Ottos, sprinkled through the zones of actuality— What were the others doing now? The goldfish gliding, gliding, within the severe perimeter of water; William pausing to introduce himself . . .

Yes, so of course one felt incomplete; of course one felt obstructed and blind. And perhaps every creature on earth, on all the earths, was straining at the obdurate membranes to reunite as its own original entity, the spark of unique consciousness allocated to each being, only then to be irreconcilably refracted through world after world by the prism of time. No wonder one tended to feel so fragile. It was infuriating enough just trying to have contact with a few other people, let alone with all of one's selves!

To think there could be an infinitude of selves, and not an iota of latitude for any of them! An infinitude of Ottos, lugging around that personality, those circumstances, that appearance. Not only once dreary and pointless, but infinitely so.

Oh, was there no escape? Perhaps if one could only concentrate hard enough they could be collected, all those errant, enslaved selves. And in the triumphant instant of their reunification, purified to an unmarked essence, the suffocating Otto-costumes dissolving, a true freedom at last. Oh, how tired he was! But why not make the monumental effort?

Because Naomi and Margaret were arriving at nine to show off this baby of theirs, that was why not.

But anyhow, what on earth was he thinking?

Still, at least he could apologize to William. He was himself, but at least he could go fling that inadequate self at William's feet!

No. At the *very* least he could let poor, deserving William practice undisturbed. He'd wait—patiently, patiently—and when William was finished, William would come downstairs. Then Otto could apologize abjectly, spread every bit of his worthless being at William's feet, comfort him and be comforted, reassure him and be reassured . . .

At a few minutes before nine, William appeared, whistling.

Whistling! "Good practice session?" Otto said. His voice came out cracked, as if it had been hurled against the high prison walls of himself.

"Terrific," William said, and kissed him lightly on the forehead.

Otto opened his mouth. "You know—" he said.

"Oh, listen—" William said. "There really is a baby!" And faintly interspersed among Naomi and Margaret's familiar creakings and bumpings in the hall Otto heard little chirps and gurgles.

"Hello, hello!" William cried, flinging open the door. "Look, isn't she fabulous?"

"We think so," Naomi said, her smile renewing and renewing itself. "Well, she is."

"I can't see if you do that," Margaret said, disengaging the earpiece of her glasses and a clump of her red, crimpy hair from the baby's fist as she attempted to transfer the baby over to William.

"Here." Naomi held out a bottle of champagne. "Take this, too. Well, but you can't keep the baby. Wow, look, she's fascinated by Margaret's hair. I mean, who isn't?"

Otto wasn't, despite his strong feelings about hair in general. "Should we open this up and drink it?" he said, his voice a mechanical voice, his hand a mechanical hand accepting the bottle.

"That was the idea," Naomi said. She blinked up at Otto, smiling hopefully, and rocking slightly from heel to toe.

"Sit. Sit everyone," William said. "Oh, she's sensational!"

Otto turned away to open the champagne and pour it into the lovely glasses somebody or another had given to them sometime or another.

"Well, cheers," William said. "Congratulations. And here's to—"

"Molly," Margaret said. "We decided to keep it simple."

"We figured she's got so much working against her already," Naomi said, "including a couple of geriatric moms with a different ethnicity, and God only knows what infant memories, or whatever you call that stuff you don't remember. We figured we'd name her something nice, that didn't set up all kinds of expectations. Just a nice, friendly, pretty name. And she can take it from there."

"She'll be taking it from there in any case," Otto said, grimly.

The others looked at him.

"I love Maggie," Naomi said. "I always wanted a Maggie, but Margaret said—"

"Well." Margaret shrugged. "I mean—"

"No, I know," Naomi said. "But."

Margaret rolled a little white quilt out on the rug. Plunked down on it, the baby sat, wobbling, with an expression of surprise.

"Look at her!" William said.

"Here's hoping," Margaret said, raising her glass.

So, marvelous. Humans were born, they lived. They glued themselves together in little clumps, and then they died. It was no more, as William had once cheerfully explained, than a way for genes to perpetuate themselves. "The selfish gene," he'd said, quoting, probably detrimentally, someone; you were put on earth to fight for your DNA.

Let the organisms chat. Let them talk. Their voices were

as empty as the tinklings of a player-piano. Let the organisms talk about this and that; it was what (as William had so trenchantly pointed out) this particular carbon-based life form did, just as its cousin (according to William) the roundworm romped ecstatically beneath the surface of the planet.

He tried to intercept the baby's glossy, blurry stare. The baby was actually attractive, for a baby, and not bald at all, as it happened. Hello, Otto thought to it, let's you and I communicate in some manner far superior to the verbal one.

The baby ignored him. Whatever she was making of the blanket, the table legs, the shod sets of feet, she wasn't about to let on to Otto. Well, see if he cared.

William was looking at him. So, what was he supposed to do? Oh, all right, he'd contribute. Despite his current clarity of mind.

"And how was China?" he asked. "Was the food as bad as they say?"

Naomi looked at him blankly. "Well, I don't know, actually," she said. "Honey, how was the food?"

"The food," Margaret said. "Not memorable, apparently."

"The things people have to do in order to have children," Otto said.

"We toyed with the idea of giving birth," Margaret said. "That is, Naomi toyed with it."

"At first," Naomi said, "I thought, what a shame to miss an experience that nature intended for us. And, I mean, there was this guy at work, or of course there's always— But then I thought, what, am I an idiot? I mean, just because you've got arms and legs, it doesn't mean you have to—"

"No," William said. "But still. I can understand how you felt."

"Have to what?" Margaret said.

"I can't," Otto said.

"Have to what?" Margaret said.

"I *can't* understand it," Otto said. "I've just never envied the capacity. Others are awestruck, not I. I've never even remotely wished I were able to give birth, and, in fact, I've never wanted a baby. Of course it's inhuman not to want one, but I'm just not human. I'm not a human being. William is a human being. Maybe William wanted a baby. I never thought to ask. Was that what you were trying to tell me the other day, William? Were you trying to tell me that I've ruined your life? *Did* you want a baby? *Have* I ruined your life? Well, it's too bad. I'm sorry. I was too selfish ever to ask if you wanted one, and I'm too selfish to want one myself. I'm more selfish than my own genes. I'm not fighting *for* my DNA, I'm fighting against it!"

"I'm happy as I am," William said. He sat, his arms wrapped tightly around himself, looking at the floor. The baby coughed. "Who needs more champagne?"

"You see?" Otto said into the tundra of silence William left behind him as he retreated into the kitchen. "I really am a monster."

Miles away, Naomi sat blushing, her hands clasped in her lap. Then she scooped up the baby. "There, there," she said.

But Margaret sat back, eyebrows raised in semicircles, contemplating something that seemed to be hanging a few feet under the ceiling. "Oh, I don't know," she said, and the room shuttled back into proportion. "I suppose you could say it's human to want a child, in the sense that it's biologically mandated. But I mean, you could say that, or you could say it's simply unimaginative. Or you could say it's unselfish or you could say it's selfish, or you could say pretty much anything about it at all. Or you could just say, well, I want one.

But when you get right down to it, really, one what? Because, actually—I mean, well, look at Molly. I mean, actually, they're awfully specific."

"I suppose I meant, like, crawl around on all fours, or something," Naomi said. "I mean, just because you've got— But look, there they already are, all these babies, so many of them, just waiting, waiting, waiting on the shelves for some-one to take care of them. We could have gone to Romania, we could have gone to Guatemala, we could have gone almost anywhere—just, for various reasons, we decided to go to China."

"And we both really liked the idea," Margaret said, "that you could go as far away as you could possibly get, and there would be your child."

"Uh-huh," Naomi nodded, soberly. "How crazy is that?"

"I abase myself," Otto told William as they washed and dried the champagne glasses. "I don't need to tell you how deeply I'll regret having embarrassed you in front of Naomi and Mar-garet." He clasped the limp dishtowel to his heart. "How deeply I'll regret having been insufficiently mawkish about the miracle of life. I don't need to tell you how ashamed I'll feel the minute I calm down. How deeply I'll regret having tram-pled your life, and how deeply I'll regret being what I am. Well, that last part I regret already. I profoundly regret every tiny crumb of myself. I don't need to go into it all once again, I'm sure. Just send back the form, pertinent boxes checked: 'I intend to accept your forthcoming apology for—.'"

"Please stop," William said.

"Oh, how awful to have ruined the life of such a marvelous man! Have I ruined your life? You can tell me; we're friends."

"Otto, I'm going upstairs now. I didn't sleep well last night, and I'm tired."

"Yes, go upstairs."

"Good night," William said.

"Yes, go to sleep, why not?" Oh, it was like trying to pick a fight with a dog toy! "Just you go on off to sleep."

"Otto, listen to me. My concert is tomorrow. I want to be able to play adequately. I don't know why you're unhappy. You do interesting work, you're admired, we live in a wonderful place, we have wonderful friends. We have everything we need and most of the things we want. We have excellent lives by anyone's standard. I'm happy, and I wish you were. I know that you've been upset these last few days, I asked if you wanted to talk, and you said you didn't. Now you do, but this happens to be the one night of the year when I most need my sleep. Can it wait till tomorrow? I'm very tired, and you're obviously very tired, as well. Try and get some sleep, please."

" 'Try *and* get some sleep?' 'Try *and* get some sleep?' This is unbearable! I've spent the best years of my life with a man who doesn't know how to use the word 'and'! 'And' is not part of the infinitive! 'And' means '*in addition to*.' It's not 'Try *and* get some sleep,' it's 'Try *to* get some sleep.' *To! To! To! To! To! To! To! Please try to get some sleep!*"

Otto sat down heavily at the kitchen table and began to sob.

How arbitrary it all was, and cruel. This identity, that identity: Otto, William, Portia, Molly, the doctor . . .

She'd be up now, sitting at her own kitchen table, the white enamel table with a cup of tea, thinking about something, about numbers streaming past in stately sequences, about remote astral pageants . . . The doctor had rested his hand kindly on her shoulder. And what she must have felt then! Oh, to convert that weight of the world's compassion into something worthwhile—the taste, if only she could have lifted his hand and kissed it, the living satin feel of his skin . . . Everyone had to put things aside, to put things aside for good.

The way they had smiled at one another, she and that doctor! What can you do, their smiles had said. The handsome doctor in his handsome-doctor suit and Sharon in her disheveled-lunatic suit; what a charade. In this life, Sharon's little spark of consciousness would be costumed inescapably as a waif at the margins of mental organization and the doctor's would be costumed inescapably as a flashing exemplar of supreme competence; in this life (and, frankly, there would be no other) the hospital was where they would meet.

"Otto—"

A hand was resting on Otto's shoulder.

"William," Otto said. It was William. They were in the clean, dim kitchen. The full moon had risen high over the neighbors' buildings, where the lights were almost all out. Had he been asleep? He blinked up at William, whose face, shadowed against the light of the night sky, was as inflected, as ample in mystery as the face in the moon. "It's late, my darling," Otto said. "I'm tired. What are we doing down here?"

LIKE IT OR NOT

Kate would have a little tour of the coast, Giovanna would have the satisfaction of having provided an excursion for her American houseguest without having to interrupt her own work, and the man whom everyone called Harry would have the pleasure, as Giovanna put it, of Kate's company: demonstrably a good thing for all concerned.

"I wish this weren't happening," Kate said. "I'll be inconveniencing him. And besides—"

"No." Giovanna waved a finger. "This is the point. He goes every few months to check on this place of his. He loves to show people about, he loves to poke around the little shops. So, why not? You'll go with him as far as one of the towns, you'll give him a chance to shop, you'll give him a chance to shine, you'll spend the night at some pleasant hotel, then he'll go on and you'll find your way back here by taxi and train."

So, yes—it was hard to say just who was doing whom a favor . . .

"The coast is very beautiful," Giovanna added. "You don't feel like enjoying such things right now, I know, but right now is when your chance presents itself."

The whole thing had twisted itself into shape several days earlier at a party—a noisy roomful of Giovanna's friends. Harry had been speaking to Kate in English, but his unplace-

able accent and the wedges of other languages flashing around
Kate chopped up her concentration. She tried to follow his
voice—he was obliged to go frequently to the coast . . .

Had she left enough in the freezer? Brice and Blair were
hardly children, but whenever they came back home they reverted to sheer incompetence. Besides, they'd be so busy dealing with their father . . .

And was Kate fond of it? the person, Harry, was asking.

"Fond of . . ." She searched his face. "Oh. Well, actually
I've never . . ." and then both she and he were silenced, rounding this corner of the conversation and seeing its direction.

Giovanna had simply stood there, smiling a bright, vague
smile, as though she couldn't hear a thing. And Harry had
been polite—technically, at least; Kate gave him every opportunity to weasel out of an invitation to her, but he'd shoul-
dered the burden manfully. And so there it was, the thing that
was going to happen, like it or not. Still, Giovanna was right.
And perhaps the very fact that Kate was in no mood to do
anything proved, in fact, that she should submit gracefully to
whatever . . . *opportunity* came her way.

Over and over, now that she was visiting Giovanna, she'd
recall—the phone ringing, herself answering . . . as if, listening hard enough this time, she might hear something different. Sitting on the sofa, shoes off . . . It was December 3, the
date was on the quizzes she was grading. She'd almost knocked
over her cup of tea, answering the phone with her hands full
of papers. "Has Baker talked to you about what's going on
with him?" Norman had asked.

It was the gentleness of Norman's voice that stayed with
her, the tea swaying in her cup. What practical difference did

Baker's illness make to her life? Almost none. It was a good fifteen years since she and Baker had gotten divorced.

She'd sent out her annual Christmas letter:

> Sorry to be late this year, everyone, (as usual!) but school seems to get more and more time-consuming. Always more administrative annoyances, more student crises . . . This year we had to learn a new drill, in addition to the fire drill and the cyclone drill—a drive-by shooting drill! You can tell how old all the teachers here are by what we do when that bell goes off. Anyone else remember the atomic-bomb drill? Whenever the alarm rings I still just dive under the desk. Blair is surviving her first year of law school. Brice swears he'll never . . .

and so on. She looked at what she'd written—apparently a description of her life.

To Giovanna's copy she appended a note: "I'm fine, really, but Baker's sick. Very. And Blair and Brice are here this week spending days with him and Norman, nights with me. Blair's fiancé calls every few hours, frantically apologizing. He pleads, she storms. Grand opera! Will she just please tell him why she's angry? She's not angry, she insists—it's just all this *apologizing* . . . I guess the diva-gene skipped a generation. Speaking of which, Mother asks after you. She still talks about how that boring friend of Baker's followed you back to Europe after the wedding. She's weirdly sweet sometimes these days. Think that means she's dying? It scares me out of my wits, actually . . . ."

Giovanna faxed Kate at school: Come stay over spring break. No excuses.

It had been so many years since they'd seen each other,

letters were so rarely exchanged, that Giovanna had come to seem abstract; Kate hadn't even been aware of confiding. She stared at the fax as she went into her classroom. The map was still rolled down over the blackboard from the previous class. In fact, Giovanna was not only capable, evidently, of reading the note, she was also less than fifteen inches away.

They had met almost thirty years earlier at a college to which Kate had been sent for its patrician reputation and its august location, and to which Giovanna had been exiled for its puritanical reputation and backwater location, far removed from her own country and her customary amusements. Kate had first encountered the famous Giovanna in the hall outside her room, passed out on the floor, had dragged her inside, revived her, and from then on had joyfully assisted her in and out windows on extralegal forays, after hours, to destinations unequivocally off-limits, with scandalously older men—the more distinguished of the professors, local politicians, visiting lecturers and entertainers . . .

The two girls found one another's characteristics, both national and personal, hilarious and illuminating. They scrutinized each other—the one stolid, socially awkward, midwestern, and oblique; the other polished, European, and satirical—as if each were looking into a transforming mirror, which reflected now certain qualities, now certain others. So many possibilities had floated in that mirror!

While Giovanna worked long hours at her firm, Kate walked dutifully through the city, staring at churches, paintings, and fountains. What had she seen? She couldn't have said. She drew the line absolutely, she'd told Blair, at taking photographs. "But, Mother," Blair had said. "You'd get so much more out of your trip!" Poor Brice—how would he be faring at home with his sister? All his life Blair had been trying to turn him upside down and shake him, as if she could dislodge hidden problems from his pockets like loose change.

At night, Kate and Giovanna ate in local trattorias, then sat in Giovanna's huge apartment, sipping wine and talking lazily. How pleasant it must be to live like Giovanna, surrounded by beauty, by beautiful objects, so many of which had been in her family for generations. The years slid through their conversation, looping around, forming a fragile, shifting lace. "Is it possible?" Giovanna said. "We're older than your mother was when we met."

"Too strange," Kate said. "Too scary." When she dropped by every week or so now to check on her mother, Kate would often find her asleep in a chair, her head dropping sideways, her mouth slightly open. "Most of the time she's still fairly true to form, thank heavens. She's attached the one available old gent around and she's running him ragged. He simply beams. All the sweet local widows are still standing at his door, clutching their pies and pot roasts. They don't know what hit them. You know, all those years, when Baker and I were having so much trouble and neither of us quite understood what was happening and the kids were frantic and the house was pandemonium all the time—just as we'd all start screaming at each other, the phone would ring and there she'd be, saying, 'So, how is everyone enjoying this beautiful Sunday afternoon?' Now the phone rings and she says, 'Kate! What are you doing at home on a Saturday night?'"

"Ah, well." Giovanna lit a cigarette, kindling its forbidden fragrance. "She's having an adventure. And what about you?"

"Me!" Kate said. "Me?"

"What about that guy you wrote me about a year or two ago—Rover, Rower . . ."

"Rowan. Oh, lord. Blair was very enthusiastic about that one. One day she said to me, 'Mother, where's this going, this thing with Rowan?' I said, '*Going?* I'm almost fifty!'"

Giovanna exhaled a curtain of smoke. From behind it, her steady gaze rested on Kate. "You broke it off?"

"Give me a drag, please. Of course not. Though to tell you the truth, I just don't feel the need to put myself through all that again. I really don't. Anyhow, the day came, naturally, when he said he wasn't, guess what, ready for *commitment*—he actually used the word—so soon after his divorce. And then naturally the *next* day came, when I heard he'd married a twenty-three-year-old."

"You should live here." Giovanna yawned. "Here in Europe, you still have the chance to lose your lovers to someone your own age."

Much nicer, they'd agreed, clinking glasses.

There was no stone, arch, column, pediment, square inch of painting in the vicinity that Harry couldn't expound upon. He knew what pirates had lived in which of the caves below them, the Latin names of the trees, all twisted by wind, the composition of the rocks . . . Did Kate see the dome way off there? They didn't have time to stop, unfortunately, but it was a very important church, as no doubt she knew, built by X in the twelfth century, rebuilt by Y in the thirteenth, then built again on the orders of the Archbishop of Z . . . . Inside there was a wonderful Annunciation by A, a wonderful pietà by B, and of course she'd seen reproductions, hadn't she, of the altarpiece . . .

It wasn't fair. He expected everyone to be as yielding to beautiful objects as he was, as easily transported. Her expression, she hoped, as the avalanche of information—art gossip—rained down, was not the one she saw daily on the faces of her students. Her poor, exasperating students, so resentful, so uncomprehending . . . The truth was that most of them had so many problems in their lives that each precious, clarifying fragment Kate struggled to hand over to them was just one more intrusion. Yet there she stood, day after day, talking, talking, talking . . . And every once in a while—she could see it—it was as if a door opened in a high stone wall.

". . . but I'm boring you," Harry was saying. "You're a serious person! And my life, I'm afraid, has been devoted, frivolously, to beauty."

True, true, she was a grunting barbarian, he was a rarified esthete. She was a high-school biology teacher, he was a—well, he was a what, exactly? As far as she could gather, whatever it was he did seemed to involve finding art or rarities, oddities, for collectors and billionaires and grotesquely expensive hotels. He'd traveled all over, there'd been a wife or two, his family had come from everywhere—Central Asia, all around the Mediterranean . . .

"Mendelssohn or salsa?" He waved a handful of CD's "To— what is it? To soothe our savage— Ack!" He honked and swerved as a giant tour bus in front of them braked shudderingly on the precipitous incline. "They have no idea how to drive! Simply not a clue!"

For miles before and behind them, caravans of tour buses clogged the road, winding along the cliffs. "Is there always this much traffic?" Kate asked.

"From now through October it will be sheer hell," Harry announced with satisfaction, as though he'd only been waiting for an opening. "And why do they come here? For what? We'll see them later, shuffling around in the churches while the guides shout and flap their arms. Blinking, loading their cameras . . . They'd much prefer to be at Disney World. They are at Disney

World. Little ducks and mice frolic with them along the road of life. So why come to bother us here, on this road? Ah, we'll never know, we'll never know. And neither will they."

"Americans, I suppose," Kate said meekly.

"Not necessarily, my dear." Harry reached over and patted her hand. "Imbeciles pour in from all over."

One was supposed to get used to things, Kate thought, not find them increasingly annoying; that was the point of getting older. And how old was he, anyhow? It stood to reason that he was around her age. Probably a few years older.

Though actually, he looked no age in particular. He was wildly vigorous and agile, and an urgent, clocklike energy pulsed off him. He'd ordered wine when they'd stopped for lunch, in a restaurant overhanging the cliffs where they'd soon be driving again, and her heart had dropped along with the level of alcohol in the bottle, to the very bottom. Harry, however, showed no sign of having consumed a thing. "Don't worry," he'd said as they left—whether noting some expression she'd failed to inhibit, or engaging in a private dialogue—"I'm not drunk." And indeed, though the coastline waved back and forth beneath them like streamers and the racy little car flew out over the heart-stopping curves, it snapped back onto the road as if it were attached by elastic. Way below them, the water sparkled and ruffled, on and on and on.

It was late in the afternoon by the time they reached their destination. Majestic and serene, the hotel rose up in front of them with the terraced cliffs, the clouds, the trees, as if it had sprung from a magic seed.

Harry chivalrously swung her suitcase from the trunk and carried it into the lobby. "What on earth do you have in here?" Rowan would have asked, smiling to illustrate that he wasn't criticizing her. Harry, of course, was completely indifferent.

Or perhaps he knew perfectly well what weighed those hundreds of pounds—all the jars of things she'd taken, humiliatingly, to smearing on her skin or swallowing.

And what about Harry's elegant little accoutrement, hardly bigger than a briefcase? What could he have fitted into that? A set of tiny tools, no doubt—wrenches, screwdrivers, brushes—with which to disassemble himself and clean his parts . . .

The hotel, vast as it was, had apparently been a private villa at some time. The cool sound of bells and leaf-scented air pooled here and there in the lobby. Afternoon sunlight, yellow as wildflowers, drowsed on the floors. Marble, stone, wood seemed to breathe faintly . . .

Splendid in uniform, the men at the desk opened their arms at the sight of Harry, tilting their heads to the side and exclaiming softly with delight. As they came forward, he clasped their hands, speaking a few words to each, like the true king returning. They were now referring to her, Kate realized at a certain point. One of the men caught her look of slight confusion and addressed her in English. "We were discussing, signora, which room would be most suitable for you. It would be possible either the Rose Room, which has a fireplace and a magnificent four-poster bed. Or the room at the easternmost end of the hotel is also available, with a balcony overlooking the water."

She glanced at Harry. "It doesn't matter," he said expansively. "They're both lovely rooms." He turned to the desk clerk. "Perhaps the East Room—" He gave her a brief, inquiring smile. "—Yes. The signora might enjoy breakfasting on her balcony."

Oh, right—she'd been meant to speak, but never mind. How wonderful, just to go upstairs now, to sink back against giant feather pillows . . . A man in a red and gold jacket stood

slightly behind her with her suitcase. Well, yes, of course—
Harry wasn't going to show her to her room.

"Well—" she turned toward him and held out her hand
"—you must be exhausted."

"Not at all," he said, taking her hand absently and glancing around as if for a place to put it. "I never get tired."

Just as she'd feared. And it seemed that there were several
churches, several villas, a little museum, and an ex-convent
that were absolutely obligatory.

"And would you care to wash up?" he said instructively.
"We'll find one another in the bar." As she followed the bellman out of the lobby, she glimpsed, from the corner of her
eye, Harry bending to kiss the beringed claw of an ancient
lady in black, almost hidden within the wings of an enormous brocaded chair.

Kate followed, up a flowing staircase and along silent corridors. The bellman opened the massive wooden door to her
room, and then the French doors onto her balcony. Lordy! No
wonder no one else in the lobby looked much like a schoolteacher. Water gleams fleeted in, rocking the room gently;
the high ceiling curved above her, and the stone floors floated
underfoot.

Though she took as little time as possible, only slipping
her few things onto the satiny hangers and splashing at her
face, when she reached the bar Harry had almost emptied a
glass of something. "Ah!" he said, leaping to his feet as though
she'd been dawdling for an hour. "Oh. But forgive me—will
you have something to drink before we set off, or would you
prefer a look around before the light goes completely?"

He led her rapidly through the churches, the ex-convent,
the now-public villas, bounding up and down the steep town
steps and cobbled streets, providing scholarly commentary.

She was *worse*, she thought, than her students—than the tourists from the buses! Who were indeed standing around town in bewildered-looking herds, uneasily gripping their cameras as though they were passports.

"Good—" Harry said, striding through the garden leading to the little museum. "—still open!" His gesture, which swept the paintings, the small mounted sculptures, was proprietary.

He was looking at a lump of stone in a glass case. No, a head; a stone coronet sat on heavy twists of stone hair over a dreaming stone face. A real girl must have modeled for it, Kate thought—an actual princess, or a young queen.

Or possibly some girl right off the streets for whom the artist had conceived a passion. Had she lived to be old? It was hard to imagine this girl old. Trouble, she looked like; pure trouble. A provocative reserve emanated from the faint stone smile, sending a hiss of fire through the stone-cooled air. Trouble even now, Kate thought. This girl had seen to it that the sculptor's obsession would be inflicted on whoever saw her for all time to come.

Kate glanced at Harry for a translation of the bit of text on the glass case, but he had turned away, to an elaborate marble, whose racing lines were taking a moment to resolve in front of her. A faun, or possibly a satyr, something with furry haunches and little hooves and horns had seized a young woman from behind. Her head was arched way back against him and her long hair whipped around her face, which was slightly contorted. Her eyes were almost closed. One of the creature's hands was splayed out between the girl's sharp pelvic bones, and the other pinned her own hand to one of her adolescent breasts. Her free arm reached out, with what intent it was impossible to guess—it had broken off at the elbow. Kate stumbled slightly on an uneven stone underfoot. "Goodness me," she said.

"Yes, marvelous—" Harry glanced at his watch. "Second century after Christ, probably a copy of a Greek piece. Are we through here? The church I particularly want you to see closes in minutes."

In the lobby, the delicate afternoon had given way to a rich, deep twinkling. More people had arrived; the bellboys, in their red and gold, were loading huge leather cases onto trolleys. The tapping of high heels echoed faintly from the corridors. "Dinner at eight-thirty?" Harry said. "By the way, how did you find your room—satisfactory?"

"Glorious," Kate said. "It's . . . *glorious . . .*"

"Glorious." He smiled at her and briefly her arms and legs seemed to need rearrangement; what did one generally do with them? "Well, very good then. We'll have a bit of a rest, yes? And meet in the bar."

Dinner at eight-thirty. Once again, they'd be sitting at a table together. But what had she imagined was going to happen? They could hardly have dinner separately.

She found her room waiting; the crisp linen had been turned down, mysteriously, the heavy shutters drawn. She was being attended to, as if she—of all people, she thought—had come upon the palace where the poor Beast waited for his release. She sat for a while on the balcony, watching ribbons of mist twine below her through the trees and listening to distant bells from hidden fields and towns. Grass, petal, wave, stone turned to velvet—indistinct glowing patches—as veil on veil of twilight dropped over them.

A jar of aromatic bath salts had been provided. She poured them like a libation under the faucet—why not? They represented her salary—and took a long soak, moving from time to time to solicit the water's musical response.

One assumed there was such a thing as chance; when one

was young, one assumed that the way one's life was to express itself was one of many possible ways, and later, one assumed that this had been true.

Of course, even if she hadn't married Baker, she'd never have been living like this. She'd never have been living like Giovanna, casually surrounded by silk-covered furniture and lovely, old pieces of glass and silver, entertaining herself in her spare time with one admirer or another. Those things were probably not within the compass of her particular possibilities.

But surely it was within that compass—surely, with one degree's alteration here or there—that she and Baker would not have married. And if they had not, if they hadn't had children, one thing was certain—that Baker would now mean no more to her than any young man she might have met in the course of her school duties; she'd have a harmless memory of a nice young man.

And from all the years with him? You couldn't feel love once it was gone. What you could feel for a long time was the sorrow of its fading, like the burning afterimage of a setting sun. And then that was gone, too. What she would remember for the rest of her life was the fact, at least, of the shocking pain they'd been forced to inflict on one another. Eventually when they'd touched, it was like touching a wound.

When both the children had left for school, she'd expected a long period of lonely freedom, an expansion. But now that Baker was sick, Blair and Brice hovered closely, as if it were she who needed consolation, not they. Blair asked questions continuously. *Why did you and Dad . . . How did you feel when . . .*

They'd been over and over it all from the children's adolescence on. "I've told you what I can," Kate said. "I'm sorry. It was moving very fast back then."

But at the time it hadn't felt fast. There were long days of paralysis, sleepless nights. How could so much anguish have been expended on something that now seemed so remote?

"What can I say to you?" she told Blair. "I had a reasonably civil relationship with my parents, but I never understood them. I don't suppose their life together was entirely without chaos and misery, but I have no idea what went on between them. Or within either of them, actually. Of course you don't understand us. No one has ever understood their parents. And what, for that matter, do I know about you?"

Blair stared at Kate, tears spilling up into her eyes. "You knew it was me from the *back* that time, going by in Jeffrey's car at about *eighty*, even though I was supposedly at *Jennifer's*!"

Kate sighed. "That's different," she'd said.

She wrapped herself in a vast, soft towel and contemplated her clothing. A faint breeze came through the French doors and the black dress swayed slightly on its hanger.

It was a dress that she'd recklessly allowed Blair to talk her into buying from a terrifying shop in Chicago. That evening she'd thought of its cost and actually covered her face in embarrassment—of course she'd return it. But then, the sight of it swathed in its tissue paper . . . .

It was a little daring, that dress. Nonetheless, she'd gone out in it several times, before Rowan came to his senses and married an infant.

She reached over to the hanger. It was now or never. She slipped the dress over her head and breathed in; the zipper climbed, cinching her tightly. She turned to challenge the mirror: now or never.

All right, then—never, the mirror said, coolly. And what did she think this was—a *date*?

The bar was almost filled. The tender glimmer from candles and lamps embraced the encampments of guests; bright little clusters of laughter bloomed here and there amid clinking glass and conversation. Harry was sitting at the far end of the room, his back to her.

Kate's hands went cold. He was with people. A family, it seemed. A pretty girl, just a little older, Kate judged, than her students, was stretched out on a recamier, in a display of intense boredom. The father was a great, blocky affair, wearing a blazer with gold buttons, and a little boy in an identical blazer perched stiffly on a settee.

The woman next to the boy leaned toward Harry, her red-nailed fingers playing with a large solitaire at her throat. "Really!" Kate heard her exclaim, and she laughed gaily. Her toenails were the fevered red of her fingernails and her lipstick. Her little white suit was as tense as an origami construction, but a snippet of lace peeked out aggressively from under the jacket.

Harry was gesticulating; his voice came into focus: ". . . insisted, but *insisted*—" he was saying, "—that I jump on the Concorde. What could I do? A call from Dubzhinski. In New York I literally scampered to make my connection. I fell off the plane in Los Angeles, and was at the Polo Lounge in seconds. I took her out of my case, unwrapped her, and set her down in front of us on the bar. There she was, with her little chin thrust forward and her hands clasped behind her back, and those astonishing legs. Dubzhinski was trembling. I could actually hear that tiny, hard heart of his. It was hammering away like a cash register at Christmastime. He was paralyzed, he stared, and then he reached out and upended her to look under her tutu. 'Go ahead,' I said, 'we can authenticate her right here.' And the next—"

The wife was glancing sidelong at Kate with slight alarm, as though Kate might be hoping to sell them pencils. Harry swiveled in his chair, looked at her blankly, then sprang to his feet. "My dear!" he said. "Ah, we're a chair short! What shall, what shall, what shall we do, eh?"

For a moment everyone except the girl was standing and bobbing about and pushing one another toward seats. "Oh," Kate began. "Well, I could just—" Just what? But then a murmuring waiter in a white coat was there with a smile of compassion for her that pierced her like a bayonet.

Harry and the Reitzes had met several years before, in Paris, it was explained, at the home of a mutual friend, about whom they'd just been reminiscing.

"Oh, Franz and I couldn't really claim that M. Dubzhinski is a *friend*. We just happened to be with the LaRues. But you know—" Mrs. Reitz addressed Kate "—that house is even more gorgeous than in the pictures." She turned back to Harry, but her perfume continued to loiter thuggishly around Kate. "I know there are people who say M. Dubzhinski is . . . Well. But he was charming to me that time. Simply charming."

"'Charming . . .'" Mr. Reitz tried out the word and smiled pityingly. "I wouldn't entirely agree. But harmless enough at bottom. Colorful, as the expression goes. I believe it was one of your countrymen—" he nodded at Kate "—who put it so well: *I've never met a man I didn't like.*"

The girl sat up slowly, fluffing her long hair back. "Really?" she glanced at him. "I have."

Mrs. Reitz's eyes were not quite closed. Her face was more unresponsive than if she hadn't heard at all. But Mr. Reitz was speaking to Kate. "My wife, too, is American."

Was the girl's arrogance affected, or was it entirely real? As cocky as Kate's students could be, as irritating, they were actually, for all their show, quite humble. Of course, Kate had never encountered a child as privileged as this girl, with this hard candy gloss . . . "Texas," Mrs. Reitz was saying, leaning over to touch Kate's wrist, her own flashing and clanging with jewelry. "But I guess you heard that, right off! I wouldn't change Zurich for anything, but I get homesick. I miss Los Angeles. I miss Dallas. I miss New York."

"I'm from Cincinnati," Kate said.

"Oh." Mrs. Reitz's smile was puzzled. "I see."

"I'm really just visiting," Kate said.

"Ah," Mrs. Reitz said archly.

"No," Kate said. "A friend in Rome."

"A mutual friend," Harry said fussily, as he snagged a waiter. "Champagne? Champagne, my dear?" he asked Kate and then the girl, who had been drinking nothing. "Good. And another round for the rest of us, thank you. Yes, this kind lady has been good enough to accompany me thus far and have a little look at the area. Tomorrow she returns, I believe, do you not?"

"How nice," Mrs. Reitz said. Her gaze swept Kate's flowered dress, her face, her cardigan, and lapsed from Kate like a cat's.

"We're going up to Rome ourselves tomorrow or Sunday," Mr. Reitz said.

"We're doing the palaces on the kids' spring break," Mrs. Reitz explained.

"The question is," Mr. Reitz said, "which day exactly will we travel? We're told that the traffic is quite terrible on Saturday. But also we're told that the traffic is quite terrible on Sunday."

"That is true," Harry said. He looked at one child, then the other. "Are you glad to be on holiday?"

The boy nodded vigorously. "Yes, thank you."

"And you?" Harry asked.

The girl, who was reclining again, opened her eyes and looked steadily at him. "Not madly." She closed her eyes again and crossed her arms over her chest, as though she were sunbathing, or dying.

"Sit up, sweetheart," Mrs. Reitz murmured. "Well!" she said, casting a misty look at the room in general. "At least we've been lucky with the weather. They said it's been raining and raining and raining," she explained to Kate. "I was afraid it was going to rain today."

"But it didn't," Mr. Reitz said.

"No," Mrs. Reitz agreed. "It didn't."

"We have good luck with the weather," Mr. Reitz said, "but bad luck with the traffic. It took us all day to get here. We expected to arrive at three o'clock. But we arrived almost at seven."

The girl emitted a small sigh, which floated down among them like a feather.

"Now, *you've* determined it's best to drive up tomorrow . . ." Mrs. Reitz furrowed deferentially at Kate, as though Kate were a senior scholar of traffic.

"I'll be taking the train," Kate said.

"The train!" Mrs. Reitz said. "What a *marvelous*—"

"I want to take the train," the little boy said mournfully. "I wanted to take the train," he explained to Kate. "But we can't because of the Porsche."

"That's the problem, sweetie," Mrs. Reitz said absently, reaching over to a small silver bowl of mixed nuts, which Harry was nervously plundering. "Excuse me!" he said, retracting his hand as though it had been bitten.

"I am so sorry!" Mrs. Reitz exclaimed. "Oh, I am simply starving."

"I can imagine," Harry said distractedly.

"And I suppose spring holidays are the reason for all this damned, if you'll pardon me, traffic," Mr. Reitz said. "Yes, the only occasions on which one has the opportunity to travel with one's family, others are traveling with theirs. What a paradox!"

The boy's straw slurped among the ice at the bottom of his drink.

"Darling," Mrs. Reitz said. "Your father was merely making an observation."

The boy blushed red. "My baby," Mrs. Reitz said. She drew him to her and stroked his silky hair, smiling first at her husband, then at Harry. "You know, I absolutely adore this place. It's so romantic. Don't you just keep imagining all the things that must have gone on in these rooms? Oh, my. For hundreds of years!" The boy sat stock still until his mother released him, recrossing her legs and primly readjusting the hem of her little skirt.

"Good heavens—" Harry glanced at his watch "—they'll have been waiting with our table! I do wish we could ask you to join us, but, that is, they're very strict. Please excuse us."

"What an ordeal!" he said to Kate as they were seated. "How horrible! Was I terribly rude? I suppose I should have invited them to dine with us. And why not? Would it be possible for them to bore us any more than they already have? But yes, on reflection, yes. I feel I might still recover."

The dining room was an aerie, a bower, hung with a playful lattice of garlands. Its white tile floors were adorned with painted baskets of fruit, and there were real ones scattered here and there on stands. But even as the waiters glided by with trays of glossy roasted vegetables and platters of fish, even while Harry took it upon himself to order for her, knowledgeably and solicitously, Kate felt tainted. Despite the room's conceit that eating was a pastime for elves and fairies,

Mrs. Reitz's carnality had disclosed the truth: this aggrega-
tion of hairy vertebrates, scrubbed, scented, prancing about
on hind legs, was ruthlessly bent on physical gratifications—
tactile, visual, gustatory, genital . . . The candles! The flowers! A trough providing mass feedings for naked guests would
be less pornographic.

The Reitzes were being led to their own table. Mrs. Reitz
waggled one set of fingers in their direction, holding her
jacket closed beneath her collarbones with the other, as if an
enormous wind were about to whip it open, exposing her.

"One encounters these terrible people wherever one
goes," Harry said. "They all know me—it's the unfortunate
side of my work, if I can use such an elevated term for, actually, my little hobby . . . They're all clients, or friends of clients. Clients of clients . . ."

Despite Mrs. Reitz's speedy (and uncalled for!) assessment
of Kate as out of the running, Kate thought, Mrs. Reitz was
probably not much younger, really. The bouncing gold hair,
the vivacity, the strained skin suggested it . . .

All those years ago, when she'd finally confessed to her
mother about Baker and Norman, Kate had waited quietly
through her mother's initial monologue. "Don't worry," her
mother said grimly. "I won't say I told you so."

In fact, she never had told Kate so. On the contrary, she'd
been elated by Baker's family, his appearance, his education,
his law firm . . . "I can't say I'm overly surprised about . . .
this other person, but does he have to move *out*? Why can't
people of your generation set aside your personal appetites for
one instant? The children are going to be confused enough as
it is! Oh, I simply can't believe he's leaving you for— for—
for *an electrician*! Well, but I'm sure he'll continue to support
you."

Kate had smiled faintly. "You are? He's going into public-interest law."

"My God, my God!" her mother cried. "Oh, I suppose I should feel compassion for him. He was always so weak, so lost. But why did he have to marry you? Why did he feel he had the right to ruin your life while he was working things out for himself? Well, and yet I can understand it. I suppose he thought you could help him. You were always such a sweet girl. And not, if you don't mind my saying so, very threatening, sexually."

"And the worst thing," Harry was saying, "is that they all seem to want something from me. I don't know what! Perhaps they imagine I'll be able to pick up some piece for a song, something to transform a salon from the ordinarily to the spectacularly vulgar. Some great, blowsy, romping nymph with an enormous behind . . ."

Kate contemplated him as he talked decoratively on. One had to acknowledge, even admire, such energy, so strong a will to enjoy, to entertain, even if, as was clearly the case, it was only to entertain himself.

"Giovanna tells me you're a teacher," he said unexpectedly, laying down his fork and knife as if her response required his full attention.

"Nothing very exalted, I'm afraid," Kate said. "Just high school biology."

"It sounds rather exalted to me," he said. "I should think it would be rather a beautiful subject."

Kate glanced at him. "It is, actually. Hmmm . . ." She noted the sudden haloed clarity of her thought, the detailed vibrancy of her awareness, and concluded she was drunk. Natural enough—she'd certainly been drinking. "I have to admit that I do find it beautiful. Of course, what I teach is very rudimentary—basic evolutionary theory, simple genetic principles, taxonomies, a lot of structural stuff. Pretty much what I learned myself in school. You know, an oak tree, a tadpole, the shape of its growth, the way the organism works . . .."

"I understand nothing about biology," he said. "Nothing, nothing, nothing at all . . ."

"Oh, well. Neither do I, really." Kate found she was laughing loudly. She composed herself. "I mean, not what's going on now, all the fantastic molecular frontiers, the borders with chemistry, physics . . . the real mysteries . . ."

He rested his chin on the backs of his clasped hands and gazed at her. "What seems so simple to you—a tree, a tadpole—those things are completely mysterious to me!"

"Actually, I'm not being at all—" Was he, in fact, interested? Well, it wasn't her place to judge. At least he was pretending to be. At least he was— Stop that, she told herself; a conversation was something that humans had. "I mean, I'm not being . . . Because actually it's all hugely . . . It brings you to your knees, really, doesn't it? You know, it's really quite funny—there are my students, rows of little humans, staring at me. And there I am, a human, staring right back. And I'm holding up pictures! Charts! Of what's inside us. And the students write things down in their notebooks. Our hearts are pumping, the blood is going round and round, our lungs are bringing air in and out . . . *Class, look at the pictures. These are our lungs, our kidneys, our stomachs, our veins and arteries, our spleens, our brains, our hearts* . . . There we are, looking at *pictures* of what's going on every instant inside our very own bodies!"

"I don't even yet have it straight. Where any of those things are," Harry said ruefully. "My kidneys, my spleen, my heart . . ."

Kate shook her head. "It's a wonder we can understand anything at all about ourselves . . . We can't even see our own kidneys."

"Ah!" Harry grunted. "So I have recovered, after all." He summoned the waiter to order for Kate a little chalice of raspberries and scented froth, then sat back to observe as she took the first spoonful. "Extraordinary, no?" he said. "It's up to you. I'm not allowed." He smiled briefly and shallowly, then rubbed his forehead. "To tell you the truth, it's a rather stressful trip for me, always—going back to this little farmhouse of mine. I spent summers there in my childhood . . . Really, I'm very glad to have had a pretext for stopping here overnight."

Harsh tears shot up to Kate's eyes. Fatigue, she thought. "Tell me . . ."

"Yes?"

"Tell me . . . Oh—well, tell me, then . . . Have you known Giovanna long?"

"For many centuries. Our families are vaguely intertwined, though I never met her until I was a young man. There was a party, very grand, and in all the enormous crowd, women in spectacular gowns, I caught a glimpse of a young girl. I remember every detail of that glimpse—the exact posture, the smile, every button on the dress. She was scarcely thirteen. There were eight years between us."

His hand was resting on the table, three, maybe four inches from hers. "There were?" The cuff of his shirt was very white. She raised her eyes from it to smile at him. "Aren't there still?"

He sat back and studied her, amusement and sorrow competing in his own smile. "Well, now it's a different eight years." He sighed, and signaled for the check.

"Oh, please, let me. You did lunch, and drinks. You've taken all this time—"

"Madam," he said gently. "You will put your purse away for this one evening, please. But will you join me for a last drink in the bar? A digestif. And I will have, if you won't find it too disgusting, a cigar."

But the Reitzes were already ensconced again in the bar, and waved them over. Kate glanced at Harry, but he had gone completely unreadable; he had simply disappeared.

Mrs. Reitz slid to one side of her settee and patted the space next to her. Again, there was a scuffle. Harry won, and Kate found herself sitting with Mrs. Reitz, suffocating under a dome of her perfume like a dying bug, while he went off to commandeer a chair.

Well. All right. Fine. And a very good thing it was, actually, that Norman was an electrician! He'd completely rewired her little house. And that at a time when she was barely getting by, even with the money Baker managed to scrape up for the kids.

The waiter was already prepared with a cigar for Harry, undoubtedly in accord with ancient custom. "Here, please," Mr. Reitz said. "One of those for me, too."

"Oh, dear—" Mrs. Reitz fluttered toward Kate. "I know men have to have them, but I never get used to them, do you?"

"I never get used to anything—" Kate was startled by her own slightly swaggering tone. "I mean, except for the things that aren't happening any longer."

"That's an interesting way of putting it . . ." Mrs. Reitz said cautiously.

Good. Kate had frightened her. But heavens! What was her— Why was she so— After all, Harry had stated quite clearly that he was repentant about having snubbed these people before dinner. The girl was slung out sullenly upon a curvy white and gold chair, far above the juvenile sniping of her elders.

"Ooch," Mr. Reitz said, patting the prairielike region of his stomach. "It's impossible to speak after such a meal. But, really, have you no good advice for us? Saturday, or Sunday, to Rome."

"Whichever you choose—" Harry exhaled with pleasure "—you will wish you had chosen the other."

"Let us be prudent," Mr. Reitz said. "We will play the early bird. Let us be ready to make our final decision at breakfast. *If*—" he turned to the girl "—we think we can get up in good time, for a change."

The girl lifted a long, shining hair from her dress and considered it. "We'll do our best," she said.

"I surely do envy you," Mrs. Reitz said. "This little girl of mine has a talent for sleep. But I can never sleep near the sea at all. It makes me so *restless* . . ."

"The sea?" Mr. Reitz said. "Restless? How very original. One is always learning the most surprising new things about one's spouse! But it's a good thing then about our room. I must say, I was quite annoyed earlier with the staff. I had my secretary specifically request the view. They swore she never did, but a people which is known for its charm is not often known also for its honesty."

"I have a terrible time sleeping in hotels, myself," Harry said. "Unfortunately, I'm always in hotels these days . . . . How did it happen, how did it happen? Oh, it's hard to believe, isn't it, that it's the same person who has lived each bit of one's life. Yes, an hour or two of sleep, and then I'm up again, wandering around all night. In fact, I'd best go up now and try to get some sleep before I lose my chance."

Kate attempted to smile pleasantly. "I think I'll go up now, too."

"And how is your room, my dear?" Harry asked.

Kate looked at him. Why hadn't she just gone directly up after dinner?

"Good heavens, yes, where is my brain!" he said. "Glorious. Of course, you said—glorious."

He did in fact lie in his room for an hour or so, letting images of the girl play over his nerves. Her exquisite throat, the curve of her cheek . . . the clear, poreless skin, so close in color to the brows, the lashes, the light, long hair . . . her startling greenish blue eyes. She was clever about clothes, obviously—that mother surely hadn't chosen the dress, simple, and stylishly long, stopping just at narrow shins. On her feet she wore elegant straw sandals.

When the buzzing of the girl in his head grew unbearable, he would convert it into thoughts of the astonishing Russian sleigh bed he had come across in an antique store that he would pass by again on his way to the farmhouse tomorrow. Things, things—at his age! But it seemed that age only increased his appetite to acquire.

The shop was one of several in the area he returned to often, ostensibly to pick up an item for one client or another. These places sometimes came into possession of surprisingly good pieces—occasionally an object that perhaps would have been consigned to a museum had it not, fortunately, fallen into ignorant hands, to be rescued then by him.

He had bought the most fetching little Madonna at one of them on his last trip. He noted the bed at the time, but the Madonna had simply absorbed all his attention, until he got her settled into the right spot. Only then did he begin to remember the bed—its fluent maple curves, its allusion to careless pleasure . . . . This time he would buy it for certain. Assuming it was still there! Oh, why hadn't he called weeks ago, when he realized how badly he wanted it?

But the problem remained: Where to put it—Rome? Paris? Both places were small, and he already had remarkable beds in each . . .

He could move one of them out here, to the farmhouse. But that was the point. He always meant to be emptying the place out so he could sell it. And yet, each time he saw it . . . Those summers, when he was ten, eleven, twelve . . . Those were happy years, insofar as years could be said to be happy. Years filled with sensations so potent they seemed like clues to a riddle.

The place wouldn't bring much of anything, once the money was divided between himself and his surviving brother. It was a nuisance; it would simply eat cash if it were to be kept from falling to bits. His brother, and his own sons, one in Istanbul, one in London, showed no particular interest in it. Only he, only he was enslaved by the memory of the sun on the leaves around the door, the way the fruit tasted in the morning . . .

It was dark when you entered. As you opened the shutters, grand, churchly prisms turned everything in their path to phantoms. The cool aroma of the waxed stone floors blended with the smell of sun-warmed herbs. First the big room, then the room they'd used informally as a library, then the huge kitchen . . . At the long wooden table, almost transparent in the light falling from the high window, sat the girl. Water dripped slowly somewhere, onto crockery or stone. He turned, re-adjusting his pillow. Perhaps he had slept for some minutes.

The bar was now empty except for a sprawling group of five or six men and a woman, which was scaling peaks of drunken happiness—a TV crew, the waiter told him; they had filmed a commercial nearby that day. One of them was pounding away on a small piano in a corner, and the others sang along, loudly and terribly, arms around shoulders. Harry sipped a cognac and regarded them with melancholy affection. They were still young, almost young. For an instant he could see, as if it were incandescently mapped, the path of years that lay ahead of each of them, its particular sorrows, joys, terrors . . . He'd have one drink, and return to his room.

When the girl appeared in the doorway, he restrained himself from jumping to his feet. For a moment he hadn't understood that she was real.

She approached; he stood and bent over her hand.

"I thought I might find Mother down here," she said vaguely.

Wordlessly, he pulled out a chair for her.

"Huh. Well, I guess Franz has learned to sleep with his eyes open," she said. "May I have a drink, please?"

He was glad for the excuse to walk over to the bar and stand there for some moments while glasses were warmed and cognacs were poured; his brains were in such a clamor that he'd hardly been able to hear what she had said, let alone make sense of it. The TV crew was now singing an American popular song, stumbling over the words and filling in with la-la-las. Harry had read somewhere recently about the woman who'd written the song and recorded it. She'd grown up in a ghetto, he recalled, impoverished; the song was the story of her life.

The girl stared down at the little candle on the table, in an aureole of her own silence, impervious to the racket of the TV crew. After a few minutes he dared to speak. "Do you go to school in Zurich?"

She lifted an eyebrow. "Fortunately not. I'm at a boarding school in the States. One more year, and I'm free."

Tears kept coming to his eyes, as if he had been broken open; impressions, almost visible, were floating up around him, released from the hidden world by an enchanted touch: damp leaves and earth, a dappled meadow—treasure no doubt collected by his yielding and ravenous childhood senses, and stored. Every once in a while, some magic girl could unlock it. Then how to keep aloft in the radiant ether?

"Actually, I've hardly lived in Zurich at all," she said. "Mother married Franz when I was eleven, and they shipped me off to school when I was thirteen. I spent summers with my father, anyhow."

"And where does he live, my dear?"

"Oh, he's still near Dallas. Bossing a bunch of cows around. He's got some new kids . . ." She propped herself up at the table on her elbows, her long, delicate forearms together, her chin in her palms. "Mother and Franz! What a joke."

He smiled gently. "It's quite mysterious, what attracts one human being to another . . ."

"Not in this case," she said. "I mean, did you notice the size of his bank account?" She frowned, studying the small flame in front of her. "So . . . Mother said you have places all over."

"Really," he said. "All over?"

"But— I mean, where do you live?"

"Here and there. Like you."

Her green-blue gaze lingered on him, then withdrew. "She said you've got a title, too."

"Oh, lying around in a drawer somewhere."

She poked at the soft wax of the candle for a few moments, allowing him to watch her. "So, why don't you use it?" she asked.

"Evidently it's not necessary!"

She glanced at him quizzically, then smiled to herself and poked again at the candle. "Okay . . . Well, your turn . . ."

"My turn . . . All right . . . Well, why off to school at such a tender age?"

"Want to guess? Or want me to tell you."

He was sorry he'd raised the question. Any number of scenarios, all of them sordid, sprang to mind.

"I bet you can guess."

"No," he said. "You needn't—"

"Because Mother thought I was having an affair. With my piano teacher."

How many more years was his heart going to stand the sort of strain to which he was subjecting it now? "And were you?" he asked, against his will.

"Not exactly. You know. I'd go over to his apartment after school with my schoolbooks and my sheet music and my little uniform. Mother loved it that I had to wear a uniform, obviously. She'd still have me in anklets and hair ribbons if she could. And one day Mr. Schulte sort of wrestled me off the piano bench onto the floor. I mean, he left my uniform on. I guess he liked it, too. And then we'd work on Brahms. So that's sort of how it went every Tuesday. He hardly ever spoke to me, except for, you know, you should practice more, watch the tempo here, don't hold your wrists like that, this is legato . . ." She glanced at Harry speculatively, then sat back demurely with her drink.

How pitiable she was. Her bravado, her coarseness, her self-involvement—completely innocent. Perhaps never again would she be so dazzled by the primacy of her own life. "Was he—"

"The first, uh-huh. Not Franz, if that's what you were thinking. No slummy boys in an alley . . ."

It was not what he'd intended to ask. No matter. He closed his eyes and listened to her clear voice; behind the shining veil, she continued to talk.

". . . The sad fact is that Mother had this humongous crush on Schulte, it was totally obvious. He was always sort of kissing her hand and, you know, *gazing* at her with big, soulful eyes . . ." The girl sighed languorously. "Actually, I have to admit he was kind of attractive, in a creepy kind of way . . ."

One of the singers had toppled off her heights of drunken joy and was now crying; a few of the others were embracing her, mussing her hair, singing into her ear, and attempting to rock her to the music, such as it was. The girl directed an abstracted stare of distaste in their direction, then looked away, obliterating them. The word "kidney," throbbing on a flat, stylized shape, hung for an instant in Harry's mind. Then the girl dangled her empty glass by the stem and Harry caught his breath, seeing her in her flouncy bedroom, dangling a pen, with which she was about to record her most intimate feelings. A gilt-edged diary, a heart-shaped lock . . .

"Are you happy enough, my dear?" The question leapt urgently from him.

"Enough for what? Oh, well. It lies ahead, right?"

"It does," he said passionately, tears coming again to his eyes. "It does . . ."

An expression of pure derision passed quickly across her face.

"Ahead or behind," he amended, and the candle between them received a tiny smile. "Ahead or behind. That you can count on . . ."

Just beyond the cordial room, the world was whispering. Harry—it had been a long time since he had thought of himself as anything other than Harry, though what offhand joke or misunderstanding had landed him with the name he no longer quite remembered—closed his eyes to let the shimmering air, the faint ruffling of the sea from outside the open windows reach him, embrace him. "It's a remarkable night," he said. "Shall we walk for just a bit?"

She sighed and sat herself up in her chair, throwing her hair back over her shoulders again.

No, he must send his afflicted princess up to sleep. He would lie down, himself, drifting along on whatever currents her inebriating presence had conjured up.

"I don't know," she said, dreamily. "I was thinking. We could go upstairs. Don't you think? I mean, you could authenticate me . . ."

It seemed to him that she blushed faintly, though more likely it was only the flames that had roared up in front of his eyes. "I guess my room would be better," she continued. "When and if Franz ever starts to snore, Mother is sure to be out prowling for you."

They had put her in what they called the Rose Room, though except for the faint pinkish tone of the walls and the splendid four-poster, it was deliciously austere.

He perched on the chaise, in the muted light of the small lamp next to it, his lovely, dark farmhouse floating near him, the night just beyond the room's closed shutters . . . Perhaps the nervous American schoolteacher was sitting on her balcony like a sentinel at the prow of a ship keeping them from harm . . . How many wonders there used to be for him! The miraculous human landscapes! Long, brilliant nights . . . Was there never to be one of those again? Whatever role he'd been assigned in the girl's drama—her drama of triumph, her drama of degradation—it was certain to be a despicable or ridiculous one. There was no chance—at least almost no chance—that she would receive from him what he so longed to provide: even a tiny portion of pleasure or solace. And when she remembered him, no doubt she would remember him with contempt.

Briefly he closed his eyes, luxuriating in the purity of her face and body, the glowing skein of sensation she was causing the air to spin out around him, his sharp thrill of longing—everything, in short, he was waiting (like a bride!) to lose. Lazily, as though moving into a trance, she dropped one piece of clothing, then another, on the floor.

When Kate awoke, it was already late. She opened her shutters and brightness was everywhere.

The night before, she'd sat for a long while on her balcony. The sky was extraordinary—terrifying, really, with great, flaring starbursts. How long had all those blades of cold light traveled in order to cross here and pass on through this one night's heart? she wondered. Trillions and trillions of years.

She would have liked to be able to return to the cozy bar for the comfort of voices around her and a glass of something soothing. But for all she knew, the Reitzes were still there.

And the fact is, women of her age were conspicuous on their own. People tended to pity, even fear you. In any case, she was hardly the sort of person who could sit alone in such a room at this hour; one more drink could be a disaster. Oh, and worst of all—the kindness of the waiters!

So she listened to the sea altering the rocks below her, the wind around her shaping the trees, as the starlight shot past. Time itself made no sound at all.

Baker had told her about Norman—he was desperately

sorry, he said, his beautiful, dark eyes imploring her not to turn away; but there was nothing to be done. And there she was at the edge of a cliff. She'd been walking along, and just where she was about to take her next step, in that instant there was nothing.

So she went back to school to get a teaching degree, and then there was far too much to do to brood about Baker. Only sometimes at night she'd awaken as if falling from a ledge, crying out—landing hard against what her life had turned out to be, her bedclothes limp with sweat and tears.

After Baker had been living with Norman for a while, it was as if he'd always lived with Norman. There was only a residue of feeling when she and Baker met, exchanging the children or going about their separate lives—a sort of cold ash that faintly recorded their footsteps.

She had been luckier than a lot of her friends, as she learned bit by bit; Norman was wonderful with the children—so forthcoming, so understanding . . . and often when he came by to drop them off he'd sit in the kitchen with her, chatting over a leisurely beer. Through the years, in fact, they'd become truly close.

Terrible, the body's yearning, terrible. But you could always outwait it. First, there had been nothing in front of her, then—however ineptly—she, the children, Baker, and Norman wove together a swaying bridge, crossing step by cautious step over the awful chasm. And here, on the other side, Baker was dying.

The morning lobby was bright and busy. Harry was waiting to say goodbye to her, evidently, and the Reitzes were there, too. Harry put down the newspaper he seemed to have been trying to read, and stood to greet her, his arms open. "My dear! We've only just finished breakfast. We kept hoping you'd deign to join us."

"Yes, I slept and slept," she said.

"The sleep of the just!" Mr. Reitz said. "Like me!"

"And will we meet again?" Harry said to Kate. "Ah, who can say, who can say . . ."

In the bright light Mrs. Reitz's skin looked dry and fragile, as she lingered near Harry. "Now, promise me," she was saying to him, "the next time you're in Zurich—"

"Can we go now?" The girl, who had been standing at the door watching the cars pull up and depart, turned. "I'm sorry," she said to Kate, "but they always say I'm holding them up. And I've been waiting for hours!"

Kate smiled at the childish intensity of the girl's distress, and just caught herself before smoothing back the girl's hair as she used to Blair's when Blair would get herself into a state over some passing trifle. "Be patient," she used to say. "Be patient. It will be over soon, it will be better tomorrow, next week you won't even remember . . ."

WINDOW

Noah is settled down on his little blanket, and Alma has given him some spoons to play with. High up, a few feet away, Alma and Kristina drink coffee at the kitchen table. Noah, thank heavens, has been subdued since Alma opened the door to them, no trouble at all.

In this new place he seems peculiarly vivid—not entirely familiar, as if the way Alma sees him were trickling into Kristina's vision. Kristina contemplates his look of gentle inquiry, his delicate eyebrows, gold against his darker skin, his springy little ringlets. He looks distantly monumental in his beauty, like an idol at the center of a serene pond, sending out quiet ripples.

"You better do something about that cold of his. He looks like he's got a little fever," Alma says, exhaling smoke carefully away from him. "Or is that asthma?"

Kristina's gaze transfers to Alma's face.

"Does he have asthma?" Alma says.

"He'll be better now we're out of the car," Kristina says.

Yesterday afternoon and last night, and most of today, too, nothing but driving in rain, pulling over for patchy sleep, Noah waking again and again, crying, as he does these days coming out of naps, bad dreams sticking to him. Or maybe he's torn from good ones.

Or maybe dreams are new to him in general and it's frightening—one life sinking into the shadows, the forgotten one rising up. How would she know? He's talking pretty well now—he's got new words every day—but he doesn't quite have the idea yet of conversation and its uses.

Driving up, Kristina saw water just out back of the house, and tangled brush still bare of leaves, but Alma has taped plastic over her kitchen window to keep out the cold, and the plastic is blurry, and denting in the wind. All that's visible are vague, dark blotches, spreading, twisting, and disappearing. Anyone could be walking along the shore out in the gathering dark, looking in, and you wouldn't know.

Alma's saying that her friend Gerry is going to come by and then they're going out to grab a bite. "I won't be back too late, I guess." She glances at Kristina as impersonally as if she were checking something on a chart. "I'll pick up something at work tomorrow for the baby's cough." A psychiatric facility is what she called the place she works, but it sounds like a hospital.

A clattering over by the fridge makes Kristina's heart bounce, and there's a large man—stopping short in the doorway.

"Gerry, my sister Kristina," Alma says. "Kristina, Gerry."

"Your sister?" is what the man finds to say.

Alma reddens fast to an unpleasant color and looks down at her coffee cup. "Close enough. The guy who was my dad? Seems he was her dad, too."

"Hey," Gerry says, and gives Alma a little pat. But it's too late. Kristina was always the pretty one.

Gerry has a full, frowzy beard and a sheepish, tentative manner, as if it's his lot to knock over liquids or splinter chairs when he sits. Kristina picks up Noah to get him out from underfoot. "Can you say hi?" she asks him.

He observes Gerry soberly while Gerry waves, then burrows his head against her shoulder.

"Cute," Gerry says to Kristina. "Yours?"

Alma sighs. "No, ours." And then it's Gerry's turn to become red.

"Is there a store near here where I can get some milk and things for him?" Kristina asks. "We kind of ran out on the way."

Alma grinds her cigarette out on her saucer, staring at it levelly. "I would have stocked up if I'd known you were coming," she says.

"I tried to call from the road," Kristina says.

"McClure's will still be open," Gerry says.

Alma looks at him without altering her expression, and turns back to Kristina. "Gas station type place a few miles down. Not the answer to your dreams, maybe, but you'll find the essentials."

"Which way do I go?" Kristina asks.

Alma looks at her for a long moment. "If the car goes glub glub? Try turning around."

By the time Kristina returns from McClure's, Alma and Gerry are gone. Entering the house for a second time, this time with a key, juggling Noah and a bag of supplies, Kristina could practically be coming home. The mailbox says she is; that's her name there—a durable memento from the man who slid out of Alma's life soon after Alma was born and about a decade later, when Kristina was born, slid out of hers.

When Kristina first saw the house this afternoon, she had felt the sort of shame that accompanies making an error. She hadn't realized she'd been expecting anything specific, but clearly there'd been a dwelling in her mind that was larger or brighter—more cheerful. Still, it's what a person needs, four walls and a roof, shelter.

She supplements the graham crackers from McClure's with a festive-looking package of microwave lasagna that was sitting in the freezer. "Isn't this fun?" she says to Noah. "All we have to do is push the button."

Noah stares intently. Behind the window in the glossy white box, plastic wrap and Styrofoam revolve turbulently as intense, artificial smells pour out into the room. Shadows move in Noah's dark eyes, and he turns away.

"What?" she says.

He leans against her leg and says something. She has to bend down to hear.

"Not today. Thumb, Noah," she says as he puts his into his mouth. "No doggies today."

Alma might have thought of canceling her date with Gerry, Kristina thinks. It's been years since the two of them have seen each other, and it would be awfully nice to have some company. But there's Noah to concentrate on, anyhow. She urges him to eat, but he doesn't seem to be hungry. For that matter, neither is she. She spreads a sheet out on the futon that she and Alma dragged from the couch frame onto the floor, and there—she and Noah have their bed.

Outside, the wind is still hurtling clumsily by, thrashing through the branches and low, twiggy growth, groaning and pleading in the language of another world. But she and Noah are hidden under the blankets. She'll turn out the light, the night will be a deep blue swatch, Noah's cold will die down, and in the morning the wind will be gone and the sun will shine. She reaches up to the switch.

The whoosh of darkness brings Eli—surging around her

from the four corners of the earth, bursting Alma's tinny little house apart.

She gasps for breath and flings aside the churning covers; she stumbles into the kitchen where she stands naked at the window. A dull splotch of moonlight on the plastic expands and contracts in the wind.

"Kissy?" a tiny, hoarse voice says behind her.

The small form hovers in the shifting darkness. It holds out its arms to be picked up. The blank dark pools of its eye sockets face her.

"Go back to sleep," she says as calmly as she can. Fatigue is making her heart race and stirring up a muddy swirl of worries. Little discomforts and pains are piping up here and there in her body. "Now, please." She turns resolutely away and sits down at the kitchen table. After a few seconds she hears him pad away.

Fortunately, there's an open pack of Alma's cigarettes out on the table. Her hands shake slightly but manage to activate a match. Flame from sulfur, matter into clouds . . .

Everything that happens is out there waiting for you to come to it. One little turn, then another, then another—and by the time you think to wonder where you are and how you got there, it's dark.

She can't see back. It's like looking into a well. She sees her long hair ripple forward. There's nothing in front of her. But then rising up behind her, the moving shadows of trees, of the muddy road, of cars, of faces—Nonie, Roger, Liz, the girls from the distant farms, Eli . . . At the dark center of the water her own face is indistinct.

And then there she is, standing indecisively at the bus

station, over a year and a half ago, in the grimy little city where she grew up. She was a whole year out of high school, and there had been nothing but dead-end clubs and drugs, and dead-end jobs. Years before, Alma had told her, go to college, go to college, but when the time came she couldn't see it—the loans and the drudgery to repay them and then what, anyhow. There was talk of modeling—someone she met—but she was too lanky and maybe a little strange for catalog work, it turned out, and too something else for serious fashion. Narrow shoulders, and the wrong attitude, they said; no attitude, apparently. So for a while, instead of putting clothes on for the photos it had been taking them off, and after that it was working in a store that sold shoes and purses.

When she was little there had been moments like promises, disclosures—glimpses of radiant things to come that were so clear and sharp they seemed like erupting memories. A sudden scent, a sudden slant of light, and a blur of pictures would stream past. It was as if she'd been born out of a bright, fragrant world into the soiled, boarded up room of her life. She chose the town for its name from the list of destinations at the bus station.

Soft hills flowed in distant rings around the little country town, and a chick-colored sun shone over it. Out in front of the pretty white houses were bright, round-petaled flowers. Sheep drifted across the meadows like clouds.

Every day she awoke to the white houses and the gentle hills, and it was like looking down at a tender, miniature world. The sky was pure; the planet spun in it brightly, like a marble.

Tourists came on the weekends for the charged air, and the old-fashioned inns. With so many people coming to play, it had been easy to get work.

The White Rabbit . . . with that poor animal, its petrified red glass eyes staring down at her and Nonie from over the bar. It wasn't enough they shot it and stuffed it, Nonie had said; they had to plunk it down right here to listen to Frank's sickening jokes.

A pouty Angora mewed up at them from its cushion near Kristina's ankle. Good thing they didn't call this place The White Cat, huh, you, she'd said, and just then Frank craned into the dining room. Girls—ladies. A lull is not a holiday. A lull is when we wipe down tables, make salads, roll silver . . .

Or The White Guy, Nonie said.

Nonie—all that crazy, crimpy hair—energy crackling right out from it! Her new friend. Nonie had a laugh like little colored blocks of wood toppling.

It wasn't long before she moved into a room in the pretty white house Nonie and Munsen were renting. Nonie was still waiting tables on weekends then, saving up; she was planning to buy a bakery. Nonie and Munsen were hoping to have a baby.

How nice it had been when Munsen came home on his lunch breaks to hang out in the kitchen, and they were all three together. Munsen, looking for all the world like a stoopy plant, draped in the aroma of butter, smiling, blinking behind his gold-rimmed specs, drinking his coffee, sometimes a beer.

And Nonie—that was a sight to see! Little Nonie, slapping

the dough around, waking the dormant yeast as if she were officiating at the beginning of the world.

How had Nonie figured out to do that, she'd wanted to know.

No figuring involved, Nonie told her; when she was a kid she was always just sort of rolling around in the flour.

She'd given Kristina a little hug. Never mind, she said. You'll find something to roll around in.

Anyhow, Munsen said, it's overrated.

Sure, Nonie said, but it what?

Munsen had sighed. It all, he said.

One star and then another detached from its place and flamed across the dark. The skies were dense with constellations. Whole galaxies streamed toward the porch where she sat with Nonie and Munsen on her nights off, watching the coded messages from her future, light years away.

She helped, but maybe she slowed things down a bit. Well, she did, though Nonie never would have said. So while Nonie carried on in the kitchen, she would take Nonie's rattly old car and deliver orders of bread and pastries to various inns and restaurants. And Nonie and Munsen let her have her room for free.

Save those pennies! Nonie said.

For what? she had thought; uh-oh.

Every day there were new effects, modulations of colors and light, as if something were being perfected at the core. Going from day to day was like unwrapping the real day from other days made out of splendid, fragile, colored tissue.

The tourists started swarming in for the drama of the changing leaves. Every weekend the town bulged with tourists. Someone named Roger took her to dinner on one of her nights off, to The Mill Wheel, where she subbed sometimes.

Roger had waxy, poreless skin, as if he'd spent years packed in a box, and his blue eyes shone with joyous, childlike gluttony, lighting now on booty, now on tribute.

It had come to him, he told her, that it was time to make some changes. He was living in the city—toiling, as he put it, in the engine rooms of finance, but one day not long ago his company had vanished, along with so many others, in a little puff of dirty smoke. What was he to do? His portfolio had been laid waste. So, the point was, he could scrounge for something else, but it had occurred to him, why not just pull up stakes and live in some reasonably gratifying way? There wasn't any money to speak of out there these days, anyhow.

Money to speak of. A different kind of money than the money her mother had counted out for groceries.

So why not look at this period of being broke as an opportunity, he was saying, that might not come again. Because this was, he'd informed her, one's life.

The waiter poured a little wine into Roger's glass. How is that, sir? the waiter said.

Fine, Roger said, very good. He beamed as the waiter poured out a full glass for Kristina.

Thanks, Artie, she said, and Artie had bowed.

You know everyone! Roger observed.

Yeah, well, she knew Artie, unfortunately. A tiny chapter her history would have been better off without.

What is it? Roger asked. He'd smiled quizzically and taken her hand. What are you thinking?

She'd looked at him, smiled back, and withdrawn her hand.

Roger's marriage, for better or worse, had come to its natural end, he was saying. And while he looked for the occasion to make that clear, in a sensitive manner, to his wife, he was scouting out arenas in which to mine his stifled and neglected capacities.

As he talked, he gazed at her raptly, as though she were a mirror. When he reached for his wallet, to show her pictures of his children, she withdrew her hand from his again, and concentrated on drinking the very good wine. By the time they had polished off nearly two bottles and Roger was willing to throw in the towel, The Mill Wheel had almost emptied out, and Artie was lounging at the bar, staring at her evilly.

After that evening, she turned down dinner invitations, and eventually she started wearing a ring. At some point it came to her attention that Roger had indeed moved to town. In fact, he was increasingly to be seen in the afternoons hanging out at one of the bars or another, brainstorming his next move in life with the help of the bartenders.

The brilliant autumn days graded into a dazzling, glassy winter with skies like prisms, and then spring drifted down, as soft as pale linen. She painted her room a deep, mysterious blue.

Where on earth was she going to go if Nonie and Munsen had this baby they kept talking about?

She kept seeing women around her age, or anyway not much older, coming into town in their beat-up cars or pickups, to stock up. They looked sunburned and hardy and ready for the next thing, as if they were climbing out of water after a swim. Big, friendly dogs frisked around them.

Where could they be coming from? From out in the country, of course—way out, from the wild, ramshackle farms, where the weeds shot up and burst into sizzling flowers.

The kitchen is freezing. She goes into the bedroom and selects a worn chenille robe from Alma's closet. Alma's clock, with the big, reproving green numbers, says ten thirty.

So, where is Alma? Way back, when they were growing up almost next door to each other in the projects, and their mothers let Alma exercise her fierce affections on the little girl she knew to be her half-sister, Alma took care of her while their mothers worked.

And young as Kristina was, Alma confided in her. Back then, Kristina felt Alma's suffering over boys like the imprint of a slap on her own skin. Evidently things haven't changed much for Alma, and it's saddening now to picture Alma's history with Gerry: the big guy on the next bar stool, a few annihilating hours of alcohol, a messy, urgent interval at his place or hers, the sequence recapitulated now and again—an uneasy companionability hemmed about with recriminations and contingencies . . .

In her peripheral vision, Eli appears.

It was busy, and she didn't get a good look at him right away, but even at the other end of the room, sitting and talking to Frank, he was conspicuous, as if he were surrounded by his own splendid night.

Yes. She'd felt the active density right away, the gravitational pull.

It must have been several weeks later that he was there again with Frank. And when Frank got up to strut, and sniff around for mistakes, Eli looked right at her over Frank's shoulder and smiled—not the usual sort of stranger's smile, like a fence marking a divide. Not a stranger's smile at all.

It was a Friday night; the tourists started to pour in, and when she had a chance to peek back at him he was gone. He didn't reappear.

Then one night she glanced up from the table where she was taking an order and he was sitting at the bar. A little shock rippled through her. Evidently she'd been waiting.

He was looking for Frank again of course, but, as she explained, it was Frank's night off. Too bad you didn't call first, she said.

No phone, he told her, lightly.

No phone. Okay, but how did he find people when he wanted to?

Finding people is easy, he'd said; it's not getting found that's hard.

It was a slow evening, and early. They stood side by side at the bar. She could feel his gaze; she let herself float on it. How long had he and Frank been friends, she'd asked.

He'd seemed amused. Strictly business, he said. And what about her? Who was she? Where was she from?

As she spoke, he looked at her consideringly, and sorrow rose up, closing over her. How little she had to show for her eighteen years on the planet! In an hour or so the room would be filled with frenetic diners, killing time until it killed them. They might as well be shot and stuffed themselves.

I don't know about this town, though, she'd said. I'm starting to feel like I'm asleep.

So, maybe you need your sleep, he said. This isn't a bad place for a nap. Why not nap? Soon you'll be refreshed and ready to move on out.

She took to sitting at her window. Haze covered the hills in the distance; the sky had become opaque, and close. Where had that real day gone?

Sometimes after she finished delivering the orders in Nonie's old car she'd just drive around, down the small highways to the shady dirt roads. Sometimes she thought she'd caught a glimpse of Eli in town, just rounding a corner, disappearing through a doorway; she wasn't well, she thought—it seemed that maybe she never had been.

Maybe I'll try to find myself a place out in the country, she told Nonie, and get my own car.

That would be great, Nonie said. I'll help you look, if you want.

Wouldn't you even miss me? she'd said.

Of course, Nonie said. But you wouldn't be far. You'd come see us all the time.

And I'd keep helping you, she'd said.

And you'd keep helping me, Nonie said.

———

She can still see in perfect detail Zoe's face as she saw it in the The White Rabbit, for the first and only time. Truly she could only have glimpsed it—in profile as Zoe and Eli left, or in the mirror over the bar—but she might as well have scrutinized it for hours. It's almost as if she had been inside Zoe, looking into that mirror over the bar herself, seeing herself in the perfect dark skin, the perfect head, her hair almost shorn. She can feel Zoe's delicate body working as if it were her own, and she can feel the weight of the sleeping baby strapped to Zoe's back.

The lovely face with its long, wide-set eyes floats in Alma's plastic-covered window now, unsmiling, distant.

Eli had waved as he and Zoe left, but it was as if she was watching him from behind dark glass; she didn't wave back, or smile.

And Zoe appeared not to have seen her. The fact is, Zoe appeared not to see anything at all; Zoe had looked unearthly and singular, as if she were a blind woman.

Nonie was five months pregnant by the time she and Munsen told Kristina. She was superstitious, she said, and she'd had trouble before. She chuckled and patted her stomach. But this is getting pretty obvious, she said. I figured you were just being polite.

For months Munsen and Nonie had been aware there was a baby in the house.

Oh, her blue room! It had been pretty poor comfort that day.

Of course, it hadn't really been her room for the five previous months.

———

And the lady at the real estate office! Irritably raking back the streaky hair, the rectangular glasses in their thin frames, the expectant expression that went blank when Kristina spoke, or changed to a hurried smile . . .

A little less than fifteen hundred dollars! Every penny she'd saved. Not quite enough, was it, even for some crumbling hut out there, all made out of candy.

While Nonie baked rolls and Munsen sanded down to satin the cradle he'd built for the invisible baby, she'd flipped through Munsen's atlas. Chicago, Maine, Seattle, Atlanta—or why not go to one of those places really far away, where people spoke languages she couldn't understand at all? Because that was the point—this direction or that—apparently it didn't matter where she went.

The end of summer was already sweeping through town, hectic with color and heat, as if it were making a desperate stand against the darkness and cold ahead. Nearly a year had passed.

He was watching her as she walked right by him at the bar. Hey, he said, and held his hand out. No handshakes? No greetings, no how are yous, none of the customary effusions?

She had blushed deeply; she shook her hair back. All right, she said, greetings.

She remembers standing there, waiting for the blush to calm while he stretched lazily.

Well, since you ask, he'd said, here's the data. A lot of travel, recently, a lot of work. And my girlfriend is gone.

It was as if there were other words inside those, in the way there are with jokes. That's too bad, she said.

Why, exactly? he said, and the mortifying blush flared again.

To tell you the truth, he was saying, it was obvious almost from the beginning that there were going to be problems.

That woman had looked like someone with problems, she remembers having thought; that woman in the mirror looked like she was drifting there between the land of the living and the land of the dead.

And what was she up to herself these days, he'd wanted to know.

She took a deep breath to establish some poise in her thoughts. Since you ask, she said, I think nap time is just about up for me.

That very night, when she got back after work, he was there in the kitchen. He and Munsen were drinking beer, and he must have just finished saying something that made Nonie and Munsen laugh. She'd stood in the doorway, silenced.

There she is, Nonie said. How come you never brought this guy around? He's okay.

Guess I don't need to introduce anyone, she'd said.

Nonie and Munsen were sitting at the table, but he was lounging against the wall, looking at her, not quite smiling. It seemed I might not have a whole lot of time, he said. So I thought I'd drop on by to ask for your hand.

He waited for her to approach. She couldn't feel herself moving. She laughed a little, breathlessly, as he removed her ring, looking at her. Dollar store, she said, and he dropped it into the ashtray on the kitchen table.

Wow! Munsen said. Okay!

There's some stuff I have to deal with tonight, Eli said. Sit tight. I'll be back in for you at noon.

Roger was already at the bar of The White Rabbit when she went in to leave a note for Frank the next morning. His arm was around one of the new waitresses. His wife and kids were where by then, she wondered. Probably living in his abandoned SUV on just the same street where she and Alma grew up, all those years ago. Hey, she'd said. Hey, he said cheerfully. Actually, he hadn't seemed to quite remember who she was.

Wear something pretty, Eli had said the night before as he left, and so she was wearing her favorite dress, with its little straps and bare back. Her hair was pinned up. He swung her satchel into the back of the truck and then they climbed in.

Beyond the windshield, the hills had an arresting, detailed look. Red and gold were beginning to edge into the leaves. The hills were like inverted bowls or gentle cones, covered with trees. She had the impression that she could see each and every tree. The trees, like the hills, were shaped like gentle cones or inverted bowls. Would you look at that, she said.

Huh, he said, that's right. A nice little volumetric exercise.

He reached over and unpinned her hair.

This is a very crazy thing to do, she said.

Which is crazier? he said. This, or not this?

She must have been smiling, because he'd laughed. What a skeptic, he'd said. So, it's a risk, yes? Okay, but a risk of what? Look, here's the alternative, we meet, we like each other, we say hello, we say goodbye. Now there's an *actual* risk. That's pure recklessness. We're scared—is that so bad?

Because when you're scared, you can be pretty sure you're on to something.

She remembers a sudden, panicked sensation that something was wrong, and then all her relief because it was only the ring—she wasn't wearing her dime store ring.

It's pretty clear, he was saying, the things people know about each other in an instant are the important things. But all right, let's say the important things aren't everything. Let's say the unimportant things count, too—even a lot. The point is, though, we can spend as long as we like learning those unimportant things about each other. We can spend years, if we want, or we can spend a few hours. If you want, I can bring you back here tomorrow. We can say goodbye now, if you want.

They watched each other, smiling faintly. The silence raced through her over and over.

Say the word, he'd told her, and you're back where you were.

Past the gorge, where she went to swim sometimes with Nonie and Munsen, past the old foundry, past the quarry, the hills flowing around them, mile after mile, so little traffic on the highway, the sweet air pouring by and the sun ringing through the sky like trumpets. Then they were in the woods, among the woven streamers of sunlight and shadow. The dirt road was studded with rocks, and grooved, tossing her around as if she were on the high seas.

None of her drives in Nonie's car had taken her in that direction, or nearly that far. There were no other people to be seen. Every leaf and twig signified, like a sound, or a letter of the alphabet.

By the way, she said, how did you know where to look for me last night?

Hey, he said. In a town that size?

Light brimmed and quivered through the leaves in trembling drops. All around was a faint, high, glittering sound. The cabin was a maze of light and shadow—all logs, with polished plank floors, and porches. And with the attic and lofts and little ladders and stairs, you hardly knew whether you were inside or up in a tree house.

There was running water, and there was even electricity, which he used mainly for the washing machine and the big freezer at the back. He brought her out past a group of sheds to the vegetable garden he'd been clearing and tending, and to the shiny little creek. If you walked into the woods, within just a couple of minutes you couldn't even see the cabin. When the sun began to set they came back, and he showed her how to light the kerosene lanterns and the temperamental little dragon of a stove.

There was a lot of game in the freezer, Eli said; hunters often gave him things. But he'd kept it simple tonight—for all he knew, she might be the fainthearted sort.

He had opened a bottle of rich red wine and they ate wonderful noodles, with mushrooms from the woods and herbs, and a salad from the garden. He watched, with evident satisfaction, her astonishment at the bright, living flavors.

You have to live like this to taste anything like this, he said. Streamline yourself. Clear away the junk. Prepare for an encounter.

But anyhow, she'd said, and in the stillness she'd felt like a dancer, balancing—I'm not fainthearted.

How on earth was she accounting in those first hours, she wonders now, for the baby she had seen at the bar with Eli?

Well, if she'd thought of too many questions out front, she'd probably still be rotting away in that little town, living in somebody's spare room. She'd been in no position at that moment to be thinking of the sort of questions whose answers are, Go back to sleep.

They were finishing off the bottle of wine when he explained that his partner Hollis and Hollis's girlfriend, Liz, were taking care of Noah right now, as they did from time to time. It was all kind of improvisational, not ideal, but Zoe had been erratic and moody, so anyhow it was an improvement over that situation.

He rested his hand on her neck, and stars shot from it. If it had been up to her, the dishes would have stayed in the sink till morning—till winter. But Eli just held her against him for a blinding moment. Here's some of that new stuff to learn about me, he said. I am very, very disciplined.

And what had she been dreaming about that first morning? She was hidden behind something. Something was about to happen to someone very far away, who was her. There were showers of burning debris. The noise that woke her came into the dream as an alarm, she thinks, but it all dissolved like a screen over the morning light, and there was Eli lying next to her, his eyes still closed, shadows of leaves moving across him like a rich, patterned cloak.

A mechanical growl was pushing through the racket of birds and leaves. She peered out and a mottled green truck came into view. The sun must have been up for some time—it was so bright! The door of the truck slammed, and Eli groaned. Hollis, he said, and opened his eyes.

She wrapped herself around him, but he kissed her, untangled himself, and drew his jeans on. There were dogs barking. Powder! T-bone! someone yelled. Down!

Well, they're here, Eli said, and tossed her dress to her.

She'd watched from the top of the stairs as Liz transferred the baby over to him. The baby whimpered, and Eli put him on his shoulders.

A cigarette dangled from Hollis's mouth, and a line of smoke swayed up past his gray eyes. Would you mind kindly keeping that shit out of the house, please? Eli said. And away from my kid in general?

Hollis pinched the cigarette out with his fingers and flicked it through the door. So how about some coffee? he said.

The dogs were milling and bumping at things. Don't rush me, don't rush me, Eli said. He stretched, then, and reached over to tousle Hollis's floppy brown hair. I just got up.

Hollis inclined his head. Impressive, he said. Outstanding.

They'd looked like a tribe, Hollis and Liz and Eli, tall and slouchy and elastic. She sat on the stairs, rags of her dream still clinging to her, until he called for her.

It was Hollis who tracked down the guns and kept on top of the orders and sales. Because this guy's too pure in heart to have a computer in his place, Hollis had said, tilting back to appraise her.

No phone line, Eli said, unruffled.

My point, Hollis said to her. So I'm stuck with it. He shook his head. Too fucking poetic, this guy.

You are so jealous, Liz told Hollis, sliding her hand inside the back of his jeans.

The good weather continued, and there was the garden and clearing away the persistent brush. There was plenty else, too—cleaning, and dealing with the wood for the stove, and endless laundry.

Mostly, of course, there was Noah. Eli was doing a lot of things to the cabin, and the wood chips and splinters and chemicals were flying around everywhere. And there were always tools, and work on the guns going on in the sheds.

You've really got to watch him every second, Eli said. And I mean every second.

It was true; if she turned around for a *second* he'd have gotten himself over to the stove or the door or a pail of something. So she watched and she watched. But at night, when Noah was asleep, she had Eli to herself and that was well worth the trouble of the day, and more.

Usually, it was he who cooked. Sometimes just vegetables, but sometimes rabbit or venison or little birds. Often, as evening came, the sky turned greenish—a dissipating, regretful color.

She remembers his voice coming through that color from outside, asking her to get the stove going. But when he came in almost a half an hour later, she hadn't managed. I'm sorry, she said. How tired she used to get, back at the beginning! And she'd actually started to cry.

He looked at her and sighed. Here, he said. I'll show you again.

Sometimes the woods shook and flared with thunder and lightning. The deer came crashing through the trees. Way down in the valley the little foxes jumped straight up from the grass. Sometimes, walking near the creek with Eli, Noah on his shoulders or back, she would hear just a little whisper or rustle somewhere, or there would be a streak in the corner of her eye. Are there snakes? she asked.

He folded his arms around her and explored her ear with his tongue. Not to worry. They won't bother you unless you do something to stir them up.

At first Noah would go rigid when she tried to hold him. He'd swat at her if she bent down for him, and he'd scream when it seemed he thought Eli was in earshot.

And then Eli had to come in from outside and hold him or swing him around while she looked on. There we go, Eli would say when Noah calmed down. And sometimes he'd go back out hardly looking at her.

Noah was still only a baby then, but every day he was looking more like a little boy; every day he figured out new ways to resist and defeat her.

Just pick him up like a big ham, Eli said. Look. Like this, right, Noah?

He smiled at her as he went out, but later he'd taken her by the shoulders and looked at her very seriously. I know it's hard, he said. But you've got to start taking some more responsibility around here. She averted her face as he leaned over to kiss her; she'd just sneaked a cigarette.

It was early on that they talked about Zoe. She wasn't ready, Eli said; it wasn't her fault. In fact, there was a lot that was his fault, really a lot, he hated to think about it. But anyhow, it was just the way she was constituted—she lacked courage.

She was always dissatisfied. And she always would be, because she didn't have the courage to face the fact that what happens to you is largely of your own choosing.

He turned back, then, to whatever it was he'd been doing. But she was still listening, she remembers; something was still flickering in what he'd said.

Does she want to see Noah? She'd asked after a moment.

That's not a possibility, he said. His back was to her.

She was willing to leave her kid, he said. And that one's on her.

Noah isn't sounding so good. She can hear him snuffling from the kitchen. She goes to check. He's a bit sweaty—maybe Alma's right, that he's got a little fever. But little kids get sick all the time. Anyhow, what makes Alma the authority? The hospital she works at is for crazy people, not for little kids.

Tomorrow she'll get him some kind of treat—a fuzzy doggie toy, maybe. Or something. Not that there's money to burn.

She remembers once trying chocolate syrup in his milk, trying a story, promising maybe a trip into town later with Eli, but Noah still whining and crying hour after hour. All right, that's it, you behave now, she'd said. Or you're going right in your crib and you're not going to be seeing that bottle of yours anytime soon.

He let out a little yelp of fury.

Fine, then, scream, she said. Go ahead and scream. Just cry until you melt yourself away for all I care. You know he's not going to hear you out there over all that noise. They'd stared at each other. He is not going to hear you.

She turned away from him and opened one of Eli's books. When she glanced back Noah was still standing there, looking at her. What? she said.

He'd wobbled for a moment on his feet, and then plopped down on his rear end, crying again.

Eli went into town to get supplies and took Noah with him. To give her a break, he said.

She'd listened to the truck heaving itself out on the rutted road. It was the first time she'd been truly alone in the cabin for more than a few minutes. Sunlight and silence shimmered down through the leaves all around it. In the sparkling dimness the floor shone like a lake. All around her there was a tingling quiet. She shivered, then sat very still, to enter it.

It was like a garden, or park, that opened out forever. Peaceful, clever animals, invisible in the abundance, paused to take note of her. She had found her way, through patience and good fortune.

How's it been going—Eli said, when he returned, looking around at the cabin. She'd finished the dishes and tidied up. —Any lions or tigers?

Hollis's green truck pulled up, waking her. The sheets still noted Eli's place, but they were cold. She'd watched from a window upstairs. The dogs were huffing and circling in back, and Hollis and Liz got out. Eli was carrying Noah. He handed Noah over to Liz. He called something up to Kristina, and then he and Hollis got into Eli's truck and pulled back out onto the dirt road.

She heard Liz downstairs with Noah. After a while she came down herself. Hi, Liz said. Eli told me you might want some help with Noah today.

Oh, thanks, she'd said. But we'll be fine.

That's okay, Liz said, flopping herself down on the couch. Just toss me out when you get sick of me.

Sorry not to have given you a heads-up, Eli said later. But we had an unexpected opportunity. To do an errand for your old pal, Frank.

Frank, she said. What did Frank want?

He's into Mausers these days, I'm sorry to tell you. He had his tender heart set on a 1944 Kreigsmodell, and we just happened to come across one at a reasonable price. Oh, give me the sweet old American revolver guys any day. Or the Derringer guys, or the Winchester guys. Anyone at all—the Finnish military model guys. I've got to admit it's not necessarily a super high IQ clientele, but Frank is special. It's amazing he hasn't already blown his brains out by mistake.

Frank! To think of the way that freak had gotten her to scurry around. Like a rabbit! She'd let out a little whoop.

What, Eli said. Oh, right—like how would anyone know if he had.

I don't really need Liz to come help, she said the next time he'd had to go off for the day.

He'd looked at her. It doesn't hurt to have reinforcements, he said. And I'll have her bring any stuff you might need from town.

The leaves were truly turning when she first went back into town with Eli. The cycle of the year had locked tight, but she'd slipped out in time.

Past the quarry and the foundry and the gorge, into the painted, prissy town. She'd lived there only months ago, and yet it didn't look like a real place any longer—it just looked like a picture of a place.

She cast her mind back and saw Zoe—the way Zoe had looked carrying Noah, gliding and regal.

Want me to carry you? she said. Noah protested, but Eli slung him onto her back.

He was heavy, and she had to cede him to Eli pretty soon, but for a while as they went about their errands, buying food and batteries and seeds, she felt, in the weight of him, her elevated station. And when they went to the diner for lunch, people she had barely spoken to in the old days came over to admire him.

They went to one of the fancy tourist stores, and Eli picked out two dresses for her. Back in the truck, with Noah settled on her lap, she felt in the bag at the slippy, lovely fabric.

Anything you particularly want to do before we head home? Eli said.

Home. The way she had lived at Nonie and Munsen's— like a little animal! I bet Nonie and Munsen would enjoy seeing Noah, she said.

Are you saying you'd like to stop by there now? he said.

She'd glanced at him, then shrugged. We're here.

He was looking at her steadily. Do you want to see them? It's been awhile, she said.

All you have to say, he said. All you have to say is that you'd like to see them.

But neither Munsen's car nor Nonie's was out in front. Well, too bad, Eli said.

Eli had so many books. How nice it had been to take them down from the shelves and look at them. In the one about the ocean, the prettiest fish imaginable hovered so weightlessly you could almost see them moving—rising, lingering, darting down with the flick of a tail. And the gorgeous plants and flowers around them were really other animals.

How did he get out? Eli was saying. He was in front of her, holding his machete in one hand and Noah by the other, and rage was flashing off him in sheets, like lightning. *It was just luck I didn't kill him with this.*

She was still shaking when Eli returned outside. She could hardly stand. Her hand was clamped around Noah's shoulder. If you want something you come to me, do you hear? she told him, her voice tight. You come to me. You do not go outside to bother your father. Try some stunt like that again and I'll— I don't know what I'll do—

On rainy days when Eli wasn't working, she curled up against him while he read out loud. Noah curled up at his other side, or played quietly nearby. Eli read from books about history or animals or the earth and other planets. The world was living and breathing, each bit in its place. When the weather was good the three of them played together in the woods.

Whenever Eli went away for the day, Liz came in her pickup, and stayed on and on. Noah would go rigid with joy when the big, patient dogs, with their amazing tails and fur and tongues came huffling toward him through the door, but Kristina set herself to endure some bad hours.

Sometimes for days afterward, Kristina felt like a swan that had gotten caught in an oil slick—sticky and polluted, not fit to be near Eli. How could he deal with Liz? Her loudness, her opinions about every pointless thing, her gossipy chattering, the way she made everything ordinary . . . Eli had shrugged: she was an old, old friend, there was a lot of history, she was as loyal as a person could be . . .

Noah was making his way toward them, holding his empty bottle. Hey, Noah— Liz said. You're really getting that locomotion thing down! Wow, I can't believe how fast he's growing, look at him. Noah! she grabbed him up and tickled him, blowing hard into his hair.

Kristina remembers watching as Noah exploded into giggles.

Does he still cry for Zoe all the time? Liz said, when Noah had run back to the dogs.

For Zoe? she'd said.

Wow, it used to be Mama, Mama, Mama the whole fucking time, Liz said. Poor little sweetie. It used to drive Eli nuts.

I guess he's forgotten about her, she'd said.

That's great, good for you, she was a major pain, if you ask me, Liz had said, Miss Too Gorgeous for this World. I always felt like smacking her myself, to tell you the truth. She didn't appreciate what she had in Eli. Eli's intense, so what? He's got his own way of looking at things. He's more evolved than other people. Plus, he gave her everything. He was fucking great to her, and he put up with her shit a long, long time before he even *began* to lose patience. Liz was holding one of the dish towels, creasing it absently and fiercely.

They've been gone so long, Kristina remembers saying. Did they say when they were planning to get back?

Oh, you never know with those two, Liz said. She tossed the towel onto the table. They take their time with the custom work. Of course that's why they've got such a great reputation, obviously. Hollis can find just about anything, and Eli can convert just about anything. He's got great hands. She pushed her hair back and eased a pack of cigarettes from her pocket. Great, great hands. . . . She lit a cigarette and inhaled, closing her eyes.

Kristina watched her for a while. Liz— she'd said, and her voice came out fuzzy. Can I take one of those?

Help yourself. Liz opened her eyes; she'd sounded almost angry. I won't tell.

The next time Eli and Hollis went off, Noah played happily with the dogs while Liz talked on, but then suddenly Liz exclaimed, and put her hands to her forehead.

Are you okay? Kristina asked.

Sorry, Liz said. I've been getting these crucifying migraines.

Do you want to lie down? she'd asked. Then her breath caught for a moment. Do you want to leave?

Would you mind? Liz said. You don't have to mention to Eli it was so early, though. But if I don't get out of here fast, basically, I'm not going to be able to drive till probably tomorrow.

That afternoon, with Liz and the dogs gone so early, no matter how often Kristina explained that Eli was coming back soon, Noah cried and fussed, swatting at her with his little hands.

You'd be less cranky if you ate something, she said. What about some applesauce?

No, Noah said.

Well, then, a graham cracker. Don't you like your graham crackers anymore?

No, he said.

Such a tiny word. Such a tiny voice.

Do you know how furious your father's going to be if I have to tell him you refused to eat one single thing all day? Do you know how angry he's going to be with you? Are you going to make me tell him?

He looked at her, swaying a bit on his feet. Bad Kissy, he said.

Not bad me, bad you! Bad you! Do you want me to smack you? Because I'm just about ready to.

Bad Kissy, he said. Bad Kissy.

Don't you talk to me like that! Don't you look at me like that! Do you think I like picking up after you all day? And getting you your food when you do deign to eat? And cleaning up all your mess? I know you don't like having me around. And do you know what? I think I've just about had it with you! One more sassy word and I'm going to walk right out that door, and you'll just have to take care of yourself. Now, you eat your graham cracker this minute, or I'm out of here.

But then he was screaming and kicking and banging his head against the wall.

It was the moment; it was their chance, and thank God she'd recognized that. But just remembering the struggle, she starts to sweat—scooping him up and trying to hold him still, and all the time he was kicking at her and screaming. And clinging to her so fiercely she could hardly get him over to the sofa to sit down with him.

It must have been over an hour that she was holding on to him before he was calm enough for her to speak. All right then, Noah, she said.

He had gone limp. She held him steadily on her lap and broke the graham cracker in half. She wouldn't let him avoid her eyes.

I'm not going to leave you alone, she said. Listen to me. This is a promise. I am not going to leave you alone.

Tears were still rolling down his cheeks, and he hiccuped.

They watched each other as she ate her half of the cracker. She nodded, and held the other half of the cracker out to him. Slowly, gulping back the last of his sobs, still watching her, he chewed it laboriously down.

When Eli returned, Noah was still in her lap, asleep. Where's Liz? he said.

You just missed her, she said.

Huh, Eli said. And this one—trouble?

She rested her cheek against Noah's springy hair and tightened her hold on him for a moment before handing him over. No, she said. No trouble.

The cold came and kept them frequently inside. Eli was working in the shed a lot, and from time to time he'd have to take a trip or go to a show with Hollis. When they were away, Liz arrived for the daylight hours. When her truck finally pulled away, darkness folded in over the cabin.

When Eli was home, he was quiet. He read to Noah, and when he grew tired of it he turned to his own reading. He was looking a little pale, she'd thought. Eli? she said.

What's that? he'd said, pausing on his way up to the loft.

She shook her head: nothing.

Noah pined and clamored for his friends the dogs. Shh, she told him, and took him where he could play without disturbing Eli.

Once in a while a car would pull up, and some man or other would get out and Eli would take him around back to the sheds. She stayed upstairs then with Noah.

While Noah played with the blocks Eli had made him, she watched out the window as the men returned to their trucks or cars and headed off to the hills, or the hills beyond them, or the hills and cities beyond those—glinting pins springing up on the map.

And she watched Noah as he concerned himself with the blocks or with his crayons. Playing, it was called—the deep, sweet concentration, the massive effort to familiarize himself with the things of the world. Can she remember that, being so little herself, being so lost? Probably Alma had already been around, looking out for her, but she can't find a trace of that time in her mind. It was her basis, and yet it was gone.

Want me to carry you? she'd ask, and he'd raise up his little arms to her. She held him as he woke from his naps, and felt the damp heat coming off his gold skin and little ringlets. He snuggled against her, and in an attic dark area of her sleeping thoughts, things clarified for a moment, and aligned.

He never fussed anymore. He had made his choice; he had forgotten.

Sometimes Kristina felt Zoe hovering nearby, drawn by

her need, watching along with her as Noah played. But Noah never even looked up.

Yes, he had surely forgotten. Poor little thing—he was a prisoner.

Are you not talking to me? Eli said one day.

Not talking to you? she said. She looked up. He was sitting across the room, looking at her. The book he'd been reading was closed, resting on his lap.

You don't seem to be talking to me.

You were reading, she said.

Now I'm not reading, he said.

She looked at him for a clue. Is there something you want me to talk about?

He sighed and opened his book again, but a moment later he looked up at her again. You're happy, he said.

Yes, she said. He seemed to be gazing back at her sadly from some time in the future. I'm happy.

Well, good, then. He walked over to her and stroked the back of her neck, looking at her thoughtfully. He kissed her temple and then he returned to his book.

He picked up some yeast for her in town. She baked bread the way Nonie had showed her to, and the companionable aroma brought Nonie to visit.

She remembers the way she imagined showing Nonie around the cabin. It was as if she were unfolding it and spreading it out flat, like a map, so she could see all of it at once herself.

How's Eli these days? Liz said.

Fine, she'd said.

Well, I'm glad one of them is keeping it together, Liz said. Hollis is fried. But everything always happens all at once, doesn't it.

I guess, Kristina had said.

Well, but I mean what kind of dickhead doesn't back up the files? Liz said. I guess that genius they found, I hate to think where, is still saying he can resurrect the hard drive, but who believes that's going to happen? And anyhow, who cares, it's the thing with that Coffield lunatic, obviously, that's really putting him around the bend.

Yes? Kristina said. The room darkened for a moment, and she'd sat down.

Well, it's sure getting enough attention. Eli must have told you. You literally can't turn on the TV for one second without seeing the pictures. God, those kids must have been cute! With that red hair?

Kristina had let out a little sound.

But they don't usually go after the source, Liz said. Unless like it's a kid putting holes in his parents or at school, something like that. And anyhow, according to Hollis for whatever that's worth, he did check the guy out, and there was no history.

Sleet coated the trees and power lines, and froze. For a day or two the woods were shining glass, and the branches snapped and fell under the weight of the ice. Nights were mostly bundled up in silence; you could hear the world breathing in its sleep. When she closed her eyes, she'd see the animals outside in the stark, brilliant moonlight, huddled, or wandering for food—the foxes and the deer, the badgers and the possums and the pretty black bear. The stars overhead contracted in the cold. From bed she could watch them oscillating with intensified light, as if they were about to burst into sharp, glittering fragments.

Is everything all right? she asked him.

Fine, he said.

Can I help with anything?

Can you help? he said. Can you do a conversion with a broken drill press on a 1911 automatic while some drooling trog breathes down your neck?

She went into town with him, and when they passed the old house, both cars were out front. Would you like to drop by? he asked.

I don't really care, she said.

It might be nice for you, he said. You probably miss your friends.

She reached over and stroked his beautiful hair. He could drop her and Noah off, she suggested, while he did errands.

We're in no rush, he said. I'll go in with you.

Nonie was practically a sphere. She greeted Kristina with a little shriek of joy, and cried a bit.

How fussy the kitchen looked to Kristina now, with its shiny appliances and painted walls.

Nonie cut up pieces of her bread with homemade jam for everyone, and Munsen took a couple of beers from the fridge. Eli? he said.

No, thanks, Eli said.

Kristina?

Not for me, either, Munsen—thanks.

Munsen put one bottle back and opened the other for himself. Well, better a full bottle in front of me than a prefrontal lobotomy, he said, ruefully. Then he set Noah on his lap, and while Nonie recounted goings on at The White Rabbit, which were exactly the same old thing, it seemed, Munsen told Noah the true-life adventures of a lonely bottle of beer.

What a fuss Nonie made over Noah! He's going to have a friend, soon, she said.

Kristina had glanced at Eli. He was standing, leaning against the door with his head bowed.

Nonie gave Noah one of the soft little rag dolls she'd made for her own baby, with a little plastic ring in its navel. Noah looked at it with great seriousness, and then rubbed it against his cheek. He looked up at Nonie, who laughed happily and knelt down to give him a squeeze.

So little real time had passed, but she might as well have spent it living at the bottom of the sea with its creaturely landscape, or on the white polar tundras. And all the while Nonie and Munsen had been confined to the little painted town. Goodbye, she thought. Goodbye.

They had almost reached the cabin when Eli finally spoke. That is one inane guy, he said. I wonder how your friend can stand having him around.

The next morning, Kristina couldn't find Noah's new rag doll anywhere.

She was searching through a heap of laundry for it when she realized Eli was in the doorway, watching her. Everything okay? he said.

She turned and they looked at one another. Fine, she said.

Look, I've got to go away tomorrow for a few days, Eli said. But Liz will come over during the days and help.

Eli, she said.

What?

Eli, she said again.

What? he said. Speak to me.

Do you have to go?

Yes, he said. Obviously. Yes, I have to go.

Eli, can't I come with you?

And do what with him?

Bring him along. Can't we come?

No, you cannot come.

Why not?

Why not? It goes without saying why not.

She was twisting one of Noah's little T-shirts in her hands, she realized. But maybe I could be helpful.

Maybe you could, he said. Maybe you could bring a little sunshine into the lives of some lonely gun collectors.

She looked at him, but he was sealed up tight. But don't send Liz at least, please.

Fine, he said. No Liz. And you'll do what for food? You'll do what if you need something? You don't have a phone. You don't have a car.

If you're worried about us, we could go stay with Nonie and Munsen.

With Nonie and Munsen, he said. Would you be happier there?

It's just— she was saying, and then all she really remembers is her surprise, as if his fists were a brand-new part of his body.

A little blood was coming from somewhere; she'd felt something on her face, then checked her hand. There was some blood in her mouth, too. Was that tooth going to come out? she'd wondered idly.

She heard the bare branches clacking together outside in a slight breeze. Then he picked her up from where she'd fallen back.

She remembers Noah's eyes, enormous and blurry-looking. He was sucking at his blanket as Eli carried her upstairs.

He postponed his trip for a few days and stayed with her, curled up next to her in the loft, holding her hands, looking through his books with her. He taught her the names of all the little birds that lived in the leaves around them. He brought her meals on a tray. Noah played quietly downstairs, and sometimes Eli brought him up to be with her. He'd wake her urgently in the night, and after they made love, he kissed her ankles, her toes, her fingertips. Whatever barrier had been between them was gone now, completely.

She stroked his thick, coarse hair. She can feel it under her hand now—almost feel it. Sometimes as he slept she ran her hands over his beautiful face. Poor Eli. He lived with danger all the time.

It wasn't long before the swelling went way down, and she could get around pretty comfortably, as well. The day he left, she found a tube of makeup out on the bureau. Evidently he'd picked it up in town, for the bruises.

She's sure there were marks but nothing too conspicuous by the time she'd finished applying it. She watched carefully for Liz's expression when she opened the door in her sunglasses.

She's reviewed it so often she's worn away the original, but she knows perfectly well what it was.

She saw Liz register the sunglasses, the masked bruises. She saw Liz politely covering her surprise. And then she saw the thing that she had hoped so fervently that she would not see: she saw that Liz was not very surprised at all.

What did they talk about that morning? Not Eli, that's for sure. Or Hollis, or themselves. They did not, of course, allude to Zoe, though Kristina felt Zoe's volatile essence, as a slight trembling in the air. Eventually, she remembers, Liz began leafing through some trashy magazine she'd brought in with her and paused to study the picture of two pretty faces, empty of anything except a pitiful falseness. They broke up! she exclaimed, looking up at Kristina. Can you believe it? How sad is that!

It was the next day—the second of the three he was to be gone—that Zoe's sorrowing angel spirit passed her hand across Liz's brow, and Liz winced, pressing her hand to her eyes.

And there it was. The opportunity that was as clear as a command. For a moment Kristina had just stood there.

Migraine? she had asked then quietly. Want to go home and lie down?

It was a hard trip into town, and of course you always had to worry about who it was who would stop. But thank heavens it wasn't raining, at least. Feel better, she'd called to Liz, waving from the door as the pickup pulled out, and then as fast as humanly possible, she'd thrown a few necessities for Noah and a change of clothing for herself into her satchel. It wasn't heavy, but progress down the muddy road out to the highway was arduous; something in her side still hurt a lot when she tried to carry Noah.

Hey, it's you, Nonie said when she opened the door. And then her smile was gone. Wuh! Take off those sunglasses for a moment, girl.

Noah let himself be transferred over, and clung to Nonie as she put juice into a bottle for him. Come see the baby, she said.

The baby was red and gummy. Could Noah ever have looked like that? That's incredible, Kristina said.

So, could Nonie and Munsen manage with one car, she'd asked? She could give them over a thousand dollars for Nonie's. She hadn't spent so much as a dime the whole time she'd been with Eli, she realized; he'd taken care of her completely.

Well, you could pay me down the line somewhere, Nonie said. But I'm not really sure I want to know you've got it, if you see what I mean.

That was a good point.

I guess you could report it stolen, Kristina had said. But maybe not for a while? And I guess I'll have to figure out about changing the plates . . .

They'd looked at each other, frowning. Damn, Nonie said. You'd think a person would know how to steal her own car.

And for just a moment, Kristina remembered the way she'd felt sitting around that kitchen in the old days.

Dull moonlight sloshes around like rainwater in the plastic over the window. Alma hasn't come in yet. But Kristina's just as glad to have had this time with Eli.

This afternoon, when Alma answered the door she looked silently for a moment at Kristina, with her bruises and the beautiful, dark child. Then she stood aside to let them in. Heaven knows what she thinks—she didn't ask questions.

When Kristina was young she idolized Alma. It was Alma who looked out for her, and she never doubted for a moment that Alma would gladly take her in if the time came. It hardly matters now that it seems not to be the case. She looks around at Alma's cheap, carelessly ugly place—home for nobody, really. Oh, those shining floors, that quiet, the breathing shadows! Will she ever see it again?

Noah coughs raspily in his sleep. She puts her hand to his hot forehead, and he opens his eyes, just for a moment.

Stolen car! Kidnapped child! How can those words mean her? The deer come crashing through the woods, Zoe holds her breath, Eli's rage is all around them, the red net casting wide. What's right outside? Keys hanging from the warden's belt? The men with the guns? Just guns, or guns and badges . . .

No one looks at anyone—really completely looks—the way he looked at her. She never imagined, or even dared hope, that she would meet such a man or have such a time in her life. Better keep moving. New names, new histories, a nondescript room in a busy city where she'll be able to lose herself and Noah. Watching, hiding, running—that way at least she'll be with Eli for good.

REVENGE OF THE DINOSAURS

Hi, Barbara, I said. You're Barbara?

Eileen, said the nurse who answered the door. Nights.

I'm the granddaughter, I said.

I figured, Eileen said. Barbara told me you'd be showing up. So where's that handsome brother of yours?

Bill? I said, I beat Bill? That's a first.

Traffic must be bad, she said.

Traffic, traffic . . . I was goggling past Eileen at Nana's apartment—the black-and-white tile, the heavy gold-framed mirror, the enormous vases or whatever they are, the painting I'd loved so much from the time I was a child of a mysterious, leafy glade, the old silver-dust light of Nana's past. I was always shocked into sleepiness when I saw the place, as if a little mallet had bonked me on the head, sending me far away.

Or in Connecticut, Eileen said. I looked at her. Isn't that where they drive in from? she said. He's a wonderful man, your brother. So kind and thoughtful. And his wife, too. They always know just how to cheer your grandmother up. And that's one cute little girl they've got.

How's Nana doing? I asked.

A while since you've seen her, Eileen commented.

I live on the other side of the country! I said.

I know that, dear, Eileen said. I've seen your picture. With the trees. Before the second stroke she liked me to sit with her and go over the pictures.

I stared. Nana? Bill had told me to prepare myself, but still—family souvenirs with the nurse? It's supposed to mean something to be one person rather than another.

Eileen accompanied me into the living room. Nana was dozing in one of the velvet chairs. I sneezed. Soldiers were marching silently toward us across the black-and-white desert of an old television screen. An attractively standardized smiling blond woman in a suit replaced them. Does Nana watch this? I asked. She seems to like having it on, Eileen said. I keep the sound off, though. She can't really hear it, and I'd rather not. Wake up, dear, your granddaughter's here to see you. Don't be surprised if she doesn't recognize you right off, Eileen told me. Dear, it's your granddaughter.

It's Lulu, Nana, I said, loudly. Nana surveyed me, then Eileen. Neither Bill nor I had inherited those famous blue eyes that can put holes right through you, though our father had, exactly, and so had our brother, Peter. Where does all that beauty go when someone finishes with it? If something exists how can it stop existing, I mused aloud to Jeff recently. Things take their course, Jeff said (kind of irritably, frankly). Well, what does *that* mean, really—*things take their course*? Jeff always used to be (his word) charmed that I wasn't a (his word) sucker for received (his phrase) structures of logic. Anyhow, if something exists, it exists, is what I think, but when Nana turned back to the TV she did actually look like just any sweet old lady, all shrunk into her little blanket. I bent and kissed her cheek.

She winced. It's Lulu, dear, Eileen shouted. One of Nana's hands lifted from the pale cashmere blanket across her lap in a little wave, as if there were a gnat. I'll be in the kitchen,

Eileen said. Call me if you need me. I sat down near Nana on the sofa. I was not the gnat. Nana, I said, you look fabulous.

Did she hear anything at all? Well, anyhow, she'd never gone in for verbal expressions of affection. Someone sighed loudly. I looked around. The person who had sighed was me.

The last time I'd seen Nana, her hearing was perfect and she was going out all the time, looking if not still stunning, still seriously good, with the excellent clothes and hair and so on. She was older, obviously, than she had been, but that was all: older. It's too drastic to take in—a stroke! One teensy moment, total eclipse. In my opinion, all moments ought to contain uniform amounts of change: X many moments equal strictly X much increase in age equal strictly X much change. Of course, it would be better if it were X much *decrease* in age.

Oh, where on earth was Bill? Though actually, I was early. Because last week when I'd called my old friend Juliette and said I was coming to the city to see Nana, she said sure I could stay at her place and naturally I assumed I'd be hanging out there a bit when I got in from the airport and we'd catch up and so on. But when I arrived, some guy, Juliette's newish boy-friend, evidently—Wendell, I think his name might be—whom she'd sort of mentioned on the phone, turned out to be there, too. *Sure, let's just kill them, why not just kill them all,* he was shouting. Juliette was peeling an orange. I'm not saying kill *extra* people, she said. I'm just frightened; there are a lot of crazy, angry maniacs out there who want to kill us, and I'm frightened. *You're frightened,* he yelled. *No one else in the world is frightened?* Juliette raised her eyebrows at me and shrugged. The orange smelled fantastic. I was completely dehydrated from the flight because they hardly even bring you water anymore, though when I was little it was all so fun and special, with the pretty stewardesses and trays of little wrapped things, and I was just dying to tear open Juliette's fridge and see if there was another orange in there, but Wendell, if that's what his name is, was standing right in front of it shouting, *What are you saying? Are you saying we should kill everyone in the world to make sure there are no angry people left who want to hurt anyone?* So I waited a few minutes for him to finish up with what he wanted to get across and he didn't (and no one had ever gotten anything across to Juliette) and I just dropped that idea about the orange and said see you later and tossed my stuff under the kitchen table and plunged into the subway. When Juliette and I were at art school together, all her boyfriends had been a lot of fun, but that was five or six years ago.

Happy laundry danced across the screen on a line. Little kids ate ice cream. A handsome man pumped gasoline into a car, jauntily twirled the cap back on the gas tank, and turned to wink at me. A different standardly attractive woman in a suit appeared. It was hard to tell on this ancient black-and-white set what color we were supposed to believe her hair was. Red, maybe. She was standing on the street, and a small group of people, probably a family, was gathered around her. They were black, or anyhow not specifically white, and they were noticeably fatigued and agitated. Their breath made lovely vapor in the cold. One of them spoke distractedly into a microphone. The others jogged up and down, rubbing their arms. Someone was lying on the pavement. The possibly redheaded newscaster looked serene; she and the family appeared to have arrived at the very same corner from utterly different planets by complete coincidence. She had a pretty good job, actually. A lot better than selling vintage clothing, anyhow. And maybe she was getting some kind of injections. Then it was the blond newscaster again, bracketing a few seconds in which a large structure burst slowly open like a flower, spraying debris and, kind of, limbs, maybe. The blond newscaster was probably getting injections herself. I'd been noticing lines maybe trying to creep up around near my eyes, lately. But even when I was a little child I felt that people who worry about that sort of thing are petty. Of course, when I was a little child I wasn't about to be getting sneak attacks from lines anytime soon. Hi, Nana, I said, sure you're okay with this stuff? But she just kept gazing at the images supplanting each other in front of her.

One way or another it had gotten to be a few months since Bill had called to tell me about Nana's initial stroke. I'd intended to come right out to see her, but it wasn't all that easy to arrange for a free week, and Jeff and I were having sort of vaguely severe money problems, and I just didn't manage to put a trip together until Bill called again and said that this time it was really serious. I reached over and rested my hand on Nana's. Nana had pretty much looked out for us—me and Bill and Peter—when our mother got sick (well, died, really) and our father started spending all his money on cars and driving them into things. If it hadn't been for Nana, who knows what would have happened to us.

Nana gave my hand a brief, speculative look that detached it from hers, and then she turned back to the TV. From what closet had that old apparatus been unearthed? Nana had always gotten her news from the *Times*, as far as I knew, and other periodicals. I wondered what she was seeing. Was it just that the shifting black-and-white patterns engaged her attention, or did she recognize them as information and find solace in an old habit of receiving it? Or did she still have some comprehension of what was happening in front of her?

Enormous crowds were streaming through streets. Refugees! I thought for an instant, my hands tingling. Evacuations! But a lot of the people were carrying large placards or banners,

I saw, and I realized this must be one of the protests—there was the capitol building, and then something changed and the Eiffel Tower was in the distance, and then there was something that looked like Parliament, and then for a second, a place I couldn't identify at all, and then another where there were mostly Asians. The apartment was stifling! Despite the horrible freezing weather I got up to open the window a crack. When I sat down again, Nana spoke. Her voice used to have a penetrating, rather solid sound, something like an oboe's, but now there were a lot of new threadlike cracks in it—it was hoarse, and strange. I suppose you have no idea how I happen to be here, she said. This is where you live, Nana, I said, in case she'd been speaking to me; this is your home. Nana examined my face—dispassionately, I think would be the exact right word. No wonder my father had been terrified of her when he was growing up! *Thank you*, she said, apropos of what, who could say. She folded her hands primly and ceased to see me.

My brain rolled up into a tube and my childhood rushed through it, swift pictures of coming here to this apartment with my mother and father and Peter and Bill—swift-moving, decisive Nana, smelling simply beautiful when she leaned down to me, and her big, pretty teeth, and all the shiny, silver hair she could twist up and pin in place in a second with some fantastic ornament. The ornate silver tea service, the delicate slice of lemon floating and dreaming away in the fragile cup, the velvet chairs, the painting of the mysterious, beautiful, leafy world on the wall that you could practically just *enter* . . . the light, as soon as you opened the door, of a different time, the lovely, strange, tarnished light that had existed before I was born . . . Translucent scraps of coming to see Nana went whirling through the tube and were gone. Nana, I said.

Doll-like figures sprayed into the air, broke open and

poured out blackness. There was a bulldozer, and stuff crumbling. Eileen came in. Would I like a cup of tea, she asked me. Thanks, I told her, no. She paused for a moment before she went away again, squinting at the screen. Well, who knows, she said. But I'm glad I don't have sons.

Nana had come into the world at the end of one war and lived through part of another before she left Europe, so she must have seen plenty of swarming crowds in her time and crumbling stuff and men in uniforms and little black pinpricks puncturing the clear sky and swelling right up. Jeff and I don't have a TV. Jeff doesn't like anything about TV. The way the sets look, or the sound it makes, or what it does to your brain. He says he's not so dumb that he thinks he can outsmart the brainwashing. He likes to keep his brain clean all by himself, and it does have a sparkly, pristine quality, despite the fact that it's a bit squashed by events at the moment, which occasionally causes him to make remarks that could be considered vaguely inappropriate. For example, the other day we were going up in the elevator of the office building where Jeff and his team do their research, and there was a guy standing next to us, wearing a light blue kind of churchy suit, and Jeff turned and said, sort of to him, in a low voice, It's sunset.

The guy glanced at Jeff and then at his watch. He had really nice eyes—candid, I think you'd say. He glanced at Jeff again and said, Would you mind pushing seven? Jeff said, Yup, the sun is setting, you guys at the helm. He pushed seven and turned back to the guy. See it sink toward the horizon, he said, feel the planet turn? Hear the big bones crunch at the earth's hot core? The woolly mammoths, the dinosaurs, hear that? The fossil fuels sloshing? Crunch, crunch, slosh, slosh, Dinosaur Sunset Lullaby? I nodded to the guy when he got out at seven, but he wasn't looking. Normally, Jeff is very cogent, and

REVENGE OF THE DINOSAURS

he's amazingly quick to spot the specious remark or spurious explanation, especially, these days, if I'm the one who's made it. I don't especially mind having a TV around myself, but my concentration isn't all that terrific in certain ways and I really can't get myself to sit down and follow what's going on in that little square window, so maybe I'm not as vulnerable to assault as Jeff is. But if someone turns a TV on in a bar, for example, I don't just have to run out screaming.

So obviously, I never actually see a TV unless we happen to go out, which we really can't spare the money to do these days, even if we were to feel like it (which Jeff certainly doesn't). But TV or not, I had no trouble recognizing those faces appearing in front of me as I sat there next to Nana. I suppose everyone knows those faces as well as if they were tattooed on the inside of one's eyelids. There they are, those guys, whether your eyes are open or shut.

Gigantic helicopters were nosing at some mountains. I felt worn out. Flying is no joke at all these days! The interrogations at the airport, and worrying about the nail scissors, and those dull boomings, even though you know it's only luggage getting vaporized, and then when you finally do get mashed into place on the clanking, rickety old thing, with your blood clotting up, and the awful artificial, recirculated whatever it is, air or what-ever, who doesn't think of great chunks of charred metal falling from the sky. Oh, well. I'd gotten to Nana's in any case.

A recollection of my father and Nana sitting in this room back when they were on viable terms, drinking something from fragile, icy little shot glasses, pressed itself urgently upon me. Though of course, when Bill finally did stride in, allow-ing his overcoat to slip off into Eileen's hands, Peggy behind him, I was glad enough not to be sprawled out hiccuping. You beat me, Bill said, and kind of whacked me a bit on the back, that's a first. Unfair, I said, when am I ever late these days? How would I know? Bill said. You live on the other side of the country.

Peggy was carrying an enormous vase full of lilies, a funereal flower if ever there was one. Hi, Peggy, I said. Some flowers you've got there. Melinda here, too? Hi, Aunt Lulu, Melinda called from the hall, where she was studying the magical glade. I had a sudden memory of the guy who'd given Nana that painting—Mr. Berman. What a handsome old man! He was one of Nana's suitors after she booted out Dad's dad. Dad used to refer to Mr. Berman as the Great Big Jew. Mr. Berman was very nice, as I remember, and rich and handsome, but Nana was sick of getting married, so he moved on, and Nana never looked back, I think. It wasn't in her nature.

Peggy was staring at the TV. Goodness me, she said, and picked up the remote. A few sluttish teenagers flounced around a room with studio decor. That's better, Peggy said. She chuckled wanly. I calculated: the big gloomy bouquet must have cost about what I make in a week. Hey, Melinda, I said, as she wandered into the room; they brought you along, great. My sitter's mad at me, she said, they didn't have any choice. She looked at me—Alternative? Sure, I said, that's fine: they didn't have any alternative. The hell we didn't, Bill said. We could have left her on a mountain with her ankles pierced. Melinda swiveled her head toward him, then swiveled it back. Your father's just being funny, I said. You thought that was funny, Aunt Lulu? Melinda said. Cute outfit, hon, Peggy told me, fanciful; the fun shirt is what? Pucci, I said, early seventies? An as-is—there's a cigarette burn, see?

Hey, Granana, Melinda said, watchin' a show, huh. She peered at Nana scientifically and waggled her fingers in a little wave. Then she walked backward into the sofa and plopped

down, showing her teeth for a moment as though she'd performed a trick. So what's going on? she asked no one in particular.

There were about five teenagers. One was a boy. They
were all making faces and pausing for the silent audience to
laugh, apparently. Peggy, who had a gift, rubbed Nana's hands
and sort of chattered. Nana looked around and spoke in the
strange voice that sounded like it had been shut away, gathering dust. Everyone, she said. Hi, Nana! we all said. Hello,
Lulu, dear, she said, are you here? She blinked once, like a
cat, and yawned. It was an odd sight, our elegant Nana's body
and its needs taking precedence that way. She looked back at
the TV, and said, What.

What the hell is this? Bill said, squinting at the flouncing,
mugging teenagers. He flicked the remote, and there were those
familiar guys again, standing around a podium beneath a huge
flag. Bill grunted, and set the remote back on the table with a
sharp little click. He forgot about the TV and started ranging
around the room, absently picking up objects and turning them
over, as though he was expecting to see price tags. Poor Bill. He
was frowning a frown, which he'd no doubt perfected in front
of his clients, that clearly referred to weighty matters. Terrible,
he was muttering; terrible, terrible, terrible, terrible. His feelings for Nana were complicated, I knew (though he didn't seem
to), heavily tinged with rage and resentment, like his feelings for
everyone else. Our brother Peter was the quote unquote outstanding one, so Bill, as the other boy, had naturally suffered a
lot growing up and was kind of arrested, being so compensato-
rily dutiful. He looked as if he was incredibly tired, too. Poor
Nana, he said. Poor, poor, poor Nana.

Trip okay, hon? Peggy asked me. Where are you staying?
One-two punch, huh, I said. You're so funny, Peggy said

vaguely. You always make me laugh. She looked tired herself. Outside, someone was making some sort of commotion. Screaming or something. Bill went to the window and closed it. Listen, he said to me, thank you for coming. He had already acquired a drink, I noticed—how had he managed that? I'm glad to be here, I said; it's natural, isn't it? You don't have to thank me. Good, he said. He frowned his frown again. I'm glad you decided to come. Because decisions have to be made, and I wanted us to be united. Against? I said.

Against? he said. Decisions have to be made and I wanted you to be part of the process.

I've had a lot of practice in not getting pissed off at Bill, who can't help his patronizing, autocratic nature. I reminded myself severely (a) that he's just a poor trembling soul, trying to keep himself together in whatever way he can, that I should appreciate that it was Bill, obviously, who was dealing with Nana's whole thing here, and (b) that I wouldn't want to start regressing all over the place. Thanks, I said. Thanks for including me.

Bill nodded, I nodded.

Thanks for including me, I said again. But I don't have anything to contribute, remember?

I never *said* that, he said. I *never* said that you don't have anything to contribute. Be straightforward for a moment. Do you think you could be straightforward for a moment? That's merely the construction you chose to put on a perfectly harmless suggestion I made once—once!—that you might try just a little harder, in certain circumstances. We'll go into another room for a minute, shall we, you and I?

Melinda and I will stay right here with your nana, said Peggy, who has a sort of genius for pointless remarks. Bill and I strolled down the long hall to the dining room. I don't sup-

pose you happen to know where the, um, liquor cabinet is, I
said. What is it you require, Bill said, absinthe? There's not
enough stuff right over there on the credenza? Huh? I said.
He said, That's what it's called, a credenza—is that all right
with you? I said, Maybe you could be a little straightforward
yourself. He said, Sorry. I'm under a lot of, um . . .

Poor Bill. Obviously Dad wasn't going to be pitching in
here. Or Peter, who's in Melbourne these days. Peter left the
whole scene practically as soon as he could *walk*. When Peter
was little everyone thought he'd be the one to find a cure for
cancer, but he became sort of an importer instead, of things that
are rare wherever he happens to be living, so he can be away all
the time. From anywhere. Away, away. Away away away away
away. Bill at least gets some satisfaction in thinking Peter's work
is trivial—which really makes Jeff snicker, since Bill works for
insurance companies, basically figuring out why they don't have
to pay the policyholders. Now, *there's* something trivial, Jeff
said. But then he said no, actually, that it wasn't trivial at all, was
it, it was huge. And that Peggy was even worse than Bill, because Bill was born exploitative and venal and he can't help it,
but Peggy actually *cultivates* those qualities.

I remember once, in this very apartment, overhearing
Nana telling my father that he was weak and that he resorted
to the weapon of the weak—violent rage—and that he used
his charm to disguise the fact that he was always just about to
do whatever would make everyone most miserable. I provided you with grandchildren, Dad told her. Does that make
you miserable? I thought that was what every mother wanted
from her child. How can you complain about your grandchildren?

How? Nana said. Peter is brilliant, but damaged. Lucille
is certainly well meaning, and she isn't a ninny, despite

appearances, but she's afraid of reality just like you. Only *she* expresses it in immaturity, laziness, confusion, and mental passivity.

Well, that was a long, long time ago, of course, but I still remember feeling kind of sick and how quiet it was. It was so quiet I could hear the foliage in the painting rustle and the silvery dust particles clashing together. What about Bill, my father said. Surely you don't intend to spare Bill? Even from behind the door where I was hiding, I could hear Nana sigh. Poor Bill, she said. That poor, poor Bill.

Hey, that's my brother you're talking about, I told Jeff when he criticized Bill, but the fact is, I guess I did that thing that people say people do. Which is that one quality I evidently sought out in my lover is a quality that runs in my family—the quality of having a lot of opinions about other people. Low opinions, specifically.

And Nana would have to recognize now, if she were only compos, that Bill had taken charge of her well-being all by himself, and that he was doing a pretty good job of it. Eileen, for example. Eileen seemed terrific, nothing wrong with Eileen. Listen! I said to Bill. Listen, I want to tell you this with complete sincerity: I know you've had to deal with a lot here, and I'm really, truly sorry I haven't been much help. How could you have been any help? Bill said. You live on the other side of the country.

And besides, I said.

Bill did something with his jaw that made it click. There were dust covers over the chairs. He pulled one aside and sat down. Then he got up and pulled another aside for me. When did she stop going out? I said. When did she stop going out, he said, hooking the words up like the cars of a little toy train, when did she stop going out. When she stopped being able to walk, Lucille? After her first stroke? Kind of hard to get around if you can't walk.

Well, I guess I assumed she'd use a wheelchair or something, I said. Or that someone would take her. A driver, or someone.

Anyhow, she didn't want to see anyone, he said. I told you that, I know I told you that. And more to the point I suppose, she didn't want anyone to see her.

Bill was looking stricken. The fact is, Nana was an amazing person, even if she had been pretty rough with our father, who obviously deserved it anyway. She had seen a lot in her life, she'd experienced a lot, but from all those experiences there weren't going to be many, you might say, artifacts, except for, oh, the tea service and maybe a bit of jewelry and a few pamphlets or little books, I guess, that she'd written for the institute (foundation?) she worked with. At. With. At. *The tradition of liberal humanism,* I remember Dad saying once, with hatred, as though something or other. Anyhow, there wasn't going to be much for the world to remember our shiny Nana by, except for example her small, hard, rectangular book on currency. It's incredible, I can't ever quite wrap my head around it—that each life is amazingly abundant, no matter what, and every moment of experience is so intense. But so little evidence of that exists outside the living body! Billions of intense, abundant human lives on this earth, Nana's among them, vanishing. Leaving nothing more than inscrutable little piles of commemorative trash.

I could see that Bill was suffering from those thoughts, too. I put a hand on his arm and said, She didn't want people to see her, but she let *you* see her.

Bill flushed. I don't count, he said.

As far back as I can remember, he was subject to sudden

flashes of empathy that made him almost ill for a moment, after which he was sure to behave as if someone had kicked the KICK ME sign on his rear end. Anyhow, you and I have to make some decisions, he said. Like what? I said.

He gave me plenty of time to observe his expression.

Do you know how much this sort of private care costs? he said. Sure, she was well-to-do by your standards. And by mine. But you might pause to consider what will have happened to her portfolio in this last year or so. Mine will go back up in due course, yours will go back up— Portfolio? I said. But hers won't, Bill said. She doesn't have the time. In another year, if she lives, she'll be propped up over a subway grating in the freezing cold with a paper cup to collect change. So the point is that every single thing here has to be decided. And it has to be decided either by *us*, or by *me*. None of it's going to happen automatically. Honestly, Lulu—you still don't seem to get it. How do you think Nana came by her nurses? Do you think they just showed up on the doorstep one morning?

Bill rubbed the bridge of his nose as if *I* were the one having the tantrum. The point is, he said, there seems to be no chance of significant recovery. So what will happen with her things, for example? Who will go through her papers? Can we find a better place for her to be? These are decisions.

These were *not* decisions, I didn't bother to point out to Bill, who was looking really *so* pathetic with his silly jacket and premature potbelly, they were questions. This is Nana's apartment, I said. This is where she lives. We can't just, what, send her off on an ice floe.

I appreciate your horror of the sordid mechanics, Bill said. But stay on task, please, focus. I mean, driver! Good lord, Lulu. *What* driver? You know, Geoff is a fine man, I like Geoff, and it's a big relief to see you settled down, finally, with someone other than a blatant madman. But Geoff is as impractical as you are. More impractical, if possible. He takes an extreme view of things, and I know he encourages you in that as well.

I'm capable of forming my own extreme views, I said. And if you're referring to the tree painting project, it was hardly *extreme*. We all just picked one tree that was going to be deforested, and commemorated that particular tree in paint. I don't call that *extreme*.

I agree, Bill said. It's perfectly harmless. And that's great, because you have to be prudent. Courage is one thing, and simplistic rashness is another. There are lists, you know. Lists, lists, lists.

Simplistic *rashness*? I said. You know what Jeff has been doing, you know what he's been studying! I was shouting at Bill but I was thinking about poor Jeff, lying in bed this last month or so, scrawling on sheets of paper. When I'd urge him to eat, he'd start intoning statistics—how many babies born with this, how many babies born with that. I know, I said the other day, I know; don't tell *me*, tell *them*. We've *told* them, he said, that's why they cut off the funding! He did manage to write a song or two about it, at least, and he sang one on his friend Bobby Baines's 6 a.m. radio slot. You'd be surprised what Jeff can wrap a good tune around. I wish he'd get back to his music. It used to be so much fun, hanging out with his band. My mouth was still open, I noticed, and yelling at my brother. The funding's been cut off, my mouth was yelling. For the whole study! And now they're saying, Depleted uranium, wow, it's great for you, sprinkle it on your breakfast cereal! Is it any wonder Jeff isn't a barrel of laughs these days? Is it any wonder he's on a short fuse? Extreme! You're the one who's extreme! I can absolutely *hear* how you're trying to pretend his name is spelled! Jeff is *Jewish*, okay? Do you think you can handle it? His name is Jeff with a J, not Waspy, Waspy Geoff with a G, but every time you send us so much as a note, it's Dear Lulu and Geoff with a G!

Bill was just standing there with his arms folded. At least I send the occasional note, he said. And please don't pretend you don't know what a portfolio is. Please, please don't.

We looked at each other for a long, empty moment. The Corot will have to be sold, he said.

Sold, I said.

Well, I don't know why it should have made a difference to me. Sold, not sold—it wasn't as if I could have hung the thing up on our stained, peeling wall or whatever. But still! That word—sold! It's like inadvertently knocking over a glass!

Sold, Bill said. The jewelry's already been sold. Eek, I said. Who knew. Oops, sorry, you did, I get it, I get it, I get it, I abase myself and so on. Bill cleared his throat. Anyhow, he said.

He gestured at the cloth-draped room. Obviously, there's a lot of stuff left, but none of it's worth anything to speak of. Peggy's researched pretty thoroughly. Still, if there's anything you want, now's the time to claim it.

Now's the time. Now's the time. Who wants to hear that about anything? Thanks, I said.

Was there anything of Nana's I'd ever particularly coveted? I closed my eyes. Wow, to think that Nana had been showing Eileen that clipping of me and and my tree and my painting! Okay, so maybe the project hadn't been so effective, but at least there'd been a clipping! Had Nana been proud? Did she think I looked nice? Wait a minute, I said, Nana's still alive! You get no argument from me there, Bill said. But how much of this stuff do you think she's going to be using from now on? Do you think she'll be using the tea service, for example?

The tea service? I said. Do you want the tea service? he said. The tea service! I said. That great, big, hulking, silver thing? What on earth would I do with the tea service? How on earth do you think Jeff and I are living, out there in the woods? Calm down, Lucille, Bill said, for heaven's sake. Please don't go Dad's route.

Why on earth are we talking about the tea service? I yelled. Excuse me a minute.

I went into the kitchen, where Eileen was sitting, grabbed a glass from the cupboard, and clattered some ice cubes into it from a tray in the freezer. Excuse me, I said. Help yourself, dear, Eileen said.

There was a printed notice stuck to the door of the fridge with a magnet that looked like a cherry. Do Not Resuscitate, the notice said. Oh, shit, I said.

Eileen nodded. She's a lovely lady, your grandmother, she said, but I just kept looking at her, as though I were going to see something other than a nurse in a white uniform sitting there.

When I went back out to the dining room it appeared that Bill had gone back to the others, so I made a pit stop at the cruh-*den*-za to fill my glass and returned to the living room myself.

Anyhow, we weren't talking about the tea service, Bill said, *you* were talking about the tea service.

The tea service? Peggy said.

Want it? I said.

That's so sweet of you, hon, Peggy said.

Bill flashed an expression just like one of Dad's—pure gleeful, knowing malevolence. He'd obviously stopped by the good old credenza himself again and was gulping away at his tumbler. Eileen came in and helped Nana drink a glass of water with something in it to make it thick enough for her to swallow, and gave her a pill. A little water dribbled from the corner of Nana's mouth. Nana didn't appear to notice it. Eileen wiped it away, and then wiped at something leaking from Nana's eye. Melinda had her hands over her ears. Those *airplanes!* she said, I can't stand the sound of those *airplanes!* Why are there so many airplanes here?

Oh, don't fuss, Melinda, Peggy said, there are airports in New York City, and so naturally there are airplanes. And in any case, that's a helicopter, Bill said. Is it going to drop a bomb on us? Melinda said. Don't be silly, sweetie, Peggy said, they're not dropping bombs on us, we're dropping bombs on them.

Helicopters don't drop bombs, Melinda, Bill said, they're probably looking for someone. Who? Melinda said. The police, Bill said, hear those sirens? No, but who are the policemen looking *for?* Melinda said with her hands over her ears again. How would your mother and I know who the policemen are looking for? Bill said. Some criminal, I suppose.

Melinda flopped over, facedown onto the sofa, and let out a muffled wail. Just calm down, please, Melinda, Peggy said. You're upsetting your great-grandmother. Melinda cast a glance at Nana, who was gazing levelly at the images I'd seen earlier of the gracefully exploding building. I wondered where the building was—what country, for instance.

Things were always occurring suddenly and decisively inside the TV. Another building, for example, was just getting sheared off as we watched, from an even taller one standing next to it. Why is everyone always so mad at me? Melinda said.

I'm not mad at you, I said. Are you mad at Melinda? I asked Bill and Peggy. Of course not, Peggy said. You are, too, Melinda said. We are not *angry* with you, Peggy said. And I've told you repeatedly that when you pay for the paint job, you can put tape wherever you like.

I was doing it for you! Melinda said. I was just doing it for you! She turned to me. It said to do it, she said. It said to get tape and put plastic over the windows because of the poison, and my sitter was up in my room with her boyfriend so I got the tape from the drawer and some garbage bags, and then Stacy was mad at me, too, even though I didn't tell that she and Brett were upstairs having—

I don't want you talking like that, Peggy said. About Stacy or anyone else, young lady. Girls in real life don't behave like television floozies. I'm limiting your viewing time.

What did I *say*, what did I *say*? Melinda said and lapsed into loud, tearing wails that sounded like she was ripping up a piece of rotting fabric. Stop it, Melinda! Peggy said. Stop that right this instant— You're getting hysterical!

She's so theatrical, Peggy said to me, rolling her eyes. She put her arms around Melinda, who continued crying loudly. There's no reason to get so *excited*, Melinda, she said, you're just overtired.

Soldiers were marching across the screen again. Peggy was gazing at them absently, her chin resting on Melinda's soft hair. Was Melinda going to be a numbskull like her parents? I wondered, but then I reminded myself how much stress Peggy and Bill were under, worrying about Nana all the time, and whatever. Peggy was looking so tired and sad, just gazing droopily at the screen. She sighed. I sighed. She sighed. Do you remember when people could have veal chops whenever they wanted? she said. Bill had a yen for veal chops yesterday, so I went to the market and I practically had to take out a *mortgage*.

Are we poor? Melinda said, and hiccuped. Ask your mother, Bill said, looking like Dad again. Peggy glared at him.

I was trying to remember what Nana wrote in her little book on currency . . . *fixed, floating, imports, exports, economies* . . . And then I tried to remember what exactly had happened in the last wars we'd fought, or anyhow, in the last vaguely recent ones—just who exactly was involved, and so on. So many facts! So much new information always coming out about these things, after they've occurred. It's pretty hard to keep straight just what's been destroyed where and how many were killed. Well, I guess it's not that hard for the people who live in those places. And Jeff always has a pretty solid grasp on that stuff, and Nana sure used to . . . I wondered what she thought she was looking at now, if she thought she was actually seeing back, seeing pictures from her own life—memories, the inside of her own head . . . She seemed to be focusing on the screen so intently, as if she were concentrating on some taxing labor. Really working out what that screen was showing. Well, that was Nana! Always work work work work work. There was the sheared-off building, and the tall one still standing right next to it. I wondered what that tall building was, and I wondered what she thought it was. It looked like an office building, with black windows. Maybe Nana thought Death's office was there, behind those black windows. Maybe she pictured Death as a handsome old man in uniform, sitting at his desk and going over his charts and graphs. Behind him she'd be seeing a huge map with pins in it and his generals, with those familiar, familiar faces. He'd look tired—so much to do!—and sad. He wouldn't notice the glass tear leaking from his glass eye.

Guess we'll all be going together one of these days, Bill said. Swell, I said. You know, guys, I'm really tired. I'm going to go back downtown to Juliette's. We can talk over everything tomorrow, okay?

Do you have enough money for a taxi, Lulu? Bill said.

Do I have enough money for a taxi? Of course I have enough money for a taxi, I said. I was wishing I hadn't spent most of my last check before Jeff's funding was cut on those white Courrèges go-go boots. But discounts are about the only perk of my job, and I do have to say that the boots look pretty fabulous. Anyhow, I said, I'm going to take the subway.

The subway! Peggy said. Don't be *insane*, Lulu.

Don't die, Aunt Lulu! Melinda said.

For pity's sake, Melinda, Peggy said. No one's going to *die*.

Was I ever hoping that Wendell had finished trying to tenderize Juliette and I could just flop down on her futon! *No rest for the wicked,* Dad used to say, chortling, as he'd head out for a night on the town. (Or for the saintly, is what Jeff has to say about *that*, or for the morally indecipherable.)

Oh, look—Peggy said, pointing to the screen, where a grinning person in a white coat was standing near some glass beakers and holding what looked like a little spool—I think they must be talking about that new thread!

What new thread, what new thread? Melinda said.

That new thread, Peggy said. I read an article about this new thread that's electronic. Electronic? I think that's right. Anyhow, they've figured out how to make some kind of thread that's able to sense your skin temperature and chemical changes and things. And they're going to be able to make clothes that can monitor your body for trouble, so that if you have conditions, like diabetes, I think, or some kind of dangerous conditions, your clothes will be able to register what's going on and protect you.

That's *great*, huh, Granana, Melinda said. She threw her little arms around Nana, who closed her eyes as if she were finally taking a break.

THE FLAW IN THE DESIGN

I float back in.

The wall brightens, dims, brightens faintly again—a calm pulse, which mine calms to match, of the pale sun's beating heart. Outside, the sky is on the move—windswept and pearly—spring is coming from a distance. In its path, scraps of city sounds waft up and away like pages torn out of a notebook. Feather pillows, deep carpet, the mirror a lake of pure light—no imprints, no traces; the room remembers no one but us. "Do we have to be careful about the time?" he says.

The voice is exceptional, rich and graceful. I turn my head to look at him. Intent, reflective, he traces my brows with his finger, and then my mouth, as if I were a photograph he's come across, mysteriously labeled in his own hand-writing.

I reach for my watch from the bedside table and consider the dial—its rectitude, its innocence—then I understand the position of the hands and that, yes, rush-hour traffic will already have begun.

I pull into the driveway and turn off the ignition. Evening is descending, but inside no lights are on. The house looks unfamiliar.

It looks to me much the way it did when I saw it for the first time, years ago, before it was ours, when it was just a house the Realtor brought us to look at, all angles and sweep—flashy, and rather stark. John took to it immediately— I saw the quick alliance, his satisfaction as he ran his hand across the granite and steel. I remember, now, my faint embarrassment; I'd been taken by surprise to discover that this was what he wanted, that this was something he must have more or less been longing for.

I can just make out the shadowy figure upstairs in our bedroom. I allow myself to sit for a minute or so, then I get out of the car and close the door softly behind me.

John is at the roll-top desk, going over some papers. He might have heard me pull into the drive, or he might not have. He doesn't turn as I pause in the bedroom doorway, but he glances up when I approach to kiss him lightly on the temple. His tie is loosened; he's still in his suit. The heavy crystal tumbler is nearly full.

I turn on the desk light. "How can you see what you're doing?" I say.

I rest my hand on his shoulder and he reaches up to pat it. "Hello, sweetheart," he says. He pats my hand again, terminating, and I withdraw it. "Absolutely drowning in this stuff . . ." He rubs the bridge of his nose under his glasses frames, then directs a muzzy smile my way.

"Wouldn't it be wonderful to live in a tree," I say. "In a cave, with no receipts, no bills, no records—just no paper at all . . ." I close my eyes for a moment. Good. Eclipsed—the day has sealed up behind me. "Oh, darling—did you happen to feed Pod?"

John blinks. "No one told me."

"It's all right. I didn't expect to be so late. Maybe Oliver thought to."

Gingerly, I stroke back John's thin, pale hair. He waits rigidly. "Any news?" I ask.

"News," he says. "Nothing to speak of, really." He turns back to the desk.

"John?" I say.

"Hello, darling," he says.

"Lamb chops," Oliver observes pleasantly.

"I'm sorry, sweetie," I say. "I'm sure there's a plain pizza in the freezer, and there's some of that spinach thing left. If I had thought you'd be home tonight, I would have made something else."

"Don't I always come home, Mom?"

"'Always'?" I smile at him. "I assumed you'd be at Katie's again tonight."

"But don't I always *actually* come home? Don't I always come home *eventually*, Mom, to you?"

He seems to want me to laugh, or to pretend to, and I do. I can't ever disguise the pleasure I take in looking at him. How did John and I ever make this particular child, I always wonder. He looks absolutely nothing like either of us, with his black eyes and wild, black hair—though he does bear some resemblance to the huge oil portrait of John's grandfather that his parents have in their hallway. John's father once joked to me, are you sure you're the mother? I remember the look on John's face then—his look of reckoning, the pure coldness, as if he were calculating his disdain for his father in orderly columns. John's father noted that look, too—with a sort of gratification, I thought—then turned to me and winked.

"You're seriously not going to have any of these?" John says.

Oliver looks at the platter.

This only started recently, after Oliver went off to school. "You don't have to, darling," I say.

"You don't know what you're missing," John says.

"Hats off, Dad." Oliver nods earnestly at his father. "Philosophically watertight."

Recently, John has developed an absent little laugh to carry him past these moments with Oliver, and it does seem to me healthier, better for both of them, if John at least appears to rise above provocation.

"But don't think I'm not grateful, Mom, Dad, for the fact that we can have this beautiful dinner, in our beautiful, architecturally unimpeachable open-plan . . . *area*. And actually, Dad, I want to say how grateful I am to you in general. Don't think, just because I express myself awkwardly and my vocabulary's kind of fucked up—"

John inclines his head, with the faint, sardonic smile of expectations met.

"—Sorry, Dad. That I'm not grateful every single day for how we're able to preside as a *family* over the things of this world, and that owing to the fantastic education you've secured for me, I'll eventually be able—I mean of course with plenty of initiative and hard work or maybe with a phone call to someone from you—to follow in your footsteps and assume my rightful place on the planet, receiving beautiful Mother Earth's bounty—her crops, her oil, her precious metals and diamonds, and to cast my long, dark shadow over—"

"Darling," I say. "All right. And when you're at home, you're expected to feed Pod. We've talked about this."

Oliver clasps my wrist. "Wow, Mom, don't you find it poignant, come to think of it? I really think there's a poignancy here in this divergence of paths. Your successful son, home for a flying visit from his glamorous institution of higher education, and Pod, the companion of your son's youth, who stayed on and turned into a dog?"

"That's why you might try to remember to feed him," I say.

Oliver flashes me a smile, then ruffles grateful Pod's fur. "Poor old Pod," he says, "hasn't anyone fed you since I went away?"

"Not when you're handling food, please, Oliver," John says.

"Sorry, Dad," Oliver says, holding up his hands like an apprehended robber. "Sorry, Mom, sorry, Pod."

And there's the radiant smile again. It's no wonder that the girls are crazy about Oliver. His phone rings day and night. There are always a few racy, high-tech types running after him, as well as the attractive, well-groomed girls, so prevalent around here, who absolutely shine with poise and self-confidence—perfect girls, who are sure of their value. And yet the girls he prefers always seem to be in a bit of disarray. Sensitive, I once commented to John. "Grubby," he said.

"Don't you want the pizza?" I say. "I checked the label *scrupulously*—I promise."

"Thanks, Mom. I'm just not really hungry, though."

"I wish you would eat something," I can't help saying.

"Oh—but listen, you guys!" Oliver says. "Isn't it sad about Uncle Bob?"

"Who?" John says. He gets up to pour himself another bourbon.

"Uncle Bob? Bob? Uncle Bob, your old friend Bob Alpers?"

"Wouldn't you rather have a glass of wine, darling?" I ask.

"No," John says.

"Was Alpers testifying today?" I ask John. "I didn't realize. Did you happen to catch any of it?"

John shrugs. "A bit. All very tedious. When did this or

that memo come to his attention, was it before or after such and such a meeting, and so on."

"Poor Bob," I say. "Who can remember that sort of thing?"

"Who indeed," John says.

"We used to see so much of Uncle Bob and Aunt Caroline," Oliver says.

"That's life," John says. "Things change."

"That's a wise way to look at things, Dad." Oliver nods seriously. "It's, really, I mean . . . *wise*."

"I'm astonished that you remember Bob Alpers," I say. "It's been a long time since he and your father worked together. It's been years."

"We never did work together," John says. "Strictly speaking."

Oliver turns to me. "That was back when Uncle Bob was in the whatsis, Mom, right? The private sector? And Dad used to consult?"

John's gaze fixes on the table as if he were just daring it to rise.

"But I guess you still do that, don't you, Dad—don't you still consult?"

"As you know. I consult. People who know something about something 'consult,' if you will. People hire people who know things about things. What are we saying here?"

"I'm just saying, poor Uncle Bob—"

"Where did this 'uncle' business come from?" John says.

"Let me give you some salad at least, darling. You'll eat some salad, won't you?" I put a healthy amount on Oliver's plate for him.

"I mean, picture the future, the near, desolate future," Oliver says. He shakes his head and trails off, then reaches over, sticks a finger absently right into a trickle of blood on the platter, and resumes. "There's Uncle Bob, wandering around in the night and fog, friendless and alone . . ."

John's expression freezes resolutely over as Oliver walks his fingers across the platter, leaving a bloody track.

"A pariah among all his former friends," Oliver continues, getting up to wash his hands. "Doors slam in his face, the faithless sycophants flee . . . How is poor Uncle Bob supposed to live? He can't get a job, he can't get a job bussing tables! And all just because of these . . . phony *allegations*." John and I reflexively look over at one another, but our glances bounce apart. "I mean, wow, Dad, you must know what it's like out there! You must be keeping up with the unemployment stats! It's *fierce*. Of course *I'll* be fine, owing to my outrageous abundance of natural merit or possibly to the general, um, esteem, Dad, in which you're held, but gee whiz, I mean, some of my ridiculous friends are worried to the point of throwing really up about what they're all going to do when they graduate, and yet their problems *pale* in comparison to Uncle *Bob's*."

"Was there some dramatic episode I missed today?" I say.

"Nothing," John says. "Nothing at all. Just nonsense."

"I just don't see that Bob could have been expected to foresee the problems," I say.

"Well, that's the *reasonable* view," John says. "But some of the regulations are pretty arcane, and if people are out to get you, they can make fairly routine practices look very bad."

"Oh, dear," I say. "What Caroline must be going through!"

"There's no way this will stick," John says. "It's just grandstanding."

"Gosh, Dad, that's great. Because I was somehow under the impression, from the— I mean, due to the— That is, because of the—"

"Out with it, Oliver," John says. "We're all just people, here."

"—the *evidence*, I guess is what I mean, Dad, that Bob *knew* what that land was being used for. But I guess it was all, just, what did you call that, Dad? 'Standard practice,' right?"

John looks at him. "What I said was—"

"Oops, right, you said '*routine practices*,' didn't you. Sorry, that's *different*! And anyhow, you're right. How on earth could poor Bob have guessed that those silly peasants would make such a fuss, when KGS put the land to such better use than they ever had? *Beans?* I mean, *please*. Or that KGS would be so sensitive about their lousy, peasant sportsmanship and maybe overreact a bit? You know what? We should console Uncle Bob in his travails, open up our family to receive him in the warmth of our love, let him know that we feel his pain. Would Uncle Bob ever hurt a fly? He would not! Things just have a way of *happening*, don't they! And I think we should invite Uncle Bob over, for one last piece of serious *meat*, before he gets hauled off to the slammer."

John continues simply to look at Oliver, whose eyes gleam with excitement. When I reach over and touch John's hand, he speaks. "I applaud your compassion, Oliver. But no need to squander it. I very much doubt it's going to come to that."

"Really?" Oliver says. "You do? Oh, I see what you mean. That's great, Dad. You mean that if it seems like Uncle Bob might start naming names, he'll be able to retire in style, huh."

"*Ooo*okay," John says. "*All* right," and a white space cleaves through my brain as if I'd actually slapped Oliver, but in fact Oliver is turning to me with concern, and he touches my face. "What's the matter, Mom? Are you all right?"

"I'm fine, darling," I say. He reaches for my hand and holds it.

"You went all pale," he says.

"I applaud your interest in world affairs," John says. "But as the situation is far from simple, and as neither you nor I were *there* at the time, perhaps we should question, just this once—this once!—whether we actually have the right to sit in judgment. This will blow over in no time, Oliver, I'm happy to be able to promise you, and no one will be the worse for it. And should the moment arrive in which reason reasserts its check on your emotions, you will see that this spectacle is nothing more than a witch hunt."

"Well, *that's* good," Oliver says. "I mean, it's bad. Or it's good, it's bad, it's—"

"Do you think we might cross off and move on?" John says.

"Sure thing, Dad," Oliver says, dropping my hand.

John and Oliver appear to ripple briefly, and then a cottony silence drops over us. Even if I tried, I doubt I would be able to remember what we'd just been saying.

Oliver prongs some salad, and John and I watch as he lifts it slowly toward his mouth. It actually touches his lips, when he puts it down abruptly, as if he's just remembered something important. "So!" He beams at us. "What did you gentle people do today?"

John pauses, then gathers himself. "The office, naturally. Then I caught a bit of the hearings, as I have to surmise that you and Kate did."

"We did, Dad, that's very astute." Oliver nods seriously again, then turns to me with that high-watt smile. "Your turn, Mom."

"I went into town," I say. I stand up suddenly and walk over to the fridge, balancing myself on my fingertips against the reflective steel surface, in which I appear as a smudge. "I had an urge to go to the museum." I open the fridge as if I were looking for something, let the cool settle against me for a moment, close the door, and return to the table.

"You look so pretty, Mom!" Oliver says childishly. "Isn't Mom pretty, Dad?"

"Your mother was the prettiest girl at all the schools around," John says wearily. For a moment, we all just sit there again, as if someone had turned off the current, disengaging us.

"And what about you, Oliver?" John asks. "What news?"

"None," Oliver says, spearing some salad again.

"None?" John says. "Nothing at all happened today."

Oliver rests the fork on his plate and squints into the distance. "Gosh, Dad." He turns to John, wide-eyed. "I think that's right—nothing at all! Oh, unless you count my killing spree in Katie's physics class."

"Seriously not funny," John says.

"Whoops, sorry," Oliver says, standing up and stretching. "Anyhow, don't worry, Dad—I cleaned your gun and put it nicely back in the attic."

"*Enough,*" John says.

"You bet, Dad." Oliver bends down to kiss first John and then me. "I'm going upstairs now, to download some pornography. See you fine folks later."

The moon is a cold, sizzling white tonight, caustically bright. Out the window everything looks like an X-ray; the soft world of the day is nowhere to be seen.

"When did you last talk to him about seeing Molnar?"

John is sitting at the desk again. I glance at him then turn back to the window.

"He won't," I say.

"What are you looking at?" John says.

I close the blinds. "He won't see Dr. Molnar. He won't agree to see anyone. He doesn't want to take anything. He seems to be afraid it will do something to his mind." I sit down on the bed. Then I get up and sit down at the dressing table.

"Do something to his mind?" John says. "Isn't that desirable? I treat him with kid *gloves*. I'm *concerned*. But this is getting out of hand, don't you think? The raving, the grandiosity, the needling—wallow, wallow, atone, atone, avenge, avenge. And this morbid obsession with the hearings! Thank you, I do not understand what this is all about—what are we all supposed to be so tainted with? We may none of us be perfect, but one tries; one does, in my humble opinion, one's best. And explain to me, please, what the kid is doing here—what's his excuse? He should be at school."

"Darling, it's normal for a college student to want to come home from time to time."

"He's hardly 'home' in any case. For the last three days he's been with Kate every second she's not at school or asleep. I wouldn't be surprised if he actually did go to her physics class today. Why the Ericksons put up with it, I can't imagine. Have you seen that girl lately? She looks positively, what . . . *furtive*. Furtive and drained, as though she were . . . feeding some beast on the sly. What does he do to them? These wounded birds of his! It's as if he's running a hospital, providing charity transfusions to ailing vampires. That Schaeffer girl last year—my god! And before her that awful creature who liked to take razor blades to herself."

"Darling," I say. "Darling? This is a hard world for young people."

"If any human being leads an easy life, it's that boy. Attention, education, privilege—what does he lack? He lacks nothing. The whole planet was designed for his well-being."

"Well, it's stressful to be away at school. To be studying all the time and encountering so many new ideas. And all young people like to dramatize themselves."

"I didn't," John says. "And you didn't."

That's true, I realize. John took pains, in fact, to behave unexceptionably, and I was so shy I would hardly have wanted to call attention to myself with so much as a hair ribbon. I certainly didn't want drama! I wanted a life very much like the one I'd grown up with, a life like my parents'—a cozy old house on a sloping lawn, magnolias and lilacs, the sun like a benign monarch, the fragrance of a mown lawn, the pear tree a gentle torch against the blue fall sky, sleds and the children's bicycles out front, no more than that, a music box life, the chiming days.

"Young people go through things. I don't think we should allow ourselves to become alarmed. He hasn't lost his sense of humor, after all, and—"

"His—ex*cuse* me?"

"—and his grades certainly don't reflect a problem. I know you're thinking of what's best for him, I know you've benefited, but he's very afraid of medication. I don't think he should be forced to—"

"No one's forcing anyone to do anything here," John says. "*Jesus.*"

"John, we don't really have a gun in the house, do we?"

"Oh for god's sake," John says. "We don't even *really* have an attic."

"Just try to be patient with him," I say. "He loves you, darling—he respects you."

"I rue the day I ever agreed to work outside of the country," John says.

"Oh, John, don't say that darling! Even when it was difficult, it was a fascinating life for us all. And Oliver was very happy."

"I *curse* the day," John says.

Strange . . . Yes, strange to think that we used to move around so much. And then we came back and settled down here, in a government town, where everyone else is always moving. Every four years, every eight years, a new population. And yet, everyone who arrives always looks just the same as the ones who left—as if it were all a giant square dance.

"What?" John says.

"How did Bob look?" I ask.

"Bob?" he says. "Older."

Driving back along the highway this afternoon, flowing along in the reflections on the windshield, the shadows of the branches—it was like being underwater. Morning, evening, from one shore to the other, the passage between them is your body.

I stroke Oliver's hair, but his jaw is clamped tightly shut and he's staring up at the ceiling, his eyes glazed with tears.

When he was little, he and I used to lie on his bed like this and often I'd read to him, or tell him stories, and he liked to pretend that he and I were characters from the stories—an enchanted prince and a fairy, the fairy who put the spell on him or the one who removes it, or Hansel and Gretel, and we would hide under the covers from whatever wicked witch. His imagination was so vivid that sometimes I even became frightened myself.

Yesterday I was sorting through some papers upstairs at my desk, when I noticed him and Kate outside on the lawn. He was holding the lapels of her jacket and they were clearly talking, as they always seem to be, with tremendous serious-ness, as if they were explorers calculating how to survive on their last provisions. I could see Kate's round, rather sweet face—at least it's sweet when it's not flickering with doubts, worries, fears—and then Oliver held her to him, and all I could see of her was her shiny, taffy-colored hair, pinned loosely up.

It's an affecting romance. It's not likely to last long, though—none of Oliver's romances do, however intense they seem to be. Oliver is way too young. In any case, I can't help imagining a warm young woman as a daughter-in-law, some-one who would be glad for my company, rather than someone beset, as Kate always seems to be, by suspicion and resentment.

They came inside, and I could hear Oliver talking. The house was so silent I didn't have to make any effort to hear the story he was telling, a story I'd certainly never told him myself, which he must have heard from the help someplace we'd lived or stayed during our time away, a strange, winding folk tale, it seemed to be, about a man who had been granted the power to understand the language of the animals.

Oliver spoke slowly, in a searching way, as if vivid but puzzling events were being disclosed to him one by one. Kate said not a word, and I was sure that the two of them were touching in some way, lying on the sofa feet to feet, or hold-ing hands, or clasped together, looking over one another's shoulders into the glimmering mist that fans out from a story. And in the long silences I could feel her uneasiness as she waited for him to find the way to proceed.

It was as if they were sleeping, making something to-gether in their sleep—an act of memory. But I was a stranger to it, following on my own as morning after morning the poor farmer discovers the broken pots, the palm wine gone—as finally one night he waits in the dark, watching, then chases the thieving deer through the fields and hills all the way to the council of the animals—as the Leopard King, in reparations, grants him the spectacular power on condition that he never reveal it—as the farmer and his wife prosper from this power, year after year.

The story spiraled in until the farmer, now wealthy, is forced to face an enraged accuser: "I was not laughing at you," he says in desperation. "I laughed because I heard a little mouse say, *I'm so hungry—I'm going into the kitchen to steal a bit of the master's grain.*"

Oliver paused to let the story waver on its fulcrum and the shame of eavesdropping broke over me in a wave, but before I could get up and shut the door of the room or make some other alerting noise, Kate spoke. Her voice was blurred and sorrowful. "What happened then?" she said, but it was clearly less a question than a ritual acknowledgment of the impending.

"Then?" Oliver said. "So—" He seemed to awaken, and shed the memory. "—then, as all the people of the village watched, the man's lifeless body fell to the ground."

All that time we were away, during his childhood—which seems as remote to me now as the places where we were—and John was working so hard, Oliver was my companion, my darling, my *heart*. And I was shocked, I suppose, to be reminded yesterday that his childhood could not have been more different from mine, that he and I—who hardly even have to speak, often, to understand one another completely—are divided by that reality, by the differences between our earliest, most fundamental sense of the world we live in. I had never stopped to think, before, that he had heard stories from beyond the boundaries of my world. And I was really *shocked*, actually, that it was one of those stories, a story I never could have told him, that he had chosen to recount to Kate.

My gaze wanders around his pristine room, as orderly as a tribute. When he's away, no one would think of disturbing anything he has here, of course, any of his possessions. But I do sometimes come in and sit on his bed.

He's still focused at the ceiling as though he were urgently counting. "Shall I leave you alone darling?" I say. "Would you like me to leave you alone?" But he reaches for my hand.

"Oliver?" I say. "Darling?"

He blinks. His startling, long, thick eyelashes sweep down and up; his eyes glisten. "Darling, Katie is a dear girl, but sometimes I worry that she's too dependent on you. You can't be responsible for her, you know."

He draws a breath and licks his dry lips. "I can't be responsible for anything, Ma, haven't you noticed?"

"That's not true, darling. You're a very responsible person. But I just want to be sure that you and Katie are using protection."

He laughs, without lifting his head or closing his eyes, and I can tell how shallowly he's breathing. "Protection against what, Ma? Protection against Evildoers?"

"I don't want to pry, darling. I just want to set myself at ease on that score."

"Be at ease, Ma. Be very at ease. You can put down your knitting, because whatever you're fantasizing just isn't the case."

Well, I don't know. I remember, when we returned to the States, how it seemed to me, the onslaught of graphic images that are used to sell things—everywhere the perfect, shining, powerful young bodies, nearly naked, the flashing teeth, the empty, perfect, predatory faces, the threat of sexual ridicule, the spectre of sexual inadequacy if you fail to buy the critical brand of plastic wrap or insurance or macaroni and cheese.

Either the images really had proliferated and coarsened during our absence or else I had temporarily lost something that had once kept the assault from affecting me.

I became accustomed to it again soon enough, though, and I don't know that I would have remembered the feeling now, that feeling of being battered and soiled, unless I'd just been reminded of Oliver's expression when, for example, we would turn on the television and that harsh, carnal laughter would erupt.

Maybe Oliver's fastidiousness, his severity, is typical of his generation. These things come in waves, and I know that many of Oliver's friends have seen older brothers and sisters badly damaged by all sorts of excesses. And it is a fact that Oliver spent his early childhood in places where there was a certain amount of hostility toward us—not us personally, of course, but toward our culture, I suppose, as it was perceived, and it wouldn't be all that remarkable, I suppose, if his view of his native country had been tarnished before he ever really came to live in it.

There were a lot of changes occurring in all the places where John had to go, and foreigners, like ourselves, from developed countries, were seen to represent those changes. Fortunately, most of the people we encountered personally received us, and the changes that accompanied us, with great enthusiasm.

In time, it came to feel to me as though we were standing in a shrinking pool of light, with shapes moving at the edges, but, especially at first, I was delighted by the kindness, the hospitality of the local officials, by parties at the embassies. Everyone was always kind to Oliver, in any case—more than kind.

And there were always children around for Oliver to play with, the children of other people who had come to help, the engineers and agronomists and contractors of various sorts and people who were conducting studies or surveys, and children of the government officials to whose parties we went and so on, who invariably spoke English. And sometimes there would be a maid on the premises, or a gardener, who had children. But when we would drive by local markets or compounds, or even fenced-off areas, Oliver would cry—he would *scream*—to play with the children he saw outside the car window.

John would explain, quietly and tirelessly, about languages, about customs, about illnesses. We brought Oliver up to share—naturally—but how does a child *share* with another child who has nothing at all? I always thought, and I still think, that John was absolutely right to be cautious, but the fact is, when Oliver was a bit older and John was away for some days, I would sometimes relent and let Oliver play with some of the children whom, for whatever reason, he found so alluring.

Oliver had spent so little time on the planet, so all those places we went were really his life—his entire life until we came back—and maybe I didn't take adequate account of that. Sometimes now, when I hear one of those names— Nigeria, or Burma, or Ecuador—any of the names of places where we spent time—it is as lustrous to me as it was before I had ever traveled. But usually what those names bring to my mind now are only the houses where we stayed, all the houses, arranged for us by the various companies John was attached to, similarly well equipped and comfortable, where I spent so much time waiting for John and working out how to bring up a child in an unfamiliar place.

Oh, there were beautiful things, of course—many beautiful and exciting things. Startling landscapes, and the almost physical thrill of encountering unaccustomed languages and unaccustomed people, their music, their clothing, their faces, the food—the sharp, dizzying flash of possibilities revealed—trips into the hectic, noisy, astonishing towns and cities.

Sometimes, on a Sunday afternoon, when he wasn't traveling around, John liked to go to a fancy hotel if there was one in our area, and have a comically lavish lunch. Or, if we were someplace where the English had had a significant presence, a tea—which was Oliver's favorite, because of the little cakes and all the different treats and the complicated silver services.

There was the most glamorous hotel, so serene, so grand. The waiters were handsome—truly glorious—all in white linen uniforms that made their skin look like satin, dark satin. And their smiles—well, those smiles made you feel that life was worth living! And of course they were charming to Oliver, they could not have been more charming.

And there were elegant, tall windows overlooking the street, with heavy, shining glass that was very effective against the heat and noise, with long, white drapes hanging at their sides. It was really bliss to stop at that hotel, such a feeling of well-being to sip your tea, watching the silent bustle of the street outside the window. And then one afternoon, beyond the heavy glass—I was just pouring John a second cup, which I remember because I upset it, saucer and all, and could never get the spot out of my lovely yellow dress—there was a sort of explosion, and there was that dull, vast, sound of particles, unified, rising like an ocean wave, and everyone on the street was running.

Well, we were all a bit paralyzed, apparently, transfixed in our velvety little chairs—but immediately there was a *whoosh*, and the faint high ringing of the drapery hardware as the waiters rushed to draw the long, white drapes closed.

Early on, John would sometimes describe to me his vision of the burgeoning world—lush mineral fields that lie beneath the surface of the earth and the plenitude they could generate, great arteries of oil that could be made to flow to every part of the planet, immense hydroelectric dams producing cascades of energy. A degree of upheaval was inevitable, he said, painful adjustments were inevitable, but one had to keep firmly in mind the long-term benefits—the inevitable increases in employment and industry, the desperately needed revenues.

Well, in practice things are never as clear, I suppose, as they are in the abstract; things that are accomplished have to *get* accomplished in one way or another. And in fairly fluid situations, certain sorts of people will always find opportunities. And that, of course, is bound to affect everyone involved, to however slight a degree.

In any case, eventually there was a certain atmosphere. And there were insinuations in the press and rumors about the company John was working with, and it just wasn't fun for John anymore.

It was an uncomfortable, silent ride to the airport when we finally did come back for good. I remember Oliver staring out the window at the shanties and the scrub and the barbed wire as John drove. There was a low, black billowing in the sky to one side of us, fire in the distance, whether it was just brush or something more—crops or a village or an oil field, I really don't know. And after we returned, there was a very bad patch for John, for all of us, though John certainly had done well enough financially. Many people had done very well.

"What is it, darling?" I ask Oliver. "Please tell me. Is one of your courses troubling you?"

He turns to gaze at me. "One of my courses?" His face is damp.

"You're not eating at all. I'm so worried about you, sweet-heart."

"Ma, can't you see me? I can see you. I can see everything, Ma. Sometimes I feel like I can see through skin, through bone, through the surface of the earth. I can see cells doing their work, Ma—I can see thoughts as they form. I can hear everything, everything that's happening. Don't you hear the giant footfalls, the marauder coming, cracking the earth, shaking the roots of the giant trees? What can we do, Ma? We can't hide."

"Darling, there's nothing to be frightened of. We're not in any danger."

"His brain looks like a refinery at night, Ma. The little bolts of lightning combusting, shooting between the towers, all the lights blinking and moving . . ."

"Darling—" I smile, but my heart is pounding. "Your father loves you dearly."

"Mother!" He sits bolt upright and grabs me by the shoulders. "Mother, I've got one more minute—can't you see me, there, way off in the distance, coming apart, flailing up the hill, all the gears and levers breaking apart, falling off—flailing up the hill at the last moment, while the tight little ball of fire hisses and spits and falls toward the sea? He'll close his fist, Ma, he'll snuff it out. Are you protected by a magic cloak? The cloak of the prettiest girl at school?"

"Please, darling—" I try to disengage myself gently, and he flops back down. "Oh, God," he says.

"What, darling? Tell me. Please try to tell me so that I can understand. So that I can understand what is happening. So I can try to help you."

"It's all breaking up, Ma. How long do I have? I'm jump-ing from floe to floe. Do I have a minute? Do I have another minute after that? Do I have another minute after that?"

I run my hands over his face, to clear the tears and sweat. "This is a feeling, darling," I say. My heart is lodged high up near my throat, pounding, as if it's trying to exit my body. "It's just a feeling of pressure. We've all experienced something like it at one time or another. You have to remember that it's not possible for you to fix every problem in the world. Frankly, darling, no one has appointed you king of the planet." I force myself to smile.

"Every breath I take is a theft," he says.

"Oliver!" I say. "Please! Oh, darling, listen. Do you want to stay home for a while? Do you want to drop one of your courses? Tell me how to help you, sweetheart, and I will."

"It's no use, Ma. There's no way out. It was settled for me so long ago, and now here's your poor boy, his head all in pieces, just howling at the moon."

During that whole, long time, when we were away, I used to dream that I was coming home. Almost every night, for a long time, I dreamed that I was coming home. I still dream that I am coming home.

I stand, for a moment, outside the bedroom door.

"Well, there you are," John says, when I bring myself to open it. "I was calling for you. Didn't you hear me?"

"I was . . . Do we have any aspirin?"

"Come in," he says. "Why don't you come in?"

The blinds are drawn, the house is a thin shell. The acid moonlight pours down, scalding.

"Talking to your son?" he asks.

"John?" I say. "Do you remember if Oliver ever had a nurse—maybe in Africa—who told him stories?"

"A 'nurse'?" John says. "Is he having some sort of nineteenth-century European colonial hallucination?"

I sit down at the dressing table. In the mirror, I watch John pacing slowly back and forth. "He needs reassurance from you, darling," I say. "He needs your approval."

"My approval? Actually, it seems that I need *his* approval. After all, I'm an arch criminal, he must have mentioned it—he's not one to let the opportunity slip by. I'm responsible for every ill on the planet, didn't he spell it out for you? Poverty? My fault. Injustice? My fault. War somewhere? Secret prisons? Torture? My fault. Falling rate of literacy? Rising rate of infant mortality? Catastrophic climate change? New lethal viruses? My fault, whatever is wrong, whatever might some-day go wrong, whatever some nut thinks might someday go wrong, it's all my fault, did he not happen to mention that? The whole world, the future, whose fault can any of it be? Must be dear old Dad's."

I rest my head in my hands and close my eyes. When I open them again, John is looking at me in the mirror.

After a moment, he shakes his head and looks away. "I noticed we're running low on coffee," he says.

I turn around, stricken, to face him. A neat, foil packet, weighing exactly a pound—such a simple thing to have failed at! "I meant to pick some up today—I completely for-got, I'm so sorry, darling. But there's enough for you in the morning."

He looks back at me, sadly, almost pityingly, as if he had just read a dossier describing all my shortcomings. "Enough for me?" he says. "But what about you? What will you do?"

"I don't mind," I say. "It doesn't matter—it's fine. I'll get some later—I have to do a big shop tomorrow, anyhow."

"No," he says. "I'll go out now. Someplace will still be open."

John's car pulls out. The sound shrinks into a tiny dot and I feel it vanish with a little, inaudible *pop*. I listen, but I can't hear a thing from Oliver's room—no music, or sounds of movement. I'll check on him later, after John has gone to sleep. I begin to brush my hair. It's surprisingly soothing—it always has been; it's like an erasure.

It's extreme to say, "I do my best." That can never quite be true, and in my opinion it's often just a pretext for self-pity, or self-congratulation—an excuse to give yourself lee-way. Still, I do *try*. I try reasonably hard to be sincerely cheerful, and to do what I can. Of course I understand Oliver's feeling—that he's lashed to the controls of some machine that eats up whatever is in its path. But this is something he'll grow out of. As John says, this is some sort of performance Oliver is putting on for himself, some melodrama. And ultimately, people learn to get on with things. At least in your personal life, your life among the people you know and live with, you try to live responsibly. And when you have occasion to observe the difficult lives that others have to bear, you try to feel gratitude for your own good fortune.

I did manage to throw out his card. I couldn't help seeing the name; the address of his office twinkled by. But I made an effort to cleanse them from my mind right away, and I think I'd succeeded by the time the card landed in the trash basket.

There's no chance that he would turn out to be the person who appeared to me this afternoon, really no chance at all. And I doubt I'm the person he was imagining, either—which for all I know, actually, was simply a demented slut.

And the fact is, that while I might not be doing Oliver or John much good, I'm certainly in a position to do them both a great deal of harm.

I'd intended to stay in today, to run some errands, to get down to some paperwork myself. But there we are. The things that are hidden! I felt such a longing to go into town, to go to the museum. It's not something I often do, but it's been a difficult week, grueling, really, with Oliver here, ranging about as if he were in a cage, talking talking talking about those hearings and heaven only knows what—and I kept picturing the silent, white galleries.

Looking at a painting takes a certain composure, a certain resolve, but when you really do look at one it can be like a door swinging open, a sensation, however brief, of vaulting freedom. It's as if, for a moment, you were a different person, with different eyes and different capacities and a different history—a sensation, really, that's a lot like hope.

It was probably around eleven when I parked the car and went down into the metro. There was that awful, artificial light, like a disinfectant, and the people, silhouettes, standing and walking, the shapeless, senseless sounds. The trains pass through in gray streaks, and it's as if you've always been there and you always will be. You can sense the cameras, now, too—that's all new, I think, or relatively new—and you can even see some of them, big, empty eyes that miss nothing. You could be anywhere, anywhere at all; you could be an unknowing participant in a secret experiment. And with all those lives streaking toward you and streaking away, you feel so strongly, don't you, the singularity and the accidentalness of your own life.

We passed each other on the platform. I hadn't particularly noticed him until that second, and yet in some way he'd impressed himself so forcibly upon me it was as if I'd known him elsewhere.

I walked on for what seemed to be a long interval before I allowed myself to turn around—and he was turning, too, of course, at just the same instant. We looked at each other, and we smiled, just a little, and then I turned and went on my way again.

When I reached the end of the platform, I turned back, and he was waiting.

He was handsome, yes, and maybe that was all it was about, really. And maybe it was just that beautiful appearance of his that caused his beautiful clothing, too, his beautiful overcoat and scarf and shoes to seem, themselves, like an expression of merit, of integrity, of something attended to properly and tenderly, rather than an expression of mere vanity, for instance, or greed.

Because, there are a lot of attractive men in this world, and if one of them happens to be standing there, well, that's nice, but that's that. This is a different thing. The truth is that people's faces contain specific messages, people's faces are secret messages for certain other people. And when I saw this particular face, I thought, oh, yes—so that's it.

The sky was scudding by out the taxi window, and we hardly spoke—just phrases, streamers caught for an instant as they flashed past in the bright, tumultuous air. And no one at the reception desk looked at us knowingly or scornfully, despite the absence of luggage and the classically suspect hour. It was as solemn and grand, in its way, as a wedding.

We had taken the taxi, had stood at the desk; *we had done it*—the thought kept tumbling over me like pealing bells as we rose up in the elevator, our hands lightly clasped. And we were solemn, and so happy, or at least I was, as we entered our room, the beautiful room that we might as well have been the first people ever to see—elated as if by some solution, when just minutes before we'd been on the metro platform, clinging fiercely, as if before a decisive separation, the way lovers do in wartime.